CRIME NOVELS

AMERICAN NOIR
OF THE 1950S

CRIME NOVELS

AMERICAN NOIR

OF THE 1950S

The Killer Inside Me
Jim Thompson

The Talented Mr. Ripley
Patricia Highsmith

Pick-Up
Charles Willeford

Down There
David Goodis

The Real Cool Killers
Chester Himes

THE LIBRARY OF AMERICA

The Killer Inside Me copyright 1952 by Jim Thompson. *The Talented
Mr. Ripley* copyright 1955 by Patricia Highsmith. Reprinted by
permission of Alfred A. Knopf, a division of Random House, Inc.
Pick-Up copyright 1967 by Softcover Library, Inc. Reprinted by
permission of the Estate of Charles Willeford. *Down There* copyright
1956 by Fawcett Publications, Inc. Reprinted by permission of the
Estate of David Goodis and Scott Meredith Literary Agency, L.P.
The Real Cool Killers copyright 1959 by Chester Himes. Reprinted by
permission of The Roslyn Targ Literary Agency.

The paper used in this publication meets the
minimum requirements of the American National Standard for
Information Sciences—Permanence of Paper for Printed
Library Materials, ANSI z39.48—1984.

Distributed to the trade in the United States
by Penguin Books USA Inc
and in Canada by Penguin Books Canada Ltd.

Library of Congress Catalog Number: 97-2487
For cataloging information, see end of Notes.
ISBN 1-883011-49-3
———
First Printing
The Library of America—95

Manufactured in the United States of America

Robert Polito

SELECTED THE CONTENTS AND WROTE
THE NOTES FOR THIS VOLUME

Contents

THE KILLER INSIDE ME

by Jim Thompson

One

I'D FINISHED my pie and was having a second cup of coffee when I saw him. The midnight freight had come in a few minutes before; and he was peering in one end of the restaurant window, the end nearest the depot, shading his eyes with his hand and blinking against the light. He saw me watching him, and his face faded back into the shadows. But I knew he was still there. I knew he was waiting. The bums always size me up for an easy mark.

I lit a cigar and slid off my stool. The waitress, a new girl from Dallas, watched as I buttoned my coat. "Why, you don't even carry a gun!" she said, as though she was giving me a piece of news.

"No," I smiled. "No gun, no blackjack, nothing like that. Why should I?"

"But you're a cop—a deputy sheriff, I mean. What if some crook should try to shoot you?"

"We don't have many crooks here in Central City, ma'am," I said. "Anyway, people are people, even when they're a little misguided. You don't hurt them, they won't hurt you. They'll listen to reason."

She shook her head, wide-eyed with awe, and I strolled up to the front. The proprietor shoved back my money and laid a couple of cigars on top of it. He thanked me again for taking his son in hand.

"He's a different boy now, Lou," he said, kind of running his words together like foreigners do. "Stays in nights; gets along fine in school. And always he talks about you—what a good man is Deputy Lou Ford."

"I didn't do anything," I said. "Just talked to him. Showed a little interest. Anyone else could have done as much."

"Only you," he said. "Because you are good, you make others so." He was all ready to sign off with that, but I wasn't. I leaned an elbow on the counter, crossed one foot behind the other and took a long slow drag on my cigar. I liked the guy—as much as I like most people, anyway—but he was too good to let go. Polite, intelligent: guys like that are my meat.

"Well, I tell you," I drawled. "I tell you the way I feel,

3

Max. A man doesn't get any more out of life than what he puts into it."

"Umm," he said, fidgeting. "I guess you're right, Lou."

"I was thinking the other day, Max; and all of a sudden I had the doggonedest thought. It came to me out of a clear sky—the boy is father to the man. Just like that. The boy is father to the man."

The smile on his face was getting strained. I could hear his shoes creak as he squirmed. If there's anything worse than a bore, it's a corny bore. But how can you brush off a nice friendly fellow who'd give you his shirt if you asked for it?

"I reckon I should have been a college professor or something like that," I said. "Even when I'm asleep I'm working out problems. Take that heat wave we had a few weeks ago; a lot of people think it's the heat that makes it so hot. But it's not like that, Max. It's not the heat, but the humidity. I'll bet you didn't know that, did you?"

He cleared his throat and muttered something about being wanted in the kitchen. I pretended like I didn't hear him.

"Another thing about the weather," I said. "Everyone talks about it, but no one does anything. But maybe it's better that way. Every cloud has its silver lining, at least that's the way I figure it. I mean, if we didn't have the rain we wouldn't have the rainbows, now would we?"

"Lou . . ."

"Well," I said, "I guess I'd better shove off. I've got quite a bit of getting around to do, and I don't want to rush. Haste makes waste, in my opinion. I like to look before I leap."

That was dragging 'em in by the feet, but I couldn't hold 'em back. Striking at people that way is almost as good as the other, the real way. The way I'd fought to forget—and had almost forgot—until I met her.

I was thinking about her as I stepped out into the cool West Texas night and saw the bum waiting for me.

Two

CENTRAL CITY was founded in 1870, but it never became a city in size until about ten-twelve years ago. It was shipping point for a lot of cattle and a little cotton; and Chester Conway, who was born here, made it headquarters for the Conway Construction Company. But it still wasn't much more than a wide place in a Texas road. Then, the oil boom came, and almost overnight the population jumped to 48,000.

Well, the town had been laid out in a little valley amongst a lot of hills. There just wasn't any room for the newcomers, so they spread out every whichway with their homes and businesses, and now they were scattered across a third of the county. It's not an unusual situation in the oil-boom country—you'll see a lot of cities like ours if you're ever out this way. They don't have any regular city police force, just a constable or two. The sheriff's office handles the policing for both city and county.

We do a pretty good job of it, to our own way of thinking at least. But now and then things get a little out of hand, and we put on a clean-up. It was during a clean-up three months ago that I ran into her.

"Name of Joyce Lakeland," old Bob Maples, the sheriff, told me. "Lives four-five miles out on Derrick Road, just past the old Branch farm house. Got her a nice little cottage up there behind a stand of blackjack trees."

"I think I know the place," I said. "Hustlin' lady, Bob?"

"We-el, I reckon so but she's bein' mighty decent about it. She ain't running it into the ground, and she ain't takin' on no roustabouts or sheepherders. If some of these preachers around town wasn't rompin' on me, I wouldn't bother her a-tall."

I wondered if he was getting some of it, and decided that he wasn't. He wasn't maybe any mental genius, but Bob Maples was straight. "So how shall I handle this Joyce Lakeland?" I said. "Tell her to lay off a while, or to move on?"

"We-el"—he scratched his head, scowling—"I dunno, Lou. Just—well, just go out and size her up, and make your own decision. I know you'll be gentle, as gentle and pleasant as you can be. An' I know you can be firm if you have to. So go on out, an' see how she looks to you. I'll back you up in whatever you want to do."

It was about ten o'clock in the morning when I got there. I pulled the car up into the yard, curving it around so I could swing out easy. The county license plates didn't show, but that wasn't deliberate. It was just the way it had to be.

I eased up on the porch, knocked on the door and stood back, taking off my Stetson.

I was feeling a little uncomfortable. I hardly knew what I was going to say to her. Because maybe we're kind of old-fashioned, but our standards of conduct aren't the same, say, as they are in the east or middle-west. Out here you say yes ma'am and no ma'am to anything with skirts on; anything white, that is. Out here, if you catch a man with his pants down, you apologize . . . even if you have to arrest him afterwards. Out here you're a man, a man and a gentleman, or you aren't anything. And God help you if you're not.

The door opened an inch or two. Then, it opened all the way and she stood looking at me.

"Yes?" she said coldly.

She was wearing sleeping shorts and a wool pullover; her brown hair was as tousled as a lamb's tail, and her unpainted face was drawn with sleep. But none of that mattered. It wouldn't have mattered if she'd crawled out of a hog-wallow wearing a gunny sack. She had that much.

She yawned openly and said "Yes?" again, but I still couldn't speak. I guess I was staring open-mouthed like a country boy. This was three months ago, remember, and I hadn't had the sickness in almost fifteen years. Not since I was fourteen.

She wasn't much over five feet and a hundred pounds, and she looked a little scrawny around the neck and ankles. But that was all right. It was perfectly all right. The good Lord had known just where to put that flesh where it would *really* do some good.

"Oh, my goodness!" She laughed suddenly. "Come on in. I don't make a practice of it this early in the morning, but . . ." She held the screen open and gestured. I went in and she closed it and locked the door again.

"I'm sorry, ma'am," I said, "but—"

"It's all right. But I'll have to have some coffee first. You go on back."

I went down the little hall to the bedroom, listening uneasily as I heard her drawing water for the coffee. I'd acted like a chump. It was going to be hard to be firm with her after a start like this, and something told me I should be. I didn't know why; I still don't. But I knew it right from the beginning. Here was a little lady who got what she wanted, and to hell with the price tag.

Well, hell, though; it was just a feeling. She'd acted all right, and she had a nice quiet little place here. I decided I'd let her ride, for the time being anyhow. Why not? And then I happened to glance into the dresser mirror and I knew why not. I knew I couldn't. The top dresser drawer was open a little, and the mirror was tilted slightly. And hustling ladies are one thing, and hustling ladies with guns are something else.

I took it out of the drawer, a .32 automatic, just as she came in with the coffee tray. Her eyes flashed and she slammed the tray down on a table. "What," she snapped, "are you doing with that?"

I opened my coat and showed her my badge. "Sheriff's office, ma'am. What are *you* doing with it?"

She didn't say anything. She just took her purse off the dresser, opened it and pulled out a permit. It had been issued in Fort Worth, but it was all legal enough. Those things are usually honored from one town to another.

"Satisfied, copper?" she said.

"I reckon it's all right, miss," I said. "And my name's Ford, not copper." I gave her a big smile, but I didn't get any back. My hunch about her had been dead right. A minute before she'd been all set to lay, and it probably wouldn't have made any difference if I hadn't had a dime. Now she was set for something else, and whether I was a cop or Christ didn't make any difference either.

I wondered how she'd lived so long.

"Jesus!" she jeered. "The nicest looking guy I ever saw and you turn out to be a lousy snooping copper. How much? I don't jazz cops."

I felt my face turning red. "Lady," I said, "that's not very polite. I just came out for a little talk."

"You dumb bastard," she yelled. "I asked you what you wanted."

"Since you put it that way," I said, "I'll tell you. I want you out of Central City by sundown. If I catch you here after that I'll run you in for prostitution."

I slammed on my hat and started for the door. She got in front of me, blocking my way.

"You lousy son-of-a-bitch. You—"

"Don't you call me that," I said. "Don't do it, ma'am."

"I did call you that! And I'll do it again! You're a son-of-a-bitch, bastard, pimp . . ."

I tried to push past her. I had to get out of there. I knew what was going to happen if I didn't get out, and I knew I couldn't let it happen. I might kill her. It might bring *the sickness* back. And even if I didn't and it didn't, I'd be washed up. She'd talk. She'd yell her head off. And people would start thinking, thinking and wondering about that time fifteen years ago.

She slapped me so hard that my ears rang, first on one side then the other. She swung and kept swinging. My hat flew off. I stooped to pick it up, and she slammed her knee under my chin.

I stumbled backward on my heels and sat down on the floor. I heard a mean laugh, then another laugh sort of apologetic. She said, "Gosh, sheriff, I didn't mean to—I—you made me so mad I—I—"

"Sure," I grinned. My vision was clearing and I found my voice again. "Sure, ma'am, I know how it was. Used to get that way myself. Give me a hand, will you?"

"You-you won't hurt me?"

"Me? Aw, now, ma'am."

"No," she said, and she sounded almost disappointed. "I know you won't. Anyone can see you're too easy-going." And she came over to me slowly and gave me her hands.

I pulled myself up. I held her wrists with one hand and swung. It almost stunned her; I didn't want her completely stunned. I wanted her so she would understand what was happening to her.

"No, baby"—my lips drew back from my teeth. "I'm not going to hurt you. I wouldn't think of hurting you. I'm just going to beat the ass plumb off of you."

I said it, and I meant it and I damned near did.

I jerked the jersey up over her face and tied the end in a knot. I threw her down on the bed, yanked off her sleeping shorts and tied her feet together with them.

I took off my belt and raised it over my head . . .

I don't know how long it was before I stopped, before I came to my senses. All I know is that my arm ached like hell and her rear end was one big bruise, and I was scared crazy— as scared as a man can get and go on living.

I freed her feet and hands, and pulled the jersey off her head. I soaked a towel in cold water and bathed her with it. I poured coffee between her lips. And all the time I was talking, begging her to forgive me, telling her how sorry I was.

I got down on my knees by the bed, and begged and apologized. At last her eyelids fluttered and opened.

"D-don't," she whispered.

"I won't," I said. "Honest to God, ma'am, I won't ever—"

"Don't talk." She brushed her lips against mine. "Don't say you're sorry."

She kissed me again. She began fumbling at my tie, my shirt; starting to undress me after I'd almost skinned her alive.

I went back the next day and the day after that. I kept going back. And it was like a wind had been turned on a dying fire. I began needling people in that dead-pan way—needling 'em as a substitute for something else. I began thinking about settling scores with Chester Conway, of the Conway Construction Company.

I won't say that I hadn't thought of it before. Maybe I'd stayed on in Central City all these years, just in the hopes of getting even. But except for her I don't think I'd ever have done anything. She'd made the old fire burn again. She even showed me how to square with Conway.

She didn't know she was doing it, but she gave me the answer. It was one day, one night rather, about six weeks after we'd met.

"Lou," she said, "I don't want to go on like this. Let's pull out of this crummy town together, just you and I."

"Why, you're crazy!" I said. I said it before I could stop myself. "You think I'd—I'd—"

"Go on, Lou. Let me hear you say it. Tell me"—she began to drawl—"what a fine ol' family you-all Fords is. Tell me, we-all Fords, ma'am, we wouldn't think of livin' with one of you mizzable ol' whores, ma'am. Us Fords just ain't built that way, ma'am."

That was part of it, a big part. But it wasn't the main thing. I knew she was making me worse; I knew that if I didn't stop soon I'd never be able to. I'd wind up in a cage or the electric chair.

"Say it, Lou. Say it and I'll say something."

"Don't threaten me, baby," I said. "I don't like threats."

"I'm not threatening you. I'm telling you. You think you're too good for me—I'll—I'll—"

"Go on. It's your turn to do the saying."

"I wouldn't want to, Lou, honey, but I'm not going to give you up. Never, never, never. If you're too good for me now, then I'll make it so you won't be."

I kissed her, a long hard kiss. Because baby didn't know it, but baby was dead, and in a way I couldn't have loved her more.

"Well, now, baby," I said, "you've got your bowels in an uproar and all over nothing. I was thinking about the money problem."

"I've got some money. I can get some more. A lot of it."

"Yeah?"

"I can, Lou. I know I can! He's crazy about me and he's dumb as hell. I'll bet if his old man thought I was going to marry him, he—"

"Who?" I said. "Who are you talking about, Joyce?"

"Elmer Conway. You know who he is, don't you? Old Chester—"

"Yeah," I said. "Yeah, I know the Conways right well. How do you figure on hookin' 'em?"

We talked it over, lying there on her bed together, and off in the night somewhere a voice seemed to whisper to forget it, *forget it, Lou, it's not too late if you stop now.* And I did try, God knows I tried. But right after that, right after the voice, her hand gripped one of mine and kneaded it into her breasts; and she moaned and shivered . . . and so I didn't forget.

"Well," I said, after a time, "I guess we can work it out. The way I see it is, if at first you don't succeed, try, try again."

"Mmm, darling?"

"In other words," I said, "where there's a will there's a way."

She squirmed a little, and then she snickered. "Oh, Lou, you corny so and so! You slay me!"

. . . The street was dark. I was standing a few doors above the cafe, and the bum was standing and looking at me. He was a young fellow, about my age, and he was wearing what must have been a pretty good suit of clothes at one time.

"Well, how about it, bud?" he was saying. "How about it, huh? I've been on a hell of a binge, and by God if I don't get some food pretty soon—"

"Something to warm you up, eh?" I said.

"Yeah, anything at all you can help me with, I'll . . ."

I took the cigar out of my mouth with one hand and made like I was reaching into my pocket with the other. Then, I grabbed his wrist and ground the cigar butt into his palm.

"Jesus, bud!"—He cursed and jerked away from me. "What the hell you tryin' to do?"

I laughed and let him see my badge. "Beat it," I said.

"Sure, bud, sure," he said, and he began backing away. He didn't sound particularly scared or angry; more interested than anything. "But you better watch that stuff, bud. You sure better watch it."

He turned and walked off toward the railroad tracks.

I watched him, feeling sort of sick and shaky; and then I got in my car and headed for the labor temple.

Three

THE Central City Labor Temple was on a side street a couple of blocks off of the courthouse square. It wasn't much of a building, an old two-story brick with the downstairs rented out to a pool hall and the union offices and meeting hall on the second floor. I climbed the stairs, and went down the dark corridor to the end where a door opened into several of the best and largest offices in the place. The sign on the glass read

CENTRAL CITY, TEXAS
Building Trades Council
Joseph Rothman, Pres.

and Rothman opened the door before I could turn the knob.

"Let's go back here in the rear," he said, shaking hands. "Sorry to ask you to come around so late, but you being a public official and all I thought it might be best."

"Yeah," I nodded, wishing I could have ducked seeing him entirely. The law is pretty much on one side of the fence out here; and I already knew what he wanted to talk about.

He was a man of about forty, short and stocky, with sharp black eyes and a head that seemed too big for his body. He had a cigar in his mouth, but he laid it down after he sat down at his desk, and began rolling a cigarette. He lit it and blew smoke over the match, his eyes shying away from mine.

"Lou," the labor leader said, and hesitated. "I've got something to tell you—in the strictest confidence, you understand—but I'd like you to tell me something first. It's probably a pretty touchy subject with you, but . . . well, how did you feel about Mike Dean, Lou?"

"Feel? I'm not sure I know what you mean, Joe," I said.

"He was your foster brother, right? Your father adopted him?"

"Yes. Dad was a doctor, you know—"

"And a very good one, I understand. Excuse me, Lou. Go on."

So that's the way it was going to be. Spar and counter-spar. Each of us feeling the other out, each of us telling things he knows damn well the other fellow has heard a thousand times. Rothman had something important to tell me, and it looked as though he was going to do it the hard—and careful—way. Well, I didn't mind; I'd play along with him.

"He and the Deans were old friends. When they got wiped out in that big flu epidemic, he adopted Mike. My mother was dead—had been dead since I was a baby. Dad figured Mike and me would be company for each other, and the housekeeper could take care of two of us as easily as one."

"Uh-huh. And how did that strike you, Lou? I mean, you're the only son and heir and your dad brings in another son. Didn't that rub you a little the wrong way?"

I laughed. "Hell, Joe, I was four years old at the time, and Mike was six. You're not much concerned with money at that age, and, anyway, Dad never had any. He was too soft-hearted to dun his patients."

"You liked Mike, then?" He sounded like he wasn't quite convinced.

"Like isn't the word for it," I said. "He was the finest, swellest guy that ever lived. I couldn't have loved a real brother more."

"Even after he did what he did?"

"And just what," I drawled, "would that be?"

Rothman raised his eyebrows. "I liked Mike myself, Lou, but facts are facts. The whole town knows that if he'd been a little older he'd have gone to the chair instead of reform school."

"No one *knows* anything. There was never any proof."

"The girl identified him."

"A girl less than three years old! She'd have identified anyone they showed her."

"And Mike admitted it. And they dug up some other cases."

"Mike was scared. He didn't know what he was saying."

Rothman shook his head. "Let it go, Lou. I'm not really interested in that as such; only in your feelings about Mike . . . Weren't you pretty embarrassed when he came back to Central City? Wouldn't you have rather he'd stayed away?"

"No," I said. "Dad and I knew Mike hadn't done it. I mean"—I hesitated—"knowing Mike, we were sure he couldn't be guilty." *Because I was. Mike had taken the blame for me.* "I wanted Mike to come back. So did Dad." *He wanted him here to watch over me.* "My God, Joe, Dad pulled strings for months to get Mike his job as city building inspector. It wasn't easy to do, the way people felt about Mike, as popular and influential as Dad was."

"That all checks," Rothman nodded. "That's my understanding of things. But I have to be sure. You weren't sort of relieved when Mike got killed?"

"The shock killed Dad. He never recovered from it. As for me, well all I can say is that I wish it had been me instead of Mike."

Rothman grinned. "Okay, Lou. Now it's my turn . . . Mike was killed six years ago. He was walking a girder on the eighth floor of the New Texas Apartments, a Conway Construction job, when he apparently stepped on a loose rivet. He threw himself backward so he'd fall inside the building, onto the decking. But the floors hadn't been decked in properly; there were just a few planks scattered here and there. Mike fell all the way through to the basement."

I nodded. "So," I said. "What about it, Joe?"

"What about it!" Rothman's eyes flashed. "You ask me what about it when—"

"As President of the building unions, you know that the Ironworkers are under your jurisdiction, Joe. It's their obligation, and yours, to see that each floor is decked in as a building goes up."

"Now you're talking like a lawyer!" Rothman slapped his desk. "The Ironworkers are weak out here. Conway wouldn't put in the decking, and we couldn't make him."

"You could have struck the job."

"Oh, well," Rothman shrugged. "I guess I made a mistake, Lou. I understood you to say that you—"

"You heard me right," I said. "And let's not kid each other. Conway cut corners to make money. You let him—to make money. I'm not saying you're at fault, but I don't reckon he was either. It was just one of those things."

"Well," Rothman hesitated, "that's a kind of funny attitude for you to take, Lou. It seems to me you're pretty impersonal about it. But since that's the way you feel, perhaps I'd better—"

"Perhaps *I'd* better," I said. "Let me do the talking and then you won't have to feel funny about it. There was a riveter up there with Mike at the time he took his dive. Working after hours. Working by himself. But it takes two men to rivet— one to run the gun and one on the bucking iron. You're going to tell me that he didn't have any rightful business there, but I think you're wrong. He didn't have to be riveting. He could have been gathering up tools or something like that."

"But you don't know the whole story, Lou! This man—"

"I know. The guy was an iron tramp, working on a permit. He blew into town without a dime. Three days after Mike's death he left in a new Chevvy which he paid cash on the line for. That looks bad, but it doesn't really need to mean anything. He might have won the dough in a crap game or—"

"But you still don't know it all, Lou! Conway—"

"Let's see if I don't," I said. "Conway's company was the architect on that job as well as the contractor. And he hadn't allowed enough space for the boilers. To get 'em in, he was going to have to make certain alterations which he knew damned well Mike would never allow. It was either that or lose several hundred thousand dollars."

"Go on, Lou."

"So he took the loss. He hated it like hell, but he went ahead and did it."

Rothman laughed shortly. "He did, huh? I pushed iron on that job, myself, and—and—"

"Well." I gave him a puzzled look. "He did, didn't he? No matter what happened to Mike, your locals couldn't close their eyes to a dangerous situation like that. You're responsible. You can be sued. You could be tried for criminal collusion. You—"

"Lou." Rothman cleared his throat. "You're a hundred per cent right, Lou. Naturally we wouldn't stick our necks out for any amount of money."

"Sure," I smiled stupidly. "You just haven't thought this deal through, Joe. You've been getting along pretty good with Conway, and now he's taken a notion to go non-union, and naturally you're kind of upset about it. I reckon if you thought there'd really been a murder you wouldn't have waited six years to speak up."

"Yeah, I mean certainly not. Certainly, I wouldn't." He began rolling another cigarette. "Uh, how did you find out all these things, Lou, if you don't mind telling me?"

"Well, you know how it is. Mike was a member of the family, and I get around a lot. Any talk that's going around, I'd naturally hear it."

"Mmmm. I didn't realize there'd been so much gossip. In

fact, I didn't know there'd been any. And you never felt in-clined to take any action?"

"Why should I?" I said. "It was just gossip. Conway's a big business man—just about the biggest contractor in West Texas. He wouldn't get mixed up in a murder any more'n you people would keep quiet about one."

Rothman gave me another sharp look, and then he looked down at his desk. "Lou," he said softly, "do you know how many days a year an ironworker works? Do you know what his life expectancy is? Did you ever see an old ironworker? Did you ever stop to figure that there's all kinds of ways of dying, but only one way of being dead?"

"Well, no. I reckon not," I said. "I guess I don't know what you're driving at, Joe."

"Let it go. It's not really relevant."

"I suppose the boys don't have it too easy," I said. "But here's the way I look at it, Joe. There's no law says they have to stick to one line of work. If they don't like it they can do something else."

"Yeah," he nodded, "that's right, isn't it? It's funny how it takes an outsider to see through these problems . . . If they don't like it let 'em do something else. That's good, that's very good."

"Aw," I said, "it wasn't anything much."

"I disagree. It's very enlightening. You really surprise me, Lou. I've been seeing you around town for years and frankly you hardly struck me as a deep thinker . . . Do you have any solution for our larger problems, the Negro situation for ex-ample?"

"Well, that's pretty simple," I said. "I'd just ship 'em all to Africa."

"Uh-huh. I see, I see," he said, and he stood up and held out his hand. "I'm sorry I troubled you for nothing, Lou, but I've certainly enjoyed our talk. I hope we can get together again sometime."

"That would be nice," I said.

"Meanwhile, of course, I haven't seen you. Understand?"

"Oh, sure," I said.

We talked for a minute or two more, and then we walked to the outside door together. He glanced at it sharply, looked at me. "Say," he said. "Didn't I close that damned thing?"

"I thought you did," I said.

"Well, no harm done, I guess," he said. "Could I make a suggestion to you, Lou, in your own interests?"

"Why, sure you can, Joe. Anything at all."

"Save that bullshit for the birds."

He nodded, grinning at me; and for a minute you could have heard a pin drop. But he wasn't going to say anything. He wasn't ever going to let on. So, finally, I began to grin, too.

"I don't know the why of it, Lou—I don't know a thing, understand? Not a thing. But watch yourself. It's a good act but it's easy to overdo."

"You kind of asked for it, Joe," I said.

"And now you know why. And I'm not very bright or I wouldn't be a labor skate."

"Yeah," I said. "I see what you mean."

We shook hands again and he winked and bobbed his head. And I went down the dark hall and down the stairs.

Four

AFTER Dad died I'd thought about selling our house. I'd had several good offers for it, in fact, since it was right on the edge of the downtown business district; but somehow I couldn't let it go. The taxes were pretty high and there was ten times as much room as I needed, but I couldn't bring myself to sell. Something told me to hold on, to wait.

I drove down the alley to our garage. I drove in and shut off the lights. The garage had been a barn; it still was, for that matter; and I sat there in the doorway, sniffing the musty odors of old oats and hay and straw, dreaming back through the years. Mike and I had kept our ponies in those two front stalls, and back here in the box-stall we'd had an outlaws' cave. We'd hung swings and acting bars from these rafters; and we'd made a swimming pool out of the horse trough. And up overhead in the loft, where the rats now scampered and scurried, Mike had found me with the little gi—

A rat screamed suddenly on a high note.

I got out of the car and hurried out of the big sliding door of the barn, and into the backyard. I wondered if that was why I stayed here: To punish myself.

I went in the back door of the house and went through the house to the front, turning on all the lights, the downstairs lights I mean. Then I came back into the kitchen and made coffee and carried the pot up into Dad's old office. I sat in his big old leather chair, sipping coffee and smoking, and gradually the tension began to leave me.

It had always made me feel better to come here, back from the time I was kneehigh to a grasshopper. It was like coming out of the darkness into sunlight, out of a storm into calm. Like being lost and found again.

I got up and walked along the bookcases, the endless files of psychiatric literature, the bulky volumes of morbid psychology. . . . Krafft-Ebing, Jung, Freud, Bleuler, Adolf Meyer, Kretschmer, Kraepelin . . . All the answers were here, out in the open where you could look at them. And no one was terrified or horrified. I came out of the place I was hiding in—that I always had to hide in—and began to breathe.

I took down a bound volume of one of the German periodicals and read a while. I put it back and took down one in French. I skimmed through an article in Spanish and another in Italian. I couldn't speak any of those languages worth a doggone, but I could understand 'em all. I'd just picked 'em up with Dad's help, just like I'd picked up some higher mathematics and physical chemistry and half a dozen other subjects.

Dad had wanted me to be a doctor, but he was afraid to have me go away to school so he'd done what he could for me at home. It used to irritate him, knowing what I had in my head, to hear me talking and acting like any other rube around town. But, in time, when he realized how bad I had *the sickness*, he even encouraged me to do it. That's what I was going to be; I was going to have to live and get along with rubes. I wasn't ever going to have anything but some safe, small job, and I'd have to act accordingly. If Dad could have swung anything else that paid a living, I wouldn't even have been as much as a deputy sheriff.

I fiddled around Dad's desk, working out a couple of problems in calculus just for the hell of it. Turning away from the desk, I looked at myself in the mirrored door of the laboratory.

I was still wearing my Stetson, shoved a little to the back of my head. I had on a kind of pinkish shirt and a black bow tie, and the pants of my blue serge suit were hitched up so as to catch on the tops of my Justin boots. Lean and wiry; a mouth that looked all set to drawl. A typical Western-country peace officer, that was me. Maybe friendlier looking than the average. Maybe a little cleaner cut. But on the whole typical.

That's what I was, and I couldn't change. Even if it was safe, I doubted if I could change. I'd pretended so long that I no longer had to.

"Lou . . ."

I jumped and whirled.

"Amy!" I gasped. "What in the— You shouldn't be here! Where—"

"Upstairs, waiting for you. Now, don't get excited, Lou. I slipped out after the folks went to sleep and you know them."

"But someone might—"

"No one did. I slipped down the alley. Aren't you glad?"

I wasn't, although I suppose I should have been. She didn't have the shape that Joyce did, but it was a big improvement over anything else around Central City. Except when she stuck her chin out and narrowed her eyes, like she was daring you to cross her, she was a mighty pretty girl.

"Well, sure," I said. "Sure, I'm glad. Let's go back up, huh?"

I followed her up the stairs and into my bedroom. She kicked off her shoes, tossed her coat on a chair with her other clothes, and flopped down backwards on the bed.

"My!" she said, after a moment; and her chin began to edge outward. "Such enthusiasm!"

"Oh," I said, giving my head a shake. "I'm sorry, Amy. I had something on my mind."

"S-something on your mind!" Her voice quavered. "I strip myself for him, I shed my decency and my clothes for him and h-he stands there with 'something' on his m-mind!"

"Aw, now, honey. It's just that I wasn't expecting you, and—"

"No! And why should you? The way you avoid me and make excuses for not seeing me. If I had any pride left I'd— I'd—"

She buried her head in the pillow and began to sob, giving me an A-1 view of what was probably the second prettiest rear end in West Texas. I was pretty sure she was faking; I'd picked up a lot of pointers on women from Joyce. But I didn't dare give her the smacking she deserved. Instead I threw off my own clothes and crawled into bed with her, pulling her around facing me.

"Now, cut it out, honey," I said. "You know I've just been busy as a chigger at a picnic."

"I don't know it! I don't know anything of the kind! You don't want to be with me, that's what!"

"Why, that's plumb crazy, honey. Why wouldn't I want to?"

"B-because. Oh, Lou, darling, I've been so miserable . . ."

"Well, now that's a right foolish way to act, Amy," I said.

She went on whimpering about how miserable she'd been, and I went on holding her, listening—you got to do plenty of listening around Amy—and wondering how it had all started.

To tell the truth, I guess it hadn't started anywhere. We'd just drifted together like straws in a puddle. Our families had grown up together, and we'd grown up together, right here in this same block. We'd walked back and forth to school together, and when we went to parties we were paired off together. We hadn't needed to do anything. It was all done for us.

I suppose half the town, including her own folks, knew we were knocking off a little. But no one said anything or thought anything about it. After all we were going to get married . . . even if we were kind of taking our time.

"Lou!" she nudged me. "You aren't listening to me!"

"Why, sure, I am, honey."

"Well, answer me then."

"Not now," I said. "I've got something else on my mind, now."

"But . . . Oh, *darling* . . ."

I figured she'd been gabbing and nagging about nothing, as usual, and she'd forget about whatever I was supposed to answer. But it didn't work out that way. As soon as it was over and I'd reached her cigarettes for her, taking one for myself, she gave me another one of her looks and another, "Well, Lou?"

"I hardly know what to say," I said, which was exactly the case.

"You want to marry me, don't you?"

"Mar—but, sure," I said.

"I think we've waited long enough, Lou. I can go on teaching school. We'll get by a lot better than most couples."

"But . . . but that's all we'd do, Amy. We'd never get anywhere!"

"What do you mean?"

"Well, I don't want to go on being a deputy sheriff all of my life. I want to—well—be somebody."

"Like what, for example?"

"Oh, I don't know. There's no use in talking about it."

"A doctor, perhaps? I think that would be awfully nice. Is that what you had in mind, Lou?"

"I know it's crazy, Amy. But—"

She laughed. She rolled her head on the pillow, laughing. "Oh, Lou! I never heard of such a thing! You're twenty-nine years old, and y-you don't even speak good English, and—and—oh, ha, ha, ha . . ."

She laughed until she was gasping, and my cigarette burned down between my fingers and I never knew it until I smelled the scorching flesh.

"I'm s-sorry, darling. I didn't mean to hurt your feelings, but— Were you teasing me? Were you joking with your little Amy?"

"You know me," I said. "Lou the laughing boy."

She began to quiet down at the tone of my voice. She turned away from me and lay on her back, picking at the quilt with her fingers. I got up and found a cigar, and sat down on the bed again.

"You don't want to marry me, do you, Lou?"

"I don't think we should marry now, no."

"You don't want to marry me at all."

"I didn't say that."

She was silent for several minutes, but her face talked for her. I saw her eyes narrow and a mean little smile twist her lips, and I knew what she was thinking. I knew almost to a word what she was going to say.

"I'm afraid you'll have to marry me, Lou. You'll have to, do you understand?"

"No," I said, "I won't have to. You're not pregnant, Amy. You've never gone with anyone else, and you're not pregnant by me."

"I'm lying, I suppose?"

"Seems as though," I said. "I couldn't get you pregnant if I wanted to. I'm sterile."

"*You?*"

"Sterile isn't the same thing as impotent. I've had a vasectomy."

"Then why have we always been so—why do you use—?"

I shrugged. "It saved a lot of explanations. Anyway, you're not pregnant, to get back to the subject."

"I just don't understand," she said, frowning. She wasn't at all bothered by my catching her in a lie. "Your father did it? Why, Lou?"

"Oh, I was kind of run down and nervous, and he thought—"

"Why, you were not! You were never that way!"

"Well," I said, "he thought I was."

"He *thought!* He did a terrible thing like that—made you so we can never have children—just because he thought something! Why, it's terrible! It makes me sick! . . . When was it, Lou?"

"What's the difference?" I said. "I don't really remember. A long time ago."

I wished I'd kept my mouth shut about her not being pregnant. Now I couldn't back up on my story. She'd know I was lying and she'd be more suspicious than ever.

I grinned at her and walked my fingers up the curving plane of her belly. I squeezed one of her breasts, and then I moved my hand up until it was resting against her throat.

"What's the matter?" I said. "What have you got that pretty little face all puckered up for?"

She didn't say anything. She didn't smile back. She just lay there, staring, adding me up point by point, and she began to look more puzzled in one way and less in another. The answer was trying to crash through and it couldn't make it—quite. I was standing in the way. It couldn't get around the image she had of gentle, friendly easy-going Lou Ford.

"I think," she said slowly, "I'd better go home now."

"Maybe you'd better," I agreed. "It'll be dawn before long."

"Will I see you tomorrow? Today, I mean."

"Well, Saturday's a pretty busy day for me," I said. "I reckon we might go to church together Sunday or maybe have dinner together, but—"

"But you're busy Sunday night."

"I really am, honey. I promised to do a favor for a fellow, and I don't see how I can get out of it."

"I see. It never occurs to you to think about me when you're making all your plans, does it? Oh, no! I don't matter."

"I won't be tied up too long Sunday," I said. "Maybe until eleven o'clock or so. Why don't you come over and wait for me like you did tonight? I'd be tickled to death to have you."

Her eyes flickered, but she didn't break out with a lecture like she must have wanted to. She motioned for me to move so she could get up; and then she got up and began dressing.

"I'm awfully sorry, honey," I said.

"Are you?" She pulled her dress over her head, patted it down around her hips, and buttoned the collar. Standing first on one foot then the other, she put on her pumps. I got up and held her coat for her, smoothing it around her shoulders as I helped her into it.

She turned inside my arms and faced me. "All right, Lou," she said briskly. "We'll say no more tonight. But Sunday we'll have a good long talk. You're going to tell me why you've acted as you have these last few months, and no lying or evasions. Understand?"

"Ma'am, Miss Stanton," I said. "Yes, ma'am."

"All right," she nodded, "that's settled. Now you'd better put some clothes on or go back to bed before you catch cold."

Five

THAT DAY, Saturday, was a busy one. There were a lot of payday drunks in town, it being the middle of the month, and drunks out here mean fights. All of us deputies and the two constables and Sheriff Maples had our hands full keeping things under control.

I don't have much trouble with drunks. Dad taught me they were touchy as all-hell and twice as jumpy, and if you didn't ruffle 'em or alarm 'em they were the easiest people in the world to get along with. You should never bawl a drunk out, he said, because the guy had already bawled himself out to the breaking point. And you should never pull a gun or swing on a drunk because he was apt to feel that his life was in danger and act accordingly.

So I just moved around, friendly and gentle, taking the guys home wherever I could instead of to jail, and none of them got hurt and neither did I. But it all took time. From the time I went on at noon until eleven o'clock, I didn't so much as stop for a cup of coffee. Then around midnight, when I was already way over shift, I got one of the special jobs Sheriff Maples was always calling me in on.

A Mexican pipeliner had got all hayed up on marijuana and stabbed another Mexican to death. The boys had roughed him up pretty badly bringing him in and now, what with the hay and all, he was a regular wild man. They'd managed to get him off into one of the "quiet" cells, but the way he was cutting up he was going to take it apart or die in the attempt.

"Can't handle the crazy Mex the way we ought to," Sheriff Bob grumbled. "Not in a murder case. I miss my guess, we've already given some shyster defense attorney enough to go yellin' third-degree."

"I'll see what I can do," I said.

I went down to the cell and I stayed there three hours, and I was busy every minute of it. I hardly had time to slam the door before the Mex dived at me. I caught his arms and held him back, letting him struggle and rave; and then I turned him loose and he dived again. I held him back again, turned him loose again. It went on and on.

I never slugged him or kicked him. I never let him struggle hard enough to hurt himself. I just wore him down, little by little, and when he quieted enough to hear me I began talking to him. Practically everyone in this area talks some Mex, but I do it better than most. I talked on and on, feeling him relax; and all the time I was wondering about myself.

This Mex, now, was about as defenseless as a man could be. He was hopped up and crazy. With the booting around he'd had, a little bit more would never have been noticed. I'd taken a lot bigger chance with what I'd done to that bum. The bum could have caused trouble. This Mex, alone in a cell with me, couldn't.

Yet I didn't so much as twist a finger. I'd never hurt a prisoner, someone that I could harm safely. I didn't have the slightest desire to. Maybe I had too much pride in my reputation for not using force. Or maybe I figured subconsciously that the prisoners and I were on the same side. But however it was, I'd never hurt 'em. I didn't want to, and pretty soon I wouldn't want to hurt anyone. I'd get rid of her, and it would all be over for all time.

After three hours, like I say, the Mex was willing to behave. So I got him his clothes back and a blanket for his bunk, and let him smoke a cigarette while I tucked him in. Sheriff Maples peeped in as I was leaving, and shook his head wonderingly.

"Don't see how you do it, Lou," he swore. "Dagnab it, if I see where you get the patience."

"You've just got to keep smiling," I said. "That's the answer."

"Yeah? Do tell," he drawled.

"That's right," I said. "The man with the grin is the man who will win."

He gave me a funny look; and I laughed and slapped him on the back. "Just kidding, Bob," I said.

What the hell? You can't break a habit overnight. And what was the harm in a little kidding?

The sheriff wished me a good Sunday, and I drove on home. I fixed myself a big platter of ham and eggs and French fries, and carried it into Dad's office. I ate at his desk, more at peace with myself than I'd been in a long time.

I'd made up my mind about one thing. Come hell or high water, I wasn't going to marry Amy Stanton. I'd been holding off on her account; I didn't feel I had the right to marry her. Now, though, I just wasn't going to do it. If I had to marry someone, it wouldn't be a bossy little gal with a tongue like barbed-wire and a mind about as narrow.

I carried my dishes into the kitchen, washed them up, and took a long hot bath. Then I turned in and slept like a log until ten in the morning.

While I was having breakfast, I heard gravel crunch in the driveway; and looking out I saw Chester Conway's Cadillac.

He came right in the house without knocking—people had got in the habit of that when Dad was practicing—and back into the kitchen.

"Keep your seat, boy, keep your seat," he said, though I hadn't made any move to get up. "Go right on with your breakfast."

"Thanks," I said.

He sat down, craning his neck so that he could look at the food on my plate. "Is that coffee fresh? I think I'll have some. Hop up and get me a cup, will you?"

"Yes, sir," I drawled. "Right away, Mr. Conway, sir."

That didn't faze him, of course; that was the kind of talk he felt he was entitled to. He took a noisy swill of coffee, then another. The third time he gulped the cup was emptied. He said he wouldn't take any more, without my offering him any, and lighted a cigar. He dropped the match on the floor, puffed, and dusted ashes into his cup.

West Texans as a whole are a pretty high-handed lot, but they don't walk on a man if he stands up; they're quick to respect the other fellow's rights. Chester Conway was an exception. Conway had been *the* big man in town before the oil boom. He'd always been able to deal with others on his own terms. He'd gone without opposition for so many years that, by this time, he hardly knew it when he saw it. I believe I could have cussed him out in church and he wouldn't have turned a hair. He'd have just figured his ears were playing tricks on him.

It had never been hard for me to believe he'd arranged Mike's murder. The fact that *he* did it would automatically make it all right.

"Well," he said, dusting ashes all over the table. "Got everything fixed for tonight, have you? No chance of any slip-ups? You'll wind this thing right on up so it'll stay wound?"

"I'm not doing anything," I said. "I've done all I'm going to."

"Don't think we'd better leave it that way, Lou. 'Member I told you I didn't like the idea? Well, I still don't. That damned crazy Elmer sees her again no telling what'll happen. You take the money yourself, boy. I've got it all ready, ten thousand in small bills, and—"

"No," I said.

"—pay her off. Then bust her around a little, and run her across the county line."

"Mr. Conway," I said.

"That's the way to do it," he chuckled, his big pale jowls jouncing. "Pay her, bust her and chase her . . . You say something?"

I went through it again, real slowly, dealing it out a word at a time. Miss Lakeland insisted on seeing Elmer one more time before she left. She insisted on his bringing the dough, and she didn't want any witnesses along. Those were her terms, and if Conway wanted her to leave quietly he'd have to meet 'em. We could have her pinched, of course, but she was bound to talk if we did and it wouldn't be pretty talk.

Conway nodded irritably. "Understand all that. Can't have a lot of dirty publicity. But I don't see—"

"I'll tell you what you don't see, Mr. Conway," I said. "You don't see that you've got a hell of a lot of gall."

"Huh?" His mouth dropped open. "Wha-at?"

"I'm sorry," I said. "Stop and think a minute. How would it look if it got around that an officer of the law had made a blackmail pay-off—that is, if she was willing to accept it from me? How do you think I feel being mixed up in a dirty affair of this kind? Now, Elmer got into this trouble and he came to me—"

"Only smart thing he ever did."

"—and I came to you. And you asked me to see what could be done about getting her out of town quietly. I did it. That's all I'm going to do. I don't see how you can ask me to do anything more."

"Well, uh"—He cleared his throat—"Maybe not, boy. Reckon you're right. But you will see that she leaves after she gets the money?"

"I'll see to that," I said. "If she's not gone within an hour, I'll move her along myself."

He got up, fidgeting around nervously, so I walked him to the door to get rid of him. I couldn't take him much longer. It would have been bad enough if I hadn't known what he'd done to Mike.

I kept my hands in my pockets, pretending like I didn't see him when he started to shake hands. He opened the screen, then hesitated a moment.

"Better not go off anywhere," he said. "I'm sending Elmer over as soon as I can locate him. Want you to give him a good talking-to; see that he's got everything down straight. Make him know what's what, understand?"

"Yes, sir," I said. "It's mighty nice of you to let me talk to him."

"That's all right. No trouble at all," he said; and the screen slammed behind him.

A couple hours later Elmer showed up.

He was big and flabby-looking like his old man, and he tried to be as overbearing but he didn't quite have the guts for it. Some of our Central City boys had flattened him a few times, and it had done him a world of good. His blotched face was glistening with sweat; his breath would have tested a hundred and eighty proof.

"Getting started pretty early in the day, aren't you?" I said.

"So what?"

"Not a thing," I said. "I've tried to do you a favor. If you ball it up, it's your headache."

He grunted and crossed his legs. "I dunno, Lou," he frowned. "Dunno about all this. What if the old man never cools off? What'll me and Joyce do when the ten thousand runs out?"

"Well, Elmer," I said. "I guess there's some misunderstanding. I understood that you were sure your father would come around in time. If that isn't the case, maybe I'd better tell Miss Lakeland and—"

"No, Lou! Don't do that! . . . Hell, he'll get over it. He always gets over the things I do. But—"

"Why don't you do this?" I said. "Don't let your ten thousand run out. Buy you some kind of business; you and Joyce can run it together. When it's going good, get in touch with your Dad. He'll see that you've made a darned smart move, and you won't have any trouble squaring things."

Elmer brightened a little—doggoned little. Working wasn't Elmer's idea of a good solution to any problem.

"Don't let me talk you into it," I said. "I think Miss Lakeland has been mighty badly misjudged—she convinced me and I'm not easy to convince. I've stuck my neck out a mile to give you and her a fresh start together, but if you don't want to go—"

"Why'd you do it, Lou? Why'd you do all this for me and her?"

"Maybe money," I said, smiling. "I don't make very much. Maybe I figured you'd do something for me in a money way."

His face turned a few shades redder. "Well . . . I could give you a little something out of the ten thousand, I guess."

"Oh, I wouldn't take any of that!" *You're damned right I wouldn't.* "I figured a man like you must have a little dough of his own. What do you do for your cigarettes and gas and whiskey? Does your Dad buy 'em for you?"

"Like hell!" He sat up and jerked out a roll of bills. "I got plenty of money."

He started to peel off a few bills—they were all twenties, it looked like—and then he caught my eye. I gave him a grin. It told him, plain as day, that I expected him to act like a cheapskate.

"Aw, hell," he said, and he wadded the roll together and tossed the whole thing to me. "See you tonight," he said, hoisting himself up.

"At ten o'clock," I nodded.

There were twenty-five twenties in the roll. Five hundred dollars. Now that I had it, it was welcome; I could always use a little extra money. But I hadn't planned on touching Elmer. I'd only done it to shut him up about my motives in helping him.

I didn't feel much like cooking, so I ate dinner in town. Coming home again I listened to the radio a while, read the Sunday papers and went to sleep.

Yes, maybe I was taking things pretty calmly, but I'd gone through the deal so often in my mind that I'd gotten used to it. *Joyce and Elmer were going to die. Joyce had asked for it. The Conways had asked for it. I wasn't any more cold-blooded than the dame who'd have me in hell to get her own way. I wasn't any more cold-blooded than the guy who'd had Mike knocked from an eight-story building.*

Elmer hadn't done it, of course; probably he didn't even know anything about it. But I had to get to the old man through him. It was the only way I could, and it was the way it should be. I'd be doing to him what he'd done to Dad.

. . . It was eight o'clock when I waked up—eight of the dark, moonless night I'd been waiting for. I gulped a cup of coffee, eased the car down the alley and headed for Derrick Road.

Six

HERE in the oil country you see quite a few places like the old Branch house. They were ranch houses or homesteads at one time; but wells were drilled around 'em, right up to their doorsteps sometimes, and everything nearby became a mess of oil and sulphur water and red sun-baked drilling mud. The grease-black grass dies. The creeks and springs disappear. And then the oil is gone and the houses stand black and abandoned, lost and lonely-looking behind the pest growths of sunflowers and sage and Johnson grass.

The Branch place stood back from Derrick Road a few

hundred feet, at the end of a lane so overgrown with weeds that I almost missed it. I turned into the lane, killed the motor after a few yards and got out.

At first I couldn't see a thing; it was that dark. But gradually my eyes became used to it. I could see all I needed to see. I opened the trunk compartment and located a tire tool. Taking a rusty spike from my pocket, I drove it into the right rear tire. There was a *poof!* and a *whish-ss!* The springs squeaked and whined as the car settled rapidly.

I got a jack under the axle, and raised it a foot or so. I rocked the car and slid it off the jack. I left it that way and headed up the lane.

It took maybe five minutes to reach the house and pull a plank from the porch. I leaned it against the gate post where I could find it in a hurry, and headed across the fields to Joyce's house.

"Lou!" She stood back from the door, startled. "I couldn't imagine who—where's your car? Is something wrong?"

"Nothing but a flat tire," I grinned. "I had to leave the car down the road a piece."

I sauntered into the living room, and she came around in front of me, gripping her arms around my back and pressing her face against my shirt. Her negligee fell open, accidentally on purpose I imagine. She moved her body against mine.

"Lou, honey . . ."

"Yeah?" I said.

"It's only about nine and Stupid won't be here for another hour, and I won't see you for two weeks. And . . . well, you know."

I knew. I knew how *that* would look in an autopsy.

"Well, I don't know, baby," I said. "I'm kind of pooped out, and you're all prettied up—"

"Oh, I am not!" She squeezed me. "I'm always prettied up to hear you tell it. Hurry, so I can have my bath."

Bath. That made it okay. "You twisted my arm, baby," I said, and I swept her up and carried her into the bedroom. And, no, it didn't bother me a bit.

Because right in the middle of it, right in the middle of the sweet talk and sighing, she suddenly went still and pushed my head back and looked me in the eye.

"You *will* join me in two weeks, Lou? Just as soon as you sell your house and wind up your affairs?"

"That's the understanding," I said.

"Don't keep me waiting. I want to be sweet to you, but if you won't let me I'll be the other way. I'll come back here and raise hell. I'll follow you around town and tell everyone how you—"

"—robbed you of your bloom and cast you aside?" I said.

"Crazy!" she giggled. "But just the same, Lou . . ."

"I know. I won't keep you waiting, baby."

I lay on the bed while she had her bath. She came back in from it, wiping herself with a big towel, and got some panties and a brassiere out of a suitcase. She stepped into the panties, humming, and brought the brassiere over to me. I helped her put it on, giving her a pinch or two, and she giggled and wiggled.

I'm going to miss you, baby, I thought. You've got to go, but I'm sure going to miss you.

"Lou . . . You suppose Elmer will make any trouble?"

"I already told you," I said. "What can he do? He can't squawk to his Dad. I'll tell him I changed my mind, and we'll have to keep faith with the old man. And that'll be that."

She frowned. "It seems so—oh, so complicated! I mean it looks like we could have got the money without dragging Elmer into it."

"Well. . . ." I glanced at the clock.

Nine-thirty-three. I didn't need to stall any longer. I sat up beside her, swinging my feet to the floor; casually drawing on my gloves.

"Well, I'll tell you, baby," I said. "It *is* kind of complicated, but it has to be that way. You've probably heard the gossip about Mike Dean, my foster brother? Well, Mike didn't do that. He took the blame for me. So if you should do your talking around town, it would be a lot worse than you realized. People would start thinking, and before it was all over . . ."

"But, Lou. I'm not going to say anything. You're going to join me and—"

"Better let me finish," I said. "I told you how Mike fell from that building? Only he didn't fall; he was murdered. Old man Conway arranged it and—"

"Lou"—she didn't get it at all. "I won't let you do anything to Elmer! You mustn't, honey. They'll catch you and you'll go to jail and—oh, honey, don't even think about it!"

"They won't catch me," I said. "They won't even suspect me. They'll think he was half-stiff, like he usually is, and you got to fighting and you both got killed."

She still didn't get it. She laughed, frowning a little at the same time. "But, Lou—that doesn't make sense. How could I be dead when—"

"Easy," I said, and I gave her a slap. And still she didn't get it.

She put a hand to her face and rubbed it slowly. "Y-you'd better not do that, now, Lou. I've got to travel, and—"

"You're not going anywhere, baby," I said, and I hit her again.

And at last she got it.

She jumped up and I jumped with her. I whirled her around and gave her a quick one-two, and she shot backwards across the room and bounced and slumped against the wall. She staggered to her feet, weaving, mumbling, and half-fell toward me. I let her have it again.

I backed her against the wall, slugging, and it was like pounding a pumpkin. Hard, then everything giving away at once. She slumped down, her knees bent under her, her head hanging limp; and then, slowly, an inch at a time, she pushed herself up again.

She couldn't see; I don't know how she could. I don't know how she could stand or go on breathing. But she brought her head up, wobbling, and she raised her arms, raised them and spread them and held them out. And then she staggered toward me, just as a car pulled into the yard.

"Guhguh-guhby . . . kiss guhguh-guh—"

I brought an uppercut up from the floor. There was a sharp *cr-aack!* and her whole body shot upward, and came down in a heap. And that time it stayed down.

I wiped my gloves on her body; it was her blood and it belonged there. I took the gun from the dresser, turned off the light and closed the door.

Elmer was coming up the steps, crossing the porch. I got to the front door and opened it.

"Hiya, Lou, ol' boy, ol' boy, ol' boy," he said. "Right on time, huh? Thass Elmer Conway, always right on time."

"Half-stiff," I said, "that's Elmer Conway. Have you got the money?"

He patted the thick brown folder under his arm. "What's it look like? Where's Joyce?"

"Back in the bedroom. Why don't you go on back? I'll bet she won't say no if you try to slip it to her."

"Aw," he blinked foolishly. "Aw, you shouldn't talk like that, Lou. You know we're gonna get married."

"Suit yourself," I shrugged. "I'd bet money though that she's all stretched out waiting for you."

I wanted to laugh out loud. I wanted to yell. I wanted to leap on him and tear him to pieces.

"Well, maybe . . ."

He turned suddenly and lumbered down the hall. I leaned against the wall, waiting, as he entered the bedroom and turned on the light.

I heard him say, "Hiya, Joyce, ol' kid, ol' ol' k-k-k . . ." I heard a heavy thump, and a gurgling, strangled sound. Then he said, he screamed, "Joyce . . . Joyce . . . *Lou!*"

I sauntered back. He was down on his knees and there was blood on his hands, and a big streak across his chin where he'd wiped it. He looked up at me, his mouth hanging open.

I laughed—I had to laugh or do something worse—and his eyes squeezed shut and he bawled. I yelled with laughter, bending over and slapping my legs. I doubled up, laughing and farting and laughing some more. Until there wasn't a laugh in me or anyone. I'd used up all the laughter in the world.

He got to his feet, smearing his face with his big flabby hands, staring at me stupidly.

"W-who did it, Lou?"

"It was suicide," I said. "A plain case of suicide."

"B-but that d-don't make—"

"It's the only thing that does make sense! It was the way it was, you hear me? Suicide, you hear me? Suicide suicide suicide! I didn't kill her. Don't you say I killed her. SHE KILLED HERSELF!"

I shot him, then, right in his gaping stupid mouth. I emptied the gun into him.

Stooping, I curved Joyce's hand around the gun butt, then dropped the gun at her side. I went out the door and across the fields again, and I didn't look back.

I found the plank and carried it down to my car. If the car had been seen, that plank was my alibi. I'd had to go up and find one to put under the jack.

I ran the jack up on the plank and put on the spare tire. I threw the tools into the car, started the motor and backed toward Derrick Road. Ordinarily, I'd no more back into a highway at night without my lights than I would without my pants. But this wasn't ordinarily. I just didn't think of it.

If Chester Conway's Cadillac had been travelling faster, I wouldn't be writing this.

He swarmed out of his car cursing, saw who I was, and cursed harder than ever. "Goddamit, Lou, you know better'n that! You trying to get killed, for Christ's sake? Huh? What the hell are you doing here, anyhow?"

"I had to pull in there with a flat tire," I said. "Sorry if I—"

"Well, come on. Let's get going. Can't stand here gabbing all night."

"Going?" I said. "It's still early."

"The hell it is! It's a quarter past eleven, and that damned Elmer ain't home yet. Promised to come right back, and he ain't done it. Probably up there working himself into another scrape."

"Maybe we'd better give him a little more time," I said. I had to wait a while. I couldn't go back in that house now. "Why don't you go on home, Mr. Conway, and I'll—"

"I'm going now!" He turned away from the car. "And you follow me!"

The door of the Cadillac slammed. He backed up and pulled around me, yelling again for me to come on. I yelled back that I would and he drove off. Fast.

I got a cigar lit. I started the motor and killed it. I started it and killed it again. Finally, it stayed running, it just wouldn't die, so I drove off.

I drove up the lane at Joyce's house and parked at the end of it. There wasn't room in the yard with Elmer's and the old man's cars there. I shut off the motor and got out. I climbed the steps and crossed the porch.

The door was open and he was in the living room, talking on the telephone. And his face was like a knife had come down it, slicing away all the flabbiness.

He didn't seem very excited. He didn't seem very sad. He was just business-like, and somehow that made it worse.

"Sure, it's too bad," he said. "Don't tell me that again. I know all about how bad it is. He's dead and that's that, and what I'm interested in is her . . . Well, do it then! Get on out here. We ain't going to let her die, get me? Not this way. I'm going to see that she burns."

Seven

IT WAS almost three o'clock in the morning when I got through talking—answering questions, mostly—to Sheriff Maples and the county attorney, Howard Hendricks; and I guess you know I wasn't feeling so good. I was kind of sick to my stomach, and I felt, well, pretty damned sore, angry. Things shouldn't have turned out this way. It was just plumb unreasonable. It wasn't right.

I'd done everything I could to get rid of a couple of undesirable citizens in a neat no-kickbacks way. And here one of 'em was still alive; and purple hell was popping about the other one.

Leaving the courthouse, I drove to the Greek's place and got a cup of coffee that I didn't want. His boy had taken a part-time job in a filling station, and the old man wasn't sure whether it was a good thing or not. I promised to drop by and look in on the lad.

I didn't want to go home and answer a lot more questions from Amy. I hoped that if I stalled long enough, she'd give up and leave.

Johnnie Pappas, the Greek's boy, was working at Slim Murphy's place. He was around at the side of the station when I drove in, doing something to the motor of his hot rod. I got out of my car and he came toward me slowly, sort of watchfully, wiping his hands on a chunk of waste.

"Just heard about your new job, Johnnie," I said. "Congratulations."

"Yeah." He was tall, good-looking; not at all like his father. "Dad send you out here?"

"He told me you'd gone to work here," I said. "Anything wrong with that?"

"Well . . . You're up pretty late."

"Well," I laughed, "so are you. Now how about filling 'er up with gas and checking the oil?"

He got busy, and by the time he was through he'd pretty much lost his suspicions. "I'm sorry if I acted funny, Lou. Dad's been kind of nagging me—he just can't understand that a guy my age needs a little real dough of his own—and I thought he was having you check up on me."

"You know me better than that, Johnnie."

"Sure, I do," he smiled, warmly. "I've got plenty of nagging from people, but no one but you ever really tried to help me. You're the only real friend I've ever had in this lousy town. Why do you do it, Lou? What's the percentage in bothering with a guy that everyone else is down on?"

"Oh, I don't know," I said. And I didn't. I didn't even know how I could stand here talking to him with the terrible load I had on my mind. "Maybe it's because I was a kid myself not so many years ago. Fathers are funny. The best ones get in your hair most."

"Yeah. Well . . ."

"What hours do you work, Johnnie?"

"Just midnight to seven, Saturdays and Sundays. Just enough to keep me in pocket money. Dad thinks I'll be too tired to go to school on Mondays, but I won't, Lou. I'll make it fine."

"Sure, you will," I said. "There's just one thing, Johnnie. Slim Murphy hasn't got a very good reputation. We've never proved that he was mixed up in any of these car-stripping jobs, but . . ."

"I know." He kicked the gravel of the driveway, uncomfortably. "I won't get into any trouble, Lou."

"Good enough," I said. "That's a promise, and I know you don't break your promises."

I paid him with a twenty dollar bill, got my change and headed toward home. Wondering about myself. Shaking my head, as I drove. I hadn't put on an act. I *was* concerned and worried about the kid. Me, worried about *his* troubles.

The house was all dark when I got home, but it would be, whether Amy was there or not. So I didn't get my hopes too high. I figured that my standing her up would probably make her all the more determined to stay; that she was a cinch to crop up at the one time I didn't want any part of her. That's the way I figured it, and that's the way it was.

She was up in my bedroom, in bed. And she'd filled two ash trays with the cigarettes she'd smoked. And mad! I've never seen one little old girl so mad in my life.

I sat down on the edge of the bed and pulled off my boots; and for about the next twenty minutes I didn't say a word. I didn't get a chance. Finally, she began to slow up a little, and I tried to apologize.

"I'm sure sorry, honey, but I couldn't help it. I've had a lot of trouble tonight."

"I'll bet!"

"You want to hear about it or not? If you don't, just say so."

"Oh, go on! I've heard so many of your lies and excuses I may as well hear a few more."

I told her what had happened—that is, what was *supposed* to have happened—and she could hardly hold herself in until I'd finished. The last word was hardly out of my mouth before she'd cut loose on me again.

"How could you be so stupid, Lou? How *could* you do it? Getting yourself mixed up with some wretched prostitute and that awful Elmer Conway! Now, there'll be a big scandal and you'll probably lose your job, and—"

"Why?" I mumbled. "I didn't do anything."

"I want to know why you did it!"

"Well, it was kind of a favor, see? Chester Conway wanted me to see what I could do about getting Elmer out of this scrape, so—"

"Why did he have to come to you? Why do you always

have to be doing favors for other people? You never do any for me!"

I didn't say anything for a minute. But I thought, *That's what you think, honey. I'm doing you a favor by not beating your head off.*

"Answer me, Lou Ford!"

"All right," I said. "I shouldn't have done it."

"You shouldn't have allowed that woman to stay in this county in the first place!"

"No," I nodded. "I shouldn't have."

"Well?"

"I'm not perfect," I snapped. "I make plenty of mistakes. How many times do you want me to say it?"

"Well! All I've got to say is . . ."

All she had to say would take her the rest of her life to finish; and I wasn't even half-way in the mood for it. I reached out and grabbed her by the crotch.

"Lou! You stop that!"

"Why?" I said.

"Y-you stop it!" She shivered. "You s-stop or . . . Oh, *Lou!*"

I lay down beside her with my clothes on. I had to do it, because there was just one way of shutting Amy up.

So I laid down and she swarmed up against me. And there wasn't a thing wrong with Amy when she was like that; you couldn't have asked much more from a woman. But there was plenty wrong with me. Joyce Lakeland was wrong with me.

"Lou . . ." Amy slowed down a little. "What's the matter, dear?"

"All this trouble," I said. "I guess it's thrown me for a loop."

"You poor darling. Just forget everything but me, and I'll pet you and whisper to you, mmm? I'll . . ." She kissed me and whispered what she would do. And she did it. And, hell, she might as well have done it to a fence post.

Baby Joyce had taken care of me, but good.

Amy pulled her hand away, and began brushing it against her hip. Then she snatched up a handful of sheet, and wiped—scrubbed—her hip with it.

"You son-of-a-bitch," she said. "You dirty, filthy bastard."

"Wha-at?" I said. It was like getting a punch in the guts. Amy didn't go in for cussing. At least, I'd never heard her do much.

"You're dirty. I can tell. I can smell it on you. Smell her. You can't wash it off. It'll never come off. You—"

"Jesus Christ!" I grabbed her by the shoulders. "What are you saying, Amy?"

"You screwed her. You've been doing it all along. You've been putting her dirty insides inside of me, smearing me with her. And I'm going to make you pay for it. If it's the l-last thing I ever d-do, I'll—"

She jerked away from me, sobbing, and jumped out of bed. As I got up, she backed around a chair, putting it between me and her.

"K-keep away from me! Don't you dare touch me!"

"Why, sure, honey," I said. "Whatever you say."

She didn't see the meaning yet of what she'd said. All she could think of was herself, the insult to herself. But I knew that, given enough time—and not much time at that—she'd put all the parts of the picture together. She wouldn't have any real proof, of course. All she had to go on was guess-work—intuition—and that operation I'd had; something, thank God, which seemed to have slipped her mind for the moment. Anyway, she'd talk. And the fact that there wasn't any proof for what she said, wouldn't help me much.

You don't need proof, know what I mean? Not from what I've seen of the law in operation. All you need is a tip that a guy is guilty. From then on, unless he's a big shot, it's just a matter of making him admit it.

"Amy," I said. "Amy, honey. Look at me."

"I d-don't want to look at you."

"Look at me . . . This is Lou, honey, Lou Ford, remember? The guy you've known all your life. I ask you, now, would I do what you said I did?"

She hesitated, biting her lips. "You did do it." Her voice was just a shade uncertain. "I know you did."

"You don't know anything," I said. "Just because I'm tired and upset, you jump to a crazy conclusion. Why, why would I fool around with some chippy when I had you? What could a dame like that give me that would make me run the risk of losing a girl like you? Huh? Now, that doesn't make sense, does it, honey."

"Well . . ." That had got to her. It had hit her right in the pride, where she was tenderest. But it wasn't quite enough to jar her loose from her hunch.

She picked up her panties and began putting them on, still standing behind the chair. "There's no use arguing about it, Lou," she said, wearily. "I suppose I can thank my lucky stars that I haven't caught some terrible disease."

"But dammit . . . !" I moved around the chair, suddenly, and got her in my arms. "Dammit, stop talking that way about the girl I'm going to marry! I don't mind for myself, but you can't say it about her, get me? You can't say that the girl I'm going to marry would sleep with a guy who plays around with whores!"

"Let me go, Lou! Let . . ." She stopped struggling, abruptly. "What did you—?"

"You heard me," I said.

"B-but just two days ago—"

"So what?" I said. "No man likes to be yanked into marriage. He wants to do his own proposing, which is just what I'm doing right now. Hell, we've already put it off too long, in my opinion. This crazy business tonight proves it. If we were married we wouldn't have all these quarrels and misunderstandings like we've been having."

"Since that woman came to town, you mean."

"All right," I said. "I've done all I could. If you're willing to believe that about me, I wouldn't want—"

"Wait, Lou!" She hung on to me. "After all, you can't blame me if—" And she let it go at that. She had to give up for her own sake. "I'm sorry, Lou. Of course, I was wrong."

"You certainly were."

"When shall we do it, Lou? Get married, I mean."

"The sooner the better," I lied. I didn't have the slightest intention of marrying her. But I needed time to do some planning, and I had to keep her quiet. "Let's get together in a few days when we're both more ourselves, and talk about it."

"Huh-uh." She shook her head. "Now that you've—we've come to the decision, let's go through with it. Let's talk about it right now."

"But it's getting daylight, honey," I said. "If you're still here even a little while from now, people will see you when you leave."

"I don't care if they do, darling. I don't care a teensy-weensie little bit." She snuggled against me, burrowing her head against my chest. And without seeing her face, I knew she was grinning. She had me on the run, and she was getting a hell of a kick out of it.

"Well, I'm pretty tired," I said. "I think I ought to sleep a little while before—"

"I'll make you some coffee, darling. That'll wake you up."

"But, honey—"

The phone rang. She let go of me, not very hurriedly, and I stepped over to the writing desk and picked up the extension.

"Lou?" It was Sheriff Bob Maples.

"Yeah, Bob," I said. "What's on your mind?"

He told me, and I said, Okay, and hung up the phone again. Amy looked at me, and changed her mind about popping off.

"Your job, Lou? You've got some work to do?"

"Yeah," I nodded. "Sheriff Bob's driving by to pick me up in a few moments."

"You poor dear! And you so tired! I'll get dressed and get right out."

I helped her dress, and walked to the back door with her. She gave me a couple of big kisses and I promised to call her as soon as I got a chance. She left then, a couple of minutes before Sheriff Maples drove up.

Eight

THE county attorney, Howard Hendricks, was with him, sitting in the back seat of the car. I gave him a cold-eyed look and a nod, as I got in the front, and he gave me back the look without a nod. I'd never had much use for him. He was one of those professional patriots, always talking about what a great hero he'd been in the war.

Sheriff Bob put the car in gear, clearing his throat uncomfortably. "Sure hated to bother you, Lou," he said. "Hope I didn't interrupt anything."

"Nothing that can't wait," I said. "She—I'd already kept her waiting five-six hours."

"You had a date for last night?" asked Hendricks.

"That's right"—I didn't turn around in the seat.

"For what time?"

"For a little after ten. The time I figured I'd have the Conway business finished."

The county attorney grunted. He sounded more than a mite disappointed. "Who was the girl?"

"None of your—"

"Wait a minute, Lou!" Bob eased his foot off the gas, and turned onto Derrick Road. "Howard, you're getting way out of line. You're kind of a newcomer out this way—been here eight years now, ain't you?—but you still ought to know better'n to ask a man a question like that."

"What the hell?" said Hendricks. "It's my job. It's an important question. If Ford had himself a date last night, it—well"—he hesitated—"it shows that he planned on being there instead of—well, uh—some place else. You see what I mean, Ford?"

I saw, all right, but I wasn't going to tell him so. I was just old dumb Lou from Kalamazoo. I wouldn't be thinking about an alibi, because I hadn't done anything to need an alibi for.

"No," I drawled, "I reckon I don't know what you mean. To come right down to cases, and no offense meant, I figured you'd done all the jawing you had to do when I talked to you an hour or so ago."

"Well, you're dead wrong, brother!" He glared at me, red-faced, in the rear view mirror. "I've got quite a few more questions. And I'm still waiting for the answer to the last one I asked. Who was the—"

"Drop it, Howard!" Bob jerked his head curtly. "Don't ask Lou that again, or I'm personally going to lose my temper. I know the girl. I know her folks. She's one of the nicest little ladies in town, and I ain't got the slightest doubt Lou had a date with her."

Hendricks scowled, gave out with an irritated laugh. "I don't get it. She's not too nice to sl—well, skip it—but she's too nice to have her name mentioned in the strictest confidence. I'm damned if I can understand a deal like that. The more I'm around you people the less I can understand you."

I turned around, smiling, looking friendly and serious. For a while, anyway, it wasn't a good idea to have anyone sore at me. And a guy that's got something on his conscience can't afford to get riled.

"I guess we're a pretty stiff-necked lot out here, Howard," I said. "I suppose it comes from the fact that this country was never very thickly settled, and a man had to be doggoned careful of the way he acted or he'd be marked for life. I mean, there wasn't any crowd for him to sink into—he was always out where people could see him."

"So?"

"So if a man or woman does something, nothing bad you understand, but the kind of thing men and women have always been doing, you don't let on that you know anything about it. You don't, because sooner or later you're going to need the same kind of favor yourself. You see how it is? It's the only way we can go on being human, and still hold our heads up."

He nodded indifferently. "Very interesting. Well, here we are, Bob."

Sheriff Maples pulled off the pavement and parked on the shoulder of the road. We got out, and Hendricks nodded toward the weed-grown trail which led up to the old Branch house. He jerked his head at it, and then turned and looked at me.

"Do you see that track through there, Ford? Do you know what caused that?"

"Why, I reckon so," I said. "A flat tire."

"You admit that? You concede that a track of that kind would have to be there, *if* you had a flat tire?"

I pushed back my Stetson, and scratched my head. I looked at Bob, frowning a little. "I don't guess I see what you boys are driving at," I said. "What's this all about, Bob?"

Of course, I did see. I saw that I'd made one hell of a bonehead play. I'd guessed it as soon as I saw the track through the weeds, and I had an answer ready. But I couldn't come out with it too fast. It had to be done easy-like.

"This is Howard's show," said the sheriff. "Maybe you'd better answer him, Lou."

"Okay," I shrugged. "I've already said it once. A flat tire makes that kind of track."

"Do you know," said Hendricks slowly, "when that track was made?"

"I ain't got the slightest idea," I said. "All I know is that my car didn't make it."

"You're a damned li— *Huh?*" Hendricks' mouth dropped open foolishly. "B-but—"

"I didn't have a flat when I turned off the highway."

"Now, wait a minute! You—"

"Maybe you better wait a minute," Sheriff Bob interrupted. "I don't recollect Lou tellin' us his tire went flat here on Derrick Road. Don't recall his sayin' anything of the kind."

"If I did say it," I said, "I sure as heck didn't mean to. I knew I had a puncture, sure; I felt the car sway a little. But I turned off in the lane before the tire could really go down."

Bob nodded and glanced at Hendricks. The county attorney suddenly got busy lighting a cigarette. I don't know which was redder—his face or the sun pushing up over the hills.

I scratched my head again. "Well," I said, "I reckon it's none of my business. But I sure hope you fellows didn't chew up a good tire makin' that track."

Hendricks' mouth was working. Bob's old eyes sparkled. Off in the distance somewhere, maybe three-four miles away, there was a *suck-whush* as a mudhog drilling pump began to growl. Suddenly, the sheriff whuffed and coughed and let out a wild whoop of laughter.

"Haw, haw, haw!" he boomed. "Doggone it, Howard, if this ain't the funniest—haw, haw, haw—"

And then Hendricks started laughing, too. Restrained, uncomfortable, at first; then, plain unashamed laughter. I stood looking on, grinning puzzledly, like a guy who wanted to join in but didn't know the score.

I was glad now that I'd made that bonehead mistake. When a man's rope slides off you once, he's mighty cautious about making a second throw.

Hendricks slapped me on the back. "I'm a damned fool, Lou. I should have known better."

"Say," I said, letting it dawn on me at last. "You don't mean you thought I—"

"Of course, we didn't think so," said Bob, warmly. "Nothing of the kind."

"It was just something that had to be looked into," Hendricks explained. "We had to have an answer for it. Now, you didn't talk much to Conway last night, did you?"

"No," I said. "It didn't seem to me like a very good time to do much talking."

"Well, I talked to him, Bob, I did. Rather he talked to us. And he's really raring and tearing. This woman—what's her name, Lakeland?—is as good as dead. The doctors say she'll never regain consciousness, so Conway isn't going to be able to lay the blame for this mess on her. Naturally, then, he'll want to stick someone else with it; he'll be snatching at straws. That's why we have to head him off on anything that looks— uh—even mildly peculiar."

"But, shucks," I said, "anyone could see what happened. Elmer'd been drinking, and he tried to push her around, and—"

"Sure. But Conway don't want to admit that. And he won't admit it, if there's any way out."

We all rode in the front seat going back to town. I was in the middle, squeezed in between the sheriff and Hendricks; and all of a sudden a crazy notion came over me. Maybe I hadn't fooled 'em. Maybe they were putting on an act, just like I was. Maybe that was why they'd put me in the middle, so I couldn't jump out of the car.

It was a crazy idea, of course, and it was gone in a moment. But I started a little before I could catch myself.

"Feelin' twitchy?" said Bob.

"Just hunger pains," I grinned. "I haven't eaten since yesterday afternoon."

"Wouldn't mind a bite myself," Bob nodded. "How about you, Howard?"

"Might be a good idea. Mind stopping by the courthouse first?"

"Huh-uh," said Bob. "We go by there and we're apt not to get away. You can call from the restaurant—call my office, too, while you're at it."

Word of what had happened was already all over town, and there was a lot of whispering and gawking as we pulled up in front of the restaurant. I mean, there was a lot of whispering and gawking from the newcomers, the oil workers and so on. The old timers just nodded and went on about their business.

Hendricks stopped to use the telephone, and Bob and I sat down in a booth. We ordered ham and eggs all around, and pretty soon Hendricks came back.

"That Conway!" he snapped, sliding in across from us. "Now he wants to fly that woman into Fort Worth. Says she can't get the right kind of medical attention here."

"Yeah?" Bob looked down at the menu, casually. "What time is he takin' her?"

"I'm not at all sure that he is! I'm the man that has the say-so on handling this case. Why, she hasn't even been booked yet, let alone arraigned. We haven't had a chance."

"Can't see that it makes much difference," said Bob, "as long as she's going to die."

"That's not the point! The point is—"

"Yeah, sure," drawled Bob. "You like to take a little trip into Fort Worth, Lou? Maybe I'll go along myself."

"Why, I guess I could," I said.

"I reckon we'll do that, then. Okay, Howard? That'll take care of the technicalities for you."

The waitress set food in front of us, and Bob picked up his knife and fork. I felt his boot kick mine under the table. Hendricks knew how things stood, but he was too much of a phony to admit it. He had to go on playing the big hero—the county attorney that didn't take orders from anyone.

"Now, see here, Bob. Maybe I'm new here, as you see it; maybe I've got a lot to learn. But, by God, I know the law and—"

"So do I," the sheriff nodded. "The one that ain't on the books. Conway wasn't asking you if he could take her to Fort Worth. He was telling you. Did he mention what time?"

"Well"—Hendricks swallowed heavily—"ten this morning, he thought. He wanted to—he's chartering one of the air-line's twin-motor jobs, and they've got to fit it up with oxygen and a—"

"Uh-huh. Well, that ought to be all right. Lou and me'll have time to scrub up a little and pack a bag. I'll drop you off at your place, Lou, as soon as we finish here."

"Fine," I said.

Hendricks didn't say anything.

After a minute or two, Bob glanced at him and raised his eyebrows. "Something wrong with your eggs, son? Better eat 'em before they get cold."

Hendricks heaved a big sigh, and began to eat.

Nine

BOB and I were at the airport quite a bit ahead of time, so we went ahead and got on the plane and made ourselves comfortable. Some workmen were pounding around in the baggage compartment, fixing things up according to the doctor's instructions, but tired as we were it would have taken more than that to keep us awake. Bob began to nod, first. Then I closed my eyes, figuring to just rest them a little. And I guess I must have gone right to sleep. I didn't even know when we took off.

One minute I was closing my eyes. The next, it seemed like, Bob was shaking me and pointing out the window.

"There she is, Lou. There's cow town."

I looked out and down. I felt kind of disappointed. I'd never been out of the county before, and now that I was sure Joyce wasn't going to live I could have enjoyed seeing the sights. As it was I hadn't seen anything. I'd wasted all my time sleeping.

"Where's Mr. Conway?" I asked.

"Back in the baggage compartment. I just went back for a look myself."

"She—she's still unconscious?"

"Uh-huh, and she ain't ever going to be any other way if

you ask me." He shook his head solemnly. "Conway don't know when he's well off. If that no-account Elmer wasn't already dead, he'd be swingin' from a tree about now."

"Yeah," I said. "It's pretty bad all right."

"Don't know what would possess a man to do a thing like that. Dogged if I do! Don't see how he could be drunk enough or mean enough to do it."

"I guess it's my fault," I said. "I shouldn't have ever let her stay in town."

"We-el . . . I told you to use your own judgment, and she was a mighty cute little trick from all I hear. I'd probably have let her stay myself if I'd been in your place."

"I'm sure sorry, Bob," I said. "I sure wish I'd come to you instead of trying to handle this blackmail deal myself."

"Yeah," he nodded slowly, "but I reckon we've been over that ground enough. It's done now, and there's nothing we can do about it. Talking and fretting about might-have-beens won't get us anywhere."

"No," I said. "I guess there's no use crying over spilled milk."

The plane began to circle and lose altitude, and we fastened our seat belts. A couple of minutes later we were skimming along the landing field, and a police car and ambulance were keeping pace with us.

The plane stopped, and the pilot came out of his compartment and unlocked the door. Bob and I got out, and watched while the doctor supervised the unloading of the stretcher. The upper part of it was closed in kind of a little tent, and all I could see was the outline of her body under the sheet. Then I couldn't even see that; they were hustling her off toward the ambulance. And a heavy hand came down on my shoulder.

"Lou," said Chester Conway. "You come with me in the police car."

"Well," I said, glancing at Bob. "I kind of figured on—"

"You come with me," he repeated. "Sheriff, you ride in the ambulance. We'll see you at the hospital."

Bob pushed back his Stetson, and gave him a hard sharp look. Then his face sort of sagged and he turned and walked away, his scuffed boots dragging against the pavement.

I'd been pretty worried about how to act around Conway.

Now, seeing the way he'd pushed old Bob Maples around, I was just plain sore. I jerked away from his hand and got into the police car. I kept my head turned as Conway climbed in and slammed the door.

The ambulance started up, and headed off the field. We followed it. Conway leaned forward and closed the glass partition between our seat and the driver's.

"Didn't like that, did you?" he grunted. "Well, there may be a lot of things you don't like before this is over. I've got the reputation of my dead boy at stake, understand? My own reputation. I'm looking out for that and nothing but that, and I ain't standing on etiquette. I'm not letting someone's tender feelings get in my way."

"I don't suppose you would," I said. "It'd be pretty hard to start in at your time of life."

I wished, immediately, that I hadn't said it; I was giving myself away, you see. But he didn't seem to have heard me. Like always, he wasn't hearing anything he didn't want to hear.

"They're operating on that woman as soon as she gets to the hospital," he went on. "If she pulls through the operation, she'll be able to talk by tonight. I want you there at that time—just as soon as she comes out of the anaesthetic."

"Well?" I said.

"Bob Maples is all right, but he's too old to be on his toes. He's liable to foul up the works right when you need him most. That's why I'm letting him go on now when it don't matter whether anyone's around or not."

"I don't know as I understand you," I said. "You mean—"

"I've got rooms reserved at a hotel. I'll drop you off there, and you stay there until I call you. Get some rest, understand? Get rested up good, so's you'll be on your toes and raring to go when the time comes."

"All right," I shrugged, "but I slept all the way up on the plane."

"Sleep some more, then. You may have to be up all night."

The hotel was on West Seventh Street, a few blocks from the hospital; and Conway had engaged a whole suite of rooms. The assistant manager of the place went up with me and the bellboy, and a couple of minutes after they left a waiter brought in a tray of whiskey and ice. And right behind him came another waiter with a flock of sandwiches and coffee.

I poured myself a nice drink, and took it over by the window. I sat down in a big easy chair, and propped my boots up on the radiator. I leaned back, grinning.

Conway was a big shot, all right. He could push you around and make you like it. He could have places like this, with people jumping sideways to wait on him. He could have everything but what he wanted—his son and a good name.

His son had beaten a whore to death, and she'd killed him; and he'd never be able to live it down. Not if he lived to be a hundred and I damned well hoped he would.

I ate part of a clubhouse sandwich, but it didn't seem to set so well. So I fixed another big drink and took it over to the window. I felt kind of restless and uneasy. I wished I could get out and wander around the town.

Fort Worth is the beginning of West Texas, and I wouldn't have felt conspicuous, dressed as I was, like I would have in Dallas or Houston. I could have had a fine time—seen something new for a change. And instead I had to stay here by myself, doing nothing, seeing nothing, thinking the same old thoughts.

It was like there was a plot against me almost. I'd done something wrong, way back when I was a kid, and I'd never been able to get away from it. I'd had my nose rubbed in it day after day until, like an overtrained dog, I'd started crapping out of pure fright. And, now, here I was—

I poured another drink . . .

—Here I was, now, but it wouldn't be like this much longer. Joyce was bound to die if she wasn't dead already. I'd got rid of her and I'd got rid of *it*—the sickness—when I did it. And just as soon as things quieted down, I'd quit my job and sell the house and Dad's practice and pull out.

Amy Stanton? Well—I shook my head—she wasn't going to stop me. She wasn't going to keep me chained there in Central City. I didn't know just how I'd break away from her, but I knew darned well that I would.

Some way. Somehow.

More or less to kill time, I took a long hot bath; and

afterwards I tried the sandwiches and coffee again. I paced around the room, eating and drinking coffee, moving from window to window. I wished we weren't up so high so's I could see a little something.

I tried taking a nap, and that was no good. I got a shine cloth out of the bathroom and began rubbing at my boots. I'd got one brushed up real good and was starting on the toe of the second when Bob Maples came in.

He said hello, casually, and fixed himself a drink. He sat down, looking into the glass, twirling the ice around and around.

"I was sure sorry about what happened there at the airport, Bob," I said. "I reckon you know I wanted to stick with you."

"Yeah," he said, shortly.

"I let Conway know I didn't like it," I said.

And he said, "Yeah," again. "Forget it. Just drop it, will you?"

"Well, sure," I nodded. "Whatever you say, Bob."

I watched him out of the corner of my eye, as I went ahead rubbing the boot. He acted mad and worried, almost disgusted you might say. But I was pretty sure it wasn't over anything I'd done. In fact, I couldn't see that Conway had done enough to upset him like this.

"Is your rheumatism bothering you again?" I said. "Why don't you face around on that straight chair where I can get at your shoulder muscles, and I'll—"

He raised his head and looked up at me. And his eyes were clear, but somehow there seemed to be tears behind them. Slowly, softly, like he was talking to himself, he began to speak.

"I know what you are, don't I, Lou? Know you backwards and forwards. Known you since you was kneehigh to a grasshopper, and I never knowed a bad thing about you. Know just what you're goin' to say and do, no matter what you're up against. Like there at the airport—seeing Conway order me around. A lot of men in your place would have got a big bang out of that, but I knew you wouldn't. I knew you'd feel a lot more hurt about it than I did. That's the way you are, and you wouldn't know how to be any other way . . ."

"Bob," I said. "You got something on your mind, Bob?"

"It'll keep," he said. "I reckon it'll have to keep for a while. I just wanted you to know that I—I—"

"Yes, Bob?"

"It'll keep," he repeated. "Like I said, it'll have to keep." And he clicked the ice in his glass, staring down at it. "That Howard Hendricks," he went on. "Now, Howard ought to've known better'n to put you through that foolishness this morning. 'Course, he's got his job to do, same as I got mine, and a man can't let friendship stand in the way of duty. But—"

"Oh, hell, Bob," I said. "I didn't think anything of that."

"Well, I did. I got to thinking about it this afternoon after we left the airport. I thought about how you'd have acted if you'd have been in my place and me in yours. Oh, I reckon you'd have been pleasant and friendly, because that's the way you're built. But you wouldn't have left any doubt as to where you stood. You'd have said, 'Look, now, Bob Maples is a friend of mine, and I know he's straight as a string. So if there's something we want to know, let's just up and ask him. Let's don't play no little two-bit sheepherders' tricks on him like he was on one side of the fence and we was on the other.' . . . That's what you'd have done. But me— Well, I don't know, Lou. Maybe I'm behind the times. Maybe I'm getting too old for this job."

It looked to me like he might have something there. He was getting old and unsure of himself, and Conway had probably given him a hell of a riding that I didn't know about.

"You had some trouble at the hospital, Bob?" I said.

"Yeah," he hesitated. "I had some trouble." He got up and poured more whiskey into his glass. Then, he moved over to the window and stood rocking on his heels, his back turned to me. "She's dead, Lou. She never came out of the ether."

"Well," I said. "We all knew she didn't stand a chance. Everyone but Conway, and he was just too stubborn to see reason."

He didn't say anything. I walked over to the window by him and put my arm around his shoulders.

"Look, Bob," I said. "I don't know what Conway said to you, but don't let it get you down. Where the hell does he get off at, anyway? He wasn't even going to have us come along on this trip; we had to deal ourselves in. Then, when we get back here, he wants us to jump whenever he hollers frog, and he raises hell when things don't go to suit him."

He shrugged a little, or maybe he just took a deep breath. I let my arm slide from his shoulders, hesitated a moment, thinking he was about to say something, then went into the bathroom and closed the door. When a man's feeling low, sometimes the best thing to do is leave him alone.

I sat down on the edge of the tub, and lighted a cigar. I sat thinking—standing outside of myself—thinking about myself and Bob Maples. He'd always been pretty decent to me, and I liked him. But no more, I suppose, than I liked a lot of other people. When it came right down to cases, he was just one of hundreds of people I knew and was friendly with. And yet here I was, fretting about his problems instead of my own.

Of course, that might be partly because I'd known my problems were pretty much settled. I'd known that Joyce couldn't live, that she wasn't going to talk. She might have regained consciousness for a while, but she sure as hell wouldn't have talked; not after what had happened to her face . . . But knowing that I was safe couldn't entirely explain my concern for him. Because I'd been damned badly rattled after the murder. I hadn't been able to reason clearly, to accept the fact that I *had* to be safe. Yet I'd tried to help the Greek's boy, Johnnie Pappas.

The door slammed open, and I looked up. Bob grinned at me broadly, his face flushed, whiskey slopping to the floor from his glass.

"Hey," he said, "you runnin' out on me, Lou? Come on in here an' keep me company."

"Sure, Bob," I said. "Sure, I will." And I went back into the living room with him. He flopped down into a chair, and he drained his drink at a gulp.

"Let's do something, Lou. Let's go out and paint old cow town red. Just me'n you, huh?"

"What about Conway?"

"T'hell with him. He's got some business here; stayin' over for a few days. We'll check our bags somewheres, so's we won't have to run into him again, and then we'll have a party."

He made a grab for the bottle, and got it on the second try. I took it away from him, and filled his glass myself.

"That sounds fine, Bob," I said. "I'd sure like to do that. But shouldn't we be getting back to Central City? I mean, with Conway feeling the way he does, it might not look good for us—"

"I said t'hell with him. Said it, an' that's what I meant."

"Well, sure. But—"

"Done enough for Conway. Done too much. Done more'n any white man should. Now, c'mon and slide into them boots an' let's go."

I said, sure, sure I would. I'd do just that. But I had a bad callus, and I'd have to trim it first. So maybe, as long as he'd have to wait, he'd better lie down and take a little nap.

He did it, after a little grumbling and protesting. I called the railroad station, and reserved a bedroom on the eight o'clock train to Central City. It would cost us a few dollars personally, since the county would only pay for first-class Pullman fare. But I figured we were going to need privacy.

I was right. I woke him up at six-thirty, to give him plenty of time to get ready, and he seemed worse off than before his nap. I couldn't get him to take a bath. He wouldn't drink any coffee or eat. Instead, he started hitting the whiskey again; and when we left the hotel he took a full bottle with him. By the time I got him on the train, I was as frazzled as a cow's hide under a branding iron. I wondered what in the name of God Conway had said to him.

I wondered, and, hell, I should have known. Because he'd as good as told me. It was as plain as the nose on my face, and I'd just been too close to it to see it.

Maybe, though, it was a good thing I didn't know. For there was nothing to be done about it, nothing I could do. And I'd have been sweating blood.

Well. That was about the size of my trip to the big town. My first trip outside the county. Straight to the hotel from the plane. Straight to the train from the hotel. Then, the long ride home at night—when there was nothing to see—closed in with a crying drunk.

Once, around midnight, a little while before he went to

sleep, his mind must have wandered. For, all of a sudden, his fist wobbled out and poked me in the chest.

"Hey," I said. "Watch yourself, Bob."

"Wash—watch y'self," he mumbled. "Stop man with grin, smile worthwhile—s-stop all a' stuff spilt milk n' so on. Wha' you do that for, anyway."

"Aw," I said. "I was only kidding, Bob."

"T-tell you somethin'," he said. "T-tell you somethin' I bet you never thought of."

"Yeah?"

"It's—it's always lightest j-just before the dark."

Tired as I was, I laughed. "You got it wrong, Bob," I said. "You mean—"

"Huh-uh," he said. "You got it wrong."

Ten

WE GOT into Central City around six in the morning, and Bob took a taxi straight home. He was sick; really sick, not just hung-over. He was too old a man to pack away the load he'd had.

I stopped by the office, but everything was pretty quiet, according to the night deputy, so I went on home, too. I had a lot more hours in than I'd been paid for. No one could have faulted me if I'd taken a week off. Which, naturally, I didn't intend to do.

I changed into some fresh clothes, and made some scrambled eggs and coffee. As I sat down to eat, the phone rang.

I supposed it was the office, or maybe Amy checking up on me; she'd have to call early or wait until four when her school-day was over. I went to the phone, trying to think of some dodge to get out of seeing her, and when I heard Joe Rothman's voice it kind of threw me.

"Know who it is, Lou?" he said. "Remember our *late* talk."

"Sure," I said. "About the—uh—building situation."

"I'd ask you to drop around tonight, but I have to take a little jaunt to San Angelo. Would you mind if I stopped by your house a few minutes?"

"Well," I said, "I guess you could. Is it something important?"

"A small thing, but important, Lou. A matter of a few words of reassurance."

"Well, maybe I could—"

"I'm sure you could, but I think I'd better *see* you," he said; and he clicked up the receiver.

I hung up my phone, and went back to my breakfast. It was still early. The chances were that no one would see him. Anyway, he wasn't a criminal, opinion in some quarters to the contrary.

He came about five minutes later. I offered him some breakfast, not putting much warmth into the invitation since I didn't want him hanging around; and he said, no, thanks, but sat down at the table with me.

"Well, Lou," he said, starting to roll a cigarette. "I imagine you know what I want to hear."

"I think so," I nodded. "Consider it said."

"The very discreet newspaper stories are correct in their hints? He tried to dish it out and got it thrown back at him?"

"That's the way it looks. I can't think of any other explanation."

"I couldn't help wondering," he said, moistening the paper of his cigarette. "I couldn't help wondering how a woman with her face caved in and her neck broken could score six bull's-eyes on a man, even one as large as the late unlamented Elmer Conway."

He looked up slowly until his eyes met mine. I shrugged. "Probably she didn't fire all the shots at one time. She was shooting him while he was punching her. Hell, she'd hardly stand there and take it until he got through, and then start shooting."

"It doesn't seem that she would, does it?" he nodded. "Yet from the smattering of information I can gather, she must have done exactly that. She was still alive after he died; and almost any one—well, two—of the bullets she put into him was enough to lay him low. Ergo, she must have acquired the broken neck et cetera, before she did her shooting."

I shook my head. I had to do something to get my eyes away from his.

"You said you wanted reassurance," I said. "You—you—"

"The genuine article, Lou; no substitutes accepted. And I'm still waiting to get it."

"I don't know where you get off at questioning me," I said. "The sheriff and the county attorney are satisfied. That's all I care about."

"That's the way you see it, eh?"

"That's the way I see it."

"Well, I'll tell you how I see it. I get off questioning you because I'm involved in the matter. Not directly, perhaps, but—"

"But not indirectly, either."

"Exactly. I knew you had it in for the Conways; in fact, I did everything I could to set you against the old man. Morally—perhaps even legally—I share the responsibility for any untoward action you might take. At any rate, we'll say, I and the unions I head could be placed in a very unfavorable light."

"You said it," I said. "It's your own statement."

"But don't ride that horse too hard, Lou. I don't hold still for murder. Incidentally, what's the score as of to date? One or two?"

"She's dead. She died yesterday afternoon."

"I won't buy it, Lou—if it was murder. Your doing. I can't say offhand what I will do, but I won't let you ride. I couldn't. You'd wind up by getting me into something even worse."

"Oh, hell," I said. "What are we—"

"The girl's dead, and Elmer's dead. So regardless of how funny things look—and this deal should have put the courthouse crowd into hysterics—they can't prove anything. If they knew what I know, about your having a motive—"

"For killing her? Why would I want to do that?"

"Well"—he began to slow down a little—"leave her out of it. Say that she was just an instrument for getting back at Conway. A piece of stage setting."

"You know that doesn't make sense," I said. "About the other, this so-called motive—I'd had it for six years; I'd known about Mike's accident that long. Why would I wait six years, and then all of a sudden decide to pull this? Beat some poor whore to a pulp just to get at Chester Conway's son. Now, tell me if that sounds logical. Just tell me, Joe."

Rothman frowned thoughtfully, his fingers drumming upon the table. "No," he said, slowly. "It doesn't sound logical. That's the trouble. The man who walked away from that job—if he walked away—"

"You know he didn't, Joe."

"So you say."

"So I say," I said. "So everyone says. You'd say so yourself, if you didn't know how I felt about the Conways. Put that out of your mind once, and what do you have? Why, just a double murder—two people getting in a brawl and killing each other—under kind of puzzling circumstances."

He smiled wryly. "I'd call that the understatement of the century, Lou."

"I can't tell you what happened," I said, "because I wasn't there. But I know there are flukes in murder the same as there are in anything else. A man crawls a mile with his brains blown out. A woman calls the police after she's shot through the heart. A man is hanged and poisoned and chopped up and shot, and he goes right on living. Don't ask me why those things are. I don't know. But I do know they happen, and so do you."

Rothman looked at me steadily. Then, his head jerked a little, nodding.

"I guess so, Lou," he said. "I guess you're clean, at least. I've been sitting here watching you, putting together everything I know about you, and I couldn't make it tally with the picture I've got of *that* guy. Screwy as things are, that would be even screwier. You don't fit the part, to coin a phrase."

"What do I say to that?" I said.

"Not a thing, Lou. I should be thanking you for lifting a considerable load from my mind. However, if you don't mind my going into your debt a little further . . . ?"

"Yes?"

"What's the lowdown, just for my own information? I'll concede that you didn't have a killing hate for Conway, but you did hate him. What were you trying to pull off?"

I'd been expecting that question since the night I'd talked to him. I had the answer all ready.

"The money was supposed to be a payoff to get her out of

town. Conway was paying her to go away and leave Elmer alone. Actually—"

"—Elmer was going to leave with her, right?" Rothman got up, and put on his hat. "Well, I can't find it in my heart to chide you for the stunt, despite its unfortunate outcome. I almost wish I'd thought of it."

"Aw," I said, "it wasn't nothing much. Just a matter of a will finding a way."

"Ooof!" he said. "What are Conway's feelings, by the way?"

"Well, I don't think he feels real good," I said.

"Probably something he ate," he nodded. "Don't you imagine? But watch that stuff, Lou. Watch it. Save it for those birds."

He left.

I got the newspapers out of the yard—yesterday afternoon's and this morning's—poured more coffee, and sat back down at the table.

As usual, the papers had given me all of the breaks. Instead of making me look like a boob or a busybody, which they could have done easily enough, they had me down as a kind of combination J. Edgar Hoover-Lombroso, "the shrewd sheriff's sleuth whose unselfish intervention in the affair came to naught, due only to the unpredictable quirks of all-too-human behavior."

I laughed, choking on the coffee I was starting to swallow. In spite of all I'd been through, I was beginning to feel nice and relaxed. Joyce was dead. Not even Rothman suspected me. And when you passed clean with *that* guy, you didn't have anything to worry about. It was sort of an acid test, you might say.

I debated calling up the newspapers and complimenting them on their "accuracy." I often did that, spread a little sunshine, you know, and they ate it up. I could say something— I laughed—I could say something about truth being stranger than fiction. And maybe add something like—well—murder will out. Or crime doesn't pay. Or . . . or the best laid plans of mice and men.

I stopped laughing.

I was supposed to be over that stuff. Rothman had warned me about it, and it'd got Bob Maples' goat. But—

Well, why shouldn't I, if I wanted to? If it helped to take the tension out of me? It was in character. It fitted in with that dull good-natured guy who couldn't do anything bad if he tried. Rothman himself had remarked that no matter how screwy things looked, seeing me as a murderer was even screwier. And my talk was a big part of me—part of the guy that had thrown 'em all off the trail. If I suddenly stopped talking that way, what would people think?

Why, I just about had to keep on whether I wanted to or not. The choice was out of my hand. But, of course, I'd take it kind of easy. Not overdo it.

I reasoned it all out, and wound up still feeling good. But I decided not to call the newspapers, after all. The stories had been more than fair to me, but it hadn't cost 'em anything; they had to fill space some way. And I didn't care too much about a number of the details; what they said about Joyce, for example. She wasn't a "shabby sister of sin." She hadn't, for Christ's sake, "loved not wisely but too well." She was just a cute little ol' gal who'd latched onto the wrong guy, or the right guy in the wrong place; she hadn't wanted anything else, nothing else. And she'd got it. Nothing.

Amy Stanton called a little after eight o'clock, and I asked her to come over that night. The best way to stall, I figured, was not to stall; not to put up any opposition to her. If I didn't hang back, she'd stop pushing me. And, after all, she couldn't get married on an hour's notice. There'd be all sorts of things to attend to, and discuss—God, how they'd have to be discussed! even the size of the douche bag to take along on our honeymoon! And long before she was through, I'd be in shape to pull out of Central City.

After I'd finished talking to her, I went into Dad's laboratory, lighted the Bunsen burner and put an intravenous needle and an ordinary hypodermic on to boil. Then, I looked along the shelves until I found a carton each of male hormone, ACTH, B-complex and sterile water. Dad's stock of drugs was getting old, of course, but the pharmaceutical houses still kept sending us samples. The samples were what I used.

I mixed up an intravenous of the ACTH, B-complex and water and put it into my right arm. (Dad had a theory that shots should never be given on the same side as the heart.) I shot the hormone into my hip . . . and I was set for the night. Amy wouldn't be disappointed again. She wouldn't have anything to wonder about. Whether my trouble had been psychosomatic or real, the result of tension or too much Joyce, I wouldn't have it tonight. Little Amy would be tamed down for a week.

I went up to my bedroom and went to sleep. I woke up at noon, when the refinery whistles began to blow; then, dozed off again and slept until after two. Some times, most of the time, I should say, I can sleep eight-ten hours and still not feel rested. Well, I'm not tired, exactly, but I hate to get up. I just want to stay where I am, and not talk to anyone or see anyone.

Today, though, it was different; just the opposite. I could hardly wait to get cleaned up, and be out and doing something.

I showered and shaved, standing under the cold water a long time because that medicine was really working. I got into a clean tan shirt, and put on a new black bow tie, and took a freshly pressed blue suit out of the closet.

I fixed and ate a bite of lunch, and called Sheriff Maples' house.

His wife answered the phone. She said that Bob was feeling kind of poorly, and that the doctor thought he'd better stay in bed for a day or two. He was asleep, right then, and she kind of hated to wake him up. But if there was anything important . . .

"I just wondered how he was," I said. "Thought I might drop by for a few minutes."

"Well, that's mighty nice of you, Lou. I'll tell him you called when he wakes up. Maybe you can come by tomorrow if he's not up and around by then."

"Fine," I said.

I tried to read a while, but I couldn't concentrate. I wondered what to do with myself, now that I did have a day off. I couldn't shoot pool or bowl. It didn't look good for a cop to hang around pool halls and bowling alleys. It didn't look good for 'em to go into bars. It didn't look good for them to be seen in a show in the daytime.

I could drive around. Take a ride by myself. That was about all.

Gradually, the good feeling began to leave me.

I got the car out, and headed for the courthouse.

Hank Butterby, the office deputy, was reading the paper, his boots up on the desk, his jaws moving on a cud of tobacco. He asked me if it was hot enough for me, and why'n hell I didn't stay home when I had a chance. I said, well, you know how it is, Hank.

"Nice goin'," he said, nodding at the paper. "Right pretty little piece they got about you. I was just fixin' to clip it out and save it for you."

The stupid son-of-a-bitch was always doing that. Not just stories about me, but everything. He'd clip out cartoons and weather reports and crappy poems and health columns. Every goddam thing under the sun. He couldn't read a paper without a pair of scissors.

"I'll tell you what," I said. "I'll autograph it for you, and you keep it. Maybe it'll be valuable some day."

"Well"—he slanted his eyes at me, and looked quickly away again—"I wouldn't want to put you to no trouble, Lou."

"No trouble at all," I said. "Here let me have it." I scrawled my name along the margin, and handed it back to him. "Just don't let this get around," I said. "If I have to do the same thing for the other fellows, it'll run the value down."

He stared at the paper, glassy-eyed, like maybe it was going to bite him. "Uh"—there it went; he'd forgot and swallowed his spit—"you really think . . . ?"

"Here's what you do," I said, getting my elbows down on the desk and whispering. "Go out to one of the refineries, and get 'em to steam you out a steel drum. Then—you know anyone that'll lend you a welding torch?"

"Yeah"—he was whispering too. "I think I can borry one."

"Well, cut the drum in two, cut it around twice, rather, so's you'll have kind of a lid. Then put that autographed clipping inside—the only one in existence, Hank!—and weld it back together again. Sixty or seventy years from now, you can take it to some museum and they'll pay you a fortune for it."

"Cripes!" he said. "You keepin' a drum like that, Lou? Want me to pick you up one?"

"Oh, I guess not," I said. "I probably won't live that long."

Eleven

I HESITATED in the corridor in front of Howard Hendricks' office, and he glanced up from his desk and waved to me.

"Hello, there, Lou. Come on in and sit a minute."

I went in, nodding to his secretary, and pulled a chair up to the desk. "Just talked to Bob's wife a little while ago," I said. "He's not feeling so good."

"So I hear." He struck a match for my cigar. "Well, it doesn't matter much. I mean there's nothing more to be done on this Conway case. All we can do is sit tight; just be available in the event that Conway starts tossing his weight around. I imagine he'll become resigned to the situation before too long."

"It was too bad about the girl dying," I said.

"Oh, I don't know, Lou," he shrugged. "I can't see that she'd have been able to tell us anything we don't already know. Frankly, and just between the two of us, I'm rather relieved. Conway wouldn't have been satisfied unless she went to the chair with all the blame pinned on her. I'd have hated to be a party to it."

"Yeah," I said. "That wouldn't have been so good."

"Though of course I would have, Lou, if she'd lived. I mean, I'd have prosecuted her to the hilt."

He was leaning backwards to be friendly since our brush the day before. I was his old pal, and he was letting me know his innermost feelings.

"I wonder, Howard . . ."

"Yes, Lou?"

"Well, I guess I'd better not say it," I said. "Maybe you don't feel like I do about things."

"Oh, I'm sure I do. I've always felt we had a great deal in common. What is it you wanted to tell me?"

His eyes strayed a second from mine, and his mouth quirked a little. I knew his secretary had winked at him.

"Well, it's like this," I said. "Now, I've always felt we were one big happy family here. Us people that work for the county . . ."

"Uh-huh. One big happy family, eh?" His eyes strayed again. "Go on, Lou."

"We're kind of brothers under the skin . . ."

"Y-yes."

"We're all in the same boat, and we've got to put our shoulders to the wheel and pull together."

His throat seemed to swell all of a sudden, and he yanked a handkerchief from his pocket. Then he whirled around in his chair, his back to me, coughing and strangling and sputtering. I heard his secretary get up, and hurry out. Her high heels went tap-tapping down the corridor, moving faster and faster toward the woman's john until she was almost running.

I hoped she pissed in her drawers.

I hoped that chunk of shrapnel under his ribs had punctured a lung. That chunk of shrapnel had cost the taxpayers a hell of a pile of dough. He'd got elected to office talking about that shrapnel. Not cleaning up the county and seeing that everyone got a fair shake. Just shrapnel.

He finally straightened up and turned around, and I told him he'd better take care of that cold. "I'll tell you what I always do," I said. "I take the water from a boiled onion, and squeeze a big lemon into it. Well, maybe a middling-size lemon and a small one if—"

"Lou!" he said sharply.

"Yeah?" I said.

"I appreciate your sentiments—your interest—but I'll have to ask you to come to the point. What did you wish to tell me, anyway?"

"Oh, it wasn't any—"

"Please, Lou!"

"Well, here's what I was wondering about," I said. And I told him. The same thing that Rothman had wondered about. I put it into my words, drawling it out, slow and awkward.

That would give him something to worry over. Something

besides flat-tire tracks. And the beauty of it was he couldn't do much but worry.

"Jesus," he said, slowly. "It's right there, isn't it? Right out in the open, when you look at it right. It's one of those things that are so plain and simple you don't see 'em. No matter how you turn it around, he just about had to kill her after he was dead. After he couldn't do it!"

"Or vice versa," I said.

He wiped his forehead, excited but kind of sick-looking. Trying to trap old simple Lou with the tire tracks was one thing. That was about his speed. But this had him thrown for a loop.

"You know what this means, Lou?"

"Well, it doesn't necessarily mean that," I said, and I gave him an out. I rehashed the business about fluke deaths that I'd given to Rothman. "That's probably the way it was. Just one of those damned funny things that no one can explain."

"Yeah," he said. "Of course. That's bound to be it. You—uh—you haven't mentioned this to anyone, Lou?"

I shook my head. "Just popped into my mind a little while ago. 'Course, if Conway's still riled up when he gets back, I—"

"I don't believe I would, Lou. I really don't think that'd be wise, at all."

"You mean I should tell Bob, first? Oh, I intended to do that. I wouldn't go over Bob's head."

"No, Lou," he said, "that isn't what I mean. Bob isn't well. He's already taken an awful pounding from Conway. I don't think we should trouble him with anything else. Something which, as you point out, is doubtless of no consequence."

"Well," I said, "if it doesn't amount to anything, I don't see why—"

"Let's just keep it to ourselves, Lou, for the time being, at least. Just sit tight and see what happens. After all, what else can we do? What have we got to go on?"

"Nothing much," I said. "Probably nothing at all."

"Exactly! I couldn't have stated it better."

"I tell you what we might do," I said. "It wouldn't be too hard to round up all the men that visited her. Probably ain't more than thirty or forty of 'em, her being a kind of high-priced gal. Bob and us, our crowd, we could round 'em up, and you could . . ."

I wish you could have seen him sweat. Rounding up thirty or forty well-to-do citizens wouldn't be any skin off our ass, the sheriff's office. He'd be the one to study the evidence, and ask for indictments. By the time he was through, he'd be *through*. He couldn't be elected dog-catcher, if shrapnel was running out his eyeballs.

Well, though, I didn't really want him to do it any more than he wanted to. The case was closed, right on Elmer Conway's neck, and it was a darned good idea to leave it that way. So, that being the case, and seeing it was about supper time, I allowed him to convince me. I said I didn't have much sense about such things, and I was sure grateful for his setting me straight. And that's the way it ended. Almost.

I gave him my recipe for curing coughs before I left.

I sauntered down to my car, whistling; thinking of what a fine afternoon it had been, after all, and what a hell of a kick there'd be in talking about it.

Ten minutes later I was out on Derrick Road, making a U-turn back toward town.

I don't know why. Well, I do know. She was the only person I could have talked to, who'd have understood what I was talking about. But I knew she wasn't there. I knew she'd never be there again, there or anywhere. She was gone and I knew it. So . . . I don't know why.

I drove back toward town, back toward the rambling old two-story house and the barn where the rats squealed. And once I said, "I'm sorry, baby." I said it out loud. "You'll never know how sorry I am." Then I said, "You understand, don't you? In a few months more I couldn't have stopped. I'd have lost all control and . . ."

A butterfly struck lightly against the wind-screen, and fluttered away again. I went back to my whistling.

It had sure been a fine afternoon.

I was about out of groceries, so I stopped at a grocery and picked up a few, including a steak for my dinner. I went home and fixed myself a whopping big meal, and ate every bite of it. That B-complex was really doing its job. So was the other stuff. I began to actually look forward to seeing Amy. I began to want her bad.

I washed and wiped the dishes. I mopped the kitchen floor, dragging the job out as long as I could. I wrung the mop out and hung it up on the back porch, and came back and looked at the clock. The hands seemed to have been standing still. It would be at least a couple hours yet before she'd dare to come over.

There wasn't any more work I could do, so I filled a big cup with coffee and took it up into Dad's office. I set it on his desk, lighted a cigar and started browsing along the rows of books.

Dad always said that he had enough trouble sorting the fiction out of so-called facts, without reading fiction. He always said that science was already too muddled without trying to make it jibe with religion. He said those things, but he also said that science in itself could be a religion, that a broad mind was always in danger of becoming narrow. So there was quite a bit of fiction on the shelves, and as much Biblical literature, probably, as a lot of ministers had.

I'd read some of the fiction. The other I'd left alone. I went to church and Sunday school, living as I had to live, but that was the end of it. Because kids are kids; and if that sounds pretty obvious, all I can say is that a lot of supposedly deep thinkers have never discovered the fact. A kid hears you cussing all the time, and he's going to cuss, too. He won't understand if you tell him it's wrong. He's loyal, and if you do it, it must be all right.

As I say, then, I'd never looked into any of the religious literature around the house. But I did tonight. I'd already read almost everything else. And I think it was in my mind that, since I was going to sell this place, I'd better be checking things over for value.

So I reached down a big leather-bound concordance to the Bible and blew the dust off of it. And I carried it over to the desk and opened it up; it kind of slid open by itself when I laid it down. And there was a picture in it, a little two-by-four snapshot, and I picked it up.

I turned it around one way, then another. I turned it sideways and upside down—what I thought was upside down. And I kind of grinned like a man will, when he's interested and puzzled.

It was a woman's face, not pretty exactly, but the kind that gets to you without your knowing why. But where the hell it was, what she was doing, I couldn't make out. Offhand, it looked like she was peering through the crotch of a tree, a white maple, say, with two limbs tapering up from the bole. She had her hands clasped around the limbs, and . . . But I knew that couldn't be right. Because the bole was divided at the base, and there were stumps of chopped off limbs almost tangent to the others.

I rubbed the picture against my shirt, and looked at it again. That face was familiar. It was coming back to me from some faraway place, like something coming out of hiding. But it was old, the picture I mean, and there were kind of crisscross blurs—of age, I supposed—scarring whatever she was looking through.

I took a magnifying glass and looked at it. I turned it upside down, as it was supposed to be turned. Then, I kind of dropped the glass and shoved it away from me; and I sat staring into space. At nothing and everything.

She was looking through a crotch, all right. But it was her own.

She was on her knees, peering between them. And those crisscross blurs on her thighs weren't the result of age. They were scars. The woman was Helene, who had been Dad's housekeeper so long ago.

Dad . . .

Twelve

I WAS only like that for a few minutes, sitting there and staring, but a world of things, most of my kid life, came back to me in that time. *She* came back to me, the housekeeper, and she had been so much of that life.

"Want to fight, Helene? Want to learn how to box . . . ?"
And:

"Oh, I'm tired. You just hit me . . ."

And:

"But you'll like it, darling. All the big boys do it . . ."

I lived back through it all, and then I came to the end of it. That last terrible day, with me crouched at the foot of the stairs, sick with fear and shame, terrified, aching with the first and only whipping in my life; listening to the low angry voices, the angry and contemptuous voices, in the library.

"I am not arguing with you, Helene. You're leaving here tonight. Consider yourself lucky that I don't prosecute you."

"Oh, ye-ss? I'd like to see you try it!"

"Why, Helene? How in the world could you do such a thing?"

"Jealous?"

"You—a mere child, and—"

"Yes! That's right! A mere child. Why not remember that? Listen to me, Daniel. I—"

"Don't say it, please. I'm at fault. If I hadn't—"

"Has it hurt you any? Have you harmed anyone? Haven't you, in fact—I should ask!—gradually lost all interest in it?"

"But a child! My child. My only son. If anything should happen—"

"Uh-huh. That's what bothers you, isn't it? Not him, but you. How it would reflect on you."

"Get out! A woman with no more sensibilities than—"

"I'm white trash, that's the term isn't it? Riffraff. I ain't got that ol' quality. All right, and when I see some hypocritical son-of-a-bitch like you, I'm damned glad of it!"

"Get out or I'll kill you!"

"Tsk-tsk! But think of the disgrace, Doctor . . . Now, I'm going to tell you something . . ."

"Get—"

"Something that you above all people should know. This didn't need to mean a thing. Absolutely nothing. But now it will. You've handled it in the worst possible way. You—"

"I . . . please, Helene."

"You'll never kill anyone. Not you. You're too damned smug and self-satisfied and sure of yourself. You like to hurt people, but—"

"No!"

"All right. I'm wrong. You're the great, good Dr. Ford, and I'm white trash, so that makes me wrong . . . I hope."

That was all.

I'd forgotten about it, and now I forgot it again. There are things that have to be forgotten if you want to go on living. And somehow I did want to; I wanted to more than ever. If the Good Lord made a mistake in us people it was in making us want to live when we've got the least excuse for it.

I put the concordance back on the shelf. I took the picture into the laboratory and burned it, and washed the ashes down the sink. But it was a long time burning, it seemed like. And I couldn't help noticing something:

How much she looked like Joyce. How there was even a strong resemblance between her and Amy Stanton.

The phone rang. I wiped my hands against my pants, and answered it, looking at myself in the laboratory-door mirror—at the guy in the black bow tie and the pink-tan shirt, his trouser legs hooked over his boot tops.

"Lou Ford speakin'," I said.

"Howard, Lou. Howard Hendricks. Look. I want you to come right down . . . down to the courthouse, yeah."

"Well, I don't know about that," I said. "I kind of—"

"She'll have to wait, Lou. This is important!" It had to be the way he was sputtering. "Remember what we were talking about this afternoon? About the—you know—the possibility of an outside party being the murderer. Well, you, we were dead right. Our hunch was right!"

"Huh!" I said. "But it couldn't—I mean—"

"We've got him, Lou! We've got the son-of-a-bitch! We've got the bastard cold, and—"

"You mean he's admitted it? Hell, Howard, there's always some crank confessing to—"

"He's not admitting anything! He won't even talk! That's why we need you. We can't, uh, work on him, you know, but you can make him talk. You can soften him up if anyone can. I think you know him, incidentally."

"W-who—yeah?"

"The Greek's kid, Johnnie Pappas. You know him; he's

been in plenty of trouble before. Now, get down here, Lou. I've already called Chester Conway and he's flying out from Fort Worth in the morning. I gave you full credit—told him how we'd worked on this idea together and we'd been sure all along that Elmer wasn't guilty, and . . . and he's pleased as punch, Lou. Boy, if we can just crack this, get a confession right—"

"I'll come down," I said. "I'll be right down, Howard."

I lowered the receiver hook for a moment, figuring out what had happened, what must have happened. Then, I called Amy.

Her folks were still up so she couldn't talk much; and that was a help. I made her understand that I really wanted to see her—and I did—and I shouldn't be gone too long.

I hung up and took out my wallet, and spread all the bills out on the desk.

I hadn't had any twenties of my own, just the twenty-five Elmer'd given me. And when I saw that five of them were gone, I went limp clear down to my toenails. Then I remembered that I'd used four in Fort Worth on my railroad ticket, and that I'd only broken one here in town where it would matter. Only the one . . . with Johnnie Pappas. So . . .

So I got out the car, and drove down to the courthouse.

Office Deputy Hank Butterby gave me a hurt look, and another deputy that was there, Jeff Plummer, winked and said howdy to me. Then Howard bustled in and grabbed me by the elbow, and hustled me into his office.

"What a break, huh, Lou?" He was almost slobbering with excitement. "Now, I'll tell you how to handle it. Here's what you'd better do. Sweet talk him, know what I mean, and get his guard down; then tighten up on him. Tell him if he'll cooperate we'll get him off with manslaughter—we can't do it, of course, but what you say won't be binding on me. Otherwise, tell him, it'll be the chair. He's eighteen years old, past eighteen, and—"

I stared at him. He misread my look.

"Oh, hell," he said, jabbing me in the ribs with his thumb. "Who am I to be telling you what to do? Don't I know how you handle these guys? Haven't I—"

"You haven't told me anything yet," I said. "I know Johnnie's kind of wild, but I can't see him as a murderer. What are you supposed to have on him?"

"Supposed, hell! We've got"—he hesitated—"well, here's the situation, Lou. Elmer took ten thousand bucks out there to that chippy's house. He was supposed to have taken that much. But when we counted it up, five hundred dollars was missing . . ."

"Yeah?" I said. It was like I'd figured. That damned Elmer hadn't wanted to admit that he didn't have any dough of his own.

"Well, we thought, Bob and I did, that Elmer had probably pissed it off in a crap game or something like that. But the bills were all marked, see, and the old man had already tipped off the local banks. If she tried to hang around town after the payoff, he was going to crack down on her for blackmail . . . That Conway! They don't put many past him!"

"It looks like they've put a few past me," I said.

"Now, Lou"—he clapped me on the back. "There's no reason to feel that way at all. We trusted you implicitly. But it was Conway's show, and—well, you *were* there in the vicinity, Lou, and . . ."

"Let it go," I said. "Johnnie spent some of the money?"

"A twenty. He broke it at a drugstore last night and it went to the bank this morning, and it was traced back to him a couple hours ago when we picked him up. Now—"

"How do you know Elmer didn't blow in the dough, and it's just now beginning to circulate?"

"None of it's shown up. Just this one twenty. So— Wait, Lou. Wait just a minute. Let me give you the whole picture, and we'll save time. I was entirely willing to concede that he'd come by the money innocently. He pays himself there at the filling station, and oddly enough that pay comes to exactly twenty dollars for the two nights. It looked all right, see what I mean? He could have taken the twenty in and paid himself with it. But he couldn't say he did—wouldn't say anything—because he damned well couldn't. There's damned few cars stopping at Murphy's between midnight and eight o'clock. He'd have to remember anyone that gave him a twenty. We could have checked the customer or customers, and he'd have been out of here—*if* he was innocent."

"Maybe it was in his cash drawer at the start of his shift?"

"Are you kidding? A twenty-dollar bill to make change with?" Hendricks shook his head. "We'd know he didn't have it, even without Slim Murphy's word. Now, wait! Hold up! We've checked on Murphy, and his alibi's airtight. The kid— huh-uh. From about nine Sunday night until eleven, his time can't be accounted for. We can't account for it, and he won't. . . . Oh, it's a cinch, Lou, anyway you look at it. Take the murders themselves—that dame beaten to a pulp. That's something a crazy kid would lose his head and do. And the money; only five hundred taken out of ten grand. He's overwhelmed by so much dough, so he grabs up a fistful and leaves the rest. A kid stunt again."

"Yeah," I said. "Yeah, I guess you're right, Howard. You think he's got the rest cached somewhere?"

"Either that or he's got scared and thrown it away. He's a set-up, Lou. Man, I've never seen one so pretty. If he dropped dead right now I'd consider it a judgment from heaven, and I'm not a religious man either!"

Well, he'd said it all. He'd proved it in black and white.

"Well, you'd better get busy, now, Lou. We've got him on ice. Haven't booked him yet, and we're not going to until he comes through. I'm not letting some shyster tell him about his rights at this stage of the game."

I hesitated. Then I said, "No, I don't reckon that would be so smart. There's nothing to be gained by that . . . Does Bob know about this?"

"Why bother him? There's nothing he can do."

"Well, I just wondered if we should ask him—if it would be all right for me to—"

"Be all right?" He frowned. "Why wouldn't it be all right? . . . Oh, I know how you feel, Lou. He's just a kid; you know him. But he's a murderer, Lou, and a damned cold-blooded one. Keep that in your mind. Think of how that poor damned woman must have felt while he was beating her face in. You saw her. You saw what her face looked like. Stew meat, hamburger—"

"Don't," I said. "For Christ's sake!"

"Sure, Lou, sure." He dropped an arm around my shoulders. "I'm sorry. I keep forgetting that you've never become hardened to this stuff. Well?"

"Well," I said. "I guess I'd better get it over with."

I walked downstairs to the basement, the jail. The turnkey let me through the gate and closed it again; and we went down past the bullpen and the regular cells to a heavy steel door. There was a small port or peephole in it, and I peered through it. But I couldn't see anything. You couldn't keep a light globe in the place, no matter what kind of guard you put over it; and the basement window, which was two-thirds below the surface of the ground, didn't let in much natural light.

"Want to borrow a flash, Lou?"

"I guess not," I said. "I can see all I need to."

He opened the door a few inches, and I slid inside, and he slammed it behind me. I stood with my back to it a moment, blinking, and there was a squeak and a scrape, and a shadow rose up and faltered toward me.

He fell into my arms, and I held him there, patting him on the back, comforting him.

"It's all right, Johnnie boy. Everything's going to be all right."

"J-jesus, Lou. Jesus Jesus Ca-Christ. I knew—I kn-new you'd come, they'd send for you. But it was so long, so long and I began to think maybe—maybe—you'd—"

"You know me better'n that, Johnnie. You know how much I think of you."

"S-sure." He drew a long breath, and let it out slowly; like a man that's made land after a hard swim. "You got a cigarette, Lou? These dirty bastards took all my—"

"Now, now," I said. "They were just doing their duty, Johnnie. Have a cigar and I'll smoke one with you."

We sat down side-by-side on the bolted-down bunk, and I held a match for our cigars. I shook the match out, and he puffed and I puffed, and the glow came and went from our faces.

"This is going to burn the old man up." He laughed jerkily. "I guess— He'll have to know, won't he?"

"Yes," I said. "I'm afraid he'll have to know, Johnnie."

"How soon can I leave?"

"Very soon. It won't be long now," I said. "Where were you Sunday night?"

"To a picture show." He drew hard on his cigar, and I could see his jaw beginning to set. "What's the difference?"

"You know what I mean, Johnnie. Where'd you go after the show—between the time you left it and started to work?"

"Well"—*puff, puff*—"I don't see what that's got to do with this. I don't ask you"—*puff*—"where you—"

"You can," I said. "I intend to tell you. I guess maybe you don't know me as well as I thought you did, Johnnie. Haven't I always shot square with you?"

"Aw, hell, Lou," he said, shamed. "You know how I feel about you, but— All right. I'd probably tell you sooner or later anyway. It was"—*puff*—"here's the way it was, Lou. I told the old man I had this hot date Wednesday, see, but I was afraid of my tires, and I could pick up a couple good ones cheap an' hand him back something each week until I got 'em paid for. And—"

"Let me sort that out," I said. "You needed tires for your hot-rod and you tried to borrow the money from your father?"

"Sure! Just like I said. And you know what he says, Lou? He tells me I don't need tires, that I gad around too much. He says I should bring this babe to the house and Mom'll make some ice cream, an' we'll all play cards or somethin'! For Christ's sake!" He shook his head bewilderedly. "How stupid can a person get?"

I laughed gently. "You got your two tires anyway, then?" I said. "You stripped a couple off of a parked car?"

"Well—uh—to tell the truth, Lou, I took four. I wasn't meaning to but I knew where I could turn a couple real quick, an'—well—"

"Sure," I said. "This gal was kind of hard to get, and you wanted to be sure of getting over with her. A really hot babe, huh?"

"Mmmph-umph! Wow! You know what I mean, Lou. One of those gals that makes you want to take your shoes off and wade around in her."

I laughed again, and he laughed. Then it was somehow awfully silent, and he shifted uneasily.

"I know who owned the car, Lou. Soon as I get squared away a little I'll send him the money for those tires."

"That's all right," I said. "Don't worry about it."

"Are we—uh—can I—?"

"In just a little," I said. "You'll be leaving in a few minutes, Johnnie. Just a few formalities to take care of first."

"Boy, will I be glad to be out of here! Gosh, Lou, I don't know how people stand it! It'd drive me crazy."

"It'd drive anyone crazy," I said. "It does drive them crazy . . . Maybe you'd better lie down a while, Johnnie. Stretch out on the bunk. I've got a little more talking to do."

"But"—he turned slowly and tried to look at me, to see my face.

"You'd better do that," I said. "The air gets kind of bad with both of us sitting up."

"Oh," he said. "Yeah." And he lay down. He sighed deeply. "Say, this feels pretty good. Ain't it funny, Lou, what a difference it makes? Having someone to talk to, I mean. Someone that likes you and understands you. If you've got that, you can put up with almost anything."

"Yes," I said. "It makes a lot of difference, and— That's that. You didn't tell 'em you got that twenty from me, Johnnie?"

"Hell, no! What do you think I am, anyway? Piss on those guys."

"Why not?" I said. "Why didn't you tell them?"

"Well, uh"—the hard boards of the bunk squeaked—"well, I figured—oh, you know, Lou. Elmer got around in some kind of funny places, an' I thought maybe—well, I know you don't make a hell of a lot of dough, and you're always tossing it around on other people—and if someone should slip you a little tip—"

"I see," I said. "I don't take bribes, Johnnie."

"Who said anything about bribes?" I could feel him shrug. "Who said anything? I just wasn't going to let 'em hit you cold with it until you figured out a—until you remembered where you found it."

I didn't say anything for a minute. I just sat there thinking about him, this kid that everyone said was no good, and a few other people I knew. Finally I said, "I wish you hadn't done it, Johnnie. It was the wrong thing to do."

"You mean they'll be sore?" He grunted. "To hell with 'em. They don't mean anything to me, but you're a square joe."

"Am I?" I said. "How do you know I am, Johnnie? How can a man ever really know anything? We're living in a funny world, kid, a peculiar civilization. The police are playing crooks in it, and the crooks are doing police duty. The politicians are preachers, and the preachers are politicians. The tax collectors collect for themselves. The Bad People want us to have more dough, and the Good People are fighting to keep it from us. It's not good for us, know what I mean? If we all had all we wanted to eat, we'd crap too much. We'd have inflation in the toilet paper industry. That's the way I understand it. That's about the size of some of the arguments I've heard."

He chuckled and dropped his cigar butt to the floor. "Gosh, Lou. I sure enjoy hearing you talk—I've never heard you talk that way before—but it's getting kind of late and—"

"Yeah, Johnnie," I said, "it's a screwed up, bitched up world, and I'm afraid it's going to stay that way. And I'll tell you why. Because no one, almost no one, sees anything wrong with it. They can't see that things are screwed up, so they're not worried about it. What they're worried about is guys like you.

"They're worried about guys liking a drink and taking it. Guys getting a piece of tail without paying a preacher for it. Guys who know what makes 'em feel good, and aren't going to be talked out of the notion . . . They don't like you guys, and they crack down on you. And the way it looks to me they're going to be cracking down harder and harder as time goes on. You ask me why I stick around, knowing the score, and it's hard to explain. I guess I kind of got a foot on both fences, Johnnie. I planted 'em there early and now they've taken root, and I can't move either way and I can't jump. All I can do is wait until I split. Right down the middle. That's all I can do and . . . But, you, Johnnie. Well, maybe you did the right thing. Maybe it's best this way. Because it would get harder all the time, kid, and I know how hard it's been in the past."

"I . . . I don't—"

"I killed her, Johnnie. I killed both of them. And don't say I couldn't have, that I'm not that kind of a guy, because you don't know."

"I"— He started to rise up on his elbow, then lay back again. "I'll bet you had a good reason, Lou. I bet they had it coming."

"No one has it coming to them," I said. "But I had a reason, yes."

Dimly in the distance, like a ghost hooting, I heard the refinery whistles blowing for the swing shifts. And I could picture the workmen plodding in to their jobs, and the other shifts plodding out. Tossing their lunch buckets into their cars. Driving home and playing with their kids and drinking beer and watching their television sets and diddling their wives and . . . Just as if nothing was happening. Just as if a kid wasn't dying and a man, part of a man, dying with him.

"Lou . . ."

"Yes, Johnnie." It was a statement, not a question.

"Y-you m-mean I—I should take the rap for you? I—"

"No," I said. "Yes."

"I d-d-don't think—I can't, Lou! Oh, Jesus, I can't! I c-couldn't go through—"

I eased him back on the bunk. I ruffled his hair, chucked him gently under the chin, tilting it back.

" 'There is a time of peace,' " I said, " 'and a time of war. A time to sow and a time to reap. A time to live and a time to die . . .' "

"L-lou . . ."

"This hurts me," I said, "worse than it does you."

And I knifed my hand across his windpipe. Then I reached down for his belt.

. . . I pounded on the door, and after a minute the turnkey came. He cracked the door open a little and I slid out, and he slammed it again.

"Give you any trouble, Lou?"

"No," I said, "he was real peaceful. I think we've broken the case."

"He's gonna talk, huh?"

"They've talked before," I shrugged.

I went back upstairs and told Howard Hendricks I'd had a long talk with Johnnie, and that I thought he'd come through all right. "Just leave him alone for an hour or so," I said. "I've done everything I can. If I haven't made him see the light, then he just ain't going to see it."

"Certainly, Lou, certainly. I know your reputation. You want me to call you after I see him?"

"I wish you would," I said. "I'm kind of curious to know if he talks."

Thirteen

I'VE LOAFED around the streets sometimes, leaned against a store front with my hat pushed back and one boot hooked back around the other—hell, you've probably seen me if you've ever been out this way—I've stood like that, looking nice and friendly and stupid, like I wouldn't piss if my pants were on fire. And all the time I'm laughing myself sick inside. Just watching the people.

You know what I mean—the couples, the men and wives you see walking along together. The tall fat women, and the short scrawny men. The teensy little women, and the big fat guys. The dames with lantern jaws, and the men with no chins. The bowlegged wonders, and the knock-kneed miracles. The . . . I've laughed—inside, that is—until my guts ached. It's almost as good as dropping in on a Chamber of Commerce luncheon where some guy gets up and clears his throat a few times and says, "Gentlemen, we can't expect to get any more out of life than what we put into it . . ." (Where's the percentage in that?) And I guess it—they—the people—those mismatched people—aren't something to laugh about. They're really tragical.

They're not stupid, no more than average anyway. They've not tied up together just to give jokers like me a bang. The truth is, I reckon, that life has played a hell of a trick on 'em. There was a time, just for a few minutes maybe, when all their differences seemed to vanish and they were just what each other wanted; when they looked at each other at exactly the right time in the right place and under the right circumstances. And everything was perfect. They had that time— those few minutes—and they never had any other. But while it lasted . . .

. . . Everything seemed the same as usual. The shades were drawn, and the bathroom door was open a little, just to let in a little light; and she was sprawled out on her stomach asleep. Everything was the same . . . but it wasn't. It was one of those times.

She woke up while I was undressing; some change dropped out of my pocket and rolled against the baseboard. She sat up, rubbing at her eyes, starting to say something sharp. But somehow she smiled, instead, and I smiled back at her. I scooped her up in my arms and sat down on the bed and held her. I kissed her, and her mouth opened a little, and her arms locked around my neck.

That's the way it started. That's the way it went.

Until, finally, we were stretched out close, side by side, her arm around my hips and mine around hers; limp, drained dry, almost breathless. And still we wanted each other—wanted something. It was like the beginning instead of the end.

She burrowed her head against my shoulder, and it was nice. I didn't feel like shoving her away. She whispered into my ear, kind of baby-talking.

"Mad at you. You hurt me."

"I did?" I said. "Gosh, I'm sorry, honey."

"Hurt real bad. 'Iss one. Punch elbow in it."

"Well, gosh—"

She kissed me, let her mouth slide off mine. "Not mad," she whispered.

She was silent then, waiting it looked like for me to say something. Do something. She pushed closer, squirming, still keeping her face hidden.

"Bet I know something . . ."

"Yeah, honey?"

"About that vas—that operation."

"What," I said, "do you think you know?"

"It was after that—after Mike—"

"What about Mike?"

"Darling"—she kissed my shoulder—"I don't care. I don't mind. But it was then, wasn't it? Your father got ex—worried and . . . ?"

I let my breath out slowly. Almost any other night I could have enjoyed wringing her neck, but this was one time when I hadn't felt that way.

"It was about that time, as I recollect," I said. "But I don't know as that had anything to do with it."

"Honey . . ."

"Yeah?"

"Why do you suppose people . . . ?"

"It beats me," I said. "I never have been able to figure it out."

"D-don't some women . . . I'll bet you would think it was awful if—"

"If what?"

She pushed against me, and it felt like she was on fire. She shivered and began to cry. "D-don't, Lou. Don't make me ask. J-just . . ."

So I didn't make her ask.

Later on, when she was still crying but in a different way, the phone rang. It was Howard Hendricks.

"Lou, kid, you really did it! You really softened him up!"

"He signed a confession?" I said.

"Better than that, boy! He hanged himself! Did it with his belt! That proves he was guilty without us having to screw around before a judge and put the taxpayers to a lot of expense, and all that crap! Goddammit, Lou, I wish I was there right now to shake your hand!"

He stopped yelling and tried to get the gloat out of his voice. "Now, Lou, I want you to promise me that you won't take this the wrong way. You mustn't get down about it. A person like that don't deserve to live. He's a lot better off dead than he is alive."

"Yeah," I said. "I guess you're right at that."

I got rid of him and hung up. And right away the phone

rang again. This time it was Chester Conway calling from Fort Worth.

"Great work, Lou. Fine job. Fine! Guess you know what this means to me. Guess I made a mistake about—"

"Yes?" I said.

"Nothing. Don't matter now . . . See you, boy."

I hung up again, and the phone rang a third time. Bob Maples. His voice came over the wire thin and shaky.

"I know how much you thought of that boy, Lou. I know you'd just about as soon it'd happened to yourself."

As soon? "Yeah, Bob," I said. "I just about would have."

"You want to come over and set a spell, Lou? Play a game of checkers or somethin'? I ain't supposed to be up or I'd offer to come over there."

"I—I reckon not, Bob," I said. "But thanks, thanks a heap."

"That's all right, son. You change your mind, come on over. No matter what time it is."

Amy'd been taking in everything; impatient, curious. I hung up and slumped down on the bed, and she sat up beside me.

"For heaven's sake! What was that all about, Lou?"

I told her. Not the truth, of course, but what was supposed to be the truth. She clapped her hands together.

"Oh, darling! That's wonderful. My Lou solving the case! . . . Will you get a reward?"

"Why should I?" I said. "Think of all the fun I had."

"Oh, well . . ." She drew away a little, and I thought she was going to pop off; and I reckon she wanted to. But she wanted something else worse. "I'm sorry, Lou. You have every right to be angry with me."

She lay back down again, turning on her stomach, spreading her arms and legs. She stretched out, waiting, and whispered:

"Very, very angry . . ."

Sure, I know. Tell me something else. Tell a hophead he shouldn't take dope. Tell him it'll kill him, and see if he stops.

She got her money's worth.

It was going to cost her plenty, and I gave her value received. Honest Lou, that was me. Let Lou Titillate Your Tail.

Fourteen

I GUESS I must have got to sweating with all that exercise, and not having any clothes on I caught a hell of a cold. Oh, it wasn't too bad; not enough to really lay me low; but I wasn't fit to do any chasing around. I had to stay in bed for a week. And it was kind of a break for me, you might say.

I didn't have to talk to a lot of people, and have 'em asking damned fool questions and slapping me on the back. I didn't have to go to Johnnie Pappas' funeral. I didn't have to call on his folks, like I'd have felt I had to do ordinarily.

A couple of the boys from the office dropped by to say hello, and Bob Maples came in a time or two. He was still looking pretty peaked, seemed to have aged about ten years. We kept off the subject of Johnnie—just talked about things in general—and the visits went off pretty well. Only one thing came up that kind of worried me for a while. It was on the first—no, I guess the second time he came by.

"Lou," he said, "why in hell don't you get out of this town?"

"Get out?" I was startled. We'd just been sitting there quietly, smoking and passing a word now and then. And suddenly he comes out with this. "Why should I get out?"

"Why've you ever stayed here this long?" he said. "Why'd you ever want to wear a badge? Why didn't you be a doctor like your dad; try to make something of yourself?"

I shook my head, staring down at the bedclothes. "I don't know, Bob. Reckon I'm kind of lazy."

"You got awful funny ways of showin' it, Lou. You ain't never too lazy to take on some extra job. You put in more hours than any man I got. An' if I know anything about you, you don't like the work. You never have liked it."

He wasn't exactly right about that, but I knew what he meant. There was other work I'd have liked a lot better. "I don't know, Bob," I said, "there's a couple of kinds of laziness. The don't-want-to-do-nothin' and the stick-in-the-rut brand. You take a job, figuring you'll just keep it a little while, and that while keeps stretchin' on and on and on. You need a little more money before you can make a jump. You can't quite make up your mind about what you want to jump to. And then maybe you make a stab at it, you send off a few letters, and the people want to know what experience you've had—what you've been doin'. And probably they don't even want to bother with you, and if they do you've got to start right at the bottom, because you don't know anything. So you stay where you are, you just about got to, and you work pretty hard because you know it. You ain't young any more and it's all you've got."

Bob nodded slowly. "Yeah . . . I kinda know how that is. But it didn't need to be that way with you, Lou! Your dad could've sent you off to school. You could've been a practicin' doctor by this time."

"Well," I hesitated, "there'd been that trouble with Mike, and Dad would've been all alone, and . . . well, I guess my mind just didn't run to medicine, Bob. It takes an awful lot of study, you know."

"There's other things you could do, and you lack a lot of bein' broke, son. You could get you a little fortune for this property."

"Yeah, but . . ." I broke off. "Well, to tell the truth, Bob, I have kind of thought about pulling up stakes, but—"

"Amy don't want to?"

"I haven't asked her. The subject never came up. But I don't reckon she would."

"Well," he said slowly, "that's sure too bad. I don't suppose you'd . . . No, you wouldn't do that. I don't expect no man in his right mind would give up Amy."

I nodded a little, like I was acknowledging a compliment; agreeing that I couldn't give her up. And even with the way I felt about her, the nod came easy. On the surface, Amy had everything plus. She was smart and she came from a good family—which was a mighty important consideration with our people. But that was only the beginning. When Amy went down the street with that round little behind twitching, with her chin tucked in and her breasts stuck out, every man under eighty kind of drooled. They'd get sort of red in the face and forget to breathe, and you could hear whispers, *"Man, if I could just have some of that."*

Hating her didn't keep me from being proud of her.

"You trying to get rid of me, Bob?" I said.

"Kind of looks as though, don't it?" he grinned. "Guess I did too much thinkin' while I was laying around the house. Wondering about things that ain't none of my business. I got to thinkin' about how riled I get sometimes, having to give in to things I don't like, and hell, I ain't really fit to do much but what I am doin'; and I thought how much harder it must be on a man like you." He chuckled, wryly. "Fact is, I reckon, you started me thinking that way, Lou. You kind of brought it on yourself."

I looked blank, and then I grinned. "I don't mean anything by it. It's just a way of joking."

"Sure," he said, easily. "We all got our little pe-cul-ye-arities. I just thought maybe you was gettin' kind of saddle-galled, and—"

"Bob," I said, "what did Conway say to you there in Fort Worth?"

"Oh, hell"—he stood up, slapping his hat against his pants—"can't even recollect what it was now. Well, I guess I better be—"

"He said something. He said or did something that you didn't like a little bit."

"You reckon he did, huh?" His eyebrows went up. Then they came down and he chuckled, and put on his hat. "Forget it, Lou. It wasn't nothing important, and it don't matter no more, anyways."

He left; and, like I said, I was kind of worried for a while. But after I'd had time to think, it looked to me like I'd fretted about nothing. It looked like things were working out pretty good.

I was willing to leave Central City; I'd been thinking about leaving. But I thought too much of Amy to go against her wishes. I sure wouldn't do anything that Amy didn't like.

If something should happen to her, though—and something *was* going to happen—why, of course, I wouldn't want to hang around the old familiar scenes any more. It would be more than a soft-hearted guy like me could stand, and there wouldn't be any reason to. So I'd leave, and it'd all seem perfectly natural. No one would think anything of it.

Amy came to see me every day—in the morning for a few

minutes on her way to school, and again at night. She always brought some cake or pie or something, stuff I reckon their dog wouldn't eat (and that hound wasn't high-tone—he'd snatch horseturds on the fly), and she hardly nagged about anything, that I remember. She didn't give me any trouble at all. She was all sort of blushy and shy and shamed like. And she had to take it kind of easy when she sat down.

Two or three nights she drew the bath tub full of warm water and sat in it and soaked; and I'd sit and watch her and think how much she looked like *her*. And afterwards she'd lie in my arms—just lie there because that was about all either of us was up to. And I could almost fool myself into thinking it was *her*.

But it wasn't *her*, and, for that matter, it wouldn't have made any difference if it had been. I'd just been right back where I started. I'd have had to do it all over again.

I'd have had to kill her the second time . . .

I was glad Amy didn't bring up the subject of marriage; she was afraid of starting a quarrel, I guess. I'd already been right in the middle of three deaths, and a fourth coming right on top of 'em might look kind of funny. It was too soon for it. Anyway, I hadn't figured out a good safe way of killing her.

You see why I had to kill her, I reckon. Or do you? It was like this:

There wasn't any evidence against me. And even if there was some, quite a bit, I'd be a mighty hard man to stick. I just wasn't that kind of guy, you see. No one would believe I was. Why, hell, they'd been seeing Lou Ford around for years, and no one could tell them that good ol' Lou would—

But Lou could do it; Lou could convict himself. All he had to do was skip out on a girl who knew just about everything about him there was to know—who, even without that one wild night, could probably have pieced some plenty-ugly stuff together—and that would be the end of Lou. Everything would fall into place, right back to the time when Mike and I were kids.

As things stood now, she wouldn't let herself think things through. She wouldn't even let herself start to think. She'd cut up some pretty cute skylarks herself, and that had put a check on her thinking. And I was going to be her husband, so everything was all right. Everything had to be all right . . . But if I ran out on her—well, I knew Amy. That mental block she'd set up would disappear. She'd have the answer that quick—and she wouldn't keep it to herself. Because if she couldn't have me, no one else would.

Yeah, I guess I mentioned that. She and Joyce seemed pretty much alike.

Well, anyway . . .

Anyway, it had to be done, as soon as it safely could be done. And knowing that, that there was just no other way out, kind of made things easier. I stopped worrying, thinking about it, I should say. I tried to be extra pleasant to her. She was getting on my nerves, hanging around so much. But she wouldn't be hanging around long, so I thought I ought to be as nice as I could.

I'd taken sick on a Wednesday. By the next Wednesday I was up, so I took Amy to prayer meeting. Being a school teacher, she kind of had to put in an appearance at those things, now and then, and I sort of enjoy 'em. I pick up lots of good lines at prayer meetings. I asked Amy, I whispered to her, how she'd like to have a little manna on her honey. And she turned red, and kicked me on the ankle. I whispered to her again, asked her if I could Mose-y into her Burning Bush. I told her I was going to take her to my bosom and cleave unto her, and anoint her with precious oils.

She got redder and redder and her eyes watered, but somehow it made her look cute. And it seemed like I'd never seen her with her chin stuck out and her eyes narrowed. Then, she doubled over, burying her face in her songbook; and she shivered and shook and choked, and the minister stood on tiptoe, frowning, trying to figure out where the racket was coming from.

It was one of the best prayer meetings I ever went to.

I stopped and bought some ice cream on the way home, and she was giggling and breaking into snickers all the way. While I made coffee, she dished up the cream; and I took part of a spoonful and chased her around and around the kitchen with it. I finally caught her and put it in her mouth, instead of down her neck like I'd threatened. A little speck of it got on her nose and I kissed it away.

Suddenly, she threw her arms around my neck and began to cry.

"Honey," I said, "don't do that, honey. I was just playing. I was just trying to give you a good time."

"Y-you—big—"

"I know," I said, "but don't say it. Let's don't have any more trouble between us."

"D-don't"—her arms tightened around me, and she looked up through the tears, smiling—"don't you understand? I'm j-just so happy, Lou. So h-happy I c-can't s-s-stand it!" And she burst into tears again.

We left the ice cream and coffee unfinished. I picked her up and carried her into Dad's office, and sat down in Dad's big old chair. We sat there in the dark, her on my lap—sat there until she had to go home. And it was all we wanted; it seemed to be enough. It was enough.

It was a good evening, even if we did have one small spat. She asked me if I'd seen Chester Conway, and I said I hadn't. She said she thought it was darned funny that he didn't so much as come by and say hello, after what I'd done, and that if she were me she'd tell him so.

"I didn't do anything," I said. "Let's not talk about it."

"Well, I don't care, darling! He thought you'd done quite a bit at the time—couldn't wait to call you up long distance! Now, he's been back in town for almost a week, and he's too busy to—I don't care for my own sake, Lou. It certainly means nothing to me. But—"

"That makes two of us, then."

"You're too easy-going, that's the trouble with you. You let people run over you. You're always—"

"I know," I said. "I think I know it all, Amy. I've got it memorized. The whole trouble is that I won't listen to you— and it seems to me like that's about all I ever got done. I've been listening to you almost since you learned how to talk, and I reckon I can do it a while longer. If it'll make you happy. But I don't think it'll change me much."

She sat up very stiff and straight. Then, she settled back again, still holding herself kind of rigid. She was silent for about the time it takes you to count to ten.

"Well, just the same, I—I—"

"Yeah?" I said.

"Oh, be quiet," she said. "Keep still. Don't say anything."
And she laughed. And it was a good evening after all.

But it *was* kind of funny about Conway.

Fifteen

How LONG should I wait? that was the question. How long
could I wait? How long was it safe?

Amy wasn't crowding me any. She was still pretty shy and
skittish, trying to keep that barbed-wire tongue of hers in her
mouth—though she wasn't always successful. I figured I could
stall her off on marriage indefinitely, but Amy . . . well, it
wasn't just Amy. There wasn't anything I could put my finger
on, but I had the feeling that things were closing in on me.
And I couldn't talk myself out of it.

Every day that passed, the feeling grew stronger.

Conway hadn't come to see me or spoken to me, but that
didn't necessarily mean anything. It *didn't* mean anything that
I could see. He was busy. He'd never given a whoop in hell
for anyone but himself and Elmer. He was the kind of a guy
that would drop you when he got a favor, then pick you up
again when he needed another one.

He'd gone back to Fort Worth, and he hadn't returned.
But that was all right, too. Conway Construction had big offices in Fort Worth. He'd always spent a lot of time there.

Bob Maples? Well, I couldn't see that he was much different
than ever. I'd study him as the days drifted by, and I couldn't
see anything to fret about. He looked pretty old and sick, but
he *was* old and he had been sick. He didn't have too much
to say to me, but what he did have was polite and friendly—he
seemed hell-bent on being polite and friendly. And he'd never
been what you'd call real talky. He'd always had spells when
you could hardly get a word out of him.

Howard Hendricks? Well . . . Well, something was sure
enough eating on Howard.

I'd run into Howard the first day I was up after my sick
spell; he'd been coming up the steps of the courthouse, just

as I was heading down them to lunch. He nodded, not quite looking at me, and mumbled out a, "H'are you, Lou?" I stopped and said I was feeling a lot better—still felt pretty weak, but couldn't really complain any.

"You know how it is, Howard," I said. "It isn't the flu so much as the after effects."

"So I've heard," he said.

"It's kind of like I always say about auty-mobiles. It's not the original cost so much as the upkeep. But I reckon—"

"Got to run," he mumbled. "See you."

But I wasn't letting him off that easy. I was really in the clear, now, and I could afford to open up a little on him. "As I was sayin'," I said, "I reckon I can't tell you much about sickness, can I, Howard? Not with that shrapnel you got in you. I got an idea about that shrapnel, Howard—what you could do with it. You could get you some X-rays taken and print 'em on the back of your campaign cards. Then on the other side you could have a flag with your name spelled out in thermometers, and maybe a upside down—what do you call them hospital piss-pots? Oh, yeah—urinal for an exclamation mark. Where'd you say that shrapnel was anyway, Howard? Seems like I just can't keep track of it, no matter how hard I try. One time it's in—"

"My ass"—he was looking at me now, all right—"it's in my ass."

I'd been holding him by the lapel to keep him from running off. He took my hand by the wrist, still staring at me, and he pulled it away and let it drop. Then, he turned and went up the steps, his shoulders sagging a little but his feet moving firm and steady. And we hadn't passed a word between us since then. He kept out of my way when he saw me coming, and I did him the same kind of favor.

So there was something wrong there; but what else could I expect? What was there to worry about? I'd given him the works, and it had probably dawned on him that I'd needled him plenty in the past. And that wasn't the only reason he had to act stiff and cold. Elections were coming up in the fall, and he'd be running as usual. Breaking the Conway case would be a big help to him, and he'd want to talk it up. But he'd feel awkward about doing it. He'd have to cut me out of the credit, and he figured I'd be sore. So he was jumping the gun on me.

There was nothing really out of the way, then. Nothing with him or Sheriff Bob or Chester Conway. There wasn't a thing . . . but the feeling kept growing. It got stronger and stronger.

I'd been keeping away from the Greek's. I'd even stayed off the street where his restaurant was. But one day I went there. Something just seemed to pull the wheels of my car in that direction, and I found myself stopping in front of it.

The windows were all soaped over. The doors were closed. But it seemed like I could hear people inside; I heard some banging and clattering.

I got out of my car and stood by the side of it a minute or two. Then, I stepped up on the curb and crossed the walk.

There was a place on one of the double doors where the soap had been scraped away. I sheltered my eyes with my hand and peered through it; rather I started to peer through it. For the door opened suddenly, and the Greek stepped out.

"I am sorry, Officer Ford," he said. "I cannot serve you. We are not open for business."

I stammered that I didn't want anything. "Just thought I'd drop by to—to—"

"Yes?"

"I wanted to see you," I said. "I wanted to see you the night it happened, and it hasn't been off my mind since. But I couldn't bring myself to do it. I couldn't face you. I knew how you'd feel, how you'd be bound to feel, and there wasn't anything I could say. Nothing. Nothing I could say or do. Because if there'd been anything . . . well, it wouldn't have happened in the first place."

It was the truth, and God—God!—what a wonderful thing truth is. He looked at me in a way I didn't like to name; and then he looked kind of baffled; and then he suddenly caught his lip under his teeth and stared down at the sidewalk.

He was a swarthy middle-aged guy in a high-crowned black hat, and a shirt with black sateen protectors pulled over the sleeves; and he stared down at the sidewalk and looked back up again.

"I am glad you did come by, Lou," he said, quietly. "It is

fitting. I have felt, at times, that he regarded you as his one true friend."

"I aimed to be his friend," I said. "There weren't many things I wanted much more. Somehow, I slipped up; I couldn't help him right when he needed help worst. But I want you to know one thing, Max. I—I didn't hurt—"

He laid a hand on my arm. "You need not tell me that, Lou. I do not know why—what—but—"

"He felt lost," I said. "Like he was all alone in the world. Like he was out of step, and he could never get back in again."

"Yes," he said. "But . . . yes. There was always trouble, and he seemed always at fault."

I nodded, and he nodded. He shook his head, and I shook mine. We stood there, shaking our heads and nodding, neither of us really saying anything; and I wished I could leave. But I didn't quite know how to go about it. Finally, I said I was sorry he was closing the restaurant.

"If there's anything I can do . . ."

"I am not closing it," he said. "Why should I close it?"

"Well, I just thought that—"

"I am remodelling it. I am putting in leather booths and an inlaid floor and air-conditioning. Johnnie would have liked those things. Many times he suggested them, and I suggested he was hardly fitted to give me advice. But now we will have them. It will be as he wanted. It is—all that can be done."

I shook my head again. I shook it and nodded.

"I want to ask you a question, Lou. I want you to answer it, and I want the absolute truth."

"The truth?" I hesitated. "Why wouldn't I tell you the truth, Max?"

"Because you might feel that you couldn't. That it would be disloyal to your position and associates. Who else visited Johnnie's cell after you left?"

"Well, there was Howard—the county attorney—"

"I know of that; he made the discovery. And a deputy sheriff and the jailor were with him. Who else?"

My heart gave a little jump. Maybe . . . But, no, it was no good. I couldn't do that. I couldn't bring myself to try it.

"I don't have any idea, Max," I said. "I wasn't there. But

I can tell you you're on the wrong track. I've known all those boys for years. They wouldn't do a thing like that any more than I would."

It was the truth again, and he had to see it. I was looking straight into his eyes.

"Well . . ." he sighed. "Well, we will talk again, Lou."

And I said, "You bet we will, Max," and I got away from him.

I drove out on Derrick Road, five-six miles out. I pulled the car off on the shoulder, up at the crest of a little hill; and I sat there looking down through the blackjacks but I didn't see a thing. I didn't see the blackjacks.

About five minutes after I'd stopped, well, maybe no more than three minutes, a car drew up behind mine. Joe Rothman got out of it, and plodded along the shoulder and looked in at me.

"Nice view here," he said. "Mind if I join you? Thanks, I knew you wouldn't." He said it like that, all run together, without waiting for me to reply. He opened the door and slid into the seat beside me.

"Come out this way often, Lou?"

"Whenever I feel like it," I said.

"Well, it's a nice view all right. Almost unique. I don't suppose you'll find more than forty or fifty thousand billboards like that one in the United States."

I grinned in spite of myself. The billboard had been put up by the Chamber of Commerce; and the words on it were:

> You Are Now Nearing
> CENTRAL CITY, TEX.
> *"Where the hand clasp's a little stronger."*
> Pop. (1932) 4,800　　　Pop. (1952) 48,000
> WATCH US GROW!!

"Yeah," I said, "that's quite a sign, all right."

"You were looking at it, then? I thought that must be the attraction. After all, what else is there to see aside from those blackjacks and a little white cottage? The murder cottage, I believe they call it."

"What do you want?" I said.

"How many times were you there, Lou? How many times did you lay her?"

"I was there quite a few times," I said. "I had reason to be. And I'm not so hard up for it that I have to lay whores."

"No?" He squinted at me thoughtfully. "No, I don't suppose you would be. Personally, I've always operated on the theory that even in the presence of abundance, it's well to keep an eye out for the future. You never can tell, Lou. You may wake up some morning and find they've passed a law against it. It'll be un-American."

"Maybe they'll put a rider on that law," I said.

"Prohibiting bullshit? I see you don't have a legal type of mind, Lou, or you wouldn't say that. There's a basic contradiction in it. Tail we can do without, as our penal institutions so righteously prove; tail of the orthodox type that is. But what could you substitute for bullshit? Where would we be without it?"

"Well," I said, "I wouldn't be listening to you."

"But you're going to listen to me, Lou. You're going to sit right here and listen, and answer up promptly when the occasion demands. Get me? Get me, Lou?"

"I get you," I said. "I got you right from the beginning."

"I was afraid you hadn't. I wanted you to understand that I can stack it up over your head, and you'll sit there and like it."

He shook tobacco into a paper, twirled it, and ran it across his tongue. He stuck it in the corner of his mouth, and seemed to forget about it.

"You were talking with Max Pappas," he said. "From what I could judge it was a reasonably friendly conversation."

"It was," I said.

"He was resigned to the fact of Johnnie's suicide? He had accepted it as suicide?"

"I can't say that he was resigned to it," I said. "He was wondering whether someone—if someone was in the cell after I left, and . . ."

"And, Lou? And?"

"I told him, no, that it couldn't have been that way. None of the boys would be up to doing such a thing."

"Which settles that," Rothman nodded. "Or does it?"

"What are you driving at?" I snapped. "What—"

"Shut up!" His voice toughened, then went smooth again. "Did you notice the remodelling he's doing? Do you know how much all that will cost? Right around twelve thousand dollars. Where do you suppose he got that kind of money?"

"How the hell do I—"

"Lou."

"Well, maybe he had it saved."

"Max Pappas?"

"Or maybe he borrowed it."

"Without collateral?"

"Well . . . I don't know," I said.

"Let me make a suggestion. Someone gave it to him. A wealthy acquaintance, we'll say. Some man who felt he owed it to him."

I shrugged, and pushed my hat back; because my forehead was sweating. But I was feeling cold inside, so cold inside.

"Conway Construction is handling the job, Lou. Doesn't it strike you as rather odd that he'd do a job for a man whose son killed his son."

"There aren't many jobs that he don't handle," I said. "Anyway, it's the company, not him; he's not in there swinging a hammer himself. More'n likely he doesn't even know about it."

"Well . . ." Rothman hesitated. Then he went on, kind of dogged. "It's a turnkey job. Conway's jobbing all the materials, dealing with the supply houses, paying off the men. No one's seen a nickel coming from Pappas."

"So what?" I said. "Conway takes all the turnkey stuff he can get. He cuts a half a dozen profits instead of one."

"And you think Pappas would hold still for it? You don't see him as the kind of guy who'd insist on bargaining for every item, who'd haggle over everything right down to the last nail? I see him that way, Lou. It's the only way I can see him."

I nodded. "So do I. But he's not in a real good position to have his own way right now. He gets his job like Conway Construction wants to give it to him, or he just don't get it."

"Yeah . . ." He shifted his cigarette from one side of his mouth to the other. He pushed it across with his tongue, his eyes narrowed on my face. "But the money, Lou. That still doesn't explain about the money."

"He lived close," I said. "He could have had it, a big enough part, anyway, so's they'd wait on the rest. It didn't need to be in a bank. He could have had it salted away around his house."

"Yeah," said Rothman, slowly. "Yeah, I suppose so . . ."

He turned back around in the seat, so that he was looking through the windshield instead of me—instead of *at* me. He flicked his cigarette away, fumbled for his tobacco and papers, and began rolling another one.

"Did you get out to the cemetery, Lou? Out to Johnnie's grave?"

"No," I said, "and I've sure got to do that, too. I'm ashamed I haven't done it before."

"Well—dammit, you mean that, don't you? You mean every word of it!"

"Who are you to ask that?" I snapped. "What did you ever do for him? I don't want any credit for it, but I'm the only man in Central City that ever tried to help that kid. I liked him. I understood him. I—"

"I know, I know," he shook his head, dully. "I was just going to say that Johnnie's buried in Sacred Ground . . . You know what that means, Lou?"

"I reckon. The church didn't call it suicide."

"And the answer, Lou? You do have an answer?"

"He was so awful young," I said, "and he hadn't ever had much but trouble. Maybe the church figured he'd been faulted enough, and tried to give him a break. Maybe they figured that it was sort of an accident; that he'd just been fooling around and went too far."

"Maybe," said Rothman. "Maybe, maybe, maybe. One more thing, Lou. The big thing . . . On the Sunday night that Elmer and the late occupant of yon cottage got it, one of my carpenters went to the last show at the Palace. He parked his car around in back at—now get this, Lou—at nine-thirty. When he came out, all four of his tires were gone . . ."

Sixteen

I WAITED and everything got pretty quiet. "Well," I said, finally, "that's sure too bad. All four tires, huh?"

"Too bad? You mean it's funny, don't you, Lou? Plumb funny?"

"Well, it is, kind of," I said. "It's funny I didn't hear anything about it at the office."

"It'd been still funnier if you had, Lou. Because he didn't report the theft. I'd hardly call it the greatest mystery of all time, but, for some reason, you fellas down at the office don't take much interest in us fellas down at the labor temple—unless you find us on a picket line."

"I can't hardly help—"

"Never mind, Lou; it's really not pertinent. The man didn't report the theft, but he did mention it to some of the boys when the carpenters and joiners held their regular Tuesday night meeting. And one of them, as it turned out, had bought two of the tires from Johnnie Pappas. They . . . Do you have a chill, Lou? Are you catching cold?"

I bit down on my cigar. I didn't say anything.

"These lads equipped themselves with a couple of piss-elm clubs, or reasonable facsimiles thereof, and went calling on Johnnie. He wasn't at home and he wasn't at Slim Murphy's filling station. In fact, he wasn't anywhere about that time; he was swinging by his belt from the window-bars of the courthouse cooler. But his hotrod was at the station, and the remaining two stolen tires were on it. They stripped them off—Murphy, of course, isn't confiding in the police either—and that ended the matter. But there's been talk about it, Lou. There's been talk even though—*apparently*—no one has attached any great significance to the event."

I cleared my throat. "I—why should they, Joe?" I said. "I guess I don't get you."

"For the birds, Lou, remember? The starving sparrows. . . . Those tires were stolen after nine-thirty on the night of Elmer's and his lady friend's demise. Assuming that Johnnie didn't go to work on them the moment the owner parked—or even assuming that he did—we are driven to the

inevitable conclusion that he was engaged in relatively innocent pursuits until well after ten o'clock. He could not, in
other words, have had any part in the horrible happenings
behind yonder blackjacks."

"I don't see why not," I said.

"You don't?" His eyes widened. "Well, of course, poor old
Descartes, Aristotle, Diogenes, Euclid et al are dead, but I
think you'll find quite a few people around who'll defend their
theories. I'm very much afraid, Lou, that they won't go along
with your proposition that a body can be in two places at the
same time."

"Johnnie ran with a pretty wild crowd," I said. "I figure
that one of his buddies stole those tires and gave 'em to him
to peddle."

"I see. I see . . . Lou."

"Why not?" I said. "He was in a good position to get rid
of them there at the station. Slim Murphy wouldn't have interfered. . . . Why, hell, it's bound to have been that way,
Joe. If he'd have had an alibi for the time of the murders,
he'd have told me so, wouldn't he? He wouldn't have hanged
himself."

"He liked you, Lou. He trusted you."

"For damned good reasons. He knew I was his friend."

Rothman swallowed, and a sort of laughing sound came out
of his throat, the kind of sound you make when you don't
quite know whether to laugh or cry or get sore.

"Fine, Lou. Perfect. Every brick is laid straight, and the
bricklayer is an honest upstanding mechanic. But still I can't
help wondering about his handiwork and him. I can't help
wondering why he feels the need to defend his structure of
perhapses and maybes, his shelter wall of logical alternatives.
I can't see why he didn't tell a certain labor skate to get the
hell on about his business."

So . . . So there it was. I was. But where was he? He nodded as though I'd asked him the question. Nodded, and drew
a little bit back in the seat.

"Humpty-Dumpty Ford," he said, "sitting right on top of
the labor temple. And how or why he got there doesn't make
much difference. You're going to have to move, Lou. Fast.
Before someone . . . before you upset yourself."

"I was kind of figuring on leaving town," I said. "I haven't done anything, but—"

"Certainly you haven't. Otherwise, as a staunch Red Fascist Republican, I wouldn't feel free to yank you from the clutches of your detractors and persecutors—your would-be persecutors, I should say."

"You think that—you think maybe—"

He shrugged. "I think so, Lou. I think you just might have a little trouble in leaving. I think it so strongly that I'm getting in touch with a friend of mine, one of the best criminal lawyers in the country. You've probably heard of him—Billy Boy Walker? I did Billy Boy a favor one time, back East, and he has a long memory for favors, regardless of his other faults."

I'd heard of Billy Boy Walker. I reckon almost everyone has. He'd been governor of Alabama or Georgia or one of those states down south. He'd been a United States senator. He'd been a candidate for president on a Divide-the-Dough ticket. He'd started getting shot at quite a bit about that time, so he'd dropped out of politics and stuck to his criminal law practice. And he was plenty good. All the high mucky-mucks cussed and made fun of him for the way he'd cut up in politics. But I noticed that when they or their kin got into trouble, they headed straight for Billy Boy Walker.

It sort of worried me that Rothman thought I needed that kind of help.

It worried me, and it made me wonder all over again why Rothman and his unions would go to all the trouble of getting me a lawyer. Just what did Rothman stand to lose if the Law started asking me questions? Then I realized that if my first conversation with Rothman should ever come out, any jury in the land would figure he'd sicked me on the late Elmer Conway. In other words, Rothman was saving two necks—his and mine—with one lawyer.

"Perhaps you won't need him," he went on. "But it's best to have him alerted. He's not a man who can make himself available on a moment's notice. How soon can you leave town?"

I hesitated. Amy. How was I going to do it? "I'll—I can't do it right away," I said. "I'll have to kind of drop a hint or two around that I've been thinking about leaving, then work up to it gradually. You know, it would look pretty funny—"

"Yeah," he frowned, "but if they know you're getting ready to jump they're apt to close in all the faster . . . Still, I can see your point."

"What can they do?" I said. "If they could close in, they'd be doing it already. Not that I've done—"

"Don't bother. Don't say it again. Just move—start moving as quickly as you can. It shouldn't take you more than a couple of weeks at the outside."

Two weeks. Two weeks more for Amy.

"All right, Joe," I said. "And thanks for—for—"

"For what?" He opened the door. "For you, I haven't done a thing."

"I'm not sure I can make it in two weeks. It may take a little—"

"It hadn't better," he said, "take much longer."

He got out and went back to his own car. I waited until he'd turned around and headed back toward Central City; and then I turned around and started back. I drove slowly, thinking about Amy.

Years ago there was a jeweler here in Central City who had a hell of a good business, and a beautiful wife and two fine kids. And one day, on a business trip over to one of the teachers' college towns he met up with a girl, a real honey, and before long he was sleeping with her. She knew he was married, and she was willing to leave it that way. So everything was perfect. He had her and he had his family and a swell business. But one morning they found him and the girl dead in a motel—he'd shot her and killed himself. And when one of our deputies went to tell his wife about it, he found her and the kids dead, too. This fellow had shot 'em all.

He'd had everything, and somehow nothing was better.

That sounds pretty mixed up, and probably it doesn't have a lot to do with me. I thought it did at first, but now that I look at it—well, I don't know. I just don't know.

I knew I had to kill Amy; I could put the reason into words. But every time I thought about it, I had to stop and think *why* again. I'd be doing something, reading a book or something, or maybe I'd be with her. And all of a sudden it would come over me that I was going to kill her, and the idea seemed so crazy that I'd almost laugh out loud. Then, I'd start thinking and I'd see it, see that it had to be done, and . . .

It was like being asleep when you were awake and awake when you were asleep. I'd pinch myself, figuratively speaking—I had to keep pinching myself. Then I'd wake up kind of in reverse; I'd go back into the nightmare I had to live in. And everything would be clear and reasonable.

But I still didn't know how to go about doing it. I couldn't figure out a way that would leave me in the clear or even reasonably in the clear. And I sure had to be on this one. I was Humpty-Dumpty, like Rothman had said, and I couldn't jiggle around very much.

I couldn't think of a way because it was a real toughie, and I had to keep remembering the *why* of it. But finally it came to me.

I found a way, because I had to. I couldn't stall any longer.

It happened three days after my talk with Rothman. It was a payday Saturday, and I should have been working, but somehow I hadn't been able to bring myself to do it. I'd stayed in the house all day with the shades drawn, pacing back and forth, wandering from room to room. And when night came I was still there. I was sitting in Dad's office, with nothing on but the little desk light; and I heard these footsteps moving lightly across the porch, and the sound of the screen door opening.

It was way too early for Amy; but I wasn't jittered any. I'd had people walk in before like this.

I stepped to the door of the office just as he came into the hall.

"I'm sorry, stranger," I said. "The doctor doesn't practice any more. The sign's just there for sentimental reasons."

"That's okay, bud"—he walked right toward me and I had to move back—"it's just a little burn."

"But I don't—"

"A cigar burn," he said. And he held his hand out, palm up.

And, at last, I recognized him.

He sat down in Dad's big leather chair, grinning at me. He

brushed his hand across the arm, knocking off the coffee cup and saucer I'd left there.

"We got some talking to do, bud, and I'm thirsty. You got some whiskey around? An unopened bottle? I ain't no whiskey hog, understand, but some places I like to see a seal on a bottle."

"I've got a phone around," I said, "and the jail's about six blocks away. Now, drag your ass out of here before you find yourself in it."

"Huh-uh," he said. "You want to use that phone, go right ahead, bud."

I started to. I figured he'd be afraid to go through with it, and if he did, well, my word was still better than any bum's. No one had anything on me, and I was still Lou Ford. And he wouldn't get his mouth open before someone smacked a sap in it.

"Go ahead, bud, but it'll cost you. It'll sure cost you. And it won't be just the price of a burned hand."

I held onto the phone, but I didn't lift the receiver. "Go on," I said, "let's have it."

"I got interested in you, bud. I spent a year stretch on the Houston pea farm, and I seen a couple guys like you there; and I figured it might pay to watch you a little. So I followed you that night. I heard some of the talk you had with that labor fellow . . ."

"And I reckon it meant a hell of a lot to you, didn't it?" I said.

"No, sir," he wagged his head, "hardly meant a thing to me. Fact is, it didn't mean much to me a couple nights later when you came up to that old farm house where I was shacked up, and then cut cross-prairie to that little white house. That didn't mean much neither, *then* . . . You say you had some whiskey, bud? An unopened bottle?"

I went into the laboratory, and got a pint of old prescription liquor from the stores cabinet. I brought it back with a glass; and he opened it and poured the glass half full.

"Have one on the house," he said, and handed it to me.

I drank it; I needed it. I passed the glass back to him, and he dropped it on the floor with the cup and saucer. He took a big swig from the bottle, and smacked his lips.

"No, sir," he went on, "it didn't mean a thing, and I couldn't stick around to figure it out. I hiked out of there early Monday morning, and hit up the pipeline for a job. They put me with a jackhammer crew way the hell over on the Pecos, so far out I couldn't make town my first payday. Just three of us there by ourselves cut off from the whole danged world. But this payday it was different. We'd finished up on the Pecos, and I got to come in. I caught up on the news, bud, and those things you'd done and said meant plenty."

I nodded. I felt kind of glad. It was out of my hands, now, and the pieces were falling into place. I knew I had to do it, and how I was going to do it.

He took another swallow of whiskey and dug a cigarette from his shirt pocket. "I'm an understandin' man, bud, and the law ain't helped me none and I ain't helpin' it none. Unless I have to. What you figure it's worth to you to go on living?"

"I—" I shook my head. I had to go slow. I couldn't give in too easily. "I haven't got much money," I said. "Just what I make on my job."

"You got this place. Must be worth a pretty tidy sum, too."

"Yeah, but, hell," I said. "It's all I've got. If I'm not going to have a window left to throw it out of, there's not much percentage in keeping you quiet."

"You might change your mind about that, bud," he said. But he didn't sound too firm about it.

"Anyway," I said, "it's just not practical to sell it. People would wonder what I'd done with the money. I'd have to account for it to the government and pay a big chunk of taxes on it. For that matter—I reckon you're in kind of a hurry—"

"You reckon right, bud."

"Well, it would take quite a while to get rid of a place like this. I'd want to sell it to a doctor, someone who'd pay for my Dad's practice and equipment. It'd be worth at least a third more that way, but the deal couldn't be swung in a hurry."

He studied me, suspiciously, trying to figure out how much if any I was stringing him. As a matter of fact, I wasn't lying more'n a little bit.

"I don't know," he said slowly. "I don't know much about them things. Maybe—you reckon you could swing a loan on it?"

"Well, I'd sure hate to do that—"

"That ain't what I asked you, bud."

"But, look," I said, making it good, "how would I pay it back out of my job? I just couldn't do it. I probably wouldn't get more than five thousand after they took out interest and brokerage fees. And I'd have to turn right around somewhere and swing another loan to pay off the first one, and—hell, that's no way to do business. Now, if you'll just give me four-five months to find someone who—"

"Huh-uh. How long it take you to swing this loan? A week?"

"Well . . ." I might have to give her a little longer than that. I wanted to give her longer. "I think that'd be a little bit quick. I'd say two weeks; but I'd sure hate—"

"Five thousand," he said, sloshing the whiskey in the bottle. "Five thousand in two weeks. Two weeks from tonight. All right, bud, we'll call that a deal. An' it'll be a deal, understand? I ain't no hog about money or nothin'. I get the five thousand and that's the last we'll see of each other."

I scowled and cussed, but I said, "Well, all right."

He tucked the whiskey into his hip pocket, and stood up. "Okay, bud. I'm goin' back out to the pipeline tonight. This ain't a very friendly place for easy-livin' men, so I'll stay out there another payday. But don't get no notions about runnin' out on me."

"How the hell could I?" I said. "You think I'm crazy?"

"You ask unpleasant questions, bud, and you may get unpleasant answers. Just be here with that five grand two weeks from tonight and there won't be no trouble."

I gave him a clincher; I still felt I might be giving in too easy. "Maybe you'd better not come here," I said. "Someone might see you and—"

"No one will. I'll watch myself like I did tonight. I ain't no more anxious for trouble than you are."

"Well," I said, "I just thought it might be better if we—"

"Now, bud"—he shook his head—"what happened the last

time you was out wanderin' around old empty farm houses? It didn't turn out so good, did it?"

"All right," I said. "Suit yourself about it."

"That's just what I aim to do." He glanced toward the clock. "We got it all straight, then. Five thousand, two weeks from tonight, nine o'clock. That's it, and don't slip up on it."

"Don't worry. You'll get it," I said.

He stood at the front door a moment, sizing up the situation outside. Then he slipped out and off of the porch, and disappeared in the trees on the lawn.

I grinned, feeling a little sorry for him. It was funny the way these people kept asking for it. Just latching onto you, no matter how you tried to brush them off, and almost telling you how they wanted it done. Why'd they all have to come to me to get killed? Why couldn't they kill themselves?

I cleaned up the broken dishes in the office. I went upstairs and lay down and waited for Amy. I didn't have long to wait.

I didn't have long; and in a way she was the same as always, sort of snappy and trying not to be. But I could sense a difference, the stiffness that comes when you want to say or do something and don't know how to begin. Or maybe she could sense it in me; maybe we sensed it in each other.

I guess that's the way it was, because we both came out with it together. We spoke at the same time:

"Lou, why don't we . . ."⎫
"Amy, why don't we . . ."⎭ we said,

We laughed and said "bread and butter," and then she spoke again.

"You do want to, don't you, darling? Honest and truly?"

"Didn't I just start to ask you?" I said.

"How—when do you—"

"Well, I was thinking a couple of weeks would—"

"Darling!" She kissed me. "That was just what I was going to say!"

There was just a little more. That last piece of the picture needed one more little push.

"What are you thinking about, darling?"

"Well, I was thinking we've always had to do kinda like people expected us to. I mean— Well, what were you thinking about?"

"You tell me first, Lou."

"No, you tell me, Amy."

"Well . . ."

"Well . . ."

"Why don't we elope," we said.

We laughed, and she threw her arms around me, snuggled up against me, sort of shivery but warm; so hard but so soft. And she whispered into my ear and I whispered into hers:

"Bread and butter . . .

"Bad luck, stay 'way from my darling."

Seventeen

HE SHOWED UP on, well, I guess it was the following Tuesday. The Tuesday after the Saturday the bum had shown up and Amy and I had decided to elope. He was a tall, stoop-shouldered guy with a face that seemed to be all bone and yellowish tightly drawn skin. He said his name was Dr. John Smith and that he was just passing through, he was just looking around in this section, and he'd heard—he'd thought, perhaps—that the house and the practice might be on the market.

It was around nine o'clock in the morning. By rights, I should have been headed for the courthouse. But I wasn't knocking myself out, these days, to get downtown; and Dad had always laid himself out for any doctors that came around.

"I've thought about selling it, off and on," I said, "but that's about as far as it's gone. I've never taken any steps in that direction. But come in, anyway. Doctors are always welcome in this house."

I sat him down in the office and brought out a box of cigars, and got him some coffee. Then, I sat down with him and tried to visit. I can't say that I liked him much. He kept staring at me out of his big hollow eyes like I was really some sort of curiosity, something to look at instead of to talk to. But—well, doctors get funny mannerisms. They live in an I'm-the-King world, where everyone else is wrong but them.

"You're a general practitioner, Doctor Smith?" I said. "I wouldn't want to discourage you, but I'm afraid the general

practice field is pretty well the monopoly here of long-estab-
lished doctors. Now—I haven't thought too much about dis-
posing of this place, but I might consider it—now, I do think
there's room for a good man in pediatrics or obstetrics . . ."

I let it hang there, and he blinked and came out of his
trance.

"As a matter of fact, I am interested in those fields, Mr.
Ford. I would—uh—hesitate to call myself a specialist, but—
uh—"

"I think you might find an opening here, then," I said.
"What's been your experience in treating nephritis, doctor?
Would you say that inoculation with measles has sufficiently
proven itself as a curative agent to warrant the inherent
danger?"

"Well, uh—uh—" He crossed his legs. "Yes and no."

I nodded seriously. "You feel that there are two sides to the
question?"

"Well—uh—yes."

"I see," I said. "I'd never thought about it quite that way,
but I can see that you're right."

"That's your—uh—specialty, Mr. Ford? Children's diseases?"

"I haven't any specialty, doctor," I laughed. "I'm living
proof of the adage about the shoemaker's son going bare-
footed. But I've always been interested in children, and I suppose the little I do know about medicine is confined to
pediatrics."

"I see. Well, uh, as a matter of fact, most of my work has
been in—uh—geriatrics."

"You should do well here, then," I said. "We have a high
percentage of elderly people in the population. Geriatrics,
eh?"

"Well, uh, as a matter of fact . . ."

"You know *Max Jacobsohn on Degenerative Diseases*? What
do you think of his theorem as to the ratio between deceler-
ated activity and progressive senility? I can understand the basic concept, of course, but my math isn't good enough to
allow me to appreciate his formulae. Perhaps you'll explain
them to me?"

"Well, I—uh—it's pretty complicated . . .''

"I see. You feel, perhaps, that Jacobsohn's approach may be a trifle empirical? Well, I was inclined to that belief myself, for a time, but I'm afraid it may have been because my own approach was too subjective. For instance. Is the condition pathological? Is it psycho-pathological? Is it psycho-pathological-psychosomatic? Yes, yes, yes. It can be one or two or all three—*but* in varying degrees, doctor. Like it or not, we must contemplate an x factor. Now, to strike an equation—and you'll pardon me for oversimplifying—let's say that our cosine is. . . .''

I went on smiling and talking, wishing that Max Jacobsohn was here to see him. From what I'd heard of Dr. Jacobsohn, he'd probably grab this guy by the seat of his pants and boot him out into the street.

"As a matter of fact," he interrupted me, rubbing a big bony hand across his forehead, "I have a very bad headache. What do you do for headaches, Mr. Ford.''

"I never have them," I said.

"Uh, oh? I thought perhaps that studying so much, sitting up late nights when you can't—uh—sleep . . .''

"I never have any trouble sleeping," I said.

"You don't worry a lot? I mean that in a town such as this where there is so much gossip—uh—malicious gossip, you don't feel that people are talking about you? It doesn't—uh—seem unbearable at times?''

"You mean," I said, slowly, "do I feel persecuted? Well, as a matter of fact, I do, doctor. But I never worry about it. I can't say that it doesn't bother me, but—''

"Yes? Yes, Mr. Ford?''

"Well, whenever it gets too bad, I just step out and kill a few people. I frig them to death with a barbed-wire cob I have. After that I feel fine.''

I'd been trying to place him, and finally it had come to me. It's been several years since I'd seen that big ugly mug in one of the out-of-town papers, and the picture hadn't been too good a resemblance. But I remembered it, now, and some of the story I'd read about him. He'd taken his degree at the University of Edinburgh at a time when we were admitting their graduates to practice. He'd killed half a dozen people before he picked up a jerkwater PhD, and edged into psychiatry.

Out on the West Coast, he'd worked himself into some staff job with the police. And then a big murder case had cropped up, and he'd gotten hog-wild raw with the wrong suspects—people who had the money and influence to fight back. He hadn't lost his license, but he'd had to skip out fast. Now, well, I knew what he'd be doing now. What he'd have to be doing. Lunatics can't vote, so why should the legislature vote a lot of money for them?

"As a matter of fact—uh—" It was just beginning to soak in on him. "I think I'd better—"

"Stick around," I said. "I'll show you that corncob. Or maybe you can show me something from your collection—those Japanese sex goods you used to flash around. What'd you do with that rubber phallus you had? The one you squirted into that high school kid's face? Didn't you have time to pack it when you jumped the Coast?"

"I'm a-afraid you have me confused w-with—"

"As a matter of fact," I said, "I *do*. But you don't have me confused. You wouldn't know how to begin. You wouldn't know shit from wild honey, so go back and sign your report that way. Sign it shitbird. And you'd better add a footnote to the effect, that the next son-of-a-bitch they send out here is going to get kicked so hard he'll be wearing his asshole for a collar."

He backed out into the hall and toward the front door, the bones in his face wobbling and twitching under the tight yellow skin. I followed him grinning.

He stuck a hand out sideways and lifted his hat from the halltree. He put it on backwards; and I laughed and took a quick step toward him. He almost fell out the door; and I picked up his briefcase and threw it into the yard.

"Take care of yourself, doc," I said. "Take good care of your keys. If you ever lose them, you won't be able to get out."

"You—you'll be . . ." The bones were jerking and jumping. He'd got down the steps, and his nerve was coming back. "If I ever get you up—"

"Me, doc? But I sleep swell. I don't have headaches. I'm not worried a bit. The only thing that bothers me is that corncob wearing out."

He snatched up the briefcase and went loping down the walk, his neck stuck out like a buzzard's. I slammed the door, and made more coffee.

I cooked a big second breakfast, and ate it all.

You see, it didn't make a bit of difference. I hadn't lost a thing by telling him off. I'd thought they were closing in on me, and now I knew it. And they'd know that I knew it. But nothing was lost by that, and nothing else had changed.

They could still only guess, suspect. They had no more to go on than they'd ever had. They still wouldn't have anything two weeks—well, ten days from now. They'd have more suspicions, they'd *feel* surer than ever. But they wouldn't have any proof.

They could only find the proof in me—in what I was—and I'd never show it to 'em.

I finished the pot of coffee, smoked a cigar, and washed and wiped the dishes. I tossed some bread scraps into the yard for the sparrows, and watered the sweet potato plant in the kitchen window.

Then, I got out the car and headed for town; and I was thinking how good it had been to talk—even if he had turned out to be a phony—for a while. To talk, really talk, for even a little while.

Eighteen

I KILLED Amy Stanton on Saturday night on the fifth of April, 1952, at a few minutes before nine o'clock.

It had been a bright, crisp spring day, just warm enough so's you'd know that summer was coming, and the night was just tolerably cool. And she fixed her folks an early dinner, and got them off to a picture show about seven. Then, at eight-thirty, she came over to my place, and . . .

Well, I saw them going by my house—her folks, I mean— and I guess she must have been standing at their gate waving to 'em, because they were looking back and waving. Then, I guess, she went back into the house and started getting ready real fast; taking her hair down and bathing, and fixing her face and getting her bags packed. I guess she must have been busy as all-hell, jumping sideways to get ready, because she hadn't been able to do much while her folks were around. I guess she must have been chasing back and forth, turning on the electric iron, shutting off the bathwater, straightening the seams in her stockings, moving her mouth in and out to center the lipstick while she jerked the pins from her hair.

Why, hell, she had dozens of things to do, dozens of 'em, and if she'd just moved a little bit slower, ever so little—but Amy was one of those quick, sure girls. She was ready with time to spare, I guess, and then—I guess—she stood in front of the mirror, frowning and smiling, pouting and tossing her head, tucking her chin in and looking up under her brows; studying herself frontwards and sidewards, turning around and looking over her shoulder and brushing at her bottom, hitching her girdle up a little and down a little and then gripping it by both sides and sort of wiggling her hips in it. Then . . . then, I guess that must have been about all; she was all ready. So she came over where I was, and I . . .

I was ready too. I wasn't fully dressed, but I was ready for her.

I was standing in the kitchen waiting for her, and she was out of breath from hurrying so fast, I guess, and her bags were pretty heavy, I guess, and I guess . . .

I guess I'm not ready to tell about it yet. It's too soon, and it's not necessary yet. Because, hell, we had a whole two weeks before then, before Saturday, April 5th, 1952, at a few minutes before nine p.m.

We had two weeks and they were pretty good ones, because for the first time in I don't remember when my mind was really free. The end was coming up, it was rushing toward me, and everything would be over soon. I could think, well, go ahead and say something, do something, and it won't matter now. I can stall you *that* long; and I don't have to watch myself any more.

I was with her every night. I took her everywhere she

wanted to go, and did everything she wanted to do. And it wasn't any trouble, because she didn't want to go much or do much. One evening we parked by the high school, and watched the baseball team work out. Another time we went down to the depot to see the Tulsa Flyer go through with the people looking out the dining car windows and the people staring back from the observation car.

That's about all we did, things like that, except maybe to drive down to the confectionery for some ice cream. Most of the time we just stayed at home, at my house. Both of us sitting in Dad's big old chair, or both of us stretched out upstairs, face to face, holding each other.

Just holding each other a lot of nights.

We'd lie there for hours, not speaking for an hour at a time sometimes; but the time didn't drag any. It seemed to rush by. I'd lie there listening to the ticking of the clock, listening to her heart beat with it, and I'd wonder why it had to tick so fast; I'd wonder *why*. And it was hard to wake up and go to sleep, to go back into the nightmare where I could remember.

We had a few quarrels but no bad ones. I just wasn't going to have them; I let her have her own way and she tried to do the same with me.

One night she said she was going to the barbershop with me some time, and see that I got a decent haircut for a change. And I said—before I remembered—whenever she felt like doing that, I'd start wearing it in a braid. So we had a little spat, but nothing bad.

Then, one night she asked me how many cigars I smoked in a day, and I said I didn't keep track of 'em. She asked me why I didn't smoke cigarettes like "everyone else" did, and I said I didn't reckon that everyone else did smoke 'em. I said there was two members of my family that never smoked 'em, Dad and me. She said, well, of course, if you thought more of him than you do of me, there's nothing more to be said. And I said, Jesus Christ, how do you figure—what's that got to do with it?

But it was just a little spat. Nothing bad at all. I reckon she forgot about it right away like she did the first one.

I think she must have had a mighty good time those two weeks. Better'n any she'd ever had before.

So the two weeks passed, and the night of April fifth came; and she hustled her folks off to a show, and scampered around getting ready, and she got ready. And at eight-thirty she came over to my place and I was waiting for her. And I . . .

But I guess I'm getting ahead of myself again. There's some other things to tell first.

I went to work every working day of those two weeks; and believe me it wasn't easy. I didn't want to face anyone—I wanted to stay there in the house with the shades drawn, and not see anyone at all, and I knew I couldn't do that. I went to work, I forced myself to, just like always.

They suspected me; and I'd let 'em know that I knew. But there wasn't a thing on my conscience; I wasn't afraid of a thing. And I proved that there wasn't by going down. Because how could a man who'd done what they thought I had, go right on about his business and look people in the eye?

I was sore, sure. My feelings were hurt. But I wasn't afraid and I proved it.

Most of the time, at first, anyway, I wasn't given much to do. And believe me that was hard, standing around with my face hanging out and pretending like I didn't notice or give a damn. And when I did get a little job, serving a warrant or something like that, there was always a reason for another deputy to go along with me. He'd be embarrassed and puzzled, because, of course, they were keeping the secret at the top, between Hendricks and Conway and Bob Maples. He'd wonder what was up but he couldn't ask, because, in our own way, we're the politest people in the world; we'll joke around and talk about everything except what's on our minds. But he'd wonder and he'd be embarrassed, and he'd try to brag me up—maybe talk me up about the Johnnie Pappas deal to make me feel better.

I was coming back from lunch one day when the hall floors had just been oiled. And they didn't make much noise when you stepped on them, and when you kind of had to pick your way along they didn't make any at all. Deputy Jeff Plummer and Sheriff Bob were talking, and they didn't hear me coming. So I stopped just short of the door and listened. I listened and I saw them: I knew them so well I could see 'em without looking.

Bob was at his desk, pretending to thumb through some papers; and his glasses were down on the end of his nose, and he was looking up over them now and then. And he didn't like what he had to say, but you'd never know it the way his eyes came up over those glasses and the way he talked. Jeff Plummer was hunkered down in one of the windows, studying his finger-nails, maybe, his jaws moving on a stick of gum. And he didn't like telling Bob off—and he didn't sound like he was; just easy-going and casual—but he was sure as hell doing it.

"No, sir, Bob," he drawled. "Been kind of studyin' things over, and I reckon I ain't going to do no spying no more. Ain't going to do it a-tall."

"You got your mind made up, huh? You're plumb set?"

"Well, now, it sure looks that way, don't it? Yes, sir, I reckon that's prob'ly the way it is. Can't rightly see it no other way."

"You see how it's possible to do a job if'n you don't follow orders? You reckon you can do that?"

"Now"—Jeff was looking—*looking*—real pleased, like he'd drawn aces to three kings—"now, I'm sure proud you mentioned that, Bob. I plain admire a man that comes square to a point."

There was a second's silence, then a *clink* as Jeff's badge hit the desk. He slid out of the window and sauntered toward the door, smiling but not with his eyes. And Bob cussed and jumped up.

"You ornery coyote! You tryin' to knock my eyes out with that thing? I ever catch you throwin' it around again, I'll whup you down to a nubbin."

Jeff scuffed his boots; he cleared his throat. He said it was a plumb purty day out, and a man'd have to be plain out of his mind to claim different.

"I reckon a man hadn't ought to ask you a question about all the hocus-pocus around here, now had he, Bob? It wouldn't be what you'd call proper."

"Well, now, I don't know as I'd put it that way. Don't reckon I'd even prod him about why he was askin'. I'd just figure he was a man, and a man just does what he has to."

I slipped into the men's john and stayed there a while. And when I went into the office, Jeff Plummer was gone and Bob gave me a warrant to serve. By myself. He didn't exactly meet my eye, but he seemed pretty happy. He had his neck out a mile—he had everything to lose and nothing to gain—and he was happy.

And I didn't know whether I felt better or not.

Bob didn't have much longer to live, and the job was all he had. Jeff Plummer had a wife and four kids, and he was just about standing in the middle of his wardrobe whenever you saw him. People like that, well, they don't make up their mind about a man in a hurry. But once it's made up they hardly ever change it. They can't. They'd almost rather die than do it.

I went on about my business every day, and things were easier for me in a sense, because people acted easier around me, and twice as hard in another way. Because the folks that trust you, that just won't hear no bad about you nor even think it, those are the ones that are hard to fool. You can't put your heart in the job.

I'd think about my—those people, so many of them, and I'd wonder *why* . I'd have to go through it all again, step by step. And just about the time I'd get it settled, I'd start wondering all over again.

I guess I got kind of sore at myself. And at them. All those people. I'd think, why, in the hell did they have to do it—I didn't ask 'em to stick their necks out; I'm not begging for friendship. But they *did* give me their friendship and they *did* stick their necks out. So, along toward the last, I was sticking mine out.

I stopped by the Greek's place every day. I looked over the work and had him explain things to me, and I'd offer him a lift when he had to go some place. I'd say it was sure going to be one up-to-date restaurant and that Johnnie would sure like it—that he did like it. Because there hadn't ever been a better boy, and now he could look on, look down, and admire things the same as we could. I said I knew he could, that Johnnie was really happy now.

And the Greek didn't have much to say for a while—he was polite but he didn't say much. Then, pretty soon, he was taking me out in the kitchen for coffee; and he'd walk me clear out to my car when I had to leave. He'd hang around me, nodding and nodding while I talked about Johnnie. And once in a while he'd remember that maybe he ought to be ashamed, and I knew he wanted to apologize but was afraid of hurting my feelings.

Chester Conway had been staying in Fort Worth, but he came back in town one day for a few hours and I made it my business to hear about it. I was driving by his offices real slow, around two in the afternoon, when he came barging out looking for a taxi. And before he knew what was happening, I had him in charge. I hopped out, took his briefcase away from him, and hustled him into my car.

It was the last thing he'd've expected of me. He was too set back to balk, and he didn't have time to say anything. And after we were headed for the airport, he didn't get a chance. Because I was doing all the talking.

I said, "I've been hoping to run into you, Mr. Conway. I wanted to thank you for the hospitality you showed me in Fort Worth. It was sure thoughtful of you at a time like that, to think of me and Bob's comfort, and I guess I wasn't so thoughtful myself. I was kind of tired, just thinkin' of my own problems instead of yours, how you must feel, and I reckon I was pretty snappy with you there at the airport. But I didn't really mean anything by it, Mr. Conway, and I've been wanting to apologize. I wouldn't blame you a bit if you were put out with me, because I ain't ever had much sense and I guess I've made a hell of a mess of things.

"Now, I knew Elmer was kind of innocent and trusting and I knew a woman like that just couldn't be much good. I shoulda done like you said and gone there with him—I don't rightly see how I could the way she was acting, but I shoulda done that anyway. And don't think I don't know it now, and if cussing me out will help any or if you want to get my job, and I know you can get it, I won't hold any grudge. No matter what you did it wouldn't be enough, it wouldn't bring Elmer back. An' . . . I never got to know him real well, but in a way kinda I felt like I did. I reckon it must've been because he looked so much like you, I'd see him from a distance some times and I'd think it was you. I guess maybe that's one

reason I wanted to see you today. It was kinda like seein'
Elmer again. I could sorta feel for a minute that he was still
here an' nothing had ever happened. An' . . ."

We'd come to the airport.

He got out without speaking or looking at me, and strode
off to the plane. Moving fast, never turning around or looking
sideways; almost like he was running away from something.

He started up the ramp, but he wasn't moving so fast now.
He was walking slower and slower, and halfway up he almost
stopped. Then he went on, plodding, dragging his feet; and
he reached the top. And he stood there for a second, blocking
the door.

He turned around, gave the briefcase a little jerk, and
ducked inside the plane.

He'd waved to me.

I drove back to town, and I guess I gave up about then. It
was no use. I'd done everything I could. I'd dropped it in
their plates, and rubbed their noses in it. And it was no use.
They wouldn't see it.

No one would stop me.

So, on Saturday night, April 5th, 1952, at a few minutes before nine o'clock, I . . .

But I guess there's another thing or two to tell you first,
and—but I *will* tell you about it. I want to tell you, and I
will, exactly how it happened. I won't leave you to figure
things out for yourself.

In lots of books I read, the writer seems to go haywire every
time he reaches a high point. He'll start leaving out punctuation and running his words together and babble about stars
flashing and sinking into a deep dreamless sea. And you can't
figure out whether the hero's laying his girl or a cornerstone.
I guess that kind of crap is supposed to be pretty deep stuff—
a lot of the book reviewers eat it up, I notice. But the way I
see it is, the writer is just too goddam lazy to do his job. And
I'm not lazy, whatever else I am. I'll tell you everything.

But I want to get everything in the right order.

I want you to understand how it was.

Late Saturday afternoon, I got Bob Maples alone for a minute and told him I wouldn't be able to work that night. I said
that Amy and me had something mighty important to do, and

maybe I wouldn't be getting in Monday or Tuesday either; and I gave him a wink.

"Well, now"—he hesitated, frowning. "Well, now, you don't think maybe that—" Then, he gripped my hand and wrung it. "That's real good news, Lou. Real good. I know you'll be happy together."

"I'll try not to lay off too long," I said. "I reckon things are, well, kind of up in the air and—"

"No, they ain't," he said, sticking his chin out. "Everything's all right, and it's going to stay that way. Now go on and buss Amy for me, and don't you worry about nothing."

It still wasn't real late in the day, so I drove out on Derrick Road and parked a while.

Then I went home, leaving the car parked out in front, and fixed dinner.

I stretched out on the bed for about an hour, letting my food settle. I drew water in the bath tub and got in.

I lay in the tub for almost an hour, soaking and smoking and thinking. Finally, I got out, looked at the clock and began laying out clothes.

I packed my gladstone, and cinched the straps on it. I put on clean underwear and socks and new-pressed pants, and my Sunday go-to-meetin' boots. I left off my shirt and tie.

I sat on the edge of the bed smoking until eight o'clock. Then, I went downstairs to the kitchen.

I turned the light on in the pantry, moving the door back and forth until I had it like I wanted it. Until there was just enough light in the kitchen. I looked around, making sure that all the blinds were drawn, and went into Dad's office.

I took down the concordance to the Bible and removed the four hundred dollars in marked money, Elmer's money. I dumped the drawers of Dad's desk on the floor. I turned off the light, pulled the door almost shut, and went back into the kitchen.

The evening newspaper was spread out on the table. I slid a butcher knife under it, and— And it was that time. I heard her coming.

She came up the back steps and across the porch, and banged and fumbled around for a minute getting the door open. She came in, out of breath kind of and out of temper,

and pushed the door shut behind her. And she saw me standing there, not saying anything because I'd forgotten *why* and
I was trying to remember. And, finally, I did remember.

So—or did I mention it already?—on Saturday night, the
fifth of April, 1952, at a few minutes before nine o'clock I killed
Amy Stanton.

Or maybe you could call it suicide.

Nineteen

SHE SAW me and it startled her for a second. Then she
dropped her two traveling cases on the floor and gave one of
'em a kick, and brushed a wisp of hair from her eyes.

"Well!" she snapped. "I don't suppose it would occur to
you to give me a little help! Why didn't you leave the car in
the garage, anyway?"

I shook my head. I didn't say anything.

"I'll swear, Lou Ford! Sometimes I think— And you're not
even ready yet! You're always talking about how slow I am,
and here you stand, on your own wedding night of all things,
and you haven't—" She stopped suddenly, her mouth shut
tight, her breasts rising and falling. And I heard the kitchen
clock tick ten times before she spoke again. "I'm sorry, darling," she said softly. "I didn't mean—"

"Don't say anything more, Amy," I said. "Just don't say
anything more."

She smiled and came toward me with her arms held out.
"I won't, darling. I won't ever say anything like that again.
But I do want to tell you how much—"

"Sure," I said. "You want to pour your heart out to me."

And I hit her in the guts as hard as I could.

My fist went back against her spine, and the flesh closed
around it to the wrist. I jerked back on it, I had to jerk, and
she flopped forward from the waist, like she was hinged.

Her hat fell off, and her head went clear down and touched
the floor. And then she toppled over, completely over, like a
kid turning a somersault. She lay on her back, eyes bulging,
rolling her head from side to side.

She was wearing a white blouse and a light cream-colored suit; a new one, I reckon, because I didn't remember seeing it before. I got my hand in the front of the blouse, and ripped it down to the waist. I jerked the skirt up over her head, and she jerked and shook all over; and there was a funny sound like she was trying to laugh.

And then I saw the puddle spreading out under her.

I sat down and tried to read the paper. I tried to keep my eyes on it. But the light wasn't very good, not good enough to read by, and she kept moving around. It looked like she couldn't lie still.

Once I felt something touch my boot, and I looked down and it was her hand. It was moving back and forth across the toe of my boot. It moved up along the ankle and the leg, and somehow I was afraid to move away. And then her fingers were at the top, clutching down inside; and I almost couldn't move. I stood up and tried to jerk away, and the fingers held on.

I dragged her two-three feet before I could break away.

Her fingers kept on moving, sliding and crawling back and forth, and finally they got ahold of her purse and held on. They dragged it down inside of her skirt, and I couldn't see it or her hands any more.

Well, that was all right. It would look better to have her hanging onto her purse. And I grinned a little, thinking about it. It was so much like her, you know, to latch onto her purse. She'd always been so tight, and . . . and I guess she'd had to be.

There wasn't a better family in town than the Stantons. But both her folks had been ailing for years, and they didn't have much any more aside from their home. She'd had to be tight, like any damned fool ought to have known; because there wasn't any other way of being, and that's all any of us ever are: what we have to be. And I guessed it hadn't been very funny when I'd kidded her dead-pan, and acted surprised when she got mad.

I guess that stuff she'd brought to me when I was sick wasn't really crap. It was as good as she knew how to fix. I guess that dog of theirs didn't have to chase horses unless'n he wanted the exercise. I—

Why the hell didn't he come? Hell, she hadn't had a real breath now in almost thirty minutes, and it was hard as hell on her. I knew how hard it was and I held my own breath a while because we'd always done things together, and . . .

He came.

I'd locked the front screen, so that he couldn't just walk in, and I heard him tugging at it.

I gave her two hard kicks in the head and she rose up off the floor, her skirt falling down off of her face, and I knew there wouldn't be any doubt about her. She was dead on the night of— Then I went and opened the door and let him in.

I pushed the roll of marked twenties on him and said, "Stick this in your pocket. I've got the rest back in the kitchen," and I started back there.

I knew he would put the money in his pocket, and you do too if you can remember back when you were a kid. You'd walk up to a guy and say, "Here, hold this," and probably he'd pulled the same gag himself; he'd know you were handing him a horse turd or a prickly pear or a dead mouse. But if you pulled it fast enough, he'd do just what you told him.

I pulled it fast, and headed right back toward the kitchen. And he was right on my heels, because he didn't want me to get too far away from him.

There was just a little light, like I've said. I was between him and her. He was right behind me, watching me instead of anything else, and we went into the kitchen and I stepped aside quickly.

He almost stepped in her stomach. I guess his foot did touch it for a split second.

He pulled it back, staring down at her like his eyes were steel and she was a magnet. He tried to tug them away, and they'd just roll, going all-white in his head, and finally he got them away.

He looked at me and his lips shook as though he'd been playing a juice-harp, and he said:

"Yeeeeeeee!"

It was a hell of a funny sound, like a siren with a slippy chain that can't quite get started. "Yeeeeee!" he said. "Yeeeeee!" It sounded funny as hell, and he looked funny as hell.

Did you ever see one of these two-bit jazz singers? You know, trying to put something across with their bodies that they haven't got the voice to do? They lean back from the waist a little with their heads hanging forward and their hands held up about even with their ribs and swinging limp. And they sort of wobble and roll on their hips.

That's the way he looked, and he kept making that damned funny noise, his lips quivering ninety to the minute and his eyes rolling all-white.

I laughed and laughed, he looked and sounded so funny I couldn't help it. Then, I remembered what he'd done and I stopped laughing, and got mad—sore all over.

"You son-of-a-bitch," I said. "I was going to marry that poor little girl. We were going to elope and she caught you going through the house and you tried to . . ."

I stopped, because he hadn't done it at all. But he *could* have done it. He could've done it just as easy as not. The son-of-a-bitch could have, but he was just like everyone else. He was too nicey-nice and pretendsy to do anything really hard. But he'd stand back and crack the whip over me, keep moving around me every way I turned so that I couldn't get away no matter what I did, and it was always now-don't-you-do-nothin'-bud; but they kept cracking that old whip all the time they were sayin' it. And they—he'd done it all right; and I wasn't going to take the blame. I could be just as tricky and pretendsy as they were.

I could . . .

I went blind ma—angry seeing him so pretendsy shocked, "Yeeeing!" and shivering and doing that screwy dance with his hands—hell, he hadn't had to watch *her* hands!—and white-rolling his eyes. What right did he have to act like that? I was the one that should have been acting that way, but, oh, no, I couldn't. That was their—his right to act that way, and I had to hold in and do all the dirty work.

I was as mad as all-hell.

I snatched the butcher-knife from under the newspaper, and made for him.

And my foot slipped where she'd been lying.

I went sprawling, almost knocking him over backwards if he hadn't moved, and the knife flew out of my hands.

I couldn't have moved a finger for a minute. I was laid out flat, helpless, without any weapon. And I could have maybe rolled a little and put my arms around her, and we'd have been together like we'd always been.

But do you think he'd do it? Do you think he'd pick up that knife and use it, just a little thing like that that wouldn't have been a bit of trouble? Oh, hell, no, oh, God, no, oh, Christ and Mary and all the Saints . . . ?

No.

All he could do was beat it, just like they always did.

I grabbed up the knife and took off after the heartless son-of-a-bitch.

He was out to the street sidewalk by the time I got to the front door; the dirty bastard had sneaked a head start on me. When I got out to the walk, he was better'n a half-block away, heading toward the center of town. I took after him as fast as I could go.

That wasn't very fast on account of the boots. I've seen plenty of men out here that never walked fifty miles altogether in their lives. But he wasn't moving very fast either. He was sort of skipping, jerky, rather than running or walking. He was skipping and tossing his head, and his hair was flying. And he still had his elbows held in at his sides, with his hands doing that funny floppy dance, and he kept saying—it was louder, now—that old siren was warming up—he kept saying, kind of screaming:

"Yeeeee! Yeeeeee! Yeeeeeeeeee. . . . !"

He was skipping and flopping his hands and tossing his head like one of those holy roller preachers at a brushwoods revival meeting. "Yeeeing!" and gone-to-Jesus and all you miserable sinners get right with Gawd like I went and done.

The dirty son-of-a-bitch! How low down can you get?

"MUR-DER!" I yelled. "Stop him, stop him! He killed Amy Stanton! MUR-DER. . . . !"

I yelled at the top of my lungs and I kept yelling. And windows started banging up and doors slammed. And people ran down off their porches. And that snapped him out of that crap—some of it.

He skipped out into the middle of the street, and started moving faster. But I moved faster, too, because it was still dirt

in this block, just one short of the business district, and boots
are meant for dirt.

He saw that I was gaining a little on him, and he tried to
come out of that floppy skippy stuff, but it didn't look like he
could quite make it. Maybe he was using too much steam with
that "Yeeeeing!"

"MURDER!" I yelled. "MUR-DER! Stop him! He killed
Amy Stanton. . . . !"

And everything was happening awful fast. It just sounds like
it was a long time, because I'm not leaving out anything. I'm
trying to tell you exactly how it was, so's you'll be sure to
understand.

Looking up ahead, into the business district, it looked like
a whole army of automobiles was bearing down on us. Then,
suddenly, it was like a big plough had come down the street,
pushing all those cars into the curb.

That's the way people are here in this section. That's the
way they get. You don't see them rushing into the middle of
a commotion to find out what's happening. There's men that
are paid to do that and they do it prompt, without any fuss
or feathers. And the folks know that no one's going to feel
sorry for 'em if they get in the way of a gun butt or a bullet.

"Yeeeeee! Yeeeeee! Yeeeeeeeeeeeeee!" he screamed, skipping and flopping.

"MUR-DER! He killed Amy Stanton. . . ."

And up ahead a little old roadster swung crossways with the
intersection and stopped, and Jeff Plummer climbed out.

He reached down on the floor and took out a Winchester.
Taking his time, easy-like. He leaned back against the fender,
one boot heel hooked through the wheel spokes, and brought
the gun up to his shoulder.

"Halt!" he called.

He called out the one time and then he fired, because the
bum had started to skip toward the side of the street; and a
man sure ought to know better than that.

The bum stumbled and went down, grabbing at his knee.
But he got up again and he was still jerking and flopping his
hands, and it looked like he was reaching into his clothes. And
a man *really* hadn't ought to do that. He hadn't even ought
to look anything like that.

Jeff fired three times, shifting his aim easy-like with each shot, and the bum was dropping with the first one but all three got him. By the time he hit the dirt he didn't have much left in the way of a head.

I fell down on top of him and began beating him, and they had their hands full dragging me off. I babbled out the story—how I'd been upstairs getting ready and I'd heard some commotion but I hadn't thought much of it. And—

And I didn't have to tell it too good. They all seemed to understand how it was.

A doctor pushed through the crowd, Dr. Zweilman, and he gave me a shot in the arm; and then they took me home.

Twenty

I WOKE UP a little after nine the next morning.

My mouth was sticky and my throat dry from the morphine—I don't know why he hadn't used hyoscin like any damned fool should have—and all I could think of right then was how thirsty I was.

I stood in the bathroom, gulping down glass after glass of water, and pretty soon it began to bounce on me. (I'm telling you almost *anything* is better than morphine.) But after a while it stopped. I drank a couple glasses more, and they stayed down. And I scrubbed my face in hot and cold water, and combed my hair.

Then I went back and sat down on the bed, wondering who'd undressed me; and all at once it hit me. Not about her. I wouldn't think about that. But—well, this.

I shouldn't have been alone. Your friends don't leave you alone at a time like that. I'd lost the girl I was going to marry, and I'd been through a terrible experience. And they'd left me alone. There wasn't anyone around to comfort me, or wait on me or just sit and shake their heads and say it was God's will and she was happy, and I—a man that's been through something like that needs those things. He needs all the help and comfort he can get, and I've never held back when one of my friends was bereaved. Why, hell, I—a man isn't himself when one of these disasters strikes. He might do something to himself, and the least people can do is have a nurse around. And . . .

But there wasn't any nurse around. I got up and looked through the other bedrooms, just to make sure.

And I wasn't doing anything to myself. They'd never done anything for me, and I wasn't doing anything for them.

I went downstairs and . . . and the kitchen had been cleaned up. There was no one there but me. I started to make some coffee, and then I thought I heard someone out in front, someone cough. And I was so all-fired glad I felt the tears come to my eyes. I turned off the coffee and went to the front door and opened it.

Jeff Plummer was sitting on the steps.

He was sitting sideways, his back to a porch post. He slanted a glance at me, then let his eyes go straight again, without turning his head.

"Gosh, Jeff," I said. "How long you been out here? Why didn't you knock?"

"Been here quite a spell," he said. And he fingered a stick of gum from his shirt pocket and began to unwrap it. "Yes, sir, I been here quite a spell."

"Well, come on in! I was just—"

"Kinda like it where I am," he said. "Air smells real good. Been smellin' real good, anyways."

He put the gum in his mouth. He folded the wrapper into a neat little square and tucked it back into his pocket.

"Yes, sir," he said, "it's been smellin' real good, and that's a fact."

I felt like I was nailed there in the doorway. I had to stand there and wait, watch his jaws move on that gum, look at him not looking at me. Never looking at me.

"Has there . . . hasn't anyone been—?"

"Told 'em you wasn't up to it," he said. "Told 'em you was all broke up about Bob Maples."

"Well, I— *Bob?*"

"Shot hisself around midnight last night. Yes, sir, pore ol' Bob killed hisself, and I reckon he had to. I reckon I know just how he felt."

And he still didn't look at me.

I closed the door.

I leaned against it, my eyes aching, my head pounding; and I ticked them off with the pounding that reached from my head to my heart . . . Joyce, Elmer, Johnnie Pappas, Amy, the . . . Him, Bob Maples . . . But he hadn't known anything! He couldn't have known, had any real proof. He'd just jumped to conclusions like they were jumping. He couldn't wait for me to explain like, hell, I'd've been glad to do. Hadn't I always been glad to explain? But he couldn't wait; he'd made up his mind without any proof, like they'd made up theirs.

Just because I'd been around when a few people got killed, just because I happened to be around . . .

They couldn't know anything, because I was the only one who could tell 'em—show 'em—and I never had.

And I sure as hell wasn't going to.

Actually, well, logically, and you can't do away with logic, there *wasn't* anything. Existence and proof are inseparables. You have to have the second to have the first.

I held onto that thought, and I fixed myself a nice big breakfast. But I couldn't eat but a little bit. That damned morphine had taken all my appetite, just like it always does. About all I could get down was part of a piece of toast and two-three cups of coffee.

I went back upstairs and lighted a cigar, and stretched out on the bed. I—a man that'd been through what I had belonged in bed.

About a quarter of eleven, I heard the front door open and close, but I stayed right where I was. I still stayed there, stretched out on the bed, smoking, when Howard Hendricks and Jeff Plummer came in.

Howard gave me a curt nod, and drew up a straight chair near the bed. Jeff sat down, sort of out of the way, in an easy chair. Howard could hardly hold himself in, but he was sure trying. He tried. He did the best he could to be stern and sorrowful, and to hold his voice steady.

"Lou," he said, "we—I'm not at all satisfied. Last night's events—these recent events—I don't like them a bit, Lou."

"Well," I said, "that's natural enough. Don't hardly see how you could like 'em. I know I sure don't."

"You know what I mean!"

"Why, sure I do. I know just how—"

"Now, this alleged robber-rapist—this poor devil you'd have us believe was a robber and rapist. We happen to know he was nothing of the kind! He was a pipeline worker. He had a pocket full of wages. And—and yes, we know he wasn't drunk because he'd just had a big steak dinner! He wouldn't have had the slightest reason to be in this house, so Miss Stanton couldn't have—"

"Are you saying he wasn't here, Howard?" I said. "That should be mighty easy to prove."

"Well—he wasn't prowling, that's a certainty! If—"

"Why is it?" I said. "If he wasn't prowling, what was he doing?"

His eyes began to glitter. "Never mind! Let that go for a minute! But I'll tell you this much. If you think you can get away with planting that money on him and making it look like—"

"What money?" I said. "I thought you said it was his wages?"

You see? The guy didn't have any sense. Otherwise, he'd have waited for me to mention that marked money.

"The money you stole from Elmer Conway! The money you took the night you killed him and that woman!"

"Now, wait a minute, wait a minute," I frowned. "Let's take one thing at a time. Let's take the woman. Why would I kill her?"

"Because—well—because you'd killed Elmer and you had to shut her up."

"But why would I kill Elmer? I'd known him all my life. If I'd wanted to do him any harm, I'd sure had plenty of chances."

"You know—" He stopped abruptly.

"Yeah?" I said, puzzled. "Why would I kill Elmer, Howard?"

And he couldn't say, of course. Chester Conway had given him his orders about that.

"You killed him all right," he said, his face reddening. "You killed her. You hanged Johnnie Pappas."

"You're sure not making much sense, Howard." I shook

my head. "You plumb insisted on me talking to Johnnie because you knew how much I liked him and how much he
liked me. Now you're saying I killed him."

"You had to kill him to protect yourself! You'd given him
that marked twenty-dollar bill!"

"Now you really ain't making sense," I said. "Let's see;
there was five hundred dollars missing, wasn't there? You
claiming that I killed Elmer and that woman for five hundred
dollars? Is that what you're saying, Howard?"

"I'm saying that—that—goddammit, Johnnie wasn't anywhere near the scene of the murders! He was stealing tires at
the time they were committed!"

"Is that a fact?" I drawled. "Someone see him, Howard?"

"Yes! I mean, well—uh—"

See what I mean? Shrapnel.

"Let's say that Johnnie didn't do those killings," I said.
"And you know it was mighty hard for me to believe that he
had, Howard. I said so right along. I always did think he was
just scared and kind of out of his mind when he hanged himself. I'd been his only friend, and now it sort of seemed like
I didn't believe in him any more, an'—"

"His friend! Jesus!"

"So I reckon he didn't do it, after all. Poor little Amy was
killed in pretty much the same way that other woman was.
And this man—you say he had a big part of the missing money
on him. Five hundred dollars would seem like a lot of money
to a man like that, an' seeing that the two killings were so
much alike . . ."

I let my voice trail off, smiling at him; and his mouth
opened and went shut again.

Shrapnel. That's all he had.

"You've got it all figured out, haven't you?" he said, softly.
"Four—five murders; six counting poor Bob Maples who
staked everything he had on you, and you sit there explaining
and smiling. You aren't bothered a bit. How can you do it,
Ford? How can—"

I shrugged. "Somebody has to keep their heads, and it sure
looks like you can't. You got some more questions, Howard?"

"Yes," he nodded, slowly. "I've got one. How did Miss
Stanton get those bruises on her body. Old bruises, not made

last night. The same kind of bruises we found on the body of the Lakeland woman. How did she get them, Ford?''

Shrap—

"Bruises?'' I said. "Gosh, you got me there, Howard. How would I know?''

"H-how''—he sputtered—"how would you know?''

"Yeah?'' I said, puzzled. "How?''

"Why, goddam you! You'd been screwing that gal for years! You—''

"Don't say that,'' I said.

"No,'' said Jeff Plummer, "don't say that.''

"But''—Howard turned on him, then turned back to me. "All right, I won't say it! I don't need to say it. That girl had never gone with anyone but you, and only you could have done that to her! You'd been beating on her just like you'd beaten on that whore!''

I laughed, sort of sadly. "And Amy just took it huh, Howard? I bruised her up, and she went right ahead seeing me? She got all ready to marry me? That wouldn't make sense with any woman, and it makes no sense minus about Amy. You sure wouldn't say a thing like that if you'd known Amy Stanton.''

He shook his head, staring, like I was some kind of curiosity. That old shrapnel wasn't doing a thing for him.

"Now, maybe Amy did pick up a bruise here and there,'' I went on. "She had all sorts of work to do, keepin' house and teaching school, and everything there was to be done. It'd been mighty strange if she didn't bang herself up a little, now and—''

"That's not what I mean. You know that's not what I mean.''

"—but if you're thinking I did it, and that she put up with it, you're way off base. You sure didn't know Amy Stanton.''

"Maybe,'' he said, "you didn't know her.''

"Me? But you just got through sayin' we'd gone together for years—''

"I—'' He hesitated, frowning. "I don't know. It isn't all clear to me, and I won't pretend that it is. But I don't think you knew her. Not as well as . . .''

"Yeah?'' I said.

He reached into his inside coat pocket, and brought out a square blue envelope. He opened it and removed one of those double sheets of stationery. I could see it was written on both sides, four pages in all. And I recognized that small neat handwriting.

Howard looked up from the paper, and caught my eye.

"This was in her purse." *Her purse.* "She'd written it at home and was planning, apparently, to give it to you after you were out of Central City. As a matter of fact"—he glanced down at the letter—"she intended to have you stop at a restaurant up the road, and have you read it while she was in the restroom. Now, it begins, 'Lou, Darling . . .'"

"Let me have it," I said.

"I'll read—"

"It's his letter," said Jeff. "Let him have it."

"Very well," Howard shrugged; and he tossed me the letter. And I knew he'd planned on having me read it all along. He wanted me to read it while he sat back and watched.

I looked down at the thick double page, holding my eyes on it.

Lou, Darling:

Now you know why I had you stop here, and why I've excused myself from the table. It was to allow you to read this, the things I couldn't somehow otherwise say to you. Please, please read carefully, darling. I'll give you plenty of time. And if I sound confused and rambling, please don't be angry with me. It's only because I love you so much, and I'm a little frightened and worried.

Darling, I wish I could tell you how happy you've made me these last few weeks. I wish I could be sure that you'd been even a tiny fraction as happy. Just a teensy-weensie bit as much. Sometimes I get the crazy, wonderful notion that you have been, that you were even as happy as I was (though I don't see how you could be!) and at others I tell myself . . . Oh, I don't know, Lou!

I suppose the trouble is that it all seemed to come about so suddenly. We'd gone on for years, and you seemed to be growing more and more indifferent; you seemed to keep drawing away from me and taking pleasure in making me follow. (Seemed,

Lou; I don't say you did do it.) I'm not trying to excuse myself, darling. I only want to explain, to make you understand that I'm not going to behave that way any more. I'm not going to be sharp and demanding and scolding and . . . I may not be able to change all at once (oh, but I will, darling; I'll watch myself; I'll do it just as fast as I can) but if you'll just love me, Lou, just act like you love me, I'm sure—

Do you understand how I felt? Just a little? Do you see why I was that way, then, and why I won't be any more? Everyone knew I was yours. Almost everyone. I wanted it to be that way; to have anyone else was unthinkable. But I couldn't have had anyone else if I'd wished to. I was yours. I'd always be yours if you dropped me. And it seemed, Lou, that you were slipping further and further away, still owning me yet not letting yourself belong to me. You were (it seemed, darling, seemed) leaving me with nothing—and knowing that you were doing it, knowing I was helpless—and apparently enjoying it. You avoided me. You made me chase you. You made me question you and beg you, and—and then you'd act so innocent and puzzled and . . . Forgive me, darling. I don't want to criticise you ever, ever again. I only wanted you to understand, and I suppose only another woman could do that.

Lou, I want to ask you something, a few things, and I want to beg you please, please, please not to take it the wrong way. Are you—oh, don't be, darling—are you afraid of me? Do you feel that you have to be nice to me? There I won't say anything more, but you know what I mean, as well as I do at least. And you will know . . .

I hope and pray I am wrong, darling. I do so hope. But I'm afraid—are you in trouble? Is something weighing on your mind? I don't want to ask you more than that, but I do want you to believe that whatever it is, even if it's what I—whatever it is, Lou, I'm on your side. I love you (are you tired of my saying that), and I know you. I know you'd never knowingly do anything wrong, you just couldn't, and I love you so much and . . . Let me help you, darling. Whatever it is, whatever help you need. Even if it should involve being separated for a while, a long while, let's—let me help you. Because I'll wait for you, however long—and it mightn't be long at all, it might be just a question of—well, it will be all right, Lou, because you wouldn't

*knowingly do anything. I know that and everyone else knows it,
and it will be all right. We'll make it all right, you and I
together. If you'll only tell me. If you'll just let me help you.*

*Now. I asked you not to be afraid of me, but I know how
you've felt, how you used to feel, and I know that asking you or
telling you might not be enough. That's why I had you stop at
this place, here at a bus stop. That's why I'm giving you so much
time. To prove to you that you don't need to be afraid.*

*I hope that when I come back to the table, you'll still be there.
But if you aren't, darling, if you feel that you can't . . . then
just leave my bags inside the door. I have money with me and I
can get a job in some other town, and—do that, Lou. If you feel
that you must. I'll understand, and it'll be perfectly all right—
honestly it will, Lou—and . . .*

*Oh, darling, darling, darling, I love you so much. I've always
loved you and I always will, whatever happens. Always, darling.
Always and always. Forever and forever.*

Always and forever,
Amy

Twenty-One

WELL. WELL?

What are you going to do? What are you going to say?

What are you going to say when you're drowning in your
own dung and they keep booting you back into it, when all
the screams in hell wouldn't be as loud as you want to scream,
when you're at the bottom of the pit and the whole world's
at the top, when it has but one face, a face without eyes or
ears, and yet it watches and listens . . .

What are you going to do and say? Why, pardner, that's
simple. It's easy as nailing your balls to a stump and falling
off backwards. Snow again, pardner, and drift me hard, because that's an easy one.

You're gonna say, they can't keep a good man down. You're
gonna say, a winner never quits and a quitter never wins.
You're gonna smile, boy, you're gonna show 'em the ol'

fightin' smile. And then you're gonna get out there an' hit 'em hard and fast and low, an'—an' Fight!

Rah.

I folded the letter, and tossed it back to Howard.

"She was sure a talky little girl," I said. "Sweet but awful talky. Seems like if she couldn't say it to you, she'd write it down for you."

Howard swallowed. "That—that's all you have to say?"

I lit a cigar, pretending like I hadn't heard him. Jeff Plummer's chair creaked. "I sure liked Miss Amy," he said. "All four of my younguns went to school to her, an' she was just as nice as if they'd had one of these oilmen for a daddy."

"Yes, sir," I said, "I reckon she really had her heart in her work."

I puffed on my cigar, and Jeff's chair creaked again, louder than the first time, and the hate in Howard's eyes seemed to lash out against me. He gulped like a man choking down puke.

"You fellows getting restless?" I said. "I sure appreciate you dropping in at a time like this, but I wouldn't want to keep you from anything important."

"You—y-you!"

"You starting to stutter, Howard? You ought to practice talking with a pebble in your mouth. Or maybe a piece of shrapnel."

"You dirty son-of-a-bitch! You—"

"Don't call me that," I said.

"No," said Jeff, "don't call him that. Don't never say anything about a man's mother."

"To hell with that crap! He—you"—he shook his fist at me—"you killed that little girl. She as good as says so!"

I laughed. "She wrote it down after I killed her, huh? That's quite a trick."

"You know what I mean. She knew you were going to kill her . . ."

"And she was going to marry me, anyway?"

"She knew you'd killed all those other people!"

"Yeah? Funny she didn't mention it."

"She did mention it! She—"

"Don't recall seeing anything like that. Don't see that she said anything much. Just a lot of woman-worry talk."

"You killed Joyce Lakeland and Elmer Conway and Johnnie Pappas and—"

"President McKinley?"

He sagged back in his chair, breathing hard. "You killed them, Ford. You killed them."

"Why don't you arrest me, then? What are you waiting on?"

"Don't worry," he nodded, grimly. "Don't you worry. I'm not waiting much longer."

"And I'm not either," I said.

"What do you mean?"

"I mean you and your courthouse gang are doing spite work. You're pouring it on me because Conway says to, just why I can't figure out. You haven't got a shred of proof but you've tried to smear me—"

"Now, wait a minute! We haven't—"

"You've tried to; you had Jeff out here this morning chasing visitors away. You'd do it, but you can't because you haven't got a shred of proof and people know me too well. You know you can't get a conviction, so you try to ruin my reputation. And with Conway backing you up you may manage it in time. You'll manage it if you have the time, and I guess I can't stop you. But I'm not going to sit back and take it. I'm leaving town, Howard."

"Oh, no you're not. I'm warning you here and now, Ford, don't you even attempt to leave."

"Who's going to stop me?"

"I am."

"On what grounds?"

"Mur—suspicion of murder."

"But who suspects me, Howard, and why? The Stantons? I reckon not. Mike Pappas? Huh-uh. Chester Conway? Well, I've got kind of a funny feeling about Conway, Howard. I've got a feeling that he's going to stay in the background, he's not going to do or say a thing, no matter how bad you need him."

"I see," he said. "I see."

"You see that opening there behind you?" I said. "Well,

that's a door, Howard, in case you were wonderin', and I can't think of a thing to keep you and Mister Plummer from walking through it."

"We're walking through it," said Jeff, "and so are you."

"Huh-uh," I said, "no I ain't. I sure ain't aimin' to do nothing like that, Mister Plummer. And that's a fact."

Howard kept his seat. His face looked like a blob of reddish dough, but he shook his head at Jeff and kept his seat. Howard was really trying hard.

"I—it's to your own interest as well as ours to get this settled, Ford. I'm asking you to place yourself—to remain available until—"

"You mean you want me to cooperate with you?" I said.

"Yes."

"That door," I said. "I wish you'd close it real careful. I'm suffering from shock, and I might have a relapse."

Howard's mouth twisted and opened, and snapped shut. He sighed and reached for his hat.

"I sure liked Bob Maples," said Jeff. "I sure liked that little Miss Amy."

"Sure enough?" I said. "Is that a fact?"

I laid my cigar down on an ashtray, leaned back on the pillow and closed my eyes. A chair creaked and squeaked real loud, and I heard Howard say, "Now, Jeff"—and there was a sound like he'd sort of stumbled.

I opened my eyes again. Jeff Plummer was standing over me.

He was smiling down at me with his lips and there was a .45 in his hand, and the hammer was thumbed back.

"You right sure you ain't coming with us?" he said. "You don't reckon you could change your mind?"

The way he sounded I knew he hoped I wouldn't change it. He was just begging, waiting for me to say no. And I reckoned I wouldn't say all of even a short word like that before I was past saying anything.

I got up and began to dress.

Twenty-Two

IF I'D KNOWN that Rothman's lawyer friend, Billy Boy Walker, was tied up in the East and was having trouble getting away, I might have felt different. I might have cracked up right off. But, on the other hand, I don't think I would have. I had a feeling that I was speeding fast down a one-way trail, that I was almost to the place I had to get to. I was almost there and moving fast, so why hop off and try to run ahead? It wouldn't have made a particle of sense, and you know I don't do things that don't make sense. You know it or you will know it.

That first day and that night, I spent in one of the "quiet" cells, but the next morning they put me on ice, down in the cooler where I'd—where Johnnie Pappas had died. They—

How's that? Well, sure they can do it to you. They can do anything they're big enough to do and you're little enough to take. They don't book you. No one knows where you are, and you've got no one on the outside that can get you out. It's not legal, but I found out long ago that the place where the law is apt to be abused most is right around a courthouse.

Yeah, they can do it all right.

So I was saying. I spent the first day and night in one of the quiet cells, and most of the time I was trying to kid myself. I couldn't face up to the truth yet, so I tried to play like there was a way around it. You know. Those kid games?

You've done something pretty bad or you want something bad, and you think, well, if I can just do such and such I can fix it. If I can count down from a thousand backwards by three and a third or recite the Gettysburg Address in pig-latin while I'm touching my little toes with my big ones, everything will be all right.

I'd play those games and their kin-kind, doing real impossible things in my imagination. I'd trot all the way from Central City to San Angelo without stopping. Or they'd grease the pipeline across the Pecos River, and I'd hop across it on one foot with my eyes blindfolded and an anvil around my neck. I'd really get to sweating and panting sometimes. My feet'd be all achy and blistered from pounding that San

Angelo Highway, and that old anvil would keep swinging and dragging at me, trying to pull me off into the Pecos; and finally I'd win through, just plumb worn out. And—and I'd have to do something still harder.

Well, then they moved me down into the cooler where Johnnie Pappas had died, and pretty soon I saw why they hadn't put me there right away. They'd had a little work to do on it first. I don't know just how they'd rigged the stunt— only that that unused light-socket in the ceiling was part of it. But I was stretched out on the bunk, fixing to shinny up the water tower without using my hands, when all at once I heard Johnnie's voice:

"Hello, you lovely people. I'm certainly having a fine time and I wish you were here. See you soon."

Yes, it was Johnnie, speaking in that sharp smart-alecky way he used a lot. I jumped up from the bunk and started turning around and looking up and down and sideways. And here his voice came again:

"Hello, you lovely people. I'm certainly having a fine time and I wish you were here. See you soon."

He kept saying the same thing over and over, about fifteen seconds between times, and, hell, as soon as I had a couple minutes to think, I knew what it was all about. It was one of those little four-bit voice recordings, like you've just about got time to sneeze on before it's used up. Johnnie'd sent it to his folks the time he visited the Dallas Fair. He'd mentioned it to me when he told me about the trip—and I'd remembered because I liked Johnnie and would remember. He'd mentioned it, apologizing for not sending me some word. But he'd lost all his dough in some kind of wheel game and had to hitch-hike back to Central City.

"Hello, you lovely people . . ."

I wondered what kind of story they'd given the Greek, because I was pretty sure he wouldn't have let 'em have it if he'd known what it was going to be used for. He knew how I felt about Johnnie and how Johnnie'd felt about me.

They kept playing that record over and over, from maybe five in the morning until midnight; I don't know just what the hours were because they'd taken away my watch. It didn't even stop when they brought me food and water twice a day.

I'd lie and listen to it, or sit and listen. And every once in a while, when I could remember to do it, I'd jump up and pace around the cell. I'd pretend like it was bothering the hell out of me, which of course it didn't at all. Why would it? But I wanted 'em to think it did, so they wouldn't turn it off. And I guess I must have pretended pretty good, because they played it for three days and part of a fourth. Until it wore out, I reckon.

After that there wasn't much but silence, nothing but those faraway sounds like the factory whistles which weren't any real company for a man.

They'd taken away my cigars and matches, of course, and I fidgeted around quite a bit the first day, thinking I wanted a smoke. Yeah, *thinking*, because I didn't actually want one. I'd been smoking cigars for—well—around eleven years; ever since my eighteenth birthday when Dad had said I was getting to be a man, so he hoped I'd act like one and smoke cigars and not go around with a coffin-nail in my mouth. So I'd smoked cigars, from then on, never admitting to myself that I didn't like them. But now I could admit it. I had to, and I did.

When life attains a crisis, man's focus narrows. *Nice lines, huh? I could talk that way all the time if I wanted to.* The world becomes a stage of immediate concern, swept free of illusion. *I used to could talk that way all the time.*

No one had pushed me around or even tried to question me since the morning they'd locked me up. No one, at all. And I'd tried to tell myself that that was a good sign. They didn't have any evidence; I'd got their goats, so they'd put me on ice, just like they'd done with plenty of other guys. And pretty soon they'd simmer down and let me go of their own accord, or Billy Boy Walker'd show up and they'd have to let me out . . . That's what I'd told myself and it made sense—all my reasoning does. But it was top-of-the-cliff sense, not the kind you make when you're down near the tag-end of the rope.

They hadn't tried to beat the truth out of me or talk it out of me for a couple of reasons. First of all, they were pretty sure it wouldn't do any good: You can't stamp on a man's corns when he's got his feet cut off. Second—the second reason was—they didn't think they had to.

They *had* evidence.

They'd had it right from the beginning.

Why hadn't they sprung it on me? Well, there were a couple of reasons behind that, too. For one thing, they weren't sure that it was evidence because they weren't sure about me. I'd thrown them off the track with Johnnie Pappas. For another thing, they *couldn't* use it—it wasn't in shape to be used.

But now they were sure of what I'd done, though they probably weren't too clear as to why I'd done it. And that evidence would be ready to be used before long. And I didn't reckon they'd let go of me until it was ready. Conway was determined to get me, and they'd gone too far to back down.

I thought back to the day Bob Maples and I had gone to Fort Worth, and how Conway hadn't invited us on the trip but had got busy ordering us around the minute we'd landed. You see? What could be clearer? He'd tipped his hand on me right there.

Then, Bob had come back to the hotel, and he was all upset about something Conway had said to him, ordered him to do. And he wouldn't tell me what it was. He just talked on and on about how long he'd known me and what a swell guy I was, and . . . Hell, don't you see? Don't you get it?

I'd let it go by me because I had to. I couldn't let myself face the facts. But I reckon you've known the truth all along.

Then, I'd brought Bob home on the train and he'd been babbling drunk, and he'd gotten sore about some of my kidding. So he'd snapped back at me, giving me a tip on where I stood at the same time. He'd said—what was it?—*"It's always lightest just before the dark . . ."*

He'd been sore and drunk so he'd come out with that. He was telling me in so many words that I might not be sitting nearly as pretty as I thought I was. And he was certainly right about that—but I think he'd got his words twisted a little. He was saying 'em to be sarcastic, but they happen to be the truth. At least it seemed so to me.

It *is* lightest just before the dark. Whatever a man is up against, it makes him feel better to know that he *is* up against it. That's the way it seemed to me, anyhow, and I ought to know.

Once I'd admitted the truth about that piece of evidence, it was easy to admit other things. I could stop inventing reasons for what I'd done, stop believing in the reasons I'd invented, and see the truth. And it sure wasn't hard to see. When you're climbing up a cliff or just holding on for dear life, you keep your eyes closed. You know you'll get dizzy and fall if you don't. But after you fall down to the bottom, you open 'em again. And you can see just where you started from, and trace every foot of your trail up that cliff.

Mine had started back with the housekeeper; with Dad finding out about us. All kids pull some pretty sorry stunts, particularly if an older person edges 'em along, so it hadn't needed to mean a thing. But Dad had made it mean something. I'd been made to feel that I'd done something that couldn't ever be forgiven—that would always lie between him and me, the only kin I had. And there wasn't anything I could do or say that would change things. I had a burden of fear and shame put on me that I could never get shed of.

She was gone, and I couldn't strike back at her, yes, kill her, for what I'd been made to feel she'd done to me. But that was all right. She was the first woman I'd ever known; she *was* woman to me; and all womankind bore her face. So I could strike back at any of them, any female, the ones it would be safest to strike at, and it would be the same as striking at her. And I did that, I started striking out . . . and Mike Dean took the blame.

Dad tightened the reins on me after that. I could hardly be out of his sight an hour without his checking up on me. So years passed and I didn't strike out again, and I was able to distinguish between women and *the* woman. Dad slacked off on the reins a little; I seemed to be normal. But every now and then I'd catch myself in that dead-pan kidding, trying to ease the terrific pressure that was building up inside of me. And even without that I knew—though I wouldn't recognize the fact—that I wasn't all right.

If I could have got away somewhere, where I wouldn't have been constantly reminded of what had happened and I'd had something I wanted to do—something to occupy my mind—

it might have been different. But I couldn't get away, and there wasn't anything here I wanted to do. So nothing had changed; I was still looking for *her*. And any woman who'd done what she had would be *her*.

I'd kept pushing Amy away from me down through the years, not because I didn't love her but because I did. I was afraid of what might happen between us. I was afraid of what I'd do . . . what I finally did.

I could admit, now, that I'd never had any real cause to think that Amy would make trouble for me. She had too much pride; she'd have hurt herself too much; and, anyway, she loved me.

I'd never had any real cause, either, to be afraid that Joyce would make trouble. She was too smart to try to, from what I'd seen of her. But if she had been sore enough to try—if she'd been mad enough so's she just didn't give a damn—she wouldn't have got anywhere. After all, she was just a whore and I was old family, quality; and she wouldn't have opened her mouth more than twice before she was run out of town.

No, I hadn't been afraid of her starting talk. I hadn't been afraid that if I kept on with her I'd lose control of myself. I'd never had any control even before I met her. No control— only luck. Because anyone who reminded me of the burden I carried, anyone who did what that first *her* had done, would get killed . . .

Anyone. Amy. Joyce. Any woman who, even for a moment, became *her*.

I'd kill them.

I'd keep trying until I did kill them.

Elmer Conway had had to suffer, too, on *her* account. Mike had taken the blame for me, and then he'd been killed. So, along with the burden, I had a terrible debt to him that I couldn't pay. I could never repay him for what he'd done for me. The only thing I could do was what I did . . . try to settle the score with Chester Conway.

That was my main reason for killing Elmer, but it wasn't the only one. The Conways were part of the circle, the town, that ringed me in; the smug ones, the hypocrites, the holier-than-thou guys—all the stinkers I had to face day in and day out. I had to grin and smile and be pleasant to them; and maybe there are people like that everywhere, but when you can't get away from them, when they keep pushing themselves at you, and you can't get away, never, never, get away . . .

Well.

The bum. The few others I'd struck out at. I don't know—I'm not really sure about them.

They were all people who didn't have to stay here. People who took what was handed them because they didn't have enough pride or guts to strike back. So maybe that was it. Maybe I think that the guy who won't fight when he can and should deserves the worst you can toss at him.

Maybe. I'm not sure of all the details. All I can do is give you the general picture; and not even the experts could do more than that.

I've read a lot of stuff by a guy—name of Kraepelin, I believe—and I can't remember all of it, of course, or even the gist of all of it. But I remember the high points of some, the most important stuff, and I think it goes something like this:

". . . difficult to study because so seldom detected. The condition usually begins around the period of puberty, and is often precipitated by a severe shock. The subject suffers from strong feelings of guilt . . . combined with a sense of frustration and persecution . . . which increase as he grows older; yet there are rarely if ever any surface signs of . . . disturbance. On the contrary, his behavior appears to be entirely logical. He reasons soundly, even shrewdly. He is completely aware of what he does and why he does it . . ."

That was written about a disease, or a condition, rather, called dementia praecox. Schizophrenia, paranoid type. Acute, recurrent, advanced.

Incurable.

It was written, you might say, about—

But I reckon you know, don't you?

Twenty-Three

I was in jail eight days, but no one questioned me and they didn't pull any more stunts like that voice recording. I kind of looked for them to do the last because they couldn't be positive about that piece of evidence they had—about my reaction to it, that is. They weren't certain that it would make me put the finger on myself. And even if they had been certain, I knew they'd a lot rather I cracked up and confessed of my own accord. If I did that they could probably send me to the chair. The other way—if they used their evidence—they couldn't.

But I reckon they weren't set up right at the jail for any more stunts or maybe they couldn't get ahold of the equipment they needed. At any rate, they didn't pull any more. And on the eighth day, around eleven o'clock at night, they transferred me to the insane asylum.

They put me in a pretty good room—better'n any I'd seen the time I'd had to take a poor guy there years before—and left me alone. But I took one look around and I knew I was being watched through those little slots high up on the walls. They wouldn't have left me in a room with cigarette tobacco and matches and a drinking glass and water pitcher unless someone was watching me.

I wondered how far they'd let me go if I started to cut my throat or wrap myself in a sheet and set fire to it, but I didn't wonder very long. It was late, and I was pretty well wornout after sleeping on that bunk in the cooler. I smoked a couple of hand-rolled cigarettes, putting the butts out real careful. Then with the lights still burning—there wasn't any switch for me to turn 'em off—I stretched out on the bed and went to sleep.

About seven in the morning, a husky-looking nurse came in with a couple of young guys in white jackets. And she took my temperature and pulse while they stood and waited. Then, she left and the two attendants took me down the hall to a shower room, and watched while I took a bath. They didn't act particularly tough or unpleasant, but they didn't say a word more than they needed to. I didn't say anything.

I finished my shower and put my short-tailed nightgown back on. We went back to my room, and one of 'em made up my bed while the other went after my breakfast. The scrambled eggs tasted pretty flat, and it didn't help my appetite any to have them cleaning up the room, emptying the enamel night-can and so on. But I ate almost everything and drank all of the weak luke-warm coffee. They were through cleaning, by the time I'd finished. They left, locking me in again.

I smoked a hand-rolled cigarette, and it tasted good.

I wondered—no I didn't, either. I didn't need to wonder what it would be like to spend your whole life like this. Not a tenth as good as this probably, because I was something pretty special right now. Right now I was a hide-out; I'd been kidnapped, actually. And there was always a chance that there'd be a hell of a stink raised. But if that hadn't been the case, if I'd been committed—well, I'd still be something special, in a different way. I'd be worse off than anyone in the place.

Conway would see to that, even if Doc Bony-face didn't have a special sort of interest in me.

I'd kind of figured that the Doc might show up with his hard-rubber playthings, but I guess he had just enough sense to know that he was out of his class. Plenty of pretty smart psychiatrists have been fooled by guys like me, and you can't really fault 'em for it. There's just not much they can put their hands on, know what I mean?

We might have the disease, the condition; or we might just be cold-blooded and smart as hell; or we might be innocent of what we're supposed to have done. We might be any one of those three things, because the symptoms we show would fit any one of the three.

So Bony-face didn't give me any trouble. No one did. The nurse checked on me night and morning, and the two attendants carried on with pretty much the same routine. Bringing my meals, taking me to the shower, cleaning up the room. The second day, and every other day after that, they let me shave with a safety razor while they stood by and watched.

I thought about Rothman and Billy Boy Walker, just thought, wondered, without worrying any. Because, hell, I didn't have anything to worry about, and they were probably doing enough worrying for all three of us. But—

But I'm getting ahead of myself.

They, Conway and the others, still weren't positive about

that piece of evidence they had; and, like I say, they preferred to have me crack up and confess. So, on the evening of my second night in the asylum, there came the stunt.

I was lying on my side in bed, smoking a cigarette, when the lights dimmed way down, down to almost nothing. Then, there was a click and a flash up above me, and Amy Stanton stood looking at me from the far wall of the room.

Oh, sure, it was a picture; one that had been made into a glass slide. I didn't need to do any figuring at all to know that they were using a slide projector to throw her picture against the wall. She was coming down the walk of her house, smiling, but looking kind of fussed like I'd seen her so many times. I could almost hear her saying, *"Well, you finally got here, did you?"* And I knew it was just a picture, but it looked so real, it seemed so real, that I answered her back in my mind. *"Kinda looks that way, don't it?"*

I guess they'd got a whole album of her pictures. Which wouldn't have been any trouble, since the old folks, the Stantons, were awfully innocent and accommodating and not given to asking questions. Anyway, after that first picture, which was a pretty recent one, there was one taken when she was about fifteen years old. And they worked up through the years from that.

They . . . I saw her the day she graduated from high school, she was sixteen that spring, wearing one of those white lacy dresses and flat-heeled slippers, and standing real stiff with her arms held close to her sides.

I saw her sitting on her front steps, laughing in spite of herself . . . *it always seemed hard for Amy to laugh* . . . because that old dog of theirs was trying to lick her on the ear.

I saw her all dressed up, and looking kind of scared, the time she started off for teachers' college. I saw her the day she finished her two-year course, standing very straight with her hand on the back of a chair and trying to look older than she was.

I saw her—and I'd taken a lot of those pictures myself; it seemed just like yesterday—I saw her working in the garden, in a pair of old jeans; walking home from church and kind of frowning up at the little hat she'd made for herself; coming out of the grocery store with both arms around a big sack; sitting in the porch swing with an apple in her hand and a book in her lap.

I saw her with her dress pulled way up high—she'd just slid off the fence where I'd taken a snap of her—and she was bent over, trying to cover herself, and yelling at me, *"Don't you dare, Lou! Don't you dare, now!"* . . . She'd sure been mad about me taking that picture, but she'd saved it.

I saw her . . .

I tried to remember how many pictures there were, to figure out how long they would last. They were sure in a hell of a hurry to get through with them, it looked like to me. They were just racing through 'em, it seemed like. I'd just be starting to enjoy a picture, remembering when it was taken and how old Amy was at the time, when they'd flash it off and put on another one.

It was a pretty sorry way to act, the way I saw it. You know, it was as though she wasn't worth looking at; like, maybe, they'd seen someone that was better to look at. And I'm not prejudiced or anything, but you wouldn't find a girl as pretty and well-built as Amy Stanton in a month of Sundays.

Aside from being a slight on Amy, it was damned stupid to rush through those pictures like they were doing . . . like they seemed to be doing. After all, the whole object of the show was to make me crack up, and how could I do it if they didn't even let me get a good look at her?

I wasn't going to crack up, of course; I felt stronger and better inside every time I saw her. But they didn't know that, and it doesn't excuse them. They were lying down on the job. They had a doggone ticklish job to do, and they were too lazy and stupid to do it right.

Well . . .

They'd started showing the pictures about eight-thirty, and they should have lasted until one or two in the morning. But they had to be in a hell of a hurry, so it was only around eleven when they came to the last one.

It was a picture I'd taken less than three weeks before, and they *did* leave it on long enough—well, not long enough, but they let me get a good look at it. She and I had fixed up a little lunch that evening, and eaten it over in Sam Houston

Park. And I'd taken this picture just as she was stepping back into the car. She was looking over her shoulder at me, wide-eyed, smiling but sort of impatient. Saying:

"Can't you hurry a little, darling?"

Hurry?

"Well, I reckon so, honey. I'll sure try to."

"When, Lou? How soon will I see you, darling?"

"Well, now, honey. I—I . . ."

I was almost glad right then that the lights came back on. I never was real good at lying to Amy.

I got up and paced around the room. I went over by the wall where they'd flashed the pictures, and I rubbed my eyes with my fists and gave the wall a few pats and tugged my hair a little.

I put on a pretty good act, it seemed to me. Just good enough to let 'em think I was bothered, but not enough to mean anything at a sanity hearing.

The nurse and the two attendants didn't have any more to say than usual the next morning. It seemed to me, though, that they acted a little different, more watchful sort of. So I did a lot of frowning and staring down at the floor, and I only ate part of my breakfast.

I passed up most of my lunch and dinner, too, which wasn't much of a chore, hungry as I was. And I did everything else I could to put on just the right kind of act—not too strong, not too weak. But I was too anxious. I had to go and ask the nurse a question when she made the night check on me, and that spoiled everything.

"Will they be showing the pictures tonight?" I said, and I knew doggone well it was the wrong thing to do.

"What pictures? I don't know anything about pictures," she said.

"The pictures of my girl. You know. Will they show 'em, ma'am?"

She shook her head, a kind of mean glint in her eye. "You'll see. You'll find out, mister."

"Well, tell 'em not to do it so fast," I said. "When they do it so fast, I don't get to see her very good. I hardly get to look at her at all before she's gone."

She frowned. She shook her head, staring at me, like

she hadn't heard me right. She edged away from the bed a little.

"You"—she swallowed—"you want to see those pictures?"

"Well—uh—I—"

"You *do* want to see them," she said slowly. "You want to see the pictures of the girl you—you—"

"Sure, I want to see 'em." I began to get sore. "Why shouldn't I want to see them? What's wrong with that? Why the hell wouldn't I want to see them?"

The attendants started to move toward me. I lowered my voice.

"I'm sorry," I said, "I don't want to cause any trouble. If you folks are too busy, maybe you could move the projector in here. I know how to run one, and I'd take good care of it."

That was a pretty bad night for me. There weren't any pictures, and I was so hungry I couldn't go to sleep for hours. I was sure glad when morning came.

So, that was the end of their stunt, and they didn't try any others. I reckon they figured it was a waste of time. They just kept me from then on; just held me without me saying any more than I had to and them doing the same.

That went on for six days, and I was beginning to get puzzled. Because that evidence of theirs should have been about ready to use, by now, if it was ever going to be ready.

The seventh day rolled around, and I was really getting baffled. And, then, right after lunch, Billy Boy Walker showed up.

Twenty-Four

"WHERE is he?" he yelled. "What have you done with the poor man? Have you torn out his tongue? Have you roasted his poor broken body over slow fires? Where is he, I say!"

He was coming down the corridor, yelling at the top of his lungs; and I could hear several people scurrying along with him, trying to shush him up, but no one had ever had much luck at that and they didn't either. I'd never seen him in my

life—just heard him a couple of times on the radio—but I
knew it was him. I reckon I'd have known he'd come even if
I hadn't heard him. You didn't have to see or hear Billy
Boy Walker to know he was around. You could just kind of
sense it.

They stopped in front of my door, and Billy Boy started
beating on it like they didn't have a key and he was going to
have to knock it down.

"Mr. Ford! My poor man!" he yelled; and, man, I'll bet
they could hear him all the way into Central City. "Can you
hear me? Have they punctured your eardrums? Are you too
weak to cry out? Be brave, my poor fellow!"

He kept it up, beating on the door and yelling, and it
sounds like it must've been funny but somehow it wasn't.
Even to me, knowing that they hadn't done a thing to me,
really, it didn't sound funny. I could almost believe that they
had put me through the works.

They managed to get the door unlocked, and he came
bounding in. And he looked as funny—he should have looked
as funny as he should have sounded—but I didn't feel the
slightest call to laugh. He was short and fat and pot-bellied;
and a couple of buttons were off his shirt and his belly-button
was showing. He was wearing a baggy old black suit and red
suspenders; and he had a big floppy black hat sitting kind of
crooked on his head. Everything about him was sort of off-
size and out-of-shape, as the saying is. But I couldn't see a
thing to laugh about. Neither, apparently, could the nurse and
the two attendants and old Doc Bony-face.

Billy Boy flung his arms around me and called me a "poor
man" and patted me on the head. He had to reach up to do
it; but he didn't seem to reach and it didn't seem funny.

He turned around, all at once, and grabbed the nurse by
the arm. "Is this the woman, Mr. Ford? Did she beat you
with chains? Fie! Fah! Abomination!" And he scrubbed his
hand against his pants, glaring at her.

The attendants were helping me into my clothes, and they
weren't losing any time about it. But you'd never have known
it to hear Billy Boy. "Fiends!" he yelled. "Will your sadistic
appetites never be satiated? Must you continue to stare and
slaver over your handiwork? Will you not clothe this poor

tortured flesh, this broken creature that was once a man built in God's own image?"

The nurse was spluttering and sputtering, her face a half-dozen different colors. The doc's bones were leaping like jumping-jacks. Billy Boy Walker snatched up the night-can, and shoved it under his nose. "You fed him from this, eh? I thought so! Bread and water, served in a slop jar! Shame, shame, fie! You did do it? Answer me, sirrah! You didn't do it? Fie, fah, paah! Perjurer, suborner! Answer, yes or no!"

The doc shook his head, and then nodded. He shook and nodded it at the same time. Billy Boy dropped the can to the floor, and took me by the arm. "Never mind your gold watch, Mr. Ford. Never mind the money and jewelry they have stolen. You have your clothes. Trust me to recover the rest—and more! Much, much more, Mr. Ford."

He pushed me out the door ahead of him, and then he turned around real slow and pointed around the room. "You," he said softly, pointing them out one by one. "You and you and you are through. This is the end for you. The end."

He looked them all in the eye, and no one said a word and none of them moved. He took me by the arm again, and we went down the corridor, and each of the three gates were open for us before we got to 'em.

He squeezed in behind the wheel of the car he'd rented in Central City. He started it up with a roar and a jerk, and we went speeding out through the main gate to the highway where two signs, facing in opposite directions, read:

WARNING! WARNING!
Hitch-hikers May Be Escaped
LUNATICS!

He lifted himself in the seat, reached into his hip pocket, and pulled out a plug of tobacco. He offered it to me and I shook my head, and he took a big chew.

"Dirty habit," he said, in just a quiet conversational voice. "Got it young, though, and I reckon I'll keep it."

He spat out the window, wiped his chin with his hand, and

wiped his hand on his pants. I found the makings I'd had at the asylum and started rolling a cigarette.

"About Joe Rothman," I said. "I didn't say anything about him, Mr. Walker."

"Why, I didn't think you had, Mr. Ford! It never occurred to me that you would," he said; and whether he meant it or not he sure sounded like it. "You know somethin', Mr. Ford? There wasn't a bit of sense in what I did back there."

"No," I said.

"No, sir, not a bit. I've been snorting and pawing up the earth around here for four days. Couldn't have fought harder getting Christ off the cross. And I reckon it was just habit like this chewing tobacco—I knew it but I kept right on chawing. I didn't get you free, Mr. Ford. I didn't have a thing to do with it. They *let* me have a writ. They *let* me know where you were. That's why you're here, Mr. Ford, instead of back there."

"I know," I said. "I figured it would be that way."

"You understand? They're not letting you go; they've gone too far to start backing water."

"I understand," I said.

"They've got something? Something you can't beat?"

"They've got it."

"Maybe you'd better tell me about it."

I hesitated, thinking, and finally I shook my head. "I don't think so, Mr. Walker. There's nothing you can do. Or I can do. You'd be wasting your time, and you might get Joe and yourself in a fix."

"Well, now, pshaw." He spat out the window again. "I reckon I might be a better judge of some things than you are, Mr. Ford. You—uh—aren't maybe a little distrustful, are you?"

"I think you know I'm not," I said. "I just don't want anyone else to get hurt."

"I see. Put it hypothetically, then. Just say that there are a certain set of circumstances which would have you licked—if they concerned you. Just make me up a situation that doesn't have anything to do with yours."

So I told him what they had and how they planned to use

it, hypothetically. And I stumbled around a lot, because describing my situation, the evidence they had, in a hypothetical way was mighty hard to do. He got it, though, without me having to repeat a word.

"That's the whole thing?" he said. "They haven't got—they can't get, we'll say, anything in the way of actual testimony?"

"I'm pretty sure they can't," I said. "I may be wrong but I'm almost positive they couldn't get anything out of this—evidence."

"Well, then? As long as you're—"

"I know," I nodded. "They're not taking me by surprise, like they figured on. I—I mean this fellow I'm talking about—"

"Go right ahead, Mr. Ford. Just keep on using the first person. It's easier to talk that way."

"Well, I wouldn't cut loose in front of 'em. I don't think I would. But I'd do it sooner or later, with someone. It's best to have it happen now, and get it over with."

He turned his head a moment to glance at me, the big black hat flopping in the wind. "You said you didn't want anyone else to get hurt. You meant it?"

"I meant it. You can't hurt people that are already dead."

"Good enough," he said; and whether he knew what I really meant and was satisfied with it, I don't know. His ideas of right and wrong didn't jibe too close with the books.

"I sure hate to give up, though," he frowned. "Just never got in the habit of giving up, I reckon."

"You can't call it giving up," I said. "Do you see that car way back behind us? And the one up in front, the one that turned in ahead of us, a while back? Those are county cars, Mr. Walker. You're not giving up anything. It's been lost for a long time."

He glanced up into the rear-view mirror, then squinted ahead through the windshield. He spat and rubbed his hand against his pants, wiped it slowly against the soiled black cloth. "Still got quite a little ride ahead of us, Mr. Ford. About thirty miles isn't it?"

"About that. Maybe a little more."

"I wonder if you'd like to tell me about it. You don't need

to, you understand, but it might be helpful, I might be able to help someone else."

"Do you think I could—that I'm able to tell you?"

"Why not?" he said. "I had a client years ago, Mr. Ford, a very able doctor. One of the most pleasant men you'd want to meet, and he had more money than he knew what to do with. But he'd performed about fifty abortions before they moved in on him, and so far as the authorities could find out every one of the abortion patients had died. He'd deliberately seen that they did die of peritonitis about a month after the operation. And he told me why—and he could've told anyone else why, when he finally faced up to the facts—he'd done it. He had a younger brother who was 'unfinished,' a prematurely born monstrosity, as the result of an attempted late-pregnancy abortion. He saw that terrible half-child die in agony for years. He never recovered from the experience— and neither did the women he aborted . . . Insane? Well, the only legal definition we have for insanity is the condition which necessitates the confinement of a person. So, since he hadn't been confined when he killed those women, I reckon he was sane. He made pretty good sense to me, anyhow."

He shifted the cud in his jaw, chewed a moment and went on. "I never had any legal schooling, Mr. Ford; picked up my law by reading in an attorney's office. All I ever had in the way of higher education was a couple years in agricultural college, and that was pretty much a plain waste of time. Crop rotation? Well, how're you going to do it when the banks only make crop loans on cotton? Soil conservation? How're you going to do terracing and draining and contour ploughing when you're cropping on shares? Purebred stock? Sure. Maybe you can trade your razorbacks for Poland Chinas . . . I just learned two things there at that college, Mr. Ford, that was ever of any use to me. One was that I couldn't do any worse than the people that were in the saddle, so maybe I'd better try pulling 'em down and riding myself. The other was a definition I got out of the agronomy books, and I reckon it was even more important than the first. It did more to revise my thinking, if I'd really done any thinking up until that time. Before that I'd seen everything in black and white, good and bad. But after I was set straight I saw that the name you put to a thing depended on where you stood and where it stood. And . . . and here's the definition, right out of the agronomy books: 'A weed is a plant out of place.' Let me repeat that. 'A weed is a plant out of place.' I find a hollyhock in my cornfield, and it's a weed. I find it in my yard, and it's a flower.

"You're in my yard, Mr. Ford."

. . . So I told him how it had been while he nodded and spat and drove, a funny pot-bellied shrimp of a guy who really had just one thing, understanding, but so much of it that you never missed anything else. He understood me better'n I understood myself.

"Yes, yes," he'd say, "you had to like people. You had to keep telling yourself you liked them. You needed to offset the deep, subconscious feelings of guilt." Or, he'd say, he'd interrupt, "And, of course, you knew you'd never leave Central City. Overprotection had made you terrified of the outside world. More important, it was part of the burden you had to carry to stay here and suffer."

He sure understood.

I reckon Billy Boy Walker's been cussed more in high places than any man in the country. But I never met a man I liked more.

I guess the way you felt about him depended on where you stood.

He stopped the car in front of my house, and I'd told him all I had to tell. But he sat there for a few minutes, spitting and sort of studying.

"Would you care to have me come in for a while, Mr. Ford?"

"I don't think it'd be smart," I said. "I got an idea it's not going to be very long, now."

He pulled an old turnip of a watch from his pocket and glanced at it. "Got a couple hours until train time, but—well, maybe you're right. I'm sorry, Mr. Ford. I'd hoped, if I couldn't do any better, to be taking you away from here with me."

"I couldn't have gone, no matter how things were. It's like you say, I'm tied here. I'll never be free as long as I live . . ."

Twenty-Five

YOU'VE GOT no time at all, but it seems like you've got forever. You've got nothing to do, but it seems like you've got everything.

You make coffee and smoke a few cigarettes; and the hands of the clock have gone crazy on you. They haven't moved hardly, they've hardly budged out of the place you last saw them, but they've measured off a half? two-thirds? of your life. You've got forever, but that's no time at all.

You've got forever; and somehow you can't do much with it. You've got forever; and it's a mile wide and an inch deep and full of alligators.

You go into the office and take a book or two from the shelves. You read a few lines, like your life depended on reading 'em right. But you know your life doesn't depend on anything that makes sense, and you wonder where in the hell you got the idea it did; and you begin to get sore.

You go into the laboratory and start pawing along the rows of bottles and boxes, knocking them on the floor, kicking them, stamping them. You find the bottle of one hundred percent pure nitric acid and you jerk out the rubber cork. You take it into the office and swing it along the rows of books. And the leather bindings begin to smoke and curl and wither—and it isn't good enough.

You go back into the laboratory. You come out with a gallon bottle of alcohol and the box of tall candles always kept there for emergencies. For *emergencies.*

You go upstairs, and then on up the little flight of stairs that leads to the attic. You come down from the attic and go through each of the bedrooms. You come back downstairs and go down into the basement. And when you return to the kitchen you are empty-handed. All the candles are gone, all the alcohol.

You shake the coffee pot and set it back on the stove burner. You roll another cigarette. You take a carving knife from a drawer and slide it up the sleeve of your pinkish-tan shirt with the black bow tie.

You sit down at the table with your coffee and cigarette,

and you ease your elbow up and down, seeing how far you can lower your arm without dropping the knife, letting it slide down from your sleeve a time or two.

You think, *"Well how can you? How can you hurt someone that's already dead?"*

You wonder if you've done things right, so's there'll be nothing left of something that shouldn't ever have been, and you know everything has been done right. You know, because you planned this moment before eternity way back yonder someplace.

You look up at the ceiling, listening, up through the ceiling and into the sky beyond. And there isn't the least bit of doubt in your mind. That'll be the plane, all right, coming in from the east, from Fort Worth. It'll be the plane she's on.

You look up at the ceiling, grinning, and you nod and say, "Long time no see. How you been doin' anyway, huh, baby? How are you, Joyce?"

Twenty-Six

JUST FOR the hell of it, I took a peek out the back door, and then I went part way into the living room and stooped down so I could look out the window. It was like I'd thought, of course. They had the house covered from every angle. Men with Winchesters. Deputies, most of 'em, with a few of the "safety inspectors" on Conway's payroll.

It would have been fun to take a real good look, to step to the door and holler howdy to 'em. But it would have been fun for them, too, and I figured they were having far too much as it was. Anyway, some of those "inspectors" were apt to be a mite trigger happy, anxious to show their boss they were on their toes, and I had a little job to do yet.

I had to get everything wrapped up to take with me.

I took one last walk through the house, and I saw that everything—the alcohol and the candles and everything—was going fine. I came back downstairs, closing all the doors behind me—*all the doors behind me* —and sat back down at the kitchen table.

The coffee pot was empty. There was just one cigarette paper left and just enough tobacco to fill it, and, yeah—*yeah!*—I was down to my last match. Things were sure working out fine.

I puffed on the cigarette, watching the red-gray ashes move down toward my fingers. I watched, not needing to, knowing they'd get just so far and no further.

I heard a car pull into the driveway. I heard a couple of its doors slam. I heard them crossing the yard and coming up the steps and across the porch. I heard the front door open; and they came in. And the ashes had burned out, the cigarette had gone dead.

And I laid it in my saucer and looked up.

I looked out the kitchen window, first, at the two guys standing outside. Then I looked at them:

Conway and Hendricks, Hank Butterby and Jeff Plummer. Two or three fellows I didn't know.

They fell back, watching me, letting her move out ahead of them. I looked at her.

Joyce Lakeland.

Her neck was in a cast that came clear up to her chin like a collar, and she walked stiff-backed and jerky. Her face was a white mask of gauze and tape, and nothing much showed of it but her eyes and her lips. And she was trying to say something—her lips were moving—but she didn't really have a voice. She could hardly get out a whisper.

"Lou . . . I didn't . . ."

"Sure," I said. "I didn't figure you had, baby."

She kept coming toward me and I stood up, my right arm raised like I was brushing at my hair.

I could feel my face twisting, my lips pulling back from my teeth. I knew what I must look like, but she didn't seem to mind. She wasn't scared. What did she have to be scared of?

". . . this, Lou. Not like this . . ."

"Sure you can't," I said. "Don't hardly see how you could."

". . . not anyway without . . ."

"Two hearts that beat as one," I said. "T-wo—ha, ha, ha,—two—ha, ha, ha, ha, ha, ha, ha,—two—J-jesus Chri—ha, ha, ha, ha, ha, ha, ha—two Jesus . . ."

And I sprang at her, I made for her just like they'd thought I would. Almost. And it was like I'd signalled, the way the smoke suddenly poured up through the floor. And the room exploded with shots and yells, and I seemed to explode with it, yelling and laughing and . . . and . . . Because they hadn't got the point. She'd got that between the ribs and the blade along with it. And they all lived happily ever after, I guess, and I guess—that's—all.

Yeah, I reckon that's all unless our kind gets another chance in the Next Place. Our kind. Us people.

All of us that started the game with a crooked cue, that wanted so much and got so little, that meant so good and did so bad. All us folks. Me and Joyce Lakeland, and Johnnie Pappas and Bob Maples and big ol' Elmer Conway and little ol' Amy Stanton. All of us.

All of us.

THE TALENTED MR. RIPLEY

by Patricia Highsmith

I.

Tom glanced behind him and saw the man coming out of the Green Cage, heading his way. Tom walked faster. There was no doubt the man was after him. Tom had noticed him five minutes ago, eyeing him carefully from a table, as if he weren't *quite* sure, but almost. He had looked sure enough for Tom to down his drink in a hurry, pay and get out.

At the corner Tom leaned forward and trotted across Fifth Avenue. There was Raoul's. Should he take a chance and go in for another drink? Tempt fate and all that? Or should he beat it over to Park Avenue and try losing him in a few dark doorways? He went into Raoul's.

Automatically, as he strolled to an empty space at the bar, he looked around to see if there was anyone he knew. There was the big man with red hair, whose name he always forgot, sitting at a table with a blond girl. The red-haired man waved a hand, and Tom's hand went up limply in response. He slid one leg over a stool and faced the door challengingly, yet with a flagrant casualness.

"Gin and tonic, please," he said to the barman.

Was this the kind of man they would send after him? Was he, wasn't he, was he? He didn't look like a policeman or a detective at all. He looked like a businessman, somebody's father, well-dressed, well-fed, graying at the temples, an air of uncertainty about him. Was that the kind they sent on a job like this, maybe to start chatting with you in a bar, and then *bang!*—the hand on the shoulder, the other hand displaying a policeman's badge. *Tom Ripley, you're under arrest.* Tom watched the door.

Here he came. The man looked around, saw him, and immediately looked away. He removed his straw hat, and took a place around the curve of the bar.

My God, what did he want? He certainly wasn't a *pervert*, Tom thought for the second time, though now his tortured brain groped and produced the actual word, as if the word could protect him, because he would rather the man be a pervert than a policeman. To a pervert, he could simply say,

"No, thank you," and smile and walk away. Tom slid back on the stool, bracing himself.

Tom saw the man make a gesture of postponement to the barman, and come around the bar toward him. Here it was! Tom stared at him, paralyzed. They couldn't give you more than ten years, Tom thought. Maybe fifteen, but with good conduct— In the instant the man's lips parted to speak, Tom had a pang of desperate, agonized regret.

"Pardon me, are you Tom Ripley?"

"Yes."

"My name is Herbert Greenleaf. Richard Greenleaf's father." The expression on his face was more confusing to Tom than if he had focused a gun on him. The face was friendly, smiling and hopeful. "You're a friend of Richard's, aren't you?"

It made a faint connection in his brain. Dickie Greenleaf. A tall blond fellow. He had quite a bit of money, Tom remembered. "Oh, Dickie Greenleaf. Yes."

"At any rate, you know Charles and Marta Schriever. They're the ones who told me about you, that you might— uh— Do you think we could sit down at a table?"

"Yes," Tom said agreeably, and picked up his drink. He followed the man toward an empty table at the back of the little room. Reprieved, he thought. Free! Nobody was going to arrest him. This was about something else. No matter what it was, it wasn't grand larceny or tampering with the mails or whatever they called it. Maybe Richard was in some kind of jam. Maybe Mr. Greenleaf wanted help, or advice. Tom knew just what to say to a father like Mr. Greenleaf.

"I wasn't quite sure you were Tom Ripley," Mr. Greenleaf said. "I've seen you only once before, I think. Didn't you come up to the house once with Richard?"

"I think I did."

"The Schrievers gave me a description of you, too. We've all been trying to reach you, because the Schrievers wanted us to meet at their house. Somebody told them you went to the Green Cage bar now and then. This is the first night I've tried to find you, so I suppose I should consider myself lucky." He smiled. "I wrote you a letter last week, but maybe you didn't get it."

"No, I didn't." Marc wasn't forwarding his mail, Tom thought. Damn him. Maybe there was a check there from Aunt Dottie. "I moved a week or so ago," Tom added.

"Oh, I see. I didn't say much in my letter. Only that I'd like to see you and have a chat with you. The Schrievers seemed to think you knew Richard quite well."

"I remember him, yes."

"But you're not writing to him now?" He looked disappointed.

"No. I don't think I've seen Dickie for a couple of years."

"He's been in Europe for two years. The Schrievers spoke very highly of you, and thought you might have some influence on Richard if you were to write to him. I want him to come home. He has responsibilities here—but just now he ignores anything that I or his mother try to tell him."

Tom was puzzled. "Just what did the Schrievers say?"

"They said—apparently they exaggerated a little—that you and Richard were very good friends. I suppose they took it for granted you were writing him all along. You see, I know so few of Richard's friends any more—" He glanced at Tom's glass, as if he would have liked to offer him a drink, at least, but Tom's glass was nearly full.

Tom remembered going to a cocktail party at the Schrievers' with Dickie Greenleaf. Maybe the Greenleafs were more friendly with the Schrievers than he was, and that was how it had all come about, because he hadn't seen the Schrievers more than three or four times in his life. And the last time, Tom thought, was the night he had worked out Charley Schriever's income tax for him. Charley was a TV director, and he had been in a complete muddle with his free-lance accounts. Charley had thought he was a genius for having doped out his tax and made it lower than the one Charley had arrived at, and perfectly legitimately lower. Maybe that was what had prompted Charley's recommendation of him to Mr. Greenleaf. Judging him from that night, Charley could have told Mr. Greenleaf that he was intelligent, level-headed, scrupulously honest, and very willing to do a favor. It was a slight error.

"I don't suppose you know of anybody else close to

Richard who might be able to wield a little influence?" Mr. Greenleaf asked rather pitifully.

There was Buddy Lankenau, Tom thought, but he didn't want to wish a chore like this on Buddy. "I'm afraid I don't," Tom said, shaking his head. "Why won't Richard come home?"

"He says he prefers living over there. But his mother's quite ill right now— Well, those are family problems. I'm sorry to annoy you like this." He passed a hand in a distraught way over his thin, neatly combed gray hair. "He says he's painting. There's no harm in that, but he hasn't the talent to be a painter. He's got great talent for boat designing, though, if he'd just put his mind to it." He looked up as a waiter spoke to him. "Scotch and soda, please. Dewar's. You're not ready?"

"No, thanks," Tom said.

Mr. Greenleaf looked at Tom apologetically. "You're the first of Richard's friends who's even been willing to listen. They all take the attitude that I'm trying to interfere with his life."

Tom could easily understand that. "I certainly wish I could help," he said politely. He remembered now that Dickie's money came from a shipbuilding company. Small sailing boats. No doubt his father wanted him to come home and take over the family firm. Tom smiled at Mr. Greenleaf, meaninglessly, then finished his drink. Tom was on the edge of his chair, ready to leave, but the disappointment across the table was almost palpable. "Where is he staying in Europe?" Tom asked, not caring a damn where he was staying.

"In a town called Mongibello, south of Naples. There's not even a library there, he tells me. Divides his time between sailing and painting. He's bought a house there. Richard has his own income—nothing huge, but enough to live on in Italy, apparently. Well, every man to his own taste, but I'm sure I can't see the attractions of the place." Mr. Greenleaf smiled bravely. "Can't I offer you a drink, Mr. Ripley?" he asked when the waiter came with his scotch and soda.

Tom wanted to leave. But he hated to leave the man sitting alone with his fresh drink. "Thanks, I think I will," he said, and handed the waiter his glass.

"Charley Schriever told me you were in the insurance business," Mr. Greenleaf said pleasantly.

"That was a little while ago. I—" But he didn't want to say he was working for the Department of Internal Revenue, not now. "I'm in the accounting department of an advertising agency at the moment."

"Oh?"

Neither said anything for a minute. Mr. Greenleaf's eyes were fixed on him with a pathetic, hungry expression. What on earth could he say? Tom was sorry he had accepted the drink. "How old is Dickie now, by the way?" he asked.

"He's twenty-five."

So am I, Tom thought. Dickie was probably having the time of his life over there. An income, a house, a boat. Why should he want to come home? Dickie's face was becoming clearer in his memory: he had a big smile, blondish hair with crisp waves in it, a happy-go-lucky face. Dickie was lucky. What was he himself doing at twenty-five? Living from week to week. No bank account. Dodging cops now for the first time in his life. He had a talent for mathematics. Why in hell didn't they pay him for it, somewhere? Tom realized that all his muscles had tensed, that the matchcover in his fingers was mashed sideways, nearly flat. He was bored, God-damned bloody bored, bored, bored! He wanted to jump up and leave the table without a word. He wanted to be back at the bar, by himself.

Tom took a gulp of his drink. "I'd be very glad to write to Dickie, if you give me his address," he said quickly. "I suppose he'll remember me. We were at a weekend party once out on Long Island, I remember. Dickie and I went out and gathered mussels, and everyone had them for breakfast." Tom smiled. "A couple of us got sick, and it wasn't a very good party. But I remember Dickie talking that weekend about going to Europe. He must have left just—"

"I remember!" Mr. Greenleaf said. "That was the last weekend Richard was here. I think he told me about the mussels." He laughed rather loudly.

"I came up to your apartment a few times, too," Tom went on, getting into the spirit of it. "Dickie showed me some ship models that were sitting on a table in his room."

"Those are only childhood efforts!" Mr. Greenleaf was beaming. "Did he ever show you his frame models? Or his drawings?"

Dickie hadn't, but Tom said brightly, "Yes! Of course he did. Pen-and-ink drawings. Fascinating, some of them." Tom had never seen them, but he could see them now, precise draftsman's drawings with every line and bolt and screw labeled, could see Dickie smiling, holding them up for him to look at, and he could have gone on for several minutes describing details for Mr. Greenleaf's delight, but he checked himself.

"Yes, Richard's got talent along those lines," Mr. Greenleaf said with a satisfied air.

"I think he has," Tom agreed. His boredom had slipped into another gear. Tom knew the sensations. He had them sometimes at parties, but generally when he was having dinner with someone with whom he hadn't wanted to have dinner in the first place, and the evening got longer and longer. Now he could be maniacally polite for perhaps another whole hour, if he had to be, before something in him exploded and sent him running out the door. "I'm sorry I'm not quite free now or I'd be very glad to go over and see if I could persuade Richard myself. Maybe I could have some influence on him," he said, just because Mr. Greenleaf wanted him to say that.

"If you seriously think so—that is, I don't know if you're planning a trip to Europe or not."

"No, I'm not."

"Richard was always so influenced by his friends. If you or somebody like you who knew him could get a leave of absence, I'd even send them over to talk to him. I think it'd be worth more than my going over, anyway. I don't suppose you could possibly get a leave of absence from your present job, could you?"

Tom's heart took a sudden leap. He put on an expression of reflection. It was a possibility. Something in him had smelt it out and leapt at it even before his brain. Present job: nil. He might have to leave town soon, anyway. He wanted to leave New York. "I might," he said carefully, with the same pondering expression, as if he were even now going over the thousands of little ties that could prevent him.

"If you did go, I'd be glad to take care of your expenses, that goes without saying. Do you really think you might be able to arrange it? Say, this fall?"

It was already the middle of September. Tom stared at the gold signet ring with the nearly worn-away crest on Mr. Greenleaf's little finger. "I think I might. I'd be glad to see Richard again—especially if you think I might be of some help."

"I do! I think he'd listen to you. Then the mere fact that you don't know him very well— If you put it to him strongly why you think he ought to come home, he'd know you hadn't any ax to grind." Mr. Greenleaf leaned back in his chair, looking at Tom with approval. "Funny thing is, Jim Burke and his wife—Jim's my partner—they went by Mongibello last year when they were on a cruise. Richard promised he'd come home when the winter began. Last winter. Jim's given him up. What boy of twenty-five listens to an old man sixty or more? You'll probably succeed where the rest of us have failed!"

"I hope so," Tom said modestly.

"How about another drink? How about a nice brandy?"

2.

IT was after midnight when Tom started home. Mr. Greenleaf had offered to drop him off in a taxi, but Tom had not wanted him to see where he lived—in a dingy brownstone between Third and Second with a ROOMS TO LET sign hanging out. For the last two and a half weeks Tom had been living with Bob Delancey, a young man he hardly knew, but Bob had been the only one of Tom's friends and acquaintances in New York who had volunteered to put him up when he had been without a place to stay. Tom had not asked any of his friends up to Bob's, and had not even told anybody where he was living. The main advantage of Bob's place was that he could get his George McAlpin mail there with the minimum chance of detection. But that smelly john down the hall that didn't lock, that grimy single room that looked as if it had been lived in by a thousand different people who had left behind their particular kind of filth and never lifted a hand to clean it, those slithering stacks of *Vogue* and *Harper's Bazaar* and those big chi-chi smoked-glass bowls all over the place, filled with tangles of string and pencils and cigarette butts and decaying fruit! Bob was a free-lance window decorator for shops and department stores, but now the only work he did was occasional jobs for Third Avenue antique shops, and some antique shop had given him the smoked-glass bowls as a payment for something. Tom had been shocked at the sordidness of the place, shocked that he even knew anybody who lived like that, but he had known that he wouldn't live there very long. And now Mr. Greenleaf had turned up. Something always turned up. That was Tom's philosophy.

Just before he climbed the brownstone steps, Tom stopped and looked carefully in both directions. Nothing but an old woman airing her dog, and a weaving old man coming around the corner from Third Avenue. If there was any sensation he hated, it was that of being followed, by *anybody*. And lately he had it all the time. He ran up the steps.

A lot the sordidness mattered now, he thought as he went into the room. As soon as he could get a passport, he'd be sailing for Europe, probably in a first-class cabin. Waiters to bring him things when he pushed a button! Dressing for dinner, strolling into a big dining room, talking with people at his table like a gentleman! He could congratulate himself on tonight, he thought. He had behaved just right. Mr. Greenleaf couldn't possibly have had the impression that he had finagled the invitation to Europe. Just the opposite. He wouldn't let Mr. Greenleaf down. He'd do his very best with Dickie. Mr. Greenleaf was such a decent fellow himself, he took it for granted that everybody else in the world was decent, too. Tom had almost forgotten such people existed.

Slowly he took off his jacket and untied his tie, watching every move he made as if it were somebody else's movements he were watching. Astonishing how much straighter he was standing now, what a different look there was in his face. It was one of the few times in his life that he felt pleased with himself. He put a hand into Bob's glutted closet and thrust the hangers aggressively to right and left to make room for his suit. Then he went into the bathroom. The old rusty showerhead sent a jet against the shower curtain and another jet in an erratic spiral that he could hardly catch to wet himself, but it was better than sitting in the filthy tub.

When he woke up the next morning Bob was not there, and Tom saw from a glance at his bed that he hadn't come home. Tom jumped out of bed, went to the two-ring burner and put on coffee. Just as well Bob wasn't home this morning. He didn't want to tell Bob about the European trip. All that crummy bum would see in it was a free trip. And Ed Martin, too, probably, and Bert Visser, and all the other crumbs he knew. He wouldn't tell any of them, and he wouldn't have anybody seeing him off. Tom began to whistle. He was invited to dinner tonight at the Greenleafs' apartment on Park Avenue.

Fifteen minutes later, showered, shaved, and dressed in a suit and a striped tie that he thought would look well in his passport photo, Tom was strolling up and down the room with a cup of black coffee in his hand, waiting for the morning mail. After the mail, he would go over to Radio City to take care of the passport business. What should he do this afternoon? Go to some art exhibits, so he could chat about them tonight with the Greenleafs? Do some research on Burke-Greenleaf Watercraft, Inc., so Mr. Greenleaf would know that he took an interest in his work?

The whack of the mailbox came faintly through the open window, and Tom went downstairs. He waited until the mailman was down the front steps and out of sight before he took the letter addressed to George McAlpin down from the edge of the mailbox frame where the mailman had stuck it. Tom ripped it open. Out came a check for one hundred and nineteen dollars and fifty-four cents, payable to the Collector of Internal Revenue. Good old Mrs. Edith W. Superaugh! Paid without a whimper, without even a telephone call. It was a good omen. He went upstairs again, tore up Mrs. Superaugh's envelope and dropped it into the garbage bag.

He put her check into a manila envelope in the inside pocket of one of his jackets in the closet. This raised his total in checks to one thousand eight hundred and sixty-three dollars and fourteen cents, he calculated in his head. A pity that he couldn't cash them. Or that some idiot hadn't paid in cash yet, or made out a check to George McAlpin, but so far no one had. Tom had a bank messenger's identification card that he had found somewhere with an old date on it that he could try to alter, but he was afraid he couldn't get away with cashing the checks, even with a forged letter of authorization for whatever the sum was. So it amounted to no more than a practical joke, really. Good clean sport. He wasn't stealing money from anybody. Before he went to Europe, he thought, he'd destroy the checks.

There were seven more prospects on his list. Shouldn't he try just one more in these last ten days before he sailed? Walking home last evening, after seeing Mr. Greenleaf, he had thought that if Mrs. Superaugh and Carlos de Sevilla paid up, he'd call it quits. Mr. de Sevilla hadn't paid up yet—he needed a good scare by telephone to put the fear of God into him, Tom thought—but Mrs. Superaugh had been so easy, he was tempted to try just *one* more.

Tom took a mauve-colored stationery box from his suitcase in the closet. There were a few sheets of stationery in the box, and below them a stack of various forms he had taken from the Internal Revenue office when he had worked there as a stockroom clerk a few weeks ago. On the very bottom was his list of prospects—carefully chosen people who lived in the Bronx or in Brooklyn and would not be too inclined to pay the New York office a personal visit, artists and writers and free-lance people who had no withholding taxes, and who made from seven to twelve thousand a year. In that bracket, Tom figured that people seldom hired professional tax men to compute their taxes, while they earned enough money to be logically accused of having made a two- or three-hundred-dollar error in their tax computations. There was William J. Slatterer, journalist; Philip Robillard, musician; Frieda Hoehn, illustrator; Joseph J. Gennari, photographer; Frederick Reddington, artist; Frances Karnegis— Tom had a hunch about Reddington. He was a comic-book artist. He probably didn't know whether he was coming or going.

He chose two forms headed NOTICE OF ERROR IN COMPUTATION, slipped a carbon between them, and began to copy rapidly the data below Reddington's name on his list. Income:

$11,250. Exemptions: 1. Deductions: $600. Credits: nil. Remittance: nil. Interest: (he hesitated a moment) $2.16. Balance
due: $233.76. Then he took a piece of typewriter paper
stamped with the Department of Internal Revenue's Lexington Avenue address from his supply in his carbon folder,
crossed out the address with one slanting line of his pen, and
typed below it:

Dear Sir:
    Due to an overflow at our regular Lexington Avenue
office, your reply should be sent to:
                    Adjustment Department
                    Attention of George McAlpin
                    187 E. 51 Street
                    New York 22, New York.
Thank you.
                            Ralph F. Fischer
                            Gen. Dir. Adj. Dept.

Tom signed it with a scrolly, illegible signature. He put the
other forms away in case Bob should come in suddenly, and
picked up the telephone. He had decided to give Mr. Reddington a preliminary prod. He got Mr. Reddington's number from information and called it. Mr. Reddington was at
home. Tom explained the situation briefly, and expressed surprise that Mr. Reddington had not yet received the notice
from the Adjustment Department.

"That should have gone out a few days ago," Tom said.
"You'll undoubtedly get it tomorrow. We've been a little
rushed around here."

"But I've *paid* my tax," said the alarmed voice at the other
end. "They were all—"

"These things can happen, you know, when the income's
earned on a free-lance basis with no withholding tax. We've
been over your return very carefully, Mr. Reddington. There's
no mistake. And we wouldn't like to slap a lien on the office
you work for or your agent or whatever—" Here he chuckled.
A friendly, personal chuckle generally worked wonders. "—but
we'll have to do that unless you pay within forty-eight hours.
I'm sorry the notice hasn't reached you before now. As I said,
we've been pretty—"

"Is there anyone there I can talk to about it if I come in?" Mr. Reddington asked anxiously. "That's a hell of a lot of money!"

"Well, there is, of course." Tom's voice always got folksy at this point. He sounded like a genial old codger of sixty-odd, who might be as patient as could be if Mr. Reddington came in, but who wouldn't yield by so much as a red cent, for all the talking and explaining Mr. Reddington might do. George McAlpin represented the Tax Department of the United States of America, suh. "You can talk to *me*, of course," Tom drawled, "but there's absolutely no mistake about this, Mr. Reddington. I'm just thinking of saving you your time. You can come in if you want to, but I've got all your records right here in my hand."

Silence. Mr. Reddington wasn't going to ask him anything about records, because he probably didn't know what to begin asking. But if Mr. Reddington were to ask him to explain what it was all about, Tom had a lot of hash about net income versus accrued income, balance due versus computation, interest at six per cent per annum accruing from due date of the tax until paid on any balance which represents tax shown on original return, which he could deliver in a slow voice as incapable of interruption as a Sherman tank. So far, no one had insisted on coming in person to hear more of that. Mr. Reddington was backing down, too. Tom could hear it in the silence.

"All right," Mr. Reddington said in a tone of collapse. "I'll read the notice when I get it tomorrow."

"All right, Mr. Reddington," he said, and hung up.

Tom sat there for a moment, giggling, the palms of his thin hands pressed together between his knees. Then he jumped up, put Bob's typewriter away again, combed his light-brown hair neatly in front of the mirror, and set off for Radio City.

3.

"HELLO-O, Tom, my boy!" Mr. Greenleaf said in a voice that promised good martinis, a gourmet's dinner, and a bed for the night in case he got too tired to go home. "Emily, this is Tom Ripley!"

"I'm so happy to meet you!" she said warmly.

"How do you do, Mrs. Greenleaf?"

She was very much what he had expected—blond, rather tall and slender, with enough formality to keep him on his good behavior, yet with the same naïve good-will-toward-all that Mr. Greenleaf had. Mr. Greenleaf led them into the living room. Yes, he had been here before with Dickie.

"Mr. Ripley's in the insurance business," Mr. Greenleaf announced, and Tom thought he must have had a few already, or he was very nervous tonight, because Tom had given him quite a description last night of the advertising agency where he had said he was working.

"Not a very exciting job," Tom said modestly to Mrs. Greenleaf.

A maid came into the room with a tray of martinis and canapés.

"Mr. Ripley's been here before," Mr. Greenleaf said. "He's come here with Richard."

"Oh, has he? I don't believe I met you, though." She smiled. "Are you from New York?"

"No, I'm from Boston," Tom said. That was true.

About thirty minutes later—just the right time later, Tom thought, because the Greenleafs had kept insisting that he drink another and another martini—they went into a dining room off the living room, where a table was set for three with candles, huge dark-blue dinner napkins, and a whole cold chicken in aspic. But first there was céleri rémoulade. Tom was very fond of it. He said so.

"So is Richard!" Mrs. Greenleaf said. "He always liked it the way our cook makes it. A pity you can't take him some."

"I'll put it in with the socks," Tom said, smiling, and Mrs. Greenleaf laughed. She had told him she would like him to take Richard some black woolen socks from Brooks Brothers, the kind Richard always wore.

The conversation was dull, and the dinner superb. In answer to a question of Mrs. Greenleaf's, Tom told her that he was working for an advertising firm called Rothenberg, Fleming and Barter. When he referred to it again, he deliberately called it Reddington, Fleming and Parker. Mr. Greenleaf didn't seem to notice the difference. Tom mentioned the firm's name the second time when he and Mr. Greenleaf were alone in the living room after dinner.

"Did you go to school in Boston?" Mr. Greenleaf asked.

"No, sir. I went to Princeton for a while, then I visited another aunt in Denver and went to college there." Tom waited, hoping Mr. Greenleaf would ask him something about Princeton, but he didn't. Tom could have discussed the system of teaching history, the campus restrictions, the atmosphere at the weekend dances, the political tendencies of the student body, anything. Tom had been very friendly last summer with a Princeton junior who had talked of nothing but Princeton, so that Tom had finally pumped him for more and more, foreseeing a time when he might be able to use the information. Tom had told the Greenleafs that he had been raised by his Aunt Dottie in Boston. She had taken him to Denver when he was sixteen, and actually he had only finished high school there, but there had been a young man named Don Mizell rooming in his Aunt Bea's house in Denver who had been going to the University of Colorado. Tom felt as if he had gone there, too.

"Specialize in anything in particular?" Mr. Greenleaf asked.

"Sort of divided myself between accounting and English composition," Tom replied with a smile, knowing it was such a dull answer that nobody would possibly pursue it.

Mrs. Greenleaf came in with a photograph album, and Tom sat beside her on the sofa while she turned through it. Richard taking his first step, Richard in a ghastly full-page color photograph dressed and posed as the Blue Boy, with long blond curls. The album was not interesting to him until Richard got to be sixteen or so, long-legged, slim, with the wave tightening in his hair. So far as Tom could see, he had hardly changed between sixteen and twenty-three or -four, when the pictures of him stopped, and it was astonishing to Tom how little the bright, naïve smile changed. Tom could not help feeling that Richard was not very intelligent, or else he loved to be photographed and thought he looked best with his mouth spread from ear to ear, which was not very intelligent of him, either.

"I haven't gotten round to pasting these in yet," Mrs. Greenleaf said, handing him a batch of loose pictures. "These are all from Europe."

They were more interesting: Dickie in what looked like a café in Paris, Dickie on a beach. In several of them he was frowning.

"This is Mongibello, by the way," Mrs. Greenleaf said, indicating the picture of Dickie pulling a rowboat up on the sand. The picture was backgrounded by dry, rocky mountains and a fringe of little white houses along the shore. "And here's the girl there, the only other American who lives there."

"Marge Sherwood," Mr. Greenleaf supplied. He sat across the room, but he was leaning forward, following the picture-showing intently.

The girl was in a bathing suit on the beach, her arms around her knees, healthy and unsophisticated-looking, with tousled, short blond hair—the good-egg type. There was a good picture of Richard in shorts, sitting on the parapet of a terrace. He was smiling, but it was not the same smile, Tom saw. Richard looked more poised in the European pictures.

Tom noticed that Mrs. Greenleaf was staring down at the rug in front of her. He remembered the moment at the table when she had said, "I wish I'd never heard of Europe!" and Mr. Greenleaf had given her an anxious glance and then smiled at him, as if such outbursts had occurred before. Now he saw tears in her eyes. Mr. Greenleaf was getting up to come to her.

"Mrs. Greenleaf," Tom said gently, "I want you to know that I'll do everything I can to make Dickie come back."

"Bless you, Tom, bless you." She pressed Tom's hand that rested on his thigh.

"Emily, don't you think it's time you went in to bed?" Mr. Greenleaf asked, bending over her.

Tom stood up as Mrs. Greenleaf did.

"I hope you'll come again to pay us a visit before you go, Tom," she said. "Since Richard's gone, we seldom have any young men to the house. I miss them."

"I'd be delighted to come again," Tom said.

Mr. Greenleaf went out of the room with her. Tom remained standing, his hands at his sides, his head high. In a large mirror on the wall he could see himself: the upright, self-respecting young man again. He looked quickly away. He was doing the right thing, behaving the right way. Yet he had a feeling of guilt. When he had said to Mrs. Greenleaf just now, *I'll do everything I can . . .* Well, he meant it. He wasn't trying to fool anybody.

He felt himself beginning to sweat, and he tried to relax. What was he so worried about? He'd felt so well tonight! When he had said that about Aunt Dottie—

Tom straightened, glancing at the door, but the door had not opened.

That had been the only time tonight when he had felt uncomfortable, unreal, the way he might have felt if he had been lying, yet it had been practically the only thing he had said that *was* true: *My parents died when I was very small. I was raised by my aunt in Boston.*

Mr. Greenleaf came into the room. His figure seemed to pulsate and grow larger and larger. Tom blinked his eyes, feeling a sudden terror of him, an impulse to attack him before he was attacked.

"Suppose we sample some brandy?" Mr. Greenleaf said, opening a panel beside the fireplace.

It's like a movie, Tom thought. In a minute, Mr. Greenleaf or somebody else's voice would say, "Okay, *cut!*" and he would relax again and find himself back in Raoul's with the gin and tonic in front of him. No, back in the Green Cage.

"Had enough?" Mr. Greenleaf asked. "Don't drink this, if you don't want it."

Tom gave a vague nod, and Mr. Greenleaf looked puzzled for an instant, then poured the two brandies.

A cold fear was running over Tom's body. He was thinking of the incident in the drugstore last week, though that was all over and he wasn't *really* afraid, he reminded himself, not now. There was a drugstore on Second Avenue whose phone number he gave out to people who insisted on calling him again about their income tax. He gave it out as the phone number of the Adjustment Department where he could be reached only between three-thirty and four on Wednesday and Friday afternoons. At these times, Tom hung around the booth in the drugstore, waiting for the phone to ring. When the druggist had looked at him suspiciously the second time he had been there, Tom had said that he was waiting for a call from his girl friend. Last Friday when he had answered the telephone, a man's voice had said, "You know what we're talking about, don't you? We know where you live, if you want us to come to your place. . . . We've got the stuff for you, if you've got it for us." An insistent yet evasive voice, so that Tom had thought it was some kind of a trick and hadn't been able to answer anything. Then, "Listen, we're coming right over. To your *house*." Tom's legs had felt like jelly when he got out of the phone booth, and then he had seen the druggist staring at him, wide-eyed, panicky-looking, and the conversation had suddenly explained itself: the druggist sold dope, and he was afraid that Tom was a police detective who had come to get the goods on *him*. Tom had started laughing, had walked out laughing uproariously, staggering as he went, because his legs were still weak from his own fear.

"Thinking about Europe?" Mr. Greenleaf's voice said.

Tom accepted the glass Mr. Greenleaf was holding out to him. "Yes, I was," Tom said.

"Well, I hope you enjoy your trip, Tom, as well as have some effect on Richard. By the way, Emily likes you a lot. She told me so. I didn't have to ask her." Mr. Greenleaf rolled his brandy glass between his hands. "My wife has leukemia, Tom."

"Oh. That's very serious, isn't it?"

"Yes. She may not live a year."

"I'm sorry to hear that," Tom said.

Mr. Greenleaf pulled a paper out of his pocket. "I've got a list of boats. I think the usual Cherbourg way is quickest, and also the most interesting. You'd take the boat train to Paris, then a sleeper down over the Alps to Rome and Naples."

"That'd be fine." It began to sound exciting to him.

"You'll have to catch a bus from Naples to Richard's village. I'll write him about you—not telling him that you're an emissary from me," he added, smiling, "but I'll tell him we've met. Richard ought to put you up, but if he can't for some reason, there're hotels in the town. I expect you and Richard'll hit it off all right. Now as to money—" Mr. Greenleaf smiled his fatherly smile. "I propose to give you six hundred dollars in traveler's checks apart from your round-trip ticket. Does that suit you? The six hundred should see you through nearly two months, and if you need more, all you have to do is wire me, my boy. You don't look like a young man who'd throw money down the drain."

"That sounds ample, sir."

Mr. Greenleaf got increasingly mellow and jolly on the brandy, and Tom got increasingly close-mouthed and sour. Tom wanted to get out of the apartment. And yet he still wanted to go to Europe, and wanted Mr. Greenleaf to approve of him. The moments on the sofa were more agonizing than the moments in the bar last night when he had been so bored, because now that break into another gear didn't come. Several times Tom got up with his drink and strolled to the fireplace and back, and when he looked into the mirror he saw that his mouth was turned down at the corners.

Mr. Greenleaf was rollicking on about Richard and himself in Paris, when Richard had been ten years old. It was not in the least interesting. If anything happened with the police in the next ten days, Tom thought, Mr. Greenleaf would take him in. He could tell Mr. Greenleaf that he'd sublet his apartment in a hurry, or something like that, and simply hide out here. Tom felt awful, almost physically ill.

"Mr. Greenleaf, I think I should be going."

"Now? But I wanted to show you— Well, never mind. Another time."

Tom knew he should have asked, "Show me what?" and been patient while he showed whatever it was, but he couldn't.

"I want you to visit the yards, of course," Mr. Greenleaf said cheerfully. "When can you come out? Only during your lunch hour, I suppose. I think you should be able to tell Richard what the yards look like these days."

"Yes—I could come in my lunch hour."

"Give me a call any day, Tom. You've got my card with my private number. If you give me half an hour's notice, I'll have a man pick you up at your office and drive you out. We'll have a sandwich as we walk through, and he'll drive you back."

"I'll call you," Tom said. He felt he would faint if he stayed one minute longer in the dimly lighted foyer, but Mr.

Greenleaf was chuckling again, asking him if he had read a certain book by Henry James.

"I'm sorry to say I haven't, sir, not that one," Tom said.

"Well, no matter." Mr. Greenleaf smiled.

Then they shook hands, a long suffocating squeeze from Mr. Greenleaf, and it was over. But the pained, frightened expression was still on his face as he rode down in the elevator, Tom saw. He leaned in the corner of the elevator in an exhausted way, though he knew as soon as he hit the lobby he would fly out the door and keep on running, running, all the way home.

4.

THE atmosphere of the city became stranger as the days went on. It was as if something had gone out of New York—the realness or the importance of it—and the city was putting on a show just for him, a colossal show with its buses, taxis, and hurrying people on the sidewalks, its television shows in all the Third Avenue bars, its movie marquees lighted up in broad daylight, and its sound effects of thousands of honking horns and human voices, talking for no purpose whatsoever. As if when his boat left the pier on Saturday, the whole city of New York would collapse with a *poof* like a lot of cardboard on a stage.

Or maybe he was afraid. He hated water. He had never been anywhere before on water, except to New Orleans from New York and back to New York again, but then he had been working on a banana boat mostly below deck, and he had hardly realized he was on water. The few times he had been on deck the sight of the water had at first frightened him, then made him feel sick, and he had always run below deck again, where, contrary to what people said, he had felt better. His parents had drowned in Boston Harbor, and Tom had always thought that probably had something to do with it, because as long as he could remember he had been afraid of water, and he had never learned how to swim. It gave Tom a sick, empty feeling at the pit of his stomach to think that in less than a week he would have water below him, miles deep, and that undoubtedly he would have to look at it most of the time, because people on ocean liners spent most of their time on deck. And it was particularly un-chic to be seasick, he felt. He had never been seasick, but he came very near it several times in those last days, simply thinking about the voyage to Cherbourg.

He had told Bob Delancey that he was moving in a week, but he hadn't said where. Bob did not seem interested, anyway. They saw very little of each other at the Fifty-first Street place. Tom had gone to Marc Priminger's house in East-Forty-fifth Street—he still had the keys—to pick up a couple of things he had forgotten, and he had gone at an hour when he had thought Marc wouldn't be there, but Marc had come in with his new housemate, Joel, a thin drip of a young man who worked for a publishing house, and Marc had put on one of his suave "Please-do-*just*-as-you-like" acts for Joel's benefit, though if Joel hadn't been there Marc would have cursed him out in language that even a Portuguese sailor wouldn't have used. Marc (his given name was, of all things, Marcellus) was an ugly mug of a man with a private income and a hobby of helping out young men in temporary financial difficulties by putting them up in his two-story, three-bedroom house, and playing God by telling them what they could and couldn't do around the place and by giving them advice as to their lives and their jobs, generally rotten advice. Tom had stayed there three months, though for nearly half that time Marc had been in Florida and he had had the house all to himself, but when Marc had come back he had made a big stink about a few pieces of broken glassware—Marc playing God again, the Stern Father—and Tom had gotten angry enough, for once, to stand up for himself and talk back to him. Whereupon Marc had thrown him out, after collecting sixty-three dollars from him for the broken glassware. The old tightwad! He should have been an old maid, Tom thought, at the head of a girls' school. Tom was bitterly sorry he had ever laid eyes on Marc Priminger, and the sooner he could forget Marc's stupid, pig-like eyes, his massive jaw, his ugly hands with the gaudy rings (waving through the air, ordering this and that from everybody), the happier he would be.

The only one of his friends he felt like telling about his European trip was Cleo, and he went to see her on the Thursday before he sailed. Cleo Dobelle was a tall, slim, dark-haired girl who could have been anything from twenty-three to thirty, Tom didn't know, who lived with her parents in Gracie Square and painted in a small way—a *very* small way, in fact, on little pieces of ivory no bigger than postage stamps that had to be viewed through a magnifying glass, and Cleo used a magnifying glass when she painted them. "But think how convenient it is to be able to carry *all* my paintings in a cigar box! Other painters have to have rooms and rooms to hold their canvases!" Cleo said. Cleo lived in her own suite of rooms with a little bath and kitchen at the back of her parents' section of the apartment, and Cleo's apartment was always rather dark since it had no exposure except to a tiny backyard overgrown with ailanthus trees that blocked out the light. Cleo always had the lights on, dim ones, which gave a nocturnal atmosphere whatever the time of day. Except for the night when he had met her, Tom had seen Cleo only in close-fitting velvet slacks of various colors and gaily striped silk shirts. They had taken to each other from the very first night, when Cleo had asked him to dinner at her apartment on the following evening. Cleo always asked him up to her apartment, and there was somehow never any thought that he might ask her out to dinner or the theatre or do any of the ordinary things that a young man was expected to do with a girl. She didn't expect him to bring her flowers or books or candy when he came for dinner or cocktails, though Tom did bring her a little gift sometimes, because it pleased her so. Cleo was the one person he could tell that he was going to Europe and why. He did.

Cleo was enthralled, as he had known she would be. Her red lips parted in her long, pale face, and she brought her hands down on her velvet thighs and exclaimed, "*Tom*-mie! How too, too marvelous! It's just like out of Shakespeare or something!"

That was just what Tom thought, too. That was just what he had needed someone to say.

Cleo fussed around him all evening, asking him if he had this and that, Kleenexes and cold tablets and woolen socks because it started raining in Europe in the fall, and his vaccinations. Tom said he felt pretty well prepared.

"Just don't come to see me off, Cleo. I don't want to be seen off."

"Of course not!" Cleo said, understanding perfectly. "Oh, Tommie, I think that's such fun! Will you write me everything that happens with Dickie? You're the only person I know who ever went to Europe for a *reason*."

He told her about visiting Mr. Greenleaf's shipyards in Long Island, the miles and miles of tables with machines making shiny metal parts, varnishing and polishing wood, the drydocks with boat skeletons of all sizes, and impressed her with the terms Mr. Greenleaf had used—coamings, inwales, keelsons, and chines. He described the second dinner at Mr. Greenleaf's house, when Mr. Greenleaf had presented him with a wristwatch. He showed the wristwatch to Cleo, not a fabulously expensive wristwatch, but still an excellent one and just the style Tom might have chosen for himself—a plain white face with fine black Roman numerals in a simple gold setting with an alligator strap.

"Just because I happened to say a few days before that I didn't own a watch," Tom said. "He's really adopted me like a son." And Cleo, too, was the only person he knew to whom he could say that.

Cleo sighed. "Men! You have all the luck. Nothing like that could ever happen to a girl. Men're so *free!*"

Tom smiled. It often seemed to him that it was the other way around. "Is that the lamb chops burning?"

Cleo jumped up with a shriek.

After dinner, she showed him five or six of her latest paintings, a couple of romantic portraits of a young man they both knew, in an open-collared white shirt, three imaginary landscapes of a junglelike land, derived from the view of ailanthus trees out her window. The hair of the little monkeys in the paintings was really astoundingly well done, Tom thought. Cleo had a lot of brushes with just one hair in them, and even these varied from comparatively coarse to ultra fine. They drank nearly two bottles of Medoc from her parents' liquor shelf, and Tom got so sleepy he could have spent the night right where he was lying on the floor—they had often slept side by side on the two big bear rugs in front of the fireplace, and it was another of the wonderful things about Cleo that she never wanted or expected him to make a pass at her, and he never had—but Tom hauled himself up at a quarter to twelve and took his leave.

"I won't see you again, will I?" Cleo said dejectedly at the door.

"Oh, I should be back in about six weeks," Tom said, though he didn't think so at all. Suddenly he leaned forward and planted a firm, brotherly kiss on her ivory cheek. "I'll miss you, Cleo."

She squeezed his shoulder, the only physical touch he could recall her ever having given him. "I'll miss you," she said.

The next day he took care of Mrs. Greenleaf's commissions at Brooks Brothers, the dozen pairs of black woolen socks and the bathrobe. Mrs. Greenleaf had not suggested a color for the bathrobe. She would leave that up to him, she had said. Tom chose a dark maroon flannel with a navy-blue belt and lapels. It was not the best-looking robe of the lot, in Tom's opinion, but he felt it was exactly what Richard would have chosen, and that Richard would be delighted with it. He put the socks and the robe on the Greenleafs' charge account. He saw a heavy linen sport shirt with wooden buttons that he liked very much, that would have been easy to put on the Greenleafs' account, too, but he didn't. He bought it with his own money.

5.

THE morning of his sailing, the morning he had looked forward to with such buoyant excitement, got off to a hideous start. Tom followed the steward to his cabin congratulating himself that his firmness with Bob about not wanting to be seen off had taken effect, and had just entered the room when a bloodcurdling whoop went up.

"Where's all the champagne, Tom? We're waiting!"

"Boy, is this a stinking room! Why don't you ask them for something decent?"

"Tommie, take *me?*" from Ed Martin's girl friend, whom Tom couldn't bear to look at.

There they all were, mostly Bob's lousy friends, sprawled on his bed, on the floor, everywhere. Bob had found out he was sailing, but Tom had never thought he would do a thing like this. It took self-control for Tom not to say in an icy voice, "There *isn't* any champagne." He tried to greet them all, tried to smile, though he could have burst into tears like a child. He gave Bob a long, withering look, but Bob was already high, on something. There were very few things that got under his skin, Tom thought self-justifyingly, but this was one of them: noisy surprises like this, the riffraff, the vulgarians, the slobs he had thought he had left behind when he crossed the gangplank, littering the very stateroom where he was to spend the next five days!

Tom went over to Paul Hubbard, the only respectable person in the room, and sat down beside him on the short, built-in sofa. "Hello, Paul," he said quietly. "I'm sorry about all this."

"Oh!" Paul scoffed. "How long'll you be gone?—What's the matter, Tom? Are you sick?"

It was awful. It went on, the noise and the laughter and the girls feeling the bed and looking in the john. Thank God the Greenleafs hadn't come to see him off! Mr. Greenleaf had had to go to New Orleans on business, and Mrs. Greenleaf, when Tom had called this morning to say good-bye, had said that she didn't feel quite up to coming down to the boat.

Finally, Bob or somebody produced a bottle of whisky, and they all began to drink out of the two glasses from the bathroom, and then a steward came in with a tray of glasses. Tom refused to have a drink. He was sweating so heavily, he took off his jacket so as not to soil it. Bob came over and rammed a glass in his hand, and Bob was not exactly joking, Tom saw, and he knew why—because he had accepted Bob's hospitality for a month, and he might at least put on a pleasant face, but Tom could not put on a pleasant face any more than if his face had been made of granite. So what if they all hated him after this, he thought, what had he lost?

"I can fit in here, Tommie," said the girl who was determined to fit in somewhere and go with him. She had wedged herself sideways into a narrow closet about the size of a broom closet.

"I'd like to see Tom caught with a girl in his room!" Ed Martin said, laughing.

Tom glared at him. "Let's get out of here and get some air," he murmured to Paul.

The others were making so much noise, nobody noticed their leaving. They stood at the rail near the stern. It was a sunless day, and the city on their right was already like some gray, distant land that he might be looking at from mid-ocean—except for those bastards inside his stateroom.

"Where've you been keeping yourself?" Paul asked. "Ed called up to tell me you were leaving. I haven't seen you in weeks."

Paul was one of the people who thought he worked for the Associated Press. Tom made up a fine story about an assign-ment he had been sent on. Possibly the Middle East, Tom said. He made it sound rather secret. "I've been doing quite a lot of night work lately, too," Tom said, "which is why I haven't been around much. It's awfully nice of you to come down and see me off."

"I hadn't any classes this morning." Paul took the pipe out of his mouth and smiled. "Not that I wouldn't have come anyway, probably. Any old excuse!"

Tom smiled. Paul taught music at a girls' school in New York to earn his living, but he preferred to compose music on his own time. Tom could not remember how he had met Paul, but he remembered going to his Riverside Drive apartment for Sunday brunch once with some other people, and Paul had played some of his own compositions on the piano, and Tom had enjoyed it immensely. "Can't I offer you a drink? Let's see if we can find the bar," Tom said.

But just then a steward came out, hitting a gong and shout-ing, "Visitors ashore, please! All visitors ashore!"

"That's me," Paul said.

They shook hands, patted shoulders, promised to write postcards to each other. Then Paul was gone.

Bob's gang would stay till the last minute, he thought, probably have to be blasted out. Tom turned suddenly and ran up a narrow, ladderlike flight of stairs. At the top of it he was confronted by a CABIN CLASS ONLY sign hanging from a chain, but he threw a leg over the chain and stepped onto the deck. They surely wouldn't object to a first-class passenger going into second-class, he thought. He couldn't bear to look at Bob's gang again. He had paid Bob half a month's rent and given him a good-bye present of a good shirt and tie. What more did Bob want?

The ship was moving before Tom dared to go down to his room again. He went into the room cautiously. Empty. The neat blue bedcover was smooth again. The ashtrays were clean. There was no sign they had ever been here. Tom relaxed and smiled. This was service! The fine old tradition of the Cunard Line, British seamanship and all that! He saw a big basket of fruit on the floor by his bed. He seized the little white envelope eagerly. The card inside said:

> Bon voyage and bless you, Tom. All our good wishes go with you.
> Emily and Herbert Greenleaf

The basket had a tall handle and it was entirely under yellow cellophane—apples and pears and grapes and a couple of candy bars and several little bottles of liqueurs. Tom had never received a bon voyage basket. To him, they had always been something you saw in florists' windows for fantastic prices and laughed at. Now he found himself with tears in his eyes, and he put his face down in his hands suddenly and began to sob.

6.

HIS mood was tranquil and benevolent, but not at all sociable. He wanted his time for thinking, and he did not care to meet any of the people on the ship, not any of them, though when he encountered the people with whom he sat at his table, he greeted them pleasantly and smiled. He began to play a role on the ship, that of a serious young man with a serious job ahead of him. He was courteous, poised, civilized and preoccupied.

He had a sudden whim for a cap and bought one in the haberdashery, a conservative bluish-gray cap of soft English wool. He could pull its visor down over nearly his whole face when he wanted to nap in his deckchair, or wanted to look as if he were napping. A cap was the most versatile of head-gears, he thought, and he wondered why he had never thought of wearing one before? He could look like a country gentleman, a thug, an Englishman, a Frenchman, or a plain American eccentric, depending on how he wore it. Tom amused himself with it in his room in front of the mirror. He had always thought he had the world's dullest face, a thoroughly forgettable face with a look of docility that he could not understand, and a look also of vague fright that he had never been able to erase. A real conformist's face, he thought. The cap changed all that. It gave him a country air, Greenwich, Connecticut, country. Now he was a young man with a private income, not long out of Princeton, perhaps. He bought a pipe to go with the cap.

He was starting a new life. Good-bye to all the second-rate people he had hung around and had let hang around him in the last three years in New York. He felt as he imagined immigrants felt when they left everything behind them in some foreign country, left their friends and relations and their past mistakes, and sailed for America. A clean slate! Whatever happened with Dickie, he would acquit himself well, and Mr. Greenleaf would know that he had, and would respect him for it. When Mr. Greenleaf's money was used up, he might not come back to America. He might get an interesting job in a hotel, for instance, where they needed somebody bright and personable who spoke English. Or he might become a representative for some European firm and travel everywhere in the world. Or somebody might come along who needed a young man exactly like himself, who could drive a car, who was quick at figures, who could entertain an old grandmother or squire somebody's daughter to a dance. He was versatile, and the world was wide! He swore to himself he would stick to a job once he got it. Patience and perseverance! Upward and onward!

"Have you Henry James' *The Ambassadors*?" Tom asked the officer in charge of the first-class library. The book was not on the shelf.

"I'm sorry, we haven't, sir," said the officer.

Tom was disappointed. It was the book Mr. Greenleaf had asked him if he had read. Tom felt he ought to read it. He went to the cabin-class library. He found the book on the shelf, but when he started to check it out and gave his cabin number, the attendant told him sorry, that first-class passengers were not allowed to take books from the cabin-class library. Tom had been afraid of that. He put the book back docilely, though it would have been easy, so easy, to make a pass at the shelf and slip the book under his jacket.

In the mornings he strolled several times round the deck, but very slowly, so that the people puffing around on their morning constitutionals always passed him two or three times before he had been around once, then settled down in his deckchair for bouillon and more thought on his own destiny. After lunch, he pottered around in his cabin, basking in its privacy and comfort, doing absolutely nothing. Sometimes he sat in the writing room, thoughtfully penning letters on the ship's stationery to Marc Priminger, to Cleo, to the Greenleafs. The letter to the Greenleafs began as a polite greeting and a thank-you for the bon voyage basket and the comfortable accommodations, but he amused himself by adding an imaginary postdated paragraph about finding Dickie and living with him in his Mongibello house, about the slow but steady progress he was making in persuading Dickie to come home, about the swimming, the fishing, the café life, and he got so carried away that it went on for eight or ten pages and he knew he would never mail any of it, so he wrote on about Dickie's not being romantically interested in Marge (he gave a complete character analysis of Marge) so it was not Marge who was holding Dickie, though Mrs. Greenleaf had thought it might be, etc., etc., until the table was covered with sheets of paper and the first call came for dinner.

On another afternoon, he wrote a polite note to Aunt Dottie:

Dear Auntie [which he rarely called her in a letter and never to her face],

As you see by the stationery, I am on the high seas. An unexpected business offer which I cannot explain now. I had to leave rather suddenly, so I was not able to get up to Boston and I'm sorry, because it may be months or even years before I come back.

I just wanted you not to worry and not to send me any more checks, thank you. Thank you very much for the last one of a month or so ago. I don't suppose you have sent any more since then. I am well and extremely happy.

Love,
Tom

No use sending any good wishes about her health. She was as strong as an ox. He added:

P.S. I have no idea what my address will be, so I cannot give you any.

That made him feel better, because it definitely cut him off from her. He needn't ever tell her where he was. No more of the snidely digging letters, the sly comparisons of him to his father, the piddling checks for the strange sums of six dollars and forty-eight cents and twelve dollars and ninety-five, as if she had had a bit left over from her latest bill-paying, or taken something back to a store and had tossed the money to him, like a crumb. Considering what Aunt Dottie might have sent him, with her income, the checks were an insult. Aunt Dottie insisted that his upbringing had cost her more than his father had left in insurance, and maybe it had, but did she have to keep rubbing it in his face? Did anybody human keep rubbing a thing like that in a child's face? Lots of aunts and even strangers raised a child for nothing and were delighted to do it.

After his letter to Aunt Dottie, he got up and strode around the deck, walking it off. Writing her always made him feel angry. He resented the courtesy to her. Yet until now he had always wanted her to know where he was, because he had always needed her piddling checks. He had had to write a score of letters about his changes of address to Aunt Dottie. But he didn't need her money now. He would hold himself independent of it, forever.

He thought suddenly of one summer day when he had been about twelve, when he had been on a cross-country trip with Aunt Dottie and a woman friend of hers, and they had gotten stuck in a bumper-to-bumper traffic jam somewhere. It had been a hot summer day, and Aunt Dottie had sent him out with the thermos to get some ice water at a filling station, and suddenly the traffic had started moving. He remembered running between huge, inching cars, always about to touch the door of Aunt Dottie's car and never being quite able to, because she had kept inching along as fast as she could go, not willing to wait for him a minute, and yelling, "Come on, come on, slowpoke!" out the window all the time. When he had finally made it to the car and gotten in, with tears of frustration and anger running down his cheeks, she had said gaily to her friend, "Sissy! He's a sissy from the ground up. Just like his father!" It was a wonder he had emerged from such treatment as well as he had. And just what, he wondered, made Aunt Dottie think his father had been a sissy? Could she, had she, ever cited a single thing? No.

Lying in his deckchair, fortified morally by the luxurious surroundings and inwardly by the abundance of well-prepared food, he tried to take an objective look at his past life. The last four years had been for the most part a waste, there was no denying that. A series of haphazard jobs, long perilous intervals with no job at all and consequent demoralization because of having no money, and then taking up with stupid, silly people in order not to be lonely, or because they could offer him something for a while, as Marc Priminger had. It was not a record to be proud of, considering he had come to New York with such high aspirations. He had wanted to be an actor, though at twenty he had not had the faintest idea of the difficulties, the necessary training, or even the necessary talent. He had thought he had the necessary talent, and that all he would have to do was show a producer a few of his original one-man skits—Mrs. Roosevelt writing "My Day" after a visit to a clinic for unmarried mothers, for instance—but his first three rebuffs had killed all his courage and his hope. He had had no reserve of money, so he had taken the job on the banana boat, which at least had removed him from New York. He had been afraid that Aunt Dottie had called the police to look for him in New York, though he hadn't done anything wrong in Boston, just run off to make his own way in the world as millions of young men had done before him.

His main mistake had been that he had never stuck to anything, he thought, like the accounting job in the department store that might have worked into something, if he had not been so completely discouraged by the slowness of department-store promotions. Well, he blamed Aunt Dottie to some extent for his lack of perseverance, never giving him credit when he was younger for anything he had stuck to—like his paper route when he was thirteen. He had won a silver medal from the newspaper for "Courtesy, Service, and Reliability." It was like looking back at another person to remember himself then, a skinny, sniveling wretch with an eternal cold in the nose, who had still managed to win a medal for courtesy, service, and reliability. Aunt Dottie had hated him when he had a cold; she used to take her handkerchief and nearly wrench his nose off, wiping it.

Tom writhed in his deckchair as he thought of it, but he writhed elegantly, adjusting the crease of his trousers.

He remembered the vows he had made, even at the age of eight, to run away from Aunt Dottie, the violent scenes he had imagined—Aunt Dottie trying to hold him in the house, and he hitting her with his fists, flinging her to the ground and throttling her, and finally tearing the big brooch off her dress and stabbing her a million times in the throat with it. He had run away at seventeen and been brought back, and he had done it again at twenty and succeeded. And it was astounding and pitiful how naïve he had been, how little he had known about the way the world worked, as if he had spent so much of his time hating Aunt Dottie and scheming how to escape her, that he had not had enough time to learn and grow. He remembered the way he had felt when he had been fired from the warehouse job during his first month in New York. He had held the job less than two weeks, because he hadn't been strong enough to lift orange crates eight hours a day, but he had done his best and knocked himself out trying to hold the job, and when they had fired him, he remembered how horribly unjust he had thought it. He remembered deciding then that the world was full of Simon Legrees, and that you had to be an animal, as tough as the gorillas who worked with him at the warehouse, or starve. He remembered that right after that, he had stolen a loaf of bread from a delicatessen counter and had taken it home and devoured it, feeling that the world owed a loaf of bread to him, and more.

"Mr. Ripley?" One of the Englishwomen who had sat on

the sofa with him in the lounge the other day during tea was bending over him. "We were wondering if you'd care to join us in a rubber of bridge in the game room? We're going to start in about fifteen minutes."

Tom sat up politely in his chair. "Thank you very much, but I think I prefer to stay outside. Besides, I'm not too good at bridge."

"Oh, neither are we! All right, another time." She smiled and went away.

Tom sank back in his chair again, pulled his cap down over his eyes and folded his hands over his waist. His aloofness, he knew, was causing a little comment among the passengers. He had not danced with either of the silly girls who kept looking at him hopefully and giggling during the after-dinner dancing every night. He imagined the speculations of the passengers: Is he an American? I *think* so, but he doesn't act like an American, does he? Most Americans are so *noisy*. He's terribly serious, isn't he, and he can't be more than twenty-three. He must have something very important on his mind.

Yes, he had. The present and the future of Tom Ripley.

7.

PARIS was no more than a glimpse out a railroad station window of a lighted café front, complete with rain-streaked awning, sidewalk tables, and boxes of hedges, like a tourist poster illustration, and otherwise a series of long station platforms down which he followed dumpy little blue-clad porters with his luggage, and at last the sleeper that would take him all the way to Rome. He could come back to Paris at some other time, he thought. He was eager to get to Mongibello.

When he woke up the next morning, he was in Italy. Something very pleasant happened that morning. Tom was watching the landscape out the window, when he heard some Italians in the corridor outside his compartment say something with the word "Pisa" in it. A city was gliding by on the other side of the train. Tom went into the corridor to get a better look at it, looking automatically for the Leaning Tower, though he was not at all sure that the city was Pisa or that the tower would even be visible from here, but there it was!—a thick white column sticking up out of the low chalky houses that formed the rest of the town, and *leaning*, leaning at an angle that he wouldn't have thought possible! He had always taken it for granted that the leaning of the Leaning Tower of Pisa was exaggerated. It seemed to him a good omen, a sign that Italy was going to be everything that he expected, and that everything would go well with him and Dickie.

He arrived in Naples late that afternoon, and there was no bus to Mongibello until tomorrow morning at eleven. A boy of about sixteen in dirty shirt and trousers and G.I. shoes latched onto him at the railroad station when he was changing some money, offering him God knew what, maybe girls, maybe dope, and in spite of Tom's protestations actually got into the taxi with him and instructed the driver where to go, jabbering on and holding a finger up as if he were going to fix him up fine, wait and see. Tom gave up and sulked in a corner with his arms folded, and finally the taxi stopped in front of a big hotel that faced the bay. Tom would have been afraid of the imposing hotel if Mr. Greenleaf had not been paying the bill.

"Santa Lucia!" the boy said triumphantly, pointing seaward.

Tom nodded. After all, the boy seemed to mean well. Tom paid the driver and gave the boy a hundred-lire bill, which he estimated to be sixteen and a fraction cents and appropriate as a tip in Italy, according to an article on Italy he had read on the ship, and when the boy looked outraged, gave him another hundred, and when he still looked outraged, waved a hand at him and went into the hotel behind the bellboys who had already gathered up his luggage.

Tom had dinner that evening at a restaurant down on the water called Zi' Teresa, which had been recommended to him by the English-speaking manager of the hotel. He had a difficult time ordering, and he found himself with a first course of miniature octopuses, as virulently purple as if they had been cooked in the ink in which the menu had been written. He tasted the tip of one tentacle, and it had a disgusting consistency like cartilage. The second course was also a mistake, a platter of fried fish of various kinds. The third course—which he had been sure was a kind of dessert—was a couple of small reddish fish. Ah, Naples! The food didn't matter. He was feeling mellow on the wine. Far over on his left, a three-quarter moon drifted above the jagged hump of Mount Vesuvius. Tom gazed at it calmly, as if he had seen it a thousand times before. Around the corner of land there, beyond Vesuvius, lay Richard's village.

He boarded the bus the next morning at eleven. The road followed the shore and went through little towns where they made brief stops—Torre del Greco, Torre Annunciata, Castellammare, Sorrento. Tom listened eagerly to the names of the towns that the driver called out. From Sorrento, the road was a narrow ridge cut into the side of the rock cliffs that Tom had seen in the photographs at the Greenleafs'. Now and then he caught glimpses of little villages down at the water's edge, houses like white crumbs of bread, specks that were the heads of people swimming near the shore. Tom saw a boulder-sized rock in the middle of the road that had evidently broken off of a cliff. The driver dodged it with a nonchalant swerve.

"Mongibello!"

Tom sprang up and yanked his suitcase down from the rack. He had another suitcase on the roof, which the bus boy took down for him. Then the bus went on, and Tom was alone at the side of the road, his suitcases at his feet. There were houses above him, straggling up the mountain, and houses below, their tile roofs silhouetted against the blue sea. Keeping an eye on his suitcases, Tom went into a little house across the road marked POSTA, and inquired of the man behind the window where Richard Greenleaf's house was. Without thinking, he spoke in English, but the man seemed to understand, because he came out and pointed from the door up the road Tom had come on the bus, and gave in Italian what seemed to be explicit directions how to get there.

"Sempre seeneestra, seeneestra!"

Tom thanked him, and asked if he could leave his two suitcases in the post office for a while, and the man seemed to understand this, too, and helped Tom carry them into the post office.

He had to ask two more people where Richard Greenleaf's house was, but everybody seemed to know it, and the third person was able to point it out to him—a large two-story house with an iron gate on the road, and a terrace that projected over the cliff's edge. Tom rang the metal bell beside the gate. An Italian woman came out of the house, wiping her hands on her apron.

"Mr. Greenleaf?" Tom asked hopefully.

The woman gave him a long, smiling answer in Italian and pointed downward toward the sea. "Jew," she seemed to keep saying. "Jew."

Tom nodded. "Grazie."

Should he go down to the beach as he was, or be more casual about it and get into a bathing suit? Or should he wait until the tea or cocktail hour? Or should he try to telephone him first? He hadn't brought a bathing suit with him, and he'd certainly have to have one here. Tom went into one of the little shops near the post office that had shirts and bathing shorts in its tiny front window, and after trying on several pairs of shorts that did not fit him, or at least not adequately enough to serve as a bathing suit, he bought a black-and-yellow thing hardly bigger than a G-string. He made a neat bundle of his clothing inside his raincoat, and started out the door barefoot. He leapt back inside. The cobblestones were hot as coals.

"Shoes? Sandals?" he asked the man in the shop.

The man didn't sell shoes.

Tom put on his own shoes again and walked across the road to the post office, intending to leave his clothes with his suitcases, but the post office door was locked. He had heard of this in Europe, places closing from noon to four sometimes. He turned and walked down a cobbled lane which he supposed led toward the beach. He went down a dozen steep stone steps, down another cobbled slope past shops and houses, down more steps, and finally he came to a level length of broad sidewalk slightly raised from the beach, where there were a couple of cafés and a restaurant with outdoor tables. Some bronzed adolescent Italian boys sitting on wooden benches at the edge of the pavement inspected him thoroughly as he walked by. He felt mortified at the big brown shoes on his feet and at his ghost-white skin. He had not been to a beach all summer. He hated beaches. There was a wooden walk that led half across the beach, which Tom knew must be hot as hell to walk on, because everybody was lying on a towel or something else, but he took his shoes off anyway and stood for a moment on the hot wood, calmly surveying the groups of people near him. None of the people looked like Richard, and the shimmering heat waves kept him from making out the people very far away. Tom put one foot out on the sand and drew it back. Then he took a deep breath, raced down the rest of the walk, sprinted across the sand, and sank his feet into the blissfully cool inches of water at the sea's edge. He began to walk.

Tom saw him from a distance of about a block—unmistakably Dickie, though he was burnt a dark brown and his crinkly blond hair looked lighter than Tom remembered it. He was with Marge.

"Dickie Greenleaf?" Tom asked, smiling.

Dickie looked up. "Yes?"

"I'm Tom Ripley. I met you in the States several years ago. Remember?"

Dickie looked blank.

"I think your father said he was going to write you about me."

"Oh, yes!" Dickie said, touching his forehead as if it was stupid of him to have forgotten. He stood up. "Tom *what* is it?"

"Ripley."

"This is Marge Sherwood," he said. "Marge, Tom Ripley."

"How do you do?" Tom said.

"How do you do?"

"How long are you here for?" Dickie asked.

"I don't know yet," Tom said. "I just got here. I'll have to look the place over."

Dickie was looking him over, not entirely with approval, Tom felt. Dickie's arms were folded, his lean brown feet planted in the hot sand that didn't seem to bother him at all. Tom had crushed his feet into his shoes again.

"Taking a house?" Dickie asked.

"I don't know," Tom said undecidedly, as if he had been considering it.

"It's a good time to get a house, if you're looking for one for the winter," the girl said. "The summer tourists have practically all gone. We could use a few more Americans around here in winter."

Dickie said nothing. He had reseated himself on the big towel beside the girl, and Tom felt that he was waiting for him to say good-bye and move on. Tom stood there, feeling pale and naked as the day he was born. He hated bathing suits. This one was very revealing. Tom managed to extract his pack of cigarettes from his jacket inside the raincoat, and offered it to Dickie and the girl. Dickie accepted one, and Tom lighted it with his lighter.

"You don't seem to remember me from New York," Tom said.

"I can't really say I do," Dickie said. "Where did I meet you?"

"I think— Wasn't it at Buddy Lankenau's?" It wasn't, but he knew Dickie knew Buddy Lankenau, and Buddy was a very respectable fellow.

"Oh," said Dickie, vaguely. "I hope you'll excuse me. My memory's rotten for America these days."

"It certainly is," Marge said, coming to Tom's rescue. "It's getting worse and worse. When did you get here, Tom?"

"Just about an hour ago. I've just parked my suitcases at the post office." He laughed.

"Don't you want to sit down? Here's another towel." She spread a smaller white towel beside her on the sand.

Tom accepted it gratefully.

"I'm going down for a dip to cool off," Dickie said, getting up.

"Me, too!" Marge said. "Coming in, Tom?"

Tom followed them. Dickie and the girl went out quite far—both seemed to be excellent swimmers—and Tom stayed near the shore and came in much sooner. When Dickie and the girl came back to the towels, Dickie said, as if he had been prompted by the girl, "We're leaving. Would you like to come up to the house and have lunch with us?"

"Why, yes. Thanks very much." Tom helped them gather up the towels, the sunglasses, the Italian newspapers.

Tom thought they would never get there. Dickie and Marge went in front of him, taking the endless flights of stone steps slowly and steadily, two at a time. The sun had enervated Tom. The muscles of his legs trembled on the level stretches. His shoulders were already pink, and he had put on his shirt against the sun's rays, but he could feel the sun burning through his hair, making him dizzy and nauseous.

"Having a hard time?" Marge asked, not out of breath at all. "You'll get used to it, if you stay here. You should have seen this place during the heat wave in July."

Tom hadn't breath to reply anything.

Fifteen minutes later he was feeling better. He had had a cool shower, and he was sitting in a comfortable wicker chair on Dickie's terrace with a martini in his hand. At Marge's suggestion, he had put his swimming outfit on again, with his shirt over it. The table on the terrace had been set for three while he was in the shower, and Marge was in the kitchen now, talking in Italian to the maid. Tom wondered if Marge lived here. The house was certainly big enough. It was sparsely furnished, as far as Tom could see, in a pleasant mixture of Italian antique and American bohemian. He had seen two original Picasso drawings in the hall.

Marge came out on the terrace with her martini. "That's my house over there." She pointed. "See it? The square-looking white one with the darker red roof than the houses just beside it."

It was hopeless to pick it out from the other houses, but Tom pretended he saw it. "Have you been here long?"

"A year. All last winter, and it was quite a winter. Rain every day except one for three whole months!"

"Really!"

"Um-hm." Marge sipped her martini and gazed out contentedly at her little village. She was back in her bathing suit, too, a tomato-colored bathing suit, and she wore a striped shirt over it. She wasn't bad-looking, Tom supposed, and she even had a good figure, if one liked the rather solid type. Tom didn't, himself.

"I understand Dickie has a boat," Tom said.

"Yes, the *Pipi*. Short for *Pipistrello*. Want to see it?"

She pointed at another indiscernible something down at the little pier that they could see from the corner of the terrace. The boats looked very much alike, but Marge said Dickie's boat was larger than most of them and had two masts.

Dickie came out and poured himself a cocktail from the pitcher on the table. He wore badly ironed white duck trousers and a terra cotta linen shirt the color of his skin. "Sorry there's no ice. I haven't got a refrigerator."

Tom smiled. "I brought a bathrobe for you. Your mother said you'd asked for one. Also some socks."

"Do you know my mother?"

"I happened to meet your father just before I left New York, and he asked me to dinner at his house."

"Oh? How was my mother?"

"She was up and around that evening. I'd say she gets tired easily."

Dickie nodded. "I had a letter this week saying she was a little better. At least there's no particular crisis right now, is there?"

"I don't think so. I think your father was more worried a few weeks ago." Tom hesitated. "He's also a little worried because you won't come home."

"Herbert's always worried about something," Dickie said.

Marge and the maid came out of the kitchen carrying a steaming platter of spaghetti, a big bowl of salad, and a plate of bread. Dickie and Marge began to talk about the enlargement of some restaurant down on the beach. The proprietor was widening the terrace so there would be room for people to dance. They discussed it in detail, slowly, like people in a small town who take an interest in the most minute changes in the neighborhood. There was nothing Tom could contribute. He spent the time examining Dickie's rings. He liked them both: a large rectangular green stone set in gold on the third finger of his right hand, and on the little finger of the other hand a signet ring, larger and more ornate than the signet Mr. Greenleaf had worn. Dickie had long, bony hands, a little like his own hands, Tom thought.

"By the way, your father showed me around the Burke-Greenleaf yards before I left," Tom said. "He told me he'd made a lot of changes since you've seen it last. I was quite impressed."

"I suppose he offered you a job, too. Always on the lookout for promising young men." Dickie turned his fork round and round, and thrust a neat mass of spaghetti into his mouth.

"No, he didn't." Tom felt the luncheon couldn't have been going worse. Had Mr. Greenleaf told Dickie that he was coming to give him a lecture on why he should go home? Or was Dickie just in a foul mood? Dickie had certainly changed since Tom had seen him last.

Dickie brought out a shiny espresso machine about two feet high, and plugged it into an outlet on the terrace. In a few moments there were four little cups of coffee, one of which Marge took into the kitchen to the maid.

"What hotel are you staying at?" Marge asked Tom.

Tom smiled. "I haven't found one yet. What do you recommend?"

"The Miramare's the best. It's just this side of Giorgio's. The only other hotel is Giorgio's, but—"

"They say Giorgio's got pulci in his beds," Dickie interrupted.

"That's fleas. Giorgio's is cheap," Marge said earnestly, "but the service is—"

"Nonexistent," Dickie supplied.

"You're in a fine mood today, aren't you?" Marge said to Dickie, flicking a crumb of gorgonzola at him.

"In that case, I'll try the Miramare," Tom said, standing up. "I must be going."

Neither of them urged him to stay. Dickie walked with him to the front gate. Marge was staying on. Tom wondered if Dickie and Marge were having an affair, one of those old, faute de mieux affairs that wouldn't necessarily be obvious from the outside, because neither was very enthusiastic. Marge was in love with Dickie, Tom thought, but Dickie couldn't have been more indifferent to her if she had been the fifty-year-old Italian maid sitting there.

"I'd like to see some of your paintings sometime," Tom said to Dickie.

"Fine. Well, I suppose we'll see you again if you're

around," and Tom thought he added it only because he remembered that he had brought him the bathrobe and the socks.

"I enjoyed the lunch. Good-bye, Dickie."

"Good-bye."

The iron gate clanged.

8.

TOM took a room at the Miramare. It was four o'clock by the time he got his suitcases up from the post office, and he had barely the energy to hang up his best suit before he fell down on the bed. The voices of some Italian boys who were talking under his window drifted up as distinctly as if they had been in the room with him, and the insolent, cackling laugh of one of them, bursting again and again through the pattering syllables, made Tom twitch and writhe. He imagined them discussing his expedition to Signor Greenleaf, and making unflattering speculations as to what might happen next.

What was he doing here? He had no friends here and he didn't speak the language. Suppose he got sick? Who would take care of him?

Tom got up, knowing he was going to be sick, yet moving slowly because he knew just when he was going to be sick and that there would be time for him to get to the bathroom. In the bathroom he lost his lunch, and also the fish from Naples, he thought. He went back to his bed and fell instantly asleep.

When he awoke, groggy and weak, the sun was still shining and it was five-thirty by his new watch. He went to a window and looked out, looking automatically for Dickie's big house and projecting terrace among the pink and white houses that dotted the climbing ground in front of him. He found the sturdy reddish balustrade of the terrace. Was Marge still there? Were they talking about him? He heard a laugh rising over the little din of street noises, tense and resonant, and as

American as if it had been a sentence in American. For an instant he saw Dickie and Marge as they crossed a space between houses on the main road. They turned the corner, and Tom went to his side window for a better view. There was an alley by the side of the hotel just below his window, and Dickie and Marge came down it, Dickie in the white trousers and terra cotta shirt, Marge in a skirt and blouse. She must have gone home, Tom thought. Or else she had clothes at Dickie's house. Dickie talked with an Italian on the little wooden pier, gave him some money, and the Italian touched his cap, then untied the boat from the pier. Tom watched Dickie help Marge into the boat. The white sail began to climb. Behind them, to the left, the orange sun was sinking into the water. Tom could hear Marge's laugh, and a shout from Dickie in Italian toward the pier. Tom realized he was seeing them on a typical day—a siesta after the late lunch, probably, then the sail in Dickie's boat at sundown. Then apéritifs at one of the cafés on the beach. They were enjoying a perfectly ordinary day, as if he did not exist. Why should Dickie want to come back to subways and taxis and starched collars and a nine-to-five job? Or even a chauffeured car and vacations in Florida and Maine? It wasn't as much fun as sailing a boat in old clothes and being answerable to nobody for the way he spent his time, and having his own house with a good-natured maid who probably took care of everything for him. And money besides to take trips, if he wanted to. Tom envied him with a heartbreaking surge of envy and of self-pity.

Dickie's father had probably said in his letter the very things that would set Dickie against him, Tom thought. How much better it would have been if he had just sat down in one of the cafés down at the beach and struck up an acquaintance with Dickie out of the blue! He probably could have persuaded Dickie to come home eventually, if he had begun like that, but this way it was useless. Tom cursed himself for having been so heavy-handed and so humorless today. Nothing he took desperately seriously ever worked out. He'd found that out years ago.

He'd let a few days go by, he thought. The first step, anyway, was to make Dickie like him. That he wanted more than anything else in the world.

9.

TOM let three days go by. Then he went down to the beach on the fourth morning around noon, and found Dickie alone, in the same spot Tom had seen him first, in front of the gray rocks that extended across the beach from the land.

"Morning!" Tom called. "Where's Marge?"

"Good morning. She's probably working a little late. She'll be down."

"Working?"

"She's a writer."

"Oh."

Dickie puffed on the Italian cigarette in the corner of his mouth. "Where've you been keeping yourself? I thought you'd gone."

"Sick," Tom said casually, tossing his rolled towel down on the sand, but not too near Dickie's towel.

"Oh, the usual upset stomach?"

"Hovering between life and the bathroom," Tom said, smiling. "But I'm all right now." He actually had been too weak even to leave the hotel, but he had crawled around on the floor of his room, following the patches of sunlight that came through his windows, so that he wouldn't look so white the next time he came down to the beach. And he had spent the remainder of his feeble strength studying an Italian conversation book that he had bought in the hotel lobby.

Tom went down to the water, went confidently up to his waist and stopped there, splashing the water over his shoulders. He lowered himself until the water reached his chin, floated around a little, then came slowly in.

"Can I invite you for a drink at the hotel before you go up to your house?" Tom asked Dickie. "And Marge, too, if she comes. I wanted to give you your bathrobe and socks, you know."

"Oh, yes. Thanks very much, I'd like to have a drink." He went back to his Italian newspaper.

Tom stretched out on his towel. He heard the village clock strike one.

"Doesn't look as if Marge is coming down," Dickie said. "I think I'll be going along."

Tom got up. They walked up to the Miramare, saying practically nothing to each other, except that Tom invited Dickie to lunch with him, and Dickie declined because the maid had his lunch ready at the house, he said. They went up to Tom's room, and Dickie tried the bathrobe on and held the socks up to his bare feet. Both the bathrobe and the socks were the right size, and, as Tom had anticipated, Dickie was extremely pleased with the bathrobe.

"And this," Tom said, taking a square package wrapped in drugstore paper from a bureau drawer. "Your mother sent you some nosedrops, too."

Dickie smiled. "I don't need them any more. That was sinus. But I'll take them off your hands."

Now Dickie had everything, Tom thought, everything he had to offer. He was going to refuse the invitation for a drink, too, Tom knew. Tom followed him toward the door. "You know, your father's very concerned about your coming home. He asked me to give you a good talking to, which of course I won't, but I'll still have to tell him something. I promised to write him."

Dickie turned with his hand on the doorknob. "I don't know what my father thinks I'm doing over here—drinking myself to death or what. I'll probably fly home this winter for a few days, but I don't intend to stay over there. I'm happier here. If I went back there to live, my father would be after me to work in Burke-Greenleaf. I couldn't possibly paint. I happen to like painting, and I think it's my business how I spend my life."

"I understand. But he said he wouldn't try to make you work in his firm if you came back, unless you wanted to work in the designing department, and he said you liked that."

"Well—my father and I have been over that. Thanks, anyway, Tom, for delivering the message and the clothes. It was very nice of you." Dickie held out his hand.

Tom couldn't have made himself take the hand. This was the very edge of failure, failure as far as Mr. Greenleaf was concerned, and failure with Dickie. "I think I ought to tell you something else," Tom said with a smile. "Your father sent me over here especially to ask you to come home."

"What do you mean?" Dickie frowned. "Paid your way?"

"Yes." It was his one last chance to amuse Dickie or to repel him, to make Dickie burst out laughing or go out and slam the door in disgust. But the smile was coming, the long corners of his mouth going up, the way Tom remembered Dickie's smile.

"Paid your way! What do you know! He's getting desperate, isn't he?" Dickie closed the door again.

"He approached me in a bar in New York," Tom said. "I told him I wasn't a close friend of yours, but he insisted I could help if I came over. I told him I'd try."

"How did he ever meet you?"

"Through the Schrievers. I hardly know the Schrievers, but there it was! I was your friend and I could do you a lot of good."

They laughed.

"I don't want you to think I'm someone who tried to take advantage of your father," Tom said. "I expect to find a job somewhere in Europe soon, and I'll be able to pay him back my passage money eventually. He bought me a round-trip ticket."

"Oh, don't bother! It goes on the Burke-Greenleaf expense list. I can just see Dad approaching you in a bar! Which bar was it?"

"Raoul's. Matter of fact, he followed me from the Green Cage." Tom watched Dickie's face for a sign of recognition of the Green Cage, a very popular bar, but there was no recognition.

They had a drink downstairs in the hotel bar. They drank to Herbert Richard Greenleaf.

"I just realized today's Sunday," Dickie said. "Marge went to church. You'd better come up and have lunch with us. We always have chicken on Sunday. You know it's an old American custom, chicken on Sunday."

Dickie wanted to go by Marge's house to see if she was still there. They climbed some steps from the main road up the side of a stone wall, crossed part of somebody's garden, and climbed more steps. Marge's house was a rather sloppy-look-ing one-story affair with a messy garden at one end, a couple of buckets and a garden hose cluttering the path to the door, and the feminine touch represented by her tomato-colored bathing suit and a bra hanging over a windowsill. Through an open window, Tom had a glimpse of a disorderly table with a typewriter on it.

"Hi!" she said, opening the door. "Hello, Tom! Where've you been all this time?"

She offered them a drink, but discovered there was only half an inch of gin in her bottle of Gilbey's.

"It doesn't matter, we're going to my house," Dickie said. He strolled around Marge's bedroom–living room with an air of familiarity, as if he lived half the time here himself. He bent over a flower pot in which a tiny plant of some sort was grow-ing, and touched its leaf delicately with his forefinger. "Tom has something funny to tell you," he said. "Tell her, Tom."

Tom took a breath and began. He made it very funny, and Marge laughed like someone who hadn't had anything funny to laugh at in years. "When I saw him coming in Raoul's after me, I was ready to climb out a back window!" His tongue rattled on almost independently of his brain. His brain was estimating how high his stock was shooting up with Dickie and Marge. He could see it in their faces.

The climb up the hill to Dickie's house didn't seem half so long as before. Delicious smells of roasting chicken drifted out on the terrace. Dickie made some martinis. Tom showered and then Dickie showered, and came out and poured himself a drink, just like the first time, but the atmosphere now was totally changed.

Dickie sat down in a wicker chair and swung his legs over one of the arms. "Tell me more," he said, smiling. "What kind of work do you do? You said you might take a job."

"Why? Do you have a job for me?"

"Can't say that I have."

"Oh, I can do a number of things—valeting, baby-sitting, accounting—I've got an unfortunate talent for figures. No matter how drunk I get, I can always tell when a waiter's cheating me on a bill. I can forge a signature, fly a helicopter, handle dice, impersonate practically anybody, cook—and do a one-man show in a nightclub in case the regular entertainer's sick. Shall I go on?" Tom was leaning forward, counting them off on his fingers. He could have gone on.

"What kind of a one-man show?" Dickie asked.

"Well—" Tom sprang up. "This, for example." He struck a pose with one hand on his hip, one foot extended. "This is Lady Assburden sampling the American subway. She's never even been in the underground in London, but she wants to take back some American experiences." Tom did it all in pantomime, searching for a coin, finding it didn't go into the slot, buying a token, puzzling over which stairs to go down, registering alarm at the noise and the long express ride, puzzling again as to how to get out of the place—here Marge came out, and Dickie told her it was an Englishwoman in the subway, but Marge didn't seem to get it and asked, "What?"—walking through a door which could only be the door of the men's room from her twitching horror of this and that, which augmented until she fainted. Tom fainted gracefully onto the terrace glider.

"Wonderful!" Dickie yelled, clapping.

Marge wasn't laughing. She stood there looking a little blank. Neither of them bothered to explain it to her. She didn't look as if she had that kind of sense of humor, anyway, Tom thought.

Tom took a gulp of his martini, terribly pleased with himself. "I'll do another for you sometime," he said to Marge, but mostly to indicate to Dickie that he had another one to do.

"Dinner ready?" Dickie asked her. "I'm starving."

"I'm waiting for the darned artichokes to get done. You know that front hole. It'll barely make anything come to a boil." She smiled at Tom. "Dickie's very old-fashioned about some things, Tom, the things *he* doesn't have to fool with. There's still only a wood stove here, and he refuses to buy a refrigerator or even an icebox."

"One of the reasons I fled America," Dickie said. "Those things are a waste of money in a country with so many servants. What'd Ermelinda do with herself, if she could cook a meal in half an hour?" He stood up. "Come on in, Tom, I'll show you some of my paintings."

Dickie led the way into the big room Tom had looked into a couple of times on his way to and from the shower, the room with a long couch under the two windows and the big easel in the middle of the floor. "This is one of Marge I'm working on now." He gestured to the picture on the easel.

"Oh," Tom said with interest. It wasn't good in his opinion, probably in anybody's opinion. The wild enthusiasm of her smile was a bit off. Her skin was as red as an Indian's. If Marge hadn't been the only girl around with blond hair, he wouldn't have noticed any resemblance at all.

"And these—a lot of landscapes," Dickie said with a deprecatory laugh, though obviously he wanted Tom to say something complimentary about them, because obviously he was proud of them. They were all wild and hasty and monotonously similar. The combination of terra cotta and electric blue was in nearly every one, terra cotta roofs and mountains and bright electric-blue seas. It was the blue he had put in Marge's eyes, too.

"My surrealist effort," Dickie said, bracing another canvas against his knee.

Tom winced with almost a personal shame. It was Marge again, undoubtedly, though with long snakelike hair, and worst of all two horizons in her eyes, with a miniature landscape of Mongibello's houses and mountains in one eye, and the beach in the other full of little red people. "Yes, I like that," Tom said. Mr. Greenleaf had been right. Yet it gave Dickie something to do, kept him out of trouble, Tom supposed, just as it gave thousands of lousy amateur painters all over America something to do. He was only sorry that Dickie fell into this category as a painter, because he wanted Dickie to be much more.

"I won't ever set the world on fire as a painter," Dickie said, "but I get a great deal of pleasure out of it."

"Yes." Tom wanted to forget all about the paintings and forget that Dickie painted. "Can I see the rest of the house?"

"Absolutely! You haven't seen the salon, have you?"

Dickie opened a door in the hall that led into a very large room with a fireplace, sofas, bookshelves, and three exposures—to the terrace, to the land on the other side of the house, and to the front garden. Dickie said that in summer he did not use the room, because he liked to save it as a change of scene for the winter. It was more of a bookish den than a living room, Tom thought. It surprised him. He had Dickie figured out as a young man who was not particularly brainy, and who probably spent most of his time playing. Perhaps he was wrong. But he didn't think he was wrong in feeling that Dickie was bored at the moment and needed someone to show him how to have fun.

"What's upstairs?" Tom asked.

The upstairs was disappointing: Dickie's bedroom in the corner of the house above the terrace was stark and empty—a bed, a chest of drawers, and a rocking chair, looking lost and unrelated in all the space—a narrow bed, too, hardly wider than a single bed. The other three rooms of the second floor were not even furnished, or at least not completely. One of them held only firewood and a pile of canvas scraps. There was certainly no sign of Marge anywhere, least of all in Dickie's bedroom.

"How about going to Naples with me sometime?" Tom asked. "I didn't have much of a chance to see it on my way down."

"All right," Dickie said. "Marge and I are going Saturday afternoon. We have dinner there nearly every Saturday night and treat ourselves to a taxi or a carrozza ride back. Come along."

"I meant in the daytime or some weekday so I could see a little more," Tom said, hoping to avoid Marge in the excursion. "Or do you paint all day?"

"No. There's a twelve o'clock bus Mondays, Wednesdays, and Fridays. I suppose we could go tomorrow, if you feel like it."

"Fine," Tom said, though he still wasn't sure that Marge wouldn't be asked along. "Marge is a Catholic?" he asked as they went down the stairs.

"With a vengeance! She was converted about six months ago by an Italian she had a mad crush on. Could that man talk! He was here for a few months, resting up after a ski accident. Marge consoles herself for the loss of Eduardo by embracing his religion."

"I had the idea she was in love with you."

"With me? Don't be silly!"

The dinner was ready when they went out on the terrace. There were even hot biscuits with butter, made by Marge.

"Do you know Vic Simmons in New York?" Tom asked Dickie.

Vic had quite a salon of artists, writers, and dancers in New York, but Dickie didn't know of him. Tom asked him about two or three other people, also without success.

Tom hoped Marge would leave after the coffee, but she didn't. When she left the terrace for a moment Tom said, "Can I invite you for dinner at my hotel tonight?"

"Thank you. At what time?"

"Seven-thirty? So we'll have a little time for cocktails?— After all, it's your father's money," Tom added with a smile.

Dickie laughed. "All right, cocktails and a good bottle of wine. Marge!" Marge was just coming back. "We're dining tonight at the Miramare, compliments of Greenleaf père!"

So Marge was coming, too, and there was nothing Tom could do about it. After all, it was Dickie's father's money.

The dinner that evening was pleasant, but Marge's presence kept Tom from talking about anything he would have liked to talk about, and he did not feel even like being witty in Marge's presence. Marge knew some of the people in the dining room, and after dinner she excused herself and took her coffee over to another table and sat down.

"How long are you going to be here?" Dickie asked.

"Oh, at least a week, I'd say," Tom replied.

"Because—" Dickie's face had flushed a little over the cheekbones. The chianti had put him into a good mood. "If you're going to be here a little longer, why don't you stay with me? There's no use staying in a hotel, unless you really prefer it."

"Thank you very much," Tom said.

"There's a bed in the maid's room, which you didn't see. Ermelinda doesn't sleep in. I'm sure we can make out with the furniture that's scattered around, if you think you'd like to."

"I'm sure I'd like to. By the way, your father gave me six hundred dollars for expenses, and I've still got about five hundred of it. I think we both ought to have a little fun on it, don't you?"

"Five hundred!" Dickie said, as if he'd never seen that much money in one lump in his life. "We could pick up a little car for that!"

Tom didn't contribute to the car idea. That wasn't his idea of having fun. He wanted to fly to Paris. Marge was coming back, he saw.

The next morning he moved in.

Dickie and Ermelinda had installed an armoire and a couple of chairs in one of the upstairs rooms, and Dickie had thumb-tacked a few reproductions of mosaic portraits from St. Mark's Cathedral on the walls. Tom helped Dickie carry up the narrow iron bed from the maid's room. They were finished before twelve, a little lightheaded from the frascati they had been sipping as they worked.

"Are we still going to Naples?" Tom asked.

"Certainly." Dickie looked at his watch. "It's only a quarter to twelve. We can make the twelve o'clock bus."

They took nothing with them but their jackets and Tom's book of traveler's checks. The bus was just arriving as they reached the post office. Tom and Dickie stood by the door, waiting for people to get off; then Dickie pulled himself up, right into the face of a young man with red hair and a loud sports shirt, an American.

"Dickie!"

"Freddie!" Dickie yelled. "What're you doing here?"

"Came to see you! And the Cecchis. They're putting me up for a few days."

"Ch'elegante! I'm off to Naples with a friend. Tom?" Dickie beckoned Tom over and introduced them.

The American's name was Freddie Miles. Tom thought he was hideous. Tom hated red hair, especially this kind of carrot-red hair with white skin and freckles. Freddie had large red-brown eyes that seemed to wobble in his head as if he were cockeyed, or perhaps he was only one of those people who never looked at anyone they were talking to. He was also overweight. Tom turned away from him, waiting for Dickie to finish his conversation. They were holding up the bus, Tom noticed. Dickie and Freddie were talking about skiing, making a date for some time in December in a town Tom had never heard of.

"There'll be about fifteen of us at Cortina by the second," Freddie said. "A real bang-up party like last year! Three weeks, if our money holds out!"

"If we hold out!" Dickie said. "See you tonight, Fred!"

Tom boarded the bus after Dickie. There were no seats, and they were wedged between a skinny, sweating man who smelled, and a couple of old peasant women who smelled worse. Just as they were leaving the village Dickie remembered that Marge was coming for lunch as usual, because they had thought yesterday that Tom's moving would cancel the Naples trip. Dickie shouted for the driver to stop. The bus stopped with a squeal of brakes and a lurch that threw everybody who was standing off balance, and Dickie put his head through a window and called, "Gino! Gino!"

A little boy on the road came running up to take the hundred-lire bill that Dickie was holding out to him. Dickie said something in Italian, and the boy said, "Subito, signor!" and flew up the road.

Dickie thanked the driver, and the bus started again. "I told him to tell Marge we'd be back tonight, but probably late," Dickie said.

"Good."

The bus spilled them into a big, cluttered square in Naples, and they were suddenly surrounded by pushcarts of grapes, figs, pastry, and watermelon, and screamed at by adolescent boys with fountain pens and mechanical toys. The people made way for Dickie.

"I know a good place for lunch," Dickie said. "A real Neapolitan pizzeria. Do you like pizza?"

"Yes."

The pizzeria was up a street too narrow and steep for cars. Strings of beads hanging in the doorway, a decanter of wine on every table, and there were only six tables in the whole place, the kind of place you could sit in for hours and drink wine and not be disturbed. They sat there until five o'clock, when Dickie said it was time to move on to the Galleria. Dickie apologized for not taking him to the art museum, which had original da Vincis and El Grecos, he said, but they could see that at another time. Dickie had spent most of the afternoon talking about Freddie Miles, and Tom had found it as uninteresting as Freddie's face. Freddie was the son of an American hotel-chain owner, and a playwright—self-styled, Tom gathered, because he had written only two plays, and neither had seen Broadway. Freddie had a house in Cagnes-sur-Mer, and Dickie had stayed with him several weeks before he came to Italy.

"This is what I like," Dickie said expansively in the Galleria, "sitting at a table and watching the people go by. It does something to your outlook on life. The Anglo-Saxons make a great mistake not staring at people from a sidewalk table."

Tom nodded. He had heard it before. He was waiting for something profound and original from Dickie. Dickie was handsome. He looked unusual with his long, finely cut face, his quick, intelligent eyes, the proud way he carried himself regardless of what he was wearing. He was wearing broken-down sandals and rather soiled white pants now, but he sat there as if he owned the Galleria, chatting in Italian with the waiter when he brought their espressos.

"Ciao!" he called to an Italian boy who was passing by.

"Ciao, Dickie!"

"He changes Marge's traveler's checks on Saturdays," Dickie explained to Tom.

A well-dressed Italian greeted Dickie with a warm hand-shake and sat down at the table with them. Tom listened to their conversation in Italian, making out a word here and there. Tom was beginning to feel tired.

"Want to go to Rome?" Dickie asked him suddenly.

"Sure," Tom said. "Now?" He stood up, reaching for money to pay the little tabs that the waiter had stuck under their coffee cups.

The Italian had a long gray Cadillac equipped with venetian blinds, a four-toned horn, and a blaring radio that he and Dickie seemed content to shout over. They reached the out-skirts of Rome in about two hours. Tom sat up as they drove along the Appian Way, especially for his benefit, the Italian told Tom, because Tom had not seen it before. The road was bumpy in spots. These were stretches of original Roman brick left bare to show people how Roman roads felt, the Italian said. The flat fields to left and right looked desolate in the twilight, like an ancient graveyard, Tom thought, with just a few tombs and remains of tombs still standing. The Italian dropped them in the middle of a street in Rome and said an abrupt good-bye.

"He's in a hurry," Dickie said. "Got to see his girl friend and get away before the husband comes home at eleven. There's the music hall I was looking for. Come on."

They bought tickets for the music-hall show that evening. There was still an hour before the performance, and they went to the Via Veneto, took a sidewalk table at one of the cafés, and ordered americanos. Dickie didn't know anybody in Rome, Tom noticed, or at least none who passed by, and they watched hundreds of Italians and Americans pass by their table. Tom got very little out of the music-hall show, but he tried his very best. Dickie proposed leaving before the show was over. Then they caught a carrozza and drove around the city, past fountain after fountain, through the Forum and around the Colosseum. The moon had come out. Tom was still a little sleepy, but the sleepiness, underlaid with excitement at being in Rome for the first time, put him into a receptive, mellow mood. They sat slumped in the carrozza, each with a sandaled foot propped on a knee, and it seemed to Tom that he was looking in a mirror when he looked at Dickie's leg and his propped foot beside him. They were the same height, and very much the same weight, Dickie perhaps a bit heavier, and they wore the same size bathrobe, socks, and probably shirts.

Dickie even said, "Thank you, Mr. Greenleaf," when Tom paid the carrozza driver. Tom felt a little weird.

They were in even finer mood by one in the morning, after a bottle and a half of wine between them at dinner. They walked with their arms around each other's shoulders, singing, and around a dark corner they somehow bumped into a girl and knocked her down. They lifted her up, apologizing, and offered to escort her home. She protested, they insisted, one on either side of her. She had to catch a certain trolley, she said. Dickie wouldn't hear of it. Dickie got a taxi. Dickie and

Tom sat very properly on the jump seats with their arms folded like a couple of footmen, and Dickie talked to her and made her laugh. Tom could understand nearly everything Dickie said. They helped the girl out in a little street that looked like Naples again, and she said, "Grazie tante!" and shook hands with both of them, then vanished into an absolutely black doorway.

"Did you hear that?" Dickie said. "She said we were the nicest Americans she'd ever met!"

"You know what most crummy Americans would do in a case like that—rape her," Tom said.

"Now where are we?" Dickie asked, turning completely around.

Neither had the slightest idea where they were. They walked for several blocks without finding a landmark or a familiar street name. They urinated against a dark wall, then drifted on.

"When the dawn comes up, we can see where we are," Dickie said cheerfully. He looked at his watch. "'S only a couple of more hours."

"Fine."

"It's worth it to see a nice girl home, isn't it?" Dickie asked, staggering a little.

"Sure it is. I like girls," Tom said protestingly. "But it's just as well Marge isn't here tonight. We never could have seen that girl home with Marge with us."

"Oh, I don't know," Dickie said thoughtfully, looking down at his weaving feet. "Marge isn't—"

"I only mean, if Marge was here, we'd be worrying about a hotel for the night. We'd be *in* the damned hotel, probably. We wouldn't be seeing half of Rome!"

"That's right!" Dickie swung an arm around his shoulder.

Dickie shook his shoulder, roughly. Tom tried to roll out from under it and grab his hand. "Dickie-e!" Tom opened his eyes and looked into the face of a policeman.

Tom sat up. He was in a park. It was dawn. Dickie was sitting on the grass beside him, talking very calmly to the policeman in Italian. Tom felt for the rectangular lump of his traveler's checks. They were still in his pocket.

"Passaporti!" the policeman hurled at them again, and again Dickie launched into his calm explanation.

Tom knew exactly what Dickie was saying. He was saying that they were Americans, and they didn't have their passports because they had only gone out for a little walk to look at the stars. Tom had an impulse to laugh. He stood up and staggered, dusting his clothing. Dickie was up, too, and they began to walk away, though the policeman was still yelling at them. Dickie said something back to him in a courteous, explanatory tone. At least the policeman was not following them.

"We do look pretty cruddy," Dickie said.

Tom nodded. There was a long rip in his trouser knee where he had probably fallen. Their clothes were crumpled and grass-stained and filthy with dust and sweat, but now they were shivering with cold. They went into the first café they came to, and had caffe latte and sweet rolls, then several Italian brandies that tasted awful but warmed them. Then they began to laugh. They were still drunk.

By eleven o'clock they were in Naples, just in time to catch the bus for Mongibello. It was wonderful to think of going back to Rome when they were more presentably dressed and seeing all the museums they had missed, and it was wonderful to think of lying on the beach at Mongibello this afternoon, baking in the sun. But they never got to the beach. They had showers at Dickie's house, then fell down on their respective beds and slept until Marge woke them up around four. Marge was annoyed because Dickie hadn't sent her a telegram saying he was spending the night in Rome.

"Not that I minded your spending the night, but I thought you were in Naples and anything can happen in Naples."

"Oh-h," Dickie drawled with a glance at Tom. He was making Bloody Marys for all of them.

Tom kept his mouth mysteriously shut. He wasn't going to tell Marge anything they had done. Let her imagine what she pleased. Dickie had made it evident that they had had a very good time. Tom noticed that she looked Dickie over with disapproval of his hangover, his unshaven face, and the drink he was taking now. There was something in Marge's eyes when she was very serious that made her look wise and old in spite of the naïve clothes she wore and her windblown hair and her general air of a Girl Scout. She had the look of a mother or an older sister now—the old feminine disapproval of the destructive play of little boys and men. La dee da! Or was it jealousy? She seemed to know that Dickie had formed a closer bond with him in twenty-four hours, just because he was another man, than she could ever have with Dickie, whether he loved her or not, and he didn't. After a few moments she loosened up, however, and the look went out of her eyes. Dickie left him with Marge on the terrace. Tom asked her about the book she was writing. It was a book about Mongibello, she said, with her own photographs. She told him she was from Ohio and showed him a picture, which she carried in her wallet, of her family's house. It was just a plain clapboard house, but it was home, Marge said with a smile. She pronounced the adjective "Clabbered," which amused Tom, because that was the word she used to describe people who were drunk, and just a few minutes before she had said to Dickie, "You look absolutely clabbered!" Her speech, Tom thought, was abominable, both her choice of words and her pronunciation. He tried to be especially pleasant to her. He felt he could afford to be. He walked with her to the gate, and they said a friendly good-bye to each other, but neither said anything about their all getting together later that day or tomorrow. There was no doubt about it, Marge was a little angry with Dickie.

10.

FOR three or four days they saw very little of Marge except down at the beach, and she was noticeably cooler toward both of them on the beach. She smiled and talked just as much or maybe more, but there was an element of politeness now, which made for the coolness. Tom noticed that Dickie was concerned, though not concerned enough to talk to Marge alone, apparently, because he hadn't seen her alone since Tom had moved into the house. Tom had been with Dickie every moment since he had moved into Dickie's house.

Finally Tom, to show that he was not obtuse about Marge, mentioned to Dickie that he thought she was acting strangely.

"Oh, she has moods," Dickie said. "Maybe she's working well. She doesn't like to see people when she's in a streak of work."

The Dickie–Marge relationship was evidently just what he had supposed it to be at first, Tom thought. Marge was much fonder of Dickie than Dickie was of her.

Tom, at any rate, kept Dickie amused. He had lots of funny stories to tell Dickie about people he knew in New York, some of them true, some of them made up. They went for a sail in Dickie's boat every day. There was no mention of any date when Tom might be leaving. Obviously Dickie was enjoying his company. Tom kept out of Dickie's way when Dickie wanted to paint, and he was always ready to drop whatever he was doing and go with Dickie for a walk or a sail or simply sit and talk. Dickie also seemed pleased that Tom was taking his study of Italian seriously. Tom spent a couple of hours a day with his grammar and conversation books.

Tom wrote to Mr. Greenleaf that he was staying with Dickie now for a few days, and said that Dickie had mentioned flying home for a while in the winter, and that probably he could by that time persuade him to stay longer. This letter sounded much better now that he was staying at Dickie's house than his first letter in which he had said he was staying at a hotel in Mongibello. Tom also said that when his money gave out he intended to try to get himself a job, perhaps at one of the hotels in the village, a casual statement that served the double purpose of reminding Mr. Greenleaf that six hundred dollars could run out, and also that he was a young man ready and willing to work for a living. Tom wanted to convey the same good impression to Dickie, so he gave Dickie the letter to read before he sealed it.

Another week went by, of ideally pleasant weather, ideally lazy days in which Tom's greatest physical exertion was climbing the stone steps from the beach every afternoon and his greatest mental effort trying to chat in Italian with Fausto, the twenty-three-year-old Italian boy whom Dickie had found in the village and had engaged to come three times a week to give Tom Italian lessons.

They went to Capri one day in Dickie's sailboat. Capri was just far enough away not to be visible from Mongibello. Tom was filled with anticipation, but Dickie was in one of his preoccupied moods and refused to be enthusiastic about anything. He argued with the keeper of the dock where they tied the *Pipistrello*. Dickie didn't even want to take a walk through the wonderful-looking little streets that went off in every direction from the plaza. They sat in a café on the plaza and drank a couple of Fernet-Brancas, and then Dickie wanted to start home before it became dark, though Tom would have willingly paid their hotel bill if Dickie had agreed to stay overnight. Tom supposed they would come again to Capri, so he wrote that day off and tried to forget it.

A letter came from Mr. Greenleaf, which had crossed Tom's letter, in which Mr. Greenleaf reiterated his arguments for Dickie's coming home, wished Tom success, and asked for a prompt reply as to his results. Once more Tom dutifully took up the pen and replied. Mr. Greenleaf's letter had been in such a shockingly businesslike tone—really as if he had been checking on a shipment of boat parts, Tom thought—that he found it very easy to reply in the same style. Tom was a little high when he wrote the letter, because it was just after lunch and they were always slightly high on wine just after lunch, a delicious sensation that could be corrected at once with a couple of espressos and a short walk, or prolonged with another glass of wine, sipped as they went about their leisurely afternoon routine. Tom amused himself by injecting a faint hope in this letter. He wrote in Mr. Greenleaf's own style:

". . . If I am not mistaken, Richard is wavering in his decision to spend another winter here. As I promised you, I shall do everything in my power to dissuade him from spending another winter here, and in time—though it may be as long as Christmas—I may be able to get him to stay in the States when he goes over."

Tom had to smile as he wrote it, because he and Dickie were talking of cruising around the Greek islands this winter, and Dickie had given up the idea of flying home even for a few days, unless his mother should be really seriously ill by then. They had talked also of spending January and February, Mongibello's worst months, in Majorca. And Marge would

not be going with them, Tom was sure. Both he and Dickie
excluded her from their travel plans whenever they discussed
them, though Dickie had made the mistake of dropping to
her that they might be taking a winter cruise somewhere.
Dickie was so damned open about everything! And now,
though Tom knew Dickie was still firm about their going
alone, Dickie was being more than usually attentive to Marge,
just because he realized that she would be lonely here by herself, and that it was essentially unkind of them not to ask her
along. Dickie and Tom both tried to cover it up by impressing
on her that they would be traveling in the cheapest and worst
possible way around Greece, cattleboats, sleeping with peas-
ants on the decks and all that, no way for a girl to travel. But
Marge still looked dejected, and Dickie still tried to make it
up by asking her often to the house now for lunch and dinner.
Dickie took Marge's hand sometimes as they walked up from
the beach, though Marge didn't always let him keep it. Sometimes she extricated her hand after a few seconds in a way that
looked to Tom as if she were dying for her hand to be held.

And when they asked her to go along with them to Her-
culaneum, she refused.

"I think I'll stay home. You boys enjoy yourselves," she
said with an effort at a cheerful smile.

"Well, if she won't, she won't," Tom said to Dickie, and
drifted tactfully into the house so that she and Dickie could
talk alone on the terrace if they wanted to.

Tom sat on the broad windowsill in Dickie's studio and
looked out at the sea, his brown arms folded on his chest. He
loved to look out at the blue Mediterranean and think of himself and Dickie sailing where they pleased. Tangiers, Sofia,
Cairo, Sevastopol . . . By the time his money ran out, Tom
thought, Dickie would probably be so fond of him and so
used to him that he would take it for granted they would go
on living together. He and Dickie could easily live on Dickie's
five hundred a month income. From the terrace he could hear
a pleading tone in Dickie's voice, and Marge's monosyllabic
answers. Then he heard the gate clang. Marge had left. She
had been going to stay for lunch. Tom shoved himself off the
windowsill and went out to Dickie on the terrace.

"Was she angry about something?" Tom asked.

"No. She feels kind of left out, I suppose."

"We certainly tried to include her."

"It isn't just this." Dickie was walking slowly up and down the terrace. "Now she says she doesn't even want to go to Cortina with me."

"Oh, she'll probably come around about Cortina before December."

"I doubt it," Dickie said.

Tom supposed it was because he was going to Cortina, too. Dickie had asked him last week. Freddie Miles had been gone when they got back from their Rome trip: he had had to go to London suddenly, Marge had told them. But Dickie had said he would write Freddie that he was bringing a friend along. "Do you want me to leave, Dickie?" Tom asked, sure that Dickie didn't want him to leave. "I feel I'm intruding on you and Marge."

"Of course not! Intruding on what?"

"Well, from her point of view."

"No. It's just that I owe her something. And I haven't been particularly nice to her lately. *We* haven't."

Tom knew he meant that he and Marge had kept each other company over the long, dreary last winter, when they had been the only Americans in the village, and that he shouldn't neglect her now because somebody else was here. "Suppose I talk to her about going to Cortina," Tom suggested.

"Then she surely won't go," Dickie said tersely, and went into the house.

Tom heard him telling Ermelinda to hold the lunch because he wasn't ready to eat yet. Even in Italian, Tom could hear that Dickie said *he* wasn't ready for lunch, in the master-of-the-house tone. Dickie came out on the terrace, sheltering his lighter as he tried to light his cigarette. Dickie had a beautiful silver lighter, but it didn't work well in the slightest breeze. Tom finally produced his ugly, flaring lighter, as ugly and efficient as a piece of military equipment, and lighted it for him. Tom checked himself from proposing a drink: it wasn't his house, though as it happened he had bought the three bottles of Gilbey's that now stood in the kitchen.

"It's after two," Tom said. "Want to take a little walk and go by the post office?" Sometimes Luigi opened the post office at two-thirty, sometimes not until four, they could never tell.

They walked down the hill in silence. What *had* Marge said about him, Tom wondered. The sudden weight of guilt made sweat come out on Tom's forehead, an amorphous yet very strong sense of guilt, as if Marge had told Dickie specifically that he had stolen something or had done some other shameful thing. Dickie wouldn't be acting like this only because Marge had behaved coolly, Tom thought. Dickie walked in his slouching, downhill gait that made his bony knees jut out in front of him, a gait that Tom had unconsciously adopted, too. But now Dickie's chin was sunk down on his chest and his hands were rammed into the pockets of his shorts. He came out of the silence only to greet Luigi and thank him for his letter. Tom had no mail. Dickie's letter was from a Naples bank, a form slip on which Tom saw typewritten in a blank space: $500.00. Dickie pushed the slip carelessly into a pocket and dropped the envelope into a wastebasket. The monthly announcement that Dickie's money had arrived in Naples, Tom supposed. Dickie had said that his trust company sent his money to a Naples bank. They walked on down the hill, and Tom assumed that they would walk up the main road to where it curved around a cliff on the other side of the village, as they had done before, but Dickie stopped at the steps that led up to Marge's house.

"I think I'll go up to see Marge," Dickie said. "I won't be long, but there's no use in your waiting."

"All right," Tom said, feeling suddenly desolate. He watched Dickie climb a little way up the steep steps cut into the wall, then he turned abruptly and started back toward the house.

About halfway up the hill he stopped with an impulse to go down to Giorgio's for a drink (but Giorgio's martinis were terrible), and with another impulse to go up to Marge's house, and, on a pretense of apologizing to her, vent his anger by surprising them and annoying them. He suddenly felt that Dickie was embracing her, or at least touching her, at this minute, and partly he wanted to see it, and partly he loathed the idea of seeing it. He turned and walked back to Marge's gate. He closed the gate carefully behind him, though her house was so far above she could not possibly have heard it, then ran up the steps two at a time. He slowed as he climbed the last flight of steps. He would say, "Look here, Marge, I'm sorry if *I've* been causing the strain around here. We asked you to go today, and we mean it. *I* mean it."

Tom stopped as Marge's window came into view: Dickie's arm was around her waist. Dickie was kissing her, little pecks on her cheek, smiling at her. They were only about fifteen feet from him, but the room was shadowed compared to the bright sunlight he stood in, and he had to strain to see. Now Marge's face was tipped straight up to Dickie's, as if she were fairly lost in ecstasy, and what disgusted Tom was that he knew Dickie didn't mean it, that Dickie was only using this cheap, obvious, easy way to hold onto her friendship. What disgusted him was the big bulge of her behind in the peasant skirt below Dickie's arm that circled her waist. And Dickie—! Tom really wouldn't have believed it possible of Dickie!

Tom turned away and ran down the steps, wanting to scream. He banged the gate shut. He ran all the way up the road home, and arrived gasping, supporting himself on the parapet after he entered Dickie's gate. He sat on the couch in Dickie's studio for a few moments, his mind stunned and blank. That kiss—it hadn't looked like a first kiss. He walked to Dickie's easel, unconsciously avoiding looking at the bad painting that was on it, picked up the kneaded eraser that lay on the palette and flung it violently out the window, saw it arc down and disappear toward the sea. He picked up more erasers from Dickie's table, pen points, smudge sticks, charcoal and pastel fragments, and threw them one by one into corners or out the windows. He had a curious feeling that his brain remained calm and logical and that his body was out of control. He ran out on the terrace with an idea of jumping onto the parapet and doing a dance or standing on his head, but the empty space on the other side of the parapet stopped him.

He went up to Dickie's room and paced around for a few moments, his hands in his pockets. He wondered when Dickie was coming back? Or was he going to stay and make an afternoon of it, really take her to bed with him? He jerked Dickie's closet door open and looked in. There was a freshly

pressed, new-looking gray flannel suit that he had never seen
Dickie wearing. Tom took it out. He took off his knee-length
shorts and put on the gray flannel trousers. He put on a pair
of Dickie's shoes. Then he opened the bottom drawer of the
chest and took out a clean blue-and-white striped shirt.

He chose a dark-blue silk tie and knotted it carefully. The
suit fitted him. He reparted his hair and put the part a little
more to one side, the way Dickie wore his.

"Marge, you must understand that I don't *love* you," Tom
said into the mirror in Dickie's voice, with Dickie's higher
pitch on the emphasized words, with the little growl in his
throat at the end of the phrase that could be pleasant or unpleasant, intimate or cool, according to Dickie's mood.
"Marge, stop it!" Tom turned suddenly and made a grab in
the air as if he were seizing Marge's throat. He shook her,
twisted her, while she sank lower and lower, until at last he
left her, limp, on the floor. He was panting. He wiped his
forehead the way Dickie did, reached for a handkerchief and,
not finding any, got one from Dickie's top drawer, then resumed in front of the mirror. Even his parted lips looked like
Dickie's lips when he was out of breath from swimming,
drawn down a little from his lower teeth. "You know why I
had to do that," he said, still breathlessly, addressing Marge,
though he watched himself in the mirror. "You were inter-
fering between Tom and me.—No, not that! But there *is* a
bond between us!"

He turned, stepped over the imaginary body, and went
stealthily to the window. He could see, beyond the bend of
the road, the blurred slant of the steps that went up to
Marge's house level. Dickie was not on the steps or on the
parts of the road that he could see. Maybe they were sleeping
together, Tom thought with a tighter twist of disgust in his
throat. He imagined it, awkward, clumsy, unsatisfactory for
Dickie, and Marge loving it. She'd love it even if he tortured
her! Tom darted back to the closet again and took a hat from
the top shelf. It was a little gray Tyrolian hat with a green-
and-white feather in the brim. He put it on rakishly. It surprised him how much he looked like Dickie with the top part
of his head covered. Really it was only his darker hair that was
very different from Dickie. Otherwise, his nose—or at least

its general form—his narrow jaw, his eyebrows if he held them right—

"What're you *doing?*"

Tom whirled around. Dickie was in the doorway. Tom realized that he must have been right below at the gate when he had looked out. "Oh—just amusing myself," Tom said in the deep voice he always used when he was embarrassed. "Sorry, Dickie."

Dickie's mouth opened a little, then closed, as if anger churned his words too much for them to be uttered. To Tom, it was just as bad as if he had spoken. Dickie advanced into the room.

"Dickie, I'm sorry if it—"

The violent slam of the door cut him off. Dickie began opening his shirt, scowling, just as he would have if Tom had not been there, because this was his room, and what was Tom doing in it? Tom stood petrified with fear.

"I wish you'd get out of my clothes," Dickie said.

Tom started undressing, his fingers clumsy with his mortification, his shock, because up until now Dickie had always said wear this and wear that that belonged to him. Dickie would never say it again.

Dickie looked at Tom's feet. "Shoes, too? Are you crazy?"

"No." Tom tried to pull himself together as he hung up the suit, then he asked, "Did you make it up with Marge?"

"Marge and I are fine," Dickie snapped in a way that shut Tom out from them. "Another thing I want to say, but clearly," he said, looking at Tom, "I'm not queer. I don't know if you have the idea that I am or not."

"Queer?" Tom smiled faintly. "I never thought you were queer."

Dickie started to say something else, and didn't. He straightened up, the ribs showing in his dark chest. "Well, Marge thinks you are."

"Why?" Tom felt the blood go out of his face. He kicked off Dickie's second shoe feebly, and set the pair in the closet. "Why should she? What've I ever done?" He felt faint. Nobody had ever said it outright to him, not in this way.

"It's just the way you act," Dickie said in a growling tone, and went out the door.

Tom hurried back into his shorts. He had been half concealing himself from Dickie behind the closet door, though he had his underwear on. Just because Dickie liked him, Tom thought, Marge had launched her filthy accusations of him at Dickie. And Dickie hadn't had the guts to stand up and deny it to her! He went downstairs and found Dickie fixing himself a drink at the bar shelf on the terrace. "Dickie, I want to get this straight," Tom began. "I'm not queer either, and I don't want anybody thinking I am."

"All right," Dickie growled.

The tone reminded Tom of the answers Dickie had given him when he had asked Dickie if he knew this person and that in New York. Some of the people he had asked Dickie about were queer, it was true, and he had often suspected Dickie of deliberately denying knowing them when he did know them. All right! Who was making an issue of it, anyway? Dickie was. Tom hesitated while his mind tossed in a welter of things he might have said, bitter things, conciliatory things, grateful and hostile. His mind went back to certain groups of people he had known in New York, known and dropped finally, all of them, but he regretted now having ever known them. They had taken him up because he amused them, but *he* had never had anything to do with any of them! When a couple of them had made a pass at him, he had rejected them—though he remembered how he had tried to make it up to them later by getting ice for their drinks, dropping them off in taxis when it was out of his way, because he had been afraid they would start to dislike him. He'd been an ass! And he remembered, too, the humiliating moment when Vic Simmons had said, *Oh, for Christ sake, Tommie, shut up!* when he had said to a group of people, for perhaps the third or fourth time in Vic's presence, "I can't make up my mind whether I like men or women, so I'm thinking of giving them *both* up." Tom had used to pretend he was going to an analyst, because everybody else was going to an analyst, and he had used to spin wildly funny stories about his sessions with his analyst to amuse people at parties, and the line about giving up men and women both had always been good for a laugh, the way he delivered it, until Vic had told him for Christ sake to shut up, and after that Tom had never said it again and never mentioned his analyst again, either. As a matter of fact, there was a lot of truth in it, Tom thought. As people went, he was one of the most innocent and clean-minded he had ever known. That was the irony of this situation with Dickie.

"I feel as if I've—" Tom began, but Dickie was not even listening. Dickie turned away with a grim look around his mouth and carried his drink to the corner of the terrace. Tom advanced toward him, a little fearfully, not knowing whether Dickie would hurl him off the terrace, or simply turn around and tell him to get the hell out of the house. Tom asked quietly, "Are you in love with Marge, Dickie?"

"No, but I feel sorry for her. I care about her. She's been very nice to me. We've had some good times together. You don't seem to be able to understand that."

"I do understand. That was my original feeling about you and her—that it was a platonic thing as far as you were concerned, and that she was probably in love with you."

"She is. You go out of your way not to hurt people who're in love with you, you know."

"Of course." He hesitated again, trying to choose his words. He was still in a state of trembling apprehension, though Dickie was not angry with him any more. Dickie was not going to throw him out. Tom said in a more self-possessed tone, "I can imagine that if you both were in New York, you wouldn't have seen her nearly so often—or at all—but this village being so lonely—"

"That's exactly right. I haven't been to bed with her and I don't intend to, but I do intend to keep her friendship."

"Well, have I done anything to prevent you? I told you, Dickie, I'd rather leave than do anything to break up your friendship with Marge."

Dickie gave him a glance. "No, you haven't done anything, specifically, but it's obvious you don't like her around. Whenever you make an effort to say anything nice to her, it's so obviously an effort."

"I'm sorry," Tom said contritely. He was sorry he hadn't made more of an effort, that he had done a bad job when he might have done a good one.

"Well, let's let it go. Marge and I are okay," Dickie said defiantly. He turned away and stared off at the water.

Tom went into the kitchen to make himself a little boiled coffee. He didn't want to use the espresso machine, because Dickie was very particular about it and didn't like anyone using it but himself. He'd take the coffee up to his room and study some Italian before Fausto came, Tom thought. This wasn't the time to make it up with Dickie. Dickie had his pride. He would be silent for most of the afternoon, then come around by about five o'clock after he had been painting for a while, and it would be as if the episode with the clothes had never happened. One thing Tom was sure of: Dickie was glad to have him here. Dickie was bored with living by himself, and bored with Marge, too. Tom still had three hundred dollars of the money Mr. Greenleaf had given him, and he and Dickie were going to use it on a spree in Paris. Without Marge. Dickie had been amazed when Tom had told him he hadn't had more than a glimpse of Paris through a railroad station window.

While he waited for his coffee, Tom put away the food that was to have been their lunch. He set a couple of pots of food in bigger pots of water to keep the ants away from them. There was also the little paper of fresh butter, the pair of eggs, the paper of four rolls that Ermelinda had brought for their breakfast tomorrow. They had to buy small quantities of everything every day, because there was no refrigerator. Dickie wanted to buy a refrigerator with part of his father's money. He had mentioned it a couple of times. Tom hoped he changed his mind, because a refrigerator would cut down their traveling money, and Dickie had a very definite budget for his own five hundred dollars every month. Dickie was cautious about money, in a way, yet down at the wharf, and in the village bars, he gave generous tips right and left, and gave five-hundred-lire bills to any beggar who approached him.

Dickie was back to normal by five o'clock. He had had a good afternoon of painting, Tom supposed, because he had been whistling for the last hour in his studio. Dickie came out on the terrace where Tom was scanning his Italian grammar, and gave him some pointers on his pronunciation.

"They don't always say 'voglio' so clearly," Dickie said. "They say 'io vo' presentare mia amica Marge,' per esempio." Dickie drew his long hand backward through the air. He always made gestures when he spoke Italian, graceful gestures as if he were leading an orchestra in a legato. "You'd better listen to Fausto more and read that grammar less. I picked my Italian up off the streets." Dickie smiled and walked away down the garden path. Fausto was just coming in the gate.

Tom listened carefully to their laughing exchanges in Italian, straining to understand every word.

Fausto came out on the terrace smiling, sank into a chair, and put his bare feet up on the parapet. His face was either smiling or frowning, and it could change from instant to instant. He was one of the few people in the village, Dickie said, who didn't speak in a southern dialect. Fausto lived in Milan, and he was visiting an aunt in Mongibello for a few months. He came, dependably and punctually, three times a week between five and five-thirty, and they sat on the terrace and sipped wine or coffee and chatted for about an hour. Tom tried his utmost to memorize everything Fausto said about the rocks, the water, politics (Fausto was a Communist, a card-carrying Communist, and he showed his card to Americans at the drop of a hat, Dickie said, because he was amused by their astonishment at his having it), and about the frenzied, catlike sex-life of some of the village inhabitants. Fausto found it hard to think of things to talk about sometimes, and then he would stare at Tom and burst out laughing. But Tom was making great progress. Italian was the only thing he had ever studied that he enjoyed and felt he could stick to. Tom wanted his Italian to be as good as Dickie's, and he thought he could make it that good in another month, if he kept on working hard at it.

II.

TOM walked briskly across the terrace and into Dickie's studio. "Want to go to Paris in a coffin?" he asked.

"What?" Dickie looked up from his watercolor.

"I've been talking to an Italian in Giorgio's. We'd start out from Trieste, ride in coffins in the baggage car escorted by some Frenchman, and we'd get a hundred thousand lire apiece. I have the idea it concerns dope."

"Dope in the coffins? Isn't that an old stunt?"

"We talked in Italian, so I didn't understand everything, but he said there'd be three coffins, and maybe the third has a real corpse in it and they've put the dope into the corpse. Anyway, we'd get the trip plus the experience." He emptied his pockets of the packs of ship's store Lucky Strikes that he had just bought from a street peddler for Dickie. "What do you say?"

"I think it's a marvelous idea. To Paris in a coffin!"

There was a funny smile on Dickie's face, as if Dickie were pulling his leg by pretending to fall in with it, when he hadn't the least intention of falling in with it. "I'm serious," Tom said. "He really is on the lookout for a couple of willing young men. The coffins are supposed to contain the bodies of French casualties from Indo-China. The French escort is supposed to be the relative of one of them, or maybe all of them." It wasn't exactly what the man had said to him, but it was near enough. And two hundred thousand lire was over three hundred dollars, after all, plenty for a spree in Paris. Dickie was still hedging about Paris.

Dickie looked at him sharply, put out the bent wisp of the Nazionale he was smoking, and opened one of the packs of Luckies. "Are you sure the guy you were talking to wasn't under the influence of dope himself?"

"You're so damned cautious these days!" Tom said with a laugh. "Where's your spirit? You look as if you don't even believe me! Come with me and I'll show you the man. He's still down there waiting for me. His name's Carlo."

Dickie showed no sign of moving. "Anybody with an offer like that doesn't explain all the particulars to you. They get a couple of toughs to ride from Trieste to Paris, maybe, but even that doesn't make sense to me."

"Will you come with me and talk to him? If you don't believe me, at least look at him."

"Sure." Dickie got up suddenly. "I might even do it for a hundred thousand lire." Dickie closed a book of poems that had been lying face down on his studio couch before he followed Tom out of the room. Marge had a lot of books of poetry. Lately Dickie had been borrowing them.

The man was still sitting at the corner table in Giorgio's when they came in. Tom smiled at him and nodded.

"Hello, Carlo," Tom said. "Posso sedermi?"

"Si, si," the man said, gesturing to the chairs at his table.

"This is my friend," Tom said carefully in Italian. "He wants to know if the work with the railroad journey is correct." Tom watched Carlo looking Dickie over, sizing him up, and it was wonderful to Tom how the man's dark, tough, callous-looking eyes betrayed nothing but a polite interest, how in a split second he seemed to take in and evaluate Dickie's faintly smiling but suspicious expression, Dickie's tan that could not have been acquired except by months of lying in the sun, his worn, Italian-made clothes and his American rings.

A smile spread slowly across the man's pale, flat lips, and he glanced at Tom.

"Allora?" Tom prompted, impatient.

The man lifted his sweet martini and drank. "The job is real, but I do not think your friend is the right man."

Tom looked at Dickie. Dickie was watching the man alertly, with the same neutral smile that suddenly struck Tom as contemptuous. "Well, at least it's true, you see!" Tom said to Dickie.

"Mm-m," Dickie said, still gazing at the man as if he were some kind of animal which interested him, and which he could kill if he decided to.

Dickie could have talked Italian to the man. Dickie didn't say a word. Three weeks ago, Tom thought, Dickie would have taken the man up on his offer. Did he have to sit there looking like a stool pigeon or a police detective waiting for reinforcements so he could arrest the man? "Well," Tom said finally, "you believe me, don't you?"

Dickie glanced at him. "About the job? How do I know?"

Tom looked at the Italian expectantly.

The Italian shrugged. "There is no need to discuss it, is there?" he asked in Italian.

"No," Tom said. A crazy, directionless fury boiled in his blood and made him tremble. He was furious at Dickie. Dickie was looking over the man's dirty nails, dirty shirt collar, his ugly dark face that had been recently shaven though not recently washed, so that where the beard had been was much lighter than the skin above and below it. But the Italian's dark eyes were cool and amiable, and stronger than Dickie's. Tom felt stifled. He was conscious that he could not express himself in Italian. He wanted to speak both to Dickie and to the man.

"Niente, grazie, Berto," Dickie said calmly to the waiter who had come over to ask what they wanted. Dickie looked at Tom. "Ready to go?"

Tom jumped up so suddenly his straight chair upset behind him. He set it up again, and bowed a good-bye to the Italian. He felt he owed the Italian an apology, yet he could not open his mouth to say even a conventional good-bye. The Italian nodded good-bye and smiled. Tom followed Dickie's long white-clad legs out of the bar.

Outside, Tom said, "I just wanted you to see that it's true at least. I hope you see."

"All right, it's true," Dickie said, smiling. "What's the matter with you?"

"What's the matter with *you*?" Tom demanded.

"The man's a crook. Is that what you want me to admit? Okay!"

"Do you have to be so damned superior about it? Did he do anything to you?"

"Am I supposed to get down on my knees to him? I've seen crooks before. This village gets a lot of them." Dickie's blond eyebrows frowned. "What the hell *is* the matter with you? Do you want to take him up on his crazy proposition? Go ahead!"

"I couldn't now if I wanted to. Not after the way you acted."

Dickie stopped in the road, looking at him. They were arguing so loudly, a few people around them were looking, watching.

"It could have been fun," Tom said, "but not the way you chose to take it. A month ago when we went to Rome, you'd have thought something like this was fun."

"Oh, no," Dickie said, shaking his head. "I doubt it."

The sense of frustration and inarticulateness was agony to

Tom. And the fact that they were being looked at. He forced himself to walk on, in tense little steps at first, until he was sure that Dickie was coming with him. The puzzlement, the suspicion, was still in Dickie's face, and Tom knew Dickie was puzzled about his reaction. Tom wanted to explain it, wanted to break through to Dickie so he would understand and they would feel the same way. Dickie had felt the same way he had a month ago. "It's the way you acted," Tom said. "You didn't have to act that way. The fellow wasn't doing you any harm."

"He looked like a dirty crook!" Dickie retorted. "For Christ sake, go back if you like him so much. You're under no obligation to do what I do!"

Now Tom stopped. He had an impulse to go back, not necessarily to go back to the Italian, but to leave Dickie. Then his tension snapped suddenly. His shoulders relaxed, aching, and his breath began to come fast, through his mouth. He wanted to say at least, "All right, Dickie," to make it up, to make Dickie forget it. He felt tongue-tied. He stared at Dickie's blue eyes that were still frowning, the sun-bleached eyebrows white and the eyes themselves shining and empty, nothing but little pieces of blue jelly with a black dot in them, meaningless, without relation to him. You were supposed to see the soul through the eyes, to see love through the eyes, the one place you could look at another human being and see what really went on inside, and in Dickie's eyes Tom saw nothing more now than he would have seen if he had looked at the hard, bloodless surface of a mirror. Tom felt a painful wrench in his breast, and he covered his face with his hands. It was as if Dickie had been suddenly snatched away from him. They were not friends. They didn't know each other. It struck Tom like a horrible truth, true for all time, true for the people he had known in the past and for those he would know in the future: each had stood and would stand before him, and he would know time and time again that he would never know them, and the worst was that there would always be the il-lusion, for a time, that he did know them, and that he and they were completely in harmony and alike. For an instant the wordless shock of his realization seemed more than he could bear. He felt in the grip of a fit, as if he would fall to the ground. It was too much: the foreignness around him, the different language, his failure, and the fact that Dickie hated him. He felt surrounded by strangeness, by hostility. He felt Dickie yank his hands down from his eyes.

"What's the matter with you?" Dickie asked. "Did that guy give you a shot of something?"

"No."

"Are you sure? In your drink?"

"No." The first drops of the evening rain fell on his head. There was a rumble of thunder. Hostility from above, too. "I want to die," Tom said in a small voice.

Dickie yanked him by the arm. Tom tripped over a doorstep. They were in the little bar opposite the post office. Tom heard Dickie ordering a brandy, specifying Italian brandy because he wasn't good enough for French, Tom supposed. Tom drank it off, slightly sweetish, medicinal-tasting, drank three of them, like a magic medicine to bring him back to what his mind knew was usually called reality: the smell of the Nazionale in Dickie's hand, the curlycued grain in the wood of the bar under his fingers, the fact that his stomach had a hard pressure in it as if someone were holding a fist against his navel, the vivid anticipation of the long steep walk from here up to the house, the faint ache that would come in his thighs from it.

"I'm okay," Tom said in a quiet, deep voice. "I don't know what was the matter. Must have been the heat that got me for a minute." He laughed a little. That was reality, laughing it off, making it silly, something that was more important than anything that had happened to him in the five weeks since he had met Dickie, maybe that had ever happened to him.

Dickie said nothing, only put the cigarette in his mouth and took a couple of hundred-lire bills from his black alligator wallet and laid them on the bar. Tom was hurt that he said nothing, hurt like a child who has been sick and probably a nuisance, but who expects at least a friendly word when the sickness is over. But Dickie was indifferent. Dickie had bought him the brandies as coldly as he might have bought them for a stranger he had encountered who felt ill and had no money. Tom thought suddenly, *Dickie doesn't want me to go to Cortina.* It was not the first time Tom had thought that. Marge was going to Cortina now. She and Dickie had bought a new giant-sized thermos to take to Cortina the last time they had been in Naples. They hadn't asked him if he had liked the thermos, or anything else. They were just quietly and gradually leaving him out of their preparations. Tom felt that Dickie expected him to take off, in fact, just before the Cortina trip. A couple of weeks ago, Dickie had said he would show him some of the ski trails around Cortina that were marked on a map that he had. Dickie had looked at the map one evening, but he had not talked to him.

"Ready?" Dickie asked.

Tom followed him out of the bar like a dog.

"If you can get home all right by yourself, I thought I'd run up and see Marge for a while," Dickie said on the road.

"I feel fine," Tom said.

"Good." Then he said over his shoulder as he walked away, "Want to pick up the mail? I might forget."

Tom nodded. He went into the post office. There were two letters, one to him from Dickie's father, one to Dickie from someone in New York whom Tom didn't know. He stood in the doorway and opened Mr. Greenleaf's letter, unfolded the typewritten sheet respectfully. It had the impressive pale green letterhead of Burke-Greenleaf Watercraft, Inc., with the ship's-wheel trademark in the center.

Nov. 10, 19——

My dear Tom,

In view of the fact you have been with Dickie over a month and that he shows no more sign of coming home than before you went, I can only conclude that you haven't been successful. I realize that with the best of intentions you reported that he is considering returning, but frankly I don't see it anywhere in his letter of October 26th. As a matter of fact, he seems more determined than ever to stay where he is.

I want you to know that I and my wife appreciate whatever efforts you have made on our behalf, and his. You need no longer consider yourself obligated to me in any way. I trust you have not inconvenienced yourself greatly by your efforts of the past month, and I sincerely hope the trip has afforded you some pleasure despite the failure of its main objective.

Both my wife and I send you greetings and our thanks.

Sincerely,
H. R. Greenleaf

It was the final blow. With the cool tone—even cooler than his usual businesslike coolness, because this was a dismissal and he had injected a note of courteous thanks in it—Mr. Greenleaf had simply cut him off. He had failed. "I trust you have not inconvenienced yourself greatly . . ." Wasn't that sarcastic? Mr. Greenleaf didn't even say that he would like to see him again when he returned to America.

Tom walked mechanically up the hill. He imagined Dickie in Marge's house now, narrating to her the story of Carlo in the bar, and his peculiar behavior on the road afterward. Tom knew what Marge would say: "Why don't you get *rid* of him, Dickie?" Should he go back and explain to them, he wondered, force them to listen? Tom turned around, looking at the inscrutable square front of Marge's house up on the hill, at its empty, dark-looking window. His denim jacket was getting wet from the rain. He turned its collar up. Then he walked on quickly up the hill toward Dickie's house. At least, he thought proudly, he hadn't tried to wheedle any more money out of Mr. Greenleaf, and he might have. He might have, even with Dickie's cooperation, if he had ever approached Dickie about it when Dickie had been in a good mood. Anybody else would have, Tom thought, anybody, but he hadn't, and that counted for *something*.

He stood at the corner of the terrace, staring out at the vague empty line of the horizon and thinking of nothing, feeling nothing except a faint, dreamlike lostness and aloneness. Even Dickie and Marge seemed far away, and what they might be talking about seemed unimportant. He was alone. That was the only important thing. He began to feel a tingling fear at the end of his spine, tingling over his buttocks.

He turned as he heard the gate open. Dickie walked up the path, smiling, but it struck Tom as a forced, polite smile.

"What're you doing standing there in the rain?" Dickie asked, ducking into the hall door.

"It's very refreshing," Tom said pleasantly. "Here's a letter for you." He handed Dickie his letter and stuffed the one from Mr. Greenleaf into his pocket.

Tom hung his jacket in the hall closet. When Dickie had finished reading his letter—a letter that had made him laugh out loud as he read it—Tom said, "Do you think Marge would like to go up to Paris with us when we go?"

Dickie looked surprised. "I think she would."

"Well, ask her," Tom said cheerfully.

"I don't know if I should go up to Paris," Dickie said. "I wouldn't mind getting away somewhere for a few days, but Paris—" He lighted a cigarette. "I'd just as soon go up to San Remo or even Genoa. That's quite a town."

"But Paris—Genoa can't compare with Paris, can it?"

"No, of course not, but it's a lot closer."

"But when *will* we get to Paris?"

"I don't know. Any old time. Paris'll still be there."

Tom listened to the echo of the words in his ears, searching their tone. The day before yesterday, Dickie had received a letter from his father. He had read a few sentences aloud and they had laughed about something, but he had not read the whole letter as he had a couple of times before. Tom had no doubt that Mr. Greenleaf had told Dickie that he was fed up with Tom Ripley, and probably that he suspected him of using his money for his own entertainment. A month ago Dickie would have laughed at something like that, too, but not now, Tom thought. "I just thought while I have a little money left, we ought to make our Paris trip," Tom persisted.

"You go up. I'm not in the mood right now. Got to save my strength for Cortina."

"Well—I suppose we'll make it San Remo then," Tom said, trying to sound agreeable, though he could have wept.

"All right."

Tom darted from the hall into the kitchen. The huge white form of the refrigerator sprang out of the corner at him. He had wanted a drink, with ice in it. Now he didn't want to touch the thing. He had spent a whole day in Naples with Dickie and Marge, looking at refrigerators, inspecting ice trays, counting the number of gadgets, until Tom hadn't been able to tell one refrigerator from another, but Dickie and Marge had kept at it with the enthusiasm of newlyweds. Then they had spent a few more hours in a café discussing the respective merits of all the refrigerators they had looked at before they decided on the one they wanted. And now Marge was popping in and out more often than ever, because she stored some of her own food in it, and she often wanted to borrow ice. Tom realized suddenly why he hated the refrigerator so much. It meant that Dickie was staying put. It finished not only their Greek trip this winter, but it meant Dickie probably never would move to Paris or Rome to live, as he and Tom had talked of doing in Tom's first weeks here. Not with a refrigerator that had the distinction of being one of only about four in the village, a refrigerator with six ice trays and so many shelves on the door that it looked like a supermarket swinging out at you every time you opened it.

Tom fixed himself an iceless drink. His hands were shaking. Only yesterday Dickie had said, "Are you going home for Christmas?" very casually in the middle of some conversation, but Dickie knew damned well he wasn't going home for Christmas. He didn't have a home, and Dickie knew it. He had told Dickie all about Aunt Dottie in Boston. It had simply been a big hint, that was all. Marge was full of plans about Christmas. She had a can of English plum pudding she was saving, and she was going to get a turkey from some contadino. Tom could imagine how she would slop it up with her saccharine sentimentality. A Christmas tree, of course, probably cut out of cardboard. "Silent Night." Eggnog. Gooey presents for Dickie. Marge knitted. She took Dickie's socks home to darn all the time. And they'd both slightly, politely, leave him out. Every friendly thing they would say to him would be a painful effort. Tom couldn't bear to imagine it. All right, he'd leave. He'd do something rather than endure Christmas with them.

12.

MARGE said she didn't care to go with them to San Remo. She was in the middle of a "streak" on her book. Marge worked in fits and starts, always cheerfully, though it seemed to Tom that she was bogged down, as she called it, about seventy-five per cent of the time, a condition that she always announced with a merry little laugh. The book must stink,

Tom thought. He had known writers. You didn't write a book with your little finger, lolling on a beach half the day, wondering what to eat for dinner. But he was glad she was having a "streak" at the time he and Dickie wanted to go to San Remo.

"I'd appreciate it if you'd try to find that cologne, Dickie," she said. "You know, the Stradivari I couldn't find in Naples. San Remo's bound to have it, they have so many shops with French stuff."

Tom could see them spending a whole day looking for it in San Remo, just as they had spent hours looking for it in Naples one Saturday.

They took only one suitcase of Dickie's between them, because they planned to be away only three nights and four days. Dickie was in a slightly more cheerful mood, but the awful finality was still there, the feeling that this was the last trip they would make together anywhere. To Tom, Dickie's polite cheerfulness on the train was like the cheerfulness of a host who has loathed his guest and is afraid the guest realizes it, and who tries to make it up at the last minute. Tom had never before in his life felt like an unwelcome, boring guest. On the train, Dickie told Tom about San Remo and the week he had spent there with Freddie Miles when he first arrived in Italy. San Remo was tiny, but it had a famous name as an international shopping center, Dickie said, and people came across the French border to buy things there. It occurred to Tom that Dickie was trying to sell him on the town and might try to persuade him to stay there alone instead of coming back to Mongibello. Tom began to feel an aversion to the place before they got there.

Then, almost as the train was sliding into the San Remo station, Dickie said, "By the way, Tom—I hate to say this to you, if you're going to mind terribly, but I really would prefer to go to Cortina d'Ampezzo alone with Marge. I think she'd prefer it, and after all I owe something to her, a pleasant holiday at least. You don't seem to be too enthusiastic about skiing."

Tom went rigid and cold, but he tried not to move a muscle. Blaming it on Marge! "All right," he said. "Of course." Nervously he looked at the map in his hands, looking des-

perately around San Remo for somewhere else to go, though
Dickie was already swinging their suitcase down from the rack.
"We're not far from Nice, are we?" Tom asked.

"No."

"And Cannes. I'd like to see Cannes as long as I'm this far.
At least Cannes is France," he added on a reproachful note.

"Well, I suppose we could. You brought your passport,
didn't you?"

Tom had brought his passport. They boarded a train for
Cannes, and arrived around eleven o'clock that night.

Tom thought it beautiful—the sweep of curving harbor extended by little lights to long thin crescent tips, the elegant
yet tropical-looking main boulevard along the water with its
rows of palm trees, its row of expensive hotels. France! It was
more sedate than Italy, and more chic, he could feel that even
in the dark. They went to a hotel on the first back street, the
Gray d'Albion, which was chic enough but wouldn't cost
them their shirts, Dickie said, though Tom would gladly have
paid whatever it cost at the best hotel on the ocean front.
They left their suitcase at the hotel, and went to the bar of
the Hotel Carlton, which Dickie said was the most fashionable
bar in Cannes. As he had predicted, there were not many
people in the bar, because there were not many people in
Cannes at this time of year. Tom proposed a second round of
drinks, but Dickie declined.

They breakfasted at a café the next morning, then strolled
down to the beach. They had their swimming trunks on under
their trousers. The day was cool, but not impossibly cool for
swimming. They had been swimming in Mongibello on colder
days. The beach was practically empty—a few isolated pairs of
people, a group of men playing some kind of game up near
the embankment. The waves curved over and broke on the
sand with a wintry violence. Now Tom saw that the group of
men were doing acrobatics.

"They must be professionals," Tom said. "They're all in
the same yellow G-strings."

Tom watched with interest as a human pyramid began
building, feet braced on bulging thighs, hands gripping fore-
arms. He could hear their "Allez!" and their "Un—deux!"

"Look!" Tom said. "There goes the top!" He stood still to watch the smallest one, a boy of about seventeen, as he was boosted to the shoulders of the center man in the three top men. He stood poised, his arms open, as if receiving applause. "Bravo!" Tom shouted.

The boy smiled at Tom before he leapt down, lithe as a tiger.

Tom looked at Dickie. Dickie was looking at a couple of men sitting nearby on the beach.

"Ten thousand saw I at a glance, nodding their heads in sprightly dance," Dickie said sourly to Tom.

It startled Tom, then he felt that sharp thrust of shame, the same shame he had felt in Mongibello when Dickie had said, *Marge thinks you are.* All right, Tom thought, the acrobats were fairies. Maybe Cannes was full of fairies. So what? Tom's fists were clenched tight in his trousers pockets. He remembered Aunt Dottie's taunt: *Sissy! He's a sissy from the ground up. Just like his father!* Dickie stood with his arms folded, looking out at the ocean. Tom deliberately kept himself from even glancing at the acrobats again, though they were certainly more amusing to watch than the ocean. "Are you going in?" Tom asked, boldly unbuttoning his shirt, though the water suddenly looked cold as hell.

"I don't think so," Dickie said. "Why don't you stay here and watch the acrobats? I'm going back." He turned and started back before Tom could answer.

Tom buttoned his clothes hastily, watching Dickie as he walked diagonally away, away from the acrobats, though the next stairs up to the sidewalk were twice as far as the stairs nearer the acrobats. Damn him anyway, Tom thought. Did he have to act so damned aloof and superior all the time? You'd think he'd never seen a pansy! Obvious what was the matter with Dickie, all right! Why didn't he break down, just for once? What did he have that was so important to lose? A half-dozen taunts sprang to his mind as he ran after Dickie. Then Dickie glanced around at him coldly, with distaste, and the first taunt died in his mouth.

They left for San Remo that afternoon, just before three o'clock, so there would not be another day to pay on the hotel bill. Dickie had proposed leaving by three, though it was Tom who paid the 3,430-franc bill, ten dollars and eight cents American, for one night. Tom also bought their railroad tickets to San Remo, though Dickie was loaded with francs. Dickie had brought his monthly remittance check from Italy and cashed it in francs, figuring that he would come out better converting the francs back into lire later, because of a sudden recent strengthening of the franc.

Dickie said absolutely nothing on the train. Under a pretense of being sleepy, he folded his arms and closed his eyes. Tom sat opposite him, staring at his bony, arrogant, handsome face, at his hands with the green ring and the gold signet ring. It crossed Tom's mind to steal the green ring when he left. It would be easy: Dickie took it off when he swam. Sometimes he took it off even when he showered at the house. He would do it the very last day, Tom thought. Tom stared at Dickie's closed eyelids. A crazy emotion of hate, of affection, of impatience and frustration was swelling in him, hampering his breathing. He wanted to kill Dickie. It was not the first time he had thought of it. Before, once or twice or three times, it had been an impulse caused by anger or disappointment, an impulse that vanished immediately and left him with a feeling of shame. Now he thought about it for an entire minute, two minutes, because he was leaving Dickie anyway, and what was there to be ashamed of any more? He had failed with Dickie, in every way. He hated Dickie, because, however he looked at what had happened, his failing had not been his own fault, not due to anything he had done, but due to Dickie's inhuman stubbornness. And his blatant rudeness! He had offered Dickie friendship, companionship, and respect, everything he had to offer, and Dickie had replied with ingratitude and now hostility. Dickie was just shoving him out in the cold. If he killed him on this trip, Tom thought, he could simply say that some accident had happened. He could— He had just thought of something brilliant: he could become Dickie Greenleaf himself. He could do everything that Dickie did. He could go back to Mongibello first and collect Dickie's things, tell Marge any damned story, set up an apartment in Rome or Paris, receive Dickie's check every month and forge Dickie's signature on it. He could step right into Dickie's shoes. He could have Mr. Greenleaf, Sr., eating out of his hand. The danger of it, even the inevitable temporariness of it which he vaguely realized, only made him more enthusiastic. He began to think of *how*.

The water. But Dickie was such a good swimmer. The cliffs. It would be easy to push Dickie off some cliff when they took a walk, but he imagined Dickie grabbing at him and pulling *him* off with him, and he tensed in his seat until his thighs ached and his nails cut red scallops in his thumbs. He would have to get the other ring off, too. He would have to tint his hair a little lighter. But he wouldn't live in a place, of course, where anybody who knew Dickie lived. He had only to look enough like Dickie to be able to use his passport. Well, he did. If he—

Dickie opened his eyes, looking right at him, and Tom relaxed, slumped into the corner with his head back and his eyes shut, as quickly as if he had passed out.

"Tom, are you okay?" Dickie asked, shaking Tom's knee.

"Okay," Tom said, smiling a little. He saw Dickie sit back with an air of irritation, and Tom knew why: because Dickie had hated giving him even that much attention. Tom smiled to himself, amused at his own quick reflex in pretending to collapse, because that had been the only way to keep Dickie from seeing what must have been a very strange expression on his face.

San Remo. Flowers. A main drag along the beach again, shops and stores and French and English and Italian tourists. Another hotel, with flowers in the balconies. Where? In one of these little streets tonight? The town would be dark and silent by one in the morning, if he could keep Dickie up that long. In the water? It was slightly cloudy, though not cold. Tom racked his brain. It would be easy in the hotel room, too, but how would he get rid of the body? The body had to *disappear*, absolutely. That left only the water, and the water was Dickie's element. There were boats, rowboats and little motorboats, that people could rent down at the beach. In each motorboat, Tom noticed, was a round weight of cement attached to a line, for anchoring the boat.

"What do you say we take a boat, Dickie?" Tom asked, trying not to sound eager, though he did, and Dickie looked at him, because he had not been eager about anything since they had arrived here.

They were little blue-and-white and green-and-white motorboats, about ten of them, lined up at the wooden pier, and the Italian was anxious for customers because it was a chilly and rather gloomy morning. Dickie looked out at the Mediterranean, which was slightly hazy though not with a presage of rain. This was the kind of grayness that would not disappear all day, and there would be no sun. It was about ten-thirty, that lazy hour after breakfast, when the whole long Italian morning lay before them.

"Well, all right. For an hour around the port," Dickie said, almost immediately jumping into a boat, and Tom could see from his little smile that he had done it before, that he was looking forward to remembering, sentimentally, other mornings or some other morning here, perhaps with Freddie, or Marge. Marge's cologne bottle bulged the pocket of Dickie's corduroy jacket. They had bought it a few minutes ago at a store very much like an American drugstore on the main drag.

The Italian boatkeeper started the motor with a yanked string, asking Dickie if he knew how to work it, and Dickie said yes. And there was an oar, a single oar in the bottom of the boat, Tom saw. Dickie took the tiller. They headed straight out from the town.

"Cool!" Dickie yelled, smiling. His hair was blowing.

Tom looked to right and left. A vertical cliff on one side, very much like Mongibello, and on the other a flattish length of land fuzzing out in the mist that hovered over the water. Offhand he couldn't say in which direction it was better to go.

"Do you know the land around here?" Tom shouted over the roar of the motor.

"Nope!" Dickie said cheerfully. He was enjoying the ride.

"Is that thing hard to steer?"

"Not a bit! Want to try it?"

Tom hesitated. Dickie was still steering straight out to the open sea. "No, thanks." He looked to right and left. There was a sailboat off to the left. "Where're you going?" Tom shouted.

"Does it matter?" Dickie smiled.

No, it didn't.

Dickie swerved suddenly to the right, so suddenly that they both had to duck and lean to keep the boat righted. A wall of white spray rose up on Tom's left, then gradually fell to show the empty horizon. They were streaking across the empty water again, toward nothing. Dickie was trying the speed, smiling, his blue eyes smiling at the emptiness.

"In a little boat it always feels so much faster than it is!" Dickie yelled.

Tom nodded, letting his understanding smile speak for him. Actually, he was terrified. God only knew how deep the water was here. If something happened to the boat suddenly, there wasn't a chance in the world that they could get back to shore, or at least that *he* could. But neither was there a chance that anybody could see anything that they did here. Dickie was swerving very slightly toward the right again, toward the long spit of fuzzy gray land, but he could have hit Dickie, sprung on him, or kissed him, or thrown him overboard, and nobody could have seen him at this distance. Tom was sweating, hot under his clothes, cold on his forehead. He felt afraid, but it was not of the water, it was of Dickie. He knew that he was going to do it, that he would not stop himself now, maybe *couldn't* stop himself, and that he might not succeed.

"You dare me to jump in?" Tom yelled, beginning to unbutton his jacket.

Dickie only laughed at this proposal from him, opening his mouth wide, keeping his eyes fixed on the distance in front of the boat.

Tom kept on undressing. He had his shoes and socks off. Under his trousers he wore his swimming trunks, like Dickie. "I'll go in if you will!" Tom shouted. "Will you?" He wanted Dickie to slow down.

"Will I? Sure!" Dickie slowed the motor abruptly. He released the tiller and took off his jacket. The boat bobbed, losing its momentum. "Come on," Dickie said, nodding at Tom's trousers that were still on.

Tom glanced at the land. San Remo was a blur of chalky white and pink. He picked up the oar, as casually as if he were playing with it between his knees, and when Dickie was shoving his trousers down, Tom lifted the oar and came down with it on the top of Dickie's head.

"Hey!" Dickie yelled, scowling, sliding half off the wooden seat. His pale brows lifted in groggy surprise.

Tom stood up and brought the oar down again, sharply, all his strength released like the snap of a rubber band.

"For God's sake!" Dickie mumbled, glowering, fierce, though the blue eyes wobbled, losing consciousness.

Tom swung a left-handed blow with the oar against the side of Dickie's head. The edge of the oar cut a dull gash that filled with a line of blood as Tom watched. Dickie was on the bottom of the boat, twisted, twisting. Dickie gave a groaning roar of protest that frightened Tom with its loudness and its strength. Tom hit him in the side of the neck, three times, chopping strokes with the edge of the oar, as if the oar were an ax and Dickie's neck a tree. The boat rocked, and water splashed over his foot that was braced on the gunwale. He sliced at Dickie's forehead, and a broad patch of blood came slowly where the oar had scraped. For an instant Tom was aware of tiring as he raised and swung, and still Dickie's hands slid toward him on the bottom of the boat, Dickie's long legs straightened to thrust him forward. Tom got a bayonet grip on the oar and plunged its handle into Dickie's side. Then the prostrate body relaxed, limp and still. Tom straightened, getting his breath back painfully. He looked around him. There were no boats, nothing, except far, far away a little white spot creeping from right to left, a speeding motorboat heading for the shore.

He stooped and yanked at Dickie's green ring. He pocketed it. The other ring was tighter, but it came off, over the bleeding scuffed knuckle. He looked in the trousers pockets. French and Italian coins. He left them. He took a keychain with three keys. Then he picked up Dickie's jacket and took Marge's cologne package out of the pocket. Cigarettes and Dickie's silver lighter, a pencil stub, the alligator wallet and several little cards in the inside breast pocket. Tom stuffed it all into his own corduroy jacket. Then he reached for the rope that was tumbled over the white cement weight. The end of the rope was tied to the metal ring at the prow. Tom tried to untie it. It was a hellish, water-soaked, immovable knot that must have been there for years. He banged at it with his fist. He had to have a knife.

He looked at Dickie. Was he dead? Tom crouched in the narrowing prow of the boat watching Dickie for a sign of life. He was afraid to touch him, afraid to touch his chest or his wrist to feel a pulse. Tom turned and yanked at the rope frenziedly, until he realized that he was only making it tighter.

His cigarette lighter. He fumbled for it in the pocket of his trousers on the bottom of the boat. He lighted it, then held a dry portion of the rope over its flame. The rope was about an inch and a half thick. It was slow, very slow, and Tom used the minutes to look all around him again. Would the Italian with the boats be able to see him at this distance? The hard gray rope refused to catch fire, only glowed and smoked a little, slowly parting, strand by strand. Tom yanked it, and his lighter went out. He lighted it again, and kept on pulling at the rope. When it parted, he looped it four times around Dickie's bare ankles before he had time to feel afraid, and tied a huge, clumsy knot, overdoing it to make sure it would not come undone, because he was not very good at tying knots. He estimated the rope to be about thirty-five or forty feet long. He began to feel cooler, and smooth and methodical. The cement weight should be just enough to hold a body down, he thought. The body might drift a little, but it would not come up to the surface.

Tom threw the weight over. It made a *ker-pluns* and sank through the transparent water with a wake of bubbles, disappeared, and sank and sank until the rope drew taut on Dickie's ankles, and by that time Tom had lifted the ankles over the side and was pulling now at an arm to lift the heaviest part, the shoulders, over the gunwale. Dickie's limp hand was warm and clumsy. The shoulders stayed on the bottom of the boat, and when he pulled, the arm seemed to stretch like rubber, and the body not to rise at all. Tom got down on one knee and tried to heave him out over the side. It made the boat rock. He had forgotten the water. It was the only thing that scared him. He would have to get him out over the stern, he thought, because the stern was lower in the water. He pulled the limp body toward the stern, sliding the rope around the gunwale. He could tell from the buoyancy of the weight in the water that the weight had not touched bottom. Now he began with Dickie's head and shoulders, turned Dickie's body on its belly and pushed him out little by little. Dickie's head was in the water, the gunwale cutting across his waist, and now the legs were a dead weight, resisting Tom's strength with their amazing weight, as his shoulders had done, as if they were magnetized to the boat bottom. Tom took a deep breath and heaved. Dickie went over, but Tom lost his balance and fell against the tiller. The idling motor roared suddenly.

Tom made a lunge for the control lever, but the boat swerved at the same time in a crazy arc. For an instant he saw water underneath him and his own hand outstretched toward it, because he had been trying to grab the gunwale and the gunwale was no longer there.

He was in the water.

He gasped, contracting his body in an upward leap, grabbing at the boat. He missed. The boat had gone into a spin. Tom leapt again, then sank lower, so low the water closed over his head again with a deadly, fatal slowness, yet too fast for him to get a breath, and he inhaled a noseful of water just as his eyes sank below the surface. The boat was farther away. He had seen such spins before: they never stopped until somebody climbed in and stopped the motor, and now in the deadly emptiness of the water he suffered in advance the sensations of dying, sank threshing below the surface again, and the crazy motor faded as the water *thugged* into his ears, blotting out all sound except the frantic sounds that he made inside himself, breathing, struggling, the desperate pounding of his blood. He was up again and fighting automatically toward the boat, because it was the only thing that floated, though it was spinning and impossible to touch, and its sharp prow whipped past him twice, three times, four, while he caught one breath of air.

He shouted for help. He got nothing but a mouthful of water.

His hand touched the boat beneath the water and was

pushed aside by the animal-like thrust of the prow. He reached out wildly for the end of the boat, heedless of the propeller's blades. His fingers felt the rudder. He ducked, but not in time. The keel hit the top of his head, passing over him. Now the stern was close again, and he tried for it, fingers slipping down off the rudder. His other hand caught the stern gunwale. He kept an arm straight, holding his body away from the propeller. With an unpremeditated energy, he hurled himself toward a stern corner, and caught an arm over the side. Then he reached up and touched the lever.

The motor began to slow.

Tom clung to the gunwale with both hands, and his mind went blank with relief, with disbelief, until he became aware of the flaming ache in his throat, the stab in his chest with every breath. He rested for what could have been two or ten minutes, thinking of nothing at all but the gathering of strength enough to haul himself into the boat, and finally he made slow jumps up and down in the water and threw his weight over and lay face down in the boat, his feet dangling over the gunwale. He rested, faintly conscious of the slipperiness of Dickie's blood under his fingers, a wetness mingled with the water that ran out of his own nose and mouth. He began to think before he could move, about the boat that was all bloody and could not be returned, about the motor that he would have to get up and start in a moment. About the direction.

About Dickie's rings. He felt for them in his jacket pocket. They were still there, and after all what could have happened to them? He had a fit of coughing, and tears blurred his vision as he tried to look all around him to see if any boat was near, or coming toward him. He rubbed his eyes. There was no boat, except the gay little motorboat in the distance, still dashing around in wide arcs, oblivious of him. Tom looked at the boat bottom. *Could* he wash it all out? But blood was hell to get out, he had always heard. He had been going to return the boat, and say, if he were asked by the boatkeeper where his friend was, that he had set him ashore at some other point. Now that couldn't be.

Tom moved the lever cautiously. The idling motor picked up and he was afraid even of that, but the motor seemed more human and manageable than the sea, and therefore less frightening. He headed obliquely toward the shore, north of San Remo. Maybe he could find some place, some little deserted cove in the shore where he could beach the boat and get out. But if they found the boat? The problem seemed immense. He tried to reason himself back to coolness. His mind seemed blocked as to how to get rid of the boat.

Now he could see pine trees, a dry empty-looking stretch of tan beach and the green fuzz of a field of olive trees. Tom cruised slowly to right and left of the place, looking for people. There were none. He headed in for the shallow, short beach, handling the throttle respectfully, because he was not sure it wouldn't flare up again. Then he felt the scrape and jolt of earth under the prow. He turned the lever to FERMA, and moved another lever that cut the motor. He got out cautiously into about ten inches of water, pulled the boat up as far as he could, then transferred the two jackets, his sandals, and Marge's cologne box from the boat to the beach. The little cove where he was—not more than fifteen feet wide— gave him a feeling of safety and privacy. There was not a sign anywhere that a human foot had ever touched the place. Tom decided to try to scuttle the boat.

He began to gather stones, all about the size of a human head because that was all he had the strength to carry, and to drop them one by one into the boat, but finally he had to use smaller stones because there were no more big ones near enough by. He worked without a halt, afraid that he would drop in a faint of exhaustion if he allowed himself to relax even for an instant, and that he might lie there until he was found by somebody. When the stones were nearly level with the gunwale, he shoved the boat off and rocked it, more and more, until water slopped in at the sides. As the boat began to sink, he gave it a shove toward deeper water, shoved and walked with it until the water was up to his waist, and the boat sank below his reach. Then he plowed his way back to the shore and lay down for a while, face down on the sand. He began to plan his return to the hotel, and his story, and his next moves: leaving San Remo before nightfall, getting back to Mongibello. And the story there.

13.

AT sundown, just the hour when the Italians and everybody else in the village had gathered at the sidewalk tables of the cafés, freshly showered and dressed, staring at everybody and everything that passed by, eager for whatever entertainment the town could offer, Tom walked into the village wearing only his swimming shorts and sandals and Dickie's corduroy jacket, and carrying his slightly bloodstained trousers and jacket under his arm. He walked with a languid casualness because he was exhausted, though he kept his head up for the benefit of the hundreds of people who stared at him as he walked past the cafés, the only route to his beachfront hotel. He had fortified himself with five espressos full of sugar and three brandies at a bar on the road just outside of San Remo. Now he was playing the role of an athletic young man who had spent the afternoon in and out of the water because it was his peculiar taste, being a good swimmer and impervious to cold, to swim until late afternoon on a chilly day. He made it to the hotel, collected the key at the desk, went up to his room and collapsed on the bed. He would allow himself an hour to rest, he thought, but he must not fall asleep lest he sleep longer. He rested, and when he felt himself falling asleep, got up and went to the basin and wet his face, took a wet towel back to his bed simply to waggle in his hand to keep from falling asleep.

Finally he got up and went to work on the blood smear on one leg of his corduroy trousers. He scrubbed it over and over with soap and a nailbrush, got tired and stopped for a while to pack the suitcase. He packed Dickie's things just as Dickie had always packed them, toothpaste and toothbrush in the back left pocket. Then he went back to finish the trouser leg. His own jacket had too much blood on it ever to be worn again, and he would have to get rid of it, but he could wear Dickie's jacket, because it was the same beige color and almost identical in size. Tom had had his suit copied from Dickie's, and it had been made by the same tailor in Mongibello. He put his own jacket into the suitcase. Then he went down with the suitcase and asked for his bill.

The man behind the desk asked where his friend was, and Tom said he was meeting him at the railroad station. The clerk was pleasant and smiling, and wished Tom "Buon' viaggio."

Tom stopped in at a restaurant two streets away and forced himself to eat a bowl of minestrone for the strength it would give him. He kept an eye out for the Italian who owned the boats. The main thing, he thought, was to leave San Remo tonight, take a taxi to the next town, if there was no train or bus.

There was a train south at ten twenty-four, Tom learned at the railroad station. A sleeper. Wake up tomorrow in Rome, and change trains for Naples. It seemed absurdly simple and easy suddenly, and in a burst of self-assurance he thought of going to Paris for a few days.

" 'Spetta un momento," he said to the clerk who was ready to hand him his ticket. Tom walked around his suitcase, thinking of Paris. Overnight. Just to see it, for two days, for instance. It wouldn't matter whether he told Marge or not. He decided abruptly against Paris. He wouldn't be able to relax. He was too eager to get to Mongibello and see about Dickie's belongings.

The white, taut sheets of his berth on the train seemed the most wonderful luxury he had ever known. He caressed them with his hands before he turned the light out. And the clean blue-gray blankets, the spanking efficiency of the little black net over his head—Tom had an ecstatic moment when he thought of all the pleasures that lay before him now with Dickie's money, other beds, tables, seas, ships, suitcases, shirts, years of freedom, years of pleasure. Then he turned the light out and put his head down and almost at once fell asleep, happy, content, and utterly, utterly confident, as he had never been before in his life.

In Naples he stopped in the men's room of the railway station and removed Dickie's toothbrush and hairbrush from the suitcase, and rolled them up in Dickie's raincoat together with his own corduroy jacket and Dickie's blood-spotted trousers. He took the bundle across the street from the station and pressed it into a huge burlap bag of garbage that leaned against an alley wall. Then he breakfasted on caffe latte and a sweet roll at a café on the bus-stop square, and boarded the old eleven o'clock bus for Mongibello.

He stepped off the bus almost squarely in front of Marge, who was in her bathing suit and the loose white jacket she always wore to the beach.

"Where's Dickie?" she asked.

"He's in Rome." Tom smiled easily, absolutely prepared. "He's staying up there for a few days. I came down to get some of his stuff to take up to him."

"Is he staying with somebody?"

"No, just in a hotel." With another smile that was half a good-bye, Tom started up the hill with his suitcase. A moment later he heard Marge's cork-soled sandals trotting after him. Tom waited. "How's everything been in our home sweet home?" he asked.

"Oh, dull. As usual." Marge smiled. She was ill at ease with him. But she followed him into the house—the gate was unlocked, and Tom got the big iron key to the terrace door from its usual place, back of a rotting wooden tub that held earth and a half-dead shrub—and they went onto the terrace together. The table had been moved a little. There was a book on the glider. Marge had been here since they left, Tom thought. He had been gone only three days and nights. It seemed to him that he had been away for a month.

"How's Skippy?" Tom asked brightly, opening the refrigerator, getting out an ice tray. Skippy was a stray dog Marge had acquired a few days ago, an ugly black-and-white bastard that Marge pampered and fed like a doting old maid.

"He went off. I didn't expect him to stay."

"Oh."

"You look like you've had a good time," Marge said, a little wistfully.

"We did." Tom smiled. "Can I fix you a drink?"

"No, thanks. How long do you think Dickie's going to be away?"

"Well—" Tom frowned thoughtfully. "I don't really know. He says he wants to see a lot of art shows up there. I think he's just enjoying a change of scene." Tom poured himself a generous gin and added soda and a lemon slice. "I suppose he'll be back in a week. By the way!" Tom reached for the suitcase, and took out the box of cologne. He had removed the shop's wrapping paper, because it had had blood smears on it. "Your Stradivari. We got it in San Remo."

"Oh, thanks—very much." Marge took it, smiling, and began to open it, carefully, dreamily.

Tom strolled tensely around the terrace with his drink, not saying a word to Marge, waiting for her to go.

"Well—" Marge said finally, coming out on the terrace. "How long are you staying?"

"Where?"

"Here."

"Just overnight. I'll be going up to Rome tomorrow. Probably in the afternoon," he added, because he couldn't get the mail tomorrow until perhaps after two.

"I don't suppose I'll see you again, unless you're at the beach," Marge said with an effort at friendliness. "Have a good time in case I don't see you. And tell Dickie to write a postcard. What hotel is he staying at?"

"Oh—uh—what's the name of it? Near the Piazza di Spagna?"

"The Inghilterra?"

"That's it. But I think he said to use the American Express as a mailing address." She wouldn't try to telephone Dickie, Tom thought. And he could be at the hotel tomorrow to pick up a letter if she wrote. "I'll probably go down to the beach tomorrow morning," Tom said.

"All right. Thanks for the cologne."

"Don't mention it!"

She walked down the path to the iron gate, and out.

Tom picked up the suitcase and ran upstairs to Dickie's bedroom. He slid Dickie's top drawer out: letters, two address books, a couple of little notebooks, a watchchain, loose keys, and some kind of insurance policy. He slid the other drawers out, one by one, and left them open. Shirts, shorts, folded sweaters and disordered socks. In the corner of the room a sloppy mountain of portfolios and old drawing pads. There was a lot to be done. Tom took off all his clothes, ran downstairs naked and took a quick, cool shower, then put on

Dickie's old white duck trousers that were hanging on a nail in the closet.

He started with the top drawer, for two reasons: the recent letters were important in case there were current situations that had to be taken care of immediately, and also because, in case Marge happened to come back this afternoon, it wouldn't look as if he were dismantling the entire house so soon. But at least he could begin, even this afternoon, packing Dickie's biggest suitcases with his best clothes, Tom thought.

Tom was still pottering about the house at midnight. Dickie's suitcases were packed, and now he was assessing how much the house furnishings were worth, what he would bequeath to Marge, and how he would dispose of the rest. Marge could have the damned refrigerator. That ought to please her. The heavy carved chest in the foyer, which Dickie used for his linens, ought to be worth several hundred dollars, Tom thought. Dickie had said it was four hundred years old, when Tom had asked him about it. Cinquecento. He intended to speak to Signor Pucci, the assistant manager of the Miramare, and ask him to act as agent for the sale of the house and the furniture. And the boat, too. Dickie had told him that Signor Pucci did jobs like that for residents of the village.

He had wanted to take all of Dickie's possessions straight away to Rome, but in view of what Marge might think about his taking so much for presumably such a short time, he decided it would be better to pretend that Dickie had later made a decision to move to Rome.

Accordingly, Tom went down to the post office around three the next afternoon, claimed one uninteresting letter for Dickie from a friend in America and nothing for himself, but as he walked slowly back to the house again he imagined that he was reading a letter from Dickie. He imagined the exact words, so that he could quote them to Marge, if he had to, and he even made himself feel the slight surprise he would have felt at Dickie's change of mind.

As soon as he got home he began packing Dickie's best drawings and best linens into the big cardboard box he had gotten from Aldo at the grocery store on the way up the hill. He worked calmly and methodically, expecting Marge to drop in at any minute, but it was after four before she came.

"Still here?" she asked as she came into Dickie's room.

"Yes. I had a letter from Dickie today. He's decided he's going to move to Rome." Tom straightened up and smiled a little, as if it were a surprise to him, too. "He wants me to pick up all his things, all I can handle."

"*Move* to Rome? For how long?"

"I don't know. The rest of the winter apparently, anyway." Tom went on tying canvases.

"He's not coming back all winter?" Marge's voice sounded lost already.

"No. He said he might even sell the house. He said he hadn't decided yet."

"Gosh!—What happened?"

Tom shrugged. "He apparently wants to spend the winter in Rome. He said he was going to write to you. I thought you might have gotten a letter this afternoon, too."

"No."

Silence. Tom kept on working. It occurred to him that he hadn't packed up his own things at all. He hadn't even been into his room.

"He's still going to Cortina, isn't he?" Marge asked.

"No, he's not. He said he was going to write to Freddie and cancel it. But that shouldn't prevent your going." Tom watched her. "By the way, Dickie said he wants you to take the refrigerator. You can probably get somebody to help you move it."

The present of the refrigerator had no effect at all on Marge's stunned face. Tom knew she was wondering whether he was going to live with Dickie or not, and that she was probably concluding, because of his cheerful manner, that he was going to live with him. Tom felt the question creeping up to her lips—she was as transparent as a child to him—then she asked: "Are you going to stay with him in Rome?"

"Maybe for a while. I'll help him get settled. I want to go to Paris this month, then I suppose around the middle of December I'll be going back to the States."

Marge looked crestfallen. Tom knew she was imagining the lonely weeks ahead—even if Dickie did make periodic little visits to Mongibello to see her—the empty Sunday mornings, the lonely dinners. "What's he going to do about Christmas? Do you think he wants to have it here or in Rome?"

Tom said with a trace of irritation, "Well, I don't think here. I have the feeling he wants to be alone."

Now she was shocked to silence, shocked and hurt. Wait till she got the letter he was going to write from Rome, Tom thought. He'd be gentle with her, of course, as gentle as Dickie, but there would be no mistaking that Dickie didn't want to see her again.

A few minutes later, Marge stood up and said good-bye in an absent-minded way. Tom suddenly felt that she might be going to telephone Dickie today. Or maybe even go up to Rome. But what if she did? Dickie could have changed his hotel. And there were enough hotels in Rome to keep her busy for days, even if she came to Rome to find him. When she didn't find him, by telephone or by coming to Rome, she would suppose that he had gone to Paris or to some other city with Tom Ripley.

Tom glanced over the newspaper from Naples for an item about a scuttled boat's having been found near San Remo. *Barca affondata vicino San Remo,* the caption would probably say. And they would make a great to-do over the bloodstains in the boat, if the bloodstains were still there. It was the kind of thing the Italian newspapers loved to write up in their melodramatic journalese: "Giorgio di Stefani, a young fisherman of San Remo, yesterday at three o'clock in the afternoon made a most terrible discovery in two meters of water. A little motorboat, its interior covered with horrible bloodstains . . ." But Tom did not see anything in the paper. Nor had there been anything yesterday. It might take months for the boat to be found, he thought. It might never be found. And if they did find it, how could they know that Dickie Greenleaf and Tom Ripley had taken the boat out together? They had not told their names to the Italian boatkeeper at San Remo. The boatkeeper had given them only a little orange ticket which Tom had had in his pocket, and had later found and destroyed.

Tom left Mongibello by taxi around six o'clock, after an espresso at Giorgio's, where he said good-bye to Giorgio,

Fausto, and several other village acquaintances of his and Dickie's. To all of them he told the same story, that Signor Greenleaf was staying in Rome for the winter, and that he sent his greetings until he saw them again. Tom said that undoubtedly Dickie would be down for a visit before long.

He had had Dickie's linens and paintings crated by the American Express that afternoon, and the boxes sent to Rome along with Dickie's trunk and two heavier suitcases, to be claimed in Rome by Dickie Greenleaf. Tom took his own two suitcases and one other of Dickie's in the taxi with him. He had spoken to Signor Pucci at the Miramare, and had said that there was a possibility that Signor Greenleaf would want to sell his house and furniture, and could Signor Pucci handle it? Signor Pucci had said he would be glad to. Tom had also spoken to Pietro, the dockkeeper, and asked him to be on the lookout for someone who might want to buy the *Pipistrello*, because there was a good chance that Signor Greenleaf would want to get rid of it this winter. Tom said that Signor Greenleaf would let it go for five hundred thousand lire, hardly eight hundred dollars, which was such a bargain for a boat that slept two people, Pietro thought he could sell it in a matter of weeks.

On the train to Rome Tom composed the letter to Marge so carefully that he memorized it in the process, and when he got to the Hotel Hassler he sat down at Dickie's Hermes Baby, which he had brought in one of Dickie's suitcases, and wrote the letter straight off.

Rome
November 28, 19——

Dear Marge,

I've decided to take an apartment in Rome for the winter, just to have a change of scene and get away from old Mongy for a while. I feel a terrific urge to be by myself. I'm sorry it was so sudden and that I didn't get a chance to say good-bye, but actually I'm not far away, and I hope I'll be seeing you now and then. I just didn't feel like going back to pack my stuff, so I threw the burden on Tom.

As to us, it can't harm anything and possibly may improve everything if we don't see each other for a while. I had a terrible feeling I was boring you, though you weren't boring *me*, and please don't think I am running away from anything. On the contrary, Rome should bring me closer to reality. Mongy certainly didn't. Part of my discontent was you. My going away doesn't solve anything, of course, but it will help me to discover how I really feel about you. For this reason, I prefer not to see you for a while, darling, and I hope you'll understand. If you don't—well, you don't, and that's the risk I run. I may go up to Paris for a couple of weeks with Tom, as he's dying to go. That is, unless I start painting right away. Met a painter named Di Massimo whose work I like very much, an old fellow without much money who seems to be very glad to have me as a student if I pay him a little bit. I am going to paint with him in his studio.

The city looks marvelous with its fountains going all night and everybody up all night, contrary to old Mongy. You were on the wrong track about Tom. He's going back to the States soon and I don't care when, though he's really not a bad guy and I don't dislike him. He has nothing to do with us, anyway, and I hope you realize that.

Write me c/o American Express, Rome until I know where I am. Shall let you know when I find an apartment. Meanwhile keep the home fires burning, the refrigerators working and your typewriter also. I'm terribly sorry about Xmas, darling, but I don't think I should see you that soon, and you can hate me or not for that.

> All my love,
> Dickie

Tom had kept his cap on since entering the hotel, and he had given Dickie's passport in at the desk instead of his own, though hotels, he had noticed, never looked at the passport photo, only copied the passport number which was on the front cover. He had signed the register with Dickie's hasty and rather flamboyant signature with the big looping capitals R and G. When he went out to mail the letter he walked to a drugstore several streets away and bought a few items of make-up that he thought he might need. He had fun with the Italian salesgirl, making her think that he was buying them for his wife who had lost her make-up kit, and who was indisposed in the hotel with the usual upset stomach.

He spent that evening practicing Dickie's signature for the bank checks. Dickie's monthly remittance was going to arrive from America in less than ten days.

14.

HE moved the next day to the Hotel Europa, a moderately priced hotel near the Via Veneto, because the Hassler was a trifle flashy, he thought, the kind of hotel that was patronized by visiting movie people, and where Freddie Miles, or people like him who knew Dickie, might choose to stay if they came to Rome.

Tom held imaginary conversations with Marge and Fausto and Freddie in his hotel room. Marge was the most likely to come to Rome, he thought. He spoke to her as Dickie, if he imagined it on the telephone, and as Tom, if he imagined her face to face with him. She might, for instance, pop up to Rome and find his hotel and insist on coming up to his room, in which case he would have to remove Dickie's rings and change his clothing.

"I don't know," he would say to her in Tom's voice. "You know how he is—likes to feel he's getting away from everything. He said I could use his hotel room for a few days, because mine happens to be so badly heated. . . . Oh, he'll be back in a couple of days, or there'll be a postcard from him saying he's all right. He went to some little town with Di Massimo to look at some paintings in a church."

("But you don't know whether he went north or south?")

"I really don't. I guess south. But what good does that do us?"

("It's just my bad luck to miss him, isn't it? Why couldn't he at least have said where he was going?")

"I know. I asked him, too. Looked the room over for a map or anything else that might have shown where he was going. He just called me up three days ago and said I could use his room if I cared to."

It was a good idea to practice jumping into his own character again, because the time might come when he would need to in a matter of seconds, and it was strangely easy to forget the exact timbre of Tom Ripley's voice. He conversed with Marge until the sound of his own voice in his ears was exactly the same as he remembered it.

But mostly he was Dickie, discoursing in a low tone with

Freddie and Marge, and by long distance with Dickie's mother, and with Fausto, and with a stranger at a dinner party, conversing in English and Italian, with Dickie's portable radio turned on so that if a hotel employee passed by in the hall and happened to know that Signor Greenleaf was alone he would not think him an eccentric. Sometimes, if the song on the radio was one that Tom liked, he merely danced by himself, but he danced as Dickie would have with a girl—he had seen Dickie once on Giorgio's terrace, dancing with Marge, and also in the Giardino degli Orangi in Naples—in long strides yet rather stiffly, not what could be called exactly good dancing. Every moment to Tom was a pleasure, alone in his room or walking the streets of Rome, when he combined sightseeing with looking around for an apartment. It was impossible ever to be lonely or bored, he thought, so long as he was Dickie Greenleaf.

They greeted him as Signor Greenleaf at the American Express, where he called for his mail. Marge's first letter said:

Dickie,

Well, it was a bit of a surprise. I wonder what came over you so suddenly in Rome or San Remo or wherever it was? Tom was most mysterious except to say that he would be staying with you. I'll believe he's leaving for America when I see it. At the risk of sticking my neck out, old boy, may I say that *I* don't like that guy? From my point of view or anybody else's he is using you for what you are worth. If you want to make some changes for your own good, for gosh sakes get *him* away from you. All right, he may not be queer. He's just a nothing, which is worse. He isn't normal enough to have *any* kind of sex life, if you know what I mean. However I'm not interested in Tom but in you. Yes, I can bear the few weeks without you, darling, and even Christmas, though I prefer not to think of Christmas. I prefer not to think about you and—as you said—let the feelings come or not. But it's impossible not to think of you here because every inch of the village is haunted with you as far as I'm concerned, and in this house, everywhere I look there is some sign of you, the hedge we planted, the fence we started repairing and never finished, the books I borrowed from you and never returned. And your chair at the table, that's the worst.

To continue with the neck-sticking, I don't say that Tom is going to do anything actively bad to you, but I know that he has a subtly bad influence on you. You act vaguely ashamed of being around him when you *are* around him, do you know that? Did you ever try to analyze it? I thought you were beginning to realize all this in the last few weeks, but now you're with him again and frankly, dear boy, I don't know what to make of it. If you really "don't care when" he takes off, for God's sake send him packing! He'll never help you or anybody else to get straightened out about anything. In fact it's greatly to his interest to keep you muddled and string you along and your father, too.

Thanks loads for the cologne, darling. I'll save it—or most of it—for when I see you next. I haven't got the refrigerator over to my house yet. You can have it, of course, any time you want it back.

Maybe Tom told you that Skippy skipped out. Should I capture a gecko and tie a string around its neck? I have to get to work on the house wall right away before it mildews completely and collapses on me. Wish you were here, darling—of course.

Lots of love and *write*,

XX
Marge

c/o American Express
Rome
Dec. 12, 19——

Dear Mother and Dad,

I'm in Rome looking for an apartment, though I haven't found exactly what I want yet. Apartments here are either too big or too small, and if too big you have to shut off every room but one in winter in order to heat it properly anyway. I'm trying to get a medium-sized, medium-priced place that I can heat completely without spending a fortune for it.

Sorry I've been so bad about letters lately. I hope to do better with the quieter life I'm leading here. I felt I needed a change from Mongibello—as you've both been saying for a long time—so I've moved bag and baggage and may even sell the house and the boat. I've met a wonderful painter called Di Massimo who is willing to give me instruction in his studio. I'm going to work like blazes for a few months and see what happens. A kind of trial period. I realize this doesn't interest you, Dad, but since you're always asking how I spend my time, this is how. I'll be leading a very quiet, studious life until next summer.

Apropos of that, could you send me the latest folders from Burke-Greenleaf? I like to keep up with what you're doing, too, and it's been a long time since I've seen anything.

Mother, I hope you haven't gone to great trouble for my Christmas. I don't really need anything I can think of. How are you feeling? Are you able to get out very much? To the theatre, etc.? How is Uncle Edward now? Send him my regards and keep me posted.

With love,
Dickie

Tom read it over, decided there were probably too many commas, and retyped it patiently and signed it. He had once seen a half-finished letter of Dickie's to his parents in Dickie's typewriter, and he knew Dickie's general style. He knew that Dickie had never taken more than ten minutes writing any letter. If this letter was different, Tom thought, it could be different only in being a little more personal and enthusiastic than usual. He felt rather pleased with the letter when he read it over for the second time. Uncle Edward was a brother of Mrs. Greenleaf, who was ill in an Illinois hospital with some kind of cancer, Tom had learned from the latest letter to Dickie from his mother.

A few days later he was off to Paris by plane. He had called the Inghilterra before he left Rome: no letters or phone calls for Richard Greenleaf. He landed at Orly at five in the afternoon. The passport inspector stamped his passport after only a quick glance at him, though Tom had lightened his hair slightly with a peroxide wash and had forced some waves into it, aided by hair oil, and for the inspector's benefit he had put on the rather tense, rather frowning expression of Dickie's passport photograph. Tom checked in at the Hôtel du Quai-Voltaire, which had been recommended to him by some Americans with whom he had struck up an acquaintance at a Rome café, as being conveniently located and not too full of Americans. Then he went out for a stroll in the raw, foggy December evening. He walked with his head up and a smile on his face. It was the atmosphere of the city that he loved, the atmosphere that he had always heard about, crooked streets, gray-fronted houses with skylights, noisy car horns, and everywhere public urinals and columns with brightly colored theatre notices on them. He wanted to let the atmosphere seep in slowly, perhaps for several days, before he visited the Louvre or went up in the Eiffel Tower or anything like that. He bought a *Figaro*, sat down at a table in the Dôme, and ordered a fine à l'eau, because Dickie had once said that fine à l'eau was his usual drink in France. Tom's French was limited, but so was Dickie's, Tom knew. Some interesting people stared at him through the glass-enclosed front of the café, but no one came in to speak to him. Tom was prepared for someone to get up from one of the tables at any moment, and come over and say, "Dickie Greenleaf! Is it really you?"

He had done so little artificially to change his appearance, but his very expression, Tom thought, was like Dickie's now. He wore a smile that was dangerously welcoming to a stranger, a smile more fit to greet an old friend or a lover. It was Dickie's best and most typical smile when he was in a good humor. Tom was in a good humor. It was Paris. *Wonderful* to sit in a famous café, and to think of tomorrow and tomorrow and tomorrow being Dickie Greenleaf! The cuff links, the white silk shirts, even the old clothes—the worn brown belt with the brass buckle, the old brown grain-leather shoes, the kind advertised in *Punch* as lasting a lifetime, the old mustard-colored coat sweater with the sagging pockets, they were all his and he loved them all. And the black fountain pen with little gold initials. And the wallet, a well-worn alligator wallet from Gucci's. And there was plenty of money to go in it.

By the next afternoon he had been invited to a party in the Avenue Kléber by some people—a French girl and an American young man—with whom he had started a conversation in a large café-restaurant on the Boulevard Saint-Germain. The party consisted of thirty or forty people, most of them middle-aged, standing around rather frigidly in a huge, chilly, formal apartment. In Europe, Tom gathered, inadequate heating was a hallmark of chic in winter, like the iceless martini in summer. He had moved to a more expensive hotel in Rome, finally, in order to be warmer, and had found that the more expensive hotel was even colder. In a gloomy, old-fashioned way the house was chic, Tom supposed. There were a butler and a maid, a vast table of pâtés en croûte, sliced turkey, and petits fours, and quantities of champagne, although the upholstery of the sofa and the long drapes at the windows were threadbare and rotting with age, and he had seen mouseholes in the hall by the elevator. At least half a dozen of the guests he had been presented to were counts and countesses. An

American informed Tom that the young man and the girl who had invited him were going to be married, and that her parents were not enthusiastic. There was an atmosphere of strain in the big room, and Tom made an effort to be as pleasant as possible to everyone, even the severer-looking French people, to whom he could say little more than "C'est très agréable, n'est-ce pas?" He did his very best, and won at least a smile from the French girl who had invited him. He considered himself lucky to be there. How many Americans alone in Paris could get themselves invited to a French home after only a week or so in the city? The French were especially slow in inviting strangers to their homes, Tom had always heard. Not a single one of the Americans seemed to know his name. Tom felt completely comfortable, as he had never felt before at any party that he could remember. He behaved as he had always wanted to behave at a party. This was the clean slate he had thought about on the boat coming over from America. This was the real annihilation of his past and of himself, Tom Ripley, who was made up of that past, and his rebirth as a completely new person. One Frenchwoman and two of the Americans invited him to parties, but Tom declined with the same reply to all of them: "Thank you very much, but I'm leaving Paris tomorrow."

It wouldn't do to become too friendly with any of these, Tom thought. One of them might know somebody who knew Dickie very well, someone who might be at the next party.

At eleven-fifteen, when he said good-bye to his hostess and to her parents, they looked very sorry to see him go. But he wanted to be at Notre Dame by midnight. It was Christmas Eve.

The girl's mother asked his name again.

"Monsieur Granelafe," the girl repeated for her. "Deekie Granelafe. Correct?"

"Correct," Tom said, smiling.

Just as he reached the downstairs hall he remembered Freddie Miles' party at Cortina. December second. Nearly a month ago! He had meant to write to Freddie to say that he wasn't coming. Had Marge gone, he wondered? Freddie would think it very strange that he hadn't written to say he wasn't coming, and Tom hoped Marge had told Freddie, at least. He must write Freddie at once. There was a Florence address for Freddie in Dickie's address book. It was a slip, but nothing serious, Tom thought. He just mustn't let such a thing happen again.

He walked out into the darkness and turned in the direction of the illuminated, bone-white Arc de Triomphe. It was strange to feel so alone, and yet so much a part of things, as he had felt at the party. He felt it again, standing on the outskirts of the crowd that filled the square in front of Notre Dame. There was such a crowd he couldn't possibly have got into the cathedral, but the amplifiers carried the music clearly to all parts of the square. French Christmas carols whose names he didn't know. "Silent Night." A solemn carol, and then a lively, babbling one. The chanting of male voices. Frenchmen near him removed their hats. Tom removed his. He stood tall and straight, sober-faced, yet ready to smile if anyone had addressed him. He felt as he had felt on the ship, only more intensely, full of good will, a gentleman, with nothing in his past to blemish his character. He was Dickie, good-natured, naïve Dickie, with a smile for everyone and a thousand francs for anyone who asked him. An old man did ask him for money as Tom was leaving the cathedral square, and he gave him a crisp blue thousand-franc bill. The old man's face exploded in a smile, and he tipped his hat.

Tom felt a little hungry, though he rather liked the idea of going to bed hungry tonight. He would spend an hour or so with his Italian conversation book, he thought, then go to bed. Then he remembered that he had decided to try to gain about five pounds, because Dickie's clothes were just a trifle loose on him and Dickie looked heavier than he in the face, so he stopped at a bar-tabac and ordered a ham sandwich on long crusty bread and a glass of hot milk, because a man next to him at the counter was drinking hot milk. The milk was almost tasteless, pure and chastening, as Tom imagined a wafer tasted in church.

He came down in a leisurely way from Paris, stopping overnight in Lyon and also in Arles to see the places that Van Gogh had painted there. He maintained his cheerful equanimity in the face of atrociously bad weather. In Arles, the rain borne on the violent mistral soaked him through as he tried to discover the exact spots where Van Gogh had stood to paint from. He had bought a beautiful book of Van Gogh reproductions in Paris, but he could not take the book out in the rain, and he had to make a dozen trips back to his hotel to verify the scenes. He looked over Marseille, found it drab except for the Cannebière, and moved on eastward by train, stopping for a day in St. Tropez, Cannes, Nice, Monte Carlo, all the places he had heard of and felt such affinity for when he saw them, though in the month of December they were overcast by gray winter clouds, and the gay crowds were not there, even on New Year's Eve in Menton. Tom put the people there in his imagination, men and women in evening clothes descending the broad steps of the gambling palace in Monte Carlo, people in bright bathing costumes, light and brilliant as a Dufy watercolor, walking under the palms of the Boulevard des Anglais at Nice. People—American, English, French, German, Swedish, Italian. Romance, disappointment, quarrels, reconciliations, murder. The Côte d'Azur excited him as no other place he had yet seen in the world excited him. And it was so tiny, really, this curve in the Mediterranean coastline with the wonderful names strung like beads— Toulon, Fréjus, St. Rafaël, Cannes, Nice, Menton, and then San Remo.

There were two letters from Marge when he got back to Rome on the fourth of January. She was giving up her house on the first of March, she said. She had not quite finished the first draft of her book, but she was sending three-quarters of it with all the photographs to the American publisher who had been interested in her idea when she wrote him about it last summer. She wrote:

When am I going to see you? I hate passing up a summer in Europe after I've weathered another awful winter, but I think I'll go home early in March. Yes, I'm *homesick*, finally, *really*. Darling, it would be so wonderful if we could go home on the same boat together. Is there a possibility? I don't suppose there *is*. You're not going back to the U.S. even for a short visit this winter?

I was thinking of sending all my stuff (eight pieces of luggage, two trunks, three boxes of books and miscellaneous!) by slow boat from Naples and coming up through Rome and if you were in the mood we could at least go up the coast again and see Forte dei Marmi and

Viareggio and the other spots we like—a last look. I'm not in the mood to care about the weather, which I know will be *horrid*. I wouldn't ask you to accompany me to Marseille, where I catch the boat, but from *Genoa*??? What do you think? . . .

The other letter was more reserved. Tom knew why: he had not sent her even a postcard for nearly a month. She said:

Have changed my mind about the Riviera. Maybe this damp weather has taken away my enterprise or my book has. Anyway, I'm leaving from Naples on an earlier boat—the *Constitution* on Feb. 28th. Imagine—back to America as soon as I step aboard. American food, Americans, dollars for drinks and the horseraces— Darling, I'm sorry not to be seeing you, as I gather from your silence you still don't want to see me, so don't give it a thought. Consider me off your hands.

Of course I do hope I see you again, in the States or anywhere else. Should you possibly be inspired to make a trip down to Mongy before the 28th, you know damned well you are welcome.

As ever,

Marge

P.S. I don't even know if you're still in Rome.

Tom could see her in tears as she wrote it. He had an impulse to write her a very considerate letter, saying he had just come back from Greece, and had she gotten his two postcards? But it was safer, Tom thought, to let her leave without being sure where he was. He wrote her nothing.

The only thing that made him uneasy, and that was not very uneasy, was the possibility of Marge's coming up to see him in Rome before he could get settled in an apartment. If she combed the hotels she could find him, but she could never find him in an apartment. Well-to-do Americans didn't have to report their places of residence at the questura, though, according to the stipulations of the Permesso di Soggiorno, one was supposed to register every change of address with the police. Tom had talked with an American resident of Rome who had an apartment and who had said he never bothered with the questura, and it never bothered him. If Marge did come up to Rome suddenly, Tom had a lot of his own clothing hanging ready in the closet. The only thing he had changed about himself, physically, was his hair, but that could always be explained as being the effect of the sun. He wasn't really worried. Tom had at first amused himself with an eyebrow pencil—Dickie's eyebrows were longer and turned up a little at the outer edges—and with a touch of putty at the end of his nose to make it longer and more pointed, but he abandoned these as too likely to be noticed. The main thing about impersonation, Tom thought, was to maintain the mood and temperament of the person one was impersonating, and to assume the facial expressions that went with them. The rest fell into place.

On the tenth of January Tom wrote Marge that he was back in Rome after three weeks in Paris alone, that Tom had left Rome a month ago, saying he was going up to Paris and from there to America though he hadn't run into Tom in Paris, and that he had not yet found an apartment in Rome but he was looking and would let her know his address as soon as he had one. He thanked her extravagantly for the Christmas package: she had sent the white sweater with the red V stripes that she had been knitting and trying on Dickie for size since October, as well as an art book of quattrocento painting and a leather shaving kit with his initials, H.R.G., on the lid. The package had arrived only on January sixth, which was the main reason for Tom's letter: he didn't want her to think he hadn't claimed it, imagine that he had vanished into thin air, and then start a search for him. He asked if she had received a package from him? He had mailed it from Paris, and he supposed it was late. He apologized. He wrote:

I'm painting again with Di Massimo and am reasonably pleased. I miss you, too, but if you can still bear with my experiment, I'd prefer not to see you for several more weeks (unless you do suddenly go home in February, which I still doubt!) by which time you may not care to see me again. Regards to Giorgio and wife and Fausto if he's still there and Pietro down at the dock . . .

It was a letter in the absent-minded and faintly lugubrious tone of all Dickie's letters, a letter that could not be called warm or unwarm, and that said essentially nothing.

Actually he had found an apartment in a large apartment

house in the Via Imperiale near the Pincian Gate, and had signed a year's lease for it, though he did not intend to spend most of his time in Rome, much less the winter. He only wanted a home, a base somewhere, after years of not having any. And Rome was chic. Rome was part of his new life. He wanted to be able to say in Majorca or Athens or Cairo or wherever he was: "Yes, I live in Rome. I keep an apartment there." "Keep" was the word for apartments among the international set. You kept an apartment in Europe the way you kept a garage in America. He also wanted his apartment to be elegant, though he intended to have the minimum of people up to see him, and he hated the idea of having a telephone, even an unlisted telephone, but he decided it was more of a safety measure than a menace, so he had one installed. The apartment had a large living room, a bedroom, a kind of sitting room, kitchen, and bath. It was furnished somewhat ornately, but it suited the respectable neighborhood and the respectable life he intended to lead. The rent was the equivalent of a hundred and seventy-five dollars a month in winter including heat, and a hundred and twenty-five in summer.

Marge replied with an ecstatic letter saying she had just received the beautiful silk blouse from Paris which she hadn't expected *at all* and it fitted to perfection. She said she had had Fausto and the Cecchis for Christmas dinner at her house and the turkey had been divine, with marrons and giblet gravy and plum pudding and blah blah blah and everything but *him*. And what was he doing and thinking about? And was he happier? And that Fausto would look him up on his way to Milan if he sent an address in the next few days, otherwise leave a message for Fausto at the American Express, saying where Fausto could find him.

Tom supposed her good humor was due mostly to the fact that she now thought Tom had departed for America via Paris. Along with Marge's letter came one from Signor Pucci, saying that he had sold three pieces of his furniture for a hundred and fifty thousand lire in Naples, and that he had a prospective buyer for the boat, a certain Anastasio Martino of Mongibello, who had promised to pay the first down payment within a week, but that the house probably couldn't be sold until summer when the Americans began coming in again. Less fifteen per cent for Signor Pucci's commission, the furniture sale amounted to two hundred and ten dollars, and Tom celebrated that night by going to a Roman nightclub and ordering a superb dinner which he ate in elegant solitude at a candlelit table for two. He did not at all mind dining and going to the theatre alone. It gave him the opportunity to concentrate on being Dickie Greenleaf. He broke his bread as Dickie did, thrust his fork into his mouth with his left hand as Dickie did, gazed off at the other tables and at the dancers in such a profound and benevolent trance that the waiter had to speak to him a couple of times to get his attention. Some people waved to him from a table, and Tom recognized them as one of the American couples he had met at the Christmas Eve party in Paris. He made a sign of greeting in return. He even remembered their name, Souders. He did not look at them again during the evening, but they left before he did and stopped by his table to say hello.

"All by yourself?" the man asked. He looked a little tipsy.

"Yes. I have a yearly date here with myself," Tom replied. "I celebrate a certain anniversary."

The American nodded a little blankly, and Tom could see that he was stymied for anything intelligent to say, as uneasy as any small-town American in the presence of cosmopolitan poise and sobriety, money and good clothes, even if the clothes were on another American.

"You said you were living in Rome, didn't you?" his wife asked. "You know, I think we've forgotten your name, but we remember you very well from Christmas Eve."

"Greenleaf," Tom replied. "Richard Greenleaf."

"*Oh*, yes!" she said, relieved. "Do you have an apartment here?"

She was all ready to take down his address in her memory. "I'm staying at a hotel at the moment, but I'm planning to move into an apartment any day, as soon as the decorating's finished. I'm at the Elisio. Why don't you give me a ring?"

"We'd love to. We're on our way to Majorca in three more days, but that's plenty of time!"

"Love to see you," Tom said. "Buona sera!"

Alone again, Tom returned to his private reveries. He ought to open a bank account for Tom Ripley, he thought, and from time to time put a hundred dollars or so into it. Dickie Green-leaf had two banks, one in Naples and one in New York, with about five thousand dollars in each account. He might open the Ripley account with a couple of thousand, and put into it the hundred and fifty thousand lire from the Mongibello fur-niture. After all, he had two people to take care of.

15.

HE visited the Capitoline and the Villa Borghese, explored the Forum thoroughly, and took six Italian lessons from an old man in his neighborhood who had a tutoring sign in his window, and to whom Tom gave a false name. After the sixth lesson, Tom thought that his Italian was on a par with Dickie's. He remembered verbatim several sentences that Dickie had said at one time or another which he now knew were incorrect. For example, "Ho paura che non c'e arrivata, Giorgio," one evening in Giorgio's, when they had been wait-ing for Marge and she had been late. It should have been "sia arrivata" in the subjunctive after an expression of fearing. Dickie had never used the subjunctive as often as it should be used in Italian. Tom studiously kept himself from learning the proper uses of the subjunctive.

Tom bought dark red velvet for the drapes in his living room, because the drapes that had come with the apartment offended him. When he had asked Signora Buffi, the wife of the house superintendent, if she knew of a seamstress who could make them up, Signora Buffi had offered to make them herself. Her price was two thousand lire, hardly more than three dollars. Tom forced her to take five thousand. He bought several minor items to embellish his apartment, though he never asked anyone up—with the exception of one attractive but not very bright young man, an American, whom he had met in the Café Greco when the young man had asked him how to get to the Hotel Excelsior from there. The Excelsior was on the way to Tom's house, so Tom asked him to come up for a drink. Tom had only wanted to impress him for an hour and then say good-bye to him forever, which he did, after serving him his best brandy and strolling about his apartment discoursing on the pleasures of life in Rome. The young man was leaving for Munich the following day.

Tom carefully avoided the American residents of Rome who might expect him to come to their parties and ask them to his in return, though he loved to chat with Americans and Italians in the Café Greco and in the students' restaurants in the Via Margutta. He told his name only to an Italian painter named Carlino, whom he met in a Via Margutta tavern, told him also that he painted and was studying with a painter called Di Massimo. If the police ever investigated Dickie's activities in Rome, perhaps long after Dickie had disappeared and become Tom Ripley again, this one Italian painter could be relied upon to say that he knew Dickie Greenleaf had been painting in Rome in January. Carlino had never heard of Di Massimo, but Tom described him so vividly that Carlino would probably never forget him.

He felt alone, yet not at all lonely. It was very much like the feeling on Christmas Eve in Paris, a feeling that everyone was watching him, as if he had an audience made up of the entire world, a feeling that kept him on his mettle, because to make a mistake would be catastrophic. Yet he felt absolutely confident he would not make a mistake. It gave his existence a peculiar, delicious atmosphere of purity, like that, Tom thought, which a fine actor probably feels when he plays an important role on a stage with the conviction that the role he is playing could not be played better by anyone else. He was himself and yet not himself. He felt blameless and free, despite the fact that he consciously controlled every move he made. But he no longer felt tired after several hours of it, as he had at first. He had no need to relax when he was alone. Now, from the moment when he got out of bed and went to brush his teeth, he was Dickie, brushing his teeth with his right elbow jutted out, Dickie rotating the eggshell on his spoon for the last bite, Dickie invariably putting back the first tie he pulled off the rack and selecting a second. He had even produced a painting in Dickie's manner.

By the end of January Tom thought that Fausto must have come and gone through Rome, though Marge's last letters had not mentioned him. Marge wrote, care of the American

Express, about once a week. She asked if he needed any socks or a muffler, because she had plenty of time to knit, besides working on her book. She always put in a funny anecdote about somebody they knew in the village, just so Dickie wouldn't think she was eating her heart out for him, though obviously she was, and obviously she wasn't going to leave for the States in February without making another desperate try for him in person, Tom thought, hence the investments of the long letters and the knitted socks and muffler which Tom knew were coming, even though he hadn't replied to her letters. Her letters repelled him. He disliked even touching them, and after he glanced through them he tore them up and dropped them into the garbage.

He wrote finally:

I'm giving up the idea of an apartment in Rome for the time being. Di Massimo is going to Sicily for several months, and I may go with him and go on somewhere from there. My plans are vague, but they have the virtue of freedom and they suit my present mood.

Don't send me any socks, Marge. I really don't need a thing. Wish you much luck with "Mongibello."

He had a ticket for Majorca—by train to Naples, then the boat from Naples to Palma over the night of January thirty-first and February first. He had bought two new suitcases from Gucci's, the best leather goods store in Rome, one a large, soft suitcase of antelope hide, the other a neat tan canvas with brown leather straps. Both bore Dickie's initials. He had thrown the shabbier of his own two suitcases away, and the remaining one he kept in a closet of his apartment, full of his own clothes, in case of an emergency. But Tom was not expecting any emergencies. The scuttled boat in San Remo had never been found. Tom looked through the papers every day for something about it.

While Tom was packing his suitcases one morning his doorbell rang. He supposed it was a solicitor of some kind, or a mistake. He had no name on his doorbell, and had told the superintendent that he did not want his name on the doorbell because he didn't like people to drop in on him. It rang for the second time, and Tom still ignored it, and went on with his lackadaisical packing. He loved to pack, and he took a long time about it, a whole day or two days, laying Dickie's clothes affectionately into suitcases, now and then trying on a good-looking shirt or a jacket in front of the mirror. He was standing in front of the mirror, buttoning a blue-and-white seahorse-patterned sport shirt of Dickie's that he had never worn, when there came a knock at his door.

It crossed his mind that it might be Fausto, that it would be just like Fausto to hunt him down in Rome and try to surprise him.

That was silly, he told himself. But his hands were cool with sweat as he went to the door. He felt faint, and the absurdity of his faintness, plus the danger of keeling over and being found prostrate on the floor, made him wrench the door open with both hands, though he opened it only a few inches.

"Hello!" the American voice said out of the semidarkness of the hall. "Dickie? It's Freddie!"

Tom took a step back, holding the door open. "He's— Won't you come in? He's not here right now. He should be back a little later."

Freddie Miles came in, looking around. His ugly, freckled face gawked in every direction. How in hell had he found the place, Tom wondered. Tom slipped his rings off quickly and pocketed them. And what else? He glanced around the room.

"You're staying with him?" Freddie asked with that wall-eyed stare that made his face look idiotic and rather scared.

"Oh, no. I'm just staying here for a few hours," Tom said, casually removing the seahorse shirt. He had another shirt on under it. "Dickie's out for lunch. Otello's, I think he said. He should be back around three at the latest." One of the Buffis must have let Freddie in, Tom thought, and told him which bell to press, and told him Signor Greenleaf was in, too. Freddie had probably said he was an old friend of Dickie's. Now he would have to get Freddie out of the house without running into Signora Buffi downstairs, because she always sang out, "Buon' giorno, Signor Greenleaf!"

"I met you in Mongibello, didn't I?" Freddie asked. "Aren't you Tom? I thought you were coming to Cortina."

"I couldn't make it, thanks. How was Cortina?"

"Oh, fine. What happened to Dickie?"

"Didn't he write to you? He decided to spend the winter in Rome. He told me he'd written to you."

"Not a word—unless he wrote to Florence. But I was in Salzburg, and he had my address." Freddie half sat on Tom's long table, rumpling the green silk runner. He smiled. "Marge told me he'd moved to Rome, but she didn't have any address except the American Express. It was only by the damnedest luck I found his apartment. I ran into somebody at the Greco last night who just happened to know his address. What's his idea of—"

"Who?" Tom asked. "An American?"

"No, an Italian fellow. Just a young kid." Freddie was looking at Tom's shoes. "You've got the same kind of shoes Dickie and I have. They wear like iron, don't they? I bought my pair in London eight years ago."

They were Dickie's grain-leather shoes. "These came from America," Tom said. "Can I offer you a drink or would you rather try to catch Dickie at Otello's? Do you know where it is? There's not much use in your waiting, because he generally takes till three with his lunches. I'm going out soon myself."

Freddie had strolled toward the bedroom and stopped, looking at the suitcases on the bed. "Is Dickie leaving for somewhere or did he just get here?" Freddie asked, turning.

"He's leaving. Didn't Marge tell you? He's going to Sicily for a while."

"When?"

"Tomorrow. Or late tonight, I'm not quite sure."

"Say, what's the matter with Dickie lately?" Freddie asked, frowning. "What's the idea of all the seclusion?"

"He says he's been working pretty hard this winter," Tom said in an offhand tone. "He seems to want privacy, but as far as I know he's still on good terms with everybody, including Marge."

Freddie smiled again, unbuttoning his big polo coat. "He's not going to stay on good terms with me if he stands me up a few more times. Are you sure he's on good terms with Marge? I got the idea from her that they'd had a quarrel. I thought maybe that was why they didn't go to Cortina." Freddie looked at him expectantly.

"Not that I know of." Tom went to the closet to get his jacket, so that Freddie would know he wanted to leave, then realized just in time that the gray flannel jacket that matched his trousers might be recognizable as Dickie's, if Freddie knew Dickie's suit. Tom reached for a jacket of his own and for his own overcoat that were hanging at the extreme left of the closet. The shoulders of the overcoat looked as if the coat had been on a hanger for weeks, which it had. Tom turned around and saw Freddie staring at the silver identification bracelet on his left wrist. It was Dickie's bracelet, which Tom had never seen him wearing, but had found in Dickie's stud box. Freddie was looking at it as if he had seen it before. Tom put on his overcoat casually.

Freddie was looking at him now with a different expression, with a little surprise. Tom knew what Freddie was thinking. He stiffened, sensing danger. You're not out of the woods yet, he told himself. You're not out of the house yet.

"Ready to go?" Tom asked.

"You do live here, don't you?"

"No!" Tom protested, smiling. The ugly, freckle-blotched face stared at him from under the garish thatch of red hair. If they could only get out without running into Signora Buffi downstairs, Tom thought. "Let's go."

"Dickie's loaded you up with all his jewelry, I see."

Tom couldn't think of a single thing to say, a single joke to make. "Oh, it's a loan," Tom said in his deepest voice. "Dickie got tired of wearing it, so he told me to wear it for a while." He meant the identification bracelet, but there was also the silver clip on his tie, he realized, with the G on it. Tom had bought the tieclip himself. He could feel the belligerence growing in Freddie Miles as surely as if his huge body were generating a heat that he could feel across the room. Freddie was the kind of ox who might beat up somebody he thought was a pansy, especially if the conditions were as propitious as these. Tom was afraid of his eyes.

"Yes, I'm ready to go," Freddie said grimly, getting up. He walked to the door and turned with a swing of his broad shoulders. "That's the Otello not far from the Inghilterra?"

"Yes," Tom said. "He's supposed to be there by one o'clock."

Freddie nodded. "Nice to see you again," he said unpleasantly, and closed the door.

Tom whispered a curse. He opened the door slightly and listened to the quick *tap-tap—tap-tap* of Freddie's shoes descending the stairs. He wanted to make sure Freddie got out without speaking to one of the Buffis again. Then he heard Freddie's "Buon' giorno, signora." Tom leaned over the stairwell. Three stories down, he could see part of Freddie's coat-sleeve. He was talking in Italian with Signora Buffi. The woman's voice came more clearly.

". . . only Signor Greenleaf," she was saying. "No, only one. . . . Signor Chi? . . . No, signor. . . . I do not think he has gone out today at all, but I could be wrong!" She laughed.

Tom twisted the stair rail in his hands as if it were Freddie's neck. Then Tom heard Freddie's footsteps running up the stairs. Tom stepped back into the apartment and closed the door. He could go on insisting that he didn't live here, that Dickie was at Otello's, or that he didn't know where Dickie was, but Freddie wouldn't stop now until he had found Dickie. Or Freddie would drag him downstairs and ask Signora Buffi who he was.

Freddie knocked on the door. The knob turned. It was locked.

Tom picked up a heavy glass ashtray. He couldn't get his hand across it, and he had to hold it by the edge. He tried to think just for two seconds more: wasn't there another way out? What would he do with the body? He couldn't think. This was the only way out. He opened the door with his left hand. His right hand with the ashtray was drawn back and down.

Freddie came into the room. "Listen, would you mind telling—"

The curved edge of the ashtray hit the middle of his forehead. Freddie looked dazed. Then his knees bent and he went down like a bull hit between the eyes with a hammer. Tom kicked the door shut. He slammed the edge of the ashtray into the back of Freddie's neck. He hit the neck again and again, terrified that Freddie might be only pretending and that one of his huge arms might suddenly circle his legs and pull him down. Tom struck his head a glancing blow, and blood came. Tom cursed himself. He ran and got a towel from the bathroom and put it under Freddie's head. Then he felt Freddie's wrist for a pulse. There was one, faint, and it seemed to flutter away as he touched it as if the pressure of his own fingers stilled it. In the next second it was gone. Tom listened for any sound behind the door. He imagined Signora Buffi standing behind the door with the hesitant smile she always had when she felt she was interrupting. But there wasn't any sound. There hadn't been any loud sound, he thought, either from the ashtray or when Freddie fell. Tom looked down at Freddie's mountainous form on the floor and felt a sudden disgust and a sense of helplessness.

It was only twelve-forty, hours until dark. He wondered if Freddie had people waiting for him anywhere? Maybe in a car downstairs? He searched Freddie's pockets. A wallet. The American passport in the inside breast pocket of the overcoat. Mixed Italian and some other kind of coins. A keycase. There were two car keys on a ring that said FIAT. He searched the wallet for a license. There it was, with all the particulars: FIAT 1400 nero–convertible–1955. He could find it if it was in the neighborhood. He searched every pocket, and the pockets in the buff-colored vest, for a garage ticket, but he found none. He went to the front window, then nearly smiled because it was so simple: there stood the black convertible across the street almost directly in front of the house. He could not be sure, but he thought there was no one in it.

He suddenly knew what he was going to do. He set about arranging the room, bringing out the gin and vermouth bottles from his liquor cabinet, and on second thought the pernod because it smelled so much stronger. He set the bottles on the long table and mixed a martini in a tall glass with a couple of ice cubes in it, drank a little of it so that the glass would be soiled, then poured some of it into another glass, took it over to Freddie and crushed his limp fingers around it and carried it back to the table. He looked at the wound, and found that it had stopped bleeding or was stopping and had not run through the towel onto the floor. He propped Freddie up against the wall, and poured some straight gin from the bottle down his throat. It didn't go down very well, most of it went onto his shirtfront, but Tom didn't think the Italian police would actually make a blood test to see how drunk Freddie had been. Tom let his eyes rest absently on Freddie's limp, messy face for a moment, and his stomach contracted sickeningly and he quickly looked away. He mustn't do that again. His head had begun ringing as if he were going to faint.

That'd be a fine thing, Tom thought as he wobbled across the room toward the window, to faint now! He frowned at the black car down below, and breathed the fresh air in deeply. He wasn't going to faint, he told himself. He knew exactly what he was going to do. At the last minute, the pernod, for both of them. Two other glasses with their fingerprints and pernod. And the ashtrays must be full. Freddie smoked Chesterfields. Then the Appian Way. One of those dark places behind the tombs. There weren't any street lights for long stretches on the Appian Way. Freddie's wallet would be missing. Objective: robbery.

He had hours of time, but he didn't stop until the room was ready, the dozen lighted Chesterfields and the dozen or so Lucky Strikes burnt down and stabbed out in the ashtrays, and a glass of pernod broken and only half cleaned up from the bathroom tiles, and the curious thing was that as he set his scene so carefully, he pictured having hours more time to clean it up—say between nine this evening when the body might be found, and midnight, when the police just might decide he was worth questioning, because somebody just might have known that Freddie Miles was going to call on Dickie Greenleaf today—and he knew that he *would* have it all cleaned up by eight o'clock, probably, because according to the story he was going to tell, Freddie would have left his house by seven (as indeed Freddie was going to leave his house by seven), and Dickie Greenleaf was a fairly tidy young man, even with a few drinks in him. But the point of the messy house was that the messiness substantiated merely for his own benefit the story that he was going to tell, and that therefore he had to believe himself.

And he would still leave for Naples and Palma at ten-thirty tomorrow morning, unless for some reason the police detained him. If he saw in the newspaper tomorrow morning that the body had been found, and the police did not try to contact him, it was only decent that he should volunteer to tell them that Freddie Miles had been at his house until late afternoon, Tom thought. But it suddenly occurred to him that a doctor might be able to tell that Freddie had been dead since noon. And he couldn't get Freddie out now, not in broad daylight. No, his only hope was that the body wouldn't be found for so many hours that a doctor couldn't tell exactly how long he had been dead. And he must try to get out of the house without *anybody* seeing him—whether he could carry Freddie down with a fair amount of ease like a passed-out drunk or not—so that if he had to make any statement, he could say that Freddie left the house around four or five in the afternoon.

He dreaded the five- or six-hour wait until nightfall so much that for a few moments he thought he *couldn't* wait. That mountain on the floor! And he hadn't wanted to kill him at all. It had been so unnecessary. Freddie and his stinking, filthy suspicions. Tom was trembling, sitting on the edge of a chair cracking his knuckles. He wanted to go out and take a walk, but he was afraid to leave the body lying here. There had to be noise, of course, if he and Freddie were supposed to be talking and drinking all afternoon. Tom turned the radio on to a station that played dance music. He could have a drink, at least. That was part of the act. He made another couple of martinis with ice in the glass. He didn't even want it, but he drank it.

The gin only intensified the same thoughts he had had. He stood looking down at Freddie's long, heavy body in the polo coat that was crumpled under him, that he hadn't the energy or the heart to straighten out, though it annoyed him, and thinking how sad, stupid, clumsy, dangerous and unnecessary his death had been, and how brutally unfair to Freddie. Of course, one could loathe Freddie, too. A selfish, stupid bastard, who had sneered at one of his best friends—Dickie certainly was one of his best friends—just because he suspected him of sexual deviation. Tom laughed at that phrase "sexual deviation." Where was the sex? Where was the deviation? He looked at Freddie and said low and bitterly: "Freddie Miles, you're a victim of your own dirty mind."

16.

HE waited after all until nearly eight, because around seven there were always more people coming in and out of the house than at other times. At ten to eight, he strolled downstairs to make sure that Signora Buffi was not pottering around in the hall and that her door was not open, and to make sure there really was no one in Freddie's car, though he had gone down in the middle of the afternoon to look at the car and see if it was Freddie's. He tossed Freddie's polo coat into the back seat. He came back upstairs, knelt down and pulled Freddie's arm around his neck, set his teeth, and lifted. He staggered, jerking the flaccid weight higher on his shoulder. He had lifted Freddie earlier that afternoon, just to see if he could, and he had seemed barely able to walk two steps in the room with Freddie's pounds pressing his own feet against the floor, and Freddie was exactly as heavy now, but the difference was that he knew he had to get him out now. He let Freddie's feet drag to relieve some of his weight, managed to pull his door shut with his elbow, then began to descend the stairs. Halfway down the first flight, he stopped, hearing someone come out of an apartment on the second floor. He waited until the person had gone down the stairs and out the front door, then recommenced his slow, bumping descent. He had pulled a hat of Dickie's well down over Freddie's head so that the bloodstained hair would not show. On a mixture of gin and pernod, which he had been drinking for the last hour, Tom had gotten himself to a precisely calculated state of intoxication in which he thought he could move with a certain nonchalance and smoothness and at the same time be courageous and even foolhardly enough to take chances without flinching. The first chance, the worst thing that could happen, was that he might simply collapse under Freddie's weight before he got him to the car. He had sworn that he would not stop to rest going down the stairs. He didn't. And nobody else came out of any of the apartments, and nobody came in the front door. During the hours upstairs, Tom had imagined so tortuously everything that might happen—Signora Buffi or her husband coming out of their apartment just as he reached the bottom of the stairs, or himself fainting so that both he and Freddie would be discovered sprawled on the stairs together, or being unable to pick Freddie up again if he had to put him down to rest—imagined it all with such intensity, writhing upstairs in his apartment, that to have descended all the stairs without a single one of his imaginings happening made him feel he was gliding down under a magical protection of some kind, with ease in spite of the mass on his shoulder.

He looked out the glass of the two front doors. The street looked normal: a man was walking on the opposite sidewalk, but there was always someone walking on one sidewalk or the other. He opened the first door with one hand, kicked it aside and dragged Freddie's feet through. Between the doors, he shifted Freddie to the other shoulder, rolling his head under Freddie's body, and for a second a certain pride went through him at his own strength, until the ache in his relaxing arm staggered him with its pain. The arm was too tired even to circle Freddie's body. He set his teeth harder and staggered down the four front steps, banging his hip against the stone newel post.

A man approaching him on the sidewalk slowed his steps as if he were going to stop, but he went on.

If anyone came over, Tom thought, he would blow such a breath of pernod in his face there wouldn't be any reason to ask what was the matter. Damn them, damn them, damn them, he said to himself as he jolted down the curb. Passersby, innocent passersby. Four of them now. But only two of them so much as glanced at him, he thought. He paused a moment for a car to pass. Then with a few quick steps and a heave he thrust Freddie's head and one shoulder through the open window of the car, far enough in that he could brace Freddie's body with his own body while he got his breath. He looked around, under the glow of light from the street lamp across the street, into the shadows in front of his own apartment house. At that instant the Buffis' youngest boy ran out the door and down the sidewalk without looking in Tom's direction. Then a man crossing the street walked within a yard of the car with only a brief and faintly surprised look at Freddie's bent figure, which did look almost natural now, Tom thought, practically as if Freddie were only leaning into the car talking to someone, only he really *didn't* look quite natural, Tom knew. But that was the advantage of Europe, he thought. Nobody helped anybody, nobody meddled. If this had been America—

"Can I help you?" a voice asked in Italian.

"Ah, no, no, grazie," Tom replied with drunken good cheer. "I know where he lives," he added in mumbled English.

The man nodded, smiling a little, too, and walked on. A tall thin man in a thin overcoat, hatless, with a mustache. Tom hoped he wouldn't remember. Or remember the car.

Tom swung Freddie out on the door, pulled him around the door and onto the car seat, came around the car and pulled Freddie into the seat beside the driver's seat. Then he put on the pair of brown leather gloves he had stuck into his overcoat pocket. He put Freddie's key into the dashboard. The car started obediently. They were off. Down the hill to the Via Veneto, past the American Library, over to the Piazza Venezia, past the balcony on which Mussolini used to stand to make his speeches, past the gargantuan Victor Emmanuel Monument and through the Forum, past the Colosseum, a grand tour of Rome that Freddie could not appreciate at all. It was just as if Freddie were sleeping beside him, as sometimes people did sleep when you wanted to show them scenery.

The Via Appia Antica stretched out before him, gray and ancient in the soft lights of its infrequent lamps. Black fragments of tombs rose up on either side of the road, silhouetted against the still not quite dark sky. There was more darkness than light. And only a single car ahead, coming this way. Not many people chose to take a ride on such a bumpy, gloomy road after dark in the month of January. Except perhaps lovers. The approaching car passed him. Tom began to look around for the right spot. Freddie ought to have a handsome tomb to lie behind, he thought. There was a spot ahead with three or four trees near the edge of the road and doubtless a tomb behind them, or part of a tomb. Tom pulled off the road by the trees and shut off his lights. He waited a moment, looking at both ends of the straight, empty road.

Freddie was still as limp as a rubber doll. What was all this about rigor mortis? He dragged the limp body roughly now, scraping the face in the dirt, behind the last tree and behind the little remnant of tomb that was only a four-feet-high, jagged arc of wall, but which was probably a remnant of the tomb of a patrician, Tom thought, and quite good enough for this pig. Tom cursed his ugly weight and kicked him suddenly in the chin. He was tired, tired to the point of crying, sick of the sight of Freddie Miles, and the moment when he could turn his back on him for the last time seemed never to come. There was still the God-damned coat! Tom went back to the car to get it. The ground was hard and dry, he noticed as he walked back, and should not leave any traces of his steps. He flung the coat down beside the body and turned away quickly and walked back to the car on his numb, staggering legs, and turned the car around toward Rome again.

As he drove, he wiped the outside of the car door with his gloved hand to get the fingerprints off, the only place he had touched the car before he put his gloves on, he thought. On the street that curved up to the American Express, opposite the Florida nightclub, he parked the car and got out and left it with the keys in the dashboard. He still had Freddie's wallet in his pocket, though he had transferred the Italian money to his own billfold and had burnt a Swiss twenty-frank note and some Austrian schilling notes in his apartment. Now he took the wallet out of his pocket, and as he passed a sewer grate he leaned down and dropped it in.

There were only two things wrong, he thought as he walked toward his house: robbers would logically have taken the polo coat, because it was a good one, and also the passport, which was still in the overcoat pocket. But not every robber was logical, he thought, maybe especially an Italian robber. And not every murderer was logical, either. His mind drifted back to the conversation with Freddie. "*. . . an Italian fellow. Just a young kid . . .*" Somebody had followed him home at some time, Tom thought, because he hadn't told *anybody* where he lived. It shamed him. Maybe two or three delivery boys might know where he lived, but a delivery boy wouldn't be sitting in a place like the Café Greco. It shamed him and made him shrink inside his overcoat. He imagined a dark, panting young face following him home, staring up to see which window had lighted up after he had gone in. Tom hunched in his overcoat and walked faster, as if he were fleeing a sick, passionate pursuer.

17.

TOM went out before eight in the morning to buy the papers. There was nothing. They might not find him for days, Tom thought. Nobody was likely to walk around an unimportant tomb like the one he had put Freddie behind. Tom felt quite confident of his safety, but physically he felt awful. He had a hangover, the terrible, jumpy kind that made him stop halfway in everything he began doing, even stop halfway in brushing his teeth to go and see if his train really left at ten-thirty or at ten-forty-five. It left at ten-thirty.

He was completely ready by nine, dressed and with his overcoat and raincoat out on the bed. He had even spoken to Signora Buffi to tell her he would be gone for at least three weeks and possibly longer. Signora Buffi had behaved just as usual, Tom thought, and had not mentioned his American visitor yesterday. Tom tried to think of something to ask her, something quite normal in view of Freddie's questions yesterday, that would show him what Signora Buffi really thought about the questions, but he couldn't think of anything, and decided to let well enough alone. Everything was fine. Tom tried to reason himself out of the hangover, because he had had only the equivalent of three martinis and three pernods at most. He knew it was a matter of mental suggestion, and that he had a hangover because he had intended to pretend that he had been drinking a great deal with Freddie. And now when there was no need of it, he was still pretending, uncontrollably.

The telephone rang, and Tom picked it up and said "Pronto" sullenly.

"Signor Greenleaf?" asked the Italian voice.

"Si."

"Qui parla la stazione polizia numero ottantatre. Lei e un amico di un' americano chi se chiama Fred-derick Mee-lays?"

"Frederick Miles? Si," Tom said.

The quick, tense voice stated that the corpse of Fred-derick Mee-lays had been found that morning on the Via Appia Antica, and that Signor Mee-lays had visited him at some time yesterday, was that not so?

"Yes, that is so."

"At what time exactly?"

"From about noon to—perhaps five or six in the afternoon, I am not quite sure."

"Would you be kind enough to answer some questions? . . . No, it is not necessary that you trouble yourself to come to the station. The interrogator will come to you. Will eleven o'clock this morning be convenient?"

"I'll be very glad to help if I can," Tom said in a properly excited voice, "but can't the interrogator come now? It is necessary for me to leave the house at ten o'clock."

The voice made a little moan and said it was doubtful, but they would try it. If they could not come before ten o'clock, it was very important that he should not leave the house.

"Va bene," Tom said acquiescently, and hung up.

Damn them! He'd miss his train *and* boat now. All he wanted to do was get out, leave Rome and leave his apartment. He started to go over what he would tell the police. It was all so simple, it bored him. It was the absolute truth. They had had drinks, Freddie had told him about Cortina, they had talked a lot, and then Freddie had left, maybe a little high but in a very good mood. No, he didn't know where Freddie had been going. He had supposed Freddie had a date for the evening.

Tom went into the bedroom and put a canvas, which he had begun a few days ago, on the easel. The paint on the palette was still moist because he had kept it under water in a pan in the kitchen. He mixed some more blue and white and began to add to the grayish-blue sky. The picture was still in Dickie's bright reddish-browns and clear whites—the roofs and walls of Rome out his window. The sky was the only departure, because the winter sky of Rome was so gloomy, even Dickie would have painted it grayish-blue instead of blue, Tom thought. Tom frowned, just as Dickie frowned when he painted.

The telephone rang again.

"God damn it!" Tom muttered, and went to answer it. "Pronto!"

"Pronto! Fausto!" the voice said. "Come sta?" And the familiar bubbling, juvenile laugh.

"Oh-h! Fausto! Bene, grazie! Excuse me," Tom continued in Italian in Dickie's laughing, absent voice, "I've been trying to paint—trying." It was calculated to be possibly the voice of Dickie after having lost a friend like Freddie, and also the voice of Dickie on an ordinary morning of absorbing work.

"Can you have lunch?" Fausto asked. "My train leaves at four-fifteen for Milano."

Tom groaned, like Dickie. "I'm just taking off for Naples. Yes, immediately, in twenty minutes!" If he could escape Fausto now, he thought, he needn't let Fausto know that the police had called him at all. The news about Freddie wouldn't be in the papers until noon or later.

"But I'm here! In Roma! Where's your house? I'm at the railroad station!" Fausto said cheerfully, laughing.

"Where'd you get my telephone number?"

"Ah! allora, I called up information. They told me you didn't give the number out, but I told the girl a long story about a lottery you won in Mongibello. I don't know if she believed me, but I made it sound very important. A house and a cow and a well and even a refrigerator! I had to call her back three times, but finally she gave it to me. Allora, Deekie, where are you?"

"That's not the point. I'd have lunch with you if I didn't have this train, but—"

"Va bene, I'll help you carry your bags! Tell me where you are and I'll come over with a taxi for you!"

"The time's too short. Why don't I see you at the railroad station in about half an hour? It's the ten-thirty train for Naples."

"Okay!"

"How is Marge?"

"Ah—inamorata di te," Fausto said, laughing. "Are you going to see her in Naples?"

"I don't think so. I'll see you in a few minutes, Fausto. Got to hurry. Arrividerch."

" 'Rividerch, Deekie! Addio!" He hung up.

When Fausto saw the papers this afternoon, he would understand why he hadn't come to the railroad station, otherwise Fausto would just think they had missed each other somehow. But Fausto probably would see the papers by noon, Tom thought, because the Italian papers would play it up big—the murder of an American on the Appian Way. After the interview with the police, he would take another train to Naples—after four o'clock, so Fausto wouldn't be still around the station—and wait in Naples for the next boat to Majorca.

He only hoped that Fausto wouldn't worm the address out of information, too, and decide to come over before four o'clock. He hoped Fausto wouldn't land here just when the police were here.

Tom shoved a couple of suitcases under the bed, and carried the other to a closet and shut the door. He didn't want the police to think he was just about to leave town. But what was he so nervous about? They probably hadn't any clues. Maybe a friend of Freddie's had known that Freddie was going to try to see him yesterday, that was all. Tom picked up a brush and moistened it in the turpentine cup. For the benefit of the police, he wanted to look as if he was not too upset by the news of Freddie's death to do a little painting while he waited for them, though he was dressed to go out, because he had said he intended to go out. He was going to be a friend of Freddie's, but not too close a friend.

Signora Buffi let the police in at ten-thirty. Tom looked down the stairwell and saw them. They did not stop to ask her any questions. Tom went back into his apartment. The spicy smell of turpentine was in the room.

There were two: an older man in the uniform of an officer, and a younger man in an ordinary police uniform. The older man greeted him politely and asked to see his passport. Tom produced it, and the officer looked sharply from Tom to the picture of Dickie, more sharply than anyone had ever looked at it before, and Tom braced himself for a challenge, but there was none. The officer handed him the passport with a little bow and a smile. He was a short, middle-aged man who looked like thousands of other middle-aged Italians, with heavy gray-and-black eyebrows and a short, bushy gray-and-black mustache. He looked neither particularly bright nor stupid.

"How was he killed?" Tom asked.

"He was struck on the head and in the neck by some heavy instrument," the officer replied, "and robbed. We think he was drunk. Was he drunk when he left your apartment yesterday afternoon?"

"Well—somewhat. We had both been drinking. We were drinking martinis and pernod."

The officer wrote it down in his tablet, and also the time that Tom said Freddie had been there, from about twelve until about six.

The younger policeman, handsome and blank of face, was strolling around the apartment with his hands behind him, bending close to the easel with a relaxed air as if he were alone in a museum.

"Do you know where he was going when he left?" the officer asked.

"No, I don't."

"But you thought he was able to drive?"

"Oh, yes. He was not too drunk to drive or I would have gone with him."

The officer asked another question that Tom pretended not quite to grasp. The officer asked it a second time, choosing different words, and exchanged a smile with the younger officer. Tom glanced from one to the other of them, a little resentfully. The officer wanted to know what his relationship to Freddie had been.

"A friend," Tom said. "Not a very close friend. I had not seen or heard from him in about two months. I was terribly upset to hear about the disaster this morning." Tom let his anxious expression make up for his rather primitive vocabulary. He thought it did. He thought the questioning was very perfunctory, and that they were going to leave in another minute or so. "At exactly what time was he killed?" Tom asked.

The officer was still writing. He raised his bushy eyebrows. "Evidently just after the signor left your house, because the doctors believe that he had been dead at least twelve hours, perhaps longer."

"At what time was he found?"

"At dawn this morning. By some workmen who were walking along the road."

"Dio mio!" Tom murmured.

"He said nothing about making an excursion yesterday to the Via Appia when he left your apartment?"

"No," Tom said.

"What did you do yesterday after Signor Mee-lays left?"

"I stayed here," Tom said, gesturing with open hands as Dickie would have done, "and then I had a little sleep, and later I went out for a walk around eight or eight-thirty." A man who lived in the house, whose name Tom didn't know, had seen him come in last night at about a quarter to nine, and they had said good evening to each other.

"You took a walk alone?"

"Yes."

"And Signor Mee-lays left here alone? He was not going to meet anybody that you know of?"

"No. He didn't say so." Tom wondered if Freddie had had friends with him at his hotel, or wherever he had been staying? Tom hoped that the police wouldn't confront him with any of Freddie's friends who might know Dickie. Now his name—Richard Greenleaf—would be in the Italian newspapers, Tom thought, and also his address. He'd have to move. It was hell. He cursed to himself. The police officer saw him, but it looked like a muttered curse against the sad fate that had befallen Freddie, Tom thought.

"So—" the officer said, smiling, and closed his tablet.

"You think it was—" Tom tried to think of the word for hoodlum "—violent boys, don't you? Are there any clues?"

"We are searching the car for fingerprints now. The murderer may have been somebody he picked up to give a ride to. The car was found this morning in the vicinity of the Piazza di Spagna. We should have some clues before tonight. Thank you very much, Signor Greenleaf."

"Di niente! If I can be of any further assistance—"

The officer turned at the door. "Shall we be able to reach you here for the next few days, in case there are any more questions?"

Tom hesitated. "I was planning to leave for Majorca to-morrow."

"But the questions may be, who is such-and-such a person who is a suspect," the officer explained. "You may be able to tell us who the person is in relation to the deceased." He gestured.

"All right. But I do not think I knew Signor Miles that well. He probably had closer friends in the city."

"Who?" The officer closed the door and took out his tablet.

"I don't know," Tom said. "I only know he must have had several friends here, people who knew him better than I did."

"I am sorry, but we still must expect you to be in reach for the next couple of days," he repeated quietly, as if there were no question of Tom's arguing about it, even if he was an American. "We shall inform you as soon as you may go. I am sorry if you have made travel plans. Perhaps there is still time to cancel them. Good day, Signor Greenleaf."

"Good day." Tom stood there after they had closed the door. He could move to a hotel, he thought, if he told the police what hotel it was. He didn't want Freddie's friends or any friends of Dickie's calling on him after they saw his address in the newspapers. He tried to assess his behavior from the polizia's point of view. They hadn't challenged him on anything. He had not acted horrified at the news of Freddie's death, but that jibed with the fact that he was not an especially close friend of Freddie's, either. No, it wasn't bad, except that he had to be on tap.

The telephone rang, and Tom didn't answer it, because he had a feeling that it was Fausto calling from the railroad station. It was eleven-five, and the train for Naples would have departed. When the phone stopped ringing, Tom picked it up and called the Inghilterra. He reserved a room, and said he would be there in about an hour. Then he called the police station—he remembered that it was number eighty-three—and after nearly ten minutes of difficulties because he couldn't find anyone who knew or cared who Richard Greenleaf was, he succeeded in leaving a message that Signor Richard Green-leaf could be found at the Albergo Inghilterra, in case the police wanted to speak to him.

He was at the Inghilterra before an hour was up. His three suitcases, two of them Dickie's and one his own, depressed him: he had packed them for such a different purpose. And now this!

He went out at noon to buy the papers. Every one of the papers had it: AMERICANO MURDERED ON THE VIA APPIA ANTICA . . . SHOCKING MURDER OF RICCISSIMO AMERICANO FREDERICK MILES LAST NIGHT ON THE VIA APPIA . . . VIA APPIA MURDER OF AMERICANO WITHOUT CLUES . . . Tom read every word. There really were no clues, at least not yet, no tracks, no fingerprints, no suspects. But every paper carried the name Herbert Richard Greenleaf and gave his address as the place where Freddie had last been seen by anybody. Not one of the papers implied that Herbert Richard Greenleaf was under suspicion, however. The papers said that Miles had apparently had a few drinks and the drinks, in typical Italian journalistic style, were all enumerated and ran from americanos through Scotch whisky, brandy, champagne, even grappa. Only gin and pernod were omitted.

Tom stayed in his hotel room over the lunch hour, walking the floor and feeling depressed and trapped. He telephoned the travel office in Rome that had sold him his ticket to Palma, and tried to cancel it. He could have twenty per cent of his money back, they said. There was not another boat to Palma for about five days.

Around two o'clock his telephone rang urgently.

"Hello," Tom said in Dickie's nervous, irritable tone.

"Hello, Dick. This is Van Houston."

"Oh-h," Tom said, as if he knew him, yet the single word conveyed no excess of surprise or warmth.

"How've you been? It's been a long time, hasn't it?" the hoarse, strained voice asked.

"Certainly has. Where are you?"

"At the Hassler. I've been going over Freddie's suitcases with the police. Listen, I want to see you. What was the matter with Freddie yesterday? I tried to find you all last evening, you know, because Freddie was supposed to be back at the hotel by six. I didn't have your address. What happened yesterday?"

"I wish I knew! Freddie left the house around six. We both had taken on quite a lot of martinis, but he looked capable of driving or naturally I wouldn't have let him go off. He said he had his car downstairs. I can't imagine what happened, except that he picked up somebody to give them a lift, and they pulled a gun on him or something."

"But he wasn't killed by a gun. I agree with you somebody must have forced him to drive out there, or he blotted out, because he'd have had to get clear across town to get to the Appian Way. The Hassler's only a few blocks from where you live."

"Did he ever black out before? At the wheel of a car?"

"Listen, Dickie, can I see you? I'm free now, except that I'm not supposed to leave the hotel today."

"Neither am I."

"Oh, come on. Leave a message where you are and come over."

"I can't, Van. The police are coming over in about an hour and I'm supposed to be here. Why don't you call me later? Maybe I can see you tonight."

"All right. What time?"

"Call me around six."

"Right. Keep your chin up, Dickie."

"You too."

"See you," the voice said weakly.

Tom hung up. Van had sounded as if he were about to cry at the last. "Pronto?" Tom said, clicking the telephone to get the hotel operator. He left a message that he was not in to anybody except the police, and that they were to let nobody up to see him. Positively no one.

After that the telephone did not ring all afternoon. At about eight, when it was dark, Tom went downstairs to buy the evening papers. He looked around the little lobby and into the hotel bar whose door was off the main hall, looking for anybody who might be Van. He was ready for anything, ready even to see Marge sitting there waiting for him, but he saw no one who looked even like a police agent. He bought the evening papers and sat in a little restaurant a few streets away, reading them. Still no clues. He learned that Van Houston was a close friend of Freddie's, aged twenty-eight, traveling with him from Austria to Rome on a holiday that was to have ended in Florence, where both Miles and Houston had residences, the papers said. They had questioned three Italian youths, two of them eighteen and one sixteen, on suspicion of having done the "horrible deed," but the youths had been later released. Tom was relieved to read that no fingerprints that could be considered fresh or usable had been found on Miles' "bellissimo Fiat 1400 convertibile."

Tom ate his costoletta di vitello slowly, sipped his wine, and glanced through every column of the papers for the last-minute items that were sometimes put into Italian papers just before they went to press. He found nothing more on the Miles case. But on the last page of the last newspaper he read:

BARCA AFFONDATA CON MACCHIE DI SANGUE TROVATA
NELL' ACQUA POCO FONDO VICINO SAN REMO

He read it rapidly, with more terror in his heart than he had felt when he had carried Freddie's body down the stairs, or when the police had come to question him. This was like a nemesis, like a nightmare come true, even the wording of the headline. The boat was described in detail and it brought the scene back to him, Dickie sitting in the stern at the throttle, Dickie smiling at him, Dickie's body sinking through the water with its wake of bubbles. The text said that the stains were believed to be bloodstains, not that they were. It did not say what the police or anybody else intended to do about them. But the police would do something, Tom thought. The boat-keeper could probably tell the police the very day the boat was lost. The police could then check the hotels for that day. The Italian boatkeeper might even remember that it was two Americans who had not come back with the boat. If the police bothered to check the hotel registers around that time, the name Richard Greenleaf would stand out like a red flag. In which case, of course, it would be Tom Ripley who would be missing, who might have been murdered that day. Tom's imagination went in several directions: suppose they searched for Dickie's body and found it? It would be assumed to be Tom Ripley's now. Dickie would be suspected of murder. Ergo, Dickie would be suspected of Freddie's murder, too. Dickie would become overnight "a murderous type." On the other hand, the Italian boatkeeper might not remember the day that one of his boats had not been brought back. Even if he did remember, the hotels might not be checked. The Italian police just might not be that interested. Might, might, *might* not.

Tom folded up his papers, paid his check, and went out.

He asked at the hotel desk if there were any messages for him.

"Si, signor. Questo e questo e questo—" The clerk laid them out on the desk before him like a card player laying down a winning straight.

Two from Van. One from Robert Gilbertson. (Wasn't there a Robert Gilbertson in Dickie's address book? Check on that.) One from Marge. Tom picked it up and read its Italian carefully: Signorina Sherwood had called at three-thirty-five P.M. and would call again. The call was long distance from Mongibello.

Tom nodded, and picked them up. "Thanks very much." He didn't like the looks of the clerk behind the desk. Italians were so damned curious!

Upstairs he sat hunched forward in an armchair, smoking and thinking. He was trying to figure out what would logically happen if he did nothing, and what he could make happen by his own actions. Marge would very likely come up to Rome. She had evidently called the Rome police to get his address. If she came up, he would have to see her as Tom, and try to convince her that Dickie was out for a while, as he had with Freddie. And if he failed— Tom rubbed his palms together nervously. He mustn't see Marge, that was all. Not now with the boat affair brewing. Everything would go haywire if he saw her. It'd be the end of everything! But if he could only sit tight, nothing at all would happen. It was just this moment, he thought, just this little crisis with the boat story and the unsolved Freddie Miles murder, that made things so difficult. But absolutely nothing would happen to him, if he could keep on doing and saying the right things to everybody. Afterwards it could be smooth sailing again. Greece, or India. Ceylon. Some place far, far away, where no old friend could possibly come knocking on his door. What a fool he had been to think he could stay in Rome! Might as well have picked Grand Central Station, or put himself on exhibition in the Louvre!

He called the Stazione Termini, and asked about the trains for Naples tomorrow. There were four or five. He wrote down the times for all of them. It would be five days before a boat left from Naples for Majorca, and he would sit the time out in Naples, he thought. All he needed was a release from the police, and if nothing happened tomorrow he should get it. They couldn't hold a man forever, without even any grounds for suspicion, just in order to throw an occasional question at him! He began to feel he would be released tomorrow, that it was absolutely logical that he should be released.

He picked up the telephone again, and told the clerk that if Miss Marjorie Sherwood called again, he would accept the call. If she called again, he thought, he could convince her in two minutes that everything was all right, that Freddie's murder didn't concern him at all, that he had moved to a hotel just to avoid annoying telephone calls from total strangers and yet still be within reach of the police in case they wanted him to identify any suspects they picked up. He would tell her that he was flying to Greece tomorrow or the next day, so there was no use in her coming to Rome. As a matter of fact, he thought, he could fly to Palma from Rome. He hadn't even thought of that before.

He lay down on the bed, tired, but not ready to undress, because he felt that something else was going to happen tonight. He tried to concentrate on Marge. He imagined her at this moment sitting in Giorgio's, or treating herself to a long, slow Tom Collins in the Miramare bar, and debating whether to call him up again. He could see her troubled eyebrows, her tousled hair as she sat brooding about what might be happening in Rome. She would be alone at the table, not talking to anyone. He saw her getting up and going home, taking a suitcase and catching the noon bus tomorrow. He was there on the road in front of the post office, shouting to her not to go, trying to stop the bus, but it pulled away . . .

The scene dissolved in swirling yellow-grayness, the color of the sand in Mongibello. Tom saw Dickie smiling at him, dressed in the corduroy suit that he had worn in San Remo.

The suit was soaking wet, the tie a dripping string. Dickie bent over him, shaking him. "I swam!" he said. "Tom, wake up! I'm all right! I swam! I'm alive!" Tom squirmed away from his touch. He heard Dickie laugh at him, Dickie's happy, deep laugh. *"Tom!"* The timbre of the voice was deeper, richer, *better* than Tom had ever been able to make it in his imitations. Tom pushed himself up. His body felt leaden and slow, as if he were trying to raise himself out of deep water.

"I swam!" Dickie's voice shouted, ringing and ringing in Tom's ears as if he heard it through a long tunnel.

Tom looked around the room, looking for Dickie in the yellow light under the bridge lamp, in the dark corner by the tall wardrobe. Tom felt his own eyes stretched wide, terrified, and though he knew his fear was senseless, he kept looking everywhere for Dickie, below the half-drawn shades at the window, and on the floor on the other side of the bed. He hauled himself up from the bed, staggered across the room, and opened a window. Then the other window. He felt drugged. *Somebody put something in my wine,* he thought suddenly. He knelt below the window, breathing the cold air in, fighting the grogginess as if it were something that was going to overcome him if he didn't exert himself to the utmost. Finally he went into the bathroom and wet his face at the basin. The grogginess was going away. He knew he hadn't been drugged. He had let his imagination run away with him. He had been out of control.

He drew himself up and calmly took off his tie. He moved as Dickie would have done, undressed himself, bathed, put his pajamas on and lay down in bed. He tried to think about what Dickie would be thinking about. His mother. Her last letter had enclosed a couple of snapshots of herself and Mr. Greenleaf sitting in the living room having coffee, the scene he remembered from the evening he had had coffee with them after dinner. Mrs. Greenleaf had said that Herbert had taken the pictures himself by squeezing a bulb. Tom began to compose his next letter to them. They were pleased that he was writing more often. He must set their minds at rest about the Freddie affair, because they knew of Freddie. Mrs. Greenleaf had asked about Freddie Miles in one of her letters. But Tom was listening for the telephone while he tried to compose the letter, and he couldn't really concentrate.

18.

THE first thing he thought of when he woke up was Marge. He reached for the telephone and asked if she had called during the night. She had not. He had a horrible premonition that she was coming up to Rome. It shot him out of bed, and then as he moved in his routine of shaving and bathing, his feeling changed. Why should he worry so much about Marge? He had always been able to handle her. She couldn't be here before five or six, anyway, because the first bus left Mongibello at noon, and she wasn't likely to take a taxi to Naples.

Maybe he would be able to leave Rome this morning. At ten o'clock he would call the police and find out.

He ordered caffe latte and rolls sent up to his room, and also the morning papers. Very strangely, there was not a thing in any of the papers about either the Miles case or the San Remo boat. It made him feel odd and frightened, with the same fear he had had last night when he had imagined Dickie standing in the room. He threw the newspapers away from him into a chair.

The telephone rang and he jumped for it obediently. It was either Marge or the police. "Pronto?"

"Pronto. There are two signori of the police downstairs to see you, signor."

"Very well. Will you tell them to come up?"

A minute later he heard their footsteps in the carpeted hall. It was the same older officer as yesterday, with a different younger policeman.

"Buon' giorno," said the officer politely, with his little bow.

"Buon' giorno," Tom said. "Have you found anything new?"

"No," said the officer on a questioning note. He took the chair that Tom offered him, and opened his brown leather briefcase. "Another matter has come up. You are also a friend of the American Thomas Reepley?"

"Yes," Tom said.

"Do you know where he is?"

"I think he went back to America about a month ago."

The officer consulted his paper. "I see. That will have to be confirmed by the United States Immigration Department. You see, we are trying to find Thomas Reepley. We think he may be dead."

"Dead? Why?"

The officer's lips under his bushy iron-gray mustache compressed softly between each statement so that they seemed to be smiling. The smile had thrown Tom off a little yesterday, too. "You were with him on a trip to San Remo in November, were you not?"

They had checked the hotels. "Yes."

"Where did you last see him? In San Remo?"

"No. I saw him again in Rome." Tom remembered that Marge knew he had gone back to Rome after Mongibello, because he had said he was going to help Dickie get settled in Rome.

"When did you last see him?"

"I don't know if I can give you the exact date. Something like two months ago, I think. I think I had a postcard from— from Genoa from him, saying that he was going to go back to America."

"You think?"

"I know I had," Tom said. "Why do you think he is dead?"

The officer looked at his form paper dubiously. Tom glanced at the younger policeman, who was leaning against the bureau with his arms folded, staring impersonally at him.

"Did you take a boat ride with Thomas Reepley in San Remo?"

"A boat ride? Where?"

"In a little boat? Around the port?" the officer asked quietly, looking at Tom.

"I think we did. Yes, I remember. Why?"

"Because a little boat has been found sunken with some kind of stains on it that may be blood. It was lost on November twenty-fifth. That is, it was not returned to the dock from which it was rented. November twenty-fifth was the day you were in San Remo with Signor Reepley." The officer's eyes rested on him without moving.

The very mildness of the look offended Tom. It was dishonest, he felt. But Tom made a tremendous effort to behave in the proper way. He saw himself as if he were standing apart from himself and watching the scene. He corrected even his stance, and made it more relaxed by resting a hand on the end post of the bed. "But nothing happened to us on that boat ride. There was no accident."

"Did you bring the boat back?"

"Of course."

The officer continued to eye him. "We cannot find Signor Reepley registered in any hotel after November twenty-fifth."

"Really?—How long have you been looking?"

"Not long enough to search every little village in Italy, but we have checked the hotels in the major cities. We find you registered at the Hassler on November twenty-eighth to thirtieth, and then—"

"Tom didn't stay with me in Rome—Signor Ripley. He went to Mongibello around that time and stayed for a couple of days."

"Where did he stay when he came up to Rome?"

"At some small hotel. I don't remember which it was. I didn't visit him."

"And where were you?"

"When?"

"On November twenty-sixth and twenty-seventh. That is, just after San Remo."

"In Forte dei Marmi," Tom replied. "I stopped off there on the way down. I stayed at a pension."

"Which one?"

Tom shook his head. "I don't recall the name. A very small place." After all, he thought, through Marge he could prove that Tom was in Mongibello, alive, after San Remo, so why should the police investigate what pension Dickie Greenleaf had stayed at on the twenty-sixth and twenty-seventh? Tom sat down on the side of his bed. "I do not understand yet why you think Tom Ripley is dead."

"We think *somebody* is dead," the officer replied, "in San

Remo. Somebody was killed in that boat. That was why the boat was sunk—to hide the bloodstains."

Tom frowned. "They are sure they are bloodstains?"

The officer shrugged.

Tom shrugged, too. "There must have been a couple of hundred people renting boats that day in San Remo."

"Not so many. About thirty. It's quite true, it could have been any one of the thirty—or any pair of the fifteen," he added with a smile. "We don't even know all their names. But we are beginning to think Thomas Reepley is missing." Now he looked off at a corner of the room, and he might have been thinking of something else, Tom thought, judging from his expression. Or was he enjoying the warmth of the radiator beside his chair?

Tom recrossed his legs impatiently. What was going on in the Italian's head was obvious: Dickie Greenleaf had twice been on the scene of a murder, or near enough. The missing Thomas Ripley had taken a boat ride November twenty-fifth with Dickie Greenleaf. Ergo— Tom straightened up, frowning. "Are you saying that you do not believe me when I tell you that I saw Tom Ripley in Rome around the first of December?"

"Oh, no, I didn't say that, no, indeed!" The officer gestured placatingly. "I wanted to hear what you would say about your—your traveling with Signor Ripley after San Remo, because we cannot find him." He smiled again, a broad, conciliatory smile that showed yellowish teeth.

Tom relaxed with an exasperated shrug. Obvious that the Italian police didn't want to accuse an American citizen outright of murder. "I'm sorry that I can't tell you exactly where he is right now. Why don't you try Paris? Or Genoa? He'd always stay in a small hotel, because he prefers them."

"Have you got the postcard that he sent you from Genoa?"

"No, I haven't," Tom said. He ran his fingers through his hair, as Dickie sometimes did when he was irritated. He felt better, concentrating on being Dickie Greenleaf for a few seconds, pacing the floor once or twice.

"Do you know any friends of Thomas Reepley?"

Tom shook his head. "No, I don't even know him very well, at least not for a very long time. I don't know if he has many friends in Europe. I think he said he knew someone in Faenza. Also in Florence. But I don't remember their names." If the Italian thought he was protecting Tom's friends from a lot of police questioning by not giving their names, then let him, Tom thought.

"Va bene, we shall inquire," the officer said. He put his papers away. He had made at least a dozen notations on them.

"Before you go," Tom said in the same nervous, frank tone, "I want to ask when I can leave the city. I was planning to go to Sicily. I should like very much to leave today if it is possible. I intend to stay at the Hotel Palma in Palermo. It will be very simple for you to reach me if I am needed."

"Palermo," the officer repeated. "Ebbene, that may be possible. May I use the telephone?"

Tom lighted an Italian cigarette and listened to the officer asking for Capitano Aulicino, and then stating quite impassively that Signor Greenleaf did not know where Signor Reepley was, and that he might have gone back to America, or he might be in Florence or Faenza in the opinion of Signor Greenleaf. "Faenza," he repeated carefully, "vicino Bologna." When the man had that, the officer said that Signor Greenleaf wished to go to Palermo today. "Va bene. Benone." The officer turned to Tom, smiling. "Yes, you may go to Palermo today."

"Benone. Grazie." He walked with the two to the door. "If you find where Tom Ripley is, I wish you would let me know, too," he said ingenuously.

"Of course! We shall keep you informed, signor. Buon' giorno!"

Alone, Tom began to whistle as he repacked the few things he had taken from his suitcases. He felt proud of himself for having proposed Sicily instead of Majorca, because Sicily was still Italy and Majorca wasn't, and naturally the Italian police would be more willing to let him leave if he stayed in their territory. He had thought of that when it had occurred to him that Tom Ripley's passport did not show that he had been to France again after the San Remo–Cannes trip. He remembered he had told Marge that Tom Ripley had said he was going up to Paris and from there back to America. If they ever questioned Marge as to whether Tom Ripley was in Mongibello after San Remo, she might also add that he later went to Paris. And if he ever had to become Tom Ripley again, and show his passport to the police, they would see that he hadn't been to France again after the Cannes trip. He would just have to say that he had changed his mind after he told Dickie that, and had decided to stay in Italy. That wasn't important.

Tom straightened up suddenly from a suitcase. Could it all be a trick, really? Were they just letting him have a little more rope in letting him go to Sicily, apparently unsuspected? A sly little bastard, that officer. He'd said his name once. What was it? Ravini? Roverini? Well, what could be the advantage of letting him have a little more rope? He'd told them exactly where he was going. He had no intention of trying to run away from anything. All he wanted was to get out of Rome. He was frantic to get out! He threw the last items into his suitcase and slammed the lid down and locked it.

The phone again!

Tom snatched it up. "Pronto?"

"Oh, Dickie—!" breathlessly.

It was Marge and she was downstairs, he could tell from the sound. Flustered, he said in Tom's voice, "Who's this?"

"Is this Tom?"

"Marge! Well, hello! Where are you?"

"I'm downstairs. Is Dickie there? Can I come up?"

"You can come up in about five minutes," Tom said with a laugh. "I'm not quite dressed yet." The clerks always sent people to a booth downstairs, he thought. The clerks wouldn't be able to overhear them.

"Is Dickie there?"

"Not at the moment. He went out about half an hour ago, but he'll be back any minute. I know where he is, if you want to find him."

"Where?"

"At the eighty-third police station. No, excuse me, it's the eighty-seventh."

"Is he in any trouble?"

"No, just answering questions. He was supposed to be there at ten. Want me to give you the address?" He wished he hadn't started talking in Tom's voice: he could so easily have pretended to be a servant, some friend of Dickie's, any-body, and told her that Dickie was out for hours.

Marge was groaning. "No-o. I'll wait for him."

"Here it is!" Tom said as if he had found it. "Twenty-one Via Perugia. Do you know where that is?" Tom didn't, but he was going to send her in the opposite direction from the American Express, where he wanted to go for his mail before he left town.

"I don't want to go," Marge said. "I'll come up and wait with you, if it's all right."

"Well, it's—" He laughed, his own unmistakable laugh that Marge knew well. "The thing is, I'm expecting somebody any minute. It's a business interview. About a job. Believe it or not, old believe-it-or-not Ripley's trying to put himself to work."

"Oh," said Marge, not in the least interested. "Well, how is Dickie? Why does he have to talk to the police?"

"Oh, just because he had some drinks with Freddie that day. You saw the papers, didn't you? The papers make it ten times more important than it was for the simple reason that the dopes haven't got any clues at all about anything."

"How long has Dickie been living here?"

"Here? Oh, just overnight. I've been up north. When I heard about Freddie, I came down to Rome to see him. If it hadn't been for the police, I'd never have found him!"

"You're telling me! I went to the police in desperation! I've been so worried, Tom. He might at least have phoned me— at Giorgio's or somewhere—"

"I'm awfully glad you're in town, Marge. Dickie'll be tick-led pink to see you. He's been worried about what you might think of all this in the papers."

"Oh, has he?" Marge said disbelievingly, but she sounded pleased.

"Why don't you wait for me in Angelo's? It's that bar right down the street in front of the hotel going toward the Piazza di Spagna steps. I'll see if I can sneak out and have a drink or a coffee with you in about five minutes, okay?"

"Okay. But there's a bar right here in the hotel."

"I don't want to be seen by my future boss in a bar."

"Oh, all right. Angelo's?"

"You can't miss it. On the street straight in front of the hotel. Bye-bye."

He whirled around to finish his packing. He really was finished except for the coats in the closet. He picked up the telephone and asked for his bill to be prepared, and for somebody to carry his luggage. Then he put his luggage in a neat heap for the bellboys and went down via the stairs. He wanted to see if Marge was still in the lobby, waiting there for him, or possibly still there making another telephone call. She couldn't have been downstairs waiting when the police were here, Tom thought. About five minutes had passed between the time the police left and Marge called up. He had put on a hat to conceal his blonder hair, a raincoat which was new, and he wore Tom Ripley's shy, slightly frightened expression.

She wasn't in the lobby. Tom paid his bill. The clerk handed him another message: Van Houston had been here. The message was in his own writing, dated ten minutes ago.

Waited for you half an hour. Don't you ever go out for a walk? They won't let me up. Call me at the Hassler.

Van

Maybe Van and Marge had run into each other, if they knew each other, and were sitting together in Angelo's now.

"If anybody else asks for me, would you say that I've left the city?" Tom said to the clerk.

"Va bene, signor."

Tom went out to his waiting taxi. "Would you stop at the American Express, please?" he asked the driver.

The driver did not take the street that Angelo's was on. Tom relaxed and congratulated himself. He congratulated himself above all on the fact that he had been too nervous to stay in his apartment yesterday and had taken a hotel room. He never could have evaded Marge in his apartment. She had the address from the newspapers. If he had tried the same trick, she would have insisted on coming up and waiting for Dickie in the apartment. Luck was with him!

He had mail at the American Express—three letters, one from Mr. Greenleaf.

"How are you today?" asked the young Italian girl who had handed him his mail.

She'd read the papers, too, Tom thought. He smiled back at her naïvely curious face. Her name was Maria. "Very well, thanks, and you?"

As he turned away, it crossed his mind that he could never use the Rome American Express as an address for Tom Ripley. Two or three of the clerks knew him by sight. He was using the Naples American Express for Tom Ripley's mail now, though he hadn't claimed anything there or written them to forward anything, because he wasn't expecting anything important for Tom Ripley, not even another blast from Mr. Greenleaf. When things cooled off a little, he would just walk into the Naples American Express some day and claim it with Tom Ripley's passport, he thought.

He couldn't use the Rome American Express as Tom Ripley, but he had to keep Tom Ripley with him, his passport and his clothes in order for emergencies like Marge's telephone call this morning. Marge had come damned close to being right in the room with him. As long as the innocence of Dickie Greenleaf was debatable in the opinion of the police, it was suicidal to think of leaving the country as Dickie, because if he had to switch back suddenly to Tom Ripley, Ripley's passport would not show that he had left Italy. If he wanted to leave Italy—to take Dickie Greenleaf entirely away from the police—he would have to leave as Tom Ripley, and re-enter later as Tom Ripley and become Dickie again once the police investigations were over. That was a possibility.

It seemed simple and safe. All he had to do was weather the next few days.

19.

THE boat approached Palermo harbor slowly and tentatively, nosing its white prow gently through the floating orange peels, the straw and the pieces of broken fruit crates. It was the way Tom felt, too, approaching Palermo. He had spent two days in Naples, and there had been nothing of any interest in the papers about the Miles case and nothing at all about the San Remo boat, and the police had made no attempt to reach him that he knew of. But maybe they had just not bothered to look for him in Naples, he thought, and were waiting for him in Palermo at the hotel.

There were no police waiting for him on the dock, anyway. Tom looked for them. He bought a couple of newspapers, then took a taxi with his luggage to the Hotel Palma. There were no police in the hotel lobby, either. It was an ornate old lobby with great marble supporting columns and big pots of palms standing around. A clerk told him the number of his reserved room, and handed a bellboy the key. Tom felt so much relieved that he went over to the mail counter and asked boldly if there was any message for Signor Richard Greenleaf.

The clerk told him there was not.

Then he began to relax. That meant there was not even a message from Marge. Marge would undoubtedly have gone to the police by now to find out where Dickie was. Tom had imagined horrible things during the boat trip: Marge beating him to Palermo by plane, Marge leaving a message for him at the Hotel Palma that she would arrive on the next boat. He had even looked for Marge on the boat when he got aboard in Naples.

Now he began to think that perhaps Marge had given Dickie up after this episode. Maybe she'd caught onto the idea that Dickie was running away from her and that he wanted to be with Tom, alone. Maybe that had even penetrated *her* thick skull. Tom debated sending her a letter to that effect as he sat in his deep warm bath that evening, spreading soapsuds luxuriously up and down his arms. Tom Ripley ought to write the letter, he thought. It was about time. He would say that he'd wanted to be tactful all this while, that he hadn't wanted to come right out with it on the telephone in Rome, but that by now he had the feeling she understood, anyway. He and Dickie were very happy together, and that was that. Tom began to giggle merrily, uncontrollably, and squelched himself by slipping all the way under the water, holding his nose.

Dear Marge, he would say. I'm writing this because I don't think Dickie ever will, though I've asked him to many times.

You're much too fine a person to be strung along like this for so long . . .

He giggled again, then sobered himself by deliberately concentrating on the little problem that he hadn't solved yet: Marge had also probably told the Italian police that she had talked to Tom Ripley at the Inghilterra. The police were going to wonder where the hell he went to. The police might be looking for him in Rome now. The police would certainly look for Tom Ripley around Dickie Greenleaf. It was an added danger—if they were, for instance, to think that he was Tom Ripley now, just from Marge's description of him, and strip him and search him and find both his and Dickie's passports. But what had he said about risks? Risks were what made the whole thing fun. He burst out singing:

> *Papa non vuole, Mama ne meno,*
> *Come faremo far' l'amor'?*

He boomed it out in the bathroom as he dried himself. He sang it in Dickie's loud baritone that he had never heard, but he felt sure Dickie would have been pleased with his ringing tone.

He dressed, put on one of his new nonwrinkling traveling suits, and strolled out into the Palermo dusk. There across the plaza was the great Norman-influenced cathedral he had read about, built by the English archbishop Walter-of-the-Mill, he remembered from a guidebook. Then there was Siracusa to the south, scene of a mighty naval battle between the Latins and the Greeks. And Dionysius' Ear. And Taormina. And Etna! It was a big island and brand-new to him. Sicilia! Stronghold of Giuliano! Colonized by the ancient Greeks, invaded by Norman and Saracen! Tomorrow he would commence his tourism properly, but this moment was glorious, he thought as he stopped to stare at the tall, towered cathedral in front of him. Wonderful to look at the dusty arches of its façade and to think of going inside tomorrow, to imagine its musty, sweetish smell, composed of the uncounted candles and incense-burnings of hundreds and hundreds of years. Anticipation! It occurred to him that his anticipation was more pleasant to him than his experiencing. Was it always going to be like that? When he spent evenings alone, handling Dickie's possessions, simply looking at his rings on his own fingers, or his woolen ties, or his black alligator wallet, was that experiencing or anticipation?

Beyond Sicily came Greece. He definitely wanted to see Greece. He wanted to see Greece as Dickie Greenleaf with Dickie's money, Dickie's clothes, Dickie's way of behaving with strangers. But would it happen that he couldn't see Greece as Dickie Greenleaf? Would one thing after another come up to thwart him—murder, suspicion, *people*? He hadn't wanted to murder, it had been a necessity. The idea of going to Greece, trudging over the Acropolis as Tom Ripley, American tourist, held no charm for him at all. He would as soon not go. Tears came in his eyes as he stared up at the campanile of the cathedral, and then he turned away and began to walk down a new street.

There was a letter for him the next morning, a fat letter from Marge. Tom squeezed it between his fingers and smiled. It was what he had expected, he felt sure, otherwise it wouldn't have been so fat. He read it at breakfast. He savored every line of it along with his fresh warm rolls and his cinnamon-flavored coffee. It was all he could have expected, and more.

. . . If you really *didn't* know that I had been by your hotel, that only means that Tom didn't tell you, which leaves the same conclusion to be drawn. It's pretty obvious now that you're running out and can't face me. Why don't you admit that you can't live without your little chum? I'm only sorry, old boy, that you didn't have the courage to tell me this before and *outright*. What do you think I am, a small-town hick who doesn't know about such things? *You're* the only one who's acting small-town! At any rate, I hope my telling you what you hadn't the courage to tell me relieves your conscience a little bit and lets you hold your head up. There's nothing like being proud of the person you love, is there? Didn't we once talk about this?

Accomplishment Number Two of my Roman holiday is informing the police that Tom Ripley is with you. They seemed in a perfect tizzy to find him. (I wonder why? What's he done now?) I also informed the police in my best Italian that you and Tom are inseparable and how they could have found you and still missed *Tom*, I could not imagine.

Changed my boat and I'll be leaving for the States around the end of March, after a short visit to Kate in Munich, after which I presume our paths will never cross again. No hard feelings, Dickie boy. I'd just given you credit for a lot more guts.

Thanks for all the wonderful memories. They're like something in a museum already or something preserved in amber, a little unreal, as you must have felt yourself always to me.

Best wishes for the future,
Marge

Ugh! That corn at the end! Ah, Clabber Girl! Tom folded the letter and stuck it into his jacket pocket. He glanced at the two doors of the hotel restaurant, automatically looking for police. If the police thought that Dickie Greenleaf and Tom Ripley were traveling together, they must have checked the Palermo hotels already for Tom Ripley, he thought. But he hadn't noticed any police watching him, or following him. Or maybe they'd given the whole boat scare up, since they were sure Tom Ripley was alive. Why on earth should they go on with it? Maybe the suspicion against Dickie in San Remo and in the Miles murder, too, had already blown over. Maybe.

He went up to his room and began a letter to Mr. Greenleaf on Dickie's portable Hermes. He began by explaining the Miles affair very soberly and logically, because Mr. Greenleaf would probably be pretty alarmed by now. He said that the police had finished their questioning, and that all they conceivably might want now was for him to try to identify any suspects they might find, because the suspect might be a mutual acquaintance of his and Freddie's.

The telephone rang while he was typing. A man's voice said that he was a Tenente Somebody of the Palermo police force.

"We are looking for Thomas Phelps Ripley. Is he with you in your hotel?" he asked courteously.

"No, he is not," Tom replied.

"Do you know where he is?"

"I think he is in Rome. I saw him just three or four days ago in Rome."

"He has not been found in Rome. You do not know where he might have been going from Rome?"

"I'm sorry, I haven't the slightest idea," Tom said.

"Peccato," sighed the voice, with disappointment. "Grazie tante, signor."

"Di niente." Tom hung up and went back to his letter.

The dull yards of Dickie's prose came out more fluently now than Tom's own letters ever had. He addressed most of the letter to Dickie's mother, told her the state of his wardrobe, which was good, and his health, which was also good, and asked if she had received the enamel triptych he had sent her from an antique store in Rome a couple of weeks ago. While he wrote, he was thinking of what he had to do about Thomas Ripley. The quest was apparently very courteous and lukewarm, but it wouldn't do to take wild chances. He shouldn't have Tom's passport lying right in a pocket of his suitcase, even if it was wrapped up in a lot of old income tax papers of Dickie's so that it wasn't visible to a custom inspector's eyes. He should hide it in the lining of the new antelope suitcase, for instance, where it couldn't be seen even if the suitcase were emptied, yet where he could get at it on a few minutes' notice if he had to. Because some day he might have to. There might come a time when it would be more dangerous to be Dickie Greenleaf than to be Tom Ripley.

Tom spent half the morning on the letter to the Greenleafs. He had a feeling that Mr. Greenleaf was getting restless and impatient with Dickie, not in the same way that he had been impatient when Tom had seen him in New York, but in a much more serious way. Mr. Greenleaf thought his removal from Mongibello to Rome had been merely an erratic whim, Tom knew. Tom's attempt to make his painting and studying in Rome sound constructive had really been a failure. Mr. Greenleaf had dismissed it with a withering remark: something about his being sorry that he was still torturing himself with painting at all, because he should have learned by now that it took more than beautiful scenery or a change of scene to make a painter. Mr. Greenleaf had also not been much impressed by the interest Tom had shown in the Burke-Greenleaf folders that Mr. Greenleaf had sent him. It was a far cry from what Tom had expected by this time: that he would have Mr. Greenleaf eating out of his hand, that he would have made up for all Dickie's negligence and unconcern for his parents in the past, and that he could ask Mr. Greenleaf for some extra money and get it. He couldn't possibly ask Mr. Greenleaf for money now.

Take care of yourself, moms [he wrote]. Watch out for those colds. [She had said she'd had four colds this winter, and had spent Christmas propped up in bed, wearing the pink woolen shawl he had sent her as one of his Christmas presents.] If you'd been wearing a pair of those wonderful woolen socks you sent me, you never would have caught the colds. I haven't had a cold this winter, which is something to boast about in a European winter. . . . Moms, can I send you anything from here? I enjoy buying things for you . . .

20.

FIVE days passed, calm, solitary but very agreeable days in which he rambled about Palermo, stopping here and there to sit for an hour or so in a café or a restaurant and read his guidebooks and the newspapers. He took a carrozza one gloomy day and rode all the way to Monte Pelligrino to visit the fantastic tomb of Santa Rosalia, the patron saint of Palermo, depicted in a famous statue, which Tom had seen pictures of in Rome, in one of those states of frozen ecstasy that are given other names by psychiatrists. Tom found the tomb vastly amusing. He could hardly keep from giggling when he saw the statue: the lush, reclining female body, the groping hands, the dazed eyes, the parted lips. It was all there but the actual sound of the panting. He thought of Marge. He visited a Byzantine palace, the Palermo library with its paintings and old cracked manuscripts in glass cases, and studied the formation of the harbor, which was carefully diagrammed in his guidebook. He made a sketch of a painting by Guido Reni, for no particular purpose, and memorized a long inscription by Tasso on one of the public buildings. He wrote letters to Bob Delancey and to Cleo in New York, a long letter to Cleo describing his travels, his pleasures, and his multifarious acquaintances with the convincing ardor of Marco Polo describing China.

But he was lonely. It was not like the sensation in Paris of being alone yet not alone. He had imagined himself acquiring a bright new circle of friends with whom he would start a new life with new attitudes, standards, and habits that would be far better and clearer than those he had had all his life. Now he realized that it couldn't be. He would have to keep a distance from people, always. He might acquire the different standards and habits, but he could never acquire the circle of friends—not unless he went to Istanbul or Ceylon, and what was the use of acquiring the kind of people he would meet in those places? He was alone, and it was a lonely game he was playing. The friends he might make were most of the danger, of course. If he had to drift about the world entirely alone, so much the better: there was that much less chance that he would be found out. That was one cheerful aspect of it, anyway, and he felt better having thought of it.

He altered his behavior slightly, to accord with the role of a more detached observer of life. He was still courteous and smiling to everyone, to people who wanted to borrow his newspaper in restaurants and to clerks he spoke to in the hotel, but he carried his head even higher and he spoke a little less when he spoke. There was a faint air of sadness about him now. He enjoyed the change. He imagined that he looked like a young man who had had an unhappy love affair or some kind of emotional disaster, and was trying to recuperate in a civilized way, by visiting some of the more beautiful places on the earth.

That reminded him of Capri. The weather was still bad, but Capri was Italy. That glimpse he had had of Capri with Dickie had only whetted his appetite. Christ, had Dickie been a bore *that* day! Maybe he should hold out until summer, he thought, hold the police off until then. But even more than Greece and the Acropolis, he wanted one happy holiday in Capri, and to hell with culture for a while. He had read about Capri in winter—wind, rain, and solitude. But still Capri! There was Tiberius' Leap and the Blue Grotto, the plaza without people but still the plaza, and not a cobblestone changed. He might even go today. He quickened his steps toward his hotel. The lack of tourists hadn't detracted from the Côte d'Azur. Maybe he could fly to Capri. He had heard of a sea-plane service from Naples to Capri. If the seaplane wasn't running in February, he could charter it. What was money for?

"Buon' giorno! Come sta?" He greeted the clerk behind the desk with a smile.

"A letter for you, signor. Urgentissimo," the clerk said, smiling, too.

It was from Dickie's bank in Naples. Inside the envelope was another envelope from Dickie's trust company in New York. Tom read the letter from the Naples bank first.

Feb. 10, 19——

Most esteemed signor:

It has been called to our attention by the Wendell Trust Company of New York, that there exists a doubt whether your signature of receipt of your remittance of five hundred dollars of January last is actually your own. We hasten to inform you so that we may take the necessary action.

We have already deemed it proper to inform the police, but we await your confirmation of the opinion of our Inspector of Signatures and of the Inspector of Signatures of the Wendell Trust Company of New York. Any information you may be able to give will be most appreciated, and we urge you to communicate with us at your earliest possible convenience.

Most respectfully and obediently yours,
Emilio di Braganzi
Segretario Generale della Banca di Napoli

P.S. In the case that your signature is in fact valid, we urge you despite this to visit our offices in Naples as soon as possible in order to sign your name again for our permanent records. We enclose a letter to you sent in our care from the Wendell Trust Company.

Tom ripped open the trust company's letter.

Feb. 5, 19——

Dear Mr. Greenleaf:

Our Department of Signatures has reported to us that in its opinion your signature of January on your regular monthly remittance, No. 8747, is invalid. Believing this may for some reason have escaped your notice, we are hastening to inform you, so that you may confirm the signing of the said check or confirm our opinion that the said check has been forged. We have called this to the attention of the Bank of Naples also.

Enclosed is a card for our permanent signature file which we request you to sign and return to us.

Please let us hear from you as soon as possible.

Sincerely,
Edward T. Cavanach
Secretary

Tom wet his lips. He'd write to both banks that he was not missing any money at all. But would that hold them off for long? He had signed three remittances, beginning in December. Were they going to go back and check on all his signatures now? Would an expert be able to tell that all three signatures were forged?

Tom went upstairs and immediately sat down at the typewriter. He put a sheet of hotel stationery into the roller and sat there for a moment, staring at it. They wouldn't rest with this, he thought. If they had a board of experts looking at the signatures with magnifying glasses and all that, they probably would be able to tell that the three signatures were forgeries. But they were such damned good forgeries, Tom knew. He'd signed the January remittance a little fast, he remembered, but it wasn't a bad job or he never would have sent it off. He would have told the bank he lost the remittance and would have had them send him another. Most forgeries took months to be discovered, he thought. Why had they spotted this one in four weeks? Wasn't it because they were checking on him in every department of his life, since the Freddie Miles murder and the San Remo boat story? They wanted to see him personally in the Naples bank. Maybe some of the men there knew Dickie by sight. A terrible, tingling panic went over his shoulders and down his legs. For a moment he felt weak and helpless, too weak to move. He saw himself confronted by a dozen policemen, Italian and American, asking him where Dickie Greenleaf was, and being unable to produce Dickie Greenleaf or tell them where he was or prove that he existed. He imagined himself trying to sign H. Richard Greenleaf under the eyes of a dozen handwriting experts, and going to pieces suddenly and not being able to write at all. He brought his hands up to the typewriter keys and forced himself to begin. He addressed the letter to the Wendell Trust Company of New York.

Feb. 12, 19———

Dear Sirs:

In regard to your letter concerning my January remittance:

I signed the check in question myself and received the money in full. If I had missed the check, I should of course have informed you at once.

I am enclosing the card with my signature for your permanent record as you requested.

Sincerely,
H. Richard Greenleaf

He signed Dickie's signature several times on the back of the trust company's envelope before he signed his letter and then the card. Then he wrote a similar letter to the Naples bank, and promised to call at the bank within the next few days and sign his name again for their permanent record. He marked both envelopes "Urgentissimo," went downstairs and bought stamps from the porter and posted them.

Then he went out for a walk. His desire to go to Capri had vanished. It was four-fifteen in the afternoon. He kept walking, aimlessly. Finally, he stopped in front of an antique shop window and stared for several minutes at a gloomy oil painting of two bearded saints descending a dark hill in moonlight. He went into the shop and bought it for the first price the man quoted to him. It was not even framed, and he carried it rolled up under his arm back to his hotel.

21.

83 Stazione Polizia
Roma
Feb. 14, 19———

Most esteemed Signor Greenleaf:

You are urgently requested to come to Rome to answer some important questions concerning Thomas Ripley. Your presence would be most appreciated and would greatly expedite our investigations.

Failure to present yourself within a week will cause us to take certain measures which will be inconvenient both to us and to you.

> Most respectfully yours,
> Cap. Enrico Farrara

So they were still looking for Tom. But maybe it meant that something had happened on the Miles case, too, Tom thought. The Italians didn't summon an American in words like these. That last paragraph was a plain threat. And of course they knew about the forged check by now.

He stood with the letter in his hand, looking blankly around the room. He caught sight of himself in the mirror, the corners of his mouth turned down, his eyes anxious and scared. He looked as if he were trying to convey the emotions of fear and shock by his posture and his expression, and because the way he looked was involuntary and real, he became suddenly twice as frightened. He folded the letter and pocketed it, then took it out of his pocket and tore it to bits.

He began to pack rapidly, snatching his robe and pajamas from the bathroom door, throwing his toilet articles into the leather kit with Dickie's initials that Marge had given him for Christmas. He stopped suddenly. He had to get rid of Dickie's belongings, all of them. Here? Now? Should he throw them overboard on the way back to Naples?

The question didn't answer itself, but he suddenly knew what he had to do, what he was going to do when he got back to Italy. He would not go anywhere near Rome. He could go straight up to Milan or Turin, or maybe somewhere near Venice, and buy a car, secondhand, with a lot of mileage on it. He'd say he'd been roaming around Italy for the last two or three months. He hadn't heard anything about the search for Thomas Ripley. Thomas Reepley.

He went on packing. This was the end of Dickie Greenleaf, he knew. He hated becoming Thomas Ripley again, hated being nobody, hated putting on his old set of habits again, and feeling that people looked down on him and were bored with him unless he put on an act for them like a clown, feeling incompetent and incapable of doing anything with himself except entertaining people for minutes at a time. He hated going back to himself as he would have hated putting on a shabby suit of clothes, a grease-spotted, unpressed suit of clothes that had not been very good even when it was new. His tears fell on Dickie's blue-and-white-striped shirt that lay uppermost in the suitcase, starched and clean and still as new-looking as when he had first taken it out of Dickie's drawer in Mongibello. But it had Dickie's initials on the pocket in little red letters. As he packed he began to reckon up defiantly the things of Dickie's that he could still keep because they had no initials, or because no one would remember that they were Dickie's and not his own. Except maybe Marge would re-member a few, like the new blue leather address book that Dickie had written only a couple of addresses in, and that Marge had very likely given to him. But he wasn't planning to see Marge again.

Tom paid his bill at the Palma, but he had to wait until the next day for a boat to the mainland. He reserved the boat ticket in the name of Greenleaf, thinking that this was the last time he would ever reserve a ticket in the name of Greenleaf, but that maybe it wouldn't be, either. He couldn't give up the idea that it might all blow over. Just might. And for that reason it was senseless to be despondent. It was senseless to be despondent, anyway, even as Tom Ripley. Tom Ripley had never really been despondent, though he had often looked it. Hadn't he learned something from these last months? If you wanted to be cheerful, or melancholic, or wistful, or thought-ful, or courteous, you simply had to *act* those things with every gesture.

A very cheerful thought came to him when he awoke on the last morning in Palermo: he could check all Dickie's clothes at the American Express in Venice under a different name and reclaim them at some future time, if he wanted to or had to, or else never claim them at all. It made him feel much better to know that Dickie's good shirts, his studbox with all the cuff links and the identification bracelet and his wristwatch would be safely in storage somewhere, instead of at the bottom of the Tyrrhenian Sea or in some ashcan in Sicily.

So, after scraping the initials off Dickie's two suitcases, he sent them, locked, from Naples to the American Express Company, Venice, together with two canvases he had begun painting in Palermo, in the name of Robert S. Fanshaw, to be stored until called for. The only things, the only revealing things, he kept with him were Dickie's rings, which he put into the bottom of an ugly little brown leather box belonging to Thomas Ripley, that he had somehow kept with him for years everywhere he traveled or moved to, and which was otherwise filled with his own uninteresting collection of cuff links, collar pins, odd buttons, a couple of fountain-pen points, and a spool of white thread with a needle stuck in it.

Tom took a train from Naples up through Rome, Florence, Bologna, and Verona, where he got out and went by bus to the town of Trento about forty miles away. He did not want to buy a car in a town as big as Verona, because the police might notice his name when he applied for his license plates, he thought. In Trento he bought a secondhand cream-colored Lancia for the equivalent of about eight hundred dollars. He bought it in the name of Thomas Phelps Ripley, as his passport read, and took a hotel room in that name to wait the twenty-four hours until his license plates should be ready. Six hours later nothing had happened. Tom had been afraid that even this small hotel might recognize his name, that the office that took care of the applications for plates might also notice his name, but by noon the next day he had his plates on his car and nothing had happened. Neither was there anything in the papers about the quest for Thomas Ripley, or the Miles case, or the San Remo boat affair. It made him feel rather strange, rather safe and happy, and as if perhaps all of it were unreal. He began to feel happy even in his dreary role as Thomas Ripley. He took a pleasure in it, overdoing almost the old Tom Ripley reticence with strangers, the inferiority in every duck of his head and wistful, sidelong glance. After all, would anyone, *anyone*, believe that such a character had ever done a murder? And the only murder he could possibly be suspected of was Dickie's in San Remo, and they didn't seem to be getting very far on that. Being Tom Ripley had one compensation, at least: it relieved his mind of guilt for the stupid, unnecessary murder of Freddie Miles.

He wanted to go straight to Venice, but he thought he should spend one night doing what he intended to tell the police he had been doing for several months: sleeping in his car on a country road. He spent one night in the back seat of the Lancia, cramped and miserable, somewhere in the neighborhood of Brescia. He crawled into the front seat at dawn with such a painful crick in his neck he could hardly turn his head sufficiently to drive, but that made it authentic, he thought, that would make him tell the story better. He bought a guidebook of Northern Italy, marked it up appropriately with dates, turned down corners of its pages, stepped on its covers and broke its binding so that it fell open at Pisa.

The next night he spent in Venice. In a childish way Tom had avoided Venice simply because he expected to be disappointed in it. He had thought only sentimentalists and American tourists raved over Venice, and that at best it was only a town for honeymooners who enjoyed the inconvenience of not being able to go anywhere except by a gondola moving at two miles an hour. He found Venice much bigger than he had supposed, full of Italians who looked like Italians anywhere else. He found he could walk across the entire city via the narrow streets and bridges without setting foot in a gondola, and that the major canals had a transportation system of motor launches just as fast and efficient as the subway system, and that the canals did not smell bad, either. There was a tremendous choice of hotels, from the Gritti and the Danieli, which he had heard of, down to crummy little hotels and pensions in back alleys so off the beaten track, so removed from the world of police and American tourists, that Tom could imagine living in one of them for months without being noticed by anybody. He chose a hotel called the Costanza, very near the Rialto bridge, which struck the middle between the famous luxury hotels and the obscure little hostelries on the back streets. It was clean, inexpensive, and convenient to points of interest. It was just the hotel for Tom Ripley.

Tom spent a couple of hours pottering around in his room, slowly unpacking his old familiar clothes, and dreaming out the window at the dusk falling over the Canale Grande. He imagined the conversation he was going to have with the police before long. . . . Why, I haven't any idea. I saw him in Rome. If you've any doubt of that, you can verify it with Miss Marjorie Sherwood. . . . Of course I'm Tom Ripley! (He would give a laugh.) I can't understand what all the fuss is about! . . . San Remo? Yes, I remember. We brought the boat back after an hour. . . . Yes, I came back to Rome after Mongibello, but I didn't stay more than a couple of nights. I've been roaming around the north of Italy. . . . I'm afraid I haven't any idea where he is, but I saw him about three weeks ago. . . . Tom got up from the windowsill smiling, changed his shirt and tie for the evening, and went out to find a pleasant restaurant for dinner. A good restaurant, he thought. Tom Ripley could treat himself to something expensive for once. His billfold was so full of long ten- and twenty-thousand-lire notes it wouldn't bend. He had cashed a thousand dollars' worth of traveler's checks in Dickie's name before he left Palermo.

He bought two evening newspapers, tucked them under his arm and walked on, over a little arched bridge, through a long street hardly six feet wide full of leather shops and men's shirt shops, past windows glittering with jeweled boxes that spilled out necklaces and rings like the boxes Tom had always imagined that treasures spilled out of in fairy tales. He liked the fact that Venice had no cars. It made the city human. The streets were like veins, he thought, and the people were the blood, circulating everywhere. He took another street back and crossed the great quadrangle of San Marco's for the second time. Pigeons everywhere, in the air, in the light of shops—even at night, pigeons walking along under people's feet like sightseers themselves in their own home town! The chairs and tables of the cafés spread across the arcade into the plaza itself, so that people and pigeons had to look for little aisles through them to get by. From either end of the plaza blaring phonographs played in disharmony. Tom tried to imagine the place in summer, in sunlight, full of people tossing handfuls of grain up into the air for the pigeons that fluttered down for it. He entered another little lighted tunnel of a street. It was full of restaurants, and he chose a very substantial and respectable-looking place with white tablecloths and brown wooden walls, the kind of restaurant which experience had taught him by now concentrated on food and not the passing tourist. He took a table and opened one of his newspapers.

And there it was, a little item on the second page:

POLICE SEARCH FOR MISSING AMERICAN
Dickie Greenleaf, Friend of the Murdered Freddie Miles,
Missing After Sicilian Holiday

Tom bent close over the paper, giving it his full attention, yet he was conscious of a certain sense of annoyance as he read it, because in a strange way it seemed silly, silly of the police to be so stupid and ineffectual, and silly of the newspaper to waste space printing it. The text stated that H. Richard ("Dickie") Greenleaf, a close friend of the late Frederick Miles, the American murdered three weeks ago in Rome, had disappeared after presumably taking a boat from Palermo to Naples. Both the Sicilian and Roman police had been alerted and were keeping a vigilantissimo watch for him. A final paragraph said that Greenleaf had just been requested by the Rome police to answer questions concerning the disappearance of Thomas Ripley, also a close friend of Greenleaf. Ripley had been missing for about three months, the paper said.

Tom put the paper down, unconsciously feigning so well the astonishment that anybody might feel on reading in a newspaper that he was "missing," that he didn't notice the waiter trying to hand him the menu until the menu touched his hand. This was the time, he thought, when he ought to go straight to the police and present himself. If they had nothing against him—and what could they have against Tom Ripley?—they wouldn't likely check as to when he had bought the car. The newspaper item was quite a relief to him, because it meant that the police really had not picked up his name at the bureau of automobile registration in Trento.

He ate his meal slowly and with pleasure, ordered an espresso afterward, and smoked a couple of cigarettes as he thumbed through his guidebook on Northern Italy. By then he had had some different thoughts. For example, why should he have seen an item this small in the newspaper? And it was in only one newspaper. No, he oughtn't to present himself until he had seen two or three such items, or one big one that would logically catch his attention. They probably would come out with a big item before long: when a few days passed and Dickie Greenleaf still had not appeared, they would begin to suspect that he was hiding away because he had killed Freddie Miles and possibly Tom Ripley, too. Marge might have told the police she spoke with Tom Ripley two weeks ago in Rome, but the police hadn't seen him yet. He leafed through the guidebook, letting his eyes run over the colorless prose and statistics while he did some more thinking.

He thought of Marge, who was probably winding up her house in Mongibello now, packing for America. She'd see in the papers about Dickie's being missing, and Marge would blame him, Tom knew. She'd write to Dickie's father and say that Tom Ripley was a vile influence, at very least. Mr. Greenleaf might decide to come over.

What a pity he couldn't present himself as Tom Ripley and quiet them down about that, then present himself as Dickie Greenleaf, hale and hearty, and clear up that little mystery, too!

He might play up Tom a little more, he thought. He could stoop a little more, he could be shyer than ever, he could even wear horn-rimmed glasses and hold his mouth in an even sadder, droopier manner to contrast with Dickie's tenseness. Because some of the police he might talk to might be the ones who had seen him as Dickie Greenleaf. What was the name of that one in Rome? Rovassini? Tom decided to rinse his hair again in a stronger solution of henna, so that it would be even darker than his normal hair.

He looked through all the papers a third time for anything about the Miles case. Nothing.

22.

THE next morning there was a long account in the most important newspaper, saying in only a small paragraph that Thomas Ripley was missing, but saying very boldly that Richard Greenleaf was "exposing himself to suspicion of participation" in the murder of Miles, and that he must be considered as evading the "problem," unless he presented himself to be cleared of suspicion. The paper also mentioned the forged check. It said that the last communication from Richard Greenleaf had been his letter to the Bank of Naples, attesting that no forgeries had been committed against him. But two experts out of three in Naples said that they believed Signor Greenleaf's January and February checks were forgeries, concurring with the opinion of Signor Greenleaf's American bank, which had sent photostats of his signatures back to Naples. The newspaper ended on a slightly facetious note: "Can anybody commit a forgery against himself? Or is the wealthy American shielding one of his friends?"

To hell with them, Tom thought. Dickie's own handwriting changed often enough: he had seen it on an insurance policy among Dickie's papers, and he had seen it in Mongibello, right in front of his eyes. Let them drag out everything he had signed in the last three months, and see where it got them! They apparently hadn't noticed that the signature on his letter from Palermo was a forgery, too.

The only thing that really interested him was whether the police had found anything that actually incriminated Dickie in the murder of Freddie Miles. And he could hardly say that that really interested him, personally. He bought *Oggi* and *Epoca* at a news stand in the corner of San Marco's. They were tabloid-sized weeklies full of photographs, full of anything from murder to flagpole-sitting, anything spectacular that was happening anywhere. There was nothing in them yet about the missing Dickie Greenleaf. Maybe next week, he thought. But they wouldn't have any photographs of him in them, anyway. Marge had taken pictures of Dickie in Mongibello, but she had never taken one of him.

On his ramble around the city that morning he bought some rimmed glasses at a shop that sold toys and gadgets for practical jokers. The lenses were of plain glass. He visited San Marco's cathedral and looked all around inside it without seeing anything, but it was not the fault of the glasses. He was thinking that he had to identify himself, immediately. It would look worse for him, whatever happened, the longer he put it off. When he left the cathedral he inquired of a policeman where the nearest police station was. He asked it sadly. He felt sad. He was not afraid, but he felt that identifying himself

as Thomas Phelps Ripley was going to be one of the saddest
things he had ever done in his life.

"*You* are Thomas Reepley?" the captain of police asked,
with no more interest than if Tom had been a dog that had
been lost and was now found. "May I see your passport?"

Tom handed it to him. "I don't know what the trouble is,
but when I saw in the papers that I am believed missing—"
It was all dreary, dreary, just as he had anticipated. Policemen
standing around blank-faced, staring at him. "What happens
now?" Tom asked the officer.

"I shall telephone to Rome," the officer answered calmly,
and picked up the telephone on his desk.

There was a few minutes' wait for the Rome line, and then,
in an impersonal voice, the officer announced to someone in
Rome that the American, Thomas Reepley, was in Venice.
More inconsequential exchanges, then the officer said to Tom,
"They would like to see you in Rome. Can you go to Rome
today?"

Tom frowned. "I wasn't planning to go to Rome."

"I shall tell them," the officer said mildly, and spoke into
the telephone again.

Now he was arranging for the Rome police to come to him.
Being an American citizen still commanded certain privileges,
Tom supposed.

"At what hotel are you staying?" the officer asked.

"At the Costanza."

The officer gave this piece of information to Rome. Then
he hung up and informed Tom politely that a representative
of the Rome police would be in Venice that evening after eight
o'clock to speak to him.

"Thank you," Tom said, and turned his back on the dismal
figure of the officer writing on his form sheet. It had been a
very boring little scene.

Tom spent the rest of the day in his room, quietly thinking,
reading, and making further small alterations in his appearance. He thought it quite possible that they would send the
same man who had spoken to him in Rome, Tenente Rovassini or whatever his name was. He made his eyebrows a trifle
darker with a lead pencil. He lay around all afternoon in his

brown tweed suit, and even pulled a button off the jacket.
Dickie had been rather on the neat side, so Tom Ripley was
going to be notably sloppy by contrast. He ate no lunch, not
that he wanted any, anyway, but he wanted to continue losing
the few pounds he had added for the role of Dickie Greenleaf.
He would make himself thinner than he had even been before
as Tom Ripley. His weight on his own passport was one hundred and fifty-five. Dickie's was a hundred and sixty-eight,
though they were the same height, six feet one and one-half.

At eight-thirty that evening his telephone rang, and the
switchboard operator announced that Tenente Roverini was
downstairs.

"Would you have him come up, please?" Tom said.

Tom went to the chair that he intended to sit in, and drew
it still farther back from the circle of light cast by the standing
lamp. The room was arranged to look as if he had been reading and killing time for the last few hours—the standing lamp
and a tiny reading lamp were on, the counterpane was not
smooth, a couple of books lay open face down, and he had
even begun a letter on the writing table, a letter to Aunt
Dottie.

The tenente knocked.

Tom opened the door in a languid way. "Buona sera."

"Buona sera. Tenente Roverini della Polizia Romana." The
tenente's homely, smiling face did not look the least surprised
or suspicious. Behind him came another tall, silent young police officer—not another, Tom realized suddenly, but the one
who had been with the tenente when Tom had first met Roverini in the apartment in Rome. The officer sat down in the
chair Tom offered him, under the light. "You are a friend of
Signor Richard Greenleaf?" he asked.

"Yes." Tom sat down in the other chair, an armchair that
he could slouch in.

"When did you last see him and where?"

"I saw him briefly in Rome, just before he went to Sicily."

"And did you hear from him when he was in Sicily?" The
tenente was writing it all down in the notebook that he had
taken from his brown briefcase.

"No, I didn't hear from him."

"Ah-hah," the tenente said. He was spending more time

looking at his papers than at Tom. Finally, he looked up with a friendly, interested expression. "You did not know when you were in Rome that the police wanted to see you?"

"No, I did not know that. I cannot understand why I am said to be missing." He adjusted his glasses, and peered at the man.

"I shall explain later. Signor Greenleaf did not tell you in Rome that the police wanted to speak to you?"

"No."

"Strange," he remarked quietly, making another notation. "Signor Greenleaf knew that we wanted to speak to you. Signor Greenleaf is not very cooperative." He smiled at Tom.

Tom kept his face serious and attentive.

"Signor Reepley, where have you been since the end of November?"

"I have been traveling. I have been mostly in the north of Italy." Tom made his Italian clumsy, with a mistake here and there, and with quite a different rhythm from Dickie's Italian.

"Where?" The tenente gripped his pen again.

"Milano, Torino, Faenza—Pisa—"

"We have inquired at the hotels in Milano and Faenza, for example. Did you stay all the time with friends?"

"No, I—slept quite often in my car." It was obvious that he hadn't a great deal of money, Tom thought, and also that he was the kind of young man who would prefer to rough it with a guidebook and a volume of Silone or Dante, than to stay in a fancy hotel. "I am sorry that I did not renew my permiso di soggiorno," Tom said contritely. "I did not know that it was such a serious matter." But he knew that tourists in Italy almost never took the trouble to renew their soggiorno, and stayed for months after stating on entering the country that they intended to be here for only a few weeks.

"*Permesso* di soggiorno," the tenente said in a tone of gentle, almost paternal correction.

"Grazie."

"May I see your passport?"

Tom produced it from his inside jacket pocket. The tenente studied the picture closely, while Tom assumed the faintly anxious expression, the faintly parted lips, of the passport photograph. The glasses were missing from the photograph, but his hair was parted in the same manner, and his tie was tied in the same loose, triangular knot. The tenente glanced at the few stamped entries that only partially filled the first two pages of the passport.

"You have been in Italy since October second, except for the short trip to France with Signor Greenleaf?"

"Yes."

The tenente smiled, a pleasant Italian smile now, and leaned forward on his knees. "Ebbene, this settles one important matter—the mystery of the San Remo boat."

Tom frowned. "What is that?"

"A boat was found sunken there with some stains that were believed to be bloodstains. Naturally, when you were missing, so far as we knew, immediately after San Remo—" He threw his hands out and laughed. "We thought it might be advisable to ask Signor Greenleaf what had happened to you. Which we did. The boat was missed the same day that you two were in San Remo!" He laughed again.

Tom pretended not to see the joke. "But did not Signor Greenleaf tell you that I went to Mongibello after San Remo? I did some—" he groped for a word "—little labors for him."

"Benone!" Tenente Roverini said, smiling. He loosened his brass-buttoned overcoat comfortably, and rubbed a finger back and forth across the crisp, bushy mustache. "Did you also know Fred-derick Mee-lays?" he asked.

Tom gave an involuntary sigh, because the boat incident was apparently closed. "No. I only met him once when he was getting off the bus in Mongibello. I never saw him again."

"Ah-hah," said the tenente, taking this in. He was silent a minute, as if he had run out of questions, then he smiled. "Ah, Mongibello! A beautiful village, is it not? My wife comes from Mongibello."

"Ah, indeed!" Tom said pleasantly.

"Si. My wife and I went there on our honeymoon."

"A most beautiful village," Tom said. "Grazie." He accepted the Nazionale that the tenente offered him. Tom felt that this was perhaps a polite Italian interlude, a rest between rounds. They were surely going to get into Dickie's private life, the forged checks and all the rest. Tom said seriously in his plodding Italian, "I have read in a newspaper that the police think that Signor Greenleaf may be guilty of the murder of Freddie Miles, if he does not present himself. Is it true that they think he is guilty?"

"Ah, no, no, no!" the tenente protested. "But it is imperative that he present himself! Why is he hiding from us?"

"I don't know. As you say—he is not very cooperative," Tom commented solemnly. "He was not enough cooperative to tell me in Rome that the police wanted to speak with me. But at the same time—I cannot believe it is possible that he killed Freddie Miles."

"*But*—you see, a man has said in Rome that he saw two men standing beside the car of Signor Mee-lays across the street from the house of Signor Greenleaf, and that they were both drunk or—" he paused for effect, looking at Tom "—perhaps one man was dead, because the other was holding him up beside the car! Of course, we cannot say that the man who was being supported was Signor Mee-lays or Signor Greenleaf," he added, "but if we could find Signor Greenleaf, we could at least ask him if he was so drunk that Signor Mee-lays had to hold him up!" He laughed. "Yes."

"It is a very serious matter."

"Yes, I can see that."

"You have absolutely no idea where Signor Greenleaf might be at this moment?"

"No. Absolutely no."

The tenente mused. "Signor Greenleaf and Signor Mee-lays had no quarrel that you know of?"

"No, but—"

"But?"

Tom continued slowly, doing it just right. "I know that Dickie did not go to a ski party that Freddie Miles had invited him to. I remember that I was surprised that he had not gone. He did not tell me why."

"I know about the ski party. In Cortina d'Ampezzo. Are you sure there was no woman involved?"

Tom's sense of humor tugged at him, but he pretended to think this one over carefully. "I do not think so."

"What about the girl, Marjorie Sherwood?"

"I suppose it is *possible*," Tom said, "but I do not think so. I am perhaps not the person to answer questions about Signor Greenleaf's personal life."

"Signor Greenleaf never talked to you about his affairs of the heart?" the tenente asked with a Latin astonishment.

He could lead them on indefinitely, Tom thought. Marge would back it up, just by the emotional way she would react to questions about Dickie, and the Italian police could never get to the bottom of Signor Greenleaf's emotional involvements. He hadn't been able to himself! "No," Tom said. "I cannot say that Dickie ever talked to me about his most personal life. I know he is very fond of Marjorie." He added, "She also knew Freddie Miles."

"How well did she know him?"

"Well—" Tom acted as if he might say more if he chose.

The tenente leaned forward. "Since you lived for a time with Signor Greenleaf in Mongibello, you are perhaps in a position to tell us about Signor Greenleaf's attachments in general. They are most important."

"Why don't you speak to Signorina Sherwood?" Tom suggested.

"We have spoken to her in Rome—before Signor Greenleaf disappeared. I have arranged to speak to her again when she comes to Genoa to embark for America. She is now in Munich."

Tom waited, silent. The tenente was waiting for him to contribute something more. Tom felt quite comfortable now. It was going just as he had hoped in his most optimistic moments: the police held nothing against him at all, and they suspected him of nothing. Tom felt suddenly innocent and strong, as free of guilt as his old suitcase from which he had carefully scrubbed the *Deponimento* sticker from the Palermo baggage room. He said in his earnest, careful, Ripley-like way, "I remember that Marjorie said for a while in Mongibello that she would *not* go to Cortina, and later she changed her mind. But I do not know why. If that could mean anything—"

"But she never went to Cortina."

"No, but only because Signor Greenleaf did not go, I think. At least, Signorina Sherwood likes him so much that she would not go alone on a holiday after she expected to go on the holiday with him."

"Do you think they had a quarrel, Signors Mee-lays and Greenleaf, about Signorina Sherwood?"

"I cannot say. It is possible. I know that Signor Miles was very fond of her, too."

"Ah-hah." The tenente frowned, trying to figure all that out. He glanced up at the younger policeman, who was evidently listening, though, from his immobile face, he had nothing to contribute.

What he had said gave a picture of Dickie as a sulking lover, Tom thought, unwilling to let Marge go to Cortina to have some fun, because she liked Freddie Miles too much. The idea of anybody, Marge especially, liking that wall-eyed ox in preference to Dickie made Tom smile. He turned the smile into an expression of noncomprehension. "Do you actually think Dickie is running away from something, or do you think it is an accident that you cannot find him?"

"Oh, no. This is too much. First, the matter of the checks. You perhaps know about that from the newspapers."

"I do not completely understand about the checks."

The officer explained. He knew the dates of the checks and the number of people who believed they were forged. He explained that Signor Greenleaf had denied the forgeries. "But when the bank wishes to see him again about a forgery against himself, and also the police in Rome wish to see him again about the murder of his friend, and he suddenly vanishes—" The tenente threw out his hands. "That can only mean that he is running away from us."

"You don't think someone may have murdered *him?*" Tom said softly.

The officer shrugged, holding his shoulders up under his ears for at least a quarter of a minute. "I do not think so. The facts are not like that. Not quite. Ebbene—we have checked by radio every boat of any size with passengers which has left from Italy. He has either taken a small boat, and it must have been as small as a fishing boat, or else he is hiding in Italy. Or of course, anywhere else in Europe, because we do not ordinarily take the names of people leaving our country, and Signor Greenleaf had several days in which to leave. In any case, he is hiding. In any case, he acts guilty. *Something* is the matter."

Tom stared gravely at the man.

"Did you ever *see* Signor Greenleaf sign any of those remittances? In particular, the remittances of January and February?"

"I saw him sign one of them," Tom said. "But I am afraid it was in December. I was not with him in January and February. —Do you seriously suspect that he might have killed Signor Miles?" Tom asked again, incredulously.

"He has no actual alibi," the officer replied. "He says he was taking a walk after Signor Mee-lays departed, but nobody saw him taking the walk." He pointed a finger at Tom suddenly. "*And*—we have learned from the friend of Signor Mee-lays, Signor Van Houston, that Signor Mee-lays had a difficult time finding Signor Greenleaf in Rome—as if Signor Greenleaf were trying to hide from him. Signor Greenleaf might have been angry with Signor Mee-lays, though, according to Signor Van Houston, Signor Mee-lays was not at all angry with Signor Greenleaf!"

"I see," Tom said.

"Ecco," the tenente said conclusively. He was staring at Tom's hands.

Or at least Tom imagined that he was staring at his hands. Tom had his own ring on again, but did the tenente possibly notice some resemblance? Tom boldly thrust his hand forward to the ashtray and put out his cigarette.

"Ebbene," the tenente said, standing up. "Thank you so much for your help, Signor Reepley. You are one of the very few people from whom we can find out about Signor Greenleaf's personal life. In Mongibello, the people he knew are extremely quiet. An Italian trait, alas! You know, afraid of the police." He chuckled. "I hope we can reach you more easily the next time we have questions to ask you. Stay in the cities a little more and in the country a little less. Unless, of course, you are addicted to our countryside."

"I am!" Tom said heartily. "In my opinion, Italy is the most beautiful country of Europe. But if you like, I shall keep in touch with you in Rome so you will always know where I am. I am as much interested as you in finding my friend." He said it as if his innocent mind had already forgotten the possibility that Dickie could be a murderer.

The tenente handed him a card with his name and the address of his headquarters in Rome. He bowed. "Grazie tante, Signor Reepley. Buona sera!"

"Buona sera," Tom said.

The younger policeman saluted him as he went out, and Tom gave him a nod and closed the door.

He could have flown—like a bird, out the window, with spread arms! The idiots! All around the thing and never guessing it! Never guessing that Dickie was running from the forgery questions because he wasn't Dickie Greenleaf in the first place! The one thing they were bright about was that Dickie Greenleaf might have killed Freddie Miles. But Dickie Greenleaf was dead, dead, deader than a doornail and he, Tom Ripley, was safe! He picked up the telephone.

"Would you give me the Grand Hotel, please," he said in Tom Ripley's Italian. "Il ristorante, per piacere. —Would you reserve a table for one for nine-thirty? Thank you. The name is Ripley. R-i-p-l-e-y."

Tonight he was going to have a dinner. And look out at the moonlight on the Grand Canal. And watch the gondolas drifting as lazily as they ever drifted for any honeymooner, with the gondoliers and their oars silhouetted against the moonlit water. He was suddenly ravenous. He was going to have something luscious and expensive to eat—whatever the Grand Hotel's specialty was, breast of pheasant or petto di pollo, and perhaps cannelloni to begin with, creamy sauce over delicate pasta, and a good valpolicella to sip while he dreamed about his future and planned where he went from here.

He had a bright idea while he was changing his clothes: he ought to have an envelope in his possession, on which should be written that it was not to be opened for several months to come. Inside it should be a will signed by Dickie, bequeathing him his money and his income. Now that was an idea.

23.

Venice
Feb. 28, 19—

Dear Mr. Greenleaf,

I thought under the circumstances you would not take it amiss if I wrote you whatever personal information I have in regard to Richard—I being one of the last people, it seems, who saw him.

I saw him in Rome around February 2nd at the Inghilterra Hotel. As you know, this was only two or three days after the death of Freddie Miles. I found Dickie upset and nervous. He said he was going to Palermo as soon as the police finished their questioning him in regard to Freddie's death, and he seemed eager to get away, which was understandable, but I wanted to tell you that there was a certain depression underlying all this that troubled me much more than his obvious nervousness. I had the feeling he would try to do something violent—perhaps to himself. I knew also that he didn't want to see his friend Marjorie Sherwood again, and he said he would try to avoid her if she came up from Mongibello to see him because of the Miles affair. I tried to persuade him to see her. I don't know if he did. Marge has a soothing effect on people, as perhaps you know.

What I am trying to say is that I feel Richard may have killed himself. At the time of this writing he has not been found. I certainly hope he will be before this reaches you. It goes without saying that I am sure Richard had nothing to do, directly or indirectly, with Freddie's death, but I think the shock of it and the questioning that followed did do something to upset his equilibrium. This is a depressing message to send to you and I regret it. It may be all completely unnecessary and Dickie may be (again understandably, according to his temperament) simply in hiding until these unpleasantnesses blow over. But as the time goes on, I begin to feel more uneasy myself. I thought it my duty to write you this, simply by way of letting you know. . . .

Munich
March 3, 19—

Dear Tom,

Thanks for your letter. It was very kind of you. I've answered the police in writing, and one came up to see me. I won't be coming by Venice, but thanks for your invitation. I am going to Rome day after tomorrow to meet Dickie's father, who is flying over. Yes, I agree with you that it was a good idea for you to write to him.

I am so bowled over by all this, I have come down with something resembling undulant fever, or maybe what the Germans call Foehn, but with some kind of virus thrown in. Literally unable to get out of bed for four days, otherwise I'd have gone to Rome before now. So please excuse this disjointed and probably feeble-minded letter which is such a bad answer to your very nice one. But I did want to say I don't agree with you at all that Dickie might have committed suicide. He just isn't the type, though I know all you're going to say about people never acting like they're going to do it, etc. No, anything else but this for Dickie. He might have been murdered in some back alley of Naples—or even Rome, because who knows whether he got up to Rome or not after he left Sicily? I can also imagine him running out on obligations to such an extent that he'd be *hiding* now. I think that's what he's doing.

I'm glad you think the forgeries are a mistake. Of the bank, I mean. So do I. Dickie has changed so much since November, it could easily have changed his handwriting, too. Let's hope something's happened by the time you get this. Had a wire from Mr. Greenleaf about Rome—so must save all my energy for that.

Nice to know your address finally. Thanks again for your letter, your advice, and invitations.

Best,
Marge

P.S. I didn't tell you my *good* news. I've got a publisher interested in "Mongibello"! Says he wants to see the whole thing before he can give me a contract, but it really sounds hopeful! Now if I can only finish the damn thing!

M.

She had decided to be on good terms with him, Tom supposed. She'd probably changed her tune about him to the police, too.

Dickie's disappearance was stirring up a great deal of excitement in the Italian press. Marge, or somebody, had provided the reporters with photographs. There were pictures in *Epoca* of Dickie sailing his boat in Mongibello, pictures of Dickie in *Oggi* sitting on the beach in Mongibello and also on Giorgio's terrace, and a picture of Dickie and Marge—"girl friend of both il sparito Dickie and il assassinato Freddie"—smiling, with their arms around each other's shoulders, and there was even a businesslike portrait of Herbert Greenleaf, Sr. Tom had gotten Marge's Munich address right out of a newspaper. *Oggi* had been running a life story of Dickie for the past two weeks, describing his school years as "rebellious" and embroidering his social life in America and his flight to Europe for the sake of his art to such an extent that he emerged as a combination of Errol Flynn and Paul Gauguin. The illustrated weeklies always gave the latest police reports, which were practically nil, padded with whatever theorizing the writers happened to feel like concocting that week. A favorite theory was that he had run off with another girl—a girl who might have been signing his remittances—and was having a good time, incognito, in Tahiti or South America or Mexico. The police were still combing Rome and Naples and Paris, that was all. No clues as to Freddie Miles' killer, and nothing about Dickie Greenleaf's having been seen carrying Freddie Miles, or vice versa, in front of Dickie's house. Tom wondered why they were holding that back from the newspapers. Probably because they couldn't write it up without subjecting themselves to charges of libel by Dickie. Tom was gratified to find himself described as "a loyal friend" of the missing Dickie Greenleaf, who had volunteered everything he knew as to Dickie's character and habits, and who was as bewildered by his disappearance as anybody else. "Signor Ripley, one of the young well-to-do American visitors in Italy," said *Oggi*, "now lives in a palazzo overlooking San Marco in Venice." That pleased Tom most of all. He cut out that write-up.

Tom had not thought of it as a "palace" before, but of course it was what the Italians called a palazzo—a two-story house of formal design more than two hundred years old, with a main entrance on the Grand Canal approachable only by gondola, with broad stone steps descending into the water, and iron doors that had to be opened by an eight-inch-long key, besides the regular doors behind the iron doors which also took an enormous key. Tom used the less formal "back door" usually, which was on the Viale San Spiridione, except when he wanted to impress his guests by bringing them to his home in a gondola. The back door—itself fourteen feet high like the stone wall that enclosed the house from the street—led into a garden that was somewhat neglected but still green, and which boasted two gnarled olive trees and a birdbath made of an ancient-looking statue of a naked boy

holding a wide shallow bowl. It was just the garden for a
Venetian palace, slightly run down, in need of some restora-
tion which it was not going to get, but indelibly beautiful
because it had sprung into the world so beautiful more than
two hundred years ago. The inside of the house was Tom's
ideal of what a civilized bachelor's home should look like, in
Venice, at least: a checkerboard black-and-white marble floor
downstairs extending from the formal foyer into each room,
pink-and-white marble floor upstairs, furniture that did not
resemble furniture at all but an embodiment of cinquecento
music played on hautboys, recorders, and violas da gamba. He
had his servants—Anna and Ugo, a young Italian couple who
had worked for an American in Venice before, so that they
knew the difference between a Bloody Mary and a crème de
menthe frappé—polish the carved fronts of the armoires and
chests and chairs until they seemed alive with dim lustrous
lights that moved as one moved around them. The only thing
faintly modern was the bathroom. In Tom's bedroom stood
a gargantuan bed, broader than it was long. Tom decorated
his bedroom with a series of panoramic pictures of Naples
from 1540 to about 1880, which he found at an antique store.
He had given his undivided attention to decorating his house
for more than a week. There was a sureness in his taste now
that he had not felt in Rome, and that his Rome apartment
had not hinted at. He felt surer of himself now in every way.

His self-confidence had even inspired him to write to Aunt
Dottie in a calm, affectionate and forbearing tone that he had
never wanted to use before, or had never before been able to
use. He had inquired about her flamboyant health, about her
little circle of vicious friends in Boston, and had explained to
her why he liked Europe and intended to live here for a while,
explained so eloquently that he had copied that section of his
letter and put it into his desk. He had written this inspired
letter one morning after breakfast, sitting in his bedroom in
a new silk dressing gown made to order for him in Venice,
gazing out the window now and then at the Grand Canal and
the Clock Tower of the Piazza San Marco across the water.
After he had finished the letter he had made some more coffee
and on Dickie's own Hermes he had written Dickie's will,
bequeathing him his income and the money he had in various

banks, and had signed it Herbert Richard Greenleaf, Jr. Tom thought it better not to add a witness, lest the banks or Mr. Greenleaf challenge him to the extent of demanding to know who the witness was, though Tom had thought of making up an Italian name, presumably someone Dickie might have called into his apartment in Rome for the purpose of witnessing the will. He would just have to take his chances on an unwitnessed will, he thought, but Dickie's typewriter was so in need of repair that its quirks were as recognizable as a particular handwriting, and he had heard that holograph wills required no witnesses. But the signature was perfect, exactly like the slim, tangled signature on Dickie's passport. Tom practiced for half an hour before he signed the will, relaxed his hands, then signed a piece of scrap paper, then the will, in rapid succession. And he would defy anybody to prove that the signature on the will wasn't Dickie's. Tom put an envelope into the typewriter and addressed it To Whom It May Concern, with a notation that it was not to be opened until June of this year. He tucked it into a side pocket of his suitcase, as if he had been carrying it there for some time and hadn't bothered unpacking it when he moved into the house. Then he took the Hermes Baby in its case downstairs and dropped it into the little inlet of the canal, too narrow for a boat, which ran from the front corner of his house to the garden wall. He was glad to be rid of the typewriter, though he had been unwilling to part with it until now. He must have known, subconsciously, he thought, that he was going to write the will or something else of great importance on it, and that was the reason why he had kept it.

Tom followed the Italian newspapers and the Paris edition of the *Herald-Tribune* on the Greenleaf and Miles cases with the anxious concern befitting a friend of both Dickie and Freddie. The papers were suggesting by the end of March that Dickie might be dead, murdered by the same man or men who had been profiting by forging his signature. A Rome paper said that one man in Naples now held that the signature on the letter from Palermo, stating that no forgeries had been committed against him, was also a forgery. Others, however, did not concur. Some man on the police force, not Roverini, thought that the culprit or culprits had been "intimo" with

Greenleaf, that they had had access to the bank's letter and had had the audacity to reply to it themselves. "The mystery is," the officer was quoted, "not only who the forger was but how he gained access to the letter, because the porter of the hotel remembers putting the registered bank letter into Greenleaf's hands. The hotel porter also recalls that Greenleaf was always alone in Palermo. . . ."

More hitting around the answer without ever hitting it. But Tom was shaken for several minutes after he read it. There remained only one more step for them to take, and wasn't somebody going to take it today or tomorrow or the next day? Or did they really already know the answer, and were they just trying to put him off guard—Tenente Roverini sending him personal messages every few days to keep him abreast of what was happening in the search for Dickie—and were they going to pounce on him one day soon with every bit of evidence they needed?

It gave Tom the feeling that he was being followed, especially when he walked through the long, narrow street to his house door. The Viale San Spiridione was nothing but a functional slit between vertical walls of houses, without a shop in it and with hardly enough light for him to see where he was going, nothing but unbroken housefronts and the tall, firmly locked doors of the Italian house gates that were flush with the walls. Nowhere to run to if he were attacked, no house door to duck into. Tom did not know who would attack him, if he were attacked. He did not imagine police, necessarily. He was afraid of nameless, formless things that haunted his brain like the Furies. He could go through San Spiridione comfortably only when a few cocktails had knocked out his fear. Then he walked through swaggering and whistling.

He had his pick of cocktail parties, though in his first two weeks in his house he went to only two. He had his choice of people because of a little incident that had happened the first day he had started looking for a house. A rental agent, armed with three huge keys, had taken him to see a certain house in San Stefano parish, thinking it would be vacant. It had not only been occupied but a cocktail party had been in progress, and the hostess had insisted on Tom and the rental agent, too, having a cocktail by way of making amends for their inconvenience and her remissness. She had put the house up for rent a month ago, had changed her mind about leaving, and had neglected to inform the rental agency. Tom stayed for a drink, acted his reserved, courteous self, and met all her guests, who he supposed were most of the winter colony of Venice and rather hungry for new blood, judging from the way they welcomed him and offered their assistance in finding a house. They recognized his name, of course, and the fact that he knew Dickie Greenleaf raised his social value to a degree that surprised even Tom. Obviously they were going to invite him everywhere and quiz him and drain him of every last little detail to add some spice to their dull lives. Tom behaved in a reserved but friendly manner appropriate for a young man in his position—a sensitive young man, unused to garish publicity, whose primary emotion in regard to Dickie was anxiety as to what had happened to him.

He left that first party with the addresses of three other houses he might look at (one being the one he took) and invitations to two other parties. He went to the party whose hostess had a title, the Condessa Roberta (Titi) della Latta-Cacciaguerra. He was not at all in the mood for parties. He seemed to see people through a mist, and communication was slow and difficult. He often asked people to repeat what they had said. He was terribly bored. But he could use them, he thought, to practice on. The naïve questions they asked him ("Did Dickie drink a lot?" and "But he *was* in love with Marge, wasn't he?" and "Where do you *really* think he went?") were good practice for the more specific questions Mr. Greenleaf was going to ask him when he saw him, if he ever saw him. Tom began to be uneasy about ten days after Marge's letter, because Mr. Greenleaf had not written or telephoned him from Rome. In certain frightened moments, Tom imagined that the police had told Mr. Greenleaf that they were playing a game with Tom Ripley, and had asked Mr. Greenleaf not to talk to him.

Each day he looked eagerly in his mailbox for a letter from Marge or Mr. Greenleaf. His house was ready for their arrival. His answers to their questions were ready in his head. It was like waiting interminably for a show to begin, for a curtain to rise. Or maybe Mr. Greenleaf was so resentful of him (not to

mention possibly being actually suspicious) that he was going
to ignore him entirely. Maybe Marge was abetting him in that.
At any rate, he couldn't take a trip until *something* happened.
Tom wanted to take a trip, the famous trip to Greece. He had
bought a guidebook of Greece, and he had already planned
his itinerary over the islands.

Then, on the morning of April fourth, he got a telephone
call from Marge. She was in Venice, at the railroad station.

"I'll come and pick you up!" Tom said cheerfully. "Is Mr.
Greenleaf with you?"

"No, he's in Rome. I'm alone. You don't have to pick me
up. I've only got an overnight bag."

"Nonsense!" Tom said, dying to do something. "You'll
never find the house by yourself."

"Yes, I will. It's next to della Salute, isn't it? I take the
motoscafo to San Marco's, then take a gondola across."

She knew, all right. "Well, if you insist." He had just
thought that he had better take one more good look around
the house before she got here. "Have you had lunch?"

"No."

"Good! We'll lunch together somewhere. Watch your step
on the motoscafo!"

They hung up. He walked soberly and slowly through the
house, into both large rooms upstairs, down the stairs and
through his living room. Nothing, anywhere, that belonged
to Dickie. He hoped the house didn't look too plush. He took
a silver cigarette box, which he had bought only two days ago
and had had initialed, from the living-room table and put it
in the bottom drawer of a chest in the dining room.

Anna was in the kitchen, preparing lunch.

"Anna, there'll be one more for lunch," Tom said. "A
young lady."

Anna's face broke into a smile at the prospect of a guest.
"A young American lady?"

"Yes. An old friend. When the lunch is ready, you and Ugo
can have the rest of the afternoon off. We can serve ourselves."

"Va bene," Anna said.

Anna and Ugo came at ten and stayed until two, ordinarily.
Tom didn't want them here when he talked with Marge. They

understood a little English, not enough to follow a conversation perfectly, but he knew both of them would have their ears out if he and Marge talked about Dickie, and it irritated him.

Tom made a batch of martinis, and arranged the glasses and a plate of canapés on a tray in the living room. When he heard the door knocker, he went to the door and swung it open.

"Marge! Good to see you! Come in!" He took the suitcase from her hand.

"How are you, Tom? My! —Is all this yours?" She looked around her, and up at the high coffered ceiling.

"I rented it. For a song," Tom said modestly. "Come and have a drink. Tell me what's new. You've been talking to the police in Rome?" He carried her topcoat and her transparent raincoat to a chair.

"Yes, and to Mr. Greenleaf. He's very upset—naturally." She sat down on the sofa.

Tom settled himself in a chair opposite her. "Have they found anything new? One of the police officers there has been keeping me posted, but he hasn't told me anything that really matters."

"Well, they found out that Dickie cashed over a thousand dollars' worth of traveler's checks before he left Palermo. *Just* before. So he must have gone off somewhere with it, like Greece or Africa. He couldn't have gone off to kill himself after just cashing a thousand dollars, anyway."

"No," Tom agreed. "Well, that sounds hopeful. I didn't see that in the papers."

"I don't think they put it in."

"No. Just a lot of nonsense about what Dickie used to eat for breakfast in Mongibello," Tom said as he poured the martinis.

"Isn't it awful! It's getting a little better now, but when Mr. Greenleaf arrived, the papers were at their worst. Oh, thanks!" She accepted the martini gratefully.

"How is he?"

Marge shook her head. "I feel so sorry for him. He keeps saying the American police could do a better job and all that, and he doesn't know any Italian, so that makes it twice as bad."

"What's he doing in Rome?"

"Waiting. What can any of us do? I've postponed my boat again. —Mr. Greenleaf and I went to Mongibello, and I questioned everyone there, mostly for Mr. Greenleaf's benefit, of course, but they can't tell us anything. Dickie hasn't been back there since November."

"No." Tom sipped his martini thoughtfully. Marge was optimistic, he could see that. Even now she had that energetic buoyance that made Tom think of the typical Girl Scout, that look of taking up a lot of space, of possibly knocking something over with a wild movement, of rugged health and vague untidiness. She irritated him intensely suddenly, but he put on a big act, got up and patted her on the shoulder, and gave her an affectionate peck on the cheek. "Maybe he's sitting in Tangiers or somewhere living the life of Riley and waiting for all this to blow over."

"Well, it's damned inconsiderate of him if he is!" Marge said, laughing.

"I certainly didn't mean to alarm anybody when I said what I did about his depression. I felt it was a kind of duty to tell you and Mr. Greenleaf."

"I understand. No, I think you were right to tell us. I just don't think it's true." She smiled her broad smile, her eyes glowing with an optimism that struck Tom as completely insane.

He began asking her sensible, practical questions about the opinions of the Rome police, about the leads that they had (they had none worth mentioning), and what she had heard on the Miles case. There was nothing new on the Miles case, either, but Marge did know about Freddie and Dickie's having been seen in front of Dickie's house around eight o'clock that night. She thought the story was exaggerated.

"Maybe Freddie was drunk, or maybe Dickie just had an arm around him. How could anybody tell in the dark? Don't tell me Dickie murdered him!"

"Have they any concrete clues at all that would make them think Dickie killed him?"

"Of course not!"

"Then why don't the so-and-so's get down to the business

of finding out who really did kill him? And also where Dickie is?"

"*Ecco!*" Marge said emphatically. "Anyway, the police are sure now that Dickie at least got from Palermo to Naples. A steward remembers carrying his bags from his cabin to the Naples dock."

"Really," Tom said. He remembered the steward, too, a clumsy little oaf who had dropped his canvas suitcase, trying to carry it under one arm. "Wasn't Freddie killed hours after he left Dickie's house?" Tom asked suddenly.

"No. The doctors can't say exactly. And it seems Dickie didn't have an alibi, of course, because he was undoubtedly alone. Just more of Dickie's bad luck."

"They don't actually *believe* Dickie killed him, do they?"

"They don't say it, no. It's just in the air. Naturally, they can't make rash statements right and left about an American citizen, but as long as they haven't any suspects and Dickie's disappeared— Then also his landlady in Rome said that Freddie came down to ask her who was living in Dickie's apartment or something like that. She said Freddie looked angry, as if they'd been quarreling. She said he asked if Dickie was living alone."

Tom frowned. "I wonder why?"

"I can't imagine. Freddie's Italian wasn't the best in the world, and maybe the landlady got it wrong. Anyway, the mere fact that Freddie was angry about something looks bad for Dickie."

Tom raised his eyebrows. "I'd say it looked bad for Freddie. Maybe Dickie wasn't angry at all." He felt perfectly calm, because he could see that Marge hadn't smelled out anything about it. "I wouldn't worry about that unless something concrete comes out of it. Sounds like nothing at all to me." He refilled her glass. "Speaking of Africa, have they inquired around Tangiers yet? Dickie used to talk about going to Tangiers."

"I think they've alerted the police everywhere. I think they ought to get the French police down here. The French are terribly good at things like this. But of course they can't. This is Italy," she said with the first nervous tremor in her voice.

"Shall we have lunch here?" Tom asked. "The maid is functioning over the lunch hour and we might as well take advantage of it." He said it just as Anna was coming in to announce that the lunch was ready.

"Wonderful!" Marge said. "It's raining a little, anyway."

"Pronta la collazione, signor," Anna said with a smile, staring at Marge.

Anna recognized her from the newspaper pictures, Tom saw. "You and Ugo can go now if you like, Anna. Thanks."

Anna went back into the kitchen—there was a door from the kitchen to a little alley at the side of the house, which the servants used—but Tom heard her pottering around with the coffee maker, stalling for another glimpse, no doubt.

"And Ugo?" Marge said. "Two servants, no less?"

"Oh, they come in couples around here. You may not believe it, but I got this place for fifty dollars a month, not counting heat."

"I don't believe it! That's practically like Mongibello rates!"

"It's true. The heating's fantastic, of course, but I'm not going to heat any room except my bedroom."

"It's certainly comfortable here."

"Oh, I opened the whole furnace for your benefit," Tom said, smiling.

"What happened? Did one of your aunts die and leave you a fortune?" Marge asked, still pretending to be dazzled.

"No, just a decision of my own. I'm going to enjoy what I've got as long as it lasts. I told you that job I was after in Rome didn't pan out, and here I was in Europe with only about two thousand dollars to my name, so I decided to live it up and go home—broke—and start over again." Tom had explained to her in his letter that the job he had applied for had been selling hearing aids in Europe for an American company, and he hadn't been able to face it, and the man who had interviewed him, he said, hadn't thought him the right type, either. Tom had also told her that the man had appeared one minute after he spoke to her, which was why he had been unable to keep his appointment with her in Angelo's that day in Rome.

"Two thousand dollars won't last you long at this rate."

She was probing to see if Dickie had given him anything, Tom knew. "It will last till summer," Tom said matter-of-factly. "Anyway, I feel I deserve it. I spent most of the winter going around Italy like a gypsy on practically no money, and I've had about enough of that."

"Where *were* you this winter?"

"Well, not with Tom. I mean, not with Dickie," he said laughing, flustered at his slip of the tongue. "I know you probably thought so. I saw about as much of Dickie as you did."

"Oh, come on now," Marge drawled. She sounded as if she were feeling her drinks.

Tom made two or three more martinis in the pitcher. "Except for the trip to Cannes and the two days in Rome in February, I haven't seen Dickie at all." It wasn't quite true, because he had written her that "Tom was staying" with Dickie in Rome for several days after the Cannes trip, but now that he was face to face with Marge he found he was ashamed of her knowing, or thinking, that he had spent so much time with Dickie, and that he and Dickie might be guilty of what she had accused Dickie of in her letter. He bit his tongue as he poured their drinks, hating himself for his cowardice.

During lunch—Tom regretted very much that the main dish was cold roast beef, a fabulously expensive item on the Italian market—Marge quizzed him more acutely than any police officer on Dickie's state of mind while he was in Rome. Tom was pinned down to ten days spent in Rome with Dickie after the Cannes trip, and was questioned about everything from Di Massimo, the painter Dickie had worked with, to Dickie's appetite and the hour he got up in the morning.

"How do you think he felt about *me?* Tell me honestly. I can take it."

"I think he was worried about you," Tom said earnestly. "I think—well, it was one of those situations that turn up quite often, a man who's terrified of marriage to begin with—"

"But I never asked him to marry me!" Marge protested.

"I know, but—" Tom forced himself to go on, though the subject was like vinegar in his mouth. "Let's say he couldn't face the responsibility of your caring so much about him. I think he wanted a more casual relationship with you." That told her everything and nothing.

Marge stared at him in that old, lost way for a moment, then rallied bravely and said, "Well, all that's water under the bridge by now. I'm only interested in what Dickie might have done with himself."

Her fury at his apparently having been with Dickie all winter was water under the bridge, too, Tom thought, because she hadn't wanted to believe it in the first place, and now she didn't have to. Tom asked carefully, "He didn't happen to write to you when he was in Palermo?"

Marge shook her head. "No. Why?"

"I wanted to know what kind of state you thought he was in then. Did you write to him?"

She hesitated. "Yes—matter of fact, I did."

"What kind of a letter? I only ask because an unfriendly letter might have had a bad effect on him just then."

"Oh—it's hard to say what kind. A fairly friendly letter. I told him I was going back to the States." She looked at him with wide eyes.

Tom enjoyed watching her face, watching somebody else squirm as they lied. That had been the filthy letter in which she said she had told the police that he and Dickie were always together. "I don't suppose it matters then," Tom said, with sweet gentleness, sitting back.

They were silent a few moments, then Tom asked her about her book, who the publisher was, and how much more work she had to do. Marge answered everything enthusiastically. Tom had the feeling that if she had Dickie back and her book published by next winter, she would probably just explode with happiness, make a loud, unattractive *ploop!* and that would be the end of her.

"Do you think I should offer to talk to Mr. Greenleaf, too?" Tom asked. "I'd be glad to go to Rome—" Only he wouldn't be so glad, he remembered, because Rome had simply too many people in it who had seen him as Dickie Greenleaf. "Or do you think he would like to come here? I could put him up. Where's he staying in Rome?"

"He's staying with some American friends who have a big apartment. Somebody called Northup in Via Quattro Novembre. I think it'd be nice if you called him. I'll write the address down for you."

"That's a good idea. He doesn't like me, does he?"

Marge smiled a little. "Well, frankly, no. I think he's a little hard on you, considering. He probably thinks you sponged off Dickie."

"Well, I didn't. I'm sorry the idea didn't work out about my getting Dickie back home, but I explained all that. I wrote him the nicest letter I could about Dickie when I heard he was missing. Didn't that help any?"

"I think it did, but— Oh, I'm terribly sorry, Tom! All over this wonderful tablecloth!" Marge had turned her martini over. She daubed at the crocheted tablecloth awkwardly with her napkin.

Tom came running back from the kitchen with a wet cloth. "Perfectly all right," he said, watching the wood of the table turn white in spite of his wiping. It wasn't the tablecloth he cared about, it was the beautiful table.

"I'm so sorry," Marge went on protesting.

Tom hated her. He suddenly remembered her bra hanging over the windowsill in Mongibello. Her underwear would be draped over his chairs tonight, if he invited her to stay here. The idea repelled him. He deliberately hurled a smile across the table at her. "I hope you'll honor me by accepting a bed for the night. Not mine," he added, laughing, "but I've got two rooms upstairs and you're welcome to one of them."

"Thanks a lot. All right, I will." She beamed at him.

Tom installed her in his own room—the bed in the other room being only an outsized couch and not so comfortable as his double bed—and Marge closed her door to take a nap after lunch. Tom wandered restlessly through the rest of the house, wondering whether there was anything in his room that he ought to remove. Dickie's passport was in the lining of a suitcase in his closet. He couldn't think of anything else. But women had sharp eyes, Tom thought, even Marge. She might snoop around. Finally he went into the room while she was still asleep and took the suitcase from the closet. The floor squeaked, and Marge's eyes fluttered open.

"Just want to get something out of here," Tom whispered. "Sorry." He continued tiptoeing out of the room. Marge probably wouldn't even remember, he thought, because she hadn't completely waked up.

Later he showed Marge all around the house, showed her the shelf of leather-bound books in the room next to his bedroom, books that he said had come with the house, though they were his own, bought in Rome and Palermo and Venice. He realized that he had had about ten of them in Rome, and that one of the young police officers with Roverini had bent close to them, apparently studying their titles. But it was nothing really to worry about, he thought, even if the same police officer were to come back. He showed Marge the front entrance of the house, with its broad stone steps. The tide was low and four steps were bared now, the lower two covered with thick wet moss. The moss was a slippery, long-filament variety, and hung over the edges of the steps like messy dark-green hair. The steps were repellent to Tom, but Marge thought them very romantic. She bent over them, staring at the deep water of the canal. Tom had an impulse to push her in.

"Can we take a gondola and come in this way tonight?" she asked.

"Oh, sure." They were going out to dinner tonight, of course. Tom dreaded the long Italian evening ahead of them, because they wouldn't eat until ten, and then she'd probably want to sit in San Marco's over espressos until two in the morning.

Tom looked up at the hazy, sunless Venetian sky, and watched a gull glide down and settle on somebody else's front steps across the canal. He was trying to decide which of his new Venetian friends he would telephone and ask if he could bring Marge over for a drink around five o'clock. They would all be delighted to meet her, of course. He decided on the Englishman Peter Smith-Kingsley. Peter had an Afghan, a piano, and a well-equipped bar. Tom thought Peter would be best because Peter never wanted anybody to leave. They could stay there until it was time for them to go to dinner.

24.

Tom called Mr. Greenleaf from Peter Smith-Kingsley's house at about seven o'clock. Mr. Greenleaf sounded friendlier than Tom had expected, and sounded pitifully hungry for the little crumbs Tom gave him about Dickie. Peter and Marge and the Franchettis—an attractive pair of brothers from Trieste whom Tom had recently met—were in the next room and able to hear almost every word he said, so Tom did it better than he would have done it completely alone, he felt.

"I've told Marge all I know," he said, "so she'll be able to tell you anything I've forgotten. I'm only sorry that I can't contribute anything of real importance for the police to work on."

"These police!" Mr. Greenleaf said gruffly. "I'm beginning to think Richard is dead. For some reason the Italians are reluctant to admit he might be. They act like amateurs or—or old ladies playing at being detectives."

Tom was shocked at Mr. Greenleaf's bluntness about Dickie's possibly being dead. "Do *you* think Dickie might have killed himself, Mr. Greenleaf?" Tom asked quietly.

Mr. Greenleaf sighed. "I don't know. I think it's possible, yes. I never thought much of my son's stability, Tom."

"I'm afraid I agree with you," Tom said. "Would you like to talk to Marge? She's in the next room."

"No, no, thanks. When's she coming back?"

"I think she said she'd be going back to Rome tomorrow. If you'd possibly like to come to Venice, just for a slight rest, Mr. Greenleaf, you're very welcome to stay at my house."

But Mr. Greenleaf declined the invitation. It wasn't necessary to bend over backwards, Tom realized. It was as if he were really inviting trouble, and couldn't stop himself. Mr. Greenleaf thanked him for his telephone call and said a very courteous good night.

Tom went back into the other room. "There's no more news from Rome," he said dejectedly to the group.

"Oh." Peter looked disappointed.

"Here's for the phone call, Peter," Tom said, laying twelve hundred lire on top of Peter's piano. "Thanks very much."

"I have an idea," Pietro Franchetti began in his English-accented English. "Dickie Greenleaf has traded passports with a Neapolitan fisherman or maybe a Roman cigarette peddler, so that he can lead the quiet life he always wanted to. It so happens that the bearer of the Dickie Greenleaf passport is not so good a forger as he thought he was, and he had to disappear suddenly. The police should find a man who can't produce his proper carta d'identità, find out who he is, then look for a man with his name, who will turn out to be Dickie Greenleaf!"

Everybody laughed, and Tom loudest of all.

"The trouble with that idea," Tom said, "is that lots of people who knew Dickie saw him in January and February—"

"*Who?*" Pietro interrupted with that irritating Italian belligerence in conversation that was doubly irritating in English.

"Well, I did, for one. Anyway, as I was going to say, the forgeries now date from December, according to the bank."

"Still, it's an idea," Marge chirruped, feeling very good on her third drink, lolling back on Peter's big chaise-longue. "A very Dickie-like idea. He probably would have done it right after Palermo, when he had the bank forgery business on top of everything else. I don't believe those forgeries for one minute. I think Dickie'd changed so much that his handwriting changed."

"I think so, too," Tom said. "The bank isn't unanimous, anyway, in saying they're all forged. America's divided about it, and Naples fell right in with America. Naples never would have noticed a forgery if the U.S. hadn't told them about it."

"I wonder what's in the papers tonight?" Peter asked brightly, pulling on the slipperlike shoe that he had half taken off because it probably hurt. "Shall I go out and get them?"

But one of the Franchettis volunteered to go, and dashed out of the room. Lorenzo Franchetti was wearing a pink embroidered waistcoat, all' inglese, and an English-made suit and heavy-soled English shoes, and his brother was dressed in much the same way. Peter, on the other hand, was dressed in Italian clothes from head to foot. Tom had noticed, at parties and at the theatre, that if a man was dressed in English clothes he was bound to be an Italian, and vice versa.

Some more people arrived just as Lorenzo came back with the papers—two Italians and two Americans. The papers were passed around. More discussion, more exchanges of stupid speculation, more excitement over today's news: Dickie's house in Mongibello had been sold to an American for twice the price he originally asked for it. The money was going to be held by a Naples bank until Greenleaf claimed it.

The same paper had a cartoon of a man on his knees, looking under his bureau. His wife asked, "Collar button?" And his answer was, "No, I'm looking for Dickie Greenleaf."

Tom had heard that the Rome music halls were taking off the search in skits, too.

One of the Americans who had just come in, whose name was Rudy something, invited Tom and Marge to a cocktail party at his hotel the following day. Tom started to decline, but Marge said she would be delighted to come. Tom hadn't thought she would be here tomorrow, because she had said something at lunch about leaving. The party would be deadly, Tom thought. Rudy was a loud-mouthed, crude man in flashy clothes who said he was an antique dealer. Tom maneuvered himself and Marge out of the house before she accepted any more invitations that might be further into the future.

Marge was in a giddy mood that irritated Tom throughout their long five-course dinner, but he made the supreme effort and responded in kind—like a helpless frog twitching from an electric needle, he thought—and when she dropped the ball, he picked it up and dribbled it a while. He said things like, "Maybe Dickie's suddenly found himself in his painting, and he's gone away like Gauguin to one of the South Sea Islands." It made him ill. Then Marge would spin a fantasy about Dickie and the South Sea Islands, making lazy gestures with her hands. The worst was yet to come, Tom thought: the gondola ride. If she dangled those hands in the water, he hoped a shark bit them off. He ordered a dessert that he hadn't room for, but Marge ate it.

Marge wanted a private gondola, of course, not the regular ferry-service gondola that took people over ten at a time from San Marco's to the steps of Santa Maria della Salute, so they engaged a private gondola. It was one-thirty in the morning. Tom had a dark-brown taste in his mouth from too many espressos, his heart was fluttering like bird wings, and he did not expect to be able to sleep until dawn. He felt exhausted, and lay back in the gondola's seat about as languidly as Marge, careful to keep his thigh from touching hers. Marge was still in ebullient spirits, entertaining herself now with a monologue about the sunrise in Venice, which she had apparently seen on some other visit. The gentle rocking of the boat and the rhythmic thrusts of the gondolier's oar made Tom feel slightly sickish. The expanse of water between the San Marco boat stop and his steps seemed interminable.

The steps were covered now except for the upper two, and the water swept just over the surface of the third step, stirring its moss in a disgusting way. Tom paid the gondolier mechanically, and was standing in front of the big doors when he realized he hadn't brought the keys. He glanced around to see if he could climb in anywhere, but he couldn't even reach a window ledge from the steps. Before he even said anything, Marge burst out laughing.

"You didn't bring the key! Of all things, stuck on the doorstep with the raging waters around us, and no key!"

Tom tried to smile. Why the hell should he have thought to bring two keys nearly a foot long that weighed as much as a couple of revolvers? He turned and yelled to the gondolier to come back.

"Ah!" the gondolier chuckled across the water. "Mi dispiace, signor! Deb' ritornare a San Marco! Ho un appuntamento!" He kept on rowing.

"We have no keys!" Tom yelled in Italian.

"Mi dispiace, signor!" replied the gondolier. "Mandarò un altro gondoliere!"

Marge laughed again. "Oh, some other gondolier'll pick us up. Isn't it beautiful?" She stood on tiptoe.

It was not at all a beautiful night. It was chilly, and a slimy little rain had started falling. He might get the ferry gondola to come over, Tom thought, but he didn't see it. The only boat he saw was the motoscafo approaching the San Marco pier. There was hardly a chance that the motoscafo would trouble to pick them up, but Tom yelled to it, anyway. The motoscafo, full of lights and people, went blindly on and nosed in at the wooden pier across the canal. Marge was sitting on the top step with her arms around her knees, doing nothing. Finally, a lowslung motorboat that looked like a fishing boat of some sort slowed down, and someone yelled in Italian: "Locked out?"

"We forgot the keys!" Marge explained cheerfully.

But she didn't want to get into the boat. She said she would wait on the steps while Tom went around and opened the street door. Tom said it might take fifteen minutes or more, and she would probably catch a cold there, so she finally got in. The Italian took them to the nearest landing at the steps of the Santa Maria della Salute church. He refused to take any money for his trouble, but he accepted the rest of Tom's pack of American cigarettes. Tom did not know why, but he felt more frightened that night, walking through San Spiridione with Marge, than if he had been alone. Marge, of course, was not affected at all by the street, and talked the whole way.

25.

Tom was awakened very early the next morning by the banging of his door knocker. He grabbed his robe and went down. It was a telegram, and he had to run back upstairs to get a tip for the man. He stood in the cold living room and read it.

CHANGED MY MIND. WOULD LIKE TO SEE YE. ARRIVING 11:45 AM.
H. GREENLEAF

Tom shivered. Well, he had expected it, he thought. But he hadn't really. He dreaded it. Or was it just the hour? It was barely dawn. The living room looked gray and horrible. That "YE" gave the telegram such a creepy, archaic touch. Generally Italian telegrams had much funnier typographical errors. And what if they'd put "R." or "D." instead of the "H."? How would he be feeling then?

He ran upstairs and got back into his warm bed to try to catch some more sleep. He kept wondering if Marge would come in or knock on his door because she had heard that loud knocker, but he finally decided she had slept through it. He imagined greeting Mr. Greenleaf at the door, shaking his hand firmly, and he tried to imagine his questions, but his mind blurred tiredly and it made him feel frightened and uncomfortable. He was too sleepy to form specific questions and answers, and too tense to get to sleep. He wanted to make coffee and wake Marge up, so he would have someone to talk to, but he couldn't face going into that room and seeing the underwear and garter belts strewn all over the place, he absolutely *couldn't*.

It was Marge who woke him up, and she had already made coffee downstairs, she said.

"What do you think?" Tom said with a big smile. "I got a telegram from Mr. Greenleaf this morning and he's coming at noon."

"He *is*? When did you get the telegram?"

"This morning early. If I wasn't dreaming." Tom looked for it. "Here it is."

Marge read it. " 'Would like to see ye,' " she said, laughing a little. "Well, that's nice. It'll do him good. I hope. Are you coming down or shall I bring the coffee up?"

"I'll come down," Tom said, putting on his robe.

Marge was already dressed in slacks and a sweater, black corduroy slacks, well-cut and made to order, Tom supposed, because they fitted her gourdlike figure as well as pants possibly could. They prolonged their coffee drinking until Anna and Ugo arrived at ten with milk and rolls and the morning papers. Then they made more coffee and hot milk and sat in the living room. It was one of the mornings when there was nothing in the papers about Dickie or the Miles case. Some mornings were like that, and then the evening papers would have something about them again, even if there was no real news to report, just by way of reminding people that Dickie was still missing and the Miles murder was still unsolved.

Marge and Tom went to the railroad station to meet Mr. Greenleaf at eleven forty-five. It was raining again, and so windy and cold that the rain felt like sleet on their faces. They stood in the shelter of the railroad station, watching the people come through the gate, and finally there was Mr. Greenleaf, solemn and ashen. Marge rushed forward to kiss him on the cheek, and he smiled at her.

"Hello, Tom!" he said heartily, extending his hand. "How're you?"

"Very well, sir. And you?"

Mr. Greenleaf had only a small suitcase, but a porter was carrying it and the porter rode with them on the motoscafo, though Tom said he could easily carry the suitcase himself. Tom suggested they go straight to his house, but Mr. Greenleaf wanted to install himself in a hotel first. He insisted.

"I'll come over as soon as I register. I thought I'd try the Gritti. Is that anywhere near your place?" Mr. Greenleaf asked.

"Not too close, but you can walk to San Marco's and take a gondola over," Tom said. "We'll come with you, if you just want to check in. I thought we might all have lunch together—unless you'd rather see Marge by yourself for a while." He was the old self-effacing Ripley again.

"Came here primarily to talk to you!" Mr. Greenleaf said.

"Is there any news?" Marge asked.

Mr. Greenleaf shook his head. He was casting nervous, absent-minded glances out the windows of the motoscafo, as if the strangeness of the city compelled him to look at it, though nothing of it was registering. He had not answered Tom's question about lunch. Tom folded his arms, put a pleasant expression on his face, and did not try to talk any more. The boat's motor made quite a roar, anyway. Mr. Greenleaf and Marge were talking very casually about some people they knew in Rome. Tom gathered that Marge and Mr. Greenleaf got along very well, though Marge had said she had not known him before she met him in Rome.

They went to lunch at a modest restaurant between the Gritti and the Rialto, which specialized in seafoods that were always displayed raw on a long counter inside. One of the plates held varieties of the little purple octopuses that Dickie had liked so much, and Tom said to Marge, nodding toward the plates as they passed, "Too bad Dickie isn't here to enjoy some of those."

Marge smiled gaily. She was always in a good mood when they were about to eat.

Mr. Greenleaf talked a little more at lunch, but his face kept its stony expression, and he still glanced around as he spoke, as if he hoped that Dickie would come walking in at any moment. No, the police hadn't found a blessed thing that could be called a clue, he said, and he had just arranged for an American private detective to come over and try to clear the mystery up.

It made Tom swallow thoughtfully—he, too, must have a lurking suspicion, or illusion, perhaps, that American detectives were better than the Italian—but then the evident futility of it struck him as it was apparently striking Marge, because her face had gone long and blank suddenly.

"That may be a very good idea," Tom said.

"Do you think much of the Italian police?" Mr. Greenleaf asked him.

"Well—actually, I do," Tom replied. "There's also the advantage that they speak Italian and they can get around everywhere and investigate all kinds of suspects. I suppose the man you sent for speaks Italian?"

"I really don't know. I don't know," Mr. Greenleaf said in a flustered way, as if he realized he should have demanded that, and hadn't. "The man's name is McCarron. He's said to be very good."

He probably didn't speak Italian, Tom thought. "When is he arriving?"

"Tomorrow or the next day. I'll be in Rome tomorrow to meet him if he's there." Mr. Greenleaf had finished his vitello alla parmigiana. He had not eaten much.

"Tom has the most beautiful house!" Marge said, starting in on her seven-layer rum cake.

Tom turned his glare at her into a faint smile.

The quizzing, Tom thought, would come at the house, probably when he and Mr. Greenleaf were alone. He knew Mr. Greenleaf wanted to talk to him alone, and therefore he proposed coffee at the restaurant where they were before Marge could suggest having it at home. Marge liked the coffee that his filter pot made. Even so, Marge sat around with them in the living room for half an hour after they got home. Marge was incapable of sensing anything, Tom thought. Finally Tom frowned at her facetiously and glanced at the stairs, and she got the hint, clapped her hand over her mouth and announced that she was going up to have a wee nap. She was in her usual invincibly merry mood, and she had been talking to Mr. Greenleaf all during lunch as if *of course* Dickie wasn't dead, and he mustn't, mustn't worry so much because it wasn't good for his digestion. As if she still had hopes of being his daughter-in-law one day, Tom thought.

Mr. Greenleaf stood up and paced the floor with his hands in his jacket pockets, like an executive about to dictate a letter to his stenographer. He hadn't commented on the plushness of the house, or even much looked at it, Tom had noticed.

"Well, Tom," he began with a sigh, "this is a strange end, isn't it?"

"End?"

"Well, you living in Europe now, and Richard—"

"None of us has suggested yet that he might have gone back to America," Tom said pleasantly.

"No. That couldn't be. The immigration authorities in America are much too well alerted for that." Mr. Greenleaf continued to pace, not looking at him. "What's your real opinion as to where he may be?"

"Well, sir, he could be hiding out in Italy—very easily if he doesn't use a hotel where he has to register."

"Are there any hotels in Italy where one doesn't have to register?"

"No, not officially. But anyone who knows Italian as well as Dickie might get away with it. Matter of fact, if he bribed some little innkeeper in the south of Italy not to say anything, he could stay there even if the man knew his name was Richard Greenleaf."

"And is that your idea of what he may be doing?" Mr. Greenleaf looked at him suddenly, and Tom saw that pitiful expression he had noticed the first evening he had met him.

"No, I— It's possible. That's all I can say about it." He paused. "I'm sorry to say it, Mr. Greenleaf, but I think there's a possibility that Dickie is dead."

Mr. Greenleaf's expression did not change. "Because of that depression you mentioned in Rome? What exactly did he say to you?"

"It was his general mood." Tom frowned. "The Miles thing had obviously shaken him. He's the sort of man— He really does hate publicity of any kind, violence of any kind."

Tom licked his lips. His agony in trying to express himself was genuine. "He did say if one more thing happened, he would blow his top—or he didn't know what he would do. Also for the first time, I felt he wasn't interested in his painting. Maybe it was only temporary, but up until then I'd always thought Dickie had his painting to go to, whatever happened to him."

"Does he really take his painting so seriously?"

"Yes, he does," Tom said firmly.

Mr. Greenleaf looked off at the ceiling again, his hands behind him. "A pity we can't find this Di Massimo. He might know something. I understand Richard and he were going to go together to Sicily."

"I didn't know that," Tom said. Mr. Greenleaf had got that from Marge, he knew.

"Di Massimo's disappeared, too, if he ever existed. I'm inclined to think Richard made him up to try to convince me he was painting. The police can't find a painter called Di Massimo on their—their identity lists or whatever it is."

"I never met him," Tom said. "Dickie mentioned him a couple of times. I never doubted his identity—or his actuality." He laughed a little.

"What did you say before about 'if one more thing happened to him'? What else had happened to him?"

"Well, I didn't know then, in Rome, but I think I know what he meant now. They'd questioned him about the sunken boat in San Remo. Did they tell you about that?"

"No."

"They found a boat in San Remo, scuttled. It seems the boat was missed on the day or around the day Dickie and I were there, and we'd taken a ride in the same kind of boat. They were the little motorboats people rented there. At any rate, the boat was scuttled, and there were stains on it that they thought were bloodstains. They happened to find the boat just after the Miles murder, and they couldn't find *me* at that time, because I was traveling around the country, so they asked Dickie where I was. I think for a while, Dickie must have thought they suspected him of having murdered me!" Tom laughed.

"Good lord!"

"I only know this, because a police inspector questioned

me about it in Venice just a few weeks ago. He said he'd
questioned Dickie about it before. The strange thing is that I
didn't know I was being looked for—not very seriously, but
still being looked for—until I saw it in the newspaper in Venice. I went to the police station here and presented myself."
Tom was still smiling. He had decided days ago that he had
better narrate all this to Mr. Greenleaf, if he ever saw him,
whether Mr. Greenleaf had heard about the San Remo boat
incident or not. It was better than having Mr. Greenleaf
learn about it from the police, and be told that he had been
in Rome with Dickie at a time when he should have known
that the police were looking for him. Besides, it fitted in with
what he was saying about Dickie's depressed mood at that
time.

"I don't quite understand all this," Mr. Greenleaf said. He
was sitting on the sofa, listening attentively.

"It's blown over now, since Dickie and I are both alive.
The reason I mention it at all is that Dickie knew I was being
looked for by the police, because they had asked him where
I was. He may not have known exactly where I was at the first
interview with the police, but he did know at least that I was
still in the country. But even when I came to Rome and saw
him, he didn't tell the police he'd seen me. He wasn't going
to be that cooperative, he wasn't in the mood. I know this
because at the very time Marge talked to me in Rome at the
hotel, Dickie was out talking to the police. His attitude was,
let the police find me themselves, he wasn't going to tell them
where I was."

Mr. Greenleaf shook his head, a kind of fatherly, mildly impatient shake of the head, as if he could easily believe it of
Dickie.

"I think that was the night he said, if one more thing happened to him— It caused me a little embarrassment when I
was in Venice. The police probably thought I was a moron
for not knowing before that I was being looked for, but the
fact remains I didn't."

"Hm-m," Mr. Greenleaf said uninterestedly.

Tom got up to get some brandy.

"I'm afraid I don't agree with you that Richard committed
suicide," Mr. Greenleaf said.

"Well, neither does Marge. I just said it's a possibility. I don't even think it's the most likely thing that's happened."

"You don't? What do you think is?"

"That he's hiding out," Tom said. "May I offer you some brandy, sir? I imagine this house feels pretty chilly after America."

"It does, frankly." Mr. Greenleaf accepted his glass.

"You know, he could be in several other countries besides Italy, too," Tom said. "He could have gone to Greece or France or anywhere else after he got back to Naples, because no one was looking for him until days later."

"I know, I know," Mr. Greenleaf said tiredly.

26.

TOM had hoped Marge would forget about the cocktail party invitation of the antique dealer at the Danieli, but she didn't. Mr. Greenleaf had gone back to his hotel to rest around four o'clock, and as soon as he had gone Marge reminded Tom of the party at five o'clock.

"Do you really want to go?" Tom asked. "I can't even remember the man's name."

"Maloof. M-a-l-o-o-f," Marge said. "I'd like to go. We don't have to stay long."

So that was that. What Tom hated about it was the spectacle they made of themselves, not one but two of the principals in the Greenleaf case, conspicuous as a couple of spotlighted acrobats at a circus. He felt—he knew—they were nothing but a pair of names that Mr. Maloof had bagged, guests of honor that had actually turned up, because certainly Mr. Maloof would have told everybody today that Marge Sherwood and Tom Ripley were attending his party. It was unbecoming, Tom felt. And Marge couldn't excuse her giddiness simply by saying that she wasn't worried a bit about Dickie's being missing. It even seemed to Tom that Marge guzzled the martinis because they were free, as if she couldn't get all she wanted at his house, or as if he wasn't going to buy her several more when they met Mr. Greenleaf for dinner.

Tom sipped one drink slowly and managed to stay on the other side of the room from Marge. He was the friend of Dickie Greenleaf, when anybody began a conversation by asking him if he was, but he knew Marge only slightly.

"Miss Sherwood is my house guest," he said with a troubled smile.

"Where's Mr. Greenleaf? Too bad you didn't bring him," Mr. Maloof said, sidling up like an elephant with a huge Manhattan in a champagne glass. He wore a checked suit of loud English tweed, the kind of pattern, Tom supposed, the English made, reluctantly, especially for such Americans as Rudy Maloof.

"I think Mr. Greenleaf is resting," Tom said. "We're going to see him later for dinner."

"Oh," said Mr. Maloof. "Did you see the papers tonight?" This last politely, with a respectfully solemn face.

"Yes, I did," Tom replied.

Mr. Maloof nodded, without saying anything more. Tom wondered what inconsequential item he could have been going to report if he had said he hadn't read the papers. The papers tonight said that Mr. Greenleaf had arrived in Venice and was staying at the Gritti Palace. There was no mention of a private detective from America arriving in Rome today, or that one was coming at all, which made Tom question Mr. Greenleaf's story about the private detective. It was like one of those stories told by someone else, or one of his own imaginary fears, which were never based on the least fragment of fact and which, a couple of weeks later, he was ashamed that he *could* have believed. Such as that Marge and Dickie were having an affair in Mongibello, or were even on the brink of having an affair. Or that the forgery scare in February was going to ruin him and expose him if he continued in the role of Dickie Greenleaf. The forgery scare had blown over, actually. The latest was that seven out of ten experts in America had said that they did not believe the checks were forged. He could have signed another remittance from the American bank, and gone on forever as Dickie Greenleaf, if he hadn't let his imaginary fears get the better of him. Tom set his jaw. He was still listening with a fraction of his brain to Mr. Maloof, who was trying to sound intelligent and serious by describing his expedition to the islands of Murano and Burano that morning. Tom set his jaw, frowning, listening, and concentrating doggedly on his own life. Perhaps he should believe Mr. Greenleaf's story about the private detective coming over, until it was disproven, but he would not let it rattle him or cause him to betray fear by so much as the blink of an eye.

Tom made an absent-minded reply to something Mr. Maloof had said, and Mr. Maloof laughed with inane good cheer and drifted off. Tom followed his broad back scornfully with his eyes, realizing that he had been rude, was being rude, and that he ought to pull himself together, because behaving courteously even to this handful of second-rate antique dealers and bric-a-brac and ashtray buyers—Tom had seen the samples of their wares spread out on the bed in the room where they had put their coats—was part of the business of being a gentleman. But they reminded him too much of the people he had said good-bye to in New York, he thought, that was why they got under his skin like an itch and made him want to run. Marge was the reason he was here, after all, the only reason. He blamed *her*. Tom took a sip of his martini, looked up at the ceiling, and thought that in another few months his nerves, his patience, would be able to bear even people like this, if he ever found himself with people like this again. He had improved, at least, since he left New York, and he would improve still more. He stared up at the ceiling and thought of sailing to Greece, down the Adriatic from Venice, into the Ionian Sea to Crete. That was what he would do this summer. June. *June.* How sweet and soft the word was, clear and lazy and full of sunshine! His reverie lasted only a few seconds, however. The loud, grating American voices forced their way into his ears again, and sank like claws into the nerves of his shoulders and his back. He moved involuntarily from where he stood, moved toward Marge. There were only two other women in the room, the horrible wives of a couple of the horrible businessmen, and Marge, he had to admit, was better-looking than either of them, but her voice, he thought, was worse, like theirs only worse.

He had something on the tip of his tongue to say about their leaving, but, since it was unthinkable for a man to propose leaving, he said nothing at all, only joined Marge's group and smiled. Somebody refilled his glass. Marge was talking about Mongibello, telling them about her book, and the three gray-templed, seamy-faced, bald-headed men seemed to be entranced with her.

When Marge herself proposed leaving a few minutes later, they had a ghastly time getting clear of Maloof and his co-horts, who were a little drunker now and insistent that they *all* get together for dinner, and Mr. Greenleaf, too.

"That's what Venice is for—a good time!" Mr. Maloof kept saying idiotically, taking the opportunity to put his arm around Marge and maul her a little as he tried to make her stay, and Tom thought it was a good thing that he hadn't eaten yet because he would have lost it right then. "What's Mr. Greenleaf's number? Let's call him up!" Mr. Maloof weaved his way to the telephone.

"I think we'd better get out of here!" Tom said grimly into Marge's ear. He took a hard, functional grip on her elbow and steered her toward the door, both of them nodding and smiling good-byes as they went.

"What's the *matter*?" Marge asked when they were in the corridor.

"Nothing. I just thought the party was getting out of hand," Tom said, trying to make light of it with a smile. Marge was a little high, but not too high to see that something was the matter with him. He was perspiring. It showed on his forehead, and he wiped it. "People like that get me down," he said, "talking about Dickie all the time, and we don't even know them and I don't want to. They make me ill."

"Funny. Not a soul talked to me about Dickie or even mentioned his name. I thought it was much better than yesterday at Peter's house."

Tom lifted his head as he walked and said nothing. It was the class of people he despised, and why say that to Marge, who was of the same class?

They called for Mr. Greenleaf at his hotel. It was still early for dinner, so they had apéritifs at a café in a street near the Gritti. Tom tried to make up for his explosion at the party by being pleasant and talkative during dinner. Mr. Greenleaf was in a good mood, because he had just telephoned his wife and found her in very good spirits and feeling much better. Her doctor had been trying a new system of injections for the past ten days, Mr. Greenleaf said, and she seemed to be responding better than to anything they had tried before.

It was a quiet dinner. Tom told a clean, mildly funny joke, and Marge laughed hilariously. Mr. Greenleaf insisted on paying for the dinner, and then said he was going back to his hotel because he didn't feel quite up to par. From the fact that he carefully chose a pasta dish and ate no salad, Tom thought that he might be suffering from the tourist's complaint, and he wanted to suggest an excellent remedy, obtainable in every drugstore, but Mr. Greenleaf was not quite the person one could say a thing like that to, even if they had been alone.

Mr. Greenleaf said he was going back to Rome tomorrow, and Tom promised to give him a ring around nine o'clock the next morning to find out which train he had decided on. Marge was going back to Rome with Mr. Greenleaf, and she was agreeable to either train. They walked back to the Gritti— Mr. Greenleaf with his taut face-of-an-industrialist under his gray homburg looking like a piece of Madison Avenue walking through the narrow, zigzagging streets—and they said good night.

"I'm terribly sorry I didn't get to spend more time with you," Tom said.

"So am I, my boy. Maybe some other time." Mr. Greenleaf patted his shoulder.

Tom walked back home with Marge in a kind of glow. It had all gone awfully well, Tom thought. Marge chattered to him as they walked, giggling because she had broken a strap of her bra and had to hold it up with one hand, she said. Tom was thinking of the letter he had received from Bob Delancey this afternoon, the first word he'd gotten from Bob except one postcard ages ago, in which Bob had said that the police had questioned everybody in his house about an income tax fraud of a few months ago. The defrauder, it seemed, had used the address of Bob's house to receive his checks, and had gotten the checks by the simple means of taking the letters down from the letter-box edge where the postman had stuck them. The postman had been questioned, too, Bob had said, and remembered the name George McAlpin on the letters. Bob seemed to think it was rather funny. He described the reactions of some of the people in the house when they were questioned by the police. The mystery was, who took the letters addressed to George McAlpin? It was very reassuring. That income tax episode had been hanging over his head in a vague way, because he had known there would be an investigation at some time. He was glad it had gone this far and no further. He couldn't imagine how the police would ever, could ever, connect Tom Ripley with George McAlpin. Besides, as Bob had remarked, the defrauder had not even tried to cash the checks.

He sat down in the living room to read Bob's letter again when he got home. Marge had gone upstairs to pack her things and to go to bed. Tom was tired too, but the anticipation of freedom tomorrow, when Marge and Mr. Greenleaf would be gone, was so pleasant to relish he would not have minded staying up all night. He took his shoes off so he could put his feet up on the sofa, lay back on a pillow, and continued reading Bob's letter. "The police think it's some outsider who dropped by occasionally to pick up his mail, because none of the dopes in this house look like criminal types. . . ." It was strange to read about the people he knew in New York, Ed and Lorraine, the newt-brained girl who had tried to stow herself away in his cabin the day he sailed from New York. It was strange and not at all attractive. What a dismal life they led, creeping around New York, in and out of subways, standing in some dingy bar on Third Avenue for their entertainment, watching television, or even if they had enough money for a Madison Avenue bar or a good restaurant now and then, how dull it all was compared to the worst little trattoria in Venice with its tables of green salads, trays of wonderful cheeses, and its friendly waiters bringing you the best wine in the world! "I certainly do envy you sitting there in Venice in an old palazzo!" Bob wrote. "Do you take a lot of gondola rides? How are the girls? Are you getting so cultured you won't speak to any of us when you come back? How long are you staying, anyway?"

Forever, Tom thought. Maybe he'd never go back to the States. It was not so much Europe itself as the evenings he

had spent alone, here and in Rome, that made him feel that
way. Evenings by himself simply looking at maps, or lying
around on sofas thumbing through guidebooks. Evenings
looking at his clothes—his clothes and Dickie's—and feeling
Dickie's rings between his palms, and running his fingers over
the antelope suitcase he had bought at Gucci's. He had polished the suitcase with a special English leather dressing, not
that it needed polishing, because he took such good care of
it, but for its protection. He loved possessions, not masses of
them, but a select few that he did not part with. They gave a
man self-respect. Not ostentation but quality, and the love
that cherished the quality. Possessions reminded him that he
existed, and made him enjoy his existence. It was as simple as
that. And wasn't that worth something? He existed. Not many
people appreciated existence as he did. Not many people in
the world knew how to, even if they had the money. It really
didn't take money, masses of money, it took a certain security.
He had been on the road to it, even with Marc Priminger.
He had appreciated Marc's possessions, and they were what
had attracted him to the house, but they were not his own,
and it had been impossible to make a beginning at acquiring
anything of his own on forty dollars a week. It would have
taken him the best years of his life, even if he had economized
stringently, to buy the things he wanted. Dickie's money had
given him only an added momentum on the road he had been
traveling. The money gave him the leisure to see Greece, to
collect Etruscan pottery if he wanted to (he had recently read
an interesting book on that subject by an American living in
Rome), to join art societies if he cared to and to donate to
their work. It gave him the leisure, for instance, to read his
Malraux tonight as late as he pleased, because he did not have
to go to a job in the morning. He had just bought a two-
volume edition of Malraux's *Psychologie de l'Art* which he was
now reading, with great pleasure, in French with the aid of a
dictionary. He thought he might nap for a while, then read
some in it, whatever the hour. He felt cozy and drowsy, in
spite of the espressos. The curve of the sofa corner fitted his
shoulders like somebody's arm, or rather fitted it better than
somebody's arm. He decided he would spend the night here.

It was more comfortable than the sofa upstairs. In a few minutes he might go up and get a blanket.

"Tom?"

He opened his eyes. Marge was coming down the stairs, barefoot. Tom sat up. She had his brown leather box in her hand.

"I just found Dickie's rings in here," she said rather breathlessly.

"Oh. He gave them to me. To take care of." Tom stood up.

"When?"

"In Rome, I think." He took a step back, struck one of his shoes and picked it up, mostly in an effort to seem calm.

"What was he going to do? Why'd he give them to you?"

She'd been looking for thread to sew her bra, Tom thought. Why in hell hadn't he put the rings somewhere else, like in the lining of that suitcase? "I don't really know," Tom said. "A whim or something. You know how he is. He said if anything ever happened to him, he wanted me to have his rings."

Marge looked puzzled. "Where was he going?"

"To Palermo. Sicily." He was holding the shoe in both hands, in a position to use the wooden heel of it as a weapon. And how he would do it went quickly through his head: hit her with the shoe, then haul her out by the front door and drop her into the canal. He'd say she'd fallen, slipped on the moss. And she was such a good swimmer, he'd thought she could keep afloat.

Marge stared down at the box. "Then he *was* going to kill himself."

"Yes—if you want to look at it that way, the rings— They make it look more likely that he did."

"Why didn't you say anything about it before?"

"I think I absolutely forgot them. I put them away so they wouldn't get lost and I never thought of looking at them since the day he gave them to me."

"He either killed himself or changed his identity—didn't he?"

"Yes." Tom said it sadly and firmly.

"You'd better tell Mr. Greenleaf."

"Yes, I will. Mr. Greenleaf and the police."

"This practically *settles* it," Marge said.

Tom was wringing the shoe in his hands like a pair of gloves now, yet still keeping the shoe in position, because Marge was staring at him in a funny way. She was still thinking. Was she kidding him? Did she know now?

Marge said earnestly, "I just can't imagine Dickie ever being without his rings," and Tom knew then that she hadn't guessed the answer, that her mind was miles up some other road.

He relaxed then, limply, sank down on the sofa and pretended to busy himself with putting on his shoes. "No," he agreed, automatically.

"If it weren't so late, I'd call Mr. Greenleaf now. He's probably in bed, and he wouldn't sleep all night if I told him, I know."

Tom tried to push a foot into the second shoe. Even his fingers were limp, without strength. He racked his brain for something sensible to say. "I'm sorry I didn't mention it sooner," he brought out in a deep voice. "It was just one of those—"

"Yes, it makes it kind of silly at this point for Mr. Greenleaf to bring a private detective over, doesn't it?" Her voice shook.

Tom looked at her. She was about to cry. This was the very first moment, Tom realized, that she was admitting to herself that Dickie could be dead, that he probably was dead. Tom went toward her slowly. "I'm sorry, Marge. I'm sorry above all that I didn't tell you sooner about the rings." He put his arm around her. He fairly had to, because she was leaning against him. He smelled her perfume. The Stradivari, probably. "That's one of the reasons I felt so sure he'd killed himself—at least that he might have."

"Yes," she said in a miserable, wailing tone.

She was not crying, actually, only leaning against him with her head rigidly bent down. Like someone who has just heard the news of a death, Tom thought. Which she had.

"How about a brandy?" he said tenderly.

"No."

"Come over and sit on the sofa." He led her toward it.

She sat down, and he crossed the room to get the brandy. He poured brandy into two inhalers. When he turned around, she was gone. He had just time to see the edge of her robe and her bare feet disappear at the top of the stairs.

She preferred to be by herself, he thought. He started to take a brandy up to her, then decided against it. She was probably beyond the help of brandy. He knew how she felt. He carried the brandies solemnly back to the liquor cabinet. He had meant to pour only one back, but he poured them both back, and then let it go and replaced the bottle among the other bottles.

He sank down on the sofa again, stretched a leg out with his foot dangling, too exhausted now even to remove his shoes. As tired as after he had killed Freddie Miles, he thought suddenly, or as after Dickie in San Remo. He had come so close! He remembered his cool thoughts of beating her senseless with his shoe heel, yet not roughly enough to break the skin anywhere, of dragging her through the front hall and out the doors with the lights turned off so that no one would see them, and his quickly invented story, that she had evidently slipped, and thinking she could surely swim back to the steps, he hadn't jumped in or shouted for help until— In a way, he had even imagined the exact words that he and Mr. Greenleaf would say to each other afterward, Mr. Greenleaf shocked and astounded, and he himself just as apparently shaken, but only apparently. Underneath he would be as calm and sure of himself as he had been after Freddie's murder, because his story would be unassailable. Like the San Remo story. His stories were good because he imagined them intensely, so intensely that he came to believe them.

For a moment he heard his own voice saying: ". . . I stood there on the steps calling to her, thinking she'd come up any second, or even that she might be playing a trick on me. . . . But I wasn't *sure* she'd hurt herself, and she'd been in such good humor standing there a moment before. . . ." He tensed himself. It was like a phonograph playing in his head, a little drama taking place right in the living room that he was unable to stop. He could see himself standing with the Italian police and Mr. Greenleaf by the big doors that opened to the front hall. He could see and hear himself talking earnestly. And being believed.

But what seemed to terrify him was not the dialogue or his

hallucinatory belief that he had done it (he knew he hadn't),
but the memory of himself standing in front of Marge with
the shoe in his hand, imagining all this in a cool, methodical
way. And the fact that he had done it twice before. Those two
other times were *facts*, not imagination. He could say he
hadn't wanted to do them, but he had done them. He didn't
want to be a murderer. Sometimes he could absolutely forget
that he had murdered, he realized. But sometimes—like
now—he couldn't. He had surely forgotten for a while tonight, when he had been thinking about the meaning of
possessions, and why he liked to live in Europe.

He twisted onto his side, his feet drawn up on the sofa. He
was sweating and shaking. What was happening to him? What
had happened? Was he going to blurt out a lot of nonsense
tomorrow when he saw Mr. Greenleaf, about Marge falling
into the canal, and his screaming for help and jumping in and
not finding her? Even with Marge standing there with them,
would he go berserk and spill the story out and betray himself
as a maniac?

He had to face Mr. Greenleaf with the rings tomorrow. He
would have to repeat the story he had told to Marge. He
would have to give it details to make it better. He began to
invent. His mind steadied. He was imagining a Roman hotel
room, Dickie and he standing there talking, and Dickie taking
off both his rings and handing them to him. Dickie said: "It's
just as well you don't tell anybody about this. . . ."

27.

MARGE called Mr. Greenleaf at eight-thirty the next morning
to ask how soon they could come over to his hotel, she had
told Tom. But Mr. Greenleaf must have noticed that she was
upset. Tom heard her starting to tell him the story of the
rings. Marge used the same words that Tom had used to her
about the rings—evidently Marge had believed him—but
Tom could not tell what Mr. Greenleaf's reaction was. He
was afraid this piece of news might be just the one that would
bring the whole picture into focus, and that when they saw

Mr. Greenleaf this morning he might be in the company of a policeman, ready to arrest Tom Ripley. This possibility rather offset the advantage of his not being on the scene when Mr. Greenleaf heard about the rings.

"What did he say?" Tom asked when Marge had hung up.

Marge sat down tiredly on a chair across the room. "He seems to feel the way I do. He said it himself. It looks as if Dickie meant to kill himself."

But Mr. Greenleaf would have a little time to think about it before they got there, Tom thought. "What time are we due?" Tom asked.

"I told him about nine-thirty or before. As soon as we've had some coffee. The coffee's on now." Marge got up and went into the kitchen. She was already dressed. She had on the traveling suit that she had worn when she arrived.

Tom sat up indecisively on the edge of the sofa and loosened his tie. He had slept in his clothes on the sofa, and Marge had awakened him when she had come down a few minutes ago. How he had possibly slept all night in the chilly room he didn't know. It embarrassed him. Marge had been amazed to find him there. There was a crick in his neck, his back, and his right shoulder. He felt wretched. He stood up suddenly. "I'm going upstairs to wash," he called to Marge.

He glanced into his room upstairs and saw that Marge had packed her suitcase. It was lying in the middle of the floor, closed. Tom hoped that she and Mr. Greenleaf were still leaving on one of the morning trains. Probably they would, because Mr. Greenleaf was supposed to meet the American detective in Rome today.

Tom undressed in the room next to Marge's, then went into the bathroom and turned on the shower. After a look at himself in the mirror he decided to shave first, and he went back to the room to get his electric razor which he had removed from the bathroom, for no particular reason, when Marge arrived. On the way back he heard the telephone ring. Marge answered it. Tom leaned over the stairwell, listening.

"Oh, that's fine," she said. "Oh, that doesn't matter if we don't. . . . Yes, I'll tell him. . . . All right, we'll hurry. Tom's just washing up. . . . Oh, less than an hour. Bye-bye."

He heard her walking toward the stairs, and he stepped back because he was naked.

"Tom?" she yelled up. "The detective from America just got here! He just called Mr. Greenleaf and he's coming from the airport!"

"Fine!" Tom called back, and angrily went into the bedroom. He turned the shower off, and plugged his razor into the wall outlet. Suppose he'd been under the shower? Marge would have yelled up, anyway, simply assuming that he would be able to hear her. He would be glad when she was gone, and he hoped she left this morning. Unless she and Mr. Greenleaf decided to stay to see what the detective was going to do with him. Tom knew that the detective had come to Venice especially to see him, otherwise he would have waited to see Mr. Greenleaf in Rome. Tom wondered if Marge realized that too. Probably she didn't. That took a minimum of deduction.

Tom put on a quiet suit and tie, and went down to have coffee with Marge. He had taken his shower as hot as he could bear it, and he felt much better. Marge said nothing during the coffee except that the rings should make a great difference both to Mr. Greenleaf and the detective, and she meant that it should look to the detective, too, as if Dickie had killed himself. Tom hoped she was right. Everything depended on what kind of man the detective would be. Everything depended on the first impression he made on the detective.

It was another gray, clammy day, not quite raining at nine o'clock, but it had rained, and it would rain again, probably toward noon. Tom and Marge caught the gondola from the church steps to San Marco, and walked from there to the Gritti. They telephoned up to Mr. Greenleaf's room. Mr. Greenleaf said that Mr. McCarron was there, and asked them to come up.

Mr. Greenleaf opened his door for them. "Good morning," he said. He pressed Marge's arm in a fatherly way. "Tom—"

Tom came in behind Marge. The detective was standing by the window, a short, chunky man of about thirty-five. His face looked friendly and alert. Moderately bright, but only moderately, was Tom's first impression.

"This is Alvin McCarron," Mr. Greenleaf said. "Miss Sherwood and Mr. Tom Ripley."

They all said, "How do you do?"

Tom noticed a brand-new briefcase on the bed with some papers and photographs lying around it. McCarron was looking him over.

"I understand you're a friend of Richard's?" he asked.

"We both are," Tom said.

They were interrupted for a minute while Mr. Greenleaf saw that they were all seated. It was a good-sized, heavily furnished room with windows on the canal. Tom sat down in an armless chair upholstered in red. McCarron had installed himself on the bed, and was looking through his sheaf of papers. There were a few photostated papers, Tom saw, that looked like pictures of Dickie's checks. There were also several loose photographs of Dickie.

"Do you have the rings?" McCarron asked, looking from Tom to Marge.

"Yes," Marge said solemnly, getting up. She took the rings from her handbag and gave them to McCarron.

McCarron held them out on his palm to Mr. Greenleaf. "These are his rings?" he asked, and Mr. Greenleaf nodded after only a glance at them, while Marge's face took on a slightly affronted expression as if she were about to say, "*I* know his rings just as well as Mr. Greenleaf and probably better." McCarron turned to Tom. "When did he give them to you?" he asked.

"In Rome. As nearly as I can remember, around February third, just a few days after the murder of Freddie Miles," Tom answered.

The detective was studying him with his inquisitive, mild brown eyes. His lifted eyebrows put a couple of wrinkles in the thick-looking skin of his forehead. He had wavy brown hair, cut very short on the sides, with a high curl above his forehead, in a rather cute college-boy style. One couldn't tell a thing from that face, Tom thought; it was trained. "What did he say when he gave them to you?"

"He said that if anything happened to him he wanted me to have them. I asked him what he thought was going to happen to him. He said he didn't know, but something might." Tom paused deliberately. "He didn't seem more depressed at that particular moment than a lot of other times I'd talked to him, so it didn't cross my mind that he was going to kill himself. I knew he intended to go away, that was all."

"Where?" asked the detective.

"To Palermo, he said." Tom looked at Marge. "He must have given them to me the day you spoke to me in Rome—at the Inghilterra. That day or the day before. Do you remember the date?"

"February second," Marge said in a subdued voice.

McCarron was making notes. "What else?" he asked Tom. "What time of day was it? Had he been drinking?"

"No. He drinks very little. I think it was early afternoon. He said it would be just as well if I didn't mention the rings to anybody, and of course I agreed. I put the rings away and completely forgot about them, as I told Miss Sherwood—I suppose because I'd so impressed on myself that he didn't want me to say anything about them." Tom spoke straightforwardly, stammering a little, inadvertently, just as anybody might stammer under the circumstances, Tom thought.

"What did you do with the rings?"

"I put them in an old box that I have—just a little box I keep odd buttons in."

McCarron regarded him for a moment in silence, and Tom took the moment to brace himself. Out of that placid yet alert Irish face could come anything, a challenging question, a flat statement that he was lying. Tom clung harder in his mind to his own facts, determined to defend them unto death. In the silence, Tom could almost hear Marge's breathing, and a cough from Mr. Greenleaf made him start. Mr. Greenleaf looked remarkably calm, almost bored. Tom wondered if he had fixed up some scheme with McCarron against him, based on the rings story?

"Is he the kind of man to lend you the rings for luck for a short time? Had he ever done anything else like that?" McCarron asked.

"No," Marge said before Tom could answer.

Tom began to breathe more easily. He could see that

McCarron didn't know yet what he should make out of it. McCarron was waiting for him to answer. "He had lent me certain things before," Tom said. "He'd told me to help myself to his ties and jackets now and then. But that's quite a different matter from the rings, of course." He had felt a compulsion to say that, because Marge undoubtedly knew about the time Dickie had found him in his clothes.

"I can't imagine Dickie without his rings," Marge said to McCarron. "He took the green one off when he went swimming, but he always put it right on again. They were just like part of his dressing. That's why I think he was either intending to kill himself or he meant to change his identity."

McCarron nodded. "Had he any enemies that you know of?"

"Absolutely none," Tom said. "I've thought of that."

"Any reason you can think of why he might have wanted to disguise himself, or assume another identity?"

Tom said carefully, twisting his aching neck, "*Possibly*—but it's next to impossible in Europe. He'd have had to have a different passport. Any country he'd have entered, he would have had to have a passport. He'd have had to have a passport even to get into a hotel."

"You told me he might not have had to have a passport," Mr. Greenleaf said.

"Yes, I said that about small hotels in Italy. It's a remote possibility, of course. But after all this publicity about his disappearance, I don't see how he could still be keeping it up," Tom said. "Somebody would surely have betrayed him by this time."

"Well, he left with his passport, obviously," McCarron said, "because he got into Sicily with it and registered at a big hotel."

"Yes," Tom said.

McCarron made notes for a moment, then looked up at Tom. "Well, how do you see it, Mr. Ripley?"

McCarron wasn't nearly finished, Tom thought. McCarron was going to see him alone, later. "I'm afraid I agree with Miss Sherwood that it looks as if he's killed himself, and it looks as if he intended to all along. I've said that before to Mr. Greenleaf."

McCarron looked at Mr. Greenleaf, but Mr. Greenleaf said nothing, only looked expectantly at McCarron. Tom had the feeling that McCarron was now inclined to think that Dickie was dead, too, and that it was a waste of time and money for him to have come over.

"I just want to check these facts again," McCarron said, still plodding on, going back to his papers. "The last time Richard was seen by anyone is February fifteenth, when he got off the boat in Naples, coming from Palermo."

"That's correct," Mr. Greenleaf said. "A steward remembers seeing him."

"But no sign of him at at any hotel after that, and no communications from him since." McCarron looked from Mr. Greenleaf to Tom.

"No," Tom said.

McCarron looked at Marge.

"No," Marge said.

"And when was the last time you saw him, Miss Sherwood?"

"On November twenty-third, when he left for San Remo," Marge said promptly.

"You were then in Mongibello?" McCarron asked, pronouncing the town's name with a hard "g," as if he had no knowledge of Italian, or at least no relationship to the spoken language.

"Yes," Marge said. "I just missed seeing him in Rome in February, but the last time I saw him was in Mongibello."

Good old Marge! Tom felt almost affectionate toward her—underneath everything. He had begun to feel affectionate this morning, even though she had irritated him. "He was trying to avoid everyone in Rome," Tom put in. "That's why, when he first gave me the rings, I thought he was on some tack of getting away from everyone he had known, living in another city, and just vanishing for a while."

"Why, do you think?"

Tom elaborated, mentioning the murder of his friend Freddie Miles, and its effect on Dickie.

"Do you think Richard knew who killed Freddie Miles?"

"No. I certainly don't."

McCarron waited for Marge's opinion.

"No," Marge said, shaking her head.

"Think a minute," McCarron said to Tom. "Do you think that might have explained his behavior? Do you think he's avoiding answering the police by hiding out now?"

Tom thought for a minute. "He didn't give me a single clue in that direction."

"Do you think Dickie was afraid of something?"

"I can't imagine of what," Tom said.

McCarron asked Tom how close a friend Dickie had been of Freddie Miles, whom else he knew who was a friend of both Dickie and Freddie, if he knew of any debts between them, any girl friends— "Only Marge that I know of," Tom replied, and Marge protested that she wasn't a *girl* friend of Freddie's, so there couldn't possibly have been any *rivalry* over her—and could Tom say that he was Dickie's best friend in Europe?

"I wouldn't say that," Tom answered. "I think Marge Sherwood is. I hardly know any of Dickie's friends in Europe."

McCarron studied Tom's face again. "What's your opinion about these forgeries?"

"Are they forgeries? I didn't think anybody was sure."

"I don't think they are," Marge said.

"Opinion seems to be divided," McCarron said. "The experts don't think the letter he wrote to the bank in Naples is a forgery, which can only mean that if there is a forgery somewhere, he's covering up for someone. Assuming there is a forgery, do you have any idea who he might be trying to cover up for?"

Tom hesitated a moment, and Marge said, "Knowing him, I can't imagine him covering up for anyone. Why should he?"

McCarron was staring at Tom, but whether he was debating his honesty or mulling over all they had said to him, Tom couldn't tell. McCarron looked like a typical American automobile salesman, or any other kind of salesman, Tom thought—cheerful, presentable, average in intellect, able to talk baseball with a man or pay a stupid compliment to a woman. Tom didn't think too much of him, but, on the other hand, it was not wise to underestimate one's opponent. McCarron's small, soft mouth opened as Tom watched him, and he said, "Would you mind coming downstairs with me for a few minutes, Mr. Ripley, if you've still got a few minutes?"

"Certainly," Tom said, standing up.

"We won't be long," McCarron said to Mr. Greenleaf and Marge.

Tom looked back from the door, because Mr. Greenleaf had gotten up and was starting to say something, though Tom didn't listen. Tom was suddenly aware that it was raining, that thin, gray sheets of rain were slapping against the window-panes. It was like a last glimpse, blurred and hasty—Marge's figure looking small and huddled across the big room, Mr. Greenleaf doddering forward like an old man, protesting. But the comfortable room was the thing, and the view across the canal to where his house stood—invisible now because of the rain—which he might never see again.

Mr. Greenleaf was asking, "Are you—you are coming back in a few minutes?"

"Oh, yes," McCarron answered with the impersonal firmness of an executioner.

They walked toward the elevator. Was this the way they did it? Tom wondered. A quiet word in the lobby. He would be handed over to the Italian police, and then McCarron would return to the room just as he had promised. McCarron had brought a couple of the papers from his briefcase with him. Tom stared at an ornamental vertical molding beside the floor numbers panel in the elevator: an egg-shaped design framed by four raised dots, egg-shape, dots, all the way down. *Think of some sensible, ordinary remark to make about Mr. Greenleaf, for instance*, Tom said to himself. He ground his teeth. If he only wouldn't start sweating now. He hadn't started yet, but maybe it would break out all over his face when they reached the lobby. McCarron was hardly as tall as his shoulder. Tom turned to him just as the elevator stopped, and said grimly, baring his teeth in a smile, "Is this your first trip to Venice?"

"Yes," said McCarron. He was crossing the lobby. "Shall we go in here?" He indicated the coffee bar. His tone was polite.

"All right," Tom said agreeably. The bar was not crowded, but there was not a single table that would be out of earshot of some other table. Would McCarron accuse him in a place like this, quietly laying down fact after fact on the table? He took the chair that McCarron pulled out for him. McCarron sat with his back to the wall.

A waiter came up. "Signori?"

"Coffee," McCarron said.

"Cappuccino," Tom said. "Would you like a cappuccino or an espresso?"

"Which is the one with milk? Cappuccino?"

"Yes."

"I'll have that."

Tom gave the order.

McCarron looked at him. His small mouth smiled on one side. Tom imagined three or four different beginnings: "You killed Richard, didn't you? The rings are just too much, aren't they?" Or "Tell me about the San Remo boat, Mr. Ripley, in detail." Or simply, leading up quietly, "Where were you on February fifteenth, when Richard landed in Naples? . . . All right, but where were you living then? Where were you living in January, for instance? . . . Can you prove it?"

McCarron was saying nothing at all, only looking down at his plump hands now, and smiling faintly. As if it had been so absurdly simple for him to unravel, Tom thought, that he could hardly force himself to put it into words.

At a table next to them four Italian men were babbling away like a madhouse, screeching with wild laughter. Tom wanted to edge away from them. He sat motionless.

Tom had braced himself until his body felt like iron, until sheer tension created defiance. He heard himself asking, in an incredibly calm voice, "Did you have time to speak to Tenente Roverini when you came through Rome?" and at the same time he asked it, he realized that he had even an objective in the question: to find out if McCarron had heard about the San Remo boat.

"No, I didn't," McCarron said. "There was a message for me that Mr. Greenleaf would be in Rome today, but I'd landed in Rome so early, I thought I'd fly over and catch him—and also talk to you." McCarron looked down at his papers. "What kind of a man is Richard? How would you describe him as far as his personality goes?"

Was McCarron going to lead up to it like this? Pick out

more little clues from the words he chose to describe him? Or did he only want the objective opinion that he couldn't get from Dickie's parents? "He wanted to be a painter," Tom began, "but he knew he'd never be a very good painter. He tried to act as if he didn't care, and as if he were perfectly happy and leading exactly the kind of life he wanted to lead over here in Europe." Tom moistened his lips. "But I think the life was beginning to get him down. His father disapproved, as you probably know. And Dickie had got himself into an awkward spot with Marge."

"How do you mean?"

"Marge was in love with him, and he wasn't with her, and at the same time he was seeing her so much in Mongibello, she kept on hoping—" Tom began to feel on safer ground, but he pretended to have difficulty in expressing himself. "He never actually discussed it with me. He always spoke very highly of Marge. He was very fond of her, but it was obvious to everybody—Marge too—that he never would marry her. But Marge never quite gave up. I think that's the main reason Dickie left Mongibello."

McCarron listened patiently and sympathetically, Tom thought. "What do you mean never gave up? What did she do?"

Tom waited until the waiter had set down the two frothy cups of cappuccino and stuck the tab between them under the sugar bowl. "She kept writing to him, wanting to see him, and at the same time being very tactful, I'm sure, about not intruding on him when he wanted to be by himself. He told me all this in Rome when I saw him. He said, after the Miles murder, that he certainly wasn't in the mood to see Marge, and he was afraid that she'd come up to Rome from Mongibello when she heard of all the trouble he was in."

"Why do you think he was nervous after the Miles murder?" McCarron took a sip of the coffee, winced from the heat or the bitterness, and stirred it with the spoon.

Tom explained. They'd been quite good friends, and Freddie had been killed just a few minutes after leaving his house.

"Do you think Richard might have killed Freddie?" McCarron asked quietly.

"No, I don't."

"Why?"

"Because there was no reason for him to kill him—at least no reason that I happen to know of."

"People usually say, because so-and-so wasn't the type to kill anybody," McCarron said. "Do you think Richard was the type who could have killed anyone?"

Tom hesitated, seeking earnestly for the truth. "I never thought of it. I don't know what kind of people are apt to kill somebody. I've seen him angry—"

"When?"

Tom described the two days in Rome, when Dickie, he said, had been angry and frustrated because of the police questioning, and had actually moved out of his apartment to avoid phone calls from friends and strangers. Tom tied this in with a growing frustration in Dickie, because he had not been progressing as he had wanted to in his painting. He depicted Dickie as a stubborn, proud young man, in awe of his father and therefore determined to defy his father's wishes, a rather erratic fellow who was generous to strangers as well as to his friends, but who was subject to changes of mood—from sociability to sullen withdrawal. He summed it up by saying that Dickie was a very ordinary young man who liked to think he was extraordinary. "If he killed himself," Tom concluded, "I think it was because he realized certain failures in himself—inadequacies. It's much easier for me to imagine him a suicide than a murderer."

"But I'm not so sure that he didn't kill Freddie Miles. Are you?"

McCarron was perfectly sincere. Tom was sure of that. McCarron was even expecting him to defend Dickie now, because they had been friends. Tom felt some of his terror leaving him, but only some of it, like something melting very slowly inside him. "I'm not sure," Tom said, "but I just don't believe that he did."

"I'm not sure either. But it would explain a lot, wouldn't it?"

"Yes," Tom said. "Everything."

"Well, this is only the first day of work," McCarron said with an optimistic smile. "I haven't even looked over the re-

port in Rome. I'll probably want to talk to you again after
I've been to Rome."

Tom stared at him. It seemed to be over. "Do you speak
Italian?"

"No, not very well, but I can read it. I do better in French,
but I'll get along," McCarron said, as if it were not a matter
of much importance.

It was very important, Tom thought. He couldn't imagine
McCarron extracting everything that Roverini knew about the
Greenleaf case solely through an interpreter. Neither would
McCarron be able to get around and chat with people like
Dickie Greenleaf's landlady in Rome. It was most important.
"I talked with Roverini here in Venice a few weeks ago," Tom
said. "Give him my regards."

"I'll do that." McCarron finished his coffee. "Knowing
Dickie, what places do you think he would be likely to go if
he wanted to hide out?"

Tom squirmed back a little on his chair. This was getting
down to the bottom of the barrel, he thought. "Well, I know
he likes Italy best. I wouldn't bet on France. He also likes
Greece. He talked about going to Majorca at some time. All
of Spain is a possibility, I suppose."

"I see," McCarron said, sighing.

"Are you going back to Rome today?"

McCarron raised his eyebrows. "I imagine so, if I can catch
a few hours' sleep here. I haven't been to bed in two days."

He held up very well, Tom thought. "I think Mr. Greenleaf
was wondering about the trains. There are two this morning
and probably some more in the afternoon. He was planning
to leave today."

"We can leave today." McCarron reached for the check.
"Thanks very much for your help, Mr. Ripley. I have your
address and phone number, in case I have to see you again."

They stood up.

"Mind if I go up and say good-bye to Marge and Mr.
Greenleaf?"

McCarron didn't mind. They rode up in the elevator again.
Tom had to check himself from whistling. *Papa non vuole* was
going around in his head.

Tom looked closely at Marge as they went in, looking for

signs of enmity. Marge only looked a little tragic, he thought. As if she had recently been made a widow.

"I'd like to ask you a few questions alone, too, Miss Sherwood," McCarron said. "If you don't mind," he said to Mr. Greenleaf.

"Certainly not. I was just going down to the lobby to buy some newspapers," Mr. Greenleaf said.

McCarron was carrying on. Tom said good-bye to Marge and to Mr. Greenleaf, in case they were going to Rome today and he did not see them again. He said to McCarron, "I'd be very glad to come to Rome at any time, if I can be of any help. I expect to be here until the end of May, anyway."

"We'll have something before then," McCarron said with his confident Irish smile.

Tom went down to the lobby with Mr. Greenleaf.

"He asked me the same questions all over again," Tom told Mr. Greenleaf, "and also my opinion of Richard's character."

"Well, what is your opinion?" Mr. Greenleaf asked in a hopeless tone.

Whether he was a suicide or had run away to hide himself would be conduct equally reprehensible in Mr. Greenleaf's eyes, Tom knew. "I told him what I think is the truth," Tom said, "that he's capable of running away and also capable of committing suicide."

Mr. Greenleaf made no comment, only patted Tom's arm. "Good-bye, Tom."

"Good-bye," Tom said. "Let me hear from you."

Everything was all right between him and Mr. Greenleaf, Tom thought. And everything would be all right with Marge, too. She had swallowed the suicide explanation, and that was the direction her mind would run in from now on, he knew.

Tom spent the afternoon at home, expecting a telephone call, one telephone call at least from McCarron, even if it was not about anything important, but none came. There was only a call from Titi, the resident countess, inviting him for cock-tails that afternoon. Tom accepted.

Why should he expect any trouble from Marge, he thought. She never had given him any. The suicide was an idée fixe, and she would arrange everything in her dull imagination to fit it.

28.

McCARRON called Tom the next day from Rome, wanting the names of everyone Dickie had known in Mongibello. That was apparently all that McCarron wanted to know, because he took a leisurely time getting them all, and checking them off against the list that Marge had given him. Most of the names Marge had already given him, but Tom went through them all, with their difficult addresses—Giorgio, of course, Pietro the boatkeeper, Fausto's Aunt Maria whose last name he didn't know though he told McCarron in a complicated way how to get to her house, Aldo the grocer, the Cecchis, and even old Stevenson, the recluse painter who lived just outside the village and whom Tom had never even met. It took Tom several minutes to list them all, and it would take McCarron several days to check on them, probably. He mentioned everybody but Signor Pucci, who had handled the sale of Dickie's house and boat, and who would undoubtedly tell McCarron, if he hadn't learned it through Marge, that Tom Ripley had come to Mongibello to arrange Dickie's affairs. Tom did not think it very serious, one way or the other, if McCarron did know that he had taken care of Dickie's affairs. And as to people like Aldo and Stevenson, McCarron was welcome to all he could get out of them.

"Anyone in Naples?" McCarron asked.

"Not that I know of."

"Rome?"

"I'm sorry, I never saw him with any friends in Rome."

"Never met this painter—uh—Di Massimo?"

"No. I saw him once," Tom said, "but I never met him."

"What does he look like?"

"Well, it was just on a street corner. I left Dickie as he was going to meet him, so I wasn't very close to him. He looked about five feet nine, about fifty, grayish-black hair—that's about all I remember. He looked rather solidly built. He was wearing a light-gray suit, I remember."

"Hm-m—okay," McCarron said absently, as if he were writing all that down. "Well, I guess that's about all. Thanks very much, Mr. Ripley."

"You're very welcome. Good luck."

Then Tom waited quietly in his house for several days, just as anybody would do, if the search for a missing friend had reached its intensest point. He declined three or four invitations to parties. The newspapers had renewed their interest in Dickie's disappearance, inspired by the presence in Italy of an American private detective who had been hired by Dickie's father. When some photographers from *Europeo* and *Oggi* came to take pictures of him and his house, he told them firmly to leave, and actually took one insistent young man by the elbow and propelled him across the living room toward the door. But nothing of any importance happened for five days—no telephone calls, no letters, even from Tenente Roverini. Tom imagined the worst sometimes, especially at dusk when he felt more depressed than at any other time of day. He imagined Roverini and McCarron getting together and developing the theory that Dickie could have disappeared in November, imagined McCarron checking on the time he had bought his car, imagined him picking up a scent when he found out that Dickie had not come back after the San Remo trip and that Tom Ripley had come down to arrange for the disposal of Dickie's things. He measured and remeasured Mr. Greenleaf's tired, indifferent good-bye that last morning in Venice, interpreted it as unfriendly, and imagined Mr. Greenleaf flying into a rage in Rome when no results came of all the efforts to find Dickie, and suddenly demanding a thorough investigation of Tom Ripley, that scoundrel he had sent over with his own money to try to get his son home.

But each morning Tom was optimistic again. On the good side was the fact that Marge unquestioningly believed that Dickie had spent those months sulking in Rome, and she would have kept all his letters and she would probably bring them all out to show to McCarron. Excellent letters they were, too. Tom was glad he had spent so much thought on them. Marge was an asset rather than a liability. It was really a very good thing that he had put down his shoe that night that she had found the rings.

Every morning he watched the sun, from his bedroom window, rising through the winter mists, struggling upward over the peaceful-looking city, breaking through finally to give a couple of hours of actual sunshine before noon, and the quiet beginning of each day was like a promise of peace in the future. The days were growing warmer. There was more light, and less rain. Spring was almost here, and one of these mornings, one morning finer than these, he would leave the house and board a ship for Greece.

On the evening of the sixth day after Mr. Greenleaf and McCarron had left, Tom called him in Rome. Mr. Greenleaf had nothing new to report, but Tom had not expected anything. Marge had gone home. As long as Mr. Greenleaf was in Italy, Tom thought, the papers would carry something about the case every day. But the newspapers were running out of sensational things to say about the Greenleaf case.

"And how is your wife?" Tom asked.

"Fair. I think the strain is telling on her, however. I spoke to her again last night."

"I'm sorry," Tom said. He ought to write her a nice letter, he thought, just a friendly word while Mr. Greenleaf was away and she was by herself. He wished he had thought of it before.

Mr. Greenleaf said he would be leaving at the end of the week, via Paris, where the French police were also carrying on the search. McCarron was going with him, and if nothing happened in Paris they were both going home. "It's obvious to me or to anybody," Mr. Greenleaf said, "that he's either dead or deliberately hiding. There's not a corner of the world where the search for him hasn't been publicized. Short of Russia, maybe. My God, he never showed any liking for that place, did he?"

"Russia? No, not that I know of."

Apparently Mr. Greenleaf's attitude was that Dickie was either dead or to hell with him. During that telephone call, the to-hell-with-him attitude seemed to be uppermost.

Tom went over to Peter Smith-Kingsley's house that same evening. Peter had a couple of English newspapers that his friends had sent him, one with a picture of Tom ejecting the *Oggi* photographer from his house. Tom had seen it in the Italian newspapers too. Pictures of him on the streets of Venice and pictures of his house had also gotten to America. Bob and Cleo both had airmailed him photographs and write-ups from New York tabloids. They thought it was all terribly exciting.

"I'm good and sick of it," Tom said. "I'm only hanging around here to be polite and to help if I can. If any more reporters try to crash my house, they're going to get it with a shotgun as soon as they walk in the door." He really was irritated and disgusted, and it sounded in his voice.

"I quite understand," Peter said. "I'm going home at the end of May, you know. If you'd like to come along and stay at my place in Ireland, you're more than welcome. It's deadly quiet there, I can assure you."

Tom glanced at him. Peter had told him about his old Irish castle and had shown him pictures of it. Some quality of his relationship with Dickie flashed across his mind like the memory of a nightmare, like a pale and evil ghost. It was because the same thing could happen with Peter, he thought, Peter the upright, unsuspecting, naive, generous good fellow—except that he didn't look enough like Peter. But one evening, for Peter's amusement, he had put on an English accent and had imitated Peter's mannerisms and his way of jerking his head to one side as he talked, and Peter had thought it hilariously funny. He shouldn't have done that, Tom thought now. It made Tom bitterly ashamed, that evening and the fact that he had thought even for an instant that the same thing that had happened with Dickie could happen with Peter.

"Thanks," Tom said. "I'd better stay by myself for a while longer. I miss my friend Dickie, you know. I miss him terribly." He was suddenly near tears. He could remember Dickie's smiles that first day they began to get along, when he had confessed to Dickie that his father had sent him. He remembered their crazy first trip to Rome. He remembered with affection even that half-hour in the Carlton Bar in Cannes, when Dickie had been so bored and silent, but there had been a reason why Dickie had been bored, after all: he had dragged Dickie there, and Dickie didn't care for the Côte d'Azur. If he'd only gotten his sightseeing done all by himself, Tom thought, if he only hadn't been in such a hurry and so greedy, if he only hadn't misjudged the relationship between Dickie and Marge so stupidly, or had simply waited for them to separate of their own volition, then none of this would have happened, and he *could* have lived with Dickie for the rest of his life, traveled and lived and enjoyed living for the rest of his life. If he only hadn't put on Dickie's clothes that day—

"I understand, Tommie boy, I really do," Peter said, patting his shoulder.

Tom looked up at him through distorting tears. He was imagining traveling with Dickie on some liner back to America for Christmas holidays, imagining being on as good terms with Dickie's parents as if he and Dickie had been brothers. "Thanks," Tom said. It came out a childlike "blub."

"I'd really think something was the matter with you if you didn't break down like this," Peter said sympathetically.

29.

Venice
June 3, 19——

Dear Mr. Greenleaf,

While packing a suitcase today, I came across an envelope that Richard gave me in Rome, and which for some unaccountable reason I had forgotten until now. On the envelope was written "Not to be opened until June" and, as it happens, it is June. The envelope contained Richard's will, and he leaves his income and possessions to me. I am as astounded by this as you probably are, yet from the wording of the will (it is typewritten) he seems to have been in possession of his senses.

I am only bitterly sorry I did not remember having the envelope, because it would have proven much earlier that Dickie intended to take his own life. I put it into a suitcase pocket, and then I forgot it. He gave it to me on the last occasion I saw him, in Rome, when he was so depressed.

On second thought, I am enclosing a photostat copy of the will so that you may see it for yourself. This is the first will I have ever seen in my life, and I am absolutely unfamiliar with the usual procedure. What should I do?

Please give my kindest regards to Mrs. Greenleaf and realize that I sympathize deeply with you both, and regret the necessity of writing

this letter. Please let me hear from you as soon as possible. My next
address will be:

> c/o American Express
> Athens, Greece
>> Most sincerely yours,
>> Tom Ripley

In a way it was asking for trouble, Tom thought. It might
start a new investigation of the signatures, on the will and also
the remittances, one of the relentless investigations that insurance companies and probably trust companies also
launched when it was a matter of money out of their own
pockets. But that was the mood he was in. He had bought
his ticket for Greece in the middle of May, and the days had
grown finer and finer, making him more and more restless.
He had taken his car out of the Fiat garage in Venice and had
driven over the Brenner to Salzburg and Munich, down to
Trieste and over to Bolzano, and the weather had held everywhere, except for the mildest, most springlike shower in Munich when he had been walking in the Englischer Garten, and
he had not even tried to get under cover from it but had
simply kept on walking, thrilled as a child at the thought that
this was the first German rain that had ever fallen on him. He
had only two thousand dollars in his own name, transferred
from Dickie's bank account and saved out of Dickie's income,
because he hadn't dared to withdraw any more in so short a
time as three months. The very chanciness of trying for all of
Dickie's money, the peril of it, was irresistible to him. He was
so bored after the dreary, eventless weeks in Venice, when
each day that went by had seemed to confirm his personal
safety and to emphasize the dullness of his existence. Roverini had stopped writing to him. Alvin McCarron had gone
back to America (after nothing more than another inconsequential telephone call to him from Rome), and Tom supposed that he and Mr. Greenleaf had concluded that Dickie
was either dead or hiding of his own will, and that further
search was useless. The newspapers had stopped printing anything about Dickie for want of anything to print. Tom had a
feeling of emptiness and abeyance that had driven him nearly
mad until he made the trip to Munich in his car. When he

came back to Venice to pack for Greece and to close his house, the sensation had been worse: he was about to go to Greece, to those ancient heroic islands, as little Tom Ripley, shy and meek, with a dwindling two-thousand-odd in his bank, so that he would practically have to think twice before he bought himself even a book on Greek art. It was intolerable.

He had decided in Venice to make his voyage to Greece an heroic one. He would see the islands, swimming for the first time into his view, as a living, breathing, courageous individual—not as a cringing little nobody from Boston. If he sailed right into the arms of the police in Piraeus, he would at least have known the days just before, standing in the wind at the prow of a ship, crossing the wine-dark sea like Jason or Ulysses returning. So he had written the letter to Mr. Greenleaf and mailed it three days before he was to sail from Venice. Mr. Greenleaf would probably not get the letter for four or five days, so there would be no time for Mr. Greenleaf to hold him in Venice with a telegram and make him miss his ship. Besides, it looked better from every point of view to be casual about the thing, not to be reachable for another two weeks until he got to Greece, as if he were so unconcerned as to whether he got the money or not, he had not let the fact of the will postpone even a little trip he had planned to make.

Two days before his sailing, he went to tea at the house of Titi della Latta-Cacciaguerra, the countess he had met the day he had started looking for a house in Venice. The maid showed him into the living room, and Titi greeted him with the phrase he had not heard for many weeks: "Ah, ciao, Tomaso! Have you seen the afternoon paper? They have found Deekie's suitcases! And his paintings! Right here in the American Express in Venice!" Her gold earrings trembled with her excitement.

"*What?*" Tom hadn't seen the papers. He had been too busy packing that afternoon.

"Read it! Here! All his clothes deposited only in February! They were sent from Naples. Perhaps he is here in Venice!"

Tom was reading it. The cord around the canvases had come undone, the paper said, and in wrapping them again a clerk had discovered the signature R. Greenleaf on the paintings. Tom's hands began to shake so that he had to grip the sides of the paper to hold it steady. The paper said that the police were now examining everything carefully for fingerprints.

"Perhaps he is alive!" Titi shouted.

"I don't think—I don't see why this proves he is alive. He could have been murdered or killed himself after he sent the suitcases. The fact that it's under another name—Fanshaw—" He had the feeling the countess, who was sitting rigidly on the sofa staring at him, was startled by his nervousness, so he pulled himself together abruptly, summoned all his courage and said, "You see? They're looking through everything for fingerprints. They wouldn't be doing that if they were sure Dickie sent the suitcases himself. Why should he deposit them under Fanshaw, if he expected to claim them again himself? His passport's even here. He packed his passport."

"Perhaps he is hiding himself under the name of Fanshaw! Oh, caro mio, you need some tea!" Titi stood up. "Giustina! Il te, per piacere, subitissimo!"

Tom sank down weakly on the sofa, still holding the newspaper in front of him. What about the knot on Dickie's body? Wouldn't it be just his luck to have that come undone now?

"Ah, carissimo, you are so pessimistic," Titi said, patting his knee. "This is good news! Suppose all the fingerprints are his? Wouldn't you be happy then? Suppose tomorrow, when you are walking in some little street of Venice, you will come face to face with Deekie Greenleaf, alias Signor Fanshaw!" She let out her shrill, pleasant laugh that was as natural to her as breathing.

"It says here that the suitcases contained everything—shaving kit, toothbrush, shoes, overcoat, complete equipment," Tom said, hiding his terror in gloom. "He couldn't be alive and leave all that. The murderer must have stripped his body and deposited his clothes there because it was the easiest way of getting rid of them."

This gave even Titi pause. Then she said, "Will you not be so downhearted until you know what the fingerprints are? You are supposed to be off on a pleasure trip tomorrow. Ecco il te!"

The day after tomorrow, Tom thought. Plenty of time for Roverini to get his fingerprints and compare them with those

on the canvases and in the suitcases. He tried to remember
any flat surfaces on the canvas frames and on things in the
suitcases from which fingerprints could be taken. There was
not much, except the articles in the shaving kit, but they could
find enough, in fragments and smears, to assemble ten perfect
prints if they tried. His only reason for optimism was that they
didn't have his fingerprints yet, and that they might not ask
for them, because he was not yet under suspicion. But if they
already had Dickie's fingerprints from somewhere? Wouldn't
Mr. Greenleaf send Dickie's fingerprints from America the
very first thing, by way of checking? There could be any number of places they could find Dickie's fingerprints: on certain
possessions of his in America, in the house in Mongibello—

"Tomaso! Take your tea!" Titi said, with another gentle
press of his knee.

"Thank you."

"You will see. At least this is a step toward the truth, what
really happened. Now let us talk about something else, if it
makes you so unhappy! Where do you go from Athens?"

He tried to turn his thoughts to Greece. For him, Greece
was gilded, with the gold of warriors' armor and with its own
famous sunlight. He saw stone statues with calm, strong faces,
like the women on the porch of the Erechtheum. He didn't
want to go to Greece with the threat of the fingerprints in
Venice hanging over him. It would debase him. He would feel
as low as the lowest rat that scurried in the gutters of Athens,
lower than the dirtiest beggar who would accost him in the
streets of Salonika. Tom put his face in his hands and wept.
Greece was finished, exploded like a golden balloon.

Titi put her firm, plump arm around him. "Tomaso, cheer
up! Wait until you have reason to feel so downcast!"

"I can't see why you don't see that this is a bad sign!" Tom
said desperately. "I really don't!"

30.

THE worst sign of all was that Roverini, whose messages had
been so friendly and explicit up to now, sent him nothing at

all in regard to the suitcases and canvases having been found in Venice. Tom spent a sleepless night and then a day of pacing his house while he tried to finish the endless little chores pertaining to his departure, paying Anna and Ugo, paying various tradesmen. Tom expected the police to come knocking on his door at any hour of the day or night. The contrast between his tranquil self-confidence of five days ago and his present apprehension almost tore him apart. He could neither sleep nor eat nor sit still. The irony of Anna's and Ugo's commiseration with him, and also of the telephone calls from his friends, asking him if he had any ideas as to what might have happened in view of the finding of the suitcases, seemed more than he could bear. Ironic, too, that he could let them know that he was upset, pessimistic, desperate even, and they thought nothing of it. They thought it was perfectly normal, because Dickie after all might have been murdered: everybody considered it very significant that all Dickie's possessions had been in the suitcases in Venice, down to his shaving kit and comb.

Then there was the matter of the will. Mr. Greenleaf would get it day after tomorrow. By that time they might know that the fingerprints were not Dickie's. By that time they might have intercepted the *Hellenes*, and taken his own fingerprints. If they discovered that the will was a forgery, too, they would have no mercy on him. All three murders would come out, as naturally as ABC.

By the time he boarded the *Hellenes* Tom felt like a walking ghost. He was sleepless, foodless, full of espressos, carried along only by his twitching nerves. He wanted to ask if there was a radio, but he was positive there was a radio. It was a good-sized, triple-deck ship with forty-eight passengers. He collapsed about five minutes after the stewards had brought his luggage into his cabin. He remembered lying face down on his bunk with one arm twisted under him, and being too tired to change his position, and when he awakened the ship was moving, not only moving but rolling gently with a pleasant rhythm that suggested a tremendous reserve of power and a promise of unending, unobstructable forward movement that would sweep aside anything in its way. He felt better, except that the arm he had been lying on hung limply at his

side like a dead member, and flopped against him when he
walked through the corridor so that he had to grip it with the
other hand to hold it in place. It was a quarter of ten by his
watch, and utterly dark outside.

There was some kind of land on his extreme left, probably
part of Yugoslavia, five or six little dim white lights, and otherwise nothing but black sea and black sky, so black that there
was no trace of an horizon and they might have been sailing
against a black screen, except that he felt no resistance to the
steadily plowing ship, and the wind blew freely on his forehead as if out of infinite space. There was no one around him
on the deck. They were all below, eating their late dinner, he
supposed. He was glad to be alone. His arm was coming back
to life. He gripped the prow where it separated in a narrow
V and took a deep breath. A defiant courage rose in him.
What if the radioman were receiving at this very minute a
message to arrest Tom Ripley? He would stand up just as
bravely as he was standing now. Or he might hurl himself over
the ship's gunwale—which for him would be the supreme act
of courage as well as escape. Well, what if? Even from where
he stood, he could hear the faint *beep—beep-beep* from the
radio room at the top of the superstructure. He was not afraid.
This was it. This was the way he had hoped he would feel,
sailing to Greece. To look out at the black water all around
him and not be afraid was almost as good as seeing the islands
of Greece coming into view. In the soft June darkness ahead
of him he could construct in imagination the little islands, the
hills of Athens dotted with buildings, and the Acropolis.

There was an elderly Englishwoman on board the ship, traveling with her daughter who herself was forty, unmarried, and
so wildly nervous she could not even enjoy the sun for fifteen
minutes in her deckchair without leaping up and announcing
in a loud voice that she was "off for a walk." Her mother, by
contrast, was extremely calm and slow—she had some kind of
paralysis in her right leg, which was shorter than the other so
that she had to wear a thick heel on her right shoe and could
not walk except with a cane—the kind of person who would
have driven Tom insane in New York with her slowness and

her unvarying graciousness of manner, but now Tom was inspired to spend hours with her in the deckchairs, talking to
her and listening to her talk about her life in England and
about Greece, when she had last seen Greece in 1926. He took
her for slow walks around the deck, she leaning on his arm
and apologizing constantly for the trouble she was giving him,
but obviously she loved the attention. And the daughter was
obviously delighted that someone was taking her mother off
her hands.

Maybe Mrs. Cartwright had been a hellcat in her youth,
Tom thought, maybe she was responsible for every one of her
daughter's neuroses, maybe she had clutched her daughter so
closely to her that it had been impossible for the daughter to
lead a normal life and marry, and maybe she deserved to be
kicked overboard instead of walked around the deck and listened to for hours while she talked, but what did it matter?
Did the world always mete out just deserts? Had the world
meted his out to him? He considered that he had been lucky
beyond reason in escaping detection for two murders, lucky
from the time he had assumed Dickie's identity until now. In
the first part of his life fate had been grossly unfair, he
thought, but the period with Dickie and afterward had more
than compensated for it. But something was going to happen
now in Greece, he felt, and it couldn't be good. His luck had
held just too long. But supposing they got him on the fingerprints, and on the will, and they gave him the electric
chair—could that death in the electric chair equal in pain, or
could death itself, at twenty-five, be so tragic, that he could
not say that the months from November until now had not
been worth it? Certainly not.

The only thing he regretted was that he had not seen all
the world yet. He wanted to see Australia. And India. He
wanted to see Japan. Then there was South America. Merely
to look at the art of those countries would be a pleasant,
rewarding life's work, he thought. He had learned a lot about
painting, even in trying to copy Dickie's mediocre paintings.
At the art galleries in Paris and Rome he had discovered an
interest in paintings that he had never realized before, or perhaps that had not been in him before. He did not want to be

a painter himself, but if he had money, he thought, his greatest pleasure would be to collect paintings that he liked, and to help young painters with talent who needed money.

His mind went off on such tangents as he walked with Mrs. Cartwright around the deck, or listened to her monologues that were not always interesting. Mrs. Cartwright thought him charming. She told him several times, days before they got to Greece, how much he had contributed to her enjoyment of the voyage, and they made plans as to how they would meet at a certain hotel in Crete on the second of July, Crete being the only place their itineraries crossed. Mrs. Cartwright was traveling by bus on a special tour. Tom acquiesced to all her suggestions, though he never expected to see her again once they got off the ship. He imagined himself seized at once and taken on board another ship, or perhaps a plane, back to Italy. No radio messages had come about him—that he knew of— but would they necessarily inform him if any had come? The ship's paper, a little one-page mimeographed sheet that appeared every evening at each place on the dinner tables, was entirely concerned with international political news, and would not have contained anything about the Greenleaf case even if something important had happened. During the ten-day voyage Tom lived in a peculiar atmosphere of doom and of heroic, unselfish courage. He imagined strange things: Mrs. Cartwright's daughter falling overboard and he jumping after her and saving her. Or fighting through the waters of a ruptured bulkhead to close the breach with his own body. He felt possessed of a preternatural strength and fearlessness.

When the boat approached the mainland of Greece Tom was standing at the rail with Mrs. Cartwright. She was telling him how the port of Piraeus had changed in appearance since she had seen it last, and Tom was not interested at all in the changes. It existed, that was all that mattered to him. It wasn't a mirage ahead of him, it was a solid hill that he could walk on, with buildings that he could touch—if he got that far.

The police were waiting on the dock. He saw four of them, standing with folded arms, looking up at the ship. Tom helped Mrs. Cartwright to the very last, boosted her gently over the curb at the end of the gangplank, and said a smiling good-bye to her and her daughter. He had to wait under the R's and they under the C's to receive their luggage, and the two Cartwrights were leaving right away for Athens on their special bus.

With Mrs. Cartwright's kiss still warm and slightly moist on his cheek, Tom turned and walked slowly toward the policemen. No fuss, he thought, he'd just tell them himself who he was. There was a big newsstand behind the policemen, and he thought of buying a paper. Perhaps they would let him. The policemen stared back at him from over their folded arms as he approached them. They wore black uniforms with visored caps. Tom smiled at them faintly. One of them touched his cap and stepped aside. But the others did not close in. Now Tom was practically between two of them, right in front of the newsstand, and the policemen were staring forward again, paying no attention to him at all.

Tom looked over the array of papers in front of him, feeling dazed and faint. His hand moved automatically to take a familiar paper of Rome. It was only three days old. He pulled some lire out of his pocket, realized suddenly that he had no Greek money, but the newsdealer accepted the lire as readily as if he were in Italy, and even gave him back change in lire.

"I'll take these, too," Tom said in Italian, choosing three more Italian papers and the Paris *Herald-Tribune*. He glanced at the police officers. They were not looking at him.

Then he walked back to the shed on the dock where the ship's passengers were awaiting their luggage. He heard Mrs. Cartwright's cheerful halloo to him as he went by, but he pretended not to have heard. Under the R's he stopped and opened the oldest Italian paper, which was four days old.

NO ONE NAMED ROBERT S. FANSHAW FOUND,
DEPOSITOR OF GREENLEAF BAGGAGE

said the awkward caption on the second page. Tom read the long column below it, but only the fifth paragraph interested him:

The police ascertained a few days ago that the fingerprints on the suitcases and paintings are the same as the fingerprints found in Greenleaf's abandoned apartment in Rome. Therefore, it has been assumed that Greenleaf deposited the suitcases and the paintings himself. . . .

Tom fumbled open another paper. Here it was again:

. . . In view of the fact that the fingerprints on the articles in the suitcases are identical with those in Signor Greenleaf's apartment in Rome, the police have concluded that Signor Greenleaf packed and dispatched the suitcases to Venice, and there is speculation that he may have committed suicide, perhaps in the water in a state of total nudity. An alternative speculation is that he exists at present under the alias of Robert S. Fanshaw or another alias. Still another possibility is that he was murdered, after packing or being made to pack his own baggage—perhaps for the express purpose of confusing police inquiries through fingerprints. . . .

In any case, it is futile to search for "Richard Greenleaf" any longer, because, even if he is alive, he has not his "Richard Greenleaf" passport. . . .

Tom felt shaky and lightheaded. The glare of sunlight under the edge of the roof hurt his eyes. Automatically he followed the porter with his luggage toward the customs counter, and tried to realize, as he stared down at his open suitcase that the inspector was hastily examining, exactly what the news meant. It meant he was not suspected at all. It meant that the fingerprints really had guaranteed his innocence. It meant not only that he was not going to jail, and not going to die, but that he was not suspected at all. He was free. Except for the will.

Tom boarded the bus for Athens. One of his table companions was sitting next to him, but he gave no sign of greeting, and couldn't have answered anything if the man had spoken to him. There would be a letter concerning the will at the American Express in Athens, Tom was sure. Mr. Greenleaf had had plenty of time to reply. Perhaps he had put his lawyers onto it right away, and there would be only a polite negative reply in Athens from a lawyer, and maybe the next message would come from the American police, saying that he was answerable for forgery. Maybe both messages were awaiting him at the American Express. The will could undo it all. Tom looked out the window at the primitive, dry landscape. Nothing was registering on him. Maybe the Greek police were waiting for him at the American Express. Maybe the four men he had seen had not been police but some kind of soldiers.

The bus stopped. Tom got out, corraled his luggage, and found a taxi.

"Would you stop at the American Express, please?" he asked the driver in Italian, but the driver apparently understood "American Express" at least, and drove off. Tom remembered when he had said the same words to the taxi driver in Rome, the day he had been on his way to Palermo. How sure of himself he'd been that day, just after he had given Marge the slip at the Inghilterra!

He sat up when he saw the American Express sign, and looked around the building for policemen. Perhaps the police were inside. In Italian, he asked the driver to wait, and the driver seemed to understand this too, and touched his cap. There was a specious ease about everything, like the moment just before something was going to explode. Tom looked around inside the American Express lobby. Nothing seemed unusual. Maybe the minute he mentioned his name—

"Have you any letters for Thomas Ripley?" he asked in a low voice in English.

"Reepley? Spell it, if you please."

He spelt it.

She turned and got some letters from a cubbyhole.

Nothing was happening.

"Three letters," she said in English, smiling.

One from Mr. Greenleaf. One from Titi in Venice. One from Cleo, forwarded. He opened the letter from Mr. Greenleaf.

June 9, 19——

Dear Tom,

Your letter of June 3rd received yesterday.

It was not so much of a surprise to my wife and me as you may have imagined. We were both aware that Richard was very fond of you, in spite of the fact he never went out of his way to tell us this in any of his letters. As you pointed out, this will does, unhappily, seem to indicate that Richard has taken his own life. It is a conclusion that we here have at last accepted—the only other chance being that Richard has assumed another name and for reasons of his own has chosen to turn his back on his family.

My wife concurs with me in the opinion that we should carry out Richard's preferences and the spirit of them, whatever he may have done with himself. So you have, insofar as the will is concerned, my personal support. I have put your photostat copy into the hands of my lawyers, who will keep you informed as to their progress in making over Richard's trust fund and other properties to you.

Once more, thank you for your assistance when I was overseas. Let us hear from you.

With best wishes,
Herbert Greenleaf

Was it a joke? But the Burke-Greenleaf letterpaper in his hand felt authentic—thick and slightly pebbled and the letterhead engraved—and besides, Mr. Greenleaf wouldn't joke like this, not in a million years. Tom walked on to the waiting taxi. It was no joke. It was his! Dickie's money and his freedom. And the freedom, like everything else, seemed combined, his and Dickie's combined. He could have a house in Europe and a house in America too, if he chose. The money for the house in Mongibello was still waiting to be claimed, he thought suddenly, and he supposed he should send that to the Greenleafs, since Dickie put it up for sale before he wrote the will. He smiled, thinking of Mrs. Cartwright. He must take her a big box of orchids when he met her in Crete, if they had any orchids in Crete.

He tried to imagine landing in Crete—the long island, peaked with the dry, jagged lips of craters, the little bustle of excitement on the pier as his boat moved into the harbor, the small-boy porters, avid for his luggage and his tips, and he would have plenty to tip them with, plenty for everything and everybody. He saw four motionless figures standing on the imaginary pier, the figures of Cretan policemen waiting for him, patiently waiting with folded arms. He grew suddenly tense, and his vision vanished. Was he going to see policemen waiting for him on every pier that he ever approached? In Alexandria? Istanbul? Bombay? Rio? No use thinking about that. He pulled his shoulders back. No use spoiling his trip worrying about imaginary policemen. Even if there *were* policemen on the pier, it wouldn't necessarily mean—

"A donda, a donda?" the taxi driver was saying, trying to speak Italian for him.

"To a hotel, please," Tom said. "Il meglio albergo. Il meglio, il meglio!"

PICK-UP

by Charles Willeford

ONE

Enter Madame

It MUST have been around a quarter to eleven. A sailor came in and ordered a chile dog and coffee. I sliced a bun, jerked a frank out of the boiling water, nested it, poured a half-dipper of chile over the frank and sprinkled it liberally with chopped onions. I scribbled a check and put it by his plate. I wouldn't have recommended the unpalatable mess to a starving animal. The sailor was the only customer, and after he ate his dog he left.

That was the exact moment she entered.

A small woman, hardly more than five feet.

She had the figure of a teen-age girl. Her suit was a blue tweed, smartly cut, and over her thin shoulders she wore a fur jacket, bolero length. Tiny gold circular earrings clung to her small pierced ears. Her hands and feet were small, and when she seated herself at the counter I noticed she wasn't wearing any rings. She was pretty drunk.

"What'll it be?" I asked her.

"I believe I need coffee." She steadied herself on the stool by bracing her hands against the edge of the counter.

"Yes, you do," I agreed, "and you need it black."

I drew a cupful and set it before her. The coffee was too hot for her to drink and she bent her head down and blew on it with comical little puffs. I stood behind the counter watching her. I couldn't help it; she was beautiful. Even Benny, from his seat behind the cash register, was staring at her, and his only real interest is money. She wasn't nearly as young as I had first thought her to be. She was about twenty-six or -seven. Her fine blonde hair was combed straight back. Slightly to the right of a well-defined widow's-peak, an inch-wide strip of silver hair glistened, like a moonlit river flowing through night fields. Her oval face was unlined and very white. The only make-up she had on was lipstick; a dark shade of red, so dark it was almost black. She looked up from her coffee and noticed that I was staring at her. Her eyes were a charred sienna-brown, flecked with dancing particles of shining gold.

407

"This coffee is too hot." She smiled good-humoredly.

"Sure it is," I replied, "but if you want to sober up you should drink it hot as you can."

"My goodness! Who wants to sober up?"

Benny was signaling me from the cash register. I dropped my conversation with the girl to see what he wanted. Benny was a flat, bald, hook-nosed little man with a shaggy horseshoe of gray hair circling his head. I didn't particularly like him, but he never pushed or tried to boss me and I'd stuck it out as his counterman for more than two months. For me, this was a record. His dirty eyes were gleaming behind his gold-rimmed glasses.

"There's your chance, Harry!" He laughed a throaty, phlegmy laugh.

I knew exactly what he meant. About two weeks before a girl had entered the cafe at closing time and she had been pretty well down on her luck. She'd been actually hungry and Benny had had me fix her up with a steak and french fries. Afterwards, he had made her pay him for the meal by letting him take it out in trade in the kitchen.

"I don't need any advice from you," I said angrily.

He laughed again, deep in his chest. "It's quitting time. Better take advantage." He climbed down from his stool and walked stiffly to the door. He shot the bolt and hung the CLOSED sign from the hook. I started toward the kitchen and as I passed the woman she shook her empty cup at me.

"See? All finished. May I have another?"

I filled her cup, set it in front of her and went into the back room and slipped into my tweed jacket. The jacket was getting ratty. It was my only outer garment, with the exception of my trenchcoat, and I'd worn it for more than two years. The elbows were thin and the buttons, except one, were missing. The good button was the top one and a coat looks funny buttoned at the top. I resolved to move it to the middle in the morning. My blue gabardine trousers hadn't been cleaned for three weeks and they were spotted here and there with grease. I had another pair of trousers in my room, but they were tuxedo trousers, and I used them on waiter and busboy jobs. Sober, I was always embarrassed about my appearance, but I didn't intend to stay sober very long. I combed my hair and I was ready for the street, a bar and a drink.

She was still sitting at the counter and her cup was empty again.

"Just one more and I'll go," she said with a drunken little laugh. "I promise."

For the third time I gave her a cup of coffee. Benny was counting on his fingers and busily going over his receipts for the day. I tapped him on the shoulder.

"Benny, I need a ten until payday," I told him.

"Not again? I let you have ten last night and today's only Tuesday. By Saturday you won't have nothing coming."

"You don't have to worry about it."

He took his copy-book from under the counter and turned to my page. After he entered the advance in the book he reluctantly gave me a ten dollar bill. I folded the bill and put it in my watch pocket. I felt a hand timidly tugging at my sleeve and I turned around. The little woman was looking up at me with her big blue innocent eyes.

"I haven't any money," she said bitterly.

"Is that right?"

"Not a penny. Are you going to call a policeman?"

"Ask Mr. Freeman. He's the owner; I just work here."

"What's that?" Benny asked, at the mention of his name. He was in the middle of his count and didn't like to be disturbed.

"This young lady is unable to pay for her coffee."

"Coffee is ten cents," he said firmly.

"I'll tell you what, Benny. Just take it out of my pay."

"Don't think I won't!" He returned to his counting.

I unlocked the door, and the woman and I went outside.

"You're a free woman," I said to the girl. "You're lucky that Benny didn't notice you were without a purse when you came in. Where is your purse, by the way?"

"I think it's in my suitcase."

"All right. Where's your suitcase?"

"It's in a locker. I've got the key." She took a numbered key out of the pocket of her fur jacket. "The main trouble is that I can't seem to remember whether the locker's in the railroad station or the bus station." She was genuinely puzzled.

"If I were you I'd look in the bus station first. You're quite a ways from the railroad station. Do you know where it is?"

"The bus station?"

"Yes. It's seven blocks that way and one block that way." I pointed down Market Street. "You can't miss it. I'm going to have a drink."

"Would you mind buying me one too?"

"Sure. Come on."

She took my arm and we walked down Market. It was rather pleasant having a beautiful woman in tow and I was glad she had asked me to buy her a drink. I would never have asked her, but as long as she didn't mind, I certainly didn't mind. I shortened my stride so she could keep up with me and from time to time I looked down at her. Gin was my weakness, not women, but with a creature like her . . . well, it was enough to make a man think. We were nearing the bar where I always had my first drink after work and my mind returned to more practical things. We entered, found seats at the end of the bar.

"Say," she said brightly. "I remember being in here to-night!"

"That's fine. It's a cinch you were in some bar." The bartender knew me well, but his eyebrows lifted when he saw the girl with me.

"What'll you have, Harry?" he asked.

"Double gin and tonic." I turned to the girl.

"I'd better not have a double. Give me a little shot of bourbon and a beer chaser." She smiled at me. "I'm being smart, aren't I?"

"You bet." I lit two cigarettes and passed her one. She sucked it deeply.

"My name is Harry Jordan," I said solemnly. "I'm thirty-two years of age and when I'm not working, I drink."

Her laugh closely resembled a tinkling bell. "My name is Helen Meredith. I'm thirty-three years old and I don't work at all. I drink all of the time."

"You're not thirty-three, are you? I took you for about twenty-six, maybe less."

"I'm thirty-three all right, and I can't forget it."

"Well, you've got an advantage on me then. Married?"

"Uh huh. I'm married, but I don't work at that either."
She shrugged comically. I stared at her delicate fingers as she
handled the cigarette.

The bartender arrived with our drinks. Mine was good and
cold and the gin taste was strong. The way I like it. I love the
first drink best of all.

"Two more of the same," I told the bartender, "and see if
Mrs. Meredith's purse was left here, will you?"

"I haven't seen a purse laying around. Are you sure you
left it in here, miss?" he asked Helen worriedly.

"I'm not sure of anything," she replied.

"Well, I'll take a look around. Maybe you left it in a
booth."

"Helen Meredith," I said, when the bartender left. "Here's
to you!" We clicked our glasses together and drained them
down. Helen choked a bit and followed her shot down with
the short beer chaser.

"Ahhh," she sighed. "Harry, I'm going to tell you something while I'm still able to tell you. I haven't lived with my
husband for more than ten years, and even though I don't
wear a ring, I'm still married."

"You don't have to convince me."

"But I want to tell you. I live with my mother in San
Sienna. Do you know where that is?"

"Sure. It's a couple of hundred miles down the coast.
Noted for tourists, beaches, a mission and money. Nothing
else."

"That's right. Well as I told you, I drink. In the past two
years I've managed to embarrass Mother many times. It's a
small community and we're both well-known, so I decided
the best thing to do was get out. This morning I was half-
drunk, half-hungover, and I bought a bottle and I left. For
good. But I hit the bottle so hard I'm not sure whether I
came to San Francisco on the bus or on the train."

"I'm willing to lay odds of two to one it was the bus."

"You're probably right. I really don't remember."

The bartender brought us our second drink. He shook his
head emphatically. "You didn't leave no purse in here, miss.
You might've thought you did, but you didn't."

"Thanks for looking," I told him. "After we finish this one," I said to Helen, "we'll go back down to the bus station and I'll find your purse for you. Then you'd better head back for San Sienna and Mother."

Helen shook her head back and forth slowly. "No. I'm not going back. Never."

"That's your business. Not mine."

We finished our second drink and left the bar. It was a long walk to the bus station. Market Street blocks are long and crowded. Helen hung on to my arm possessively, and by the time we reached the station she had sobered considerably. The place was jampacked with servicemen of all kinds and a liberal sprinkling of civilians. The Greyhound station is the jumping-off place for servicemen. San Francisco is the hub for all the spokes leading to air bases, navy bases and army posts that dot the bay area.

"Does the bus station look familiar to you?"

"Of course!" She laughed. "I've been to San Francisco many times. I always come up on the bus for my Christmas shopping."

I felt a little foolish. "Let's start looking then." She handed me the numbered key. There are a lot of parcel lockers inside the Greyhound station and many more out on the waiting ramp, but in a few minutes we were able to locate the locker. It was in the first row to the left of the Ladies' Room. I inserted the key and opened the locker. I took the suitcase out of the locker and handed it to Helen. She unsnapped the two catches on the aluminum over-nighter and raised the lid. Her tiny hands ruffled deftly through the clothing. There wasn't any purse. I looked. No purse. I felt around inside the locker. No purse.

"Do you suppose I could have left it in some other bar, Harry?" she asked me worriedly. "Somewhere between here and the cafe?"

"That's probably what you did, all right. And if you did, you can kiss it goodbye. How much money did you have?"

"I don't know, but drunk or sober I wouldn't have left San Sienna broke. I know I had some traveler's checks."

I took my money out of my watch pocket. There were eight dollars and seventy cents. I gave the five dollar bill to Helen.

"This five'll get you a ticket back to San Sienna. You'd better get one."

Helen shook her head vigorously this time and firmly set her mouth. "I'm not going back, Harry. I told you I wasn't and I meant it!" She held the bill out to me. "Take it back; I don't want it."

"No, you go ahead and keep it. We'll consider it a loan. But I'm going to take you to a hotel. If I turned you loose you'd drink it up."

"It didn't take you long to get to know me, did it?" She giggled.

"I don't know you. It's just that I know what I'd do. Come on, we'll find a hotel."

I picked up the light suitcase and we left the station. We crossed Market Street and at Powell we turned and entered the first hotel that looked satisfactory to me. There are more than a dozen hotels on Powell Street, all of them adequate, and it was our best bet to find a vacancy. The hotel we entered was furnished in cheap modern furniture and the floor was covered with a rose wall-to-wall carpet. There were several green plants scattered about, all of them set in white pots with wrought-iron legs, and by each foam-cushioned lobby chair, there were skinny, black wrought-iron ash-stands. We crossed the empty lobby to the desk and I set the bag on the floor. The desk clerk was a fairly young man with sleek black hair. He looked up from his comic book with surly gray eyes.

"Sorry," he said flatly. "No doubles left. Just singles."

"That's fine," I said. "That's what I want."

Helen signed the register card. Her handwriting was cramped and it slanted to the left, almost microscopic in size. She put the pen back into the holder and folded her arms across her chest.

"The lady will pay in advance," I said to the clerk, without looking at Helen. She frowned fiercely for a second, then in spite of herself, she giggled and gave the clerk the five dollar bill. He gave her two ones in return. The night clerk also doubled as a bell boy and he came out from behind the desk with Helen's key in his hand.

"You want to go up now?" he asked Helen, pointedly ignoring me.

"I've still got two dollars," Helen said to me. "I'll buy you a drink!"

"No. You go to bed. You've had enough for one day."

"I'll buy you one tomorrow then."

"Tomorrow will be time enough," I said.

Helen's eyes were glassy and her eyelids were heavy. It was difficult for her to hold them open. In the warmth of the lobby she was beginning to stagger a little bit. The night clerk opened the door to the self-operated elevator and helped her in, holding her by the arm. I selected a comfortable chair near the desk and waited in the lobby until he returned. He didn't like it when he saw me sitting there.

"Do you think she'll manage all right?" I asked him.

"She managed to lock her door after I left," he replied dryly.

"Fine. Good night."

I left the hotel and walked up Powell as far as Lefty's, ordered a drink at the bar. It was dull, drinking alone, after drinking with Helen. She was the most attractive woman I had met in years. There was a quality about her that appealed to me. The fact that she was an alcoholic didn't make any difference to me. In a way, I was an alcoholic myself. She wasn't afraid to admit that she was a drunk; she was well aware of it, and she didn't have any intention to stop drinking. It wasn't necessary for her to tell me she was a drunk. I can spot an alcoholic in two minutes. Helen was still a good-looking woman, and she'd been drinking for a long time. I never expected to see her again. If I wanted to, I suppose it would have been easy enough. All I had to do was go down to her hotel in the morning, and . . .

I finished my drink quickly and left the bar. I didn't feel like drinking any more. I crossed the street and waited for my cable car. In a few minutes it dragged up the hill, slowed down at the corner, and I jumped on. I gave the conductor my fare and went inside where it was warmer. Usually, I sat in the outside section where I could smoke, but I was cold that night, my entire body was chilled.

On the long ride home I decided it would be best to steer clear of a woman like Helen.

TWO

Finder's Keepers

I GOT OUT of bed the next morning at ten, and still half-asleep, put the coffee pot on the two-ring gas burner. I padded next door to the bathroom, stood under the hot water of the shower for fifteen minutes, shaved, and returned to my room. It was the last one on the left, downstairs in Mrs. Frances McQuade's roominghouse. The house was on a fairly quiet street and my room was well separated from the other rooms and roomers. This enabled me to drink in my room without bothering anybody, and nobody could bother me.

I sat down at the table, poured a cup of black coffee, and let my mind think about Helen. I tried to define what there was about her that attracted me. Class. That was it. I didn't intend to do anything about the way I felt, but it was pleasant to let my mind explore the possibilities. I finished my coffee and looked around the room. Not only was it an ugly room; it was a filthy room. The walls were covered with a dull gray paper spotted with small crimson flowers. There was a sink in one corner, and next to it the gas burner in a small alcove. My bed was a double, and the head and footboard were made of brass rods, ornately twisted and tortured into circular designs. The dresser was metal, painted to look like maple or walnut, some kind of wood, and each leg rested in a small can of water. I kept my food in the bottom drawer and the cans of water kept the ants away. There were no pictures on the walls and no rug upon the floor, just a square piece of tangerine linoleum under the sink.

The room was in foul shape. Dirty shirts and dirty socks were scattered around, the dresser was messy with newspapers, book matches, my set of oil paints; and the floor was covered with gently moving dust motes. Lined up beneath the sink were seven empty gin bottles and an overflowing paper sack full of empty beer cans. The window was dirty and the sleazy cotton curtains were dusty. Dust was on everything . . .

Suppose, by some chance, I had brought Helen home with

me the night before? I sadly shook my head. Here was a project for me; I'd clean my room. A momentous decision.

I slipped into my shoes and blue gabardine slacks and
walked down the hall to Mrs. McQuade's room.

"Good morning," I said, when she opened the door. "I
want to borrow your broom and mop."

"The broom and mop are in the closet," she said, and
closed the door again.

Mrs. McQuade had a few eccentricities, but she was a kind,
motherly type of woman. Her hair was always freshly blued
and whenever I thought about it I would comment on how
nice it looked. Why women with beautiful white hair doctor
it with bluing has always been a mystery to me.

I found the broom and a rag mop and returned to my
room.

I spent the rest of the morning cleaning the room, even
going so far as to wash my window inside and out. The curtains needed washing, but I shook the dust out of them and
hung them back on the rod. Dusted and cleaned, the room
looked fairly presentable, even with its ancient, battered furniture. I was dirty again so I took another shower before I
dressed. I put my bundle of laundry under my arm, dragged
the mop and broom behind me, and leaned them up against
Mrs. McQuade's door.

I left the house and dumped my dirty laundry off at the
Spotless Cleaner on my way to the corner and Big Mike's Bar
and Grill. This was my real home, Big Mike's, and I spent
more time in his bar than anywhere else. It was a friendly
place, old-fashioned, with sawdust on the floor, and the walls
paneled in dark oak. The bar was long and narrow, extending
the length of the room, and it had a section with cushioned
stools and another section with a rail for those who preferred
to stand. There were a few booths along the wall, but there
was also a dining-room next door that could be entered either
from the street outside or from the barroom. The food was
good, reasonable, and there was plenty of it. I seldom ate
anything at Mike's. Food costs money and money spent for
food is money wasted. When I got hungry, which was seldom,
I ate at Benny's.

I took my regular seat at the end of the bar and ordered a

draught beer. It was lunch hour and very busy, but both of the bartenders knew me well and when my stein was emptied one of them would quickly fill it again. After one-thirty, the bar was clear of the lunch crowd and Big Mike joined me in a beer.

"You're a little late today, Harry," Mike said jokingly. He had a deep pleasant voice.

"Couldn't be helped."

Mike was an enormous man; everything about him was large, especially his head and hands. The habitual white shirt and full-sized apron he wore added to his look of massiveness. His face was badly scarred, but it didn't make him look hard or tough; it gave him a kindly, mellowed expression. He could be tough when it was necessary, however, and he was his own bouncer. The bar and grill belonged to him alone, and it had been purchased by his savings after ten years of professional football—all of it on the line, as a right tackle.

"How does my tab stand these days, Mike?" I asked him.

"I'll check." He looked in the credit book hanging by a string next to the cash register. "Not too bad," he smiled. "Twelve twenty-five. Worried about it?"

"When it gets to fifteen, cut me off, will you, Mike?"

"If I do you'll give me an argument."

"Don't pay any attention to me. Cut me off just the same."

"Okay." He shrugged his heavy shoulders. "We've gone through this before, we might as well go through it again."

"I'm not that bad, Mike."

"I honestly believe you don't know how bad you really are when you're loaded." He laughed to show he was joking, finished his beer, and lumbered back to the kitchen. I drank several beers, nursing them along, and at two-thirty I left the bar to go to work.

We picked up a little business from the theatre crowd when the afternoon show at the Bijou got out at three-thirty, and after that the cafe was fairly quiet until five. When things were busy, there was too much work for only one counterman, and I met myself coming and going. Benny was of no help at all. He never stirred all day from his seat behind the register. I don't know how he had the patience to sit like that from seven in the morning until eleven at night. His only enjoyment in life was obtained by eating orange gum-drops and counting his money at night. Once that day, during a lull, when no one was in the cafe, he tried to kid me about Helen. I didn't like it.

"Come on, Harry, where'd you take her last night?"

"Just forget about it, Benny. There's nothing to tell." I went into the kitchen to get away from him. I don't like that kind of talk. It's dirty. All of a sudden, all ten seats at the counter were filled, and I was too busy to think of anything except what I was doing. In addition to taking the orders, I had to prepare the food and serve it myself. It was quite a job to handle alone, even though Benny didn't run a regular lunch or dinner menu. Just when things are running well and the orders are simple things like sandwiches, bowls of chile, and coffee, a damned aesthete will come in and order soft-boiled eggs, wanting them two-and-one-half minutes in the water or something like that. But I like to work and the busier I am the better I like it. When I'm busy I don't have time to think about when I'll get my next drink.

Ten o'clock rolled around at last, the hour I liked the best of all. The traffic was always thin about this time and I only had another hour to go before I could have a drink. I felt a little hungry—I hadn't eaten anything all day—and I made myself a bacon and tomato sandwich. I walked around the counter and sat down to eat it. Benny eyed my sandwich hungrily.

"How about fixing me one of those, Harry?" he asked.

"Sure. Soon as I finish."

"Fix me one too," a feminine voice said lightly. I glanced to the left and there was Helen, standing in the doorway.

"You came back." My voice sounded flat and strained. No longer interested in food, I pushed my sandwich away from me.

"I told you I would. I owe you a drink. Remember?" She had a black patent leather purse in her hand. "See?" She shook the purse in the air. "I found it."

"Do you really want a sandwich?" I asked her, getting to my feet.

"No." She shook her head. "I was just talking."

"Wait right there," I said firmly, pointing my finger at Helen. "I'll be back in one second."

I went into the back room, and feverishly removed the dirty white jacket and leather tie. I changed into my own tie and sport jacket. Benny was ringing up thirty-one cents on the register when I came back. Helen had paid him for the coffee she had drunk the night before. Trust Benny to get his money.

I took Helen's arm, and Benny looked at us both with some surprise.

"Now just where in the hell do you think you're going?" he asked acidly.

"I quit. Come on, Helen." We walked through the open door.

"Hey!" he shouted after us, and I know that he said something else, but by that time we were walking down the street and well out of range.

THREE

First Night

"DID YOU really quit just like that?" Helen asked me as we walked down the street. Her voice was more amused than incredulous.

"Sure. You said you were going to buy me a drink. That's much more important than working."

"Here we are then." Helen pointed to the entrance door of the bar where we'd had our drinks the night before. "Is this all right?"

I smiled. "It's the nearest." We went inside and sat down at the bar. The bartender recognized Helen right away. He nodded pleasantly to me and then asked Helen: "Find your purse all right?"

"Sure did," Helen said happily.

"Now I'm glad to hear that," the bartender said. "I was afraid somebody might have picked it up and gone south with it. You know how these things happen sometimes. What'll you have?"

"Double gin and tonic for me," I said.

"Don't change it," Helen ordered, stringing along.

As soon as the bartender left to fix our drinks I took a sideways look at Helen. She wasn't tight, not even mellow, but barely under the influence; just enough under to give her a warm, rosy-cheeked color.

"Where did you find your purse, by the way?" I asked Helen.

"It was easy," she laughed merrily. "But I didn't think so this morning." She opened her purse, put enough change down on the bar to pay for the check and handed me a five dollar bill. "Now we're even, Harry."

"Thanks," I said, folding the bill and shoving it into my watch pocket, "I can use it."

"This morning," she began slowly, "I woke up in that miserable little hotel room with a hangover to end them all. God, I felt rotten! I could remember everything pretty well—you going down to the bus station with me, getting the room and so on, but the rest of the day was nothing. Did you ever get like that?"

"I recall a similar experience," I admitted.

"All I had was two dollars, as you know, so after I showered and dressed I checked out of the hotel, leaving my bag at the desk. I was hungry, so I ate breakfast and had four cups of coffee, black, and tried to figure out what to do next.

"Without money, I was in a bad way—" She quickly finished her drink and shook the ice in her glass at the bartender for another. I downed mine fast in order to join her for the next round.

"So I returned to the bus station after breakfast and started from there." She smiled slyly and sipped her drink. "Now where would you have looked for the purse, Harry?"

I thought the question over for a moment. "The nearest bar?"

"Correct!" She laughed appreciatively. "That's where I found it. The first bar to the left of the station. There was a different bartender on duty—about eleven this morning—and he didn't know me, of course, but I described my bag and it was there, under the shelf by the cash register. At first he wouldn't give it to me because there wasn't any identification inside. Like a driver's license, something like that, but my traveler's checks were in the bag and after I wrote my name on a piece of paper and he compared the signatures on the checks he gave it to me. The first thing I did was cash a check and buy him a drink, joining him, of course."

"No money at all?"

"Just the traveler's checks. I'm satisfied. Two hundred dollars in traveler's checks is better than money."

"Cash a couple then and let's get out of here," I said happily. "This isn't the only bar in San Francisco."

We went to several places that night and knowing where to go is a mighty tricky business. Having lived in San Francisco for more than a year I could just about tell and I was very careful about the places I took her to. I didn't want to embarrass Helen any—not that she would have given a damn—but I wanted to have a good time, and I wanted her to have a good time too.

The last night club we were in was The Dolphin. I had been there once before, when I was in the chips, and I knew Helen would like it. It's a club you have to know about or you can't find it. It's down an alley off Divisadero Street and I had to explain to the taxicab driver how to get there. There isn't any lettered sign over the door; just a large, blue neon fish blinking intermittently, and the fish itself doesn't look like a dolphin. But once inside you know you're in The Dolphin, because the name is in blue letters on the menu, and the prices won't let you forget where you are. We entered and luckily found a booth well away from the bar. The club is designed with a South Seas effect, and the drinks are served in tall, thick glasses, the size and shape of a vase. The booth we sat in was very soft, padded thickly with foam rubber, and both of us had had enough to drink to appreciate the atmosphere and the deep, gloomy lighting that made it almost impossible to see across the room. The waiter appeared at our table out of the darkness and handed each of us a menu. He was a Mexican, naked except for a grass skirt, and made up to look like an islander of some sort: there were blue and yellow streaks of paint on his brown face, and he wore a shark's-teeth necklace.

"Do you still have the Dolphin Special?" I asked him.

"Certainly," he said politely. "And something to eat? Poi, dried squid, bird's-nest soup, breadfruit au gratin, sago palm salad—"

Helen's laugh startled the waiter. "No thanks," she said. "I guess I'm not hungry."

"Just bring us two of the Dolphin Specials," I told him. He nodded solemnly and left for the bar. The Special is a good drink; it contains five varieties of rum, mint, plenty of snow-ice, and it's decorated with orange slices, pineapple slices and cherries with a sprinkling of sugar cane gratings floating on top. I needed at least two of them. I had to build up my nerve.

After the waiter brought our drinks I lighted cigarettes and we smoked silently, dumping the ashes into the large abalone shell on the table that served as an ash-tray. The trio hummed into action and the music floating our way gave me a wistful feeling of nostalgia. The trio consisted of chimes, theremin and electric guitar and the unusual quality of the theremin prevented me from recognizing the melody of the song although I was certain I knew what it was.

With sudden impulsive boldness I put my hand on Helen's knee. Her knee jumped under the touch of my hand, quivered and was still again. She didn't knock my hand away. I drank my drink, outwardly calm, bringing my glass up to my lips with my free hand, and wondering vaguely what to do next.

"Helen," I said, my voice a little hoarse, "I've been hoping and dreading to see you all day. I didn't really expect to see you, and yet, when I thought I wouldn't, my heart would sort of knot up."

"Why, Harry, you're a poet!"

"No, I'm serious. I'm trying to tell you how I feel about you."

"I didn't mean to be rude or flippant, Harry. I feel very close to you, and trying to talk about it isn't any good."

"I've had terrible luck with women, Helen," I said, "and for the last two years I've kept away from them. I didn't want to go through it all again—you know, the bickering, the jealousy, nagging, that sort of thing. Am I scaring you off?"

"You couldn't if you tried, Harry. You're my kind of man and it isn't hard to say so. What I mean is—you're somebody, under-neath, a person, and not just another man. See?" She shook her head impatiently. "I told you I couldn't talk about it."

"One thing I want to get straight is this," I said. "I'll never tell you that I love you."

"That word doesn't mean anything anyway."

"I never thought I'd hear a woman say that. But it's the truth. Love is in what you do, not in what you say. Couples work themselves into a hypnotic state daily by repeating to each other over and over again that they love each other. And they don't know the meaning of the word. They also say they love a certain brand of toothpaste and a certain brand of cereal in the same tone of voice."

Cautiously, I gathered the material of her skirt with my fingers until the hem was above her knee. My hand squeezed the warm flesh above her stocking. It was soft as only a woman's thigh is soft. She spread her legs at the touch of my hand and calmly sipped her drink. I tried to go a little higher and she clamped her legs on my hand.

"After all, Harry," she chided me, "we're not alone, you know."

I took my hand away from the softness of her thigh and she pulled her skirt down, smiling at me sympathetically. With trembling hands I lighted a cigarette. I didn't know what to do or what to say next. I felt as immature and inept as a teenager on his first date. And Helen wasn't helping me at all. I couldn't imagine what she was thinking about my crude and foolish passes.

"Helen," I blurted out like a schoolboy, "will you sleep with me tonight?" I felt like I had staked my life on the turn of a card.

"Why, Harry! What a thing to say." Her eyes didn't twinkle, that is impossible, but they came close to it. Very close. "Where else did you think I was going if I didn't go home with you?"

"I don't know," I said honestly.

"You didn't have to ask me like that. I thought there was an understanding between us, that it was understood."

"I don't like to take people for granted."

"In that case then, I'll tell you. I'm going home with you."

"I hope we're compatible," I said. "Then everything will be perfect."

"We are. I know it."

"I'm pretty much of a failure in life, Helen. Does it matter to you?"

"No. Nothing matters to me." Her voice had a resigned quality and yet it was quietly confident. There was a tragic look in her brown eyes, but her mouth was smiling. It was the smile of a little girl who knows a secret and isn't going to tell it. I held her hand in mine. It was a tiny, almost pudgy hand, soft and warm and trusting. We finished our drinks.

"Do you want another?" I asked her.

"Not really. After I go to the potty I want you to take me home." I helped her out of the booth. It wasn't easy for her to hold her feet, and she had had more to drink than I'd had. I watched her affectionately as she picked her way across the dimly lighted room. She was everything I ever wanted in a woman.

When she returned to the table I took the twenty she gave me and paid for the drinks. We walked to the mouth of the alley and I hailed a taxi. I gave my address to the driver and we settled back on the seat. I took Helen in my arms and kissed her.

"It makes me dizzy," she said. "Roll the windows down."

I had to laugh, but I rolled the windows down. The night air was cold and it was a long ride to my neighborhood. By the time we reached the roominghouse I knew she would be all right. I lit two cigarettes, passed one to Helen. She took one deep drag, tossed it out the window.

"I'm a little nervous, Harry."

"Why?"

"It's been a long time. Years, in fact."

"It doesn't change."

"Please don't say that! Be gentle with me, Harry."

"How could I be otherwise? You're just a little girl."

"I trust you, Harry."

The taxi pulled up in front of my roominghouse and we got out. We climbed the stairs quietly and walked down the long, dark hall to my room. There was only a single 40-watt bulb above the bathroom door to light the entire length of the hall. I unlocked my door and guided Helen inside. It took me a while to find the dangling string to the overhead light in the ceiling. Finding it at last, I flooded the room with light. I pulled the shade down and Helen looked the shabby room over with an amused smile.

"You're a good housekeeper," she said.

"Today anyway. I must have expected company," I said nervously.

Slowly, we started to undress. The more clothes we took off, the slower we got.

"Hadn't you better turn the light off?" Helen asked, timidly.

"No," I said firmly, "I don't want it that way."

We didn't hesitate any longer. Both of us undressed hurriedly. Helen crawled to the center of the bed, rolled over on her back and put her hands behind her head. She kept her eyes on the ceiling. Her breasts were small and the slenderness of her hips made her legs look longer than they were. Her skin was pale, almost like living mother-of-pearl, except for the flush that lay on her face like a delicately tinted rose. I stood in the center of the room and I could have watched her forever. I pulled the light cord and got into bed.

At first I just held her hot body against mine, she was trembling so hard. I covered her face with soft little kisses, her throat, her breasts. When my lips touched the tiny nipples of her breasts she sighed and relaxed somewhat. Her body still trembled, but it wasn't from fear. As soon as the nipples hardened I kissed her roughly on the mouth and she whimpered, dug her fingernails into my shoulders. She bit my lower lip with her sharp little teeth and I felt the blood spurt into my mouth.

"Now, Harry! Now!" she murmured softly.

It was even better than I'd thought it would be.

FOUR

Nude Model

WHEN I awoke the next morning Helen was curled up beside me. Her face was flushed with sleep and her nice hair curled all over her head. If it hadn't been for the single strand of pure silver hair she wouldn't have looked more than thirteen years old. I kissed her on the mouth and she opened her eyes. She sat up and stretched luxuriously, immediately awake, like a cat.

"I've never slept better in my entire life," she said.

"I'll fix some coffee. Then while you're in the bathroom, I'd better go down the hall and tell Mrs. McQuade you're here."

"Who is she?"

"The landlady. You'll meet her later on."

"Oh. What're you going to tell her?"

"I'll tell her we're married. We had a long, trial separation and now we've decided to try it again. It's a pretty thin story, but it'll hold."

"I feel married to you, Harry."

"For all practical purposes, we are married."

I got out of bed, crossed to the dresser, and tossed a clean, white shirt to Helen. She put it on and the shirt tail came to her knees. After she rolled up the sleeves she left the room. I put on my slacks and a T-shirt, fixed the coffee and lighted the gas burner under it, walked down the hall and knocked on Mrs. McQuade's door.

"Good morning, Mrs. McQuade," I said, when she opened the door.

"You're not going to clean your room again?" she asked with mock surprise in her voice.

"No." I laughed. "Two days in a row would be overdoing it. I just wanted to tell you my wife was back."

"I didn't even know you were married!" She raised her eyebrows.

"Oh, yes! I've been married a good many years. We were separated, but we've decided to try it again. I'll bring Helen down after a while. I want you to meet her."

"I'm very happy for you, Mr. Jordan."

"I think it'll work this time."

"Would you like a larger room?" she asked eagerly. "The front upstairs room is vacant, and if you want me to—"

"No, thanks," I said quickly, "we'll be all right where we are."

I knew Mrs. McQuade didn't believe me, but a woman running a roominghouse doesn't get surprised at anything.

She didn't mention it right then, but by the end of the week I could expect an increase in rent. That is the way those things go.

The coffee was ready and when Helen returned I finished my cup quickly and poured one for her.

"We've only got one cup," I said apologetically.

"We'll have to get another one."

After I shaved, and both of us were dressed, we finished the pot of coffee, taking turns with the cup. Helen borrowed my comb, painted her dark lipstick on with a tiny brush, and she was ready for the street.

"Don't you even use powder?" I asked her curiously.

"Uh uh. Just lipstick."

"We'd better go down and get your suitcase."

"I'm ready."

Mrs. McQuade and Miss Foxhall, a retired schoolteacher, were standing by the front door when we came down the hall. Mrs. McQuade had a broom in her hand, and Miss Foxhall held an armful of books; she was either going to or returning from the neighborhood branch public library. They both eyed Helen curiously, Mrs. McQuade with a smile, Miss Foxhall with hostility. I introduced Helen to the two older women. Mrs. McQuade wiped her hands on her apron and shook Helen's hand. Miss Foxhall snorted audibly, pushed roughly between us and hurried up the stairs without a word. I noticed that the top book in the stack she carried was *Ivanhoe*, by Sir Walter Scott.

"You're a very pretty girl, Mrs. Jordan," Mrs. McQuade said sincerely. All three of us pretended to ignore the rudeness of Miss Foxhall.

We walked down the block to Big Mike's, Helen holding my arm. The sun was shining and despite a slight persisting hangover I was a proud and happy man. Everyone who passed stared at Helen, and to know that she was mine made me straighten my back and hold my head erect. We entered Mike's and sat down at the bar. Big Mike joined us at once.

"You're on time today, Harry." He smiled.

"Mike, I want you to meet my wife. Helen Jordan, Big Mike."

"How do you do, Mrs. Jordan? This calls for one on the house. Now what'll it be?"

"Since it's on the house, Mike," Helen smiled, "I'll have a double bourbon and water."

"Double gin and tonic for me," I added.

Mike set up our drinks, drew a short beer for himself, and we raised our glasses in salute. He returned to his work table where he was slicing oranges, sticking toothpicks into cherries, and preparing generally for the noon-hour rush period. It was quite early to be drinking and Helen and I were the only people sitting at the bar. Rodney, the crippled newsboy, was eating breakfast in one of the booths along the wall. He waved to me with his fork and I winked at him.

After we finished our drinks we caught the cable car to the hotel on Powell Street and picked up Helen's suitcase. It only took a minute and we were able to catch the same car back, after it was ready to climb the hill again and turned on the Market Street turnaround. The round trip took more than an hour.

"I'm disgustingly sober," Helen said, as we stood on the curb, waiting for the light to change.

"What do you want to do? I'll give you two choices. We can drink in Big Mike's or we can get a bottle and go back to the room."

"Let's get a bottle, by all means."

At Mr. Watson's delicatessen I bought a fifth of gin, a fifth of whiskey and a cardboard carrier of six small bottles of soda. To nibble on, in case we happened to get hungry, I added a box of cheese crackers to the stack. We returned to our room and I removed my jacket and shirt. Helen took off her suit and hung it carefully in the closet. While I fixed the drinks Helen explored the room, digging into everything. She pulled out all of the dresser drawers, then examined the accumulation of junk above the sink. It was pleasant to watch her walking around the room in her slip. She discovered my box of oil paints on the shelf, brought it to the table and opened it.

"Do you paint, Harry?"

"At one time I did. That's the first time that box has been opened in three years." I handed her a drink. "There isn't any ice."

"All ice does is take up room. Why don't you paint any more?"

I looked into the opened paint box. The caps were tightly screwed on all of the tubes and most of the colors were there, all except yellow ochre and zinc white. I fingered the brushes, ran a finger over the edges of the bristles. They were in good shape, still usable, and there was a full package of charcoal sticks.

"I discovered I couldn't paint, that's why. It took me a long time to accept it, but after I found out I gave it up."

"Who told you you couldn't paint?"

"Did you ever do any painting?"

"Some. I graduated from Mills College, where they taught us something about everything. I even learned how to shoot a bow and arrow."

"I'll tell you how it is about painting, Helen, the way it was with me. It was a love affair. I used painting as a substitute for love. All painters do; it's their nature. When you're painting, the pain in your stomach drives you on to a climax of pure feeling, and if you're any good the feeling is transmitted to the canvas. In color, in form, in line and they blend together in a perfect design that delights your eye and makes your heart beat a little faster. That's what painting meant to me, and then it turned into an unsuccessful love affair, and we broke it off. I'm over it now, as much as I'll ever be, and certainly the world of art hasn't suffered."

"Who told you to give it up? Some critic?"

"Nobody had to tell me. I found it out for myself, the hard way. Before the war I went to the Art Institute in Chicago for two years, and after the war I took advantage of the GI Bill and studied another year in Los Angeles."

"Wouldn't anybody buy your work? Was that it?"

"No, that isn't it. I never could finish anything I started. I'd get an idea, block it out, start on it, and then when I'd get about halfway through I'd discover the idea was terrible. And I couldn't finish a picture when I knew it wasn't going to be any good. I taught for a while, but that wasn't any good either."

Helen wasn't looking at me. She had walked to the window and appeared to be studying the littered backyard next door with great interest. I knew exactly what she had on her mind. The Great American Tradition: *You can do anything you think you can do!* All Americans believe in it. What a joke that is! Can a jockey last ten rounds with Rocky Marciano? Can Marciano ride in the Kentucky Derby? Can a poet make his living by writing poetry? The entire premise was so false it was stupid to contemplate. Helen finished her drink, turned around, and set the empty glass on the table.

"Harry," she said seriously, "I want you to do something for me."

"I'll do anything for you."

"No, not just like that. I want you to hear what it is first."

"It sounds serious."

"It is. I want you to paint my portrait."

"I don't think I could do it." I shrugged, looked into my empty glass. "It's been more than three years since I tried to paint anything, and portraits are hard. To do a good one, anyway, and if I were to paint you, I'd want it to be perfect. It would have to be, and I'm not capable of it."

"I want you to paint it anyway."

"How about a sketch? If you want a picture of yourself, I can draw a charcoal likeness in five minutes."

"No. I want you to paint an honest-to-God oil painting of me."

"You really want me to; this isn't just a whim?"

"I really want you to." Her face was as deadly serious as her voice.

I thought it over and it made me feel a little sick to my stomach. The mere thought of painting again made me tremble. It was like asking a pilot to take an airplane up again after a bad crash; a crash that has left him horribly disfigured and frightened. Helen meant well. She wanted me to prove to myself that I was wrong . . . that I could do anything I really wanted to do. That is, as long as she was there to help me along by her inspiration and encouragement. More than anything else in the world, I wanted to please her.

"It takes time to paint a portrait," I said.

"We've got the time. We've got forever."

"Give me some money then."

"How much do you need?"

"I don't know. I'll need a canvas, an easel, linseed oil, turpentine, I don't know what all. I'll have to look around when I get to the art store."

"I'm going with you." She began to dress.

Once again, we made the long trip downtown by cable car. We went to an art store on Polk Street and I picked out a cheap metal easel, in addition to the regular supplies, and a large canvas, thirty by thirty-four inches. As long as I had decided to paint Helen's portrait, I was going to do it right. We left the store, both of us loaded down with bundles and I searched the streets for a taxi. Helen didn't want to return home immediately.

"You're doing something for me," she said, "and I want to do something for you. Before we go home I'm going to buy you a new pair of pants and a new sport coat."

"You can't do it, Helen," I protested. "We've spent too much already."

She had her way, but I didn't let her spend too much money on my new clothes. I insisted on buying a pair of gray corduroy trousers, and a dark blue corduroy jacket at the nearest Army and Navy surplus store. These were cheap clothes, but they satisfied Helen's desire to do something nice for me. I certainly needed them. Wearing my new clothes in the taxi, on the way home, and looking at all of the new art supplies piled on the floor, gave me a warm feeling inside and a pleasant tingling of anticipation.

The minute we entered our room I removed my new jacket and set up the easel. While I opened the paints and arranged the materials on a straight backed chair next to the easel, Helen fixed fresh drinks. She held up her glass and posed, a haughty expression on her face.

"Look, Harry. Woman of Distinction." We both laughed. "Do you want me to pose like this?"

The pose I wanted Helen to take wasn't difficult. The hard part was to paint her in the way I wanted to express my feelings for her. I wanted to capture the mother-of-pearl of her body, the secret of her smile, the strand of silver in her hair, the jet, arched brows, the tragedy in her brown, gold-flecked eyes. I wasn't capable of it; I knew that in advance. I placed two pillows on the floor, close to the bed, so she could lean back against the bed to support her back. The light from the window would fall across her body and create sharp and difficult shadows. The hard way, like always, I took the hard way.

"Take off your clothes, Helen, and sit down on the pillows."

After Helen had removed her clothes and settled herself comfortably I rearranged her arms, her right hand in her lap, her left arm stretched full length on the bed. Her legs were straight out, with the right ankle crossed over the other. The similarity between Helen and the woman in the *Olympia* almost took my breath away with the awesomeness of it.

"Is that comfortable?" I asked her.

"It feels all right. How long do you want me to stay like this?"

"Just remember it, that's all. When I tell you to pose, get into it, otherwise, sit any way you like. As I told you, this is going to take a long time. Drink your drink, talk, or smile that smile of yours. Okay?"

"I'm ready."

I started with the charcoal, blocking in Helen's figure. She was sitting too stiffly, eyes straight ahead, tense. To me, the drawing is everything and I wanted her to talk, to get animation in her face.

"Talk to me, Helen," I told her.

"Is it all right?"

"Sure. I want you to talk. Tell me about Mills College. What did you major in?"

"Geology."

"That's a strange subject for a woman to take. What made you major in geology?"

"I was romantic in those days, Harry. I liked rocks and I thought geology was fascinating, but secretly, I thought if I could learn geology I could get away from Mother. I used to dream about going to Tibet or South America with some archeological expedition. Mother was never in the dream, but she was with me all the way through college. I had a miserable college education. She came with me and we took an apartment together. While the other girls lived in sororities and had a good time I studied. She stood right over me, just like she did all the way through high school. My grades were fine, the highest in my class. Not that I was a brilliant student, but because I didn't do anything except study.

"In the summers we went back to San Sienna. One summer we went to Honolulu, and once to Mexico City so I could look at ruins. The trips weren't any fun, because Mother was along. No night life, no dates, no romance."

"It sounds terrible."

"It was, believe me." She lapsed into silence, brooding.

It was a pleasant day. Helen made a drink for herself once in awhile, but I didn't join her; I was much too busy. The outline shaped well and I was satisfied with the progress I had made. By the time the light failed Helen had finished the bottle of whiskey and was more than a little tight. We were both extremely tired from the unaccustomed activity. Helen would find that modeling was one of the toughest professions in the world before we were through.

We dressed and walked down the street to Big Mike's for dinner. I ordered steaks from Tommy the waiter, and while we waited we sat at the end of the bar and had a drink. There were three workmen in overalls occupying the booth opposite from where we were sitting and their table was completely covered with beer cans. They made a few choice nasty remarks about Helen and me, but I ignored them. Big Mike was a friend of mine and I didn't want to cause any trouble in his bar.

"Look at that," the man wearing white overalls said. "Ain't that the limit?" His voice was loud, coarse, and it carried the length of the barroom.

"By God," the man on the inside said, "I believe I've seen it *all* now!" He nodded his head solemnly. "Yes, sir, I've seen it *all!*" His voice had a forced quality of comic seriousness and his companions laughed.

Helen's face had changed from pale to chalky white. She quickly finished her drink, set the glass on the bar and took my arm. "Come on, Harry," she said anxiously, "let's go inside the dining room and find a table."

"All right." My voice sounded as though it belonged to someone else.

We climbed down from the stools and crossed to the dining room entrance. We paused in the doorway and I searched the room for a table. One of the men shouldered us apart and stared insolently at Helen.

"Why don't you try me for size, baby?"

His two friends were standing behind me and they snickered.

Without a word I viciously kicked the man in front of me in the crotch. The insolent smile left his face in a hurry. His puffy red face lost its color and he clutched his groin with both hands and sank to his knees. I kicked him in the mouth and blood bubbled out of his ripped cheek from the corner of his torn mouth all the way to his ear. I whirled around quickly, expecting an attack from the two men behind me, but Big Mike was holding both of them by the collar. There was a wide grin on his multi-scarred face.

"Go ahead, Harry," he said gruffly, "finish the job. These lice won't interfere."

The man was on his feet again; some of the color was back in his mutilated face. He snatched a bread knife from the waiter's work table and backed slowly across the room.

Many of the diners had left their tables and were crowded against the far wall near the kitchen. I advanced on the man cautiously, my arms widely spread. He lunged forward in a desperate attempt to disembowel me, bringing the knife up fast, aiming for my stomach. At the last moment I twisted sideways and brought my right fist up from below my knee. His jaw was wide open and my blow caught him flush below the chin. He fell forward on the floor, like a slugged ox.

My entire body was shaking with fear and excitement. I looked wildly around the room for Helen. She was standing, back to the wall, frozen with fear. She ran to my side, hugged me around the waist.

"Come on, Harry!" she said tearfully. "Let's get out of here!"

"Nothing doing," I said stubbornly. "We ordered steaks and we're going to eat them."

I guided Helen to an empty table against the wall. Big Mike had bounced the other two workmen out and now he was back in the dining-room. Two waiters, at his nod, dragged the unconscious man out of the room through the kitchen exit. Mike came over to our table.

"I saw the whole thing, Harry," Tommy said, "and if it goes to court or anything like that, I'll swear that he started the fight by pulling a knife on you!" He was so sincere I found it difficult to keep from laughing.

"Thanks, Tommy," I told him, "but I think that's the end of it."

I couldn't eat my steak and neither could Helen although both of us made a valiant try.

"The hell with it, Harry," Helen smiled. "Let's get a bottle and go home."

We left the grill, bought another fifth of whiskey at the delicatessen and returned to our room. My bottle of gin was scarcely tapped. I held it up to my lips, and drinking in short swallows, I drank until I almost passed out.

Helen had to undress me and put me to bed.

FIVE

Celebration

IF THERE was anything I didn't want to do the next morning, it was paint. My head was vibrating like a struck gong and my stomach was full of fluttering, little winged creatures. Every muscle of my body ached and all I wanted to do was stay in bed and quietly nurse my hangover.

Helen was one of those rare persons who seldom get a hangover. She felt fine. She showered, dressed, left the house and returned with a fifth of whiskey and a paper sack filled with cold bottles of beer.

"Drink this beer," she ordered, "and let's get started. You can't let a little thing like a fight and a hangover stop you." She handed me an opened bottle of beer. I sat up in bed, groaning, and let the icy beer flow down my throat. It tasted marvelous, tangy, refreshing, and I could feel its coldness all the way down. I drank some coffee, two more beers and started to work.

I had to draw slowly at first. There was still a slight tremor

in my fingers, caused partly by the hangover, but the unexpected fight the night before had a lot to do with it. I've never
been a fighter and when I thought about my vicious assault
on the man in Mike's, I could hardly believe it had happened.
Within a short time, Helen's beauty pushed the ugly memory
out of my head and I was more interested in the development
of her picture.

Painting or drawing from a nude model had never been an
exciting experience before, but Helen was something else . . .
I didn't have the feeling of detachment an artist is supposed
to have toward his model. I was definitely aware of Helen's
body as an instrument of love, and as my hangover gradually
disappeared I couldn't work any longer unless I did something
about it . . .

Helen talked about the dullness of San Sienna as I worked
and from time to time she would take a shot from the bottle
of whiskey resting on the floor, following it down with a sip
of water. As she began to feel the drinks her voice became
animated. And so did I. Unable to stand it any longer I tossed
my charcoal stick down, scooped Helen from the floor and
dropped her sideways on the bed. She laughed softly.

"It's about time," she said.

I dropped to my knees beside the bed, pressed my face into
her warm, soft belly and kissed her navel. She clutched my
hair with both hands and shoved my head down hard.

"Oh, yes, Harry! Make love to me! Make love to me . . ."

And I did. She didn't have to coax me.

It took all of the will power I could muster to work on the
picture again, but I managed, and surprisingly enough it was
much easier than it had been. With my body relaxed I could
now approach my work with the proper, necessary detachment an artist must have if he is to get anywhere. The drawing
was beginning to look very well, and by four in the afternoon,
when I couldn't stick it out any longer and quit for the day,
I was exhilarated by my efforts and Helen was pleasantly tight
from the whiskey.

After we were dressed I took a last look at the picture before
leaving for Mike's.

"This is my first portrait," I told Helen as I opened the
door for her. "And probably my last."

"I didn't know that, Harry," she said, somewhat surprised. "What kind of painting did you do? Landscapes?"

"No," I laughed. "Non-objective, or as you understand it, abstract."

"You mean these weird things with the lines going every which way, and the limp watches and stuff—"

"That's close enough." I couldn't explain what is impossible to explain. We went to Big Mike's, had dinner, and drank at the bar until closing time.

This was the pattern of our days for the next week and a half, except for one thing: I quit drinking. Not completely; I still drank beer, but I laid off whiskey and gin completely. I didn't need it any more. Painting and love were all I needed to make me happy. Helen continued to drink, and during the day, whether drunk or sober, if I told her to pose she assumed it without any trouble, and held it until I told her to relax.

For me, this was a fairly happy period. I hadn't realized how much I had missed painting. And with Helen for a model it was pure enjoyment. I seldom said anything. I was contented to merely paint and look at Helen. Often there were long silences between us when all we did was look at each other. These long periods usually ended up in bed without a word being spoken. It was as though our bodies had their own methods of communication. More relaxed, more sure of myself, I would take up my brush again and Helen would sit, very much at ease, on the two pillows beside the bed, and assume the pose I had given her. My Helen! *My Olympia!*

When I finished the drawing in charcoal I made a complete underpainting in tints and shades of burnt sienna, lightening the browns carefully with white and turpentine. The underpainting always makes me nervous. The all-important drawing which takes so many tedious hours is destroyed with the first stroke of the brush and replaced with shades of brown oil paint. The completed drawing, which is a picture worthy of framing by itself, is now a memory as the turpentine and oil soaks up the charcoal and replaces it with a tone in a different medium. But it is a base that will last through the years when the colors are applied over it. I had Helen look at the completed brown-tone painting.

"It looks wonderful, Harry! Is my figure that perfect?"

"It's the way it looks to me. Don't worry about your face. It's just drawn in a general way . . . the effects of the shadows."

"I'm not worried. It looks like me already."

"When I'm finished, it will be you," I said determinedly.

I started with the colors, boldly but slowly, in my old style. I didn't pay any attention to background, but concentrated on Helen's figure. At the time I felt that I shouldn't neglect the background, but no ideas came to me and I let it go. The painting was turning out far better than I had expected it to; it was good, very good. My confidence in my ability soared. I could paint, really paint. All I had to do was work at it, boldly but slowly.

Along with the ninth day, Helen, cramped by a long session, got up and walked around the room shaking her arms and kicking her legs. I lit two cigarettes and handed her one. She put an arm around my waist and studied the painting for several minutes.

"This is me, Harry, only it looks like me when I was a little girl."

"I'm not finished yet. I've been working on the hands. I figure a good two days to finish your face. If possible I want to paint your lips the same shade as your lipstick, but if I do I'm afraid it'll look out of place. It's a tricky business."

"What about the background?"

"I'm letting that go. It isn't important."

"But the picture won't be complete without a background."

"I'm not going to fill the empty places with that gray wallpaper and its weird pattern of pink flowers!"

"You don't have to. Can't you paint in an open sky, or the ocean and clouds behind me?"

"No. That would look lousy. Wrong light, anyway."

"You can't leave it blank!"

"I can until I get an idea. If I have to fill it with something I can paint it orange with black spots."

"You can't do that! That would ruin it!"

"Then let's not discuss it any more."

It made me a little sore. A man who's painting a picture doesn't want a layman's advice. At least I didn't. This was the best thing of its kind I had ever done and I was going to do it my way.

That night when we went down to Mike's for dinner I started to drink again. Both of us were well-loaded when we got home and for the first time we went to sleep without making love.

I slept until noon. Helen didn't wake me when she went to the delicatessen for beer and whiskey. The coffee was perking in the pot and the wonderful odor woke me. I drank two cups of it black and had one shot of whiskey followed by a beer chaser. I felt fine.

"Today and tomorrow and I'll be finished," I told Helen confidently.

"I'm sure tired of that pose."

"You don't have to hold it any longer, baby. All I have to finish is your face."

I had overestimated the time it would take me. By three-thirty there was nothing more to do. Anything else I did to the painting would be plain fiddling. Maybe I hadn't put in a proper background, but I had captured Helen and that was what I had set out to do. Enough of the bed and the two pillows were showing to lend form and solidity to the composition. The girl in the portrait was Helen, a much younger Helen, and if possible, a much prettier and delicate Helen, but it was Helen as she appeared to me. Despite my attempts to create the faint, tiny lines around her eyes and the streak of silver hair, it was the portrait of a young girl.

"It's beautiful," Helen said sincerely and self-consciously.

"It's the best I can do."

"How much could you sell this for, Harry?"

"I wouldn't sell it. It belongs to you."

"But what would it be worth to an art gallery?"

"It's hard to tell. Whatever you could get, I suppose. Twenty dollars, maybe."

"Surely, more than that!"

"It all depends upon how much somebody wants it. That's the way art works. The artist has his asking price, of course, and if a buyer wants the painting he pays the price. If they don't want it he couldn't give the picture away. My price for this picture is one hundred thousand dollars."

"I'd pay that much for it, Harry."

"And so would I." There was a drink apiece left in the bottle of whiskey. We divided it equally and toasted the portrait.

"If I never paint another," I bragged, "I've painted one picture."

"It doesn't really need a background, Harry," Helen said loyally, "it looks better the way it is."

"You're wrong, but the hell with it. Get dressed and we'll go out and celebrate."

"Let's stay in instead," Helen said quietly.

"Why? If you're tired of drinking at Big Mike's we can go some place else. We don't have to go there."

"No, that isn't it," she said hesitantly. "We're all out of money, Harry." The corners of her mouth turned down wryly. "I spent the last cent I had for that bottle."

"Okay. So we're out of money. You didn't expect two hundred dollars to last forever, did you? Our room rent's paid, anyway."

"Do you have any money, Harry?"

After searching through my wallet and my trousers I came up with two dollars and a half dollar in change. Not a large sum, but enough for a few drinks.

"This is enough for a couple at Mike's," I said, "or we can let the drinks go and I can look around for a job. It's up to you."

"I would like to have a drink . . . but while you're looking for work, and even after you find it, there'll still be several days before you get paid."

"We'll worry about that when we come to it. I've got fifteen dollars credit with Mike and it's all paid up. I paid him the other night when you cashed a traveler's check."

"We don't have a worry in the world then, do we?" Helen said brightly.

"Not one." I said it firmly, but with a confidence I didn't feel inside. I had a lot of things to worry about. The smile was back on Helen's lips. She gave me a quick, ardent kiss and dressed hurriedly, so fast I had to laugh.

When we got to Mike's we sat down in an empty booth and ordered hamburgers instead of our usual club steak. It was the only thing we had eaten all day, but it was still too much for me. After two bites I pushed my hamburger aside, left Helen in the booth, and signaled Mike to come down to the end of the bar.

"Mike," I said apprehensively, "I'm back on credit again."

"Okay." He nodded his massive head slowly. "I'm not surprised, though, the way you two been hitting it lately."

"I'm going to find a job tomorrow."

"You've always paid up, Harry. I'm not worried."

"Thanks, Mike." I turned to leave.

"Just a minute, Harry," he said seriously. "That guy you had a fight with the other night was in here earlier and I think he's looking for you. I ran him the hell out, but you'd better be on the lookout for him. His face looks pretty bad. There's about thirty stitches in his face and the way it's sewed up makes him look like he's smiling. Only he ain't smiling."

"I feel sorry for the guy, Mike. I don't know what got into me the other night."

"Well, I thought I'd better mention it."

"Thanks, Mike." I rejoined Helen in the booth. She had finished her sandwich and mine too.

"You didn't want it, did you?" she asked me.

I shook my head. We ordered whiskey with water chasers and stayed where we were, in the last booth against the wall, drinking until ten o'clock. I was in a mighty depressed mood and I unconsciously transmitted it to Helen. I should never have let her talk me into painting her portrait. I should never have tried any type of painting again. There was no use trying to kid myself that I could paint. Of course, the portrait was all right, but any artist with any academic background at all could have done as well. And my temerity in posing Helen as *Olympia* was the crowning height to my folly. Who in the hell did I think I was, anyway? What was I trying to prove? Liquor never helped me when I was in a depressed state of mind; it only made me feel worse. Helen broke the long, dead silence between us.

"This isn't much of a celebration, is it?"

"No. I guess not."

"Do you want to go home, Harry?"

"What do you want to do?"

"If I sit here much longer looking at you, I'll start crying."

"Let's go home, then."

I signed the tab that Tommy the waiter brought and we left. It was a dark, forbidding block to the roominghouse at night. Except for Big Mike's bar and grill on the corner, the light from Mr. Watson's delicatessen across the street was the only bright spot on the way home. We walked slowly, Helen holding onto my arm. Half-way up the street I stopped, fished two cigarettes out of my almost empty package and turned into the wind to light them. Helen accepted the lighted cigarette I handed her and inhaled deeply. We didn't know what to do with ourselves.

"What's ever to become of us, Harry?" Helen sighed.

"I don't know."

"Nothing seems to have much purpose, does it?"

"No, it doesn't."

A man I hadn't noticed in the darkness of the street, detached himself from the shadows of the Spotless Cleaner's storefront and walked toward us. His hat was pulled well down over his eyes and he was wearing a dark-brown topcoat. The faint light from the street lamp on the corner barely revealed a long red scar on his face and neat row of stitches. Like Mike had told me, the left corner of his mouth was pulled up unnaturally, and it made the man look like he was smiling.

With a quick movement he jerked a shiny, nickel-plated pistol out of his topcoat pocket and covered us with it. His hand was shaking violently and the muzzle of the pistol jerked up and down rapidly, as though it was keeping time to wild music.

"I've been waiting for you!" His voice was thick and muffled. His jaws were probably wired together and he was forced to talk through his teeth. I dropped my cigarette to the pavement and put my left arm protectingly around Helen's waist. She stared at the man with a dazed, fixed expression.

"I'm going to kill you," he said through his clenched teeth. "Both of you!"

"I don't blame you," I answered calmly. I felt no fear or anxiety at all, just a morbid feeling of detachment. Helen's body trembled beneath my arm, but it couldn't have been from fear, because the trembling stopped abruptly, and she took another deep drag on her cigarette.

"You may shoot me first, if you prefer," she said quietly.

"God damn the both of you!" the man said through his closed mouth. "Get down on your knees! Beg me! Beg for your lives!"

I shook my head. "No. We don't do that for anybody. Our lives aren't that important."

He stepped forward and jammed the muzzle into my stomach with a hard, vicious thrust.

"Pray, you son-of-a-bitch! Pray!"

I should have been frightened, but I wasn't. I knew that I should have been afraid and I even wondered why I wasn't.

"Go ahead," I told him. "Pull the trigger. I'm ready."

He hesitated and this hesitation, I believe, is what cost him his nerve. He backed slowly away from us, the pistol dancing in his hand, as though it had an independent movement of its own.

"You don't think I'll shoot you, do you?" It was the kind of a question for which there is no answer. We didn't reply.

"All right, bastard," he said softly, "start walking."

We started walking slowly up the sidewalk and he dodged to one side and fell in behind us. He jammed the pistol into the small of my back. I felt its pressure for ten or more steps and then it was withdrawn. Helen held my left arm with a tight grip, but neither one of us looked back as we marched up the hill. At any moment I expected a slug to tear through my body. We didn't look behind us until we reached the steps of the rooming house, and then I turned and looked over my shoulder while Helen kept her eyes straight to the front. There was no one in sight.

We entered the house, walked quietly down the dimly lighted hallway, and went into our room. I closed the door, turned on the light, and Helen sat down on the edge of the bed. Conscious of Helen's eyes on me, I walked across to the painting, and examined it for a long time.

"Did you feel sorry for him, Harry? I did."

"Yes, I did," I replied sincerely. "The poor bastard."

"I don't believe I'd have really cared if he'd killed us both . . ." Helen's voice was reflective, sombre.

"Cared?" I forced a tight smile. "It would have been a favor."

SIX

Suicide Pact

THERE was something bothering me when I got out of bed the next morning. I had a queasy, uneasy feeling in the pit of my stomach and it took me a few minutes to figure out what caused it. It was early in the morning, much too early to be getting out of bed. The sun was just coming up and the light filtering through the window was gray and cold. The sky was matted with low clouds, but an occasional bright spear broke through to stab at the messy backyards and the littered alley extending up the hill. I turned away from the window and the dismal view that looked worse by sunlight than it did by night.

I filled the coffee pot with water and put it on the burner. I took the coffee can down from the shelf above the sink and opened it. The coffee can was empty. I turned the fire out under the pot. No coffee this morning. I searched through my pockets before I put my trousers on and didn't find a dime. I didn't expect to, but I looked anyway. Not only had I spent the two and a half dollars in change, I had signed a chit besides for the drinks we had at Mike's. I opened Helen's purse and searched it thoroughly. There wasn't any money, but the purse contained a fresh, unopened package of cigarettes. After I finished dressing I sat in the straight chair by the window, smoking until Helen awoke.

Helen awoke after three cigarettes, sat up in bed and stretched her arms widely. She never yawned or appeared drowsy when she awoke in the mornings, but always appeared to be alert and fresh, as though she didn't need the sleep at all.

"Good morning, darling," she said. "How about lighting me one of those?"

I lit a fresh cigarette from the end of mine, put it between her lips, and sat down on the edge of the bed.

"No kiss?" she said petulantly, taking the cigarette out of her mouth. I kissed her and then returned to my chair by the window.

"We're out of coffee," I said glumly.

"That isn't such a great calamity, is it?"

"We're out of money too. Remember?"

"We've got credit, haven't we? Let's go down to Big Mike's for coffee. He might put a shot of bourbon in it if we ask him real nice."

"You really feel good, don't you?" I said bitterly.

Helen got out of bed and padded barefoot over to my chair. She put her arms around my neck, sat in my lap and kissed me on the neck.

"Look out," I said. "You'll burn me with your cigarette."

"No, I won't. And I don't feel a bit good. I feel rotten."

She bit me sharply on the ear, dropped her slip over her head and departed for the bathroom next door. I left my chair to examine my painting in the cold light of early morning. I twisted the easel around so the picture would face the window. A good amateur or Sunday painter would be proud of that portrait, I decided. Why wasn't I the one artist in a thousand who could earn his living by painting? Of course, I could always go back to teaching. Few men in the painting world knew as much as I did about color. The coarse thought of teaching made me shudder with revulsion. If you can't do it yourself you tell someone else how to do it. You stand behind them in the role of peer and mentor and watch them get better and better. You watch them overshadow you until you are nothing except a shadow within a shadow and then lost altogether in the unequal merger. Perhaps that was my main trouble? I could bring out talent where there wasn't any talent. Where there wasn't any ability I could bring out the semblance of ability. A fine quality for a man born to teach, but a heartbreaking quality for a man born to be an artist. No, I would never teach again. There were too many art students who thought they were artists who should have been mechanics. But a teacher was never allowed to be honest and tell them to quit. The art schools would have very few students if the teachers were allowed to be honest. But then, didn't the same thing hold true for all schools?

I threw myself across the bed and covered my ears with my hands. I didn't want to think about it any more. I didn't want to think about anything. Helen returned from the bathroom and curled up beside me on the bed.

"What's the matter, darling?" she asked solicitously. "Have you got a headache?"

"No. I was just thinking what a rotten, stinking world this is we live in. This isn't our kind of world, Helen. And we don't have the answer to it either. We aren't going to beat it by drinking and yet, the only way we can possibly face it is by drinking!"

"You're worried because we don't have any money, aren't you?"

"Not particularly."

"I could wire my mother for money if you want me to."

"Do you think she'd send it?"

"She'd probably bring it! She doesn't know where I am and I don't want her to know. But we're going to have to get money someplace."

"Why?"

"You need a cup of coffee and I need a drink. That's why."

"I don't give a damn about the coffee. Why do you have to have a drink? You don't really need it."

"Sure I do. I'm an alcoholic. Alcoholics drink."

"Suppose you were dead? You'd never need another drink. You wouldn't need anything. Everything would be blah. It doesn't make you happy to drink, and when I drink it only makes me unhappier than I am already. All it does in the long run is bring us oblivion."

"I need you when I come out of that oblivion, Harry." Her voice was solemn and barely under control.

"I need you too, Helen." This was as true a statement as I had ever made. Without Helen I was worse than nothing, a dark, faceless shadow, alone in the darkness. I had to take her with me.

"I haven't thought about suicide in a long time, Helen," I said. "Not once since we've been together. I used to think about it all of the time, but I never had the nerve. Together, maybe we could do it. I know I couldn't do it alone."

"I used to think about suicide too." Helen accepted my mood and took it for her own. "Down in San Sienna. It was such a tight, hateful little town. My bedroom overlooked the ocean, and I'd sit there all day, with the door locked, curled up on the window-seat, hiding my empty bottles in my dirty clothes hamper. Sitting there like that, looking at the golden sunshine glistening on the water, watching the breakers as they crashed on the beach . . . It made me depressed as hell. It was all so purposeless!"

"Did you ever attempt it?"

"Suicide?"

"That's what we're considering. Suicide."

"Yes, I tried it once." She smiled wryly. "On my wedding night, Harry. I was still a virgin, believe it or not. Oh, I wasn't ignorant; I knew what was expected of me and I thought I was ready for it. But I wasn't. Not for what happened, anyway. It was a virtual onslaught! My husband was a real estate man, and I'd never seen him in anything except a suit—all dressed up you know, with a clean, respectable look.

"But all of a sudden—I was in bed first, wearing my new nightgown, and shivering with apprehension—he flew out of the bathroom without a stitch on and rushed across the room. He was actually gibbering and drooling at the mouth. He tore the covers off me. He ripped my new, nice nightgown to shreds . . ." Helen's voice broke as she relived this experience and she talked with difficulty. "I fought him. I tore at his face with my nails; I bit him, hit at him, but it didn't make any difference. I'm positive now, that that's what he wanted me to do, you see. He overpowered me easily and completely. Then, in a second, it was all over. I was raped. He walked casually into the bathroom, doctored his scratches with iodine, put his pajamas on and climbed into bed as though nothing had happened."

Helen smiled grimly, crushed her cigarette in the ashtray.

"It was his first and last chance at me," she continued. "I never gave him another. Lying there beside him in the darkness I vowed that he'd never touch me again. After he was asleep I got out of bed and took the bottle of aspirins out of my overnight bag and went into the bathroom. There were twenty-six tablets. I counted them, because I didn't know for sure whether that was enough or not. But I decided it was and I took them three at a time until they were gone, washing each bunch down with a glass of water. Then I climbed back into bed—"

"That wasn't nearly enough," I said, interested in her story.

"No, it wasn't. But I fell asleep though, and I probably wouldn't have otherwise. They must have had some kind of psychological effect. But I awoke the next morning the same as ever, except for a loud ringing in my ears. The ringing lasted all day."

"What about your husband? Did he know you attempted suicide?"

"I didn't give him that satisfaction. We were staying at a beach motel in Santa Barbara, and after breakfast he went out to the country club to play golf. I begged off—told him I wanted to do some shopping—and as soon as he drove away I packed my bag and caught a bus for San Sienna and Mother. Mother was glad to have me back."

"And you never went back to him?"

"Never. I told Mother what happened. It was foolish of me, maybe, but she was determined to find out so I told her about it. Later on, when he begged me to come back to him, I was going to, but she wouldn't let me. He didn't know any better, the poor guy, and he told me so, after he found out the reason I left him. But it was too late then. I was safe in Mother's arms."

She finished her story bitterly, and her features assumed the tragic look I knew so well, the look that entered her face whenever she mentioned her mother. I kissed her tenderly on the mouth, got out of bed, and paced the floor restlessly.

"I'm glad you told me about this, Helen. That's when you started to drink, isn't it?"

"Yes, that's when I started to drink. It was as good an excuse as any other."

We were silent then, deep in our own thoughts. Helen lay on her back with her eyes closed while I paced the floor. I understood Helen a little better now. Thanks to me, and I don't know how many others, she didn't feel the same way about sex now, but she was so fixed in her drinking habits she could never change them. Not without some fierce drive from within, and she wasn't made that way. Before she could ever stop drinking she would have to have some purpose to her life, and I couldn't furnish it. Not when I didn't even have a purpose for my own life. If we continued on, in the direction we were traveling, the only thing that could possibly happen would be a gradual lowering of standards, and they were low enough already. If something happened to me, she would end up on the streets of San Francisco. The very thought of this sent a cold chill down my back. And I couldn't take care of her properly. It was too much of an effort to take care of myself . . .

"It takes a lot of nerve to commit suicide, Harry," Helen said suddenly, sitting up in bed, and swinging her feet to the floor.

"If we did it together I think we could do it," I said confidently. "Right now, we're on the bottom rung of the ladder. We're dead broke. I haven't got a job, and there's no one we can turn to for help. No whiskey, no religion, nothing."

"Do you think we'd be together afterwards?"

"Are you talking about the hereafter?"

"That's what I mean. I wouldn't care whether I went to Heaven or Hell as long as I was with you."

"I don't know anything about those things, Helen. But here's the way I look at it. If we went together, we'd be together. I'm positive of that."

The thought of death was very attractive to me. I could tell by the fixed expression in Helen's eyes that she was in the same mood I was in. She got the cigarettes from the table and sat down again on the edge of the bed. After she lit the cigarettes, I took mine and sat down beside her.

"How would we go about it, Harry?" Helen was in earnest, but her voice quavered at her voiced thought.

"There are lots of ways."

"But how, though? I can't stand being hurt. If it was all over with like that—" she snapped her fingers— "and I didn't feel anything, I think I could do it."

"We could cut our wrists with a razor blade."

"Oh, no!" She shuddered. "That would hurt terribly!"

"No it wouldn't," I assured her. "Just for one second, maybe, and then it would all be over."

"I couldn't do it, Harry!" She shook her head emphatically. "If you did it for me I could shut my eyes and—"

"No!" I said sharply. "You'll have to do it yourself. If I cut your wrists, well, then it would be murder. That's what it would be."

"Not if I asked you to."

"No. We'll have to do it together."

When we finished our cigarettes I put the ashtray back on the table. I was serious about committing suicide and determined to go through with it. There wasn't any fight left in me. As far as I was concerned the world we existed on was an overly-large, stinking cinder, a spinning, useless clinker. I didn't want any part of it. My life meant nothing to me and I wanted to go to sleep forever and forget about it. I got my shaving kit down from the shelf above the sink and took the package of razor blades out of it. I unwrapped the waxed paper from two shiny single-edged blades and laid them on the table. Helen joined me at the table and held out her left arm dramatically.

"Go ahead," she said tearfully. "Cut it!"

Her eyes were tightly squeezed shut and she was breathing rapidly. I took her hand in mine and looked at her thin little wrist. I almost broke down and it was an effort to fight back the tears.

"No, sweetheart," I said to her gently, "you'll have to do it yourself. I can't do it for you."

"Which one is mine?" she asked nervously.

"Either one. It doesn't make any difference."

"Are you going to give a signal?" She picked up a blade awkwardly.

"I'll count to three." I picked up the remaining blade.

"I'm ready!" she said bravely, raising her chin.

"One. Two. Three!"

We didn't do anything. We just stood there, looking at each other.

"It's no use, Harry. I can't do it to myself." She threw the blade down angrily on the table and turned away. She covered her face with her hands and sobbed. Her back shook convulsively.

"Do you want me to do it?" I asked her.

She nodded her head almost imperceptibly, but she didn't say anything. I jerked her left hand away from her face and with one quick decisive motion I cut blindly into her wrist. She screamed sharply, then compressed her lips, and held out her other arm. I cut it quickly, close to the heel of her hand, picked her up and carried her to the bed. I arranged a pillow under her head.

"Do they hurt much?"

She shook her head. "They burn a little bit. That's all." Her eyes were closed, but she was still crying noiselessly. The bright blood gushed from her wrists, making crimson pools on the white sheets. I retrieved the bloody blade from the table where I'd dropped it, returned to the bed and sat down. It was much more difficult to cut my own wrists. The skin was tougher, somehow, and I had to saw with the blade to cut through. My heart was beating so loud I could feel it throb through my body. I was afraid to go through with it and afraid not to go through with it. The blood frothed, finally, out of my left wrist and I transferred the blade to my other hand. It was easier to cut my right wrist, even though I was right-handed. It didn't hurt nearly as much as I had expected it to, but there was a searing, burning sensation, as though I had inadvertently touched my wrists to a hot poker. I threw the blade to the floor and got into bed beside Helen. She kissed me passionately. I could feel the life running out of my wrists and it made me happy and excited.

"Harry?"

"Yes?"

"As a woman, I'd like to have the last word. Is it all right?"

"Sure it's all right."

"I. Love. You."

It was the first time she had said the word since we had been living together. I kissed each of her closed eyes tenderly, then buried my face in her neck. I was overwhelmed with emotion and exhaustion.

SEVEN

Return to Life

MY HEAD was like a huge bubble perched on top of my shoulders, and ready for instant flight. I was afraid to move my head or open my eyes for fear it would float away into nothingness. Gradually, as I lay there fearfully, a feeling of solidity returned to my head and I opened my eyes. My arms were entwined around Helen, and she was lying on her side, facing me, her breathing soft and regular, in deep, restful sleep—but she was breathing! We were still alive, very much so! I disentangled my arms and raised my wrists so that I could see them. The blood was coagulated into little black ridges along the lengths of the shallow cuts. The bleeding had completely stopped. Oddly enough, I felt highly exhilarated and happy to be alive. It was as though I was experiencing a "cheap" drunk; I felt the way I had when I had taken a lower lip full of snuff many years before. My head was light and I was a trifle dizzy even though I was still in bed. I awakened Helen by kissing her partly open mouth. For a moment her eyes were startled and then they brightened into alertness the way they always did when she first awakened. She smiled shyly.

"I guess I didn't cut deep enough," I said ruefully. "I must have missed the arteries altogether."

"How do you feel, Harry?" Helen asked me. "I feel kind of wonderful, sort of giddy."

"I feel a little foolish. And at the same time I feel better than I have in months. I'm light-headed as hell and I feel drunk. Not gin-drunk, but drunk with life."

"I feel the same way. I've never been as drunk as I am now and I haven't had a drink. I never expected to wake up at all—not here, anyway."

"Neither did I," I said quietly.

"Are you sorry, Harry?"

"No. I'm not exactly sorry. It's too easy to quit and yet it took me a long time to reach the point when I was ready. But now that I've tried it once I guess I can face things again. It's still a lousy world, but maybe we owe it something."

"Light us a cigarette, Harry."

I got out of bed carefully and staggered dizzily to the table. I picked up the package of cigarettes and a folder of book matches and then noticed the bloody razor blade on the floor. It was unreal and cruel-looking and somehow offended me. I scooped it off the floor with the edge of the cardboard match folder and dropped it into the paper sack where we kept our trash and garbage. I couldn't bear to touch it with my hands. I was so giddy by this time it was difficult to keep my feet. Tumbling back onto the bed I lit Helen's cigarette, then mine.

"You've got a surprise coming when you try to walk," I said.

"You were actually staggering," Helen said, dragging the smoke deeply into her lungs.

"This bed is certainly a mess. Take a look at it."

"We'd better burn these sheets. I don't think the laundry would take them like this." Helen giggled.

"That is, if we could afford to take them to the laundry."

Both of us were in a strange mood, caused mostly by the blood we had lost. It wasn't a gay mood, not exactly, but it wasn't depressed either. All of our problems were still with us, but for a brief moment, out of mind. There was still no money, no job, no liquor and no prospects. I was still a bit light-headed and it was hard for me to think about our many problems. I wished, vaguely, that I had a religion or a God of some sort. It would have been so wonderful and easy to have gone to a priest or a minister and let him solve our problems for us. We could have gone anyway, religious or not, but without faith, any advice we listened to would have been worthless. The pat, standard homilies dished out by the boys in black were easy to predict.

Accept Jesus Christ as your personal Lord and Saviour and you are saved!

Any premise which bases its salvation on blind belief alone is bound to be wrong, I felt. It isn't fair to those who find it impossible to believe, those who have to be convinced, shown, who believe in nothing but the truth. But, all the same, suppose we did go to a church somewhere? What could we lose?

I rejected that false line of reasoning in a hurry.

"Let's bandage each other's wrists," I said quickly to Helen. It would at least be something to do. I left the bed and sat down for a moment in the straight chair by the easel.

"I suppose we'd better," Helen agreed, "before they get infected. If we're going to burn these sheets anyway, why don't you tear a few strips from the edge? They'll make fine bandages." Helen got out of bed wearily, and walked in tight circles, trying her legs. "Boy, am I dizzy!" she exclaimed, sat down on the foot of the bed.

I tore several strips of sheeting from the top sheet. Helen did some more circles and then sat down in a chair and fanned herself with her hands. I patted her bare shoulder reassuringly on my way to the dresser. My giddiness had all but disappeared, but my feeling of exhilaration remained. I had to dig through every drawer in the dresser before I could find the package of band-aids.

"Hold out your arms," I told Helen. The gashes in her wrists hurt me to look at them. They were much deeper than my own and the tiny blue veins in her thin wrists were closer to the surface than they had been before. I was deeply ashamed, and bound her wrists rapidly with the sheeting. I used the band-aids to hold the improvised bandages in place and then we changed places. She bandaged my wrists while I sat in the chair, but did a much neater job of it.

Without warning Helen rushed into my arms and began to sob uncontrollably. Her slender back was racked with violent, shuddering sobs and her hot flush of tears burned on my bare chest. I tried my best to comfort her.

"There, there, old girl," I said crooningly, "this won't do at all. Don't cry, baby, everything's going to be all right. There, there . . ."

She continued to sob piteously for a long time and all I could do was hold her. I was helpless, confused. It wasn't like Helen to cry about anything. At last she calmed down, smiled weakly, and wiped her streaming eyes with her fingers, like a little girl.

"I know it's childish of me, Harry, to cry like that, but I couldn't help it. The thought exploded inside my head and caught me when I wasn't expecting it."

"What did, honey?"

"Well, suppose you had died and I hadn't? And I woke up, and there you were—dead, and there I'd be, alone, still alive, without you, without anything . . ." Her tears started to flow again, but with better restraint. I held her on my lap like a frightened child; her face against my shoulder. I made no attempts to prevent her silent crying. I just patted her gently on her bare back, letting her cry it out. I knew precisely how she felt, because my feelings were exactly the same. Within a few minutes she was calm again and smiling her secret, tragic smile.

"If you'd kept up much longer, I'd have joined you," I said, attempting a smile.

"Do you know what's the matter with us, Harry?"

"Everything. Just name it."

"No." She shook her head. "We've lost our perspective. What we need is help, psychiatric help."

"At fifty bucks an hour, we can't afford one second of help."

"We can go to a hospital."

"That costs even more."

"Not a public hospital."

"Well, there's Saint Paul's, but I'm leery of it."

"Why? Is it free?" she asked eagerly.

"Sure, it's free all right, but what if they decide we're nuts and lock us up in a state institution for a few years? You in a woman's ward, me in a men's ward?"

"Oh, they wouldn't do that, Harry. We aren't crazy. This wholesale depression we're experiencing is caused strictly by alcohol. If we can get a few drugs and a little conversation from a psychiatrist, we'll be just fine again. I'll bet they wouldn't keep us more than a week at the longest."

"That isn't the way it works, baby," I told her. "A psychiatrist isn't a witch doctor with a speedy cure for driving out the devils. It's a long process, as I understand it, and the patient really cures himself. All the psychiatrist can do is help him along by guiding the thinking a little bit. He listens and says nothing. He doesn't even give the patient any sympathy. All he does is listen."

"That doesn't make any sense to me."

"But that's the way it works."

"Well . . ." She thought for a few moments. "They could get us off the liquor couldn't they?"

"If we didn't have any, and couldn't get any, yes. But even there, you have to have a genuine desire to quit drinking."

"I don't want to drink anymore, Harry. Let's take a chance on it, to see what happens. We can't lose anything, and I know they aren't going to lock us up anywhere, because it costs the state too much money for that. Both of us need some kind of help right now, and you know it!"

I caught some of Helen's enthusiasm, but for a different reason. The prospect of a good rest, a chance to sleep at night, some proper food in my stomach appealed to me. It was a place to start from . . .

"A week wouldn't be so bad at that," I said. "I could get straightened around some, maybe do a little thinking. I might come up with an idea."

"I could too, Harry. There are lots of things we could do together! You know all about art. Why, I'll bet we could start an art gallery and make a fortune right here in San Francisco! Did you ever get your G.I. loan?"

"No."

"A veteran can borrow all kinds of money! I think they loan as high as four thousand dollars."

"Maybe so, but an art gallery isn't any good. The dealers are all starving to death, even the well-established ones. People don't buy decent pictures for their homes any more. They buy pictures in the same place they get their new furniture. If the frame matches the davenport, they buy the picture, no matter what it is. No art gallery for me."

"They give business loans too."

"They may not take us in at the hospital." I brought the subject back to the business at hand.

"If we show them our wrists, I'll bet they'll take us in!"

I knew that Helen was right and yet I was afraid to turn in to Saint Paul's Hospital. But I could think of nothing better to do. Maybe a few days of peace and quiet were all we needed. I could use a new outlook on life. It was the smart thing to do, and for once in my life, why couldn't I do the smart thing?

"All right, Helen. Get dressed. We'll try it. If they take us in, fine! If they don't, they can go to hell."

After we were dressed, Helen began to roll up the bloody sheets to take them out to the incinerator. "Just a second," I said, and I tossed my box of oil paints and the rest of my painting equipment into the middle of the pile of sheets. "Burn that junk, too," I told her.

"You don't want to burn your paints!"

"Just do what I tell you. I know what I'm doing."

While Helen took the bundle out to the backyard to burn it in the incinerator, I walked down the hall to Mrs. McQuade's room and knocked on her door.

"Mrs. McQuade," I said, when she answered my insistent rapping. "My wife and I are going out of town for a few days. We're going to visit her mother down in San Sienna."

"How many days will you be gone, Mr. Jordan?" she asked suspiciously.

"I'm not sure yet. About a week, maybe not that long."

"I can't give you any refund, Mr. Jordan. You didn't give me any advance notice."

"I didn't ask for a refund, Mrs. McQuade."

"I know you didn't, but I thought it best to mention it." She fluttered her apron and smiled pleasantly. "Now you go ahead and have a nice time. Your room'll still be here when you get back."

"We will," I said grimly. "We expect to have a grand old time."

I returned to the room. Helen was packing her suitcase with her night things, cold cream, and toothbrush. All I took was my shaving kit. As we left the room she handed me the suitcase and locked the door with her key. At the bottom of the steps, outside in the street, I gave her my leather shaving kit to carry so I could have one hand free.

"How do you feel, baby?" I asked Helen as we paused in front of the house.

"A wee bit dizzy still, but otherwise I'm all right. Why?"

"We've got a long walk ahead of us, that's why." I grinned. "We don't have enough change for carfare."

"Oh!" She lifted her chin bravely. "Then let's get started," she said resolutely, looking into my eyes.

I shrugged my shoulders, Helen took my arm, and we started walking up the hill.

EIGHT

Hospital Case

SAN FRANCISCO is an old city with old buildings, and it is built on seven ancient hills. And long before Helen and I reached the grounds of Saint Paul's Hospital it seemed as though we had climbed every one of them. The narrow, twisted streets, the weathered, brown and crumbling façades of the rotted, huddled buildings frowning upon us as we labored up and down the hills, gave me poignant, bitter memories of my neighborhood in early childhood days: Chicago's sprawling South Side. There was no particular resemblance between the two cities I could put my finger on, but the feeling of similarity persisted. Pausing at the crest of a long, steep hill for rest and breath, I saw the magnificent panorama of the great harbor spreading below us. Angel Island, Alcatraz, several rusty, vagrant ships, a portion of the Golden Gate, and the land mass of Marin County, San Francisco's bedroom, were all within my vision at one time. The water of the bay, a dark and Prussian blue, was the only link with Chicago and my past.

The long walk was good for me. I saw a great many things I had been merely looking at for a long time. It was as though I was seeing the city through new eyes, for the first time.

The late, slanting, afternoon sun made long, fuzzy shadows; dark, colored shadows that dragged from the tops of the buildings like old-fashioned cloaks.

Noisy children were playing in the streets, shouting, screaming, laughing; all of them unaware of money and security and death.

Bright, shiny, new automobiles, chromium-trimmed, two-toned and silent, crept bug-like up and down the steep street.

How long had it been since I had owned an automobile? I couldn't remember.

House-wives in house-dresses, their arms loaded with groceries in brown-paper sacks, on their way home to prepare dinner for their working husbands. How long had it been since I had had a home? I had never had a home.

I saw non-objective designs created with charm and simplicity on every wall, every fence, every puddle of water we passed; the designs of unconscious forms and colors, patterns waiting to be untrapped by an artist's hand. The many-hued spot of oil and water surrounded by blue-black macadam. The tattered, blistered, peeling ochre paint, stripping limply from a redwood wall of an untenanted house. The clean, black spikes of ornamental iron-work fronting a narrow stucco beauty-shop. Arranged for composition and drawn in soft pastels, what delicate pictures these would be for a young girl's bedroom. For Helen's bedroom. For our bedroom. If we had a house and a bedroom and a kitchen and a living-room and a dining-room and maybe another bedroom and I had a job and I was among the living once again and I was painting again and neither one of us was drinking . . .

> *In a dim corner of my room for longer than my*
> *fancy thinks*
> *A beautiful and silent Sphinx has watched me*
> *through the shifting gloom.*

"Let's sit down for a while, Harry," Helen said wearily. There was a bus passenger's waiting bench nearby, and we both sat down. I took the shaving kit out of Helen's lap and put it inside the suitcase. No reason for her to carry it when there was room inside the suitcase. She was more tired than I was. She smiled wanly and patted my hand.

"Do you know what I've been thinking about, Harry?"

"No, but I've been thinking all kinds of things."

"It may be too early to make plans, Harry, but after we get out of the hospital and get some money again I'm going to get a divorce. It didn't make any difference before and it still doesn't—not the way I feel about you, I mean—but I'd like to be married to you. Legally, I mean."

"Why legally?"

"There isn't any real reason. I feel that I'd like it better and so would you."

"I like things better the way they are," I said, trying to discourage her. "Marriage wouldn't make me feel any different. But if it would make you any happier, that's what we'll do. But now is no time to talk about it."

"I know. First off, I'll have to get a divorce."

"That isn't hard. Where's your husband now?"

"Somewhere in San Diego, I think. I could find him. His parents are still living in San Sienna."

"Well, let's not talk about it now, baby. We've got plenty of time. Right now I'm concerned with getting hospital treatment for whatever's the matter with me, if there is such a thing, and there's anything the matter with me. What do you say?"

"I'm rested." Helen got to her feet. "Want me to carry the suitcase a while?"

"Of course not."

Saint Paul's Hospital is a six-story building set well back from the street and surrounded by an eight-foot cyclone wire fence. In front of the hospital a small park of unkempt grass, several rows of geraniums, and a few antlered, unpruned elms are the only greenery to be seen for several blocks. The hospital stands like a red, sore finger in the center of a residential district; a section devoted to four-unit duplexes and a fringe of new ranch-style apartment hotels. Across the street from the entrance-way a new shopping-center and parking lot stretches half-way down the block. As we entered the unraked gravel path leading across the park to the receiving entrance, Helen's tired feet lagged. When we reached the thick, glass double-doors leading into the lobby, she stopped and squeezed my hand.

"Are you sure you want to go through with this, Harry?" she asked me anxiously. "We didn't really have a chance to talk it over much. It was a kind of a spur-of-the-moment decision and we don't have to go through with it. Not if you don't want to," she finished lamely.

"I'm not going to walk the three miles back to the roominghouse," I said. I could see the tiny cylinders clicking inside her head. "You're scared, aren't you?"

"A little bit," she admitted. Her voice was husky. "Sure I am."

"They won't hurt us. It'll be a nice week's vacation," I assured her.

"Well . . . we've come this far . . ."

I pushed open the door and we timidly entered. The lobby was large and deep and the air was filled with a sharp, antiseptic odor that made my nose burn. There were many well-worn leather chairs scattered over the brown linoleum floor, most of them occupied with in-coming and out-going patients, with their poverty showing in their faces and eyes. In the left corner of the room there was a waist-high circular counter encircling two green, steel desks. Standing behind the desk, instead of the usual bald hotel clerk, was a gray-faced nurse in a white uniform so stiff with starch she couldn't have bent down to tie her shoe-laces. The austere expression on her face was so stern, a man with a broken leg would have denied having it; he would have been afraid she might want to minister to it. We crossed the room to the counter.

"Hello," I said tentatively to her unsmiling face, as I set the suitcase on the floor. "We'd like to see a doctor about admittance to the hospital . . . a psychiatrist, if possible."

"Been here before?"

"No, ma'am."

"Which one of you is entering the hospital?"

"Both of us." I took another look at her gray face. "Maybe we are, I mean. We don't have a dime."

"The money isn't the important thing. If you can pay, we charge, naturally, but if you can't, that's something else again. What seems to be the trouble?"

I looked at Helen, but she looked away, examined the yellowing leaves of a sickly potted plant with great interest. I was embarrassed. It was such a silly thing we had done I hated to blurt it out to the nurse, especially such a practical-minded nurse. I was afraid to tell her for fear she would deliver a lecture of some sort. I forced myself to say it.

"We attempted suicide. We cut our wrists." I stretched my arms over the counter so she could see my bandaged wrists.

"And now you want to see a psychiatrist? Is that right?"

"Yes, ma'am. We thought we would. We need help."

"Come here, dear," the nurse said to Helen, with a sudden change in manner. "Let me see your wrists."

Helen, blushing furiously, pulled the sleeves of her jacket back and held out her wrists to the nurse. At that moment I didn't like myself very well. It was my fault Helen was going through this degrading experience. I had practically forced her into the stupid suicide pact. The nurse deftly unwrapped the clumsy bandages I had affixed to Helen's wrists. She gave me an amused, professional smile.

"Did you fix these?"

"Yes, ma'am. You see, we were in a hurry to get here and I wrapped them rather hastily," I explained.

The nurse puckered her lips and examined the raw wounds on Helen's slender wrists. She clucked sympathetically and handed each of us a three-by-five card and pencils. "Suppose you two sit over there and fill in these cards," she waved us to a decrepit lounge, "and we'll see what we shall see."

We sat down with the cards and Helen asked me in a whisper whether we should use our right names or not. I nodded and we filled in the cards with our names, addresses, etc. The nurse talked on her telephone, so quietly we couldn't hear the conversation from where we were sitting. In a few minutes a young, earnest-faced man, wearing white trousers and a short-sleeved white jacket, got out of the elevator and walked directly to the desk. His feet, much too large for his short, squat body, looked larger than they were in heavy white shoes. He held a whispered conversation with the nurse, nodding his head gravely up and down in agreement. He crossed to our lounge and pulled a straight chair around so it faced us. He sat down on the edge of the chair.

"I am Doctor Davidson," he said briskly, unsmilingly. "We're going to admit you both to the hospital. But first of all you will have to sign some papers. The nurse tells me you have no money. Is that correct?"

"Yes, that is correct," I said. Helen said nothing. She kept her eyes averted from the doctor's face.

"The papers will be a mere formality, then." His face was quite expressionless. I had a hunch that he practiced his blank expression in the mirror whenever he had the chance. He held out his hand for our filled-in cards. "Come with me, please," he ordered. He arose from his chair, dropped the cards on the counter, and marched quickly to the elevator without looking back. We trailed in his wake. At the sixth floor we got out of the elevator, walked to the end of the corridor, and he told us to sit down in two metal folding chairs against the wall. We sat for a solid hour, not talking, and afraid to smoke because there weren't any ashtrays. A young, dark-haired nurse came to Helen, crooked her finger.

"I want you to come with me, dear," she said to Helen.

"Where am I going?" Helen asked nervously.

"To the women's ward." The nurse smiled pleasantly.

"I thought we were going to be together—" Helen tried to protest.

"I'm sorry, dear, but that's impossible."

"What'll I do, Harry?" Helen turned to me helplessly.

"You'd better go with her, I guess. Let me get my shaving kit out of the bag." I opened the suitcase, retrieved my shaving kit, snapped the bag shut. "Go on with her, sweetheart, we've come this far, we might as well go through with it."

The nurse picked up the light over-nighter and Helen followed reluctantly, looking back at me all the way down the corridor. They turned a corner, disappeared from view, and I was alone on my metal folding chair.

In a few minutes Dr. Davidson returned for me and we went down the hall in the opposite direction. We entered his office and he handed me a printed form and told me to sign it. I glanced through the fine print perfunctorily, without reading it in detail. It was a form declaring that I was a pauper. There was no denying that. I signed the paper and shoved it across the desk.

"You're entering the hospital voluntarily, aren't you?" he asked.

"That's about it."

"Fill out these forms then." He handed me three different forms in three different colors. "You can use my office to fill them out." He left the office and I looked at the printed forms. There were questions about everything; my life's history, my health, my relative's health, my schooling, and anything else the hospital would never need to know. For a moment I considered filling them in, but not seriously. I took the desk pen and made a check mark beside each of the numbered questions on all of the forms. That would show that I had read the questions, and if they didn't like it the hell with them. I didn't want to enter the hospital anyway. The doctor returned in about a half an hour and I signed the forms in his presence. Without looking at them he shoved them into a brown manila folder.

"I'm going to be your doctor while you're here," he told me in his well-rehearsed impersonal manner, "but it'll be a couple of days before I can get to you. Let me see your wrists."

I extended my arms and he snipped the bandages loose with a pair of scissors, dropped the soiled sheeting into the waste-basket by his desk.

"What exactly brought this on, Jordan, or do you know?"

"We've been drinking for quite a while and we ran out of money. I suppose that's the main reason. Not that I'm an alcoholic or anything like that, but I'm out of work at present and I got depressed. Helen, more or less—"

"You mean, Mrs. Jordan?"

"No. Mrs. Meredith. Helen Meredith. We don't happen to be married, we're just living together, but we're going to be married later on. As I was saying, Helen takes my moods as hard as I do. If it hadn't been for me—well, this is all strictly my fault."

"We aren't concerned with whose fault it is, Jordan. Our job is to make you well. Do you want a drink now?"

"I could stand one all right."

"Do you feel like you need one?"

"No. I guess not."

"We'll let the drink go then. Hungry?"

"No. Not a bit."

He stood up, patted me on the shoulder, trying to be friendly. "After we take care of those cuts we'll give you some soup, and I'll have the nurse give you a little something that'll make you sleep."

We left his office and I followed him down the corridor to Ward 3-C. There was a heavy, mesh-wire entrance door and a buzzer set into the wall at the right. Dr. Davidson pressed the buzzer and turned me over to an orderly he addressed as Conrad. Conrad dressed my wrists and assigned me to a bed. He issued me a pair of gray flannel pajamas, a blue corduroy robe, and a pair of skivvy slippers. The skivvy slippers were too large for me and the only way I could keep them on was to shuffle my feet without lifting them from the floor. He kept my shaving kit, locked it in a metal cupboard by his desk, which was at the end of the ward.

I sat down on the edge of my bed and looked around the ward. There were twenty-six beds and eleven men including myself. They all looked normal enough to me; none of them looked or acted crazy. The windows were all barred, however, with one-inch bars. I knew I was locked in, but I didn't feel like a prisoner. It was more frightening than jail. A man in jail knows what to expect. Here, I didn't.

Conrad brought me a bowl of weak vegetable soup, a piece of bread and an apple on a tray. He set the tray on my bedside stand.

"See what you can do to this," he said.

I spooned the soup down, not wanting it, but because I thought the doctor wanted me to have it. I ignored the apple and the piece of bread. When he came for the tray, he brought me some foul-tasting lavender medicine in a shot glass and I drank it. He took the tray, and said over his shoulder as he left, "You'd better hop into bed, boy. That stuff'll hit you fast. It's a legitimate Mickey."

I removed my skivvy slippers and robe and climbed into bed. It was soft and high and the sheets were like warm snow. The sun was going down and its softly fading glow came through the windows like a warm good-night kiss. The light bulbs in the ceiling, covered with heavy wire shields, glowed dully, without brightness. I fell asleep almost at once, my head falling down and down into the depths of my pillow.

It was three days before I talked to Dr. Davidson again.

NINE

Shock Treatment

AFTER getting used to it, and it is easy, a neuro-psychiatric ward can be in its own fashion a rather satisfying world within a world. It is the security. Not the security of being locked in, but the security of having everything locked out. The security that comes from the sense of no responsibility for anything. In a way, it is kind of wonderful.

And there is the silence, the peace and the quiet of the ward. The other patients kept to themselves and so did I. One of the orderlies, Conrad or Jones, brought our razors in the morning and watched us while we shaved. I would take a long, hot shower and then make my bed. That left nothing to do but sit in my chair by the side of my bed and wait for breakfast. Breakfast on a cart, was wheeled in and eaten. After breakfast we were left alone until lunch time. Then lunch would be wheeled in.

Near the door to the latrine there was a huge oak table. Spaced around the table there were shiny chromium chairs with colorful, comfortable cushions that whooshed when you first sat down. Along the wall behind the table were stack after stack of old magazines. Except for the brief interruptions for meals and blood-tests I killed the entire first day by going through them. I considered it a pleasant day. I didn't have to think about anything. I didn't have to do anything, and I didn't have anything to worry about. The first night following my admittance I slept like a dead man.

The next morning, after a plain but filling breakfast of mush, buttered toast, orange juice and coffee, I proceeded to the stacks of magazines again. I had a fresh package of king-sized cigarettes furnished by the Red Cross and I was set for another pleasant day. We were not allowed to keep matches and it was inconvenient to get a light from the orderly every time I wanted to smoke, but I knew I couldn't have every-thing.

Digging deeply into the stacks of magazines I ran across old copies of *Art Digest*, *The American Artist* and *The Modern*

Painter. This was a find that pleased me. It had been a long time since I had done any reading and, although the magazines were old, I hadn't read any of them. One at a time I read them through, cover to cover. I skipped nothing. I read the how-to-do's, the criticism, the personality sketches and the advertisements. It all interested me. I spent considerable time studying the illustrations of the pictures in the recent one-man shows, dissecting pictures in my mind and putting them together again. It was all very nice until after lunch. I was jolted into reality. Really jolted.

There was an article in *The Modern Artist* by one of my old teachers at the Chicago Art Institute. It wasn't an exceptional article: he was deploring at length the plight of the creative artist in America, and filling in with the old standby solution— *Art must have subsidy to survive*—when I read my name in the pages flat before me. It leaped off the pages, filling my eyes. Me. Harry Jordan. A would-be suicide, a resident of a free NP ward, and here was my name in a national magazine! Not that there was so much:

> "*. . . and what caused Harry Jordan to give up painting? Jordan was an artist who could do more with orange and brown than many painters can do with a full palette . . .*"

Just that much, but it was enough to dissolve my detached feelings and bring me back to a solid awareness of my true situation. My old teacher was wrong, of course. I hadn't given up painting for economic reasons. No real artist ever does. Van Gogh, Gauguin, Modigliani and a thousand others are the answer to that. But the mention of my name made me realize how far I had dropped from sight, from what I had been, and from what I might have been in my Chicago days. My depression returned full force. A nagging shred of doubt dangled in front of me. Maybe I could paint after all? Didn't my portrait of Helen prove that to me? Certainly, no painter could have captured her as well as I had done. Was I wrong? Had I wasted the years I could have been painting? Wouldn't it have been better to stay close to art, even as a teacher, where at least I would have had the urge to work from time to time? Maybe I would have overcome the block? The four early paintings I had done in orange-and-brown, the non-objective abstractions were still remembered by my old teacher—after all the elapsed time. It shook my convictions. Rocked me. My ruminations were rudely disturbed. My magazine was rudely jerked out of my hands.

"That's my magazine!" I turned in the direction of the high, reedy voice, verging on hysteria. A slight blond man stood by the table, clutching *The Modern Artist* to his pigeon breast. His face was flushed an angry red and his watery blue eyes were tortured with an inner pain.

"Sure," I said noncommittally, "I was just looking at it."

"I'll stick your arm in boiling water!" he informed me shrilly.

"No you won't." I didn't know what else to say to the man.

"I'll stick your arm in boiling water! I'll stick your arm in boiling water! I'll stick your arm in—" He kept repeating it over and over, his voice growing louder and higher, until Conrad was attracted from the end of the ward. Conrad covered the floor in quick strides, took the little man by the arm and led him away from the table.

"I want to show you something," Conrad told the man secretly.

"What are you going to show me?" The feverish face relaxed somewhat and he followed Conrad down the ward to his bed. Conrad showed him his chair and the man sat down wearily and buried his face in his hands. On the walk to his bed and chair, the magazine was forgotten, and it fell to the floor. On his way back to the table, Conrad picked up the magazine, slapped it on the table in front of me, and returned to his desk without a word of explanation. A man who had been watching the scene from the door of the latrine crossed to the table and sat down opposite me.

"Don't worry about him," he said. "He's a Schitzo."

"A what?"

"Schitzo. That's short for schizophrenic. In addition to that, he's a paranoid."

I looked the patient over carefully who was talking to me. Unlike the rest of us, he wore a pair of yellow silk pajamas, and an expensive vermillion brocade robe. His face was lined

with crinkly crescents about his eyes and mouth and a light-
ning blaze of white shot through his russet hair above each
ear. He was smiling broadly; the little scene had amused him.

"My name is Mr. Haas," he told me, reaching out to shake
hands.

"Harry Jordan," I said, shaking his hand.

"After a few years," he offered, "you get so you can tell.
I've been in and out of these places ever since the war. I'm a
Schitzo myself and also paranoid. What's the matter with
you?"

"Nothing," I said defensively.

"You're lucky then. Why are your wrists bandaged?"

"I tried suicide, but it didn't work."

"You're a manic-depressive then."

"No, I'm not," I said indignantly. "I'm nothing at all."

"Don't fight it, Jordan." Mr. Haas had a kind, pleasant
voice. "It's only a label. It doesn't mean anything. Take my
case for instance. I tried to kill my wife this time, and she had
me committed. I won't be in here long, I'm being transferred
to a V.A. hospital, and this time for good. It isn't so bad being
a Schitzo; there are many compensations. Did you ever have
hallucinations?"

"No. Never."

"I have them all the time, and the best kind. Most of us
hear voices, but my little hallucination comes to me in the
night and I can hear him, smell him and feel him. He feels
like a rubber balloon filled with warm water, and he smells
like Chanel Number Five. We carry on some of the damndest
conversations you've ever heard."

"What does he look like?" I was interested.

"The hell with you, Jordan. Get your own hallucination.
How about some chess?"

"I haven't played in a long time," I said.

"Neither have I. I'll get my board and chessmen."

For the rest of the day I played chess with Mr. Haas. I
didn't win a game.

By supper that night I was my old self again. Playing chess
had made me forget the magazine article temporarily. After a
supper of liver and new potatoes I crawled into bed. I was a
failure and I knew it. The false hopes of the early afternoon

were gone. The portrait of Helen was nothing but a lucky accident. My old orange-and-brown abstracts were nothing but experiments. Picasso's *Blue* period. Jordan's *Orange-and-Brown* period. They hadn't sold at my asking price and I'd destroyed them years ago. My name being mentioned, along with a dozen other painters, was no cause for emotion or elation. It was all padding. The prof. had to pad his article some way, and he had probably wracked his brain for enough names to make his point. But seeing my name in *The Modern Artist* had ruined my day.

It took me a long time to fall asleep.

The next morning I awoke with a slight headache and a sharp pain behind my eyeballs. I wasn't hungry, my hands were trembling slightly and my heart had a dull, dead ache. I felt terrible and even the hot water of the shower didn't relieve my depression.

I was back to normal.

At nine-thirty Conrad told me the doctor wanted to see me. He led the way and I sluffed along behind him in my slippers. Dr. Davidson's office was a small bare room, without a window, and lighted by fluorescent tubing the length of the ceiling. Two wooden chairs and a metal desk. The desk was stacked with patients' charts in aluminum covers. I sat down across from Dr. Davidson and Conrad closed the door, leaving us alone.

"Did you think I'd forgotten about you, Jordan?" The doctor tried a thin-lipped smile.

"No, sir." My fists were tightly clenched and I kept my eyes on my bandaged wrists.

"You forgot to fill in the forms I gave you."

"No, I didn't. I read the questions and that was enough."

"We need that information in order to admit you, Jordan."

"You won't get it from me. I'm ready to leave anyway." I got to my feet and half-way to the door.

"Sit down, Jordan." I sat down again. "What's the matter? Don't you want to tell me about it?"

"Not particularly. It all seems silly now. Although it seemed like a good idea at the time."

"Nothing is silly here," he said convincingly, "or strange, or secret. I'd like to hear about it."

"There's nothing really to tell. I was depressed, as I usually am, and I passed my depression on to Helen—Mrs. Meredith. We cut our wrists."

"But why are you depressed?"

"Because I'm a failure. I don't know how else to say it."

"How long had you been drinking?"

"Off and on. Mostly on. Helen drinks more than I do. I don't consider myself an alcoholic, but I suppose she is, or close to it."

"How long have you been drinking?"

"About five years."

"I mean you and Mrs. Meredith."

"Since we've been together. Three weeks, a month. Something like that."

"What have you used for money? Are you employed?"

"Not now. She had a couple of hundred dollars. It's gone now. That's part of this." I held up my arms. "No money."

"What kind of work do you do when you work?"

"Counterman, fry cook, dishwasher."

"Is that all?"

"I used to teach. Painting, drawing and so on. Fine arts."

"Why did you give it up?"

"I don't know."

"By that you mean you won't say."

"Take it any way you want."

"How were your carnal relations with Mrs. Meredith?"

"Carnal? That's a hell of a word to use, and it's none of your business!" I was as high-keyed and ill-strung as a Chinese musical instrument.

"Perhaps the word was unfortunate. How was your sex life, then?"

"How is any sex life? What kind of an answer do you want?"

"As a painter—you did paint, didn't you?" I nodded. "You should have a sharp notice for sensation, then. Where did it feel the best? The tip, the shaft, where?" He held his pencil poised over a sheet of yellow paper.

"I don't remember and it's none of your business!"

"You aren't making it easy for me to help you, Jordan," he said patiently.

"I don't need any help."

"You asked for help when you entered the hospital."

"That was my mistake. I don't need any help. I'm sorry I wasted your time. Just let me out and I'll be all right."

"All right, Jordan. I'll have you released in the morning."

I stood up, anxious to get away from him. "Thanks, Doctor. I'm sorry—"

"Sit down!" I sat down again. "I've already talked to Mrs. Meredith, but I wanted to check with you. Is Mrs. Meredith colored?"

"Helen?" My laugh was hard and brittle. "Of course not. What made you ask that?"

He hesitated for a moment before he answered. "Her expression and eyes, the bone structure of her face. She denied it too, but I thought I'd check with you."

"No," I said emphatically. "She definitely isn't colored."

"I'm going to tell you something, Jordan. I think you need help. As a rule, I don't give advice; people don't take it and it's a waste of time. But in your case I want to mention a thing or two. My own personal opinion. I don't think you and Mrs. Meredith are good for each other. All I can see ahead for you both is tragedy. That is, if you continue to live together."

"Thanks for your opinion. Can I go now?"

"Yes, you can go."

"Will you release Helen tomorrow too?"

"In a few more days."

"Can I see her?"

"No, I don't think so. It would be best for her not to have any visitors for the next few days."

"If you'll call Big Mike's Bar and Grill and ask for me, I'll pick her up when you release her."

"All right." He wrote the address on the sheet of yellow paper. "You can go back to your ward."

Conrad met me outside the office and took me back to the ward. For the rest of the day I played chess with Mr. Haas. I didn't win any games, but my skill improved. I couldn't sleep that night, and finally I got out of bed at eleven and asked the nurse to give me something. She gave me a sleeping pill that worked and I didn't awaken until morning. As soon as breakfast was over with my clothes were brought to me and I put them on. Mr. Haas talked with me while I was dressing.

"I'm sorry to see you leave so soon, Jordan. In another day or so you might have won a game." He laughed pleasantly. "And then I would have killed you." I didn't know whether he was kidding or not. "Makes you think, doesn't it?" he added. We shook hands and I started toward the door. "I'll be seeing you!" He called after me, and laughed again. This time rather unpleasantly, I thought. Conrad took me to the elevator and told me to stop at the desk in the lobby. At the desk downstairs, the nurse on duty gave me three pieces of paper to sign, and in a moment I was out on the street.

There wasn't any sun and the fog had closed down heavily over the city. I walked through the damp mist, up and down the hills, alone in my own little pocket of isolation. I walked slowly, but in what seemed like a short length of time I found myself in front of Big Mike's. I pushed through the swinging door, sat down at the bar and put my shaving kit on the seat beside me.

"Hello, Harry," Mike said jovially. "Where you been keeping yourself?"

"Little trip."

"Drink?"

I shook my head. "Mike, I need some money. No, I don't want a loan," I said when he reached for his hip pocket. "I want a job. Can you use me for a few days as a busboy or dishwasher?"

"I've got a dishwasher." Mike rubbed his chin thoughtfully. "But I don't have a busboy. Maybe the waiters would appreciate a man hustling dishes at noon and dinner. That's a busy time. But I can't pay you anything, Harry—dollar an hour."

"That's plenty. It would really help out while I look for a job."

"Want to start now?"

"Sure."

"Pick up a white jacket in the kitchen."

I started to work, grateful for the opportunity. The waiters were glad to have me clearing dishes and carrying them to the kitchen. I'm a fast worker and I kept the tables cleared for them all through the lunch hour, hot-footing it back and forth to the kitchen with a tray in each hand. By two-thirty the lunch crowd had slowed to a dribble and I was off until five. I took the time to go to my roominghouse for a shower. I straightened the room, dumped trash and beer bottles into the can in the backyard, returned to Mike's. I worked until ten that evening, returned to my room.

I found it was impossible to get to sleep. I quit trying to force it, dressed and went outside. I walked for a while and suddenly started to run. I ran around the block three times and was soon gasping for breath. I kept running. My heart thumped so hard I could feel it beating through my shirt. Bright stars danced in front of my eyes, turned gray, black. I had to stop. I leaned against a building, gasping until I got my breath back. My muscles twitched and ached as I slowly made my way back home. I took a shower and threw myself across the bed. Now I could sleep, and I did until ten the next morning.

It was three days before Dr. Davidson called me. It was in the middle of the noon rush and I was dripping wet when Mike called me to the telephone at the end of the bar. I didn't say anything, but held my hand over the mouthpiece until he walked away.

"Jordan here," I said into the phone.

"This is Doctor Davidson, Jordan. We've decided to release Mrs. Meredith in your custody. As her common-law husband you'll be responsible for her. Do you understand that?"

"What time?" I asked impatiently.

"About three this afternoon. You'll have to sign for her to take her out. Sure you want to do it?"

"Yes, sir. I'll be there." I racked the phone.

Big Mike was in the kitchen eating a salami sandwich and talking with the chef. The chef was complaining about the quality of the pork loin he was getting lately. I broke into the monologue.

"Mike, I have to quit."

"Okay."

"Can I have my money?"

"Okay." He took a roll of bills out of his hip pocket, peeled six ones and handed them to me.

"Only six bucks?"

"I took out for your tab, Harry, but I didn't charge your meals."

"Thanks, Mike. I don't like to leave you in the middle of a rush like this—" I began to apologize.

He waved me away impatiently, bit into his sandwich. "Forget it."

I hung the white mess jacket in the closet and slipped into my corduroy jacket. At the rooming house I showered and shaved for the second time that day. I rubbed my worn shoes with a towel but they were in such bad shape they didn't shine a bit. I caught a trolley, transferred to a bus, transferred to another trolley. It was one-thirty when I reached the entrance to the hospital. I sat down on a bench in the little park and watched the minute hand in the electric clock bounce to each mark, rarely taking my eyes away from it. The clock was set into the center of a Coca-Cola sign above the door of a drug store in the shopping center across the street. At three, on the head, I entered the hospital lobby. Helen was waiting for me by the circular counter, her lower lip quivering. As soon as she saw me she began to cry. I held her tight and kissed her, to the annoyance of the nurse.

"Hey," I said softly. "Cut that out. Everything's going to be all right." Her crying stopped as suddenly as it started. I signed the papers the nurse had ready, picked up Helen's bag and we went outside. We sat down on the bench in the little park.

"How'd they treat you, sweetheart?" I asked her.

"Terrible." Helen shuddered. "Simply terrible, and it was boring as hell."

"What did Dr. Davidson say to you? Anything?"

"He said I should quit drinking. That's about all."

"Anything else?"

"A lot of personal questions. He's got a filthy mind."

"Are you going to quit drinking?"

"Why should I? For him? That bastard!"

"Do you want a drink now?"

"It's all I've thought about all week, Harry," she said sincerely.

"Come on." I took her arm, helping her to her feet. "Let's go across the street."

A few doors down the street from the shopping center we found a small neighborhood bar. We entered and sat down in the last booth. I saved out enough money for carfare and we drank the rest of the six dollars. Helen was unusually quiet and drank nothing but straight shots, holding the glass in both hands, like a child holding a mug. Once in awhile she would almost cry, and then she would smile instead. We didn't talk; there was nothing to talk about. We left the bar and made the long, wearisome trip back to Big Mike's. We sat down in our old seats at the bar and started to drink on a new tab. Mike was glad to see Helen again and he saw that we always had a fresh, full glass in front of us. By midnight Helen was glassy-eyed drunk and I took her home and put her to bed. Despite the many drinks I had had, I was comparatively sober. Before going to bed myself I smoked a cigarette, crushed it savagely in the ashtray.

As far as I could tell, we were no better off than before.

TEN

Mother Love

NEXT MORNING I got out of bed early, and without waking Helen, took a long hot shower and dressed. Helen slept soundly, her lips slightly parted. I raised the blind and the room flooded with bright sunlight. A beautiful day. I shook Helen gently by the shoulder and she opened her eyes quickly, blinked them against the brightness. She was wide awake.

"I hated to wake you out of a sound sleep," I said, "but I'm leaving."

Helen sat up in bed immediately. "Leaving? Where?"

"Job hunting." I grinned at her alarm. "Not a drop of whiskey in the house."

"No money at all, huh?"

"No money, no coffee, nothing at all."

"What time will you be back?"

"I don't know. Depends on whether I can get a job, and if I do, when I get through. But I'll be back as soon as I can."

Helen got out of bed, slid her arms around my neck and kissed me hard on the mouth. "You shouldn't have to work, Harry," she said sincerely and impractically. "You shouldn't have to do anything except paint."

"Yeah," I said, disengaging her arms from my neck, "and make love to you. I'd better get going." I left the room, closing the door behind me.

There was a little change in my pocket, more than enough for carfare, and I caught the cable car downtown to Market Street. I had always been lucky finding jobs on Market, maybe I could again. There are a thousand and one cafes. One of them needed a man like me. From Turk Street I walked toward the Civic Center, looking for signs in windows. I wasn't particular. Waiter, dishwasher, anything, I didn't care. I tried two cafes without success. At last I saw a sign: FRY COOK WANTED, hanging against the inside of a window of a small cafe, attached with scotch tape. I entered the cafe. It was a dark, dingy place with an overpowering smell of fried onions. I reached over the shoulder of the peroxide blonde sitting behind the cash register and jerked the sign out of the window.

"What do you think you're doing?" she said indifferently.

"I'm the new fry cook. Where's the boss?"

"In the kitchen." She jerked her thumb toward the rear of the cafe, appraising me with blue, vacant eyes.

I made my way toward the kitchen. The counter was filled, all twelve stools, and the majority of the customers sitting on them were waiting for their food. There wasn't even a counterman working to give a glass of water or pass out a menu. The boss, a perspiring, overweight Italian, wearing suit pants and a white shirt, was gingerly dishing chile beans into a bowl. Except for the old, slow-moving dishwasher, he was the only one in the kitchen.

"Need a fry cook?" I grinned ingratiatingly, holding up the sign.

"Need one? You from the Alliance?"

"No, but I'm a fry cook."

"I been trying to get a cook from the Alliance for two days, and my waitress quit twenty minutes ago. The hell with the Alliance. Get busy."

"I'm your man." I removed my coat and hung it on a nail.

He wore a greasy, happy smile. "Sixty-five a week, meals and laundry."

"You don't have to convince me," I told him, "I'm working."

I wrapped an apron around my waist and took a look at the stove. The boss left the kitchen, rubbing his hands together, and started to take the orders. Although I was busy, I could handle things easily enough. I can take four or five orders in my head and have four or more working on the stove at the same time. When I try to go over that I sometimes run into trouble. But there was nothing elaborate to prepare. The menu offered nothing but plain food, nothing complicated. The boss was well pleased with my work. I could tell that by the way he smiled at me when he barked in his orders. And I had taken him out of a hole.

At one my relief cook came on duty, a fellow by the name of Tiny Sanders. I told him what was working and he nodded his head and started to break eggs for a Denver with one hand. I put my jacket on, found a brown paper sack, and filled it with food out of the ice-box. I don't believe in buying food when I'm working in a cafe. The boss came into the kitchen and I hit him up for a five spot. He opened his wallet and gave me the five without hesitation.

"I'm giving you the morning shift, Jordan. Five a.m. to one."

"That's the shift I want," I told him. "See you in the morning." It was the best shift to have. It would give me every afternoon and evening with Helen.

I left the cafe and on the corner I bought a dozen red carnations for a dollar from a sidewalk vendor. They were old flowers and I knew they wouldn't last for twenty-four hours, but they would brighten up our room. On the long ride home I sniffed the fragrance of the carnations and felt well-pleased with myself, revelling in my good fortune.

I was humming to myself as I ran up the stairs and down the hall to our room.

I opened my door and jagged tendrils of perfume clawed at my nostrils. Tweed. It was good perfume, but there was too much of a good thing. Helen, fully dressed in her best suit, was sitting nervously on the edge of the unmade bed. Across from her in the strongest chair was a formidable woman in her late fifties. Her hair was a streaked slate-gray and she was at least fifty pounds overweight for her height—about five-nine. Her sharp blue eyes examined me like a bug through a pair of eight-sided gold-rimmed glasses. The glasses were on a thin gold chain that led to a shiny black button pinned to the breast of a rather severe blue taffeta dress.

"Harry," there was a catch in Helen's throat, "this is my mother, Mrs. Mathews."

"How do you do?" I said. I put the carnations and sack of food on the table. "This is a pleasant surprise."

"Is it?" Mrs. Mathews sniffed.

"Well, I didn't expect you—"

"I'll bet you didn't!" She jerked her head to the right.

"The hospital notified Mother I was ill," Helen explained.

"That was very thoughtful of them," I said.

"Yes," Mrs. Mathews said sarcastically, "wasn't it? Yes, it was very thoughtful indeed. They also were thoughtful enough to inform me that my daughter was released from the hospital in the custody of her common-law husband. That was a nice pleasant surprise!"

For a full minute there was a strained silence. I interrupted it. "Helen is all right now," I said, trying a cheery note.

"Is she?" Mrs. Mathews asked.

"Yes, she is."

"Well, I don't think so." Mrs. Mathews jerked her head to the right. "I think she's out of her mind!"

"Please, Mother!" Helen was very close to tears.

"I'm taking good care of Helen," I said.

"Are you?" Mrs. Mathews hefted herself to her feet, clomped heavily across the room to the portrait. "Is this what you call taking good care of her? Forcing her to pose for a filthy, obscene picture?" Her words were like vitriolic drops of acid wrapped in cellophane, and they fell apart when they left her lips, filling the room with poison.

"It's only a portrait," I said defensively. "It isn't for public viewing."

"You bet it isn't! Only a depraved mind could have conceived it; only a depraved beast could execute it; and only a leering, concupiscent goat would look at it!"

"You're too hard on me, Mrs. Mathews. It isn't that bad," I said.

"Where have you been so long, Harry?" Helen asked me, trying to change the subject.

"I got a job, and that sack's full of groceries," I said, pointing.

"What kind of a job?" Mrs. Mathews asked. "Sweeping streets?"

"No. I'm a cook."

"I don't doubt it. Listen, er, ah, Mr. Jordan, if you think anything of Helen at all you'll talk some sense into her. I want her to come home with me, where she belongs. Look at her eyes! They look terrible."

"Now that I've got a job she'll be all right, Mrs. Mathews. Would you like a salami sandwich, Helen?"

"No thanks, Harry," Helen said politely. "Not right now."

"Why not?" Mrs. Mathews asked with mock surprise. "That's exactly what you should eat! Not fresh eggs, milk, orange juice and fruit. That stuff isn't any good for a person right out of a sick bed. Go ahead. Eat a salami sandwich. With pickles!"

"I'm not hungry, Mother!"

"Maybe it's a drink of whiskey you want? Have you got whiskey in that sack, Mr. Jordan, or is it all salami?"

"Just food," I said truthfully. "No whiskey."

"That's something. Are you aware that Helen shouldn't drink anything with alcohol in it? Do you know of her bad heart? Did she tell you she was sick in bed with rheumatic fever for three years when she was a little girl? Did she tell you she couldn't smoke?"

"I'm all right, Mother!" Helen said angrily. "Leave Harry alone!"

Again we suffered a full minute of silence. "I brought you some carnations," I said to Helen; "you'd better put them in water." I crossed to the table, unwrapped the green paper, and gave the flowers to Helen.

"They're lovely, Harry!" Helen exclaimed. She placed the carnations in the water pitcher on the dresser, arranged them quickly, inexpertly, sat down again on the edge of the bed, and stared at her mother. I sat beside her, reached over and took her hand. It was warm, almost feverish.

"Now listen to me, both of you." Mrs. Mathews spoke slowly, as though she were addressing a pair of idiots. "I can perceive that neither one of you has got enough sense to come in out of the rain. Helen has, evidently, made up what little mind she has, to remain under your roof instead of mine. All right. She's over twenty-one and there's nothing I can do about it. If you won't dissuade her and I can see you won't— not that I blame you—will you at least let me in on your plans?"

"We're going to be married soon," Helen said.

"Do you mind if I call to your attention that you're already married?" Mrs. Mathews jerked her head to the right, as though Helen's husband was standing outside the door waiting for her.

"I mean, after I get a divorce," Helen said.

"And meanwhile, while you're waiting, you intend to continue to live here in sin? Is that right?"

Helen didn't answer for a moment and I held my breath. "Yes, Mother, that's what I'm going to do. Only it isn't sin."

"I won't quibble." Mrs. Mathews sniffed, jerked her head to the right and turned her cold blue eyes on me. "How much money do you make per week, Mr. Jordan? Now that you have a job." The way she said it, I don't believe she thought I had a job.

"Sixty-five dollars a week. And I get my meals and laundry."

"That isn't enough. And I doubt in here—" she touched her mammoth left breast with her hand— "whether you can hold a position paying that much for any length of time. Here's what I intend to do. As long as my daughter won't listen to reason, I'll send her a check for twenty-five dollars a week. But under one condition: both of you, stay out of San Sienna!"

"We don't need any money from you, Mother!" Helen said fiercely. "Harry makes more than enough to support me."

"I'm not concerned with that," Mrs. Mathews said self-righteously. "I know where my duty lies. You can save the money if you don't need it, or tear up the check, I don't care. But starting right now, I'm giving you twenty-five dollars a week!"

"You're very generous," I said.

"I'm not doing it for you." Mrs. Mathews jerked her head to the right. "I'm doing it for Helen."

Mrs. Mathews removed a checkbook and ballpoint pen from the depths of a cavernous saddle-leather bag and wrote a check. She crossed the room to the dresser, drying the ink by waving the check in the air, and put the filled-in check beside the pitcher of carnations. She sniffed.

"That's all I have to say, but to repeat it one more time so there'll be no mistake: Stay out of San Sienna!"

"It was nice meeting you, Mrs. Mathews," I said. Helen remained silent.

Mrs. Mathews jerked her head to the right so hard her glasses were pulled off her nose. The little chain spring caught them up and they whirred up to the black button pinned to her dress. She closed the shirred beaver over the glasses, sniffed, and slammed the door in my face.

But the memory lingered on, in the form of a cloud of Tweed perfume.

Helen's face was pale and her upper lip was beaded with tiny drops of perspiration. She wound her arms around my waist tightly and pressed her face into my chest. I patted her on the back, kissed the top of her head.

"Oh, Harry, it was terrible!" Her voice was low and muffled against my chest. "She's been here since ten o'clock this morning. Arguing, arguing, arguing! Trying to break me down. And I almost lost! I was within that much"—she pulled away from me, held thumb and forefinger an inch apart—"of going with her." She looked at me accusingly; her face wore an almost pitiful expression. "Where were you? When I needed you the most, you weren't here!"

"I wasn't lying about the job, Helen. I found a job as a fry cook and had to go to work to get it."

"Why do you have to work? It isn't fair to leave me here all alone."

"We have to have money, sweetheart," I explained patiently. "We were flat broke when I went out this morning, if you remember."

"Can't we live on what money Mother sends us?"

"We could barely exist on twenty-five dollars a week. The room rent's ten dollars, and we'd have to buy food and liquor out of the rest. We just can't do it."

"What are we going to do, Harry? It's so unfair of Mother!" she said angrily. "She could just as easily give us two hundred and fifty a week!"

"Can't you see what she's up to, Helen? She's got it all planned out, she thinks. She doesn't want you to go hungry, but if she gave us more money, she knows damned well you'd never go back to her. This way, she figures she has a chance—"

"Well, she's wrong! I'm never going back to San Sienna!"

"That leaves it up to me then, where it belongs. I'll work this week out, anyway. Maybe another. We'll pay some room rent in advance that way, and the tab at Mike's. And maybe we can get a few loose dollars ahead. Then I'll look for some kind of part time work that'll give me more time with you."

We left it at that.

Helen picked the check up from the dresser and left for the delicatessen. She returned in a few minutes with a bottle of whiskey and a six-pack carton of canned beer. I had one drink with her and I made it last. I didn't want to drink that one. I felt that the situation was getting to be too much for me to handle. Helen drank steadily, pouring them down, one after the other, chasing the raw whiskey with sips of beer. Her mother's visit had upset her badly, and she faced it typically, the way she faced every situation.

By six that evening she sat numbly in the chair by the window. She was in a paralyzed stupor. I undressed her and put her to bed. She lay on her back, breathing with difficulty. Her eyes were like dark bruises, her face a mask of fragile, white tissue paper.

I didn't leave the room; I felt like a sentry standing guard duty. I made a salami sandwich, took one bite, and threw it down on the table. I sat in the chair staring at the wall until well past midnight.

After I went to bed, it was a long time before I fell asleep.

ELEVEN

Bottle Baby

THE LITTLE built-in, automatic alarm clock inside my head waked me at four a.m. and I hadn't even taken the trouble to set it. I tried to fight against it and go back to sleep, but I couldn't. The alarm was too persistent. I reluctantly got out of the warm bed, shiveringly grabbed a towel, and rushed next door to the bathroom. Standing beneath the hot water of the shower almost put me back to sleep. With an involuntary yelp I twisted the faucet to cold and remained under the pelting needles of ice for three minutes. On the way back to my room I dried myself, and then dressed hurriedly against the background of my chattering teeth. The room was much too cold to hang around for coffee to boil and I decided to wait and get a cup when I reached Vitale's Cafe. I got my trenchcoat out of the closet and put it on over my corduroy jacket. The trenchcoat was so filthy dirty I only wore it when I had to, but it was so cold inside the house I knew I would freeze on the street without something to break the wind.

Helen was sleeping on her side facing the wall and I couldn't see her face. Her hip made a minor mountain out of the covers and a long ski slope down to her bare round shoulder. I envied Helen's warm nest, but I pulled the blanket up a little higher and tucked it in all around her neck.

Helen had been so far under the night before when I put her to bed I thought it best to leave a note. I tore a strip of paper from the top of a brown sack and wrote in charcoal:

Dearest Angel,
Your slave has departed for the salt mine. Will be home by
one-thirty at latest. All my love,

Harry

Helen's bottle of whiskey was still a quarter full. I put the note in the center of the table and weighted it with the bottle where I knew she would find it easily when she first got out of bed. I turned out the overhead light and closed the door softly on my way out.

It was colder outside than I had anticipated it to be. A strong, steady wind huffed in from the bay, loaded heavily with salt and mist, and I couldn't make myself stand still on the corner to wait for my car. Cable cars are few and far between at four-twenty in the morning and it was far warmer to run a block, wait, run a block and wait until one came into view. I covered four blocks this way and the exertion warmed me enough to wait on the fourth corner until a car came along and slowed down enough for me to catch it. I paid my fare to the conductor and went inside. I was the only passenger for several blocks and then business picked up for the cable car when several hungry-looking longshoremen boarded it with neatly-lettered placards on their way to the docks to picket. I dismounted at the Powell Street turnaround and walked briskly down Market with my hands shoved deep in my pockets. The wide street was as nearly deserted as it can ever be. There were a few early-cruising cabs and some middle-aged paper boys on the corners waiting for the first morning editions. There was an ugly mechanical monster hugging the curbs and sploshing water and brushing it up behind as it noisily cleaned at the streets. Later on there would be the regular street cleaners with brooms and trash-cans on wheels to pick up what the monster missed. I entered Vitale's Cafe.

"Morning, Mr. Vitale," I said.

"It don't work for me," the boss said ruefully. "I poured hot water through ten times already and it won't turn dark. I have to use fresh coffee grounds after all."

"Did you dry the old grounds on the stove first?"

"No, I been adding hot water."

"That's what's the matter then. If you want to use coffee grounds two days in a row you have to dry them out on the stove in a shallow pan. Add a couple of handfuls of fresh coffee to the dried grounds and the coffee'll be as dark as cheap coffee ever gets."

I took off my jacket and lit the stove and checked on the groceries for breakfast. I wrapped an apron around my waist and stoned the grill while I waited for the coffee to be made, making a mental note to fix my own coffee the next morning before I left my room. By five a.m. I was ready for work and nobody had entered the cafe. I wondered why Vitale opened so early. I soon found out. All of a sudden the counter was jammed with breakfast eaters from the various office buildings and street, most of them ordering the Open Eye Breakfast Special: two ounces of tomato juice, one egg, one strip of bacon, one piece of toast and coffee extra. This breakfast was served for thirty-five cents and although it was meager fare it attracted the low income group. The night elevator operators, the cleaning women, the news-boys, the all-night movie crowd, and some of the policemen going off duty all seemed to go for it. Breakfast was served all day at Vitale's, but at ten-thirty I checked the pale blue menu and began to get ready for the lunch crowd. I was so busy during the noon rush I hated to look up from my full grill when Tiny, my relief, tapped me on the shoulder at one on the head. I told Tiny what was working, wrapped up two one-pound T-bones to take home with me, and left the cafe with a wave at the boss.

On the long ride home I tried to think of ways to bring Helen out of the doldrums, but every idea I thought of was an idea calling for money. By the time I reached my corner my immediate conclusion was that all Helen needed was one of my T-bone steaks, fried medium rare as only I could fry a steak and topped with a pile of french fried onion rings. I bought a dime's worth of onions at the delicatessen and hurried home with my surprise. I opened the door to my room and Helen wasn't there. My note was still under the whiskey bottle, but now the bottle was empty. There was a message from Helen written under mine and I picked it up and studied it.

Dear Harry,
I can't sit here all day waiting for you. If I don't talk to
somebody I'll go nuts. I love you.

Helen

The message was in Helen's unmistakable microscopic handwriting and it was written with the same piece of charcoal I had used and left on the table. It took me several minutes to decipher what she said and I still didn't know what she really meant. Was she leaving me for good? I opened the closet and checked her clothes, the few she had. They were all in the closet and so was her suitcase. That made me feel a little better, knowing she wasn't leaving me. I still didn't like the idea of her running around loose, half-drunk, and with nothing solid in her stomach. She had killed the rest of the whiskey, which was more than a half-pint, and she had the remainder of the twenty-five bucks her mother had given her. She could be anywhere in San Francisco—with anybody. I had to find her before she got into trouble.

I opened the window, put the steaks outside on the sill, and closed the window again. If the sun didn't break through the fog they would keep until that evening before they spoiled. I left the rooming house and walked down the street to Big Mike's Bar and Grill. After I entered the grill I made my way directly to the cash register where Big Mike was standing. By the look in his eyes I could tell he didn't want to talk to me.

"Have you seen Helen, Mike?" I asked him.

"Yeah, I saw her all right. She was in here earlier."

"She left, huh?"

"That's right, Harry. She left." His voice was surly, his expression sour. There was no use to question him any further. How was he supposed to know where she went? It was obvious something was bothering him and I waited for him to tell me about it.

"Listen, Harry," Mike said, after I waited a full minute. "I like you fine, and I suppose Helen's okay too, but from now on I don't want her in here when you ain't with her."

"What happened, Mike. I've been working since five this morning."

"I don't like to say nothing, Harry, but, you might as well know. She was in about eleven and drunker than hell. I wouldn't sell her another drink even, and when I won't sell another drink, they're drunk. She had her load on when she come in, and it was plenty. Anyway, she got nasty with me and I told her to leave. She wouldn't go and I didn't want to toss her out on her ear so I shoved her in a booth and had Tommy take her some coffee. She poured it on the floor, cussing Tommy out and after awhile three Marines took up with her. They sat down in her booth and she quieted down so I let it go. After a while they all left and that was it. I'm sorry as hell, Harry, but that's the way it was. I ain't got time to look after every drunk comes in here."

"I know it, Mike. You don't know where they went, do you?"

"As I said, after a while I looked and they were gone."

"Well, thanks, Mike." I left the bar and went out on the sidewalk. If the Marines and Helen had taken the cable car downtown I'd never find them. But if they took a cab from the hack-stand in the middle of the block, maybe I would be all right. I turned toward the hack-stand. Bud, the young Korean veteran driver for the Vet's Cab Company, was leaning against a telephone pole waiting for his phone to ring, a cigarette glued to the corner of his mouth, when I reached his stand. He had a pinched, fresh face with light beige-colored eyes, and wore his chauffeur's cap so far back on his head it looked like it would fall off. I knew him enough to nod to him, and saw him often around the corner and in Big Mike's, but I had never spoken to him before.

"I guess you're lookin' for your wife, huh, Jordan?" Bud made a flat statement and it seemed to give him great satisfaction.

"Yes, I am, Bud. Have you seen her?"

"Sure did." He ripped the cigarette out of his mouth, leaving a powdering of flaked white paper on his lower lip, and snapped the butt into the street. "She was with three Marines." This statement gave him greater satisfaction.

"Did you take them any place?"

"Sure did."

"Where?"

"Get in." Bud opened the back door of his cab.

"What's the tariff, Bud?" I was thinking of the three one dollar bills in my watch pocket and my small jingle of change.

"It'll run you about a buck and a half." He smiled with the left side of his face. "If you want to go. She was with three Marines." He held up three fingers. "Three," he repeated, "and you are one." He held up one finger. "One."

"We'll see," I said noncommittally and climbed into the back seat.

Bud drove me to The Green Lobster, a bar and grill near Fisherman's Wharf. The bar was too far away from the Wharf for the heavy tourist trade, but it was close enough to catch the overflow on busy days and there was enough fish stink in the air to provide an atmosphere for those who felt they needed it. On the way, Bud gave me a sucker ride in order to run up his buck and a half on the meter. At most the fare should have been six-bits, but I didn't complain. I rode the unnecessary blocks out of the way and paid the fare in full when he stopped at The Green Lobster.

"This is where I left 'em," he said. I waited on the curb until he pulled away. I couldn't understand Bud's attitude. He might have been a friend of the guy I had a fight with in Big Mike's or he might have resented me having a beautiful girl like Helen. I didn't know, but I resented his manner. I like everybody and it's always disconcerting when someone doesn't like me. I entered The Green Lobster and sat down at the end of the bar near the door.

A long, narrow bar hugged the right side of the room for the full length of the dimly lighted room. There were high, wrinkled red-leather stools for the patrons and I perched on one, my feet on the chromium rungs. The left wall had a row of green-curtained booths, and between the booths and the narrow bar, there were many small tables for two covering the rest of the floorspace. Each small table was covered with a green oilcloth cover and held a bud vase with an unidentifiable artificial flower. I surveyed the room in the bar mirror and spotted Helen and the three Marines in the second booth. The four of them leaned across their table, their heads together, and then they sat back and laughed boisterously. I couldn't hear them, but supposed they were taking turns telling dirty jokes. Helen's laugh was loud, clear, and carried across the room above the laughter of the Marines. I hadn't heard her laugh like that since the night I first brought her home with me. After the bartender finished with two other customers at the bar he got around to me.

"Straight shot," I told him.

"It's a dollar a shot," he said quietly, half-apologetically.

"I've got a dollar," and I fished one out of my watch pocket and slapped it on the bar.

He set an empty glass before me and filled it to the brim with bar whiskey. I sipped a little off the top, put the glass back down on the bar. At a dollar a clip the shot would have to last me. I didn't have a plan or course of action, so I sat stupidly, watching Helen and the Marines in the bar mirror, trying to think of what to do next.

If I tried a direct approach and merely asked Helen to leave with me, there would be a little trouble. Not knowing what to do, I did nothing. There was one sergeant and two corporals, all three of them bigger than me. They wore neat, bright-blue Marine uniforms and all had the fresh, well-scrubbed look that servicemen have on the first few hours of leave or pass. But in my mind I didn't see them in uniform. I saw them naked, Helen naked, and all of them cavorting obscenely in a hotel room somewhere, and as this picture formed in my mind my face began to perspire.

Helen inadvertently settled the action for me. She was in the seat against the wall, the sergeant on the outside, with the two corporals facing them across the table. After a while, Helen started out of the booth to go to the ladies' room. The sergeant goosed her as she squeezed by him and she squealed, giggled, and broke clear of the table. As she looked drunkenly around the room for the door to the ladies' room she saw me sitting at the bar.

"Harry!" she screamed joyfully across the room. "Come on over!"

I half-faced her, remaining on my stool, shaking my head. Helen crossed to the bar, weaving recklessly between the tables, and as soon as she reached me, threw her arms around my neck and kissed me wetly on the mouth. The action was swift and blurred from that moment on. An attack of Marines landed on me and I was hit a glancing blow on the jaw, my right arm was twisted cruelly behind my back, and in less than a minute I was next door on the asphalt of the parking lot. A corporal held my arms behind me and another was rounding the building. The sergeant, his white belt wrapped around his fist, the buckle dangling free, waved the man back. "Go back inside, Adams, and watch that bitch! We'll take care of this bastard. She might try and get away and I spent eight bucks on her already." The oncoming corporal nodded grimly and reentered the bar. Under the circumstances I tried to be as calm as possible.

"Before you hit me with that buckle, Sergeant," I said, "why don't you let me explain?"

Businesslike, the sergeant motioned the Marine holding my arms behind my back to stand clear, so he could get a good swing at me with the belt.

"You don't have to hold me," I said over my shoulder. "If you want to beat up a man for kissing his wife, go ahead!" I jerked away and dropped to my knees in front of the sergeant. Hopefully, I prayed loudly, trying to make my voice sound sincere:

"Oh, God above! Let no man tear asunder what You have joined in holy matrimony! Dear sweet God! Deliver this poor sinner from evil, and show these young Christian gentlemen the light of Your love and Your mercy! Sweet Son of the Holy Ghost and—" That was as far as I got.

"Are you and her really married?" the sergeant asked gruffly.

"Yes, sir," I said humbly, remaining on my knees and staring intently at my steepled fingers.

I glanced at the two Marines out of the corner of my eye. The youngest had a disgusted expression on his face, and was tugging at the sergeant's arm.

"Let it go, Sarge," he said, "we were took and the hell with it. I wouldn't get any fun out of hitting him now."

"Neither would I." The sergeant unwrapped the belt from his hand and buckled it around his waist. "I'm not even mad any more." There was a faint gleam of pity in his eyes as he looked at me. "If she's your wife, how come you let her run loose in the bars?"

"I was working, sir," I said, "and I thought she was home with the children." I hung my head lower, kept my eyes on the ground.

"Then it's your tough luck," the sergeant finished grimly. "Both of you got what you deserved." They left the parking lot and reentered the bar. I got off my knees, walked to the curb and waited. The sergeant brought Helen to the door, opened it for her politely, guided her outside, and as he released her arm, he cuffed her roughly across the face. Bright red marks leaped to the surface of her cheek and she reeled across the sidewalk. I caught her under the arms before she fell.

"That evens us up for the eight bucks." The sergeant grinned and shut the door.

Helen spluttered and cursed and then her body went limp in my arms. I lifted her sagging body and carried her down to the corner and the hack-stand. She hadn't really passed out; she was pretending so she wouldn't have to talk to me. I put her into the cab without help from the driver and gave him my address. I paid the eighty-cent fare when he reached my house, and hoped he didn't see the large, wet spot on the back seat until after he pulled away. Helen leaned weakly against me and I half carried her into our room and undressed her. She fell asleep immediately. Looking inside her purse, I found ninety cents in change. No bills.

I thought things over and came to a decision. I couldn't work any more and leave her by herself. Either I'd have to get money from some other source, or do without it. Left to herself, all alone, Helen would only get into serious trouble. Already I noticed things about her that had changed. She let her hair go uncombed. She skipped wearing her stockings. Her voice was slightly louder and she seemed to be getting deaf in one ear.

We never made love any more.

TWELVE

The Dregs

I DIDN'T sleep all night. I sat in the chair by the dark window with the lights out while Helen slept. I didn't try to think about anything, but kept my mind as blank as possible. When I did have a thought it was disquieting and ugly and I would get rid of it by pushing it to the back of my mind like a pack rat trading a rock for a gold nugget.

Vitale would be stuck again for a fry cook when I didn't show up, but it couldn't be helped. To leave Helen to her own devices would be foolish. When I thought about how close I came to losing her my heart would hesitate, skip like a rock on water and then beat faster than ever. I had a day's pay coming from Vitale that I would never collect. It would take more nerve than I possessed to ask him for it. I decided to let it go.

The night passed, somehow, and as soon as the gray light hit the window I left the room and walked down the block to the delicatessen. It wasn't quite six and I had to wait for almost ten minutes before Mr. Watson opened up. I had enough money with some left over for a half-pint of whiskey and Mr. Watson pursed his lips when he put it in a sack for me.

"Most of my customers this early buy milk and eggs, Harry," he said.

"Breakfast is breakfast," I said lightly and the bells above the door tinkled as I closed it behind me.

When I got back to the room, I brought the T-bones inside from the window sill, opened the package and smelled them. They seemed to be all right and I lit the burner and dropped one in the frying pan and sprinkled it with salt. I made coffee on the other burner and watched the steak for the exact moment to turn it. To fry a steak properly it should only be turned one time. Helen awoke after awhile, got out of bed without a word or a glance in my direction and went to the bathroom. The steak was ready when she got back and I had it on a plate at the table.

"How'd you like a nice T-bone for breakfast?" I asked her.

"Ugh!" She put her feet into slippers and wrapped a flowered robe around her shoulders. "I'll settle for coffee."

I poured two cups of coffee and Helen joined me at the table. I shoved the half-pint across the table and she poured a quarter of the bottle into her coffee. I started in on the steak. We both carefully avoided any reference to the Marines or the afternoon before.

"This a day off, Harry?" Helen asked after she downed half of her laced coffee.

"No. I quit."

"Good."

"But I'm a little worried."

"What about?" she asked cautiously.

"Damned near everything. Money, for one thing, and I'm worried about you, too."

"I'm all right."

"You're drinking more than you did before, and you aren't eating."

"I'm not hungry."

"Even so, you've got to eat."

"I'm not hungry."

"Suppose . . ." I spoke slowly, choosing my words with care, "all of a sudden, just like that," and I snapped my fingers, "we quit drinking? I can pour what's left of that little bottle down the drain and we can start from there. We make a resolution and stick to it, see, stay sober from now on, make a fresh start."

Helen quickly poured another shot into her coffee. "No, Harry. I know what you mean, but I couldn't quit if I wanted to."

"Why not? We aren't getting any place the way we're going."

"Who wants to get any place?" she said sardonically. "Do you? What great pinnacle have you set your eyes on?" She rubbed her cheek gently. It was swollen from the slap the Marine had given her.

"It was just an idea." Helen was right and I was wrong. We were too far down the ladder to climb up now. I was letting my worry about money and Helen lead me into dangerous thinking. The only thing to do was keep the same level without going down any further. If I could do that, we would be all right. "Pass me the bottle," I said.

I took a good swig and I felt better immediately. From now on I wouldn't let worry get me down. I would take things as they came and with any luck at all everything would be all right.

It didn't take much to mellow Helen. After two laced cups of coffee she was feeling the drinks and listening with intent interest to my story about Van Gogh and Gauguin and their partnership at Arles. Fingernails scratched at the door. Irritated by the interruption I jerked the door open. Mrs. McQuade stood in the doorway with a large package in her arms.

"This package came for you, Mrs. Jordan," she said, looking around me at Helen. "I signed for it. It was delivered by American Express."

"Thanks, Mrs. McQuade," I said. "I'll take it." I took the package.

"That's all right. I—" She wanted to talk some more but I closed the door with my shoulder and tossed the package on the bed. Helen untied the package and opened it. It was full of women's clothing.

"It's from Mother," she said happily, "she's sent me some of my things."

"That's fine," I said. Helen started through the package, holding up various items of clothing to show me how they looked. This didn't satisfy her, and she slipped a dress on to show me how well it looked on her, removed it, and started to put another one on. I was bored. But this pre-occupation with a fresh wardrobe would occupy her for quite a while. Long enough for me to look around town for a way to make a few dollars. The half-pint was almost empty.

"Look, sweetheart," I said, "why don't you take your time and go through these things, and I'll go out for a while and look for a part-time job."

"But I want to show them to you—"

"And I've got to pick up a few bucks or we'll be all out of whiskey."

"Oh. How long will you be gone?"

"Not long. An hour or so at the most." I kissed her good-bye and left the house. I caught the cable car downtown and got off at Polk Street. There wasn't any particular plan or idea in my mind and I walked aimlessly down the street. I passed the Continental Garage. It was a five-story building designed solely for the parking of automobiles. At the back of the building I could see two latticed elevators that took the cars up and down to the rest of the building. On impulse, I entered the side office. There were three men in white overalls sitting around on top of the desks. They stopped talking when I entered and I smiled at the man who had MANAGER embroidered in red above the left breast pocket of his spotless overalls. He was a peppery little man with a small red moustache clipped close to his lip. He looked at me for a moment, then closed his eyes. His eyelids were as freckled as the rest of his face.

"What I'm looking for, sir," I said, "is a part-time job. Do you have a rush period from about four to six when you could use another man to park cars?"

He opened his eyes and there was suspicion in them. "Yes and No. How come you aren't looking for an eight-hour day?"

"I am." I smiled. "I'm expecting an overseas job in Iraq," I lied. "It should come through any day now and I have to hang around the union hall all day. That's why I can't take anything permanent. But the job I'm expecting is taking a lot longer to come through than I expected and I'm running short on cash."

"I see." He nodded, compressed his lips. "You a mechanic?"

"No, sir. Petroleum engineer."

"College man, huh?" I nodded, but I didn't say anything. "Can you drive a car?"

I laughed politely. "Of course I can."

"Okay, I'll help you out. You can start this evening from four to six, parking and bringing them down. Buck and a half an hour. Take it or leave it. It's all the same to me."

"I'll take it," I said gratefully, "and thanks."

"Pete," the manager said to a loosed-jointed man with big

knobby hands, "show him how to run the elevator and tell him about the tickets."

Pete left the office for the elevators and I followed him. A push button worked the elevator, but parking the cars was more complicated. The tickets were stamped with a time-stamp and parked in time groups in accordance with time of entry. When the patron brought in his stub, it was checked for the time it was brought in and the serial number of the ticket. Cars brought in early to stay all day were on the top floor and so on down to the main floor. Patrons who said they would only be gone an hour or so had their cars parked down-stairs on the main floor. Five minutes after I left Pete I was on the cable car and on my way home. The fears I had in the morning were gone and I was elated. By a lucky break my part time job was solved. With the twenty-five a week coming in from Helen's mother, plus another three dollars a day from the garage, we should be able to get along fine. And counting the half-hour each way to downtown and my two hours of work, Helen would only be alone three hours.

I opened the door to our room and Helen was back in bed fast asleep. Her new clothes were scattered and thrown about the floor. Without waking her I picked them up and hung them in the closet. I wanted a shot but the little half-pint bottle was empty. I pulled the covers over Helen and lay down beside her on top of the bed. I napped fitfully till three and then I left. I started to wake her before I left, but she was sleeping so peacefully I didn't have the heart to do it.

Right after four the rush started and I hustled the cars out until six. It wasn't difficult and after a few minutes I could find the cars easily. I looked up the red-haired manager at six and he gave me three dollars and I left the garage. Going down the hallway I spread the three dollars like a fan before I opened the door to our room.

Helen was gone.

There wasn't any note so I assumed she was at Big Mike's. She had probably forgotten about the ruckus with him the day before and he was the logical man to give her a free drink, or let her sign for one. I left the roominghouse for Big Mike's. He hadn't seen her.

"If you haven't found her by now," he said, "you might as well forget about it, Harry."

"I did find her yesterday, Mike, I was with her till three this afternoon, and then I had to go to work."

"This isn't the only bar in the neighborhood." He grinned. "I wisht it was."

I made the rounds of all the neighborhood bars. She wasn't in any of them and I didn't ask any of the bartenders if she had been in them. I didn't know any of the bartenders that well. At eight-thirty I went back to the roominghouse and checked to see whether she had returned. I didn't want to miss her in case she came back on her own accord. She wasn't there and I started to check the bars outside the neighborhood. I was hoping she hadn't gone downtown, and I knew she didn't have enough carfare to go.

It was ten-thirty before I found her. She was in a little bar on Peacock Street. It was so dark inside I had to stand still for a full minute before my eyes became accustomed to the darkness. There was one customer at the bar and he and the bartender were watching a TV wrestling match. There were two shallow booths opposite the bar and Helen was in the second. A sailor was with her and she was wearing his white sailor hat on the back of her head. His left arm was about her waist, his hand cupping a breast, and his right hand was up under her dress, working furiously. Her legs were spread widely and he was kissing her on the mouth.

I ran directly to the booth, grabbed the sailor by his curly yellow hair and jerked his head back, pulling his mouth away from Helen's. Still keeping a tight grip on his hair I dragged him across her lap to the center of the floor. His body was too heavy to be supported by his hair alone and he slipped heavily to the floor, leaving me with a thick wad of curls in each hand. He mumbled something unintelligible and attempted to sit up. His slack mouth was open and there was a drunken, stupefied expression in his eyes. I wanted to hurt him; not kill him, but hurt him, mutilate his pasty, slack-jawed face. Looking for a handy weapon, I took a beer bottle from the bar and smashed it over his head. The neck of the bottle was still in my hand and the broken section ended in a long, jagged splinter. I carved his face with it, moving the sharp, glass dagger back and forth across his white face with a whipping wrist motion. Each slash opened a spurting channel of bright red blood that ran down his face and neck and splashed on the floor between his knees. My first blow with the bottle had partially stunned him but the pain brought him out of it and the high screams coming from deep inside his throat were what brought me to my senses. I dropped the piece of broken bottle, and in a way, I felt that I had made up somehow for the degradation I had suffered at the hands of the Marines.

Helen had sobered considerably and her eyes were round as saucers as she sat in the booth. I lifted her to her feet and she started for the door, making a wide detour around the screaming sailor. I opened the door for her and looked over my shoulder. The bartender was nowhere in sight, probably flat on the floor behind the bar. The solitary drinker was peering at me nervously from the safety of the doorway to the men's room. The sailor had managed to get to his knees and was crawling under the table to the first booth, the screams still pouring from his throat. I let the door swing shut behind us.

Helen was able to stand by herself, but both of her hands were pressed over her mouth. I released her arm and she staggered to the curb and vomited into the gutter. When she finished I put my arm around her waist and we walked up the hill. A taxi, coming down the hill on the opposite side of the street, made a U-turn when I signaled him and rolled to a stop beside us. I helped Helen into the cab. A block away from our roominghouse I told the driver to stop. When I opened the door to get out I noticed my hand was cut. I wrapped my handkerchief around my bleeding hand and gave a dollar to the hackie. The cold night air had revived Helen considerably, and she scarcely staggered as we walked the block to the house. As soon as we entered our room she made for the bed and curled up on her knees, pressed her arms to her sides, and ducked her head down. In this position it was difficult for me to remove her clothes, but before I finished taking them off she was asleep.

By that time I could have used a drink myself. I heated the leftover coffee and smoked a cigarette to control my uneasy stomach. I looked through Helen's purse and all I found was a crumpled package of cigarettes and a book of paper matches. Not a penny.

What was the use? I couldn't keep her. How could I work and stay home and watch her at the same time? I couldn't make enough money to meet expenses and keep Helen in liquor if I parked a million cars or fried a million eggs or waited on a million tables. I was so beaten down and disgusted with myself my mind wouldn't cope with it any longer. Sitting awake in the chair I had a dream, a strange, merging dream, where everything was unreal and the ordinary turned into the extraordinary. Nothing like it had ever happened to me before. The coffeepot, the cup, and the can of condensed milk on the table turned into a graphic composition, a depth study. It was beautiful. Everything I turned my eyes upon in the room was perfectly grouped. A professional photographer couldn't have arranged the room any better. The unshaded light in the ceiling was like a light above Van Gogh's pool table. Helen's clothing massed upon the chair swirled gracefully to the floor like drapes in a Titian drawing. The faded gray wallpaper with its unknown red flower pattern was suddenly quaint and charming. The gray background fell away from the flowers with a three-dimensional effect. Everything was lovely, lovely . . .

I don't know how long this spell lasted, but it seemed to be a long time and I didn't want it to end. I had no thought at all during this period. I merely sensed the new delights of my quiet, ordinary room. Only Helen's gentle, open-mouthed snoring furnished the hum of life to my introspection. And then, like a blinding flash of headlights striking my eyes, everything was clear to me. Simple. Plain. Clear.

I didn't have to fight any more.

For instance, a man is crossing the street and an automobile almost runs him down. He shakes his fist and curses and says to himself: "That Buick almost hit me!" But it wasn't the Buick that almost hit him; the Buick was merely a vehicle. It was the man or woman *driving* the Buick who almost hit him. Not the Buick. And that was me. I was the automobile, a machine, a well-oiled vehicle now matured to my early thirties. A machine without a driver. The driver was gone. The machine could now relax and run wherever it might, even into a smash. So what? It could function by itself, by habit, reflex, or whatever it was that made it run. Not only didn't I know, I didn't care any more. It might be interesting, for that part of me that used to think things out, to sit somewhere and watch Harry Jordan, the machine, go through the motions. The getting up in the morning, the shaving, the shower, walking, talking, drinking. I. Me. Whatever I was, didn't give a damn any more. Let the body function and the senses sense. The body felt elation. The eyes enjoyed the sudden beauty of the horrible little back bedroom. My mind felt nothing. Nothing at all.

Helen sat up suddenly in bed. She retched, a green streak of fluid burst from her lips and spread over her white breasts. I got a towel from the dresser and wiped her face and chest.

"Use this," and I handed her the towel, "if it hits you again."

"I think I'm all right now," she gasped. I brought her a glass of water and held it to her lips. She shook her head to move her lips away from the glass.

"Oh, Harry, I'm so sick, so sick, so sick, so sick . . ."

"You'll be all right." I set the glass on the table.

"Are you mad at me, Harry?"

"What for?" I was surprised at the question.

"For going out and getting drunk the way I did."

"You were fairly drunk when I left."

"I know, but I shouldn't have gone out like that. That sailor . . . the sailor who was with me didn't mean a thing—"

"Forget it. Go back to sleep."

"Harry, you're the only one I've ever loved. I've never loved anyone but you. And if you got sore at me I don't know what I'd do."

"I'm not angry. Go to sleep."

"You get in bed too."

"Not right now. I'm busy."

"Please, Harry. Please?"

"I'm thinking. You know I'm not going to live very long, Helen. No driver. There isn't any driver, Helen, and the controls are set. And I don't know how long they're going to last."

"What are you talking about?"

"Just that I'm not going to live very long. I quit."

Helen threw the covers back, got out of bed and rushed over to me. I was standing flat-footed by the table. My feet could feel the world pushing up at me from below. Black old cinder. I laughed. Cooling on the outside, fire on the inside and nothing in between. It was easy to feel the world turn beneath my feet. Helen was on her knees, her arms were clasped about my legs. She was talking feverishly, and I put my hand on her head.

"What's the matter, Harry!" she cried. "Are you going to try to kill yourself again? Are you angry with me? Please talk to me! Don't look away like that . . ."

"Yes, Helen," I said calmly. "I'm going to kill myself."

Helen pulled herself up, climbing my body, using my clothes as handholds, pressing her naked body against mine. "Oh, darling, darling," she whimpered. "Let me go first! Don't go away and leave me all alone!"

"All right," I said. I picked her up and carried her to the bed. "I won't leave you behind. I wouldn't do that." I kissed her, stroked her hair. "Go on to sleep, now." Helen closed her eyes and in a moment she was asleep. The tear-streaked lines on her face were drying. I undressed and got into bed beside her. Now I could sleep. The machine would sleep, it would wake, it would do things, and then it would crash, out of control and destroy itself. But first it must run over the little body that slept by its side. The small, pitiful creature with the big sienna eyes and the silver streak in its hair.

As I fell asleep I heard music. I didn't have a radio, but it wasn't the type of music played over the radio anyway. It was wild, cacophonous, and there was an off-beat of drums pounding. My laugh was harsh, rasping. I continued to laugh and the salty taste in my mouth came from the unchecked tears running down my cheeks.

THIRTEEN

Dream World

IN MY DREAM I was running rapidly down an enormous piano keyboard. The white keys made music beneath my hurried feet as I stepped on them, but the black keys were stuck together with glue and didn't play. Trying to escape the discordant music of the white keys I tried to run on the black keys, slipping and sliding to keep my balance. Although I couldn't see the end of the keyboard I felt that I must reach the end and that it was possible if I could only run fast enough and hard enough. My foot slipped on a rounded black key and I fell heavily, sideways, and my sprawled body covered three of the large white keys with a sharp, harsh discord. The notes were loud and ugly. I rolled away from the piano keyboard, unable to stand, and fell into a great mass of silent, swirling, billowing yellow fog and floated down, down, down. The light surrounding my head was like bright, luminous gold. The gloves on my hands were lemon yellow chamois with three black stitches on the back of each hand. I disliked the gloves, but I couldn't take them off no matter how hard I tried. They were glued to my hands; the bright orange glue oozed out of the gloves around my wrists.

I opened my eyes and I was wide awake. My body was drenched with perspiration. I got out of bed without waking Helen, found and lighted a cigarette. My mouth was so dry the smoke choked me and tasted terrible. The perspiration, drying on my body, made me shiver with cold and I put my shirt and trousers on.

What a weird, mixed-up dream to have! I recalled each sequence of the dream vividly and it didn't make any sense at all. Helen, still asleep, turned and squirmed under the covers. She missed the warmth of my body and was trying to get close to me in her sleep. I crushed my foul-tasting cigarette in the ash-tray and tucked the covers in around Helen. I turned on the overhead light and sat down.

I felt calm and contented. It was time for Harry Jordan to have another cigarette. As though I sat in a dark theatre as a spectator somewhere I observed the quiet, studied actions of Harry Jordan. The exacting, unconscious ritual of putting the cigarette in his mouth, the striking of the match on his thumbnail, the slow withdrawal of smoke, the sensuous exhalation and the obvious enjoyment. The man, Harry Jordan, was a very collected individual, a man of the world. Nothing bothered him now. He was about to withdraw his presence from the world and depart on a journey into space, into nothingness. Somewhere, a womb was waiting for him, a dark, warm place where the living was easy, where it was effortless to get by. A wonderful place where a man didn't have to work or think or talk or listen or dream or cavort or play or use artificial stimulation. A kind old gentleman with a long dark cloak was waiting for him. Death. Never had Death appeared so attractive. . . .

I looked at Helen's beautiful face. She slept peacefully, her mouth slightly parted, her pretty hair tousled. I would take Helen with me. This unfeeling world was too much for Helen too, and without me, who would care for her, look after her? And hadn't I promised to take her with me?

I crushed my cigarette decisively and crossed to the bed.

"Helen, baby," I said, shaking her gently by the shoulder. "Wake up."

She stirred under my hand, snapped her eyes open, awake instantly, the perfect animal. She wore a sweet, sleepy smile.

"What time is it?"

"I don't know," I said, "but it's time." My face was as stiff as cardboard and it felt as expressionless as uncarved stone. I didn't know and didn't want to explain what I was going to do and I hoped Helen wouldn't ask me any questions. She didn't question me. Somehow, she knew instinctively. Perhaps she read the thoughts in my eyes, maybe she could see my intentions in the stiffness of my smile.

"We're going away, aren't we, Harry?" Helen's voice was small, childlike, yet completely unafraid.

Not daring to trust my voice, I nodded. Helen's trust affected me deeply. In that instant I loved her more than I had ever loved her before. Such faith and trust were almost enough to take the curse out of the world. Almost.

"All right, Harry. I'm ready." She closed her eyes and the sleepy winsome smile remained on her lips.

I put my hands around her slender neck. My long fingers interlaced behind her neck and my thumbs dug deeply into her throat, probing for a place to stop her breathing. I gradually increased the pressure, choking her with unrelenting firmness of purpose, concentrating. She didn't have an opportunity to make a sound. At first she thrashed about and then her body went limp. Her dark sienna eyes, flecked with tiny spots of gold, stared guilelessly at me and then they didn't see me any more. I closed her eyelids with my thumb, pulled the covers down and put my ear to her chest. No sound came from her heart. I straightened her legs and folded her arms across her chest. They wouldn't stay folded and I had to place a pillow on top of them before they would stay. Later on, I supposed, when her body stiffened with cold, her arms would stay in place without the benefit of the pillow.

My legs were weak at the knees and I had to sit down to stop their trembling. My fingers were cramped and I opened and closed my hands several times to release the tension. I had taken the irrevocable step and had met Death half-way. I could feel his presence in the room. It was now my turn and, with the last tugs of primitive self-preservation, I hesitated, my conscious mind casting about for a way to renege. But I knew that I wouldn't renege; it was unthinkable. It was too late to back out now. However, I didn't have the courage and trust that Helen had possessed. There was no one kind enough to take charge of the operation or do it for me. I had to do it myself, without help from anyone. But I had to have a little something to help me along . . .

I omitted the socks and slipped into my shoes. I couldn't control my hands well enough to tie the laces and I let them hang loose. I put my jacket on and left my room, locked the door, and left for the street. It was dismally cold outside; there were little patches of fog swirling in groups like lost ghosts exploring the night streets. The traffic signals at the corner were turned off for the night; only the intermittent blinking of the yellow caution lights at the four corners of the intersection lighted the lost, drifting tufts of fog. Although it was after one, Mr. Watson's delicatessen was still open. Its brightly colored window was a warm spot on the dark line of buildings. I crossed the street and entered and the tinkling bell above the door announced my entrance. Mrs. Watson was sitting in a comfortable chair by the counter reading a magazine. She was a heavy woman with orange-tinted hair and a faint chestnut moustache. She smiled at me in recognition.

"Hello, Harry," she said. "How are you this evening?"

"Fine, Mrs. Watson, just fine," I replied. I was glad that it was Mrs. Watson instead of her husband in the shop that morning. I wanted to talk to somebody and she was much easier to talk to than her husband. He was a German immigrant and it always seemed to me like he considered it a favor when he waited on me. I fished the two one dollar bills out of my watch pocket and smoothed them out flat on the counter.

"I think I'm getting a slight cold, Mrs. Watson," I said, coughing into my curled fist, "and I thought if I made a little hot gin punch before I went to bed, it might cut the phlegm a little bit."

"Nothing like hot gin for colds." Mrs. Watson smiled and got out of the chair to cross to the liquor shelves. "What kind?"

"Gilbey's is fine—I'd like a pint, but I don't think I have enough here . . ." I pointed to the two one dollar bills.

"I think I can trust you for the rest, Harry. It wouldn't be the first time." She dropped a pint of Gilbey's into a sack, twisted the top and handed it to me. I slipped the bottle into my jacket pocket. My errand was over and I could leave, but I was reluctant to leave the warm room and the friendly, familiar delicatessen smells. Death was waiting for me in my room. I had an appointment with him and I meant to keep it, but he could wait a few minutes longer.

"What are you reading, Mrs. Watson?" I asked politely, when she had returned to her chair after ringing a No Sale on the cash register and putting my money into the drawer.

"*Cosmopolitan.*" Her pleasant laugh was tinged with irony. "Boy meets girl, loses girl, gets girl. They're all the same, but they pass the time."

"That's a mighty fine magazine, Mrs. Watson. I read it all

the time, and so does my wife. Why, Helen can hardly wait for it to come out and we always argue over who gets to read it first and all that. Yes, I guess it's my favorite magazine and I wish it was published every week instead of every month! What month is that, Mrs. Watson? Maybe I haven't read it yet."

"Do you feel all right, Harry?" She looked at me suspiciously.

"Yes, I do." My voice had changed pitch and was much too high.

"You aren't drunk, are you?"

"No, I get a little talkative sometimes. Well, that's a good magazine."

"It's all right." Mrs. Watson's voice was impatient; she wanted to get back to her story.

"Well, good night, Mrs. Watson, and thanks a lot." I opened the door.

"That's all right, Harry. Good night." She had found her place and was reading before I closed the door.

As soon as I was clear of the lighted window I jerked the gin out of the sack, tossed the sack in the gutter, and unscrewed the cap from the bottle. I took a long pull from the bottle, gulping the raw gin down until I choked on it and hot tears leaped to my eyes. It warmed me through and my head cleared immediately. I crossed the street and walked back to the house. Sitting on the outside steps I drank the rest of the gin in little sips, controlling my impulse to down it all at once. I knew that if I tried to let it all go down my throat at once it would be right back up and the effects would be gone. I finished the bottle and tossed it into the hedge by the porch. My stomach had a fire inside it, but I was sorry I hadn't charged a fifth instead of only getting a pint.

I walked down the dimly lighted hall, unlocked my door and entered my room. It rather startled me, in a way, to see Helen in the same position I had left her in. Not that I had expected her to move; I hadn't expected anything, but to see her lying so still, and uncovered in the cold room, unnerved me. Again I wished I had another pint of gin. I started to work.

I locked the door and locked the window. There were three

old newspapers under the sink, and I tore them into strips and stuffed the paper under the crack at the bottom of the door. I opened both jets on the two-ring burner and they hissed full blast. I sniffed the odor and it wasn't unpleasant at all. It was sweet and purifying. By this time the gin had hit me hard, and I found myself humming a little tune. I undressed carefully and hung my clothes neatly in the closet. I lined my shoes up at the end of the bed. Tomorrow we would be found dead and that was that. But there wasn't any note. I staggered to the table and with a piece of charcoal I composed a brief note of farewell. There was no one in particular to address it to, so I headed it:

> *To Who Finds This:*
> *We did this on purpose. It isn't accidental.*

I couldn't think of anything else to put in the note and I didn't sign it because the charcoal broke between my fingers. Leaving the note on the table I crawled into bed beside Helen and pulled the covers up over us both. I had left the overhead light on purposely and the room seemed gay and cheerful. I took Helen in my arms and kissed her. Her lips were like cold rubber. When I closed my eyes the image of the light bulb remained. I tried to concentrate on other things to induce sleep. The black darkness of the outside street, the inky San Francisco bay, outside space and starless skies. There were other thoughts that tried to force their way into my mind but I fought them off successfully.

The faint hissing of the gas jets grew louder. It filled the room like a faraway waterfall.

I was riding in a barrel and I could hear the falls far away. It was a comfortable barrel, well-padded, and it rocked gently to and fro, comforting me. It floated on a broad stream, drifting along with the current. The roar of the falls was louder in my ears. The barrel was drifting closer to the falls, moving ever faster toward the boiling steam above the lips of the overhang. I wondered how far the drop would be. The barrel hesitated for a second, plunged downward with a sickening drop.

A big, black pair of jaws opened and I dropped inside. They snapped shut.

FOURTEEN

Awakening

THERE was a lot of knocking and some shouting. I don't know whether it was the knocking or the shouting that aroused me from my deep, restful slumbers, but I awoke, and printed in large, wavering red letters on the surface of my returning consciousness was the word for Harry Jordan: *FAILURE.* Somehow, I wasn't surprised. Harry Jordan was a failure in everything he tried. Even suicide.

The sharp little raps still pounded on the door and I could hear Mrs. McQuade's anxious voice calling, "Mr. Jordan! Mr. Jordan! Open the door."

"All right!" I shouted from the bed. "Wait a minute."

I painfully got out of bed, crossed to the window, unlocked it and threw it open. The cold, damp air that rushed in from the alley smelled like old laundry. The gas continued to hiss from the two open burners and I turned them off. Again the rapping and the call from Mrs. McQuade: "Open the door!"

"In a minute!" I replied. The persistent knocking and shouting irritated me. I slipped into my corduroy trousers, buckled my belt as I crossed the room, unlocked and opened the door. Mrs. McQuade and her other two star roomers, Yoshi Endo and Miss Foxhall, were framed in the doorway. It's a composition by Paul Klee, I thought.

I had always thought of Mrs. McQuade as a garrulous old lady with her hand held out, but she took charge of the situation like a television director.

"I smelled the gas," Mrs. McQuade said quietly. "Are you all right?"

"I guess so."

"Go stand by the window and breathe some fresh air."

"Maybe I'd better." I walked to the window and took a few deep breaths which made me cough. After the coughing fit I was giddier than before. I turned and looked at Endo and Miss Foxhall. "Won't you please come in?" I asked them stupidly.

Little Endo, his dark eyes bulging like a toad's in his flat

Oriental face, stared solemnly at Helen's naked figure on the bed. Miss Foxhall had covered her face with both hands and was peering through the lattice-work of her fingers. Mrs. McQuade examined Helen for a moment at the bedside and then she pulled the covers over the body and face. Pursing her lips, she turned and made a flat, quiet statement: "She's dead."

"Yes," I said. Just to be doing something, anything, I put my shirt on, sat down in the straight chair and pulled on my socks. A shrill scream escaped Miss Foxhall and then she stopped herself by shoving all her fingers into her mouth. Her short involuntary scream brought Endo out of his trance-like state and he grabbed the old spinster's arm and began to shake her, saying over and over again in a high, squeaky voice, "No, no! No, no!"

"Leave her alone," Mrs. McQuade ordered sharply. "I'll take care of her." She put an arm around Miss Foxhall's waist. "You go get a policeman." Endo turned and ran down the hall. I heard the outside door slam. As Mrs. McQuade led Miss Foxhall away, she said over her shoulder: "You'd better get dressed, Mr. Jordan."

"Yes, M'am." I was alone with Helen and the room was suddenly, unnaturally quiet. Automatically, I finished dressing, but my hands trembled so much I wasn't able to tie my neck-tie. I let it hang loosely around my neck, sat down in the straight chair after I donned my jacket.

Why had I failed?

I sat facing the door and I looked up and saw the transom. It was open. It wasn't funny but I smiled grimly. No wonder the gas hadn't killed me. The escaping gas was too busy going out over the transom and creeping through the house calling attention to Harry Jordan in the back bedroom. How did I let it happen? To hold the gas in the room I had shoved newspaper under the bottom of the door and yet I had left the transom wide open. Was it a primeval desire to live? plain stupidity? or the effects of the gin? I'll never know.

In a few minutes Endo returned to the room with a policeman. The policeman was a slim, nervous young man and he stood in the doorway covering me with his revolver. More than a little startled by the weapon I raised my arms over my head. The policeman bit his lips while his sharp eyes roved the room, sizing up the situation. He holstered the pistol and nodded his head.

"Put your arms down," he ordered. "Little suicide pact, huh?"

"No," I replied. "I killed her. Choked her to death." I folded my hand in my lap.

The young policeman uncovered Helen's head and throat and looked carefully at her neck. Endo was at his side and the proximity of the little Japanese bothered him. He pushed Endo roughly toward the door. "Get the hell out of here," he told Endo. Leaving the room reluctantly, Endo hovered in the doorway. Muttering under his breath, the policeman shut the door in Endo's face and seated himself on the foot of the bed.

"What's your name?" he asked me, taking a small, black notebook out of his hip pocket.

"Harry Jordan."

"Her name?" He jerked his thumb over his shoulder.

"Mrs. Helen Meredith."

"You choked her. Right?"

"Yes."

"And then you turned on the gas to kill yourself?"

"Yes."

"She doesn't looked choked."

"There's the note I left," I said pointing to the table. He crossed to the table and read my charcoaled note without touching it. He made another notation in his little black book, returned it to his hip pocket.

"Okay, okay, okay," he said meaninglessly. There was uncertainty in his eyes. "I've got to get my partner," he informed me. Evidently he didn't know whether to take me along or leave me in the room by myself. He decided on the latter and handcuffed me to the radiator and hurried out of the room, closing the door behind him. The radiator was too low for me to stand and I had to squat down. Squatting nauseated me, and I got down on my knees on the floor. There was a queasy feeling in the pit of my stomach and it rumbled, but I didn't get sick enough to throw up.

In a few minutes he was back with his partner. He was a

much older, heavier policeman, with a buff-colored, neatly trimmed mustache and a pair of bright, alert hazel eyes. The older man grinned when he saw me handcuffed to the radiator.

"Take the cuffs off him, for Christ sake!" he told the younger policeman. "He won't get away."

After the first policeman uncuffed me and returned the heavy bracelets to his belt, I sat down in the chair again. By leaning over and sucking in my stomach I could keep the nausea under control. It was much better sitting down. The younger policeman left the room to make a telephone call and the older man took his place at the foot of the bed. He crossed his legs and after he got his cigarettes out he offered me one. He displayed no interest in Helen's body at all. He lit our cigarettes and then smiled kindly at me.

"You're in trouble, boy," he said, letting smoke trickle out through his nose. "Do you know that?"

"I guess I am." I took a long drag and it eased my stomach.

"Relax, boy. I'm not going to ask you any questions. I couldn't care less."

"Would it be all right with you if I kissed her goodbye?" That question slipped out in a rush, but he seemed to be easygoing, and I knew that after the police arrived in force I wouldn't be able to kiss her goodbye. This would be my last chance. He scratched his mustache, got up from the bed and strolled across the room to the window.

"I suppose it's all right," he said thoughtfully. "What do you want to kiss her for?"

"Just kiss her goodbye. That's all." I couldn't explain because I didn't know myself.

"Okay." He shrugged his shoulders and looked out the window. "Go ahead."

Walking bent over I crossed to the bed and kissed Helen's cold lips, her forehead, and on the lips again. "Goodbye, sweetheart," I whispered low enough so the policeman couldn't hear me, "I'll see you soon." I returned to the chair.

For a long time we sat quietly in the silent room. The door opened and the room was filled with people. It was hard to believe so many people could crowd into such a small room. There were the two original uniformed policemen, two more in plainclothes, a couple of hospital attendants or doctors in white—Endo got back into the room somehow—Mrs. McQuade, and a spectator who had crowded in from the group in front of the house. A small man entered the room and removed his hat. He was almost bald and wore a pair of dark glasses. At his entrance the room was quiet again and the noise and activity halted. The young policeman saluted smartly and pointed to me.

"He confessed, Lieutenant," the young man said. "Harry Jordan is his name and she isn't his wife—"

"I'll talk to him," the little man said, holding up a white, manicured hand. He removed the dark glasses and put them in the breast pocket of his jacket, crooked his finger at me and left the room. I followed him out and nobody tried to stop me. We walked down the hall and he paused at the stairway leading to the top floor.

"Want a cigarette, Jordan?"

"No, sir."

"Want to tell me about it, Jordan?" he asked with his quiet voice. "I'm always a little leery of confessions unless I hear them myself."

"Yes, sir. There isn't much to tell. I choked her last night, and then I turned on the gas. It was a suicide pact, in a way, but actually I killed Helen because she didn't have the nerve to do it herself."

"I see. About what time did it happen?"

"Around one, or after. I don't know. By this time I would have been dead myself if I hadn't left the transom open."

"You willing to put all this on paper, Jordan, or are you going to get a shyster and deny everything, or what?"

"I'm guilty, Lieutenant, and I want to die. I'll cooperate in every way I can. I don't want to see a lawyer, I just want to be executed. It'll be easier that way all around."

"Then that's the way it'll be." He raised his hand and a plainclothesman came down the hall, handcuffed me to his wrist, and we left the rooming-house. A sizeable crowd had gathered on the sidewalk and they stared at us curiously as we came down the outside steps and entered the waiting police car. A uniformed policeman drove us to the city jail.

At the desk I was treated impersonally by the booking sergeant. He filled in my name, address, age and height and then asked me to dump my stuff on the desk and remove my belt and shoelaces. There wasn't much to put on the desk. A piece of string, a thin, empty wallet, a parking stub left over from the Continental Garage, a button and a dirty handkerchief were all I had to offer. I put them on the desk and removed my belt and shoelaces, added them to the little pile. The sergeant wrote my name on a large brown manila envelope and started to fill it with my possessions.

"I'd like to keep the wallet, Sergeant," I said. He went through it carefully. All it contained was a small snapshot of Helen taken when she was seven years old. The little snapshot showed a girl in a white dress and Mary Jane slippers standing in the sunlight in front of a concrete bird-bath. Her eyes were squinted against the sun and she stood pigeontoed, with her hands behind her back. Once in a while, I liked to look at it. The sergeant tossed me the wallet with the picture and I shoved it into my pocket.

I was fingerprinted, pictures were taken of my face, profile and full-face, and then I was turned over to the jailer. He was quite old, and walked with an agonized limp. We entered the elevator, were whisked up several floors, and then he led me down a long corridor to the shower room.

After I undressed and folded my clothes neatly on the wooden bench I got under the shower and adjusted the water as hot as I could stand it. The water felt wonderful. I let the needle streams beat into my upturned face. It sluiced down over my body, warming me through and through. I soaped myself roughly with the one-pound cake of dark-brown laundry soap, stood under the hot water again.

I toweled myself with an olive drab towel and dressed in the blue pants and blue work shirt that were laid out on the bench. The trousers were too large around the waist and I had to hold them up with one hand. I followed Mr. Benson the jailer to the special block and he opened the steel door and locked it behind us. We walked down the narrow corridor to the last cell. He unlocked the door, pointed, and I entered. He clanged the door to, locked it with his key. As he turned to leave I hit him up for a smoke. He passed a cigarette through the bars, lighted it for me with his Zippo lighter.

"I suppose you've had breakfast already," he said gruffly.

"No, but I'm not hungry anyway."

"You mean you couldn't stand a cup of coffee?"

"I suppose I could drink a cup of coffee all right."

"I'll get you one then. No use playing coy with me. When you want something you gotta speak up. I ain't no mind-reader."

He limped away and I could hear the slap-and-drag of his feet all the way down the corridor. While I waited for the coffee I investigated my cell. The walls were gray, freshly-painted, but the paint didn't cover all of the obscene drawings and initials beneath the paint where former occupants had scratched their records. I read some of the inscriptions: FRISCO KID '38, H. E., J. D., KILROY WAS HERE, Smoe, DENVER JACK, and others. Along the length of the entire wall, chest high, in two inch letters, someone had cut deeply into the plaster:

UP YOUR RUSTY DUSTY WITH A FLOY FLOY

This was very carefully carved. It must have taken the prisoner a long time to complete it.

A porcelain toilet, without a wooden seat, a washbowl with one spigot of cold water, and a tier of three steel beds with thin cotton pads for mattresses completed the inventory of the cell. No window. I unfastened the chains and let the bottom bunk down. I sat down on it and finished half my cigarette. Instead of throwing the butt away I put it into my shirt pocket. It was all I had. Presently, Mr. Benson came back with my coffee and passed the gray enameled cup through the bars.

"I didn't know whether you liked it with sugar and cream so I brought it black," he said.

"That's fine." I took the cup gratefully and sipped it. It was almost boiling hot and I had to let it cool some before I could finish it, but Mr. Benson waited patiently. When I passed him the empty cup he gave me a fresh sack of tobacco and a sheaf of brown cigarette papers.

"Know how to roll 'em, Jordan?"

"Sure. Thanks a lot." I made a cigarette.

"You get issued a sack every day, but no matches. If you want a light you gotta holler. Okay?"

"Sure." Mr. Benson lit my cigarette and limped away again

down the hollow-sounding corridor. The heavy end door clanged and locked.

The reaction set in quickly, the reaction to Helen's death, my attempt at suicide, the effects of the liquor, all of it. It was the overall cumulation of events that hit me all at once. My knees, my legs, my entire body began to shake violently and I couldn't control any part of it. The wet cigarette fell apart in my hand and I dropped to my knees in a praying position. I started to weep, at first soundlessly, then blubbering, the tears rolled down my cheeks, streamed onto my shirt. Perspiration poured from my body. I prayed:

"Dear God up there! Put me through to Helen! I'm still here, baby! Do you hear me! Please hang on a little while and wait for me! I'll be with you as soon as they send me! I'm all alone now, and it's hard, hard, hard! I'll be with you soon, soon, soon! I love you! Do you you hear me, sweetheart? I love you! I LOVE YOU!"

From one of the cells down the corridor a thick, gutteral voice answered mine: "And I love you, too!" The voice paused, added disgustedly: "Why don't you take a goddam break for Christ's sake!"

I stopped praying, or talking to Helen, whatever I was doing, and stretched out full length on the concrete floor. I stretched my arms out in front of me and pressed my mouth against the cold floor. In that prone position I cried myself out, silently, and it took a long time. I didn't try to pull myself together, because I knew that I would never cry again.

Afterwards, I washed my face with the cold tap water at the washbowl and dried my wet face with my shirt tail. I sat down on the edge of my bunk and carefully tailored another cigarette. It was a good one, nice and fat and round. Getting to my feet I crossed to the barred door.

"Hey! Mr. Benson!" I shouted. "How's about a light?"

FIFTEEN

Confession

LUNCH consisted of beef stew, rice, stewed apricots and coffee. After the delayed-action emotional ordeal I had undergone I was weak physically and I ate every scrap of food on
my aluminum tray. With my stomach full, for the first time in
weeks, I lay down on the bottom bunk, covered myself with
the clean gray blanket and fell asleep immediately.

Mr. Benson aroused me at four-thirty by rattling an empty
cup along the bars of my cell. It was time to eat again. The
supper was a light one; fried mush, molasses and coffee with
a skimpy dessert of three stewed prunes. Again I cleaned the
tray, surprised at my hunger. I felt rested, contented, better
than I had felt in months. My headache had all but disappeared and the peaceful solitude of my cell was wonderful.
Mr. Benson picked up the tray and gave me a book of paper
matches before he left. He was tired of walking the length of
the corridor to light my cigarettes. I lay on my back on the
hard bunk and enjoyed my cigarette. After I stubbed it out
on the floor I closed my eyes. When I opened them again it
was morning and Mr. Benson was at the bars with my breakfast. Two pieces of bread, a thimble-sized paper cupful of
strawberry jam and a cup of coffee.

About an hour after breakfast the old jailer brought a razor
and watched me shave with the cold water and the brown
laundry soap. In another hour he brought my clothes to the
cell. My corduroy slacks and jacket had been sponged and
pressed and were fairly presentable.

"Your shirt's in the laundry," he said, "but you can wear
your tie with the blue shirt."

"Where am I going?" I asked as I changed clothes.

"The D.A. wants to talk to you. Just leave them blue work
pants on the bunk. You gotta change when you get back anyways."

"Okay," I agreed. I tied my necktie as well as I could without a mirror, just as I had shaved without a mirror. I followed
Mr. Benson's limping drag down the corridor and this time I

took an interest in the other prisoners in the special block, looking into each cell as I passed. There were eight cells, all of them along one side facing the passage wall, but only two others in addition to mine were occupied with prisoners. One held a sober-looking middle-aged man sitting on his bunk staring at his steepled fingers, and the other held a spiky-haired, blond youth with a broken nose and one cocked violet eye. He cocked it at me as I passed the cell and his sullen face was without expression. I quickly concluded that he was the one who had mocked me the day before and I had an overwhelming desire to kick his teeth in.

A plainclothes detective, wearing his hat, met us at the end of the corridor, signed for me, cuffed me to his wrist and we walked down the hall to the elevator. We silently rode the elevator down to the third floor, got out, and walked down a carpeted hallway to a milk-glass door with a block-lettered inscription. Asst District Atty San Francisco. We entered the office and the detective removed the cuff and left the room. The office was small and shabbily furnished. There was a battered, oak desk, a shelf of heavy law books, four straight chairs and a row of hunting prints on the sepia-tinted wall across from the bookshelf. The prints were all of gentlewomen, sitting their horses impossibly and following hounds over a field-stone wall. All four prints were exactly the same. I sat down in one of the chairs and a moment later two men entered. The first through the door was a young man with a very white skin and a blue-black beard hovering close to the surface of his chin. It was the kind of beard that shows, because I could tell by the scraped skin on his jaws that he had shaved that morning. He wore a shiny, blue gabardine suit and oversized glasses with imitation tortoise-shell rims. Business-like, he sat behind the desk and studied some papers in a folder. The other man was quite old. He had lank white hair drooping down over his ears and there was a definite tremor in his long, talon-like fingers. His suit coat and trousers didn't match and he carried a shorthand pad and several sharpened pencils. It seemed unusual to me that the city would employ such an old man as a stenographer. His white head nodded rapidly up and down and it never stopped its meaningless bobbing through-

out the interview, but his deepset eyes were bright and alert
and without glasses.

The younger man closed the folder and shoved it into the
top drawer of his desk. His eyes fastened on mine and without
taking them away he extracted a king-sized cigarette from the
package on the desk, flipped the desk lighter and the flame
found the end of the cigarette perfectly. He did this little business without looking away from my eyes at all. A movie gangster couldn't have done it better. After three contemplative
drags on the cigarette he crushed it out in the glass ash-tray,
rested his elbows on the desk, cradled his square chin in his
hands and leaned forward.

"My name is Robert Seely." His voice was deep and resonant with a lot of college speech training behind it. "I'm one
of the assistant District Attorneys and your case has been assigned to me." He hesitated, and for a moment I thought he
was going to shake hands with me, but he didn't make such
an offer. He changed his steady gaze to the old man.

"Are you ready, Timmy?"

The old man, Timmy, held up his pencils and notebook in
reply.

"I want to ask you a few questions," Robert Seely said.
"Your name is . . . ?"

"Harry Jordan."

"And your residence?"

I gave him my roominghouse address.

"Occupation?"

"Art teacher."

"Place of employment?"

"Unemployed."

"What was the name of the woman you murdered?"

"Helen Meredith. Mrs. Helen Meredith."

"What was she doing in your room?"

"She lived there . . . the past few weeks."

"Where is her husband, Mr. Meredith?"

"I don't know. She said something once about him living
in San Diego, but she wasn't sure of it."

"Did Mrs. Meredith have another address here in the city?"

"No. Before she moved to San Francisco she lived with her

mother in San Sienna. I don't know that address either, but her mother's name is Mrs. Mathews. I don't know the first name."

"All right. Take one." He pushed the package of cigarettes across the desk and I removed one and lighted it with the desk lighter. Mr. Seely held the open package out to the ancient stenographer.

"How can I smoke and take this down too?" the old man squeaked peevishly.

"Why did you kill Mrs. Meredith?" Mr. Seely asked me.

"Well, I . . ." I hesitated.

"Before we go any further, Jordan, I think I'd better tell you that anything you say may be held against you. Do you understand that?"

"You should've told him that before," the old man said sarcastically.

"I'm handling this interview, Timmy," Mr. Seely said coldly. "Your job is to take it down. Now, Jordan, are you aware that what you say may be held against you?"

"Of course. I don't care about that."

"Why, then, did you kill Mrs. Meredith?"

"In a way, it's a long story."

"Just tell it in your own words."

"Well, we'd been drinking, and once before we'd tried suicide and it didn't work so we went to the hospital and asked for psychiatric help."

"What hospital was that?"

"Saint Paul's. We stayed for a week, that is, Helen was in a week. I was only kept for three days."

"How did you attempt suicide?"

"With a razor blade." I held my arms over the desk, showing him the thin red scars on my wrists. "The psychiatric help we received was negligible. We started to drink as soon as we were released from the hospital. Anyway, I couldn't work very well and drink too. The small amount of money I made wouldn't stretch and I was despondent all the time."

"And was Mrs. Meredith despondent, too?"

"She always took my moods as her own. If I was happy, she was happy. We were perfectly compatible in every respect—counterparts, rather. So that's how I happened to kill her, you see. She knew all along I was going to kill myself sooner or later and she made me promise to kill her first. So I did. Afterwards I turned on the gas. The next thing I knew, Mrs. McQuade—that's my landlady—was hollering and pounding on the door. My—Helen was dead and I wasn't." With food in my stomach and a good night's sleep and a cigarette in my hand it was easy for me to talk about it.

"I have your suicide note, Jordan, and I notice it's written in charcoal. In the back of your mind, did you have an idea you could rub the charcoal away in case the suicide didn't work? Why did you use charcoal?"

"I didn't have a pencil."

Timmy chuckled at my reply, avoided Mr. Seely's icy stare and bent over his notebook.

"Then the death of Mrs. Meredith was definitely premeditated?"

"Yes, definitely. I plead guilty to everything, anything."

"Approximately what time was it when you choked her?"

"I don't know exactly. Somewhere between one and two a.m. Right afterwards I went out and got a pint of gin at the delicatessen down the street. It must have been before two or it wouldn't have been open."

"What delicatessen?"

"Mr. Watson's. Mrs. Watson sold me the gin, though. I still owe her forty-three cents."

"All right. We'll check the time with her. The police arrested you at ten minutes after eight. If you actually intended to commit suicide, why did you leave your transom open?"

"I don't know. I must have forgot about it, I guess."

"Did you drink the pint of gin?"

"It was a cold night, and I needed something to warm me up."

"I see. Where did you teach art last? You said you were an—"

"Lately I've been working around town as a counterman or fry cook."

"Do you have a particular lawyer in mind? I can get in touch with one for you."

"No. I don't need a lawyer. I'm guilty and that's the way

I plead. I don't like to go through all this red tape. I expected to be dead by now and all these questions are inconvenient. The sooner I get it over with in the gas chamber the happier I'll be."

"Are you willing to sign a confession to that effect?"

"Certainly. I'll sign anything that'll speed things up."

"How did you and Mrs. Meredith get together in the first place?"

I thought the question over and decided it was none of his business.

Timmy's head stopped bobbing up and down and wagged back and forth from side to side for a change. "He doesn't have to answer questions like that, Mr. Seely," he said in his weak whining voice. The two men stared at each other distastefully and Timmy won the battle of the eyes.

"Have you got enough for a confession, Timmy?" Mr. Seely asked the old man, at last.

"Plenty." Timmy nodded his white head up and down.

"That's all I have then, Jordan," Mr. Seely said. "No. One more question. Do you want to complain you were mentally unstable at the time? Or do you think you're mentally ill now?"

"Of course not. I'm perfectly sane and I knew what I was doing at the time. I'd planned it for several weeks."

"You'd better put that in the confession, Timmy." Mr. Seely left the desk and opened the door. The detective was waiting in the hall. "You can return Jordan to his cell now," Mr. Seely told the detective.

I was handcuffed and taken back to the special block and turned over to Mr. Benson. Back in my cell I changed back to my jail clothes and Mr. Benson took my own clothes away on a wire coat hanger. I was alone in my quiet cell.

My mind was much more at ease than it had been before. Thinking back over the interview I felt quite satisfied that the initial step was taken and the ball rolling. Blind justice would filter in and get me sooner or later. It was pleasant to look forward to the gas chamber. What a nice, easy way to die! So painless. Silent and practically odorless and clean! I would sit in a chair, wearing a pair of new black trunks, and stare back at a few rows of spectators staring at me. I would hear nothing and smell nothing. Then I would be dead. When I writhed on the floor and went into convulsions I wouldn't even know about it. Actually, it would be a much more horrible experience for the witnesses than it would be for me. This knowledge gave me a feeling of morbid satisfaction. I had to laugh.

Soon it was time for lunch. Mr. Benson brought a tray to my cell containing boiled cabbage, white meat, bread and margarine, raspberry jello and black coffee. I attacked the food with relish. Food had never tasted better. My mind was relieved now that things were underway and I wasn't eating in a greasy cafe and I hadn't had to cook the food myself. I suppose that is why it all tasted so good. After wiping up the cabbage pot-licker with the last of my bread I rolled and smoked a cigarette. Mr. Benson took the tray away and was back in a few minutes with Old Timmy.

"I've got your confession ready, boy," the old man said.

Timmy signed for me and we left the block for the elevator. After Timmy pushed the button for the third floor, he turned and smiled at me, bobbing his head up and down.

"You aren't sensitive, are you, Jordan?"

"How do you mean," I asked, puzzled.

"Well, it isn't really necessary for me to take you downstairs to sign your confession, and when you aren't in the block you're supposed to wear regular clothes instead of these . . ." He plucked at my blue jail shirt. "And I'm supposed to have a police officer along too." He laughed thinly. "But some of the girls in the office wanted to get a look at you. Funny, the way these young girls go for the *crime passionell*. I didn't think you'd mind."

We walked down the carpeted hallway of the third floor and entered a large office that held five desks, each with telephone and typewriter. Old Timmy winked at me as I nervously looked at the nine women who had crowded into the office. They were all ages, but were still considered girls by Old Timmy.

"This is the steno pool," Timmy said as we crossed to his desk.

"I see it is," I replied.

"I been in charge of this office for thirty-one years." He

had seven neatly typed copies of my confession on his desk and I signed them all with a ball point pen. He called two of the girls over to sign on the witness lines and they came forward timidly and signed where he held his talon-like finger. I had the feeling if I said boo the girls would jump through the window. After they signed their names they rejoined the other women, and the silent group stared at me boldly as we left the office. As Timmy shut the door behind us I heard the foolish giggling begin and so did the old man.

"I hope it didn't bother you, boy," he said. "They're just women."

"Yes, I know," I replied meaninglessly.

We entered the elevator again and Timmy pushed the button and looked at me friendlily.

"What do you think of our brilliant Assistant District Attorney, the eminent Mr. Seely?" There were sharp overtones of sarcasm in his thin, whining voice.

"I don't think anything of him," I said. "That is, one way or the other," I amended.

"He's an ass!" Timmy said convincingly. "I'd like to assign him a case."

"It doesn't make any difference to me," I said.

"You should have read your confession, boy. It's iron-tight, you can bet on that. It's a good habit to get into, reading what you sign."

"I'm not making any more habits, good or bad," I said.

Timmy chuckled deep in his throat. "You're right about that!"

We reached the special block and I returned to the custody of Mr. Benson. He opened the heavy end door and Old Timmy shook hands with me before he left, bobbed his head up and down.

He turned away, head bobbing, hands jerking, and tottered down the corridor, his feet silent on the concrete floor.

I settled down in my cell to wait. I would be tried as a matter of course, convicted, and go to wait some more in the death row at San Quentin. There, after a prescribed period and on a specified date, I would be executed. And that was that.

I wondered how long it all would take.

SIXTEEN

Sanity Test

I DON'T know how long I waited in my quiet cell before I was taken out of it again. It might have been three days, four days or five days. There was no outside light, just the refulgent electric bulbs in my cell and in the corridor, and if it hadn't been for the meals, I wouldn't have known the time of day. I didn't worry about the time; I let it slip by unnoticed. I was fed and I was allowed to take a shower every day. And the forty slim cigarettes that can be rolled from a sack of Bull Durham were just enough to last me one full day. Mr. Benson let me have matches when I ran out, and I got by very well. After breakfast one morning, Mr. Benson brought my clothes down to my cell.

"Get dressed, Jordan," he told me, "you're going on a little trip."

"Where to?"

"Get dressed, I said."

My white shirt, stiffly starched, was back from the laundry. I tore off the cellophane wrapping, put it on, my slacks, tied my necktie. The jailer gave me my belt and shoelaces and I put the laces in my shoes, the belt through the trouser loops, slipped into my sports jacket.

"Don't you know where I'm going?" I asked.

"Of course I know. Hospital. Observation."

I hesitated at the door of my cell. "Hell, I'm all right. I don't want to go to any hospital for observation. I signed a confession; what more do they want?"

"Don't worry about it," Mr. Benson reassured me. "It's routine. They always send murder suspects to the hospital nowadays. It's one of the rules."

"It isn't just me then?"

"No. It's routine. Come on, I ain't got all day."

I followed him down the corridor, but my mind didn't ac-cept his glib explanation. I didn't believe my stay in the hos-pital would be very long, but I didn't want them to get any ideas that I was insane. That would certainly delay my case and I wanted to get it over with as soon as possible. Right then, I made up my mind to cooperate with the psychiatrist, no matter what it cost me in embarrassment. It wouldn't do at all to be found criminally insane and to spend the rest of my life in an institution.

The detective was the same one who had taken me downstairs for my interview with Mr. Seely. He still had his hat on, and after he signed for me, and we were riding down in the elevator, I took a closer look at him. He was big and tough looking, with the inscrutable look that old time criminals and old time policemen have in common. To be friendly, I tried to start a little conversation with the man.

"Those other two guys, the ones in the special block with me; what are they in for?" I asked him.

"What do you want to know for?"

"Just curious, I suppose."

"You prisoners are all alike. You get in trouble and you want to hear about others in the same fix. If it makes you feel any better, I'll tell you this: they're in a lot worse shape than you are."

We got out of the elevator in the basement and climbed into the back of a white ambulance that was waiting at the loading ramp. The window in back was covered with drawn gray curtains and I couldn't see anything on the way to the hospital. But on the way, the detective told me about the other two prisoners, and like he said, they were in worse shape than I was in. The blond young man had killed his mother with an ax in an argument over the car keys, and the middle-aged man had killed his wife and three children with a shotgun and then had lost his nerve and failed to kill himself. It made me ill to hear about the two men and I was sorry I had asked about them.

A white-jacketed orderly met us at the hospital's receiving entrance and signed the slip the detective gave him. He was a husky, young man in his early thirties and there was a broad smile on his face. His reddish hair was closely cropped in a fresh crew-cut and there was a humorous expression in his blue eyes. The detective uncuffed me, put the slip of paper in his pocket and winked at the orderly.

"He's your baby, Hank," he said.

"We'll take good care of him, don't worry," the orderly said good-naturedly and I followed him inside the hospital. We entered the elevator and rode it up to the sixth floor. Hank had to unlock the elevator door with a key before we could leave the elevator. As soon as we were in the hallway he locked the elevator door again and we left the hallway for a long narrow corridor with locked cells on both sides of it. He unlocked the door marked Number 3, and motioned for me to enter. It was a small windowless room and the walls were of unpainted wood instead of gray plaster. There were no bunks, just a mattress on the floor without sheets, and a white, neatly folded blanket at the foot. The door was made of thick, heavy wood, several layers thick, with a small spy-hole at eye-level, about the size of a silver dollar. Hank started to close the door on me and I was terrified, irrationally so.

"Don't!" I said quickly. "Don't shut me up, please! Leave it open, I won't try to run away."

He nodded, smiling. "All right, I'll leave it open a crack. I'm going to get you some pajamas and I'll be back in a few minutes. You start undressing." He closed the door partially and walked away.

I removed my jacket, shirt and pants, and standing naked except for my shoes I waited apprehensively for Hank's return. It wasn't exactly a padded cell, but it was the next thing to it. I was really frightened. For the first time I knew actual terror. There is a great difference between being locked in a jail cell and being locked in a madman's cell. At the jail I was still an ordinary human being, a murderer, yes, but a normal man locked up in jail with other normal men. Here, in addition to being a murderer, I was under serious suspicion, like a dangerous lunatic, under observation from a tiny spy-hole, not to be trusted. Mr. Benson must have lied to me. Evidently, they thought I was crazy. Why would they lock me away in such a room if they didn't think so? I wanted a cigarette to calm my fears, but I didn't dare call out for one or rap on the door. I was even afraid to look out the open door, afraid they would think I was trying to escape, and then I would be put into a padded cell for sure. From now on I would have to watch out for everything I did, everything I said. Full cooperation. That is what they would get from me. From now on.

The orderly returned with a pair of blue broadcloth pajamas, a thin white cotton robe and a pair of skivvy slippers.

"Shoes too, Harry," he said.

I sat down on the mattress, removed my shoes and socks and slid my feet into the skivvy slippers. He dropped my clothes into a blue sack and pulled the cords tight at the top. He had a kind face and he winked at me.

"Just take it easy, Harry," he said, "I'll be back in a minute."

It was a little better having something to cover my nakedness. Still, there is a psychological effect to hospital pajamas. Wearing them, a man is automatically a patient, and a patient is a sick man or he wouldn't be in a hospital. That was the way I saw it, the only way I could see it. Hank returned with a syringe and needle and took a blood sample from my right arm. When he turned to leave I asked him timidly for a cigarette.

"Why, shore," he said and reached into his jacket pocket. He handed me a fresh package of king-sized Chesterfields and I opened it quickly, stuck a cigarette in my mouth. He flipped his lighter for me and said: "Keep the pack." I was pleased to note that my hands had stopped shaking. "I can't give you any matches," Hank continued, "but anytime you want a light or want to go to the can, just holler. My name is Hank, and I'm at the end of the hall."

"Thanks, Hank," I said appreciatively. "It's nice to smoke tailor-mades again. I've been rolling them at the jail."

"They don't cost me nothing. And when you run out let me know. I can get all I want from the Red Cross." He started to leave with the blood sample, turned and smiled. "Don't worry about the door. I know it's a little rough at first, but I'm right down the hall and if you holler I can hear you. I'll shut the door, but I won't latch it. Knowing you aren't locked in is sometimes as good as an open door."

"Will you do that for me?" I asked eagerly.

"Why shore. This maximum security business is a lotta crap anyway. The elevator's locked, there's no stairs, and the windows are all barred, and the door to the roof's locked. No reason to lock your cell." He closed the door behind him, and he didn't lock it.

I sat down on the mattress, my back to the pine wall and chain-smoked three cigarettes. It gave me something to do. If the rest of the staff was as nice to me as Hank I would be able to survive the ordeal and I knew it would be an ordeal. My short stay at Saint Paul's had given me a sample, but now I would be put through the real thing. At noon, Hank brought me my lunch on a tray. There was no knife or fork and I had to eat the lunch with a spoon. The food was better than the jail food, pork chops, french fries and ice cream, but it almost gagged me to eat it. I forced myself to clean the tray and saved the milk for the last. I gulped the milk down with one long swallow, hoping it would clear away the food that felt caught in my throat. When Hank returned for the tray he gave me a light for my smoke. He was pleased when he saw the empty tray.

"That's the way, Harry," he nodded and smiled good-naturedly. "Eat all you can. A man feels better with a full gut. The doctor'll be back after a while and he'll talk to you then. Don't let him worry you. He's a weirdie. All these psychiatrists are a little nuts themselves."

"I'll try not to let it bother me," I said. "How long are they going to keep me here, anyway?"

"I don't know." He grinned. "That all depends."

"You mean it all depends on me?"

"That's right. And the doctor." He left with the tray, closing the door.

About one-thirty or two Hank returned for me and we left the cell and corridor and entered a small office off the main hallway. The office wasn't much larger than my cell, but it contained a barred window that let in a little sunlight. Through the window I could observe the blue sky and the bright green plot of grass in the park outside the hospital. The doctor was seated behind his desk and he pointed to the chair across from it.

"Sit down, Jordan," he said. "Hank, you can wait outside."

There was a trace of accent in his voice. German, maybe Austrian. It was cultivated, but definitely foreign. That is the way it is in the United States. A native born American can't make a decent living and here was a foreigner all set to tell me what was wrong with me. He had a swarthy sunlamp tan and his black beard was so dark it looked dyed. It was an Imperial beard and it made him resemble the early photographs of Lenin.

"Your beard makes you look like Lenin," I said.

"Why thank you, thank you!" He took it as a compliment. I distrusted the man. There is something about a man with a beard I cannot stand. No particular reason for it. Prejudice, I suppose. I feel the same way about cats.

"I'm Doctor Fischbach," the doctor said unsmilingly. "You're to be here under my observation for a few days." He studied a sheaf of papers, clipped together with large-sized paper clips, for a full five minutes while I sat there under pressure feeling the perspiration rolling freely down my back and under my arms to the elbows. He wagged his bearded chin from side to side, clucked sympathetically.

"Too bad you entered Saint Paul's for help, Jordan." He continued to shake his head. "If you and Mrs. Meredith had come to me in the first place you would have been all right."

"Yeah," I said noncommittally. "You may be right."

"Did Saint Paul's give you any tests of any kind? If so, we could obtain them and save the time of taking them over."

"No, I didn't get any tests—just blood tests."

"Then let us begin with the Rorschach." Dr. Fischbach opened his untidy top desk drawer, dug around in its depths and brought out a stack of cards about six inches by six inches and set them before me, Number One on top. "These are ink blots, Jordan, as you can see. We'll go through the cards one by one and you tell me what they remind you of. Now, how about this one?" He shoved the first card across the desk and I studied it for a moment or so. It looked like nothing.

"It looks like an art student's groping for an idea," I suggested.

"Yes?" he encouraged me.

"It isn't much of anything. Sometimes, Doctor, when an artist is stuck for an idea, he'll doodle around with charcoal to see if he can come up with something. The meaningless lines and mass forms sometimes suggest an idea, and he can develop it into a picture. That's what these ink blots look like to me."

"How about right here?" He pointed with his pencil to

one of the larger blots. "Does this look like a butterfly to you?"

"Not to me. No."

"What does it look like?"

"It looks like some artist has been doodling around with black ink trying to get an idea." How many times did he want me to tell him?

"You don't see a butterfly?" He seemed to be disappointed.

"No butterfly." I wanted to cooperate, but I couldn't see any point in lying to the man. It was some kind of a trick he was trying to pull on me. I stared hard at the card again, trying to see something, some shape, but I couldn't. None of the blots made a recognizable shape. I shook my head as he went on to the next card which also had four strangely shaped blots.

"Do these suggest anything?" he asked hopefully.

"Yeah," I said. If he wanted to trick me I would play one on him. "I see a chicken in a sack with a man on its back; a bottle of rum and I'll have some; a red-winged leek, and an oversized beak; a pail of water and a farmer's daughter; a bottle of gin and a pound of tin; a false-faced friend and days without end; a big brown bear and he's going everywhere; a big banjo and a—"

He jerked the cards from the desk and shoved them into the drawer. He looked at me seriously without any expression on his dark face and twisted the point of his beard with thumb and forefinger. My thin cotton robe was oppressively warm. I smiled, hoping it was ingratiating enough to please the doctor. Like all doctors, I knew, he didn't have a sense of humor.

"I really want to cooperate with you, Doctor," I said meekly, "but I actually can't see anything in those ink blots. I'm an artist, or at least I used to be, and as an artist I can see anything I want to see in anything."

"That's quite all right, Jordan," he said quietly. "There are other tests." When he got to his feet I noticed he was slightly humpbacked and I had a strong desire to rub his hump for good luck. "Come on with me." I followed him down the hall, Hank trailing us behind. We entered another small room that was furnished with a small folding table, typing paper and a battered, standard Underwood typewriter.

"Do you know how to typewrite, Jordan?" the doctor asked me.

"Some. I haven't typed since I left high school though."

"Sit down."

I sat down at the folding table and the doctor left the room. Hank lit a cigarette for me and before I finished it the doctor was back with another stack of cards. These were about eight by ten inches. He put the stack on the table and picked up the first card to show it to me. "You'll have fun with these."

The first picture was a reproduction of an oil painting in black and white. It was a portrait of a young boy in white blouse and black knickers. His hair was long, with a Dutch bob, and he had a delicate, wistful face. He held a book in his hand. From the side of the portrait a large hand reached out from an unseen body and rested lightly on the boy's shoulder. The background was an ordinary living room with ordinary, old-fashioned furniture. Table, chairs, potted plants and two vases full of flowers made the picture a bit cluttered.

"What I want you to do is this:" Dr. Fischbach explained, "Examine each picture carefully and then write a little story about it. Anything at all, but write a story. You've got plenty of paper and all the time in the world. After you finish with each one, put the story and picture together and start on the next one. Number the story at the top with the same number the picture has and they won't get mixed up. Any questions?"

"No, but I'm not much of a story teller. I don't hardly know the difference between syntax and grammar."

"Don't let that bother you. I'm not looking for polished prose, I merely want to read the stories. Get started now, and if you want to smoke, Hank'll be right outside the door to give you a light. Right, Hank?"

"Yes, sir," Hank replied with his customary smile.

They left the room and I examined the little print for a while and then put a piece of paper into the machine. It wasn't fun, as Dr. Fischbach had suggested, but it passed the time away and I would rather have something to do, anything, rather than sit in the bleak cell they had assigned me. I wrote that the young boy was sitting for his portrait and during the long period of posing he got tired and fidgety. The hand resting on his shoulder was that of his father and it was merely comforting the boy and telling him the portrait would soon be over. In a few lines I finished the dull tale.

Each picture I tackled was progressively impressionistic and it did become fun after all, once I got interested. The last three reproductions were in color, in a surrealistic vein, and they bordered on the uncanny and weird. However, I made up stories on them all, pecking them out on the old machine, even though some of the stories were quite senseless. When I finished, I racked stories and cards together and called Hank. He was down at the end of the hall talking to a nurse. He dropped the cards and stories off at the doctor's office and we started back to my cell. I stopped him.

"Just a second, Hank," I said. "Didn't you say something about a roof?"

"I don't know. We've got a roof," and he pointed toward a set of stairs leading up, right next to the elevator.

"After being cooped up so long," I said, "I'd like to get some fresh air. Do you suppose the doc would let me go up on the roof for a smoke before I go back to that little tomb? That is, if you go along."

"I'll ask him." Hank left me in the hall and entered the little office. He was smiling when he came out a moment later. "Come on," he said, taking my arm. We climbed the short flight of stairs and Hank unlocked the door to the roof.

The roof was black tar-paper, but near the little building that housed the elevator machinery and short stairwell to the sixth floor, there were about twenty feet of duckboards scattered around and a small green bench. It was late in the afternoon and a little chilly that high above the ground, but we sat and smoked on the bench for about an hour. Hank didn't mind sitting up there with me, because, as he said, if he was sitting around he wasn't working. He was an interesting man to talk to.

"How come you stay with this line of work, Hank?" I asked him.

"I drifted into it and I haven't drifted out. But it isn't as bad as it looks. There are a lot of compensations." He winked. "As a hot-shot male nurse, I rank somewhere between a doctor and an interne. I have to take orders from internes, but my pay check is about ten times as big as theirs, almost as big as some of the resident doctors. So the nurses, the lovely frustrated nurses, come flocking around, and I mean the female nurses. An interne doesn't make the dough to take them out and the doctors are married, or else they're too careful to get mixed up with fellow workers, you know, so I do all right. I get my own room right here, my meals, laundry and my money too. Funny thing about these nurses. They all look good in clean white uniforms and nice white shoes, but they look like hell when they dress up to go out. I've never known one yet who knew how to wear clothes on a date. They seem to be self-conscious about it too. But when the clothes come off, they're women, and that's the main thing with me. Did you see that nurse I was talking to in the hall?"

"I caught a glimpse of her."

"She'll be in my room tonight at eleven. So you see, Harry, taking care of nuts like you has its compensations." He slapped me on the knee. "Come on, let's go." He laughed happily and I followed him down the stairs.

For supper that night I ate hamburger patties and boiled potatoes, lime jello and coffee. The mental work of thinking up stories had tired me and I fell asleep easily. As Hank said, having the door unlocked was almost like not being locked in.

The next morning I had another session with Dr. Fischbach. It was an easy one and didn't last very long. He gave me a written intelligence test. The questions were all fairly simple; questions like: "Who wrote *Faust*?", "How do you find the circumference of a circle?", "Who was the thirty-second president?", and so on. In the early afternoon I was given a brainwave test. It was rather painful, but interesting. After I was stretched out on a low operating table, fifty or more needles were stuck into my scalp, each needle attached with a wire to a machine. A man pushed gadgets on the machine and it made flip-flop sounds. It didn't hurt me and I didn't feel any electric shocks, but it was a little painful when the needles were inserted under the skin of my scalp. All of this procedure seemed like a great waste of time and I hated the ascetic loneliness of my wooden cell. Sleeping on the mattress without any springs made my back ache.

The next few boring days were all taken up with more tests.

X-Rays were taken of my chest, head and back.

Urine and feces specimens were taken.

More blood from my arm and from the end of my fore-finger.

My eyes, ears, nose and throat were examined.

My teeth were checked.

At last I began my series of interviews with Dr. Fischbach and these were the most painful experiences of all.

SEVENTEEN

Flashback

DOCTOR Leo Fischbach sat humped behind his desk twirling the point of his beard with thumb and forefinger. I often wondered if his beard was perfumed. It seemed to be the only link or concession between the rest of the world and his personality. If he had a personality. His large brown eyes, fixed and staring, were two dark mirrors that seemed to hold my image without interest, without curiosity, or at most, with an impersonal interest, the way one is interested in a dead, dry starfish, found on the beach. I was tense in my chair as I chain-smoked my free cigarettes and the longer I looked at Dr. Fischbach, the more I hated him. My efforts at total recollection, and he was never satisfied with less, had exhausted me. I began to speak again, my voice harsh and grating to my ears.

"The war, if anything, Doctor, was only another incident in my life. A nice long incident, but all the same, just another. I don't think it affected me at all. I was painting before I was drafted and that's all I did after I got in."

"Tell me about this, er, incident."

"Well, after I was drafted I was assigned to Fort Benning, Georgia. And after basic training I was pulled out of the group to paint murals in the mess-halls there. I was quite happy about this and I was given a free hand. Not literally, but for the army it was a good deal. Naturally, I knew the type of pictures they wanted and that's what I gave them. If I'd attempted a few non-objective pictures I'd have been handed a rifle in a hurry. So I painted army scenes. Stuff like paratroopers dropping out of the sky, a thin line of infantrymen in the field, guns, tank columns and so on."

"Did this type of thing satisfy you? Did you feel you were sacrificing your artistic principles by painting this way?"

"Not particularly. If I thought of it at all I knew I had a damned good deal. I was painting while other soldiers were drilling, running obstacle courses and getting shot at somewhere or other. I missed all that, you see. As a special duty man I was excused from everything except painting."

"You didn't paint murals for the duration of the war, did you?"

"Not at Fort Benning, no. After a year I was transferred to Camp Gordon—that's in Georgia too, at Augusta."

"What did you do there?"

"I painted murals in mess-halls."

"Didn't you have any desire for promotion?"

"No. None at all. But they promoted me anyway. I was made a T/5. Same pay as corporal but no rank or responsibilities."

"How was your reaction to the army? Did you like it?"

"I don't know."

"Did you dislike it then?"

"I don't know. I was in the army. Everybody was in the army."

"How were you treated?"

"In the army everybody is the same. Nobody bothered me, because I was on special duty. Many times the officers would come around and inspect the murals I was working on. They were well pleased, very happy about them. Knowing nothing at all about art was to their advantage. On two different occasions I was given letters of commendation for my murals. Of course, they didn't mean anything. Officers like to give letters like that; they believe it is good for morale. Maybe it is, I don't know."

"What did you do in your off-duty time in Georgia?"

Again I had to think back. What had I done? All I could

remember was a blur of days, distant and hazy days. Pine trees, sand and cobalt skies. And on pay-days, gin and a girl. The rest of the month—days on a scaffolding in a hot wooden building, painting, doing the best I could with regular house paint, finishing up at the end of the day, tired but satisfied, grateful there was no sergeant to make me change what I had done. A shower, a trip to the first movie, bed by nine. Was there nothing else?

"Well, I slept a lot. It was hot in Georgia and I slept. I worked and then I hit the sack."

"When did you get discharged?"

"November, 1945. And then instead of returning to Chicago I decided to come out to California and finish art school out here."

"Why?"

"I must have forgotten to tell you about it. I had a wife and child in Chicago."

"Yes, you did." He made a note on his pad. He made his notes in a bastard mixture of loose German script and Speed-writing. "This is the first time you've mentioned a wife and child."

"It must have slipped my mind. It was some girl I married while I was attending the Chicago Art Institute. She has a child, a boy, that's right, a boy. She named him John, after her father. John Jordan is his name. I've never seen him."

"Why didn't you return to your wife and child? Didn't you want to see your son? Sometimes a son is considered a great event in a man's life."

"Is that right? I considered it an unnecessary expense. I came to California because it was the practical thing to do. If I'd gone to Chicago I wouldn't have been able to continue with my painting. It would have been necessary for me to go to work and support Leonie and the child. And I didn't want to do it."

"Didn't you feel any responsibility for your wife? Or to the child?"

"Of course I did. That's why I didn't go back. I didn't want to live up to the responsibility. It was more important to paint instead. An artist paints and a husband works."

"Where's your family now?"

"I imagine they're still in Chicago. After I left the army I didn't write to her any more."

"Do you have any curiosity about how they're faring?"

"Not particularly."

Curiosity. That was an ill-chosen word for him to use. I could remember my wife well. She was a strong, intelligent, capable young woman. She thought she was a sculptor, but she had as much feeling for form as a steel worker. She didn't like Epstein and her middle-western mind couldn't grasp his purported intentions. If a statue wasn't pretty she didn't like it. But she was good on the pointing-apparatus and a fair copyist. Her drawings were rough but solid, workmanlike. She would get by, anywhere. And my son was only an accident anyway. I certainly didn't want a child, and she hadn't either. But she had one and as long as he was with his mother, as he should be, he was eating. I had no doubt about that, and no curiosity.

"And then you entered the L.A. Art Center," Dr. Fischbach prodded.

"That's right. I attended the Center for almost a year, under the G.I. Bill."

"Did you obtain a degree?"

"Just an A.A. Things didn't go so well for me after the war. I had difficulty returning to my non-objective style and I was unable to finish any picture I started. I still can't understand it. I could visualize, to a certain extent, what my picture would look like on canvas, but I couldn't achieve it. I began and tossed aside painting after painting. The rest of my academic work was way above the average. It was easy to paint academically and I could draw as well as anybody, but that wasn't my purpose in painting."

"So you quit."

"You might say I quit. But actually, I was offered a teaching job at a private school. I weighed things over in my mind and decided to accept it. I thought I'd have more free time to paint and a place to work as an art teacher. The Center was only a place to paint and as a teacher I'd get more money than the G.I. Bill paid."

"What school did you teach at?"

"Mansfield. It's between Oceanside and San Diego. It's a rather conservative little school. There isn't much money in the endowment and the regents wouldn't accept state aid. There were about a hundred and thirty students and most of them were working their way through. It wasn't accredited under the G.I. Bill."

"How did you like teaching?"

"Painting can't be taught, Doctor. Either a man can paint or he can't. I felt that most of the students were being duped, cheated out of their money. It's one thing to study art with money furnished by a grateful government, but it's something else to pay out of your own pocket for something you aren't getting. And every day I was more convinced that I wasn't a painter and never would be one. After a while I quit painting altogether. But I hung onto my job at Mansfield because I didn't know what else to do with myself. Without art as an emotional outlet I turned to drinking as a substitute and I've been drinking ever since."

"Why did you leave Mansfield then?"

"I was fired. After I started to drink I missed a lot of classes. And I never offered any excuses when I didn't show up. In my spare time I talked to some of the more inept students and persuaded them to quit painting and go into something else. Somehow, the school didn't like that. But I was only being honest. I was merely balancing the praise I gave to the students who were good."

"After you were fired, did you come directly to San Francisco?"

"Not directly. It kind of took me by surprise, getting fired, I mean. They thought they had every reason to fire me, but I didn't expect it. I was one of the most popular teachers at the school, that is, with the students. But I suppose drinking had dulled my rational mind to the situation."

"And you felt persecuted?"

"Oh, no, nothing like that. After I got my terminal pay I thought things out. I wanted to get away from the city and things connected with culture, back to the land. Well, not back to it, because I'd never been a farmer or field hand, always in cities, you know. But at the time I felt if I could work in the open, using my muscles, doing really hard labor,

I'd be able to sleep again. So that's what I did. I picked grapes in Fresno, and around Merced. I hit the sugar beet harvests in Chico, drifted in season, over to Utah, and I spent an entire summer in the Soledad lettuce fields."

"Were you happier doing that type of work?"

"I was completely miserable. All my life I had only wanted to paint. There isn't any substitute for painting. Coming to a sudden, brutal stop left me without anything to look forward to. I had nothing. I drank more and more and finally I couldn't hold a field hand's job, not even in the lettuce fields. That's when I came to San Francisco. It was a city and it was close. In a city a man can always live."

"And you've been here ever since?"

"That's right. I've gone from job to job, drinking when I've had the money, working for more when I ran out."

I dropped my head and sat quietly, my hands inert in my lap. I was drained. What possible good did it do the doctor to know these things about me? How could this refugee from Aachen analyze my actions for the drifting into nothingness when I didn't know myself? I was bored with my dull life. I didn't want to remember anything; all I wanted was peace and quiet. The silence that Death brings, an all-enveloping white cloak of everlasting darkness. By my withdrawal from the world I had made my own little niche and it was a dreary little place I didn't want to live in or tell about. But so was Doctor Fischbach's and his world was worse than mine. I wouldn't have traded places with him for anything. He sat across from me silently, fiddling with his idiotic beard, his dark eyes on the ceiling, evaluating my story, probing with his trained mind. I pitied him. The poor bastard thought he was a god.

Did I? This nasty thought hit me below the belt. How else could I have taken Helen's life if I didn't think so? What other justification was there for my brutal murder? I had no right or reason to take her with me into my nothingness. Harry Jordan had played the part of God too. It didn't matter that she had wanted to go with me. I still didn't have the right to kill her. But I had killed her and I had done it as though it was my right, merely because I loved her. Well, it was done now. No use brooding about it. At least I had done it unconsciously and I had been under the influence of gin. Doctor Fischbach was a different case. He was playing god deliberately. This strange, bearded individual had gone to medical school for years, deliberately studied psychiatry for another couple of years. He had been psychoanalyzed himself by some other foreigner who thought he was a god—and now satisfied, with an ego as large as Canada, he sat behind a desk digging for filth into other people's minds. What a miserable bastard he must be behind his implacable beard and face!

"During your employment as a field hand, Jordan, did you have any periods when you felt highly elated, followed by acute depression?"

"No," I said sullenly.

"Did you ever hear voices in the night, a voice talking to you?"

"No."

"As you go about the city, have you ever had the feeling you were being followed?"

"Only once. A man followed me with a gun in his hand, but he didn't shoot me."

"You saw this man with the gun?"

"That's right, but when I looked over my shoulder he was gone."

He made some rapid, scribbling notes on his pad.

"Did you ever see him again?"

"No."

"So far, you've been reluctant to tell me about your sexual relations with Mrs. Meredith. I need this information. It's important that I know about it."

"Not to me it isn't."

"I can't see why you object to telling me about it."

"Naturally, you can't. You think you're above human relationship. To tell you about my intimate life with Helen is indecent. She's dead now, and I have too much respect for her."

"Suppose we talk then about other women in your life. Your wife, for instance. You don't seem to have any attachment for her, of any great strength. Did you enjoy a normal marital relationship?"

"I always enjoy it, but not half as much as you do second-hand."

"How do you mean that?"

I got to my feet. "I'd like to go back to my cell, Doctor," I said, forcing the words through my compressed lips. "I don't feel like talking any more."

"Very well, Jordan. We'll talk some more tomorrow."

"I'd rather not."

"Why not?"

"I don't like to waste the time. I'm not crazy and you know it as well as I do. And I resent your vicarious enjoyment of my life's history and your dirty probing mind."

"You don't really think I enjoy this, Jordan?" he said with surprise.

"You must. If you didn't you'd go into some other kind of work. I can't believe anybody would sink so low just for money. I've gone down the ladder myself, but I haven't hit your level yet."

"I'm trying to help you, Jordan."

"You can help somebody that needs it then. I don't want your help." I turned abruptly and left his office. Hank got up from the bench outside the door and accompanied me to my cell.

My cell didn't frighten me any longer. It was a haven, an escape from Dr. Fischbach. I liked its bareness, the hard mattress on the floor. It no longer mattered that I didn't have a chair to sit down upon. After a while I forced my churning mind into pleasant, happier channels. I wondered what they would have for supper.

I was hungry as hell.

EIGHTEEN

The Big Fixation

WHEN I was about seven or eight years old, somebody gave me a map of the United States that was cut up into a jigsaw

puzzle. Whether I could read or not at the time I don't remember, but I had sense enough to start with the water surrounding the United States. These were the pieces with the
square edges and I realized if I got the outline all around I
could build toward the center a state at a time. This is the
way I worked it and when I came to Kansas it was the last
piece and it fitted into the center in the last remaining space.
This was using my native intelligence and it was the logical
method to put a jigsaw puzzle together. Evidently, Doctor
Fischbach did not possess my native intelligence. He skipped
around with his questions as he daily dug for more revelations
from my past and he reminded me of a door-to-door salesman
avoiding the houses with the BEWARE OF THE DOG signs.
Having started with my relationship with Helen, dropping
back to my art school days, returning to my childhood, then
back to Helen, we were back to my childhood again. I no
longer looked him in the eyes as we talked together, but focused my eyes on my hands or on the floor. I didn't want to
let him see the hate in my eyes.

"Did your mother love you?" he asked me. "Did you feel
that you got all of the attention you had coming to you?"

"Considering the fact that I had two brothers and five sisters I got my share. More than I deserved anyway, and I'm
not counting two other brothers that were stillborn."

"Did you feel left out in any way?"

"Left out of what?"

"Outside of the family. Were you always fairly treated?"

"Well, Doctor, money was always short during the depression, naturally, what with the large family and all, but I always
got my share. More, if anything. My father showed partiality
to me; I know that now. He thought I was more gifted than
my brothers and sisters."

"How did your father support the family? What type of
work did he do? Was he a professional man?"

"No. He didn't have a profession, not even a trade. He
contributed little, if anything, to our support. He worked
once in a while, but never steady. He always said that his boss,
whoever it happened to be at the time, was giving him the
dirty end of the stick. He had a very strong sense of justice
and he'd quit his job at the first sign of what he termed un-

fairness or prejudice. Even though the unfairness happened to someone else, he'd quit in protest."

"How about drinking? Did your father drink?"

"I don't know."

"Please try to remember. There might be some incidents. Surely you know whether he drank or not."

"Listen, Doctor, it was still prohibition when he was alive. I don't remember ever seeing him take a drink. And when he went out at night I was too small to go with him. So if he drank I don't know about it."

"If he didn't support your family, who did?"

"Mother. She was a beauty operator and she must have been a good one, because she always had a job. Ever since I can remember. She had some kind of a new system, and women used to come to our house on Sundays, her off-day, for treatments. It seemed to me that she never had any free time."

"What are your brothers and sisters doing now?"

"I suppose they're working. Father died first and then about a year later my mother died. From that time on we were on our own."

"How old were you then, when your mother died?"

"Sixteen."

"Weren't there any relatives to take you in with them?"

"We had relatives, yes. My mother's brother, Uncle Ralph, gathered us all together in his house about a week after her funeral. He had the insurance money by that time and it was divided equally between us. My share was two hundred and fifty dollars, which was quite a fortune in the depression. My uncle and aunt took my smallest sister to live with them, probably to get her two-fifty, but the rest of us were on our own. I got a room on the South Side, a part time job, and finished high school. I entered the Art Institute as soon as I finished high school. Luckily, I was able to snag a razor-blade-and-condom concession and this supported me and paid my tuition. I studied at the institute until I was drafted, and I've told you about my experiences in the army already."

"Sketchily."

"I told you all I could remember. I wasn't a hero. I was an ordinary soldier like all the draftees. I had a pretty good break, yes, but that was only because I had the skill to paint and also because the army gave me the opportunity to use my skill. Many other soldiers, a hell of a lot more talented than I was, were never given the same breaks."

"Do you have any desire to see your brothers and sisters again?"

"They all live in Chicago, Doctor. We used to have a saying when we were students in L.A.—'A lousy artist doesn't go to heaven or hell when he dies; his soul goes to Chicago.' If that saying turns out to be true, I'll be seeing them soon enough."

"How about sex experiences? Did you ever engage in sex-play with your brothers and sisters?" His well-trained words marched like slugs into the cemetery of my brain. He asked this monstrous question as casually as he asked them all. Appalled, I stared at him unbelievingly.

"You must have a hell of a lot of guts to ask me a filthy question like that!" I said angrily. "What kind of a person do you think I am, anyway? I've confessed to a brutal murder— I'm guilty—I've said I was guilty! Why don't you kill me? Why can't I go to the gas chamber? What you've been doing to me can be classified as cruel and inhuman treatment, and as a citizen I don't have to take it! How much do you think I can stand?" I was on my feet by this time and pounding the doctor's desk with my fists. "You've got everything out of me you're going to get!" I finished decisively. "From now on I'll tell you nothing!"

"What is it you don't want to tell me, Jordan?" he asked quietly, as he calmly twisted the point of his beard.

"Nothing. I've told you everything that ever happened to me. Not once, but time and time again. Why do you insist on asking the same things over and over?"

"Please sit down, Jordan." I sat down. "The reason I ask you these questions is because I haven't much time. I have to return you to the jail tomorrow—"

"Thank God for small favors!" I cut him off.

"So I've taken some unethical short cuts. I know it's most unfair to you and I'm sorry. Now. Tell me about your sex-play with your brothers and sisters."

"My brothers and I all married each other and all my sisters are lesbians. We all slept together in the same bed, including my mother and father and all of us took turns with each other. The relationship was so complicated and the experiences were so varied, all you have to do is attach a medical book of abnormal sex deviations to my file and you'll have it all. Does that satisfy your morbid curiosity?" This falsehood made me feel ashamed.

"You're evading my question. Why? Everything you tell me is strictly confidential. I only ask you these things to enable me to give a correct report—"

"From now on I'm evading you," I said. I got up from my chair and opened the door. Hank, as usual, was waiting for me outside, sitting on the bench. As I started briskly, happily, toward my cell, Hank fell in behind me. My mind was relieved, my step was airy, because I never intended to talk to Dr. Fischbach again. I didn't look back and I've never seen the doctor since.

That afternoon I was so ashamed of myself and so irritable I slammed my fists into the pine wall over and over again. I kept it up until my knuckles hurt me badly enough to get my mind on them instead of the other thoughts that boiled and churned inside my head. After a while, Hank opened the door and looked in on me. There was a wide smile on his lips.

"There's a lot of noise in here. What's going on, Harry?"

"It's that damned doctor, Hank," I said. I smiled in spite of myself. Hank had the most infectious smile I've ever seen.

"Let me tell you something, Harry," Hank said seriously, and he came as close to not smiling as he was able to do, "you've got to keep a cool stool. It don't go for a man to get emotionally disturbed in a place like this. Speaking for myself, I'll tell you this much; you'll be one hell of a lot better off in the gas chamber than you'd ever be in a state institution. Have you ever thought of that?"

I snorted. "Of course I've thought of it. But I'm not insane. You know it and so does the doctor."

"That's right, Harry. But besides working here, I've worked in three different state institutions. And I've seen guys a hell of a lot saner than you in all three of them." This remark made him laugh.

"I'm all right," I told him.

"The way to prove it is to keep a cool stool."

"I guess you're right. Doctor Fischbach says I go back to jail tomorrow. And if he's halfway fair he'll turn in a favorable report on me, Hank. Up till today, anyway, I've cooperated with him all the way."

"I know you have, Harry. Don't spoil it. It must be pretty rough, isn't it?"

"I've never had it any rougher."

He winked at me conspiratorily. "How'd you like to have a drink?" He held up his thumb and forefinger an inch apart.

"Man, I'd love one," I replied sincerely.

Hank reached into his hip-pocket and brought out a half-pint of gin. He unscrewed the cap and offered me the bottle. I didn't take it. Was this some kind of trap? After all, Hank was a hospital employee, when all was said and done. Sure, he had been more than nice to me so far, but maybe there had been a purpose to it, and this might be it. How did I know it was gin in the bottle? It might be some kind of dope, maybe a truth serum of some kind? It might possibly be Fischbach's way of getting me into some kind of a jam. I knew he didn't like me.

"No thanks, Hank," I said. "Maybe I'd better not."

Hank shrugged indifferently. "Suit yourself." He took a long swig, screwed the cap back on and returned the bottle to his hip pocket. He left my cell and slammed and locked the door. I was sorry I hadn't taken the drink. It might have made me feel better, and by refusing, I had hurt Hank's feelings. But it didn't make any difference. My problems were almost over. Tomorrow I would be back in jail. It would be almost like going home again.

That night I couldn't sleep. After twisting and turning on the uncomfortable mattress until eleven, I gave up the battle and banged on the door for the nurse. The night nurse gave me a sleeping pill without any argument, but even then it was a long time before I got to sleep. The next morning Hank brought me my breakfast on a tray. If he was still sore at me he didn't give any indication of it.

"This'll be your last meal here, Harry," he said, smiling.

"That's the best news I've had since I got here," I said. "Hank, I'm really sorry about not taking that drink you offered me yesterday. I was upset, nervous, and—"

"It doesn't bother me, Harry. I just thought you'd like a little shot."

"After a man's been in this place a while, he gets so he doesn't trust anybody."

"You're telling me!" He opened the door and looked down the corridor, turned and smiled broadly. "I found out something for you, Harry. Last night I managed to get a look at your chart, and Doctor Fischbach is reporting you as absolutely sane. In his report he stated that you were completely in possession of your faculties when you croaked your girl friend."

"That's really good news. Maybe Doctor Fischbach's got a few human qualities after all."

"I thought it would make you happy," Hank said pleasantly.

"What about the Sanity Board you were telling me about the other day? Won't I have to meet that?"

"Not as long as Fischbach says you're okay. He classified you as neurotic depressive, which doesn't mean a damn thing. The Sanity Board is for those guys who have a reasonable doubt. You're all right."

I tore into my breakfast with satisfaction. Now I could go back to the special block safe in the knowledge I would go to the gas chamber instead of the asylum. Hank was in a talkative mood and he chatted about hospital politics while I finished my breakfast, brought me another cup of coffee when I asked for it.

"Now that I'm leaving, Hank," I said, "tell me something. Why is it that I never get a hot cup of coffee? This is barely lukewarm."

He laughed. "I never give patients hot coffee. About two years ago I was taking a pot of hot coffee around the ward giving refills and I asked this guy if he wanted a second cup. 'No,' he says, so I said, 'Not even a half a cup?' and he says, 'Okay.' So I pours about a half-cup and he says, 'A little more.' I pours a little more, and he says, 'More yet.' This time I filled his cup all the way. He reached out then, grabbed my waistband and dumped the whole cupful of hot coffee inside my pants! Liked to have ruined me. I was in bed for three days with second degree burns!"

I joined Hank in laughter, not because it was a funny story, but he told it so well. He finished with the punch line:

"Ever since then I've never given out with hot coffee."

Hank lit my cigarette and we shook hands. He picked up my tray.

"I want to wish you the best of luck, Harry," he said at the door. "You're one of the nicest guys we've had in here in a long time."

"The same goes for you, Hank," I said sincerely. "You've made it bearable for me and I want you to know I appreciate it."

More than a little embarrassed, he turned away with the tray and walked out, leaving the door open. Smitty, another orderly, brought me my clothes and I changed into them quickly. Smitty unlocked the elevator and we rode down to the receiving entrance and I was turned over to a detective in a dark gray suit. I was handcuffed and returned to the jail in a police car instead of an ambulance. I was signed in at the jail and Mr. Benson returned me to my cell, my old cell.

Wearing my blue jail clothes again and stretched out on my bunk, I sighed with contentment. I speculated on how long it would be before the trial. It couldn't be too long, now that the returns were in; all I needed now, I supposed, was an open date on the court calendar. If I could occupy myself somehow, it would make the time pass faster. Maybe, if I asked Mr. Benson, he would get me a drawing pad and some charcoal sticks. I could do a few sketches to pass away the time. It was a better pastime than reading and it would be something to do.

That afternoon, right after lunch, I talked to Mr. Benson, and he said he would see what he could do . . .

NINETEEN

Portrait of a Killer

IT MUST have been about an hour after breakfast. The daily breakfast of two thick slices of bread and the big cup of black coffee didn't always set so well. Scrambled eggs, toast, and a glass of orange juice would have been better. No question about it; I had eaten better at the hospital. The two lumps of dough had absorbed the coffee and the mess felt like a full sponge in my stomach. Somebody was at my door and I looked up. It was Mr. Benson. He had a large drawing pad and a box of colored pencils in his hand. The old man was smiling and it revealed his worn down teeth, uppers and lowers. He stopped smiling the moment I looked at him.

"I bought you this stuff outa my own pocket," he said gruffly. "You can't lay around in here forever doin' nothin'." He passed the pad and pencil box through the bars and I took them.

"Thanks a lot, Mr. Benson," I said. "How'd you like to have me do your portrait? That is, after I practice up a little."

"You pretty good?"

"I used to be, and you've got an interesting face."

"What do you mean by that!" he bridled.

"I mean I'd enjoy trying to draw you."

"Oh." His face flushed. "I guess I wouldn't mind you doin' a picture of me. Maybe some time this afternoon?"

"Any time."

I practiced and experimented with the colored pencils all morning, drawing cones, blocks, trying for perspective. I would rather have had charcoal instead of colored pencils, I like it much better, but maybe the colored pencils gave me more things to do. The morning passed like a shot. I hadn't lost my touch, if anything, my hand was steadier than it had been before.

Mr. Benson held out until mid-afternoon, and then he brought a stool down the corridor and seated himself outside my cell. For some reason, a portrait, whether a plain drawing or a full-scale painting, is the most flattering thing you can do for a person. I've never met a person yet who didn't want an artist to paint his portrait. It is one of the holdovers from the nineteenth century that enables artists who go for that sort of thing to eat. A simple drawing, or a painting should always be done from life to be worthwhile. But this doesn't prevent an organization in New York from making thousands of dollars weekly by having well-known artists paint portraits from photographs that are sent in from all over the United States. If the person has enough money, all he has to do is state what artist he wants and send in his photographs. The artists who do this type of work are a hell of a lot hungrier for money than I ever was.

I didn't spend much time with Mr. Benson. I did a profile view and by doing a profile it is almost impossible not to get a good likeness. By using black, coral, and a white pencil for the highlights, I got the little drawing turned out well and Mr. Benson was more than pleased.

"What do I owe you, Harry?" he asked, after I tore the drawing from the pad and gave it to him.

"Nothing," I laughed. "You're helping me kill time, and besides you bought me the pad and pencils."

"How about a dollar?"

"No." I shook my head. "Nothing."

"Suit yourself." He picked up his stool and left happily with his picture.

Mr. Benson must have spread the word or showed his picture around. In the next three days I did several more drawings. Detectives came up to see me and they would sit belligerently, trying to cover their embarrassment while I whipped out a fast profile. They all offered me money, which I didn't accept, but I never refused a pack of cigarettes. The last portrait I did was that of a young girl. She was one of the stenos from the filing department, well-liked by Mr. Benson, and he let her in. She was very nervous and twitched on the stool while I did a three-quarter view. I suppose she was curious to see what I looked like, more than anything else, but it didn't matter to me. Drawing was a time-killer to me. I gave her the completed drawing and she hesitated outside my cell.

"You haven't been reading the papers have you, ah, Mr. Jordan?" she asked nervously.

"No."

She was about twenty-one or -two with thin blonde hair, glasses, and a green faille suit. Her figure was slim, almost slight, and she twisted her long, slender fingers nervously. "I don't know whether to tell you or not, but seeing you don't read the papers, maybe I'd better . . ."

"Tell me what?" I asked gently.

"Oh, it just makes me sore, that's all!" she said spiritedly. "These detectives! Here you've been decent enough to draw their pictures for nothing, and they've been selling them to the newshawks in the building. All of the papers have been running cuts, and these detectives have been getting ten dollars or more from the reporters."

"The reporters have been getting gypped then," I said, controlling my sudden anger.

"Well I think it's dirty, Mr. Jordan, and I just wanted you to know that I'm going to keep my picture."

"That's fine. Just tell Mr. Benson I'm not doing any more portraits. Tell him on your way out, will you please?"

"All right. Don't tell anybody I told you . . . huh?"

"No, I won't say anything. I'm not sore about them selling the pictures," I told her. "It's just that they aren't good enough for publication."

"*I* think they are." She gave me two packages of Camels and tripped away down the corridor. At first I was angry and then I had to laugh at the irony of the situation. Ten dollars. Nobody had ever paid me ten dollars for a picture. Of course, I had never priced a painting that low. The few I had exhibited, in the Chicago student shows, had all been priced at three hundred or more dollars, and none of them had sold. But anyway, no more portraits from Harry Jordan. The cheap Harry Jordan integrity would be upheld until the last sniff of cyanide gas. . . . Again I laughed.

The following afternoon, Mr. Benson opened the cell door and beckoned to me. He led me through a couple of corridors and into a small room sparsely furnished with a bare scratched desk, a couple of wooden chairs and, surprisingly, a leather couch without arms, but hinged at one end so that the head of it could be raised. It was the kind of a couch you sometimes see in psychiatrists' offices and doctors' examining rooms. "What's this?" I said.

"Examining room," he said, as I'd expected. I started to get angry. He left the room, moving rather furtively, I thought, and he shut the door, locking it on the outside. After a couple of minutes the door opened again. It was that stenographer.

She walked in, her arms full of the drawing stuff I had left in my cell. The door closed behind her and I heard the lock click again, shutting us in. I couldn't figure it out.

She was looking at me, kind of breathlessly. She put the colored pencils and stuff down on the desk. "I want you to draw me again," she said.

"I don't know as I want to do any more drawing."

"Please."

"Why in here?"

"You don't understand. I want you to draw me in the nude."

I looked at her. It was warm in the room, and there was plenty of light streaming in from the high, barred windows. The bars threw interesting shadows across her body. It was a good place to draw or paint, all right. But that wasn't what she wanted. I knew that much.

I sat woodenly. She laughed, kicked off her shoes, lay back on the couch. I could tell she was a little scared of me, but liking it. "I'll be pretty in the nude," she said. "I'll be wonderful to draw." She lifted a long and delicately formed leg and drew off the stocking. She did the same for her other leg. I could see that her thighs were a trifle plump. They were creamy-white, soft-looking, but the rest of her legs, especially around the knees, were faintly rosy.

She flicked a glance at me, to see what my response was. I had not moved. I was just standing there, watching. She stood up, made an eager, ungraceful gesture that unloosed a clasp, or a zipper or something. Her skimpy green skirt fell to the floor. She hesitated then, like a girl about to plunge into a cold shower, but took a deep breath, then quickly undid her blouse. It fell to the floor with the skirt. Another moment and her slip was off, and the wisps of nylon that were her underthings. I smelled their faint perfume in the warm room. She lifted her arms over her head and pirouetted proudly. "See?" she said. "See?"

I had not noticed before, even when I had been drawing her, how pretty she was. Maybe she was the kind of girl whose beauty only awakes when her clothes are off. I examined her thoughtfully, trying to think of her as a problem in art. Long legs. Plump around the hips and thighs. Narrow, long waist.

Jutting bosom, a trifle too soft, too immature. Her face was narrow and bony, but attractive enough. The lips were full and red. Her corn-colored hair fell in a graceful line to her shoulders.

"You fixed this up?" I said.

She was tense and excited. "Me and Mr. Benson," she said. "Nobody will bother us here." She giggled.

This would be the last time, I was thinking. I would never have another chance at a woman. Not on this earth.

"Don't look so surprised," she said. "All kinds of things go on in a place like this. It's just a question of how much money and influence a person has. You don't have money, and neither do I—but I've got the influence—" She giggled again. Like a high school kid. Was this her first adventure with a man, I wondered.

I sat down on the hard leather couch.

"Come here," I said.

She sat down on my lap.

I started by kissing her. First her silky hair. Then her soft parted lips. Then her neck, her shoulders, lower . . . "Harry," she said. "Harry!"

My arm was around her waist, and her skin felt creamy and smooth. I tilted her back, swinging her off my knees so that she lay supine on the couch. I stroked and kissed and fondled, slowly and easily at first, then faster and harder. Much harder. She began to breathe deeply. She was scared. I kissed her neck, at the same time taking her by the hair and drawing her head back.

"Harry," she said. "What are you going to do to me?"

"You're frightened, aren't you? That's part of the thrill. That's what you want, isn't it? To do it with a freak. A dangerous freak. And a murderer!"

"I want you, Harry!"

She was panting. She threw her arms around me, and her nails clawed my shoulders. It was my head that was pulled down now, and she was smothering me with lipstick and feverish kisses. This was the moment I had been waiting for. The moment when she would be craving ecstasy. I lifted my hand and, as hard as I could, slapped her in the face.

But instead of looking at me with consternation and fear

and disappointment, she giggled. Damn her, in her eyes I was just living up to expectations. This was what she had come for!

In cold disgust, I hit her with my fist, splitting her lip so that the blood ran. The blow rolled her from the couch to the floor. For a moment I pitied her bare, crumpled body, but as soon as the breath got back into her she sprang to her feet. I was standing now, too. She flung her arms around me in a desperate embrace. "I can't bear it. Please, Harry!"

I knocked her down again.

"Please, Harry! Now . . . Now . . . !"

"You slut. I loved a real woman. To her, I was no strange, freakish creature. She didn't come to me for cheap thrills. Get your clothes on!"

I picked up one of the chairs and swung at the door with it.

"Let me out of here," I shouted, pounding the door. "God damn it, let me out!"

Mr. Benson came, and shamefacedly opened the door. The girl, her clothes on, ran sobbing down the corridor. Mr. Benson looked at me.

"I'm sorry, Harry. I thought I was doing you a favor."

I never did find out the girl's name.

The next day was Sunday. After a heavy lunch of baked swordfish and boiled potatoes I fell asleep on my bunk for a little afternoon nap. The jailer aroused me by reaching through the bars and jerking on my foot. It wasn't Mr. Benson; it was the Sunday man, Mr. Paige.

"Come on, Jordan," he said, "wake up. You gotta visitor." Mr. Paige sold men's suits during the week, but he was a member of the Police Reserve, and managed to pick up extra money during the month by getting an active duty day of pay for Sunday work. At least, that is what Mr. Benson told me.

"I'm too sleepy for visitors," I grumbled, still partly asleep. "Who is it anyway?"

"It's a woman," he said softly, "a Mrs. Mathews." I could tell by the expression on his face and his tone of voice he knew Mrs. Mathews was Helen's mother. "Do you want to see her?"

I got off the bed in a hurry. No. Of course I didn't want to see her. But that wasn't the point. She wanted to see me and I couldn't very well refuse. She had every right to see the murderer of her daughter.

"Do you know what she wants to see me about?" I asked Mr. Paige.

He shook his head. "All I know, she's got a pass from the D.A. Even so, if you don't want, you don't have to talk to her."

"I guess it's all right. Give me a light." He lit my cigarette for me and I took several fast drags, hoping the smoke would dissipate my drowsiness. Smoking, I stood close to the barred door, listening nervously for the sound of Mrs. Mathews' footsteps in the corridor. And I heard her long before I saw her. Her step was strong, resolute, purposeful. And she appeared in front of the door, Mr. Paige, the jailer, behind her and slightly to one side.

"Here's Harry Jordan, ma'am. You can't go inside the cell, but you can talk to him for five minutes." I was grateful for the time limit Mr. Paige arbitrarily imposed. He turned away, walked a few steps down the corridor, out of earshot, beyond my range of vision.

Mrs. Mathews was wearing that same beaver coat, black walking shoes, and a green felt, off-the-face hat. Her gray hair was gathered and piled in a knot on the back of her neck. She glared at me through her gold-rimmed glasses. Her full lips curled back, showing her teeth, in a scornful, sneering grimace of disgust. There was a bright gleam of hatred in her eyes, the unreasoning kind of hate one reserves for a dangerous animal, or a loose snake. She made me extremely nervous, looking at me that way. My hands were damp and I took them away from the bars, wiped my palms on my shirt. As tightly as I could, I gripped the bars again.

"It was nice of you to come and visit me, Mrs. Mathews . . ." I said haltingly. She didn't reply to my opening remark and I didn't know what else to say. But I tried.

"I'm sorry things turned out the way they did," I said humbly, "but I want you to know that Helen was in full accord with what I did. It was the way Helen wanted it . . ." My throat was tight, like somebody was holding my windpipe, and

I had to force the words out of my mouth. "If we had it all to do over again, maybe things would have worked out differently . . ."

Mrs. Mathews worked her mouth in and out, pursed her lips.

"I've pleaded guilty, and—" I didn't get to finish my sentence.

Without warning, Mrs. Mathews spat into my face. Involuntarily, I jerked back from the bars. Ordinarily, a woman is quite awkward when she tries to spit. Mrs. Mathews was not. The wet, disgusting spittle struck my forehead, right above my eyebrows. I made no attempt to wipe it off, but came forward again, and tightly gripped the bars. I waited patiently for a stream of invective to follow, but it didn't come. Mrs. Mathews glared at me for another long moment, sniffed, jerked her head to the right, turned and lumbered away.

I sat down on my bunk, wiped off my face with the back of my hand. My legs and hands were trembling and I was as weak as if I had climbed out of a hot Turkish bath.

My mind didn't function very well. Maybe I had it coming to me. At least in her eyes, I did. I didn't know what to think. The viciousness and sudden fury of her pointless action had taken me completely by surprise. But how many times must I be punished before I was put to death? I don't believe I was angry, not even bitter. There was a certain turmoil inside my chest, but it was caused mostly by my reaction to her intense hatred of me. In addition to my disgust and loathing for the woman I also managed to feel sorry for her and I suspected she would suffer later for her impulsive action. After she reflected, perhaps shame would come and she would regret her impulsiveness. It was like kicking an unconscious man in the face. But on the other hand, she had probably planned what she would do for several days. I didn't want to think about it. Mr. Paige was outside the door and there was a contrite expression on his face.

"She didn't stay long," he said.

"No. She didn't."

"I saw what she did," Mr. Paige said indignantly. "If I'd have known what she was up to I wouldn't have let her in, even if she did have a pass from the D.A."

"That's all right, Mr. Paige. I don't blame you; I don't blame anybody. But if she comes back, don't let her in again. I don't want to see her any more. My life is too short."

"Don't worry, Jordan. She won't get in again!" He said this positively. He walked away and I was alone. I washed my face with the brown soap and cold water in my wash basin a dozen times, but my face still felt dirty.

The next day my appetite was off. I tried to draw something, anything, to pass the time away, but I couldn't keep my mind on it. Mr. Paige had told Mr. Benson what had happened and he had tried to talk to me about it, and I cut him off quickly. I didn't feel like talking. I lay on my back all day long, smoking cigarettes, one after another, and looking at the ceiling.

On Tuesday, I had another visitor. Mr. Benson appeared outside my cell with a well-fed man wearing a brown gabardine Brooks Brothers suit and a blue satin vest. His face was lobster red and his larynx gave him trouble when he talked. Mr. Benson opened the door and let the man into my cell.

"This is Mr. Dorrell, Jordan," the old jailer said. "He's an editor from *He-Men Magazine* and he's got an okay from the D.A.'s office so I gotta let him in for ten minutes."

"All right," I said, and I didn't move from my reclining position. There were no stools or chairs and Mr. Dorrell had to stand. "What can I do for you, Mr. Dorrell?" I asked.

"I'm from *He-Men*, Mr. Jordan," he began in his throaty voice. "And our entire editorial staff is interested in your case. To get directly to the point—we want an 'as-told-to' story from you, starting right at the beginning of your, ah, relationship with Mrs. Meredith."

"No. That's impossible."

"No," he smiled, "it isn't impossible. There is a lot of interest for people when a woman as prominent in society as Mrs. Meredith gets, shall we say, involved?"

"Helen wasn't prominent in society."

"Maybe not, not as you and I know it, Mr. Jordan. But certain places, like Biarritz, for instance, Venice, and in California, San Sienna, are very romantic watering places. And the doings of their inhabitants interests our readers very much."

"My answer is no."

"We'll pay you one thousand dollars for such an article."

"I don't want a thousand dollars."

"You might need it."

"What for?"

"Money comes in handy sometimes," he croaked, "and the public has a right to know about your case."

"Why do they?" I asked belligerently. "It's nobody's business but my own!"

"Suppose you consider the offer and let us know later?"

"No. I won't even consider it. I don't blame you, Mr. Dorrell. You've got a job to do. And I suppose your readers would get a certain amount of morbid enjoyment from my unhappy plight, and possibly, more copies of your magazine would be bought. But I can't allow myself to sell such a story. It's impossible."

"Well, I won't say anything more." Mr. Dorrell took a card out of his wallet and handed it to me. "If you happen to change your mind, send me a wire. Send it collect, and I'll send a feature writer to see you and he'll bring you a check, in advance."

At the door he called for Mr. Benson. The jailer let him out of the cell and locked the door again. The two of them chatted as they walked down the corridor and I tore the business card into several small pieces and threw them on the floor. If Mr. Dorrell had been disappointed by my refusal he certainly didn't show it. What kind of a world did I live in, anyway? Everybody seemed to believe that money was everything, that it could buy integrity, brains, art, and now, a man's soul. I had never had a thousand dollars at one time in my entire life. And now, when I had an opportunity to have that much money, I was in a position to turn it down. It made me feel better and I derived a certain satisfaction from the fact that I could turn it down. In my present position, I could afford to turn down ten thousand, a million . . .

I didn't eat any supper that evening. After drinking the black coffee I tried to sleep but all night long I rolled and tossed on my narrow bunk. From time to time I dozed, but I always awakened with a start, and my heart would violently pound. There was a dream after me, a bad dream, and my sleeping mind wouldn't accept it. I was grateful when morning came at last. I knew it was morning, because Mr. Benson brought my breakfast.

After breakfast, when I took my daily shower, I noticed the half-smile on the old jailer's face. He gave me my razor, handing it in to me as I stood under the hot water, and not only did I get a few extra minutes in the shower, I got a better shave with the hot water. As I toweled myself I wondered what was behind the old man's smile.

"What's the joke, Mr. Benson?" I asked.

"I've got news for you, Jordan, but I don't know whether it's good or bad." His smile broadened.

"What news?"

"You're being tried today."

"It's good news."

He brought me my own clothes and I put them on, tied my necktie as carefully as I could without a mirror. I had to wait in my cell for about a half-hour and then I was handcuffed and taken down to the receiving office and checked out. My stuff was returned and I signed the envelope to show that I had gotten it back. All of it. Button, piece of string, handkerchief, and parking stub from the Continental Garage. As the detective and I started toward the parking ramp the desk sergeant called out to the officer. We paused.

"He's minimum security, Jeff."

Jeff removed the handcuffs and we climbed into the waiting police car for the short drive to the Court House.

TWENTY

Trial

I WAITED in a small room adjacent to the courtroom. It was sparsely furnished; just a small chipped wooden table against the wall and four metal chairs. I stood by the window, looking down three stories at the gray haze of fog that palled down over the civic center. A middle-aged uniformed policeman was stationed in the room to stand guard over me, and he leaned against the wall by the door, picking at the loose threads of the buttonholes on his shiny Navy blue serge uniform. There was nothing much to see out of the window, only the fog, the dim outlines of automobiles with their lights on, in the street below, a few walking figures, their sex indistinguishable, but I looked out because it was a window and I hadn't been in a room with a window for a long time. One at a time I pulled at my fingers, cracking the joints. The middle finger of my left hand made the loudest crack.

"Don't do that," the policeman said. "I can't stand it. And besides, cracking your knuckles makes them swell."

I stopped popping my fingers and put my hands in my trousers pockets. That didn't feel right, so I put my hands in my jacket pockets. This was worse. I let my arms hang, swinging them back and forth like useless pendula. I didn't want to smoke because my mouth and throat were too dry, but I got a light from the policeman and inhaled the smoke into my lungs, even though it tasted like scraped bone dust. Before I finished the cigarette there was a hard rapping on the door and the policeman opened it.

A round, overweight man with a shiny bald head bounced into the room. He didn't come into the room, he "came on," like a TV master of ceremonies. There was a hearty falseness to the broad smile on his round face and his eyes were black and glittering, almost hidden by thick, sagging folds of flesh. His white hands were short, white, and puffy, and the scattering of paprika freckles made them look unhealthily pale. I almost expected him to say, "A funny thing happened to me on the way over to the court house today," but instead of saying anything he burst into a contagious, raucous, guffawing laugh that reverberated in the silence of the little room. It was the type of laughter that is usually infectious, but in my solemn frame of mind I didn't feel like joining him. After a moment he stopped abruptly, wiped his dry face with a white handkerchief.

"You are Harry Jordan!" He pointed a blunt fat finger at me.

"Yes, sir," I said.

"I'm Larry Hingen-Bergen." He unbuttoned his double-breasted tweed coat and sat down at the little table. He threw his battered briefcase on the table before him and indicated, by pointing to another chair, that he wanted me to sit down. I pulled up a chair, sat down, and faced him diagonally. "I'm your defense counsel, Jordan, appointed by the court. I suppose you wonder why I haven't been to see you before this?" He closed his eyes, while he waited for my answer.

"No. Not particularly, Mr. Hingen-Bergen. After I told the District Attorney I was guilty, I didn't think I'd need a defense counsel."

His eyes snapped open, glittering. "And you don't!" He guffawed loudly, with false heartiness. "And you don't!" He let the laugh loose again, slapped his heavy thigh with his hand. "You!" he pointed his finger at my nose, "are a very lucky boy! In fact," his expression sobered, "I don't know how to tell you how lucky you are. You're going to be a free man, Jordan."

"What's that?" I asked stupidly.

"Free. Here's the story." He related it in a sober, businesslike manner. "I was assigned to your case about two weeks ago, Jordan. Naturally, the first thing I did was have a little talk with Mr. Seely. You remember him?"

I nodded. "The Assistant D.A."

"My visit happened to coincide with the day the medical report came in. Now get a grip on yourself, boy. Helen Meredith was not choked to death, as you claimed; she died a natural death!" He took a small notebook out of his pocket. It was a long and narrow notebook, fastened at the top, covered with green imitation snakeskin, the kind insurance salesmen give away whether you buy any insurance or not. I sat dazed, tense, leaning forward slightly while he leafed through the little book. "Here it is," he said, smiling. "Coronary thrombosis. Know what that is?"

"It isn't true!" I exclaimed.

He gripped my arm with his right hand, his voice softened. "I'm afraid it is true, Jordan. Of course, there were bruises on her neck and throat where your hands had been, but that's all they were. Bruises. She actually died from a heart attack. Did she ever tell you she had a bad heart?"

I shook my head, scarcely hearing the question. "No. No,

she didn't. Her mother said something about it once, but I didn't pay much attention at the time. And I can't believe this, Mr. Hingen-Bergen. She was always real healthy; why she didn't hardly get a hangover when she drank."

"I'm not making this up, Jordan." He tapped the notebook with the back of his fat fingers. "This was the Medical Examiner's report. Right from the M.E.'s autopsy. There's no case against you at all. Now, the reason the D.A. didn't tell you about this was because he wanted to get a full psychiatrist's report first." Mr. Hingen-Bergen laughed, but it was a softer laugh, kind. "You *might* have been insane, you know. He had to find out before he could release you."

My mind still wouldn't accept the situation. "But if I didn't actually kill her, Mr. Hingen-Bergen, I must have at least hastened her death! And if so, that makes me guilty, doesn't it?"

"No," he replied flatly. "She'd have died anyway. I read the full M.E. report. She was in pretty bad shape. Malnutrition, I don't remember what all. You didn't have anything to do with her death."

The middle-aged policeman had been attentively following the conversation. "By God," he remarked, "this is an interesting case, Mr. Hingen-Bergen!"

"Isn't it?" The fat lawyer smiled at him. He turned to me again. "Now, Jordan, we're going into the court room and Mr. Seely will present the facts to the judge. He'll move for a dismissal of the charges and you'll be free to go."

"Go where?" My mind was in a turmoil.

"Why, anywhere you want to go, naturally. You'll be a free man! Why, this is the easiest case I've ever had. Usually my clients go to jail!" He laughed boisterously and the policeman joined him. "You just sit tight, Jordan, and the bailiff'll call you in a few minutes." He picked his briefcase up from the table and left the room.

I remained in my chair, my mind numb. If this was true, and evidently it was—the lawyer wouldn't lie to me right before the trial—I hadn't done anything! Not only had I fumbled my own suicide, I'd fumbled Helen's death too. I could remember the scene so vividly. I could remember the feel of her throat beneath my thumbs, and the anguish I had undergone . . . and all of it for nothing. Nothing. I covered my face with my hands. I felt a hand on my shoulder. It was the policeman's hand and he tried to cheer me up.

"Why, hell, boy," he said friendly, "don't take it so hard. You're lucky as hell. Here . . ." I dropped my hands to my lap. The policeman held out a package of cigarettes. "Take one." I took one and he lighted it for me. "You don't want to let this prey on your mind. You've got a chance to start your life all over again. Take it. Be grateful for it."

"It was quite a shock. I wasn't ready for it."

"So what? You're out of it, forget it. Better pull yourself together. You'll be seeing the judge pretty soon."

The bailiff and Mr. Hingen-Bergen came for me and took me into the court room. I'd never seen a regular trial before. All I knew about court room procedure was what I had seen in movies; and movie trials are highly dramatic, loud voices, screaming accusations, bawling witnesses, things like that. This was unlike anything I'd ever seen before. Mr. Hingen-Bergen and I joined the group at the long table. The judge sat at the end wearing his dark robes. And he was a young man, not too many years past thirty; he didn't look as old as Mr. Seely. Mr. Seely sat next to the judge, his face incompliant behind his glasses. It was a large room, not a regular court-room, and there were no spectators. A male stenographer, in his early twenties, made a fifth at the table. The bailiff leaned against the door, smoking a pipe.

Mr. Seely and the judge carried on what seemed to be a friendly conversation. I didn't pay any attention to what they were saying; I was waiting for the trial to get started.

"The Medical Examiner couldn't make it, your honor," Mr. Seely said quietly to the judge, "but here's his report, if that's satisfactory."

There was a long period of silence while the judge studied the typewritten sheets. The judge slid the report across the desk to Mr. Seely, and the Assistant District Attorney put it back inside his new cowhide briefcase. The judge pursed his lips and looked at me for a moment, nodding his head up and down soberly.

"I believe you're right, Mr. Seely," he said softly. "There's really no point in holding the defendant any longer. The case is dismissed." He got to his feet, rested his knuckles on the desk and stared at me. I thought he was going to say something to me, but he didn't. He gathered his robes about him, lifting the hems clear of the floor, and Mr. Hingen-Bergen and I stood up. He left the courtroom by a side door. Mr. Seely walked around the table and shook hands with me.

"I've got some advice for you, Jordan," Mr. Seely said brusquely. "Keep away from liquor, and see if you can find another city to live in."

"Yes, sir," I said.

"That's good advice," Mr. Hingen-Bergen added.

"Of course," Mr. Seely amended gravely, "you don't *have* to leave San Francisco. Larry can tell you that." He looked sideways at my fat defense counsel. "You're free to live any place you want to, but I believe my advice is sound."

"You bet!" Mr. Hingen-Bergen agreed. "Especially, not drinking. You might end up in jail again if you go on a bat."

"Thanks a lot," I said vaguely.

I didn't know what to do with myself. Mr. Seely and the bailiff followed the young stenographer out of the room and I was still standing behind the table with Mr. Hingen-Bergen. He was stuffing some papers into various compartments of his briefcase. I had been told what to do and when to do it for so long I suppose I was waiting for somebody to tell me when to leave.

"Ready to go, Jordan?" Mr. Hingen-Bergen asked me, as he hooked the last strap on his worn leather bag.

"Don't I have to sign something?" It all seemed too unreal to me.

"Nope. That's it. You've had it."

"Then I guess I'm ready to go."

"Fine. I'll buy you a cup of coffee."

I shook my head. "No thanks. I don't believe I want one."

"Suit yourself. What are your plans?"

Again I shook my head bewilderedly. "I don't know. This thing's too much of a surprise. I still can't grasp it or accept it, much less formulate plans."

"You'll be all right." He laughed his coarse hearty laugh. "Come on."

Mr. Hingen-Bergen took my arm and we left the court

room, rode the elevator down to the main floor. We stood on the marble floor of the large entrance way and he pointed to the outside door, the steep flight of stairs leading down to the street level.

"There you are, Jordan," the lawyer smiled. "The city."

I nodded, turned away and started down the steps. Because of the heavy fog I could only see a few feet ahead of me. I heard footsteps behind me and turned as Mr. Hingen-Bergen called out my name.

"Have you got any money?" the lawyer asked me kindly.

"No, sir."

"Here." He handed me a five dollar bill. "This'll help you get started maybe."

I accepted the bill, folded it, put it into my watch pocket.

"I don't know when I'll be able to pay you back . . ." I said lamely.

"Forget it! Next time you get in jail, just look me up!" He laughed boisterously, clapped me on the shoulder and puffed up the stairs into the court house.

I continued slowly down the steps and when I reached the sidewalk, turned left toward Market. I was a free man.

Or was I?

TWENTY-ONE

From Here to Eternity

AFTER I left the Court House I walked for several blocks before I realized I was walking aimlessly and without a destination in mind. So much had happened unexpectedly I was in a daze. The ugly word, "Freedom" overlapped and crowded out any nearly rational thoughts that tried to cope with it. Freedom meant nothing to me. After the time I had spent in jail and in the hospital, not only was I reconciled to the prospect of death, I had eagerly looked forward to it. I wanted to die and I deserved to die. But I was an innocent man. I was free. I was free to wash dishes again, free to smash baggage, carry a waiter's tray, dish up chile beans as a counterman. Free.

The lights on the marquee up ahead advertised two surefire movies. Two old Humphrey Bogart pictures. It was the Bijou Theatre and I had reached Benny's Bijou Beanery. This was where it had started. I looked through the dirty glass of the window. Benny sat in his customary seat behind the cash register and as I watched him he reached into the large jar of orange gum drops on the counter and popped one into his mouth. The cafe was well-filled, most of the stools taken, and two countermen were working behind the counter. Just to see the cafe brought back a vivid memory of Helen and the way she looked and laughed the night she first entered. I turned away and a tear escaped my right eye and rolled down my cheek. A passerby gave me a sharp look. I wiped my eyes with the back of my hand and entered the next bar I came to. Tears in a bar are not unusual.

The clock next to the mouldy deer antlers over the mirror read ten-fifty-five. Except for two soldiers and a B-girl between them, the bar was deserted. I went to the far end and sat down.

"Two ounces of gin and a slice of lemon," I told the bartender.

"No chaser?"

"Better give me a little ice water."

I was in better physical condition than I had enjoyed in two or three years, but after my layoff I expected the first drink to hit me like a sledge hammer. There was no effect. The gin rolled down my throat like a sweet cough syrup with a codeine base. I didn't need the lemon or the water.

"Give me another just like it," I said to the bartender.

After three more my numb feeling disappeared. I wasn't drunk, but my head was clear and I was able to think again. Not that it made any difference, because nothing mattered anymore. I unfolded the five dollar bill Mr. Hingen-Bergen had given me, paid for the drinks and returned to the street. There was a cable car dragging up the hill and it slowed down at my signal. I leaped aboard for the familiar ride to my old neighborhood and the roominghouse. I could no longer think of the ride as going home. Although the trip took a long while it seemed much too short. At my corner, I jumped down.

The well-remembered sign, BIG MIKE'S BAR & GRILL, the twisted red neon tubing, glowed and hummed above the double doors of the saloon. This was really my home, mine and Helen's. This was where we had spent our only really happy hours; hours of plain sitting, drinking, with our shoulders touching. Hours of looking into each other's eyes in the bar mirror. As I stood there, looking at the entrance, the image of Helen's loveliness was vivid in my mind.

Rodney, the crippled newsboy, left his pile of papers and limped toward me. There was surprise in his tired face and eyes.

"Hello, Harry," he said, stretching out his arm. I shook his hand.

"Hello, Rodney."

"You got out of it, huh?"

"Yes."

"Congratulations, Harry. None of us around here really expected you—I mean, well . . ." His voice trailed off.

"That's all right, Rodney. It was all a mistake and I don't want to talk about it."

"Sure, Harry. I'm glad you aren't guilty." Self-conscious, he bobbed his head a couple of times and returned to his newspapers. I pushed through the swinging doors and took the first empty seat at the bar. It was lunch hour and the bar and cafe were both busy; most of the stools were taken and all of the booths. As soon as he saw me, Big Mike left the cash register and waddled toward me.

"The usual, Harry?" he asked me quietly.

"No. I don't want a drink."

Mike's face was unfathomable and I didn't know how he would take the news.

"I didn't kill her, Mike. Helen died a natural death. It was a mistake. That's all."

"I'm glad." His broad face was almost stern. "Let's have one last drink together, Harry," he said, "and then, I think it would be better if you did your drinking somewhere else."

"Sure, Mike. I understand."

He poured a jigger of gin for me and a short draught beer for himself. I downed the shot quickly, nodded briefly and left the bar. So Big Mike was glad. Everybody was glad, everybody was happy, everybody except me.

The overcast had yarded down thickly and now was a dark billowing fog. Soon it would drizzle, and then it would rain. I turned up my coat collar and put my head down. I didn't want to talk to anybody else. On my way to Mrs. McQuade's I had to pass several familiar places, The A & P, the Spotless Cleaners, Mr. Watson's delicatessen; all of these stores held people who knew me well. I pulled my collar up higher and put my head down lower.

When I reached the roominghouse I climbed the front out-side steps and walked down the hall to Mrs. McQuade's door. I tapped twice and waited. As soon as she opened the door, Mrs. McQuade recognized me and clapped her hand to her mouth.

"It's quite all right, Mrs. McQuade," I said, "I'm a free man."

"Please come in, Mr. Jordan."

Her room was much too warm for me. I removed my jacket, sat down in a rocker and lighted one of my cigarettes to detract from the musty, close smell of the hot room. The old lady with blue hair sat down across from me in a straight-backed chair and folded her hands in her lap.

"It'll probably be in tonight's paper, Mrs. McQuade, but I didn't kill Helen. She died from a heart attack. A quite natural death. I didn't have anything to do with it."

"I'm not surprised." She nodded knowingly. "You both loved each other too much."

"Yes. We did."

Mrs. McQuade began to cry soundlessly. Her eyes searched the room, found her purse. She opened it and removed a Kleenex and blew her nose with a gentle, refined honk.

"How about Helen's things?" I asked. "Are they still here?"

"No. Her mother, Mrs. Mathews, took them. If I'd known that you . . . well, I didn't know, and she's Helen's mother, so when she wanted them, I helped her pack the things and she took them with her. There wasn't much, you know. That suitcase, now; I didn't know whether it was yours or Helen's, so I let Mrs. Mathews take it."

"How about the portrait?"

"Mr. Endo was keeping it in his room. He wasn't here, but when she asked for it, I got it out of his room. She burned it up . . . in the incinerator. As I say, I didn't—"

"That's all right. I'd have liked to have had it, but it doesn't matter. Is there anything of hers at all?"

"Not a thing, Mr. Jordan. Just a minute." The old lady got out of her chair and opened the closet. She rummaged around in the small, dark room. "These are yours." She brought forth my old trenchcoat and a gray laundry bag. I spread the trench-coat on the floor and dumped the contents of the bag onto it. There were two dirty white shirts, four dirty T-shirts, four pairs of dirty drawers, six pairs of black sox and two soiled handkerchiefs.

At the bottom of the bag I saw my brushes and tubes of paint, and I could feel the tears coming into my eyes. She hadn't thrown them out after all; she still had had faith in me as an artist!

Mrs. McQuade pretended not to notice my choked emotion.

"If I'd known you were going to be released I'd have had these things laundered, Mr. Jordan."

"That's not important, Mrs. McQuade. I owe you some money, don't I?"

"Not a thing. Mrs. Mathews paid the room rent, and if you want the room you can have it back."

"No, thanks. I'm leaving San Francisco. I think it's best."

"Where are you going?"

"I don't know yet."

"Well, when you get settled, you'd better write me so I can forward your mail."

"There won't be any mail." I got out of the chair, slipped my jacket on, then the trenchcoat.

"You can keep that laundry bag, Mr. Jordan. Seeing I gave away your suitcase I can give you that much, at least."

"Thank you."

"Would you like a cup of coffee? I can make some in a second."

"No, thanks."

I threw the light bag over my shoulder and Mrs. McQuade opened the door for me. We shook hands and she led the way down the hall to the outside door. It was raining.

"Don't you have a hat, Mr. Jordan?"

"No. I never wear a hat."

"That's right. Come to think of it, I've never seen you with a hat."

I walked down the steps to the street and into the rain. A wind came up and the rain slanted sideways, coming down at an angle of almost thirty degrees. Two blocks away I got under the awning of a drug store. It wasn't letting up any; if anything, it was coming down harder. I left the shelter of the awning and walked up the hill in the rain.

Just a tall, lonely Negro.

Walking in the rain.

DOWN THERE

by David Goodis

THERE WERE no street lamps, no lights at all. It was a narrow street in the Port Richmond section of Philadelphia. From the nearby Delaware a cold wind came lancing in, telling all alley cats they'd better find a heated cellar. The late November gusts rattled against midnight-darkened windows, and stabbed at the eyes of the fallen man in the street.

The man was kneeling near the curb, breathing hard and spitting blood and wondering seriously if his skull was fractured. He'd been running blindly, his head down, so of course he hadn't seen the telephone pole. He'd crashed into it face first, bounced away and hit the cobblestones and wanted to call it a night.

But you can't do that, he told himself. You gotta get up and keep running.

He got up slowly, dizzily. There was a big lump on the left side of his head, his left eye and cheekbone were somewhat swollen, and the inside of his cheek was bleeding where he'd bitten it when he'd hit the pole. He thought of what his face must look like, and he managed to grin, saying to himself, You're doing fine, jim. You're really in great shape. But I think you'll make it, he decided, and then he was running again, suddenly running very fast as the headlights rounded a corner, the car picking up speed, the engine noise closing in on him.

The beam of the headlights showed him the entrance to an alley. He veered, went shooting into the alley, went down the alley and came out on another narrow street.

Maybe this is it, he thought. Maybe this is the street you want. No, your luck is running good but not that good, I think you'll hafta do more running before you find that street, before you see that lit-up sign, that drinking joint where Eddie works, that place called Harriet's Hut.

The man kept running. At the end of the block he turned, went on to the next street, peering through the darkness for any hint of the lit-up sign. You gotta get there, he told himself. You gotta get to Eddie before they get to you. But I wish I knew this neighborhood better. I wish it wasn't so cold and dark around here, it sure ain't no night for traveling on foot.

Especially when you're running, he added. When you're running away from a very fast Buick with two professionals in it, two high-grade operators, really experts in their line.

He came to another intersection, looked down the street, and at the end of the street, there it was, the orange glow, the lit-up sign of the tavern on the corner. The sign was very old, separate bulbs instead of neon tubes. Some of the bulbs were missing, the letters unreadable. But enough of it remained so that any wanderer could see it was a place for drinking. It was Harriet's Hut.

The man moved slowly now, more or less staggering as he headed toward the saloon. His head was throbbing, his wind-slashed lungs were either frozen or on fire, he wasn't quite sure what it felt like. And worst of all, his legs were heavy and getting heavier, his knees were giving way. But he staggered on, closer to the lit-up sign, and closer yet, and finally he was at the side entrance.

He opened the door and walked into Harriet's Hut. It was a fairly large place, high-ceilinged, and it was at least thirty years behind the times. There was no juke box, no television set. In places the wallpaper was loose and some of it was ripped away. The chairs and tables had lost their varnish, and the brass of the bar-rail had no shine at all. Above the mirror behind the bar there was a faded and partially torn photograph of a very young aviator wearing his helmet and smiling up at the sky. The photograph was captioned "Lucky Lindy." Near it there was another photograph that showed Dempsey crouched and moving in on a calm and technical Tunney. On the wall adjacent to the left side of the bar there was a framed painting of Kendrick, who'd been mayor of Philadelphia during the Sesqui-Centennial.

At the bar the Friday night crowd was jammed three-and-four-deep. Most of the drinkers wore work pants and heavy-soled work shoes. Some were very old, sitting in groups at the tables, their hair white and their faces wrinkled. But their hands didn't tremble as they lifted beer mugs and shot glasses. They could still lift a drink as well as any Hut regular, and they held their alcohol with a certain straight-seated dignity that gave them the appearance of venerable elders at a town meeting.

The place was really packed. All the tables were taken, and there wasn't a single empty chair for a leg-weary newcomer.

But the leg-weary man wasn't looking for a chair. He was looking for the piano. He could hear the music coming from the piano, but he couldn't see the instrument. A view-blurring fog of tobacco smoke and liquor fumes made everything vague, almost opaque. Or maybe it's me, he thought. Maybe I'm just about done in, and ready to keel over.

He moved. He went staggering past the tables, headed in the direction of the piano music. Nobody paid any attention to him, not even when he stumbled and went down. At twelve-twenty on a Friday night most patrons of Harriet's Hut were either booze-happy or booze-groggy. They were Port Richmond mill workers who'd labored hard all week. They came here to drink and drink some more, to forget all serious business, to ignore each and every problem of the too-real too-dry world beyond the walls of the Hut. They didn't even see the man who was pulling himself up very slowly from the sawdust on the floor, standing there with his bruised face and bleeding mouth, grinning and mumbling, "I can hear the music, all right. But where's the goddam piano?"

Then he was staggering again, bumping into a pile of high-stacked beer cases set up against a wall. It formed a sort of pyramid, and he groped his way along it, his hands feeling the cardboard of the beer cases until finally there was no more cardboard and he almost went down again. What kept him on his feet was the sight of the piano, specifically the sight of the pianist who sat there on the circular stool, slightly bent over, aiming a dim and faraway smile at nothing in particular.

The bruised-faced, leg-weary man, who was fairly tall and very wide across the shoulders and had a thick mop of ruffled yellow hair, moved closer to the piano. He came up behind the musician and put a hand on his shoulder and said, "Hello, Eddie."

There was no response from the musician, not even a twitch of the shoulder on which the man's heavy hand applied more pressure. And the man thought, Like he's far away, he don't even feel it, he's all the way out there with his music, it's a crying shame you gotta bring him in, but that's the way it is, you got no choice.

"Eddie," the man said, louder now. "It's me, Eddie."

The music went on, the rhythm unbroken. It was a soft, easy-going rhythm, somewhat plaintive and dreamy, a stream of pleasant sound that seemed to be saying, Nothing matters.

"It's me," the man said, shaking the musician's shoulder. "It's Turley. Your brother Turley."

The musician went on making the music. Turley sighed and shook his head slowly. He thought, You can't reach this one. It's like he's in a cloud and nothing moves him.

But then the tune was ended. The musician turned slowly and looked at the man and said, "Hello, Turley."

"You're sure a cool proposition," Turley said. "You ain't seen me for six-seven years. You look at me as if I just came back from a walk around the block."

"You bump into something?" the musician inquired mildly, scanning the bruised face, the bloodstained mouth.

Just then a woman got up from a nearby table and made a beeline for a door marked *Girls*. Turley spotted the empty chair, grabbed it, pulled it toward the piano and sat down. A man at the table yelled, "Hey you, that chair is taken," and Turley said to the man, "Easy now, jim. Cantcha see I'm an invalid?" He turned to the musician and grinned again, saying, "Yeah, I bumped into something. The street was too dark and I hit a pole."

"Who you running from?"

"Not the law, if that's what you're thinking."

"I'm not thinking anything," the musician said. He was medium-sized, on the lean side, and in his early thirties. He sat there with no particular expression on his face.

He had a pleasant face. There were no deep lines, no shadows. His eyes were a soft gray and he had a soft, relaxed mouth. His light-brown hair was loosely combed, very loosely, as though he combed it with his fingers. The shirt collar was open and there was no necktie. He wore a wrinkled, patched jacket and patched trousers. The clothes had a timeless look, indifferent to the calendar and the men's fashion columns. The man's full name was Edward Webster Lynn and his sole occupation was here at the Hut where he played the piano six nights a week, between nine and two. His salary was thirty dollars, and with tips his weekly income was anywhere from thirty-five to forty. It more than paid for his requirements. He was unmarried, he didn't own a car, and he had no debts or obligations.

"Well, anyway," Turley was saying, "it ain't the law. If it was the law, I wouldn't be pulling you into it."

"Is that why you came here?" Eddie asked softly. "To pull me into something?"

Turley didn't reply. He turned his head slightly, looking away from the musician. Consternation clouded his face, as though he knew what he wanted to say but couldn't quite manage to say it.

"It's no go," Eddie said.

Turley let out a sigh. As it faded, the grin came back. "Well, anyway, how you doing?"

"I'm doing fine," Eddie said.

"No problems?"

"None at all. Everything's dandy."

"Including the finance?"

"I'm breaking even." Eddie shrugged, but his eyes narrowed slightly.

Turley sighed again.

Eddie said, "I'm sorry, Turl, it's strictly no dice."

"But listen—"

"No," Eddie said softly. "No matter what it is, you can't pull me into it."

"But Jesus Christ, the least you can do is—"

"How's the family?" Eddie asked.

"The family?" Turley was blinking. Then he picked up on it. "We're all in good shape. Mom and Dad are okay—"

"And Clifton?" Eddie said. "How's Clifton?" referring to the other brother, the oldest.

Turley's grin was suddenly wide. "Well, you know how it is with Clifton. He's still in there pitching—"

"Strikes?"

Turley didn't answer. The grin stayed, but it seemed to slacken just a little. Then presently he said, "You've been away a long time. We miss you."

Eddie shrugged.

"We really miss you," Turley said. "We always talk about you."

Eddie gazed past his brother. The far-off smile drifted across his lips. He didn't say anything.

"After all," Turley said, "you're one of the family. We never told you to leave. I mean you're always welcome at the house. What I mean is—"

"How'd you know where to find me?"

"Fact is, I didn't. Not at first. Then I remembered, that last letter we got, you mentioned the name of this place. I figured you'd still be here. Anyway, I hoped so. Well, today I was downtown and I looked up the address in the phone book—"

"Today?"

"I mean tonight. I mean—"

"You mean when things got tight you looked me up. Isn't that it?"

Turley blinked again. "Don't get riled."

"Who's riled?"

"You're plenty riled but you cover it up," Turley said. Then he had the grin working again. "I guess you learned that trick from living here in the city. All us country people, us South Jersey melon-eaters, we can't ever learn that caper. We always gotta show our hole card."

Eddie made no comment. He glanced idly at the keyboard, and hit a few notes.

"I got myself in a jam," Turley said.

Eddie went on playing. The notes were in the higher octaves, the fingers very light on the keyboard, making a cheery, babbling-brook sort of tune.

Turley shifted his position in the chair. He was glancing around, his eyes swiftly checking the front door, the side door, and the door leading to the rear exit.

"Wanna hear something pretty?" Eddie said. "Listen to this—"

Turley's hand came down on the fingers that were hitting the keys. Through the resulting discord, his voice came urgently, somewhat hoarsely. "You gotta help me, Eddie. I'm really in a tight spot. You can't turn me down."

"Can't get myself involved, either."

"Believe me, it won't get you involved. All I'm asking, lemme stay in your room until morning."

"You don't mean stay. You mean hide."

Again Turley sighed heavily. Then he nodded.

"From who?" Eddie asked.

"Two troublemakers."

"Really? You sure they made the trouble? Maybe you made it."

"No, they made it," Turley said. "They been giving me grief since early today."

"Get to it. What kind of grief?"

"Tracing me. They've been on my neck from the time I left Dock Street—"

"Dock Street?" Eddie frowned slightly. "What were you doing on Dock Street?"

"Well, I was—" Turley faltered, swallowed hard, then by-passed Dock Street and blurted, "Damn it all, I ain't askin' for the moon. All you gotta do is put me up for the night—"

"Hold it," Eddie said. "Let's get back to Dock Street."

"For Christ's sake—"

"And another thing," Eddie went on. "What're you doing here in Philadelphia?"

"Business."

"Like what?"

Turley didn't seem to hear the question. He took a deep breath. "Something went haywire. Next thing I know, I got these two on my neck. And then, what fixes me proper, I run clean outta folding money. It happens in a hash house on Delaware Avenue when some joker lifts my wallet. If it hadn't been for that, I coulda bought some transportation, at least a taxi to get past the city limits. As it was, all I had left was nickels and dimes, so every time I'm on a streetcar they're right behind me in a brand-new Buick. I tell you, it's been a mean Friday for me, jim. Of all the goddam days to get my pocket picked—"

"You still haven't told me anything."

"I'll give you the rundown later. Right now I'm pushed for time."

As Turley said it, he was turning his head to have another look at the door leading to the street. Absently he lifted his fingers to the battered left side of his face, and grimaced painfully. The grimace faded as the dizziness came again, and he weaved from side to side, as though the chair had wheels and was moving along a bumpy road. "Whatsa matter with the floor?" he mumbled, his eyes half closed now. "What kinda dump is this? Can't they even fix the floor? It won't even hold the chair straight."

He began to slide from the chair. Eddie grabbed his shoulders and steadied him.

"You'll be all right," Eddie said. "Just relax."

"Relax?" It came out vaguely. "Who wantsa relax?" Turley's arm flapped weakly to indicate the jam-packed bar and the crowded tables. "Look at all the people having fun. Why can't I have some fun? Why can't I—"

It's bad, Eddie thought. It's worse than I figured it was. He's got some real damage upstairs. I think what we'll hafta do is—

"Whatsa matter with him?" a voice said.

Eddie looked up and saw the Hut's owner, Harriet. She was a very fat woman in her middle forties. She had peroxide-blonde hair, a huge, jutting bosom and tremendous hips. Despite the excess weight, she had a somewhat narrow waistline. Her face was on the Slavic side, the nose broad-based and moderately pugged, the eyes gray-blue with a certain level look that said, You deal with me, you deal straight. I got no time for two-bit sharpies, fast-hand slicksters, or any kind of leeches, fakers, and freebee artists. Get cute or cagey and you'll wind up buying new teeth.

Turley was slipping off the chair again. Harriet caught him as he sagged sideways. Her fat hands held him firmly under his armpits while she leaned closer to examine the lump on his head.

"He's sorta banged up," Eddie said. "He's really groggy. I think—"

"He ain't as groggy as he looks," Harriet cut in dryly. "If he don't stop what he's doing he's gonna get banged up more."

Turley had sent one arm around her hip, his hand sliding onto the extra-large, soft-solid bulge. She reached back, grabbed his wrist and flung his arm aside. "You're either wine-crazy, punch-crazy, or plain crazy," she informed him. "You try that again, you'll need a brace on your jaw. Now sit still while I have a look."

"I'll have a look too," Turley said, and while the fat woman bent over him to study his damaged skull, he made a serious study of her forty-four-inch bosom. Again his arm went around her hip, and again she flung it off. "You're askin' for it," she told him, hefting her big fist. "You really want it, don't you?"

Turley grinned past the fist. "I always do, blondie. Ain't no hour of the day when I don't."

"You think he needs a doctor?" Eddie asked.

"I'll settle for a big fat nurse," Turley babbled, the grin very loose, sort of idiotic. And then he looked around, as though trying to figure out where he was. "Hey, somebody tell me somethin'. I'd simply like to know—"

"What year it is?" Harriet said. "It's Nineteen fifty-six, and the city is Philadelphia."

"You'll hafta do better than that." Turley sat up straighter. "What I really wanna know is—" But the fog enveloped him and he sat there gazing vacantly past Harriet, past Eddie, his eyes glazing over.

Harriet and Eddie looked at him, then looked at each other. Eddie said, "Keeps up like this, he'll need a stretcher."

Harriet took another look at Turley. She made a final diagnosis, saying, "He'll be all right. I've seen them like that before. In the ring. A certain nerve gets hit and they lose all track of what's happening. Then first thing you know, they're back in stride, they're doing fine."

Eddie was only half convinced. "You really think he'll be okay?"

"Sure he will," Harriet said. "Just look at him. He's made of rock. I know this kind. They take it and like it and come back for more."

"That's correct," Turley said solemnly. Without looking at Harriet, he reached out to shake her hand. Then he changed his mind and his hand strayed in another direction. Harriet shook her head in motherly disapproval. A wistful smile came onto her blunt features, a smile of understanding. She lowered her hand to Turley's head, her fingers in his mussed-up hair to muss it up some more, to let him know that Harriet's Hut

was not as mean-hard as it looked, that it was a place where
he could rest a while and pull himself together.

"You know him?" she said to Eddie. "Who is he?"

Before Eddie could answer, Turley was off on another fog-
bound ride, saying, "Look at that over there across the room.
What's that?"

Harriet spoke soothingly, somewhat clinically. "What is it,
johnny? Where?"

Turley's arm came up. He tried to point. It took considerable effort and finally he made it.

"You mean the waitress?" Harriet asked.

Turley couldn't answer. He had his eyes fastened on the
face and body of the brunette on the other side of the room.
She wore an apron and she carried a tray.

"You really like that?" Harriet asked. Again she mussed his
hair. She threw a wink at Eddie.

"Like it?" Turley was saying. "I been lookin' all over for
something in that line. That's my kind of material. I wanna
get to meet that. What's her name?"

"Lena."

"She's something," Turley said. He rubbed his hands.
"She's really something."

"So what are your plans?" Harriet asked quietly, as though
she meant it seriously.

"Four bits is all I need." Turley's tone was flat and technical. "A drink for me and a drink for her. And that'll get
things going."

"Sure as hell it will," Harriet said, saying it more to herself
and with genuine seriousness, her eyes aimed now across the
crowded Hut, focused on the waitress. And then, to Turley,
"You think you got lumps now, you'll get real lumps if you
make a pass at that."

She looked at Eddie, waiting for some comment. Eddie had
pulled away from it. He'd turned to face the keyboard. His
face showed the dim and far-off smile and nothing more.

Turley stood up to get a better look. "What's her name
again?"

"Lena."

"So that's Lena," he said, his lips moving slowly.

"That's sheer aggravation," Harriet said. "Do yourself a favor. Sit down. Stop looking."

He sat down, but he went on looking. "How come it's aggravation?" he wanted to know. "You mean it ain't for sale or rent?"

"It ain't available, period."

"Married?"

"No, she ain't married," Harriet said very slowly. Her eyes were riveted on the waitress.

"Then what's the setup?" Turley insisted on knowing. "She hooked up with someone?"

"No," Harriet said. "She's strictly solo. She wants no part of any man. A man moves in too close, he gets it from the hatpin."

"Hatpin?"

"She's got it stuck there in that apron. Some hungry rooster gets too hungry, she jabs him where it really hurts."

Turley snorted. "Is that all?"

"No," Harriet said. "That ain't all. The hatpin is only the beginning. Next thing the poor devil knows, he's getting it from the bouncer. That's her number-one protection, the bouncer."

"Who's the bouncer? Where is he?"

Harriet pointed toward the bar.

Turley peered through the clouds of tobacco smoke. "Hey, wait now, I've seen a picture somewhere. In the papers—"

"On the sports page, it musta been." Harriet's voice was queerly thick. "They had him tagged as the Harleyville Hugger."

"That's right," Turley said. "The Hugger. I remember. Sure, I remember now."

Harriet looked at Turley. She said, "You really do?"

"Sure," Turley said. "I'm a wrestling fan from way back. Never had the cabbage to buy tickets, but I followed it in the papers." He peered again toward the bar. "That's him, all right. That's the Harleyville Hugger."

"And it wasn't no fake when he hugged them, either," Harriet said. "You know anything about the game, you know what a bear hug can do. I mean the real article. He'd get them in a bear hug, they were finished." And then, significantly, "He still knows how."

Turley snorted again. He looked from the bouncer to the waitress and back to the bouncer. "That big-bellied slob?"

"He still has it, regardless. He's a crushing machine."

"He couldn't crush my little finger," Turley said. "I'd hook one short left to that paunch and he'd scream for help. Why, he ain't nothing but a worn-out—"

Turley was vaguely aware that he'd lost his listener. He turned and looked and Harriet wasn't there. She was walking toward the stairway near the bar. She mounted the stairway, ascending very slowly, her head lowered.

"Whatsa matter with her?" Turley asked Eddie. "She got a headache?"

Eddie was half turned away from the keyboard, watching Harriet as she climbed the stairs. Then he turned fully to the keyboard and hit a few idle notes. His voice came softly through the music. "I guess you could call it a headache. She got a problem with the bouncer. He has it bad for the waitress—"

"Me, too," Turley grinned.

Eddie went on hitting the notes, working in some chords, building a melody. "With the bouncer it's real bad. And Harriet knows."

"So what?" Turley frowned vaguely. "What's the bouncer to her?"

"They live together," Eddie said. "He's her common-law husband."

Then Turley sagged again, falling forward, bumping into Eddie, holding onto him for support. Eddie went on playing the piano. Turley let go and sat back in the chair. He was waiting for Eddie to turn around and look at him. And finally Eddie stopped playing and turned and looked. He saw the grin on Turley's face. Again it was the idiotic, eyes-glazed grin.

"You want a drink?" Eddie asked. "Maybe you could use a drink."

"I don't need no drink." Turley swayed from side to side. "Tell you what I need. I need some information. Wanna be straightened out on something. You wanna help me on that?"

"Help you on what?" Eddie murmured. "What is it you wanna know?"

Turley shut his eyes tightly. He opened them, shut them, opened them again. He saw Eddie sitting there. He said, "What you doin' here?"

Eddie shrugged.

Turley had his own answer. "I'll tell you what you're doing. You're wasting away—"

"All right," Eddie said gently. "All right—"

"It ain't all right," Turley said. And then the disjointed phrases spilled from the muddled brain. "Sits there at a second-hand piano. Wearing rags. When what you should be wearing is a full-dress suit. With one of them ties, the really fancy duds. And it should be a grand piano, a great big shiny grand piano, one of them Steinbergs, god-damn it, with every seat taken in the concert hall. That's where you should be, and what I want to know is—why ain't you there?"

"You really need a bracer, Turl. You're away off the groove."

"Don't study my condition, jim. Study your own. Why ain't you there in that concert hall?"

Eddie shrugged and let it slide past.

But Turley banged his hands against his knees. "Why ain't you there?"

"Because I'm here," Eddie said. "I can't be two places at once."

It didn't get across. "Don't make sense," Turley blabbered. "Just don't make sense at all. A knockout of a dame and she ain't got no boy friend. A piano man as good as they come and he don't make enough to buy new shoes."

Eddie laughed.

"It ain't comical," Turley said. "It's a screwed-up state of affairs." He spoke to some invisible third party, pointing a finger at the placid-faced musician. "Here he sits at this wreck of a piano, in this dirty old crummy old joint that oughtta be inspected by the fire marshal, or anyway by the Board of Health. Look at the floor, they still use sawdust on the goddam floor—" He cupped his hands to his mouth and called, "At least buy some new chairs, for Christ's sake—" Then referring again to the soft-eyed musician, "Sits here, night after night. Sits here wasting away in the bush leagues when he oughta be way up there in the majors, way up at the top cause he's got the stuff, he's got it in them ten fingers. He's a star, I tell you, he's the star of them all—"

"Easy, Turl—"

Turley was feeling it deep. He stood up, shouting again, "It oughtta be a grand piano, with candlesticks like that other cat has. Where's the candlesticks? Whatsa matter here? You cheap or somethin'? You can't afford no candle-sticks?"

"Aaah, close yer head," some nearby beer-guzzler offered.

Turley didn't hear the heckler. He went on shouting, tears streaming down his rough-featured face. The cuts in his mouth had opened again and the blood was trickling from his lips. "And there's something wrong somewhere," he pro-claimed to the audience that had no idea who he was or what he was talking about, "—like anyone knows that two and two adds up to four but this adds up to minus three. It just ain't right and it calls for some kind of action—"

"You really want action?" a voice inquired pleasantly.

It was the voice of the bouncer, formerly known as the Harleyville Hugger, known now in the Hut by his real name, Wally Plyne, although certain admirers still insisted it was Hugger. He stood there, five feet nine and weighing two-twenty. There was very little hair on his head, and what re-mained was clipped short, fuzzy. His left ear was somewhat out of shape, and his nose was a wreck, fractured so many times that now it was hardly a nose at all. It was more like a blob of putty flattened onto the rough-grained face. In Plyne's mouth there was considerable bridgework, and ribboning down from his chin and toward the collarbone was a poorly stitched scar, obviously an emergency job performed by some intern. Plyne was not pleased with the scar. He wore his shirt collar buttoned high to conceal it as much as possible. He was extremely sensitive about his battered face, and when anyone looked at him too closely he'd stiffen and his neck would swell and redden. His eyes would plead with the looker not to laugh. There'd been times when certain lookers had ignored the plea, and the next thing they knew, their ribs were frac-tured and they had severe internal injuries. At Harriet's Hut the first law of self-preservation was never laugh at the bouncer.

The bouncer was forty-three years old.

He stood there looking down at Turley. He was waiting for an answer. Turley looked up at him and said, "Why you buttin' in? Cantcha see I'm talkin'?"

"You're talking too loud," Plyne said. His tone remained pleasant, almost sympathetic. He was looking at the tears rolling down Turley's cheeks.

"If I don't talk loud they won't hear me," Turley said. "I want them to hear me."

"They got other things to do," Plyne said patiently. "They're drinkin' and they don't wanna be bothered."

"That's what's wrong," Turley sobbed. "Nobody wantsa be bothered."

Plyne took a deep breath. He said to Turley, "Now look, whoever messed up your face like that, you go ahead and hit him back. But not here. This here's a quiet place of business—"

"What you sellin' me?" Turley blinked the tears away, his tone changing to a growl. "Who asked you to be sorry for my goddam face? It's my face. The lumps are mine, the cuts are mine. You better worry about your own damn face."

"Worry?" Plyne was giving careful thought to the remark. "How you mean that?"

Turley's eyes and lips started a grin, his mouth started a reply. Before the grin could widen, before the words could come, Eddie moved in quickly, saying to Plyne, "He didn't mean anything, Wally. Cantcha see he's all mixed up?"

"You stay out of this," Plyne said, not looking at Eddie. He was studying Turley's face, waiting for the grin to go away.

The grin remained. At nearby tables there was a waiting quiet. The quiet spread to other tables, then to all the tables, and then to the crowded bar. They were all staring at the big man who stood there grinning at Plyne.

"Get it off," Plyne told Turley. "Get it off your face."

Turley widened the grin.

Plyne took another deep breath. Something came into his eyes, a kind of dull glow. Eddie saw it and knew what it meant.

He was up from the piano stool, saying to Plyne, "Don't, Wally. He's sick."

"Who's sick?" Turley challenged. "I'm in grade-A shape. I'm ready for—"

"He's ready for a brain examination," Eddie said to Plyne, to the staring audience. "He ran into a pole and banged his head. Look at that bump. If it ain't a fracture it's maybe a concussion."

"Call for an ambulance," someone directed.

"Lookit, he's bleeding from the mouth," another voice put in. "Could be that's from the busted head."

Plyne blinked a few times. The glow faded from his eyes.

Turley went on grinning. But now the grin wasn't aimed at Plyne or anyone or anything else. Again it was the idiotic grin.

Plyne looked at Eddie. "You know him?"

Eddie shrugged. "Sort of."

"Who is he?"

Another shrug. "I'll take him outside. Let him get some air—"

Plyne's thick fingers closed on Eddie's sleeve. "I asked you something. Who is he?"

"You hear the man?" It was Turley again, coming out of the brain-battered fog. "The man says he wantsa know. I think he's got a point there."

"Then you tell me," Plyne said to Turley. He stepped closer, peering into the glazed eyes. "Maybe you don't need an ambulance, after all. Maybe you ain't really hurt that bad. Can you tell me who you are?"

"Brother."

"Whose brother?"

"His." Turley pointed to Eddie.

"I didn't know he had a brother," Plyne said.

"Well, that's the way it goes." Turley spoke to all the nearby tables. "You learn something new every day."

"I'm willing to learn," Plyne said. And then, as though Eddie wasn't there, "He never talks about himself. There's a lota things about him I don't know."

"You don't?" Turley had the grin again. "How long has he worked here?"

"Three years."

"That's a long time," Turley said. "You sure oughtta have him down pat by now."

"Nobody's got him down pat. Only thing we know for sure, he plays the piano."

"You pay him wages?"

"Sure we pay him wages."

"To do what?"

"Play the piano."

"And what else?"

"Just that," Plyne said. "We pay him to play the piano, that's all."

"You mean you don't pay him wages to talk about himself?"

Plyne tightened his lips. He didn't reply.

Turley moved in closer. "You want it all for free, don't you? But the thing is, you can't get it for free. You wanna learn about a person, it costs you. And the more you learn, the more it costs. Like digging a well, the deeper you go, the more expenses you got. And sometimes it's a helluva lot more than you can afford."

"What you getting at?" Plyne was frowning now. He turned his head to look at the piano man. He saw the carefree smile and it bothered him, it caused his frown to darken. There was only a moment of that, and then he looked again at Turley. He got rid of the frown and said, "All right, never mind. This talk means nothing. It's jabber, and you're punchy, and I got other things to do. I can't stay here wasting time with you."

The bouncer walked away. The audience at the bar and the tables went back to drinking. Turley and Eddie were seated now, Eddie facing the keyboard, hitting a few chords and starting a tune. It was a placid, soft-sweet tune and the dreamy sounds brought a dreamy smile to Turley's lips. "That's nice," Turley whispered. "That's really nice."

The music went on and Turley nodded slowly, unaware that he was nodding. As his head came up, and started to go down again, he saw the front door open.

Two men came in.

2

"THAT'S them," Turley said.

Eddie went on making the music.

"That's them, all right," Turley said matter-of-factly.

The door closed behind the two men and they stood there turning their heads very slowly, looking from crowded tables to crowded bar, back to the tables, to the bar again, looking everywhere.

Then they spotted Turley. They started forward.

"Here they come," Turley said, still matter-of-factly. "Look at them."

Eddie's eyes stayed on the keyboard. He had his mind on the keyboard. The warm-cool music flowed on and now it was saying to Turley, It's your problem, entirely yours, keep me out of it.

The two men came closer. They moved slowly. The tables were close-packed, blocking their path. They were trying to move faster, to force their way through.

"Here they come," Turley said. "They're really coming now."

Don't look, Eddie said to himself. You take one look and that'll do it, that'll pull you into it. You don't want that, you're here to play the piano, period. But what's this? What's happening? There ain't no music now, your fingers are off the keyboard.

He turned his head and looked and saw the two men coming closer.

They were well-dressed men. The one in front was short and very thin, wearing a pearl-gray felt hat and a white silk muffler and a single-breasted, dark blue overcoat. The man behind him was thin, too, but much taller. He wore a hat of darker gray, a black-and-silver striped muffler, and his overcoat was a dark gray six-button-benny.

Now they were halfway across the room. There was more space here between the tables. They were coming faster.

Eddie jabbed stiffened fingers into Turley's ribs. "Don't sit there. Get up and go."

"Go where?" And there it was again, the idiotic grin.

"Side door," Eddie hissed at him, gave him another finger-stiffened jab, harder this time.

"Hey, quit that," Turley said. "That hurts."

"Does it?" Another jab made it really hurt, pulled the grin off Turley's face, pulled his rump off the chair. Then Turley was using his legs, going past the stacked pyramid of beer cases, walking faster and faster and finally lunging toward the side door.

The two men took a short cut, going diagonally away from the tables. They were running now, streaking to intercept Turley. It looked as though they had it made.

Then Eddie was up from the piano stool, seeing Turley aiming at the side door some fifteen feet away. The two men were closing in on Turley. They'd pivoted off the diagonal path and now they ran parallel to the pyramid of beer cases. Eddie made a short rush that took him into the high-stacked pile of bottle-filled cardboard boxes. He gave the pile a shoulder bump and a box came down and then another box, and more boxes. It caused a traffic jam as the two men collided with the fallen beer cases, tripped over the cardboard hurdles, went down and got up and tripped again. While that happened, Turley opened the side door and ran out.

Some nine beer cases had fallen off the stacked pyramid and several of the bottles had come loose to hit the floor and break. The two men were working hard to get past the blockade of cardboard boxes and broken bottles. One of them, the shorter one, was turning his head to catch a glimpse of whatever funnyman had caused this fiasco. He saw Eddie standing there near the partially crumbled pyramid. Eddie shrugged and lifted his arms in a sheepish gesture, as though to say, An accident, I just bumped into it, that's all. The short thin man didn't say anything. There wasn't time for a remark.

Eddie went back to the piano. He sat down and started to play. He hit a few soft chords, the dim and far-off smile drifting onto his lips while the two thin well-dressed men finally made it to the side door. Through the soft sound of the music he heard the hard sound of the door slamming shut behind them.

He went on playing. There were no wrong notes, no breaks in the rhythm, but he was thinking of Turley, seeing the two men going after Turley along the too-dark streets in the too-cold stillness out there that might be broken any moment now by the sound of a shot.

But I don't think so, he told himself. They didn't have that look, as though they were gunning for meat. It was more of a bargaining look, like all they want is to sit down with Turley and talk some business.

What kind of business? Well, sure, you know what kind. It's something on the shady side. He said it was Clifton's transaction and that puts it on the shady side, with Turl stooging for Clifton like he's always done. So whatever it is, they're in a jam again, your two dear brothers. It's a first-class talent they have for getting into jams, getting out, and getting in again. You think they'll get out this time? Well, we hope so. We really hope so. We wish them luck, and that about says it. So what you do now is get off the trolley. It ain't your ride and you're away from it.

A shadow fell across the keyboard. He tried not to see it, but it was there and it stayed there. He turned his head sideways and saw the bulky legs, the barrel torso and the mashed-nosed face of the bouncer.

He went on playing.

"That's pretty," Plyne said.

Eddie nodded his thanks.

"It's very pretty," Plyne said. "But it just ain't pretty enough. I don't wanna hear any more."

Eddie stopped playing. His arms came down limply at his sides. He sat there and waited.

"Tell me something," the bouncer said. "What is it with you?"

Eddie shrugged.

Plyne took a deep breath. "God damn it," he said to no one in particular. "I've known this party for three years now and I hardly know him at all."

Eddie's soft smile was aimed at the keyboard. He tapped out a few idle notes in the middle octaves.

"That's all you'll ever get from him," Plyne said to invisible listeners. "That same no-score routine. No matter what comes up, it's always I-don't-know-from-nothing."

Eddie's fingers stayed there in the middle octaves.

The bouncer's manner changed. His voice was hard. "I told you to stop playing."

The music stopped. Eddie went on looking at the keyboard. He said, "What is it, Wally? What is it bothers you?"

"You really wanna know?" Plyne said it slowly, as though he'd scored a point. "All right, take a look." His arm stretched out, the forefinger rigid and aiming at the littered floor, the overturned cardboard boxes, the bottles, the scattered glass and the spilled beer foaming on the splintered floor boards.

Eddie shrugged again. "I'll clean it up," he said, and started to rise from the piano stool. Plyne pushed him back onto it.

"Tell me," Plyne said, and pointed again at the beer-stained floor. "What's the deal on that?"

"Deal?" The piano man seemed bewildered. "No deal at all. It was an accident. I didn't see where I was going, and I bumped into—"

But it was no use going on. The bouncer wasn't buying it.

"Wanna bet?" the bouncer asked mildly. "Wanna bet it wasn't no accident?"

Eddie didn't reply.

"You won't tell me, I'll tell you," Plyne said. "A tag-team play, that's what it was."

"Could be." Eddie gave a very slight shrug. "I might have done it without thinking, I mean sort of unconscious-like. I'm really not sure—"

"Not much you ain't." Plyne showed a thick wet smile that widened gradually. "You handled that stunt like you'd planned it on paper. The timing was perfect."

Eddie blinked several times. He told himself to stop it. He said to himself, Something is happening here and you better check it before it goes further.

But there was no way to check it. The bouncer was saying, "First time I ever saw you pull that kind of caper. In all the years you been here, you never butted in, not once. No matter what the issue was, no matter who was in it. So how come you butted in tonight?"

Another slight shrug, and the words coming softly, "I might have figured he could use some help, like I said, I'm not really sure. Or, on the other hand, you see someone in a jam, you remind yourself he's a close relative—I don't know, it's something along those lines."

Plyne's face twisted in a sort of disgusted grimace, as though he knew there was no use digging any deeper. He turned and started away from the piano.

Then something stopped him and caused him to turn and come back. He leaned against the side of the piano. For some moments he said nothing, just listened to the music, his brow creased slightly in a moderately thoughtful frown. Then, quite casually, he moved his heavy hand, brushing Eddie's fingers away from the keyboard.

Eddie looked up, waiting.

"Gimme some more on this transaction," the bouncer said.

"Like what?"

"Them two men you stalled with the beer cases. What's the wire on them?"

"I don't know," Eddie said.

"You don't know why they were chasing him?"

"Ain't got the least idea."

"Come on, come on."

"I can't tell you, Wally. I just don't know."

"You expect me to buy that?"

Eddie shrugged and didn't reply.

"All right," Plyne said. "We'll try it from another angle. This brother of yours. What's his line?"

"Don't know that either. Ain't seen him for years. Last I knew, he was working on Dock Street."

"Doing what?"

"Longshoreman."

"You don't know what he's doing now?"

"If I knew, I'd tell you."

"Yeah, sure." Plyne was folding his thick arms high on his chest. "Spill," he said. "Come on, spill."

Eddie smiled amiably at the bouncer. "What's all this court-room action?" And then, the smile widening, "You going to law school, Wally? You practicing on me?"

"It ain't like that," Plyne said. He was stumped for a moment. "It's just that I wanna be sure, that's all. I mean—well, the thing of it is, I'm general manager here. Whatever happens in the Hut, I'm sorta responsible. You know that."

Eddie nodded, his eyebrows up. "That's a point."

"You're damn right it is," the bouncer pressed his advantage. "I gotta make sure this place keeps its license. It's a legitimate place of business. If I got anything to say, it's gonna stay legitimate."

"You're absolutely right," Eddie said.

"I'm glad you know it." Plyne's eyes were narrowed again. "Another thing you'd better know, I got more brains than you think. Can't play no music or write poems or anything like that, but sure as hell I can add up a score. Like with this brother of yours and them two engineers who wanted him for more than just a friendly chat."

"That adds," Eddie said.

"It adds perfect," Plyne approved his own arithmetic. "And I'll add it some more. I'll give it to you right down the line. He mighta been a longshoreman then, but it's a cinch he's switched jobs. He's lookin' for a higher income now. Whatever work he's doing, there's heavy cash involved—"

Eddie was puzzled. He was saying to himself, The dumber you play it, the better.

"Them two engineers," the bouncer was saying, "they weren't no small-timers. I gandered the way they were dressed. Them overcoats were hand-stitched; I know that custom quality when I see it. So we take it from there, we do it with arrows—"

"With what?"

"With arrows," Plyne said, his finger tracing an arrow-line on the side of the piano. "From them to your brother. From your brother to you."

"Me?" Eddie laughed lightly. "You're not adding it now. You're stretching it."

"But not too far," Plyne said. "Because it's more than just possible. Because there ain't nothing wrong with my peepers. I seen your brother sitting here and giving you that sales talk. It's like he wants you in on the deal, whatever it is—"

Eddie was laughing again.

"What's funny?" Plyne asked.

Eddie went on laughing. It wasn't loud laughter, but it was real. He was trying to hold it back and he couldn't.

"Is it me?" Plyne spoke very quietly. "You laughing at me?"

"At myself," Eddie managed to say through the laughter. "I got a gilt-framed picture of the setup. The big deal, with me the key man, that final arrow pointing at me. You must be kidding, Wally. Just take a look and see for yourself. Look at the key man."

Plyne looked, seeing the thirty-a-week musician who sat there at the battered piano, the soft-eyed, soft-mouthed nobody whose ambitions and goals aimed at exactly zero, who'd been working here three years without asking or even hinting for a raise. Who never grumbled when the tips were stingy, or griped about anything, for that matter, not even when ordered to help with the chairs and tables at closing time, to sweep the floor, to take out the trash.

Plyne's eyes focused on him and took him in. Three years, and aside from the music he made, his presence at the Hut meant nothing. It was almost as though he wasn't there and the piano was playing all by itself. Regardless of the action at the tables or the bar, the piano man was out of it, not even an observer. He had his back turned and his eyes on the keyboard, content to draw his pauper's wages and wear pauper's rags. A gutless wonder, Plyne decided, fascinated with this living example of absolute neutrality. Even the smile was something neutral. It was never aimed at a woman. It was aimed very far out there beyond all tangible targets, really far out there beyond the left-field bleachers. So where does that take it? Plyne asked himself. And of course there was no answer, not even the slightest clue.

But even so, he made a final effort. He squinted hard at the piano man, and said, "Tell me one thing. Where'd you come from?"

"I was born," Eddie said.

The bouncer thought it over for some moments. Then, "Thanks for the tipoff. I had it figured you came from a cloud."

Eddie laughed softly. Plyne was walking away, going toward the bar. At the bar the dark-haired waitress was arranging shot glasses on a tray. Plyne approached her, hesitated, then came in close and said something to her. She didn't reply. She didn't even look at him. She picked up the tray and headed for one of the tables. Plyne stood motionless, staring at her, his mouth tight, his teeth biting hard at the inside of his lip.

The soft-easy music came drifting from the piano.

3

IT was twenty minutes later and the last nightcapper had been ushered out. The bartender was cleaning the last of the glasses, and the bouncer had gone upstairs to bed. The waitress had her overcoat on and was lighting a cigarette as she leaned back against the wall and watched Eddie, who was sweeping the floor.

He finished sweeping, emptied the dust-pan, put the broom away, and took his overcoat off the hanger near the piano. It was a very old overcoat. The collar was torn and two buttons were missing. He didn't have a hat.

The waitress watched him as he walked toward the front door. He turned his head to smile at the bartender and say good night. And then, to the waitress, "See you, Lena."

"Wait," she said, moving toward him as he opened the front door.

He stood there smiling somewhat questioningly. In the four months she'd been working here, they'd never exchanged more than a friendly hello or good night. Never anything much more than that.

Now she was saying, "Can you spare six bits?"

"Sure." Without hesitation he reached into his pants pocket. But the questioning look remained. It even deepened just a little.

"I'm sorta stuck tonight," the waitress explained. "When Harriet pays me tomorrow, you'll get it back."

"No hurry," he said, giving her two quarters, two dimes and a nickel.

"It goes for a meal," Lena explained further, putting the coins into her purse. "I figured Harriet would cook me something, but she went to bed early, and I didn't want to bother her."

"Yeah, I saw her going upstairs," Eddie said. He paused a moment. "I guess she was tired."

"Well, she works hard," Lena said. She took a final puff at the cigarette and tossed it into a cuspidor. "I wonder how she does it. All that weight. I bet she's over two hundred."

"Way over," Eddie said. "But she carries it nice. It's packed in solid."

"Too much of it. She loses a little, she'll feel better."

"She feels all right."

Lena shrugged. She didn't say anything.

Eddie opened the door and stepped aside. She went out, and he followed her. She started across the pavement and he said, "See you tomorrow," and she stopped and turned and faced him. She said, "I think six bits is more than I need. A half is enough," and started to open her purse.

He said, "No, that's all right." But she came toward him, extending the quarter, saying, "At John's I can get a platter for forty. Another dime for coffee and that does it."

He waved away the silver quarter. He said, "You might want a piece of cake or something."

She came closer. "Go on, take it," pushing the coin toward him.

He grinned. "High finance."

"Will you please take it?"

"Who needs it? I won't starve."

"You sure you can spare it?" Her head was slanted, her eyes searching his face.

He went on grinning. "Quit worrying. I won't run short."

"Yeah, I know." She went on searching his face. "Your wallet gets low, you just pick up the phone and call your broker. Who's your broker?"

"It's a big firm on Wall Street. I fly to New York twice a week. Just to have a look at the board."

"When'd you eat last?"

He shrugged. "I had a sandwich—"

"When?"

"I don't know. Around four-thirty, maybe."

"Nothing in between?" And then, not waiting for an answer, "Come on, walk me to John's. You'll have something."

"But—"

"Come on, will you?" She took his arm and pulled him along. "You wanna live, you gotta eat."

It occurred to him that he was really hungry and he could use a bowl of soup and a hot platter. The wet-cold wind was getting through his thin coat and biting into him. The thought of hot food was pleasant. Then another thought came and he winced slightly. He had exactly twelve cents in his pocket.

He shrugged and went on walking with Lena. He decided to settle for a cup of coffee. At least the coffee would warm him up. But you really oughtta have something to eat, he told himself. How come you didn't eat tonight? You always grab a bite at the food counter at the Hut around twelve-thirty. But not tonight. You had nothing tonight. How come you forgot to fill your belly?

Then he remembered. That business with Turley, he told himself. You were busy with Turley and you forgot to eat.

I wonder if Turley made it or not. I wonder if he got away. He knows how to move around and he can take care of himself. Yes, I'd say the chances are he made it. You really think so? He was handicapped, you know. It's a cinch he wasn't in condition to play hare-and-hounds with him the hare. Well, what are you gonna do? You can't do anything. I wish you'd drop it.

And another thing. What is it with this one here, this waitress? What bothers her? You know there's something bothering her. You caught the slightest hint of it when she talked about Harriet. She was sorta fishing then, she had the line out. Well sure, that's what it is. She's worried about Harriet and the bouncer and their domestic difficulties, because the bouncer's got his eyes on someone else these days—this waitress here. Well, it ain't her fault. Only thing she offers Plyne is an ice-cold look whenever he tries to move in. So let him keep trying. What do you care? Say, you wanna do me a favor? Get outta my hair, you're bugging me.

But just then a queer idea came into his brain, a downright

silly notion. He couldn't understand why it was there. He was wondering how tall the waitress was, whether she was taller than he was. He tried to discard the thought, but it stayed there. It nudged him, shoved him, and finally caused him to turn his head and look at her.

He had to look down a little. He was a few inches taller than the waitress. He estimated she stood about five-six in semi-high heels. So what? he asked himself, but he went on looking as they crossed a narrow street and passed under a street lamp. The coat she wore fitted rather tightly and it brought out the lines of her body. She was high-waisted and with her slimness and her certain way of walking, it made her look taller. I guess that's it, he thought. I was just curious about it, that's all.

But he went on looking. He didn't know why he was looking. The glow from the street lamp spread out and lighted her face and he saw her profiled features that wouldn't make her a cover girl or a model for cosmetic ads, she didn't have that kind of face. Except for the skin. Her skin was clear and it had the kind of texture guaranteed in cosmetic ads, but this didn't come from cosmetics. This was from inside, and he thought, Probably she's got a good stomach, or a good set of glands, it's something along that line. There's nothing fragile about this one. That ain't a fragile nose or mouth or chin, and yet it's female, more female than them fragile-pretty types who look more like ornaments than girls. All in all, I'd say this one could give them cards and spades and still come out ahead. No wonder the bouncer tries to move in. No wonder all the roosters at the bar are always looking twice when she walks past. And still she ain't interested just in anything wears pants.

It's as though she's all finished with that. Maybe something happened that made her say, That does it, that ends it. But now you're guessing. How come you're guessing? Next thing, you'll want to know how old she is. And merely incidentally, how old you think she is? I'd say around twenty-seven. Should we ask her? If you do, she'll ask you why you want to know. And all you can say is, I just wondered. All right, stop wondering. It ain't as if you're interested. You know you're not interested.

Then what is it? What put you on this line of thinking? You oughtta get off it, it's like a road with too many turns and first thing you know, you just don't know where you are. But why is it she never has much to say? And hardly ever smiles?

Come to think of it, she's strictly on the solemn side. Not dreary, really. It's just that she's serious-solemn, and yet you've seen her laugh, she'll laugh at something that's comical. That is, when it's really comical.

She was laughing now. She was looking at him and quietly laughing.

"What is it?" he asked.

"Like Charlie Chaplin," she said.

"Like who?"

"Charlie Chaplin. In them silent movies he used to make. When something puzzled him and he wanted to ask about it and couldn't find the words, he'd get a dumb look on his face. You had it perfect just then."

"Did I?"

She nodded. Then she stopped laughing. She said, "What was it? What puzzled you?"

He smiled dimly. "If we're gonna get to John's, we oughtta keep walkin'."

She didn't say anything. They went on walking, turning a corner and coming onto a rutted pavement that bordered a cobblestoned street.

They covered another block and on the corner there was a rectangular structure that had once been a trolley car and was now an eatery that stayed open all night. Some of the windows were cracked, much of the paint was scraped off, and the entrance door slanted on loose hinges. Above the entrance door a sign read, *Best Food in Port Richmond—John's*. They went in and started toward the counter and for some reason she pulled him away from the counter and into a booth. As they sat down he saw she was looking past him, her eyes aimed at the far end of the counter. Her face was expressionless. He knew who it was down there. He knew also why she'd talked him into walking with her when they'd left the Hut. She hadn't wanted him to walk alone. She'd seen his maneuver with the beer cases when the two men had made their try for

Turley, and all that talk about you-gotta-eat was merely so that he shouldn't be on the street alone.

Very considerate of her, he thought. He smiled at her to hide his annoyance. But then it amused him, and he thought, She wants to play nursemaid, let her play nursemaid.

There weren't many people in the diner. He counted four at this section of the counter, and two couples in other booths. Behind the counter the short, chunky Greek named John was breaking eggs above the grill. So with John it comes to nine, he thought. We got nine witnesses in case they try something. I don't think they will. You had a good look at them in the Hut. They didn't look like dunces. No, they won't try anything now.

John served four fried eggs to a fat man at the counter, came out from behind the counter and went over to the booth. The waitress ordered roast pork and mashed potatoes and said she wanted an extra roll. He asked for a cup of coffee with cream. She said, "That all you gonna have?" He nodded and she said, "You know you're hungry. Order something."

He shook his head. John walked away from the booth. They sat there, not saying anything. He hummed a tune and lightly drummed his fingers on the tabletop.

Then she said, "You loaned me seventy-five cents. What you got left for yourself?"

"I'm really not hungry."

"Not much. Come on, tell me. How much change you got?"

He put his hand in his pants pocket. "I hate to break this fifty-dollar bill."

"Now, listen—"

"Forget it," he cut in mildly. Then, his thumb flicking backward, "They still there?"

"Who?"

"You know who."

She looked past him, past the side of the booth, her eyes checking the far end of the counter. Then she looked at him and nodded slowly. She said, "It's my fault. I didn't use my head. I didn't stop to think they might be here—"

"What're they doing now? They still eating?"

"They're finished. They're just sitting there. Smoking."

"Looking?"

"Not at us. They were looking this way a minute ago. I don't think it meant anything. They can't see you."

"Then I guess it's all right," he said. He grinned.

She grinned back at him. "Sure, it's nothing to worry about. Even if they see you, they won't do anything."

"I know they won't." And then, widening the grin, "You won't let them."

"Me?" Her grin faded. She frowned slightly. "What can I do?"

"I guess you can do something." Then, breezily, "You could hold them off while I cut out."

"Is that a joke? Whatcha think I am, Joan of Arc?"

"Well, now that you mention it—"

"Lemme tell you something," she interrupted. "I don't know what's happening between you and them two and I don't care. Whatever it is, I want no part of it. That clear?"

"Sure." And then, with a slight shrug, "If that's the way you really feel about it."

"I said so, didn't I?"

"Yeah. You said so."

"What's that supposed to mean?" Her head was slanted and she was giving him a look. "You think I don't mean what I say?"

He shrugged again. "I don't think anything. You're doing all the arguing."

John arrived with the tray, served the platter and the coffee, figured the price with his fingers and said sixty-five cents. Eddie took the dime and two pennies from his pocket and put the coins on the table. She pushed the coins aside and gave John the seventy-five cents. Eddie smiled at John and pointed to the twelve cents on the table. John said thanks, picked up the coins and went back to the counter. Eddie leaned low over the steaming black coffee, blew on it to cool it, and began sipping it. There was no sound from the other side of the table. He sensed that she wasn't eating, but was just sitting watching him. He didn't look up. He went on sipping the coffee. It was very hot and he sipped it slowly. Then he heard the noise of her knife and fork and he glanced up and saw that she was eating rapidly.

"What's the rush?" he murmured. She didn't reply. The noise of her knife and fork went on and then stopped suddenly and he looked up again. He saw she was looking out and away from the table, focusing again on the far end of the counter.

She frowned and resumed eating. He waited a few moments, and then murmured, "I thought you said it ain't your problem."

She let it slide past. She went on frowning. "They're still sitting there. I wish they'd get up and go out."

"I guess they wanna stay here and get warm. It's nice and warm in here."

"It's getting too warm," she said.

"It is?" He sipped more coffee. "I don't feel it."

"Not much you don't." She gave him another sideways look. "Don't give me that cucumber routine. You're sitting on a hot spot and you know it."

"Got a cigarette?"

"I'm talking to you—"

"I heard what you said." He gestured toward her handbag. "Look, I'm all outa smokes. See if you got a spare."

She opened the handbag and took out a pack of cigarettes. She gave him one, took one for herself, and struck a match. As he leaned forward to get the light, she said, "Who are they?"

"You got me."

"Ever see them before?"

"Nope."

"All right," she said. "We'll drop it."

She finished eating, drank some water, took a final puff at her cigarette and put it out in the ashtray. They got up from the booth and walked out of the eatery. Now the wind came harder and colder and it had started to snow. As the flakes hit the pavement they stayed there white instead of melting. She pulled up her coat collar, and put her hands into her pockets. She looked up and around at the snow coming down, and said she liked the snow, she hoped it would keep on snowing. He said it would probably snow all night and then some tomorrow. She asked him if he liked the snow. He said it didn't really matter to him.

They were walking along on the cobblestoned street and

he wanted to look behind him but he didn't. The wind was coming at them and they had to keep their heads down and push themselves along. She was saying he could walk her home if he wanted to. He said all right, not thinking to ask where she lived. She told him she lived in a rooming house on Kenworth Street. She was telling him the block number but he didn't hear. He was listening to the sound of his footsteps and her footsteps and wondering if that was the only sound. Then he heard the other sound, but it was only some alley cats crying. It was a small sound, and he decided they were kittens wailing for their mother. He wished there was something he could do for them, the motherless kittens. They were somewhere in that alley across the street. He heard the waitress saying, "Where you going?"

He had moved away from her, toward the curb. He was looking at the entrance to the alley across the street. She came up to him and said, "What is it?"

"The kittens," he said.

"Kittens?"

"Listen to them," he said. "Poor little kittens. They're having a sad time."

"You got it twisted," she said. "They ain't no kittens, they're grown-up cats. From what I hear, they're having a damn good time."

He listened again. This time he heard it correctly. He grinned and said, "Guess it needs a new aerial."

"No," she said. "The aerial's all right. You just got your stations mixed, that's all."

He didn't quite get that. He looked at her inquiringly.

She said, "I guess it's a habit you got. Like in the Hut. I've noticed it. You never seem to know or care what's really happening. Always tuned in on some weird kinda wave length that only you can hear. As if you ain't concerned in the least with current events."

He laughed softly.

"Quit that," she cut in. "Quit making it a joke. This ain't no joke, what's happening now. You take a look around, you'll see what I mean."

She was facing him, staring past him. He said, "We got company?"

She nodded slowly.

"I don't hear anything," he said. "Only them cats—"

"Forget the cats. You got your hands full now. You can't afford no side shows."

She's got a point there, he thought. He turned and looked down the street. Far down there the yellow-green glow from a street lamp came dripping off the tops of the parked cars. It formed a faintly lit, yellow-green pool on the cobblestones, a shimmering screen for all moving shadows. He saw two shadows moving on the screen, two creepers crouched down there behind one of the parked cars.

"They're waiting," he said. "They're waiting for us to move."

"If we're gonna move, we'd better do it fast." She spoke technically. "Come on, we'll hafta run—"

"No," he said. "There's no rush. We'll just keep walking."

Again she gave him the searching look. "You been through this sorta thing before?"

He didn't answer. He was concentrating on the distance between here and the street corner ahead. They were walking slowly toward the corner. He estimated the distance was some twenty yards. As they went on walking slowly, he looked at her and smiled and said, "Don't be nervous. There's nothing to be nervous about."

Not much there ain't, he thought.

4

THEY came to the street corner and turned onto a narrow street that had only one lamp. His eyes probed the darkness and found a splintered wooden door, the entrance to an alley-way. He tried the door and it gave, and he went through and she followed him, closing the door behind her. As they stood there, waiting for the sound of approaching footsteps, he heard a rustling noise, as though she was searching for something under her coat.

"What are you doing?" he asked.

"Getting my hatpin," she said. "They come in here, they'll have a five-inch hatpin all ready for them."

"You think it'll bother them?"

"It won't make them happy, that's for sure."

"I guess you're right. That thing goes in deep, it hurts."

"Let them try something." She spoke in a tight whisper. "Just let them try something, and see what happens."

They waited there in the pitch-black darkness behind the alley door. Moments passed, and then they heard the footsteps coming. The footsteps arrived, hesitated, went on and then stopped. Then the footsteps came back toward the alley door. He could feel the rigid stillness of the waitress, close beside him. Then he could hear the voices on the other side of the door.

"Where'd they go?" one of the voices said.

"Maybe into one of these houses."

"We shoulda moved faster."

"We played it right. It's just that they were close to home. They went into one of these houses."

"Well, whaddya want to do?"

"We can't start ringing doorbells."

"You wanna keep walking? Maybe they're somewhere up the street."

"Let's go back to the car. I'm getting cold."

"You wanna call it a night?"

"A loused-up night."

"In spades. God damn it."

The footsteps went away. He said to her, "Let's wait a few minutes," and she said, "I guess I can put the hatpin away."

He grinned and murmured, "Be careful where you put it, I don't wanna get jabbed." They were standing there in the cramped space of the very narrow alley and as her arm moved, her elbow came lightly against his ribs. It wasn't more than a touch, but for some reason he quivered, as though the hatpin had jabbed him. He knew it wasn't the hatpin. And then, moving again, shifting her position in the cramped space, she touched him again and there was more quivering. He breathed in fast through his teeth, feeling something happening. It was happening suddenly and much too fast and he tried to stop it. He said to himself, You gotta stop it. But the thing of it is, it came on you too quick, you just weren't ready for it, you had no idea it was on its way. Well, one thing you know, you can't get rid of it standing here with her so close, too close, too damn close. You think she knows? Sure she knows, she's trying not to touch you again. And now she's moving back so you'll have more room. But it's still too crowded in here. I guess we can go out now. Come on, open the door. What are you waiting for?

He opened the alley door and stepped out onto the pavement. She followed him. They walked up the street, not talking, not looking at each other. He started to walk faster, moving out in front of her. She made no attempt to catch up with him. It went on like that and he was moving far out in front of her, not thinking about it, just wanting to walk fast and get home and go to sleep.

Then presently it occurred to him that he was walking alone. He'd come to a street crossing and he turned and waited. He looked for her and didn't see her. Where'd she go? he asked himself. The answer came from very far down the street, the sound of her clicking heels, going off in the other direction.

For a moment he played with the thought of going after her. So you won't get Z for etiquette, he thought, and took a few steps. Then he stopped, and shook his head, and said to himself, You better leave it the way it is. Stay away from her.

But why? he asked himself, suddenly aware that something was happening again. It just don't figure, it can't be like that, like just the thought of her touching you is a little too much for you to handle and it gets started again. For months she's been working at the Hut, you've seen her there every night and she was nothing more than part of the scenery. And now out of nowhere comes this problem.

You calling it a problem? Come off that, you know it ain't no problem, you just ain't geared for any problems, for any issues at all. With you it's everything for kicks, the cool-easy kicks that ask for no effort at all, the soft-easy style that has you smiling all the time with your tongue in your cheek. It's been that way for a long time now and it's worked for you, it's worked out just fine. You take my advice, you'll keep it that way.

But she said she lived on Kenworth Street. Maybe you better do some scouting, just to make sure she got home all right. Yes, them two operators mighta changed their minds about calling it a night. They coulda decided to have another look around the neighborhood. Maybe they spotted her walking alone and—

Now look, you gotta stop it. You gotta think about something else. Think about what? All right, let's think about Oscar Levant. Is he really talented? Yes, he's really talented. Is Art Tatum talented? Art Tatum is very talented. And what about Walter Gieseking? Well, you never heard him play in person, so you can't say, you just don't know. Another thing you don't know is the house number on Kenworth. You don't even know the block number. Did she tell you the block number? I can't remember.

Oh for Christ's sake go home and go to sleep.

He lived in a rooming house a few blocks away from the Hut. It was a two-story house and his room was on the second floor. The room was small, the rent was five-fifty a week, and it amounted to a bargain because the landlady had a cleanliness phobia; she was always scrubbing or dusting. It was a very old house but all the rooms were spotless.

His room had a bed, a table and a chair. On the floor near the chair there was a pile of magazines. They were all musical publications, most of them dealing with classical music. The magazine on top of the pile was open and as he came into the room he picked it up and leafed through it. Then he started to read an article having to do with some new developments in contrapuntal theory.

The article was very interesting. It was written by a well-known name in the field, someone who really knew what it was all about. He lit a cigarette and stood there under the ceiling light, still wearing his snow-speckled overcoat, focusing on the magazine article. Somewhere in the middle of the third paragraph he lifted his eyes and looked at the window.

The window faced the street; the shade was halfway up. He

walked to the window and looked out. Then he opened the window and leaned out to get a wider look. The street was empty. He stayed there and watched the snow coming down. He felt the wind-whipped flakes taking cold bites at his face. The cold air sliced and chopped at him, and he thought, It's gonna feel good to get into that bed.

He undressed quickly. Then he was naked and climbing in under the sheet and the thick quilt, pulling the cord of the lamp near the bed, pulling the other cord that was a long string attached from the ceiling light to the bedpost. He sat there propped against the pillow, and lit another cigarette and continued with the magazine article.

For a few minutes he went on reading, then he just looked at the printed words without taking them in. It went that way for a while, and finally he let the magazine fall to the floor. He sat there smoking and looking at the wall across the room.

The cigarette burned low and he leaned over to smother it in the ashtray on the table near the bed. As he pressed the stub in the tray, he heard the knock on the door.

The wind whistled in through the open window and mixed with the sound that came from the door. He felt very cold, looking at the door, wondering who it was out there.

Then he smiled at himself, knowing who it was, knowing what he'd hear next because he'd heard it so many times in the three years he'd lived here.

From the other side of the door a female voice whispered. "You in there, Eddie? It's me, Clarice."

He climbed out of bed. He opened the door and the woman came in. He said, "Hello, Clarice," and she looked at him standing there naked and said, "Hey, get under that quilt. You'll catch cold."

Then she closed the door, doing it carefully and quietly. He was in the bed again, sitting there with the quilt up around his middle. He smiled at her and said, "Sit down."

She pulled the chair toward the bed and sat down. She said, "Jesus Christ, it's freezing in here," and got up and lowered the window. Then, seated again, she said, "You cold-air fiends amaze me. It's a wonder you don't get the flu. Or ammonia."

"Fresh air is good for you."

"Not this time of year," she said. "This time of year it's for the birds, and even they don't want it. Them birds got more brains than we got. They go to Florida."

"They can do it. They got wings."

"I wish to hell I had wings," the woman said. "Or at least the cash it needs for bus fare. I'd pack up and head south and get me some of that sunshine."

"You ever been south?"

"Sure, loads of times. On the carnival circuit. One time in Jacksonville I busted an ankle, trying out a new caper. They left me stranded there in the hospital, didn't even leave me my pay. Them carnival people—some of them are dogs, just dogs."

She helped herself to one of his cigarettes. She lit it with a loose, graceful motion of arm and wrist. Then she waved out the flaming match, tossing it from one hand to the other, the flame dying in mid-air, and caught the dead match precisely between her thumb and small finger.

"How's that for timing?" she asked him, as though he'd never seen the trick before.

He'd seen it countless times. She was always performing these little stunts. And sometimes at the Hut she'd clear the tables to give herself room, and do the flips and somersaults that showed she still had some of it left, the timing and the coordination and the extra-fast reflexes. In her late teens and early twenties she'd been a better-than-average acrobatic dancer.

Now, at thirty-two, she was still a professional, but in a different line of endeavor. It was all horizontal acrobatics on a mattress, her body for rent at three dollars a performance. In her room down the hall on the second floor she gave them more than their money's worth. Her contortions on the mattress were strictly circus-stunt variety. Among the barflies at the Hut, the consensus was "—really something, that Clarice. You come outa that room, you're dizzy."

Her abilities in this field, especially the fact that she never slackened the pace, were due mainly to her bent for keeping in condition. As a stunt dancer, she'd adhered faithfully to the strict training rules, the rigid diet and the daily exercises. In this present profession, she was equally devoted to certain laws and regulations of physical culture, maintaining that "it's very important, y'unnerstand. Sure, I drink gin. It's good for me. Keeps me from eating too much. I never overload my belly."

Her body showed it. She still had the acrobat's coiled-spring flexibility, and was double-jointed in so many places that it was as if she had no bones at all. She stood five-five and weighed one-five, but she didn't look skinny, just tightly packed around the frame. There wasn't much of breast or hip or thigh, just about enough to label it female. The female aspect showed mainly in her face, her fragile nose and chin, her wide-set, pale-gray eyes. She wore her hair rather short, and was always having it dyed. Right now it was somewhere between yellow and orange.

She sat there wearing a terry cloth bathrobe, one sleeve ripped halfway up to the elbow. With the cigarette still between the thumb and little finger, she lifted it to her mouth, took a small sip of smoke, let it out and said to him, "How's about it?"

"Not tonight."

"You broke?"

He nodded.

Clarice sipped more smoke. She said, "You want it on credit?"

He shook his head.

"You've had it on credit before," she said. "Your credit's always good with me."

"It ain't that," he said. "It's just that I'm tired. I'm awfully tired."

"You wanna go to sleep?" She started to get up.

"No," he said. "Sit there. Stick around a while. We'll talk."

"Okay." She settled back in the chair. "I need some company, anyway. I get so dragged in that room sometimes. They never wanna sit and talk. As if they're afraid I'll charge them extra."

"How'd you do tonight?"

She shrugged. "So-so." She put her hand in the bathrobe pocket and there was the rustling of paper, the tinkling of coins. "For a Friday night it wasn't bad, I guess. Most Friday nights there ain't much trade. They either spend their last nickel at Harriet's or they're so plastered they gotta be carried home. Or else they're too noisy and I can't chance it. The landlady warned me again last week. She said one more time and out I go."

"She's been saying that for years."

"Sometimes I wonder why she lets me stay."

"You really wanna know?" He smiled dimly. "Her room is right under yours. She could take a different room if she wanted to. After all, it's her house. But no, she keeps that room. So it figures she likes the sound it makes."

"The sound? What sound?"

"The bedsprings," he said.

"But look now, that woman is seventy-six years old."

"That's the point," he said. "They get too old for the action, they gotta have something, at least. With her it's the sound."

Clarice pondered it for a few moments. Then she nodded slowly. "Come to think of it, you got something there." And then, with a sigh, "It must be awful to get old like that."

"You think so? I don't think so. It's just a part of the game and it happens, that's all."

"It won't happen to me," she said decisively. "I hit sixty, I'll take gas. What's the point of hanging around doing nothing?"

"There's plenty to do after sixty."

"Not for this one. This one ain't joining a sewing circle, or playing bingo night after night. If I can't do no better than that, I'll just let them put me in a box."

"They put you in, you'd jump right out. You'd come out doing somersaults."

"You think I would? Really?"

"Sure you would." He grinned at her. "Double somersaults and back flips. And getting applause."

Her face lighted up, as though she could see it happening. But then her bare feet felt the solid floor and it brought her back to here and now. She looked at the man in the bed.

And then she was off the chair and onto the side of the bed. She put her hand on the quilt over his knee.

He frowned slightly. "What's the matter, Clarice?"

"I don't know, I just feel like doing something."

"But I told you—"

"That was business. This ain't business. Reminds me of one

night last summer when I came in here and we got to talking, I remember you were flat broke and I said you could have credit and you said no, so I let it drop and we went on talking about this and that and you happened to mention my hair-do. You said it looked real nice, the way I had my hair fixed. I'd fixed it myself earlier that night and I was wondering about how it looked. So of course it gimme a lift when you said that, and I said thanks. I remember saying thanks.

"But I don't know, I guess it needed more than just thanks. I guess I hadda show some real appreciation. Not exactly what you'd call a favor for a favor, but more like an urge, I'd call it. And the windup was I let you have it for free. So now I'll tell you something. I'll tell you the way it went for me. It went all the way up in the sky."

His frown had deepened. And then a grin mixed with the frown and he said, "Whatcha doing? Writing verses?"

She gave a little laugh. "Sounds that way, don't it?" And tried it for sound, mimicking herself, "—way up in the sky." She shook her head, and said, "Jesus Christ, I oughtta put that on tape and sell it to the soap people. But even so, what I'm trying to say, that night last summer was some night, Eddie. I sure remember that night."

He nodded slowly. "Me too."

"You remember?" She leaned toward him. "You really remember?"

"Sure," he said. "It was one of them nights don't come very often."

"And here's something else. If I ain't mistaken, it was a Friday night."

"I don't know," he said.

"Sure it was. It damn sure was a Friday night, cause next day at the Hut you got your pay from Harriet. She always pays you on Saturdays and that's how I remember. She paid you and then you came over to the table where I was sitting with some johns. You tried to give me three dollars. I told you to go to hell. So then you wanted to know what I was sore about, and I said I wasn't sore. And just to prove it, I bought you a drink. A double gin."

"That's right," he said, remembering that he hadn't wanted the gin, he'd accepted it just as a gesture. As they'd raised glasses, she'd been looking through her glass and through his glass, as though trying to tell him something that could only be said through the gin. He remembered that now. He remembered it very clearly.

He said, "I'm really tired, Clarice. If I wasn't—"

Her hand went away from the quilt over his knee. She gave a little shrug and said, "Well, I guess all Friday nights ain't the same."

He winced slightly.

She walked toward the door. At the door she turned and gave him a friendly smile. He started to say something, but he couldn't get it out. He saw that her smile had given way to a look of concern.

"What is it, Eddie?"

He wondered what showed on his face. He was trying to show the soft-easy smile, but he couldn't get it started. Then he blinked several times and made a straining effort and the smile came onto his lips.

But she was looking at his eyes. "You sure you're all right?"

"I'm fine," he said. "Why shouldn't I be? I got no worries."

She winked at him, as though to say, You want me to believe that, I'll believe it. Then she said good night and walked out of the room.

5

HE didn't get much sleep. He thought about Turley. He said to himself, Why think about that? You know they didn't get Turley. If they'd grabbed Turley, they wouldn't need you. They came after you because they're very anxious to have some discussion with Turley. What about? Well, you don't know, and you don't care. So I guess you can go to sleep now.

He thought about the beer cases falling onto the floor at the Hut. When you did that, he thought, you started something. Like telling them you had some connection with Turley. And naturally they snatched at that. They reasoned you could take them to Turley.

But I guess it's all right now. Item one, they don't know you're his brother. Item two, they don't know where you live. We'll skip item three because that item is the waitress and you don't want to think about her. All right, we won't think about her, we'll concentrate on Turley. You know he got away and that's nice to know. It's also nice to know they won't get you. After all, they're not the law, they can't go around asking questions. Not in this neighborhood, anyway. In this neighborhood it sure as hell ain't easy to get information. The citizens here have a closed-mouth policy when it comes to giving out facts and figures, especially someone's address. You've lived here long enough to know that. You know there's a very stiff line of defense against all bill collectors, skip tracers, or any kind of tracers. So no matter who they ask, they'll get nothing. But hold it there. You sure about that?

I'm sure of only one thing, mister. You need sleep and you can't sleep. You've started something and you're making it big, and the truth is it ain't nothing at all. That's just about the size of it, it's way down there at zero.

His eyes were open and he was looking at the window. In the darkness he could see the white dots moving on the black screen, the millions of white dots coming down out there, and he thought, They're gonna have sledding today, the kids. Say, is that window open? Sure it's open, you can see it's open. You opened it after Clarice walked out. Well, let's open it wider. We have more air in here, it might help us to fall asleep.

He got out of bed and went to the window. He opened it all the way. Then he leaned out and looked and the street was empty. In bed again, he closed his eyes and kept them closed and finally fell asleep. He slept for less than an hour and got up and went to the window and looked out. The street was empty. Then he had another couple hours of sleep before he felt the need for one more look. At the window, leaning out, he looked at the street and saw that it was empty. That's final, he told himself. We won't look again.

It was six-fifteen, the numbers yellow-white on the face of the alarm clock. We'll get some sleep now, some real sleep, he decided. We'll sleep till one, or make it one-thirty. He set the clock for one-thirty and climbed into bed and fell asleep. At eight he woke up and went to the window. Then he returned to the bed and slept until ten-twenty, at which time he made another trip to the window. The only action out there was the snow. It came down in thick flurries, and already it looked a few inches deep. He watched it for some moments, then climbed into bed and fell asleep. Two hours later he was up and at the window. There was nothing happening and he went back to sleep. Within thirty minutes he was awake and at the window. The street was empty, except for the Buick.

The Buick was brand-new, a pale green-and-cream hard-top convertible. It was parked across the street and from the angle of the window he could see them in the front seat, the two of them. He recognized the felt hats first, the pearl-gray and the darker gray. It's them, he told himself. And you knew they'd show. You've known it all night long. But how'd they get the address?

Let's find out. Let's get dressed and go out there and find out.

Getting dressed, he didn't hurry. They'll wait, he thought. They're in no rush and they don't mind waiting. But it's cold out there, you shouldn't make them wait too long, it's inconsiderate. After all, they were thoughtful of you, they were really considerate. They didn't come up here and break down the door and drag you out of bed. I think that was very nice of them.

He slipped into the tattered overcoat, went out of the room, down the steps, and out the front door. He walked across the snow-covered street and they saw him coming. He was smiling at them. As he came closer, he gave a little wave of recognition, and the man behind the wheel waved back. It was the short, thin one, the one in the pearl-gray hat.

The car window came down, and the man behind the wheel said, "Hello, Eddie."

"Eddie?"

"That's your name, ain't it?"

"Yes, that's my name." He went on smiling. His eyes were making the mild inquiry, Who told you?

Without sound the short, thin one answered, Let's skip that for now, then said aloud, "They call me Feather. It's sort of a nickname. I'm in that weight division." He indicated the other man, saying, "This is Morris."

"Pleased to meet you," Eddie said.

"Same here," Feather said. "We're very pleased to meet you, Eddie." Then he reached back and opened the rear door. "Why stand out there in the snow? Slide in and get comfortable."

"I'm comfortable," Eddie said.

Feather held the door open. "It's warmer in the car."

"I know it is," Eddie said. "I'd rather stay out here. I like it out here."

Feather and Morris looked at each other. Morris moved his hand toward his lapel, his fingers sliding under and in, and Feather said, "Leave it alone. We don't need that."

"I wanna show it to him," Morris said.

"He knows it's there."

"Maybe he ain't sure. I want him to be sure."

"All right, show it to him."

Morris reached in under his lapel and took out a small black revolver. It was chunky and looked heavy but he handled it as though it were a fountain pen. He twirled it once and it came down flat in his palm. He let it stay there for a few moments, then returned it to the holster under his lapel. Feather was saying to Eddie, "You wanna get in the car?"

"No," Eddie said.

Again Feather and Morris looked at each other. Morris said, "Maybe he thinks we're kidding."

"He knows we're not kidding."

Morris said to Eddie, "Get in the car. You gonna get in the car?"

"If I feel like it." Eddie was smiling again. "Right now I don't feel like it."

Morris frowned. "What's the matter with you? You can't be that stupid. Maybe you're sick in the head, or something." And then, to Feather, "How's he look to you?"

Feather was studying Eddie's face. "I don't know," he murmured slowly and thoughtfully. "He looks like he can't feel anything."

"He can feel metal," Morris said. "He gets a chunk of metal in his face, he'll feel it."

Eddie stood there next to the opened window, his hands going through his pockets and hunting for cigarettes. Feather asked him what he was looking for and he said, "A smoke," but there were no cigarettes and finally Feather gave him one and lit it for him and then said, "I'll give you more if you want. I'll give you an entire pack. If that ain't enough, I'll give you a carton. Or maybe you'd rather have cash."

Eddie didn't say anything.

"How's fifty dollars?" Morris said, smiling genially at Eddie.

"What would that buy me?" He wasn't looking at either of them.

"A new overcoat," Morris said. "You could use a new overcoat."

"I think he wants more than that," Feather said, again studying Eddie's face. He was waiting for Eddie to say something. He waited for some fifteen seconds, then said, "You want to quote a figure?"

Eddie spoke very softly. "For what? What am I selling?"

"You know," Feather said. And then, "A hundred?"

Eddie didn't reply. He was gazing slantwise through the opened window, through the windshield, and past the hood of the Buick.

"Three hundred?" Feather asked.

"That covers a lot of expenses," Morris put in.

"I ain't got much expenses," Eddie said.

"Then why you stalling?" Feather asked mildly.

"I'm not stalling," Eddie said. "I'm just thinking."

"Maybe he thinks we ain't got that kind of money," Morris said.

"Is that what's holding up the deal?" Feather said to Eddie. "You wanna see the roll?"

Eddie shrugged.

"Sure, let him see it," Morris said. "Let him know we're not just talking, we got the solid capital."

Feather reached into the inner pocket of his jacket and took out a shiny lizard billfold. His fingers went in and came out with a sheaf of crisp currency. He counted it aloud, as though counting it for himself, but loud enough for Eddie to hear. There were twenties and fifties and hundreds. The total was well over two thousand dollars. Feather returned the money to the billfold and put it back in his pocket.

"That's a lot of money to carry around," Eddie commented.

"That's chicken feed," Feather said.

"Depends on the annual income," Eddie murmured. "You make a bundle, you can carry a bundle. Or sometimes it ain't yours, they just give it to you to spend."

"They?" Feather narrowed his eyes. "Who you mean by they?"

Eddie shrugged again. "I mean, when you work for big people—"

Feather glanced at Morris. For some moments it was quiet. Then Feather said to Eddie, "You wouldn't be getting cute, would you?"

Eddie smiled at the short, thin man and made no answer.

"Do yourself a favor," Feather said quietly. "Don't be cute with me. I'll only get irritated and then we can't talk business. I'll be too upset." He was looking at the steering wheel. He played his thin fingers around the smooth rim of the steering wheel. "Now let's see. Where were we?"

"It was three," Morris offered. "He wouldn't sell at three. So what I think is, you offer him five—"

"All right," Feather said. He looked at Eddie. "Five hundred dollars."

Eddie glanced down at the cigarette between his fingers. He lifted it to his mouth and took a meditative drag.

"Five hundred," Feather said. "And no more."

"That's final?"

"Capped," Feather said, and reached inside his jacket, going for the billfold.

"Nothing doing," Eddie said.

Feather exchanged another look with Morris. "I don't get this," Feather said. He spoke as though Eddie weren't there. "I've seen all kinds, but this one here is new to me. What gives with him?"

"You're asking me?" Morris made a hopeless gesture, his palms out and up. "I can't reach out that far. He's moon material."

Eddie was wearing the soft-easy smile and gazing at nothing. He stood there taking small drags at the cigarette. His overcoat was unbuttoned, as though he weren't aware of wind and snow. The two men in the car were staring at him, waiting for him to say something, to give some indication that he was actually there.

And finally, from Feather, "All right, let's try it from another angle." His voice was mild. "It's this way, Eddie. All we wanna do is talk to him. We're not out to hurt him."

"Hurt who?"

Feather snapped his fingers, "Come on, let's put it on the table. You know who I'm talking about. Your brother. Your brother Turley."

Eddie's expression didn't change. He didn't even blink. He was saying to himself, Well, there it is. They know you're his brother. So now you're in it, you're pulled in and I wish you could figure a way to slide out.

He heard Feather saying, "We just wanna sit him down and have a little talk. All you gotta do is make the connection."

"I can't do that," he said. "I don't know where he is."

Then, from Morris, "You sure about that? You sure you ain't trying to protect him?"

"Why should I?" Eddie shrugged. "He's only my brother. For half a grand I'd be a fool not to hand him over. After all, what's a brother? A brother means nothing."

"Now he's getting cute again," Feather said.

"A brother, a mother, a father," Eddie said with another shrug, "they ain't important at all. Like merchandise you sell across a counter. That is," and his voice dropped just a little, "according to certain ways of thinking."

"What's he saying now?" Morris wanted to know.

"I think he's telling us to go to hell," Feather said. Then he looked at Morris, and he nodded slowly, and Morris took out the revolver. Then Feather said to Eddie. "Open the door. Get in."

Eddie stood there smiling at them.

"He wants it," Morris said, and then there was the sound of the safety catch.

"That's a pretty noise," Eddie said.

"You wanna hear something really pretty?" Feather murmured.

"First you gotta count to five," Eddie told him. "Go on, count to five. I wanna hear you count."

Feather's thin face was powder-white. "Let's make it three." But as he said it he was looking past Eddie.

Eddie was saying, "All right, we'll count to three. You want me to count for you?"

"Later," Feather said, still looking past him, and smiling now. "That is, when she gets here."

Just then Eddie felt the snow and the wind. The wind was very cold. He heard himself saying, "When who gets here?"

"The skirt," Feather said. "The skirt we saw you with last night. She's coming to pay you a visit."

He turned and saw her coming down the street. She was crossing the street diagonally, coming toward the car. He raised his hand just high enough to make the warning gesture, telling her to stay away, to please stay away. She kept advancing toward the car and he thought, She knows, she knows you're in a situation and she figures she can help. But that gun. She can't see that gun—

He heard the voice of Feather saying, "She your girl friend, Eddie?"

He didn't answer. The waitress came closer. He made another warning gesture but now she was very close and he looked away from her to glance inside the car. He saw Morris sitting slantwise with the gun moving slowly from side to side, to cover two people instead of one. That does it, he thought. That includes her in.

6

THEN she was standing there next to him and they were both looking at the gun. He waited for her to ask him what it was all about, but she didn't say anything. Feather leaned back, smiling at them, giving them plenty of time to study the gun, to think about the gun. It went on that way for perhaps half a minute, and then Feather said to Eddie, "That counting routine. You still want me to count to three?"

"No," Eddie said. "I guess that ain't necessary." He was trying not to frown. He was very much annoyed with the waitress.

"What's the seating arrangement?" Morris wanted to know.

"You in the back," Feather told him, then took the gun from Morris and opened the door and got out of the car. He held the gun close to his side as he walked with Eddie and Lena, staying just a little behind them as they went around to the other side of the car. He told them to get in the front seat. Eddie started to get in first, and Feather said, "No, I want her in the middle." She climbed in and Eddie followed her. Morris was reaching out from the back seat to take the gun from Feather. For just an instant there was a chance for interception, but it wasn't much of a chance and Eddie thought, No matter how quick you are, the gun is quicker. You go for it, it'll go for you. And you know it'll get there first. I guess we'd better face the fact that we're going on a trip somewheres.

He watched Feather climbing in behind the wheel. The waitress sat there looking straight ahead through the windshield. "Sit back," Feather said to her. "You might as well be comfortable." Without looking at Feather, she said, "Thanks," and leaned back, folding her arms. Then Feather started the engine.

The Buick cruised smoothly down the street, turned a corner, went down another narrow street and then moved onto a wider street. Feather switched on the radio. A cool jazz outfit was in the middle of something breezy. It was nicely modulated music, featuring a soft-toned saxophone and someone's light expert touch on the keyboard. That's very fine piano, Eddie said to himself. I think that's Bud Powell.

Then he heard Lena saying, "Where we going?"

"Ask your boy friend," Feather said.

"He's not my boy friend."

"Well, ask him anyway. He's the navigator."

She looked at Eddie. He shrugged and went on listening to the music.

"Come on," Feather said to him. "Start navigating."

"Where you wanna go?"

"Turley."

"Where's that?" Lena asked.

"It ain't a town," Feather said. "It's his brother. We got some business with his brother."

"The man from last night?" She put the question to Eddie. "The one who ran out of the Hut?"

He nodded. "They did some checking," he said. "First they find out he's my brother. Then they get more information. They get my address."

"Who told them?"

"I think I know," he said. "But I'm not sure."

"I'll straighten you," Feather offered. "We went back to that saloon when it opened up this morning. We buy a few drinks and then we get to talking with big-belly, I mean the one who looks like a has-been wrestler—"

"Plyne," the waitress said.

"Is that his name?" Feather hit the horn lightly and two very young sledders jumped back on the curb. "So we're there at the bar and he's getting friendly, he's telling us he's the general manager and he gives us a drink on the house. Then he talks about this and that, staying clear of the point he wants to make. He handles it all right for a while, but finally it's too much for him, and he's getting clumsy with the talk. We just stand there and look at him. Then he makes his pitch. He wants to know what our game is."

"He said it kind of hungry-like," from Morris in the back seat.

"Yeah," Feather said. "Like he has it tabbed we're big time and he's looking for an in. You know how it is with these has-beens, they all want to get right up there again."

"Not all of them," the waitress said. And just for a moment she glanced at Eddie. And then, turning again to Feather, "You were saying?"

"Well, we didn't give him anything, just some nowhere talk that only made him hungrier. And then, just tossing it away, as if it ain't too important, I mention our friend here who knocked down them beer cases. It was a long shot, sure. But it paid off." He smiled congenially at Eddie. "It paid off real nice."

"That Plyne," the waitress said. "That Plyne and his big mouth."

"He got paid off, too," Feather said. "I slipped him a half-C for the info."

"That fifty made his eyes pop," Morris said.

"And made him greedy for more." Feather laughed lightly. "He asked us to come around again. He said if there was anything more he could do, we should call on him and—"

"The pig," she said. "The filthy pig."

Feather went on laughing. He looked over his shoulder, saying to Morris, "Come to think of it, that's what he looked like. I mean, when he went for the fifty. Like a pig going for slop—"

Morris pointed toward the windshield. "Watch where you're going."

Feather stopped laughing. "Who's got the wheel?"

"You got the wheel," Morris said. "But look at all the snow, it's freezing. We don't have chains."

"We don't need chains," Feather said. "We got snow tires."

"Well, even so," Morris said, "you better drive careful."

Again Feather looked at him. "You telling me how to drive?"

"For Christ's sake," Morris said. "I'm only telling you—"

"Don't tell me how to drive. I don't like when they tell me how to drive."

"When it snows, there's always accidents," Morris said. "We wanna get where we're going—"

"That's a sensible statement," Feather said. "Except for one thing. We don't know where we're going yet."

Then he glanced inquiringly at Eddie.

Eddie was listening to the music from the radio.

Feather reached toward the instrument panel and switched off the radio. He said to Eddie, "We'd like to know where we're going. You wanna help us out on that a little?"

Eddie shrugged. "I told you, I don't know where he is."

"You haven't any idea? No idea at all?"

"It's a big city," Eddie said. "It's a very big city."

"Maybe he ain't in the city," Feather murmured.

Eddie blinked a few times. He was looking straight ahead. He sensed that the waitress was watching him.

Feather probed gently. "I said maybe he ain't in the city. Maybe he's in the country."

"What?" Eddie said. All right, he told himself. Easy, now. Maybe he's guessing.

"The country," Feather said. "Like, say, in New Jersey."

That does it, Eddie thought. That wasn't a guess.

"Or let's tighten it a little," Feather said. "Let's make it South Jersey."

Now Eddie looked at Feather. He didn't say anything. The waitress sat there between them, quiet and relaxed, her hands folded in her lap.

Morris said, sort of mockingly, with pretended ignorance, "What's this with South Jersey? What's in South Jersey?"

"Watermelons," Feather said. "That's where they grow them."

"The melons?" Morris was playing straight man. "Who grows them?"

"The farmers, stupid. There's a lotta farmers in South Jersey. There's all these little farms, these watermelon patches."

"Where?"

"Whaddya mean, where? I just told you where. In South Jersey."

"The watermelon trees?"

"Pipe that," Feather said to the two front-seat passengers. "He thinks they grow on trees." And then, to Morris, "They grow in the ground. Like lettuce."

"Well, I've seen them growing lettuce, but never watermelons. How come I ain't seen the watermelons?"

"You didn't look."

"Sure I looked. I always look at the scenery. Especially in South Jersey. I've been to South Jersey loads of times. To Cape May. To Wildwood. All down through there."

"No watermelons?"

"Not a one," Morris said.

"I guess you were driving at night," Feather told him.

"Could be," Morris said. And then, timing it, "Or maybe these farms are far off the road."

"Now, that's an angle." Feather took a quick look at Eddie, then purred, "Some of these farms are way back there in the woods. These watermelon patches, I mean. They're sorta hidden back there—"

"All right, all right," the waitress broke in. She turned to Eddie. "What are they talking about?"

"It's nothing," Eddie said.

"You wish it was nothing," Morris said.

She turned to Feather. "What is it?"

"His folks," Feather said. Again he looked at Eddie. "Go on, tell her. You might as well tell her."

"Tell her what?" Eddie spoke softly. "What's there to tell?"

"There's plenty," Morris said. "That is, if you're in on it." He moved the gun forward just a little, doing it gently, so that the barrel barely touched Eddie's shoulder. "You in on it?"

"Hey, for Christ's sake—" Eddie pulled his shoulder away.

"What's happening there?" Feather asked.

"He's afraid of the rod," Morris said.

"Sure he's afraid. So am I. Put that thing away. We hit a bump it might go off."

"I want him to know—"

"He knows. They both know. They don't have to feel it to know it's there."

"All right." Morris sounded grumpy. "All right, all right."

The waitress was looking at Feather, then at Eddie, then at Feather again. She said, "Well, if he can't tell me, maybe you can—"

"About his folks?" Feather smiled. "Sure, I got some facts. There's the mother and the father and the two brothers. There's this Turley and the other one, his name is Clifton. That right, Eddie?"

Eddie shrugged. "If you say so."

"You know what I think?" Morris said slowly. "I think he's in on it."

"In on what?" the waitress snapped. "At least you could give me some idea—"

"You'll get the idea," Feather told her. "You'll get it when we reach that house."

"What house?"

"In South Jersey," Feather said. "In them woods where it used to be a watermelon patch but the weeds closed in and now it ain't a farm any more. It's just an old wooden house with a lot of weeds around it. And then the woods. There's no other houses around for miles—"

"No roads, either," Morris put in.

"Not cement roads, anyway," Feather said. "Just wagon paths that take you deep in them woods. So all you see is trees and more trees. And finally, there it is, the house. Just that one house far away from everything. It's what I'd call a gloomy layout." He looked at Eddie. "We got no time for fooling around. You know the route, so what you do is, you give the directions."

"How come?" the waitress asked. "Why do you need directions? You pictured that house like you've been there."

"I've never been there," Feather said. He went on looking at Eddie. "I was told about it, that's all. But they left out something. Forgot to tell me how to get there."

"He'll tell you," Morris said.

"Sure he'll tell me. What else can he do?"

Morris nudged Eddie's shoulder. "Give."

"Not yet," Feather said. "Wait'll we cross the bridge into Jersey. Then he'll tell us what roads to take."

"Maybe he don't know," the waitress said.

"You kidding?" Feather flipped it at her. "He was born and raised in that house. For him it's just a trip to the country, to visit the folks."

"Like coming home for Thanksgiving," Morris said. Again he touched Eddie's shoulder. This time it was a friendly pat. "After all, there's no place like home."

"Except it ain't a home," Feather said softly. "It's a hide-out."

7

Now they were on Front Street, headed south toward the Delaware River Bridge. They were coming into heavy traffic, and south of Lehigh Avenue the street was jammed. In addition to cars and trucks, there was a slow-moving swarm of Saturday afternoon shoppers, some of them jay-walkers who kept their heads down against the wind and the snow. The Buick moved very slowly and Feather kept hitting the horn. Morris was cursing the pedestrians. In front of the Buick there was a very old car without chains. It also lacked a windshield wiper. It was traveling at approximately fifteen miles per hour.

"Give him the horn," Morris said. "Give him the horn again."

"He can't hear it," Feather said.

"Give him the goddam horn. Keep blowing it."

Feather pressed the chromed rim, and the horn blasted and kept blasting. In the car ahead the driver turned and scowled and Feather went on blowing the horn.

"Try to pass him," Morris said.

"I can't," Feather muttered. "The street ain't wide enough."

"Try it now. There's no cars coming now."

Feather steered the Buick toward the left and then out a little more. He started to cut past the old car and then a bread truck came riding in for what looked to be a head-on collision. Feather pulled hard at the wheel and got back just in time.

"You shoulda kept on," Morris said. "You had enough room."

Feather didn't say anything.

A group of middle-aged women crossed the street between the Buick and the car in front of it. They seemed utterly oblivious to the existence of the Buick. Feather slammed his foot against the brake pedal.

"What're you stopping for?" Morris yelled. "They wanna get hit, then hit them!"

"That's right," the waitress said. "Smash into them. Grind them to a pulp."

The women passed and the Buick started forward. Then a flock of children darted through and the Buick was stopped again.

Morris opened the window at his side and leaned out and shouted, "What the hell's wrong with you?"

"Drop dead," one of the children said. It was a girl about seven years old.

"I'll break your little neck for you," Morris shouted at her.

"That's all right," the child sang back. "Just stay off my blue suede shoes."

The other children began singing the rock-and-roll tune, "Blue Suede Shoes," twanging on imaginary guitars and imitating various dynamic performers. Morris closed the window, gritting, "Goddam juvenile delinquents."

"Yes, it's quite a problem," the waitress said.

"You shut up," Morris told her.

She turned to Eddie. "The trouble is, there ain't enough playgrounds. We oughtta have more playgrounds. That would get them off the street."

"Yes," Eddie said. "The people ought to do something. It's a very serious problem."

She turned her head and looked back at Morris. "What do you think about it? You got an opinion?"

Morris wasn't listening. He had the window open again and he was leaning out, concentrating on the oncoming traffic. He called to Feather, "It's clear now. Go ahead—"

Feather started to turn the wheel. Then he changed his mind and pulled back in behind the car in front. A moment later a taxicab came whizzing from the other direction. It made a yellow blur as it sped past.

"You coulda made it," Morris complained. "You had plenty of time—"

Feather didn't say anything.

"You gotta cut through while you got the chance," Morris said. "Now if I had that wheel—"

"You want the wheel?" Feather asked.

"All I said was—"

"I'll give you the wheel," Feather said. "I'll wrap it around your neck."

"Don't get excited," Morris said.

"Just leave me alone and let me drive. Is that all right?"

"Sure." Morris shrugged. "You're the driver. You know how to drive."

"Then keep quiet." Feather faced the windshield again. "If there's one thing I can do, it's handle a car. There ain't nobody can tell me about that. I can make a car do anything—"

"Except get through traffic," Morris remarked.

Again Feather's head turned. His eyes were dull-cold, aiming at the tall, thin man. "What are you doing? You trying to irritate me?"

"No," Morris said. "I'm only making talk."

Feather went on looking at him. "I don't need that talk.

You give that talk to someone else. You tell someone else how to drive."

Morris pointed to the windshield. "Keep your eyes on the traffic—"

"You just won't let up, will you?" Feather shifted slightly in his seat, to get a fuller look at the man in the rear of the car. "Now I'm gonna tell you something, Morris. I'm gonna tell you—"

"Watch the light," Morris shouted, and gestured wildly toward the windshield. "You got a red light—"

Feather kept looking at him. "I'm telling you, Morris. I'm telling you for the last time—"

"The light," Morris screeched. "It's red, it's red, it says stop—"

The Buick was some twenty feet from the intersection when Feather took his foot off the gas pedal, then lightly stepped on the brake. The car was coming to a stop and Eddie glanced at the waitress, saw that she was focusing slantwise to the other side of the intersecting street, where a black-and-white police car was double-parked, the two policemen standing out there talking to the driver of a truck parked in a no-parking zone. Eddie had seen the police car and he'd wondered if the waitress would see it and would know what to do about it. He thought, This is the time for it, there won't be another time.

The waitress moved her left leg and her foot came down full force on the accelerator. Pedestrians leaped out of the way as the Buick went shooting past the red light and narrowly missed a westbound car, then stayed southbound going across the trolley tracks and lurching now as Feather hit the brake while the waitress kept her foot on the accelerator. An eastbound trailer made a frantic turn and went up on the pavement. Some women screamed, there was considerable activity on the pavement, brakes screeched, and, finally, a policeman's whistle shrilled through the air.

The Buick was stopped on the south side of the trolley tracks. Feather sat there leaning back, looking sideways at the waitress. Eddie was watching the policeman, who was yelling at the driver of the trailer, telling him to back off the pavement. There was no one hurt, although several of the pedestrians were considerably unnerved. A few women were yelling incoherently, pointing accusingly at the Buick. Then, gradually, a crowd closed in on the Buick. In the Buick there was no talk at all. Around the car the crowd thickened. Feather was still looking at the waitress. Eddie glanced into the rearview mirror and saw Morris with his hat off. Morris had the hat in his hands and was gazing stupidly at the crowd outside the window. Some of the people in the crowd were saying things to Feather. Then the crowd moved to make a path for the policeman from the black-and-white car. Eddie saw that the other policeman was still occupied with the parking violator. He turned his head slowly and the waitress was looking at him. It seemed she was waiting for him to say something or do something. Her eyes said to him, It's your play, from here on in it's up to you. He made a very slight gesture, pointing to himself, as if saying, All right, I'll handle it, I'll do the talking.

The policeman spoke quietly to Feather. "Let's clear this traffic. Get her over there to the curb." The Buick moved slowly across the remainder of the intersection, the policeman walking along with it, guiding the driver to the southeast corner. "Cut the engine," the policeman told Feather. "Get out of the car."

Feather switched off the engine and opened the door and got out. The crowd went on making noise. A man said, "He's stewed. He's gotta be stewed to drive like that." And an elderly woman shouted, "We just ain't safe any more. We venture out we take our lives in our hands—"

The policeman moved in close to Feather and said, "How many?" and Feather answered, "All I had was two, officer. I'll drive you back to the bar, and you can ask the bartender." The policeman looked Feather up and down. "All right, so you're not drunk. Then how do you account for this?" As Feather opened his mouth to reply, Eddie cut in quickly, saying, "He just can't drive, that's all. He's a lousy driver." Feather turned and looked at Eddie. And Eddie went on, "He always gets rattled in traffic." Then he turned to the waitress, saying, "Come on, honey. We don't need this. We'll take a trolley."

"Can't hardly blame you," the policeman said to them as they got out of the car. From the back seat, Morris called out, "See you later, Eddie," and for a moment there was indecision. Eddie glanced toward the policeman, thinking, You wanna tell the cop what's happening? You figure it's better that way? No, he decided. It's probably better this way.

"Later," Morris called to them as they moved off through the crowd. The waitress stopped and looked back at Morris. "Yeah, give us a call," and she waved at the tall, thin man in the Buick, "we'll be waiting—"

They went on moving through the crowd. Then they were walking north on Front Street. The snow had slackened somewhat. It was slightly warmer now, and the sun was trying to come out. But the wind had not lessened, there was still a bite in it, and Eddie thought, There's gonna be more snow, that sky looks strictly from changeable weather. It could be a blizzard coming.

He heard the waitress saying, "Let's get off this street."

"They won't circle back."

"They might."

"I don't think they will," he said. "When that cop gets finished with them, they're gonna be awfully tired. I think they'll go to a movie or a Turkish bath or something. They've had enough for one day."

"He said he'd see us later."

"You gave him a good answer. You said we'd be waiting. That gives them something to think about. They'll really think about that."

"For how long?" She looked at him. "How long until they try again?"

He made an offhand gesture. "Who knows? Why worry?"

She mimicked his gesture, his indifferent tone. "Well, maybe you're right. Except for one little angle. That thing he had wasn't a water pistol. If they come looking for us, it might be something to worry about."

He didn't say anything. They were walking just a little faster now. "Well?" she said, and he didn't answer. She said it again. She was watching his face and waiting for an answer. "How about it?" she asked, and took hold of his arm. They came to a stop and stood facing each other.

"Now look," he said, and smiled dimly. "This ain't your problem."

She shifted her weight onto one leg, put her hand on her hip and said, "I didn't quite get that."

"It's simple enough. I'm only repeating what you said last night. I thought you meant it. Anyway, I was hoping you meant it."

"In other words," and she took a deep breath, "you're telling me to mind my own damn business."

"Well, I wouldn't put it that way—"

"Why not?" She spoke a trifle louder. "Don't be so polite."

He gazed past her, his smile very soft. "Let's not get upset—"

"You're too goddam polite," she said. "You wanna make a point, make it. Don't walk all around it."

His smile fell away. He tried to build it again. It wouldn't build. Don't look at her, he told himself. You look at her, it'll start like it started last night in that alley when she was standing close to you.

She's close now, come to think of it. She's much too close. He took a backward step, went on gazing past her, then heard himself saying, "I don't need this."

"Need what?"

"Nothing," he mumbled. "Let it ride."

"It's riding."

He winced. He took a step toward her. What are you doing? he asked himself. Then he was shaking his head, trying to clear his brain. It was no go. He felt very dizzy.

He heard her saying, "Well, I might as well know who I'm riding with."

"We're not riding now," he said, and tried to make himself believe it. He grinned at her. "We're just standing here and gabbing."

"Is that what it is?"

"Sure," he said. "That's all it is. What else could it be?"

"I wouldn't know." Her face was expressionless. "That is, I wouldn't know unless I was told."

I'll let that pass, he said to himself. I'd better let it pass. But look at her, she's waiting. But it's more than that, she's aching. She's aching for you to say something.

"Let's walk," he said. "It's no use standing here."

"You're right," she said with a little smile. "It sure ain't getting us anywhere. Come on, let's walk."

They resumed walking north on Front Street. Now they were walking slowly and there was no talk. They went on for several blocks without speaking and then she stopped again and said to him, "I'm sorry, Eddie."

"Sorry? About what?"

"Butting in. I shoulda kept my long nose out of it."

"It ain't a long nose. It's just about right."

"Thanks," she said. They were standing outside a five-and-dime. She glanced toward the display window. "I think I'll do some shopping—"

"I'd better go in with you."

"No," she said. "I can make it alone."

"Well, what I mean is, just in case they—"

"Look, you said there was nothing to worry about. You got them going to the movies or a Turkish bath—"

"Or Woolworth's," he cut in. "They might walk into this Woolworth's."

"What if they do?" She gave a little shrug. "It ain't me they want, it's you."

"That cuts it nice." He smiled at her. "Except it don't cut that way at all. They got you tabbed now. Tied up with me. Like as if we're a team—"

"A team?" She looked away from him. "Some team. You won't even tell me the score."

"On what?"

"South Jersey. That house in the woods. Your family—"

"The score on that is zero," he said. "I got no idea what's happening there."

"Not even a hint?" She gave him a side glance.

He didn't reply. He thought, What can you tell her? What the hell can you tell her when you just don't know?

"Well," she said, "whatever it is, you sure kept it away from that cop. I mean the way you played it, not telling the cop about the gun. To keep the law out of this. Or, let's say, to keep your family away from the law. Something along that line?"

"Yes," he said. "It's along that line."

"Anything more?"

"Nothing," he said. "I know from nothing."

"All right," she said. "All right, Edward."

There was a rush of quiet. It was like a valve opening and the quiet rushing in.

"Or is it Eddie?" she asked herself aloud. "Well, now it's Eddie. It's Eddie at the old piano, at the Hut. But years ago it was Edward—"

He waved his hand sideways, begging her to stop it.

She said, "It was Edward Webster Lynn, the concert pianist, performing at Carnegie Hall."

She turned away and walked into the five-and-dime.

8

So there it is, he said to himself. But how did she know? What tipped her off? I think we ought to examine that. Or maybe it don't need examining. It stands to reason she remembered something. It must have hit her all at once. That's it, that's the way it usually happens. It came all at once, the name and the face and the music. Or the music and the name and the face. All mixed in there together from seven years ago.

When did it hit her? She's been working at the Hut for four months, six nights a week. Until last night she hardly knew you were alive. So let's have a look at that. Did something happen last night? Did you pull some fancy caper on that keyboard? Just a bar or two of Bach, maybe? Or Brahms or Schumann or Chopin? No. You know who told her. It was Turley.

Sure as hell it was Turley when he went into that booby-hatch raving, when he jumped up and gave that lecture on musical appreciation and the currently sad state of culture in America, claiming that you didn't belong in the Hut, it was the wrong place, the wrong piano, the wrong audience. He screamed it oughta be a concert hall, with the gleaming grand piano, the diamonds gleaming on the white throats, the full-dress shirt fronts in the seven-fifty orchestra seats. That was what hit her.

But hold it there for just a minute. What's the hookup there? How does she come to Carnegie Hall? She ain't from the classical groove, the way she talks she's from the honky-tonk school. Or no, you don't really know what school she's from. The way a person talks has little or nothing to do with the schooling. You ought to know that. Just listen to the way you talk.

What I mean is, the way Eddie talks. Eddie spills words like "ain't" and says "them there" and "this here" and so forth. You know Edward never talked that way. Edward was educated, and an artist, and had a cultured manner of speaking. I guess it all depends where you're at and what you're doing and the people you hang around with. The Hut is a long way off from Carnegie Hall. *Yes.* And it's a definite fact that Eddie has no connection with Edward. You cut all them wires a long time ago. It was a clean split.

Then why are you drifting back? Why pick it up again? Well, just to look at it. Won't hurt to have a look. Won't hurt? You kidding? You can feel the hurt already, as though it's happening again. The way it happened.

It was deep in the woods of South Jersey, in the wooden house that overlooked the watermelon patch. His early childhood was mostly on the passive side. As the youngest of three brothers, he was more or less a small, puzzled spectator, unable to understand Clifton's knavery or Turley's rowdyism. They were always at it, and when they weren't pulling capers in the house they were out roaming the countryside. Their special meat was chickens. They were experts at stealing chickens. Or sometimes they'd try for a shoat. They were seldom caught. They'd slide out of trouble or fight their way out of it and, on a few occasions, in their middle teens, they shot their way out of it.

The mother called them bad boys, then shrugged and let it go at that. The mother was an habitual shrugger who'd run out of gas in her early twenties, surrendering to farmhouse drudgery, to the weeds and beetles and fungus that lessened the melon crop each year. The father never worried about anything. The father was a slothful, languid, easy-smiling drinker. He had a remarkable capacity for alcohol.

There was another gift the father had. The father could play
the piano. He claimed he'd been a child prodigy. Of course,
no one believed him. But at times, sitting at the ancient upright in the shabby, carpetless parlor, he did some startling
things with the keyboard.

At other times, when he felt in the mood, he'd give music
lessons to five-year-old Edward. It seemed there was nothing
else to do with Edward, who was on the quiet side, who
stayed away from his villainous brothers as though his very
life depended on it. Actually, this was far from the case. They
never bullied him. They'd tease him now and then, but mostly
they left him alone. They didn't even know he was around.
The father felt a little sorry for Edward, who wandered
through the house like some lost creature from the woods
that had gotten in by mistake.

The music lessons increased from once a week to twice a
week and finally to every day. The father became aware that
something was happening here, something really unusual.
When Edward was nine he performed for a gathering of teachers at the schoolhouse six miles away. When he was fourteen,
some people came from Philadelphia to hear him play. They
took him back to Philadelphia, to a scholarship at the Curtis
Institute of Music.

At nineteen, he gave his first concert in a small auditorium.
There wasn't much of an audience, and most of them got in
on complimentary tickets. But one of them was a man from
New York, a concert artists' manager, and his name was
Eugene Alexander.

Alexander had his office on Fifty-seventh Street, not many
doors away from Carnegie Hall. It was a small office and the
list of clients was rather small. But the furnishings of the office
were extremely expensive, and the clients were all big names
or on their way to becoming big names. When Edward signed
with Alexander, he was given to understand that he was just
a tiny drop of water in a very large pool. "And frankly,"
Alexander said, "I must tell you of the obstacles in this field.
In this field the competition is ferocious, downright ferocious.
But if you're willing to—"

He was more than willing. He was bright-eyed and anxious
to get started. He started the very next day, studying under

Gelensky, with Alexander paying for the lessons. Gelensky was a sweetly-smiling little man, completely bald, his face criss-crossed with so many wrinkles that he looked like a goblin. And, as Edward soon learned, the sweet smiles were more on the order of goblin's smiles, concealing a fiendish tendency to ignore the fact that the fingers are flesh and bone, that the fingers can get tired. "You must never get tired," the little man would say, smiling sweetly. "When the hands begin to sweat, that's good. The flow of sweat is the stream of attainment."

He sweated plenty. There were nights when his fingers were so stiff that he felt as though he was wearing splints. Nights when his eyes were seared with the strain of seven and eight and nine hours at the keyboard, the notes on the music sheets finally blurring to a gray mist. And nights of self-doubt, of discouragement. Is it worth all this? he'd ask himself. It's work, work, and more work. And so much work ahead. So much to learn. Oh, Christ, this is hard, it's really hard. It's being cooped up in this room all the time, and even if you wanted to go out, you couldn't. You're too tired. But you ought to get out. For some fresh air, at least. Or a walk in Central Park; it's nice in Central Park. Yes, but there's no piano in Central Park. The piano is here, in this room.

It was a basement apartment on Seventy-sixth Street between Amsterdam and Columbus Avenues. The rent was fifty dollars a month and the rent money came from Alexander. The money for food and clothes and all incidentals also came from Alexander. And for the piano. And for the radio-phonograph, along with several albums of concertos and sonatas. Everything was from Alexander.

Will he get it back? Edward asked himself. Do I have what he thinks I have? Well, we'll soon find out. Not really soon, though. Gelensky is certainly taking his time. He hasn't even mentioned your New York debut. You've been with Gelensky almost two years now and he hasn't said a word about a concert. Or even a small recital. What does that mean? Well, you can ask him. That is, if you're not afraid to ask him. But I think you're afraid. Coming right down to it, I think you're afraid he'll say yes, and then comes the test, the real test here in New York.

Because New York is not Philadelphia. These New York

critics are so much tougher. Look what they did last week to
Harbenstein. And Gelensky had Harbenstein for five years.
Another thing, Harbenstein is managed by Alexander. Does
that prove something?

It could. It very well could. It could prove that despite a
superb teacher and a devoted, efficient manager, the per-
former just didn't have it, just couldn't make the grade. Poor
Harbenstein. I wonder what Harbenstein did the next day
when he read the write-ups? Cried, probably. Sure, he cried.
Poor devil. You wait so long for that one chance, you aim
your hopes so high, and next thing you know it's all over and
they've ripped you apart, they've slaughtered you. But what
I think now, you're getting jumpy. And that's absurd, Edward.
There's certainly no reason to be jumpy. Your name is Edward
Webster Lynn and you're a concert pianist, you're an artist.

Three weeks later he was told by Gelensky that he'd soon
be making his New York debut. In the middle of the following
week, in Alexander's office, he signed a contract to give a
recital. It was to be a one-hour recital in the small auditorium
of a small art museum on upper Fifth Avenue. He went back
to the little basement apartment, dizzily excited and elated,
and saw the envelope, and opened it, and stood there staring
at the mimeographed notice. It was from Washington. It ordered him to report to his local draft board.

They classified him I-A. They were in a hurry and there was
no use preparing for the recital. He went to South Jersey,
spent a day with his parents, who informed him that Clifton
had been wounded in the Pacific and Turley was somewhere
in the Aleutians with the Seabees. His mother gave him a nice
dinner and his father forced him to have a drink "for good
luck." He went back to New York, then to a training camp
in Missouri, and from there he was sent to Burma.

He was with Merrill's Marauders. He got hit three times.
The first time it was shrapnel in the leg. Then it was a bullet
in the shoulder. The last time it was multiple bayonet wounds
in the ribs and abdomen, and in the hospital they doubted
that he'd make it. But he was very anxious to make it. He was
thinking in terms of getting back to New York, to the piano,
to the night when he'd put on a white tie and face the audience at Carnegie Hall.

When he returned to New York, he was informed that Alexander had died of kidney trouble and a university in Chili had given Gelensky an important professorship. They're really gone? he asked the Manhattan sky and streets as he walked alone and felt the ache of knowing it was true, that they were really gone. It meant he had to start all over.

Well, let's get started. First thing, we find a concert manager.

He couldn't find a manager. Or, rather, the managers didn't want him. Some were polite, some were kind and said they wished they could do something but there were so many pianists, the field was so crowded—

And some were blunt, some were downright brutal. They didn't even bother to write his name on a card. They made him acutely aware of the fact that he was unknown, a nobody.

He went on trying. He told himself it couldn't go on this way, and sooner or later he'd get a chance, there'd be at least one sufficiently interested to say, "All right, try some Chopin. Let's hear you play Chopin."

But none of them was interested, not the least bit interested. He wasn't much of a salesman. He couldn't talk about himself, couldn't get it across that Eugene Alexander had come to that first recital, had signed him onto a list that included some of the finest, and that Gelensky had said, "No, they won't applaud. They'll sit there stupefied. The way you're playing now, you are a master of pianoforte. You think there are many? In this world, according to my lastest count, there are nine. Exactly nine."

He couldn't quote Gelensky. There were times when he tried to describe his own ability, his full awareness of this talent he had, but the words wouldn't come out. The talent was all in the fingers and all he could say was, "If you'd let me play for you—"

They brushed him off.

It went on like that for more than a year while he worked at various jobs. He was a shipping clerk and truck driver and construction laborer, and there were other jobs that lasted for only a few weeks or a couple of months. It wasn't because he was lazy, or tardy, or lacked the muscle. When they fired him, they said it was mostly "forgetfulness" or "absentmindedness" or some of them, more perceptive, would comment, "you're only half here; you got your thoughts someplace else."

But the Purple Heart with two clusters started paying off and the disability money was enough to get him a larger room, and then an apartment, and finally an apartment just about big enough to label it a studio. He bought a piano on the installment plan, and put out a sign that stated simply, Piano Teacher.

Fifty cents a lesson. They couldn't afford more. They were mostly Puerto Ricans who lived in the surrounding tenements in the West Nineties. One of them was a girl named Teresa Fernandez, who worked nights behind the counter of a tiny fruit-drink enterprise near Times Square. She was nineteen years old, and a war widow. His name had been Luis and he'd been blown to bits on a heavy cruiser during some action in the Coral Sea. There were no children and now she lived alone in a fourth-floor-front on Ninety-third Street. She was a quiet girl, a diligent and persevering music student, and she had no musical talent whatsoever.

After several lessons, he saw the way it was, and he told her to stop wasting the money. She said she didn't care about the money, and if Meester Leen did not mind she would be most grateful to take more lessons. Maybe with some more lessons I will start to learn something. I know I am stupid, but—

"Don't say that," he told her. "You're not stupid at all. It's just—"

"I like dese lessons, Meester Leen. It is a nice way for me to pass the time in dese afternoons."

"You really like the piano?"

"Yes, yes. Very much." A certain eagerness that glowed in her eyes, and he knew what it was, he knew it had nothing to do with music. She looked away, blinking hard and trying to cover it up, and then bit her lip, as though to scold herself for letting it show. She was embarrassed and silently apologetic, her shoulders drooping just a little, her slender throat twitching as she swallowed the words she didn't dare to let out. He told himself that she was something very pleasant, very sweet, and, also, she was lonely. It was apparent that she was terribly lonely.

Her features and her body were on the fragile side, and she had a graceful way of moving. Her looks were more Castilian than Caribbean. Her hair was a soft-hued amber, her eyes were amber, and her complexion was pearl-white, the kind of complexion they try to buy in the expensive salons. Teresa had it from someone down the line a very long time ago, before they'd come over from Spain. There was a trace of deep-rooted nobility in the line of her lips and in the coloring of them. Yes, this is something real, he decided, and wondered why he'd never noticed it before. Until this moment she'd been just another girl who wanted to learn piano.

Three months later they were married. He took her to South Jersey to meet his family, and prepared her for it with a frank briefing, but it turned out to be pleasant in South Jersey. It was especially pleasant because the brothers weren't there to make a lot of noise and lewd remarks. Clifton was presently engaged in some kind of work that required him to do considerable traveling. Turley was a longshoreman on the Philadelphia waterfront. They hadn't been home for more than a year. Once every few months there'd be a post card from Turley, but nothing from Clifton, and the mother said to Teresa, "He ought to write, at least. Don't you think he ought to write?" It was as though Teresa had been a member of the family for years. They were at the table and the mother had roasted a goose. It was a very special dinner and the father made it extra-special by appearing with combed hair, a clean shirt, and scrubbed fingernails. And all day long he'd stayed off the liquor. But after dinner he was at it again and within a few hours he'd consumed the better part of a quart. He winked at Teresa and said, "Say, you're one hell of a pretty girl. Come over here and gimme a kiss." She smiled at her father-in-law and said, "To celebrate the happiness?" and went to him and gave him a kiss. He took another drink from the bottle and winked at Edward and said, "You got yourself a sweet little number here. Now what you wanna do is hold onto her. That New York's a fast town—"

They went back to the basement apartment on Ninety-third Street. He continued giving piano lessons, and Teresa remained at the fruit-drink stand. Some weeks passed, and then he asked her to quit the job. He said he didn't like this night-work routine. It was a locale that worried him, he explained, stating that although she'd never had trouble with Times Square night owls, it was nevertheless a possibility.

"But is always policemen around there," she argued. "The policemen, they protect the women—"

"Even so," he said, "I can think of safer places than Times Square late at night."

"Like what places?"

"Well, like—"

"Like here? With you?"

He mumbled, "Whenever you're not around, it's like—well, it's like I'm blindfolded."

"You like to see me all the time? You need me that much?"

He touched his lips to her forehead. "It's more than that. It's so much more—"

"I know," she breathed, and held him tightly. "I know what you mean. Is same with me. Is more each day—"

She quit the Times Square job, and found nine-to-five employment in a coffee shop on Eighty-sixth Street off Broadway. It was a nice little place, with a generally pleasant atmosphere, and some days he'd go there for lunch. They'd play a game, customer-and-waitress, pretending that they didn't know each other, and he'd try to make a date. Then one day, after she'd worked there for several months, they were playing the customer-waitress game and he was somehow aware of an interruption, a kind of intrusion.

It was a man at a nearby table. The man was watching them, smiling at them. At her? he wondered, and gazed levelly at the man. But then it was all right and he said to himself, It's me, he's smiling at me. As if he knows me—

Then the man stood up and came over and introduced himself. His name was Woodling. He was a concert manager and of course he remembered Edward Webster Lynn. "Yes, of course," Woodling said, as Edward gave his name, "you came to my office about a year ago. I was terribly busy then and couldn't give you much time. I'm sorry if I was rather abrupt—"

"Oh, that's all right. I understand the way it is."

"It shouldn't be that way," Woodling said. "But this is such a frantic town, and there's so much competition."

Teresa said, "Would the gentlemen like to have lunch?"

Her husband smiled at her, took her hand. He introduced her to Woodling, then explained the customer-waitress game. Woodling laughed and said it was a wonderful game, there were always two winners.

"You mean we both get the prize?" Teresa asked.

"Especially the customer," Woodling said, gesturing toward Edward. "He's a very fortunate man. You're really a prize, my dear."

"Thank you," Teresa murmured. "Is very kind of you to say."

Woodling insisted on paying for the lunch. He invited the pianist to visit him at his office. They made an appointment for an afternoon meeting later that week. When Woodling walked out of the coffee shop, the pianist sat there with his mouth open just a little. "What is it?" Teresa asked, and he said, "Can't believe it. Just can't—"

"He gives you a job?"

"Not a job. It's a chance. I never thought it would happen. I'd given up hoping."

"This is something important?"

He nodded very slowly.

Three days later he entered the suite of offices on Fifty-seventh Street. The furnishings were quietly elegant, the rooms large. Woodling's private office was very large, and featured several oil paintings. There was a Matisse and a Picasso and some by Utrillo.

They had a long talk. Then they went into an audition room and Edward seated himself at a mahogany Baldwin. He played some Chopin, some Schumann, and an extremely difficult piece by Stravinsky. He was at the piano for exactly forty-two minutes. Woodling said, "Excuse me a moment," and walked out of the room, and came back with a contract.

It was a form contract and it offered nothing in the way of guarantees. It merely stipulated that for a period of not less than three years the pianist would be managed and represented by Arthur Woodling. But this in itself was like starting the climb up a gem-studded ladder. In the field of classical music, the name Woodling commanded instant attention from coast to coast, from hemisphere to hemisphere. He was one of the biggest.

Woodling was forty-seven. He was of medium height and built leanly and looked as though he took very good care of himself. He had a healthy complexion. His eyes were clear and showed that he didn't go in for overwork or excessively late hours. He had a thick growth of tightly-curled black hair streaked with white and at the temples it was all white. His features were neatly sculptured, except for the left side of his jaw. It was slightly out of line, the souvenir of a romantic interlude some fifteen years before when a colaratura-soprano had ended their relationship during a South American concert tour. She'd used a heavy bronze book-end to fracture his jaw.

On the afternoon of the contract-signing ceremony with Edward Webster Lynn, the concert manager wore a stiffly starched white collar and a gray cravat purchased in Spain. His suit was also from Spain. His cuff links were emphatically Spanish, oblongs of silver engraved with conquistador helmets. The Spanish theme, especially the cuff links, had been selected specifically for this occasion.

Seven months later, Edward Webster Lynn made his New York debut. It was at Carnegie Hall. They shouted for encores. Next it was Chicago, and then New York again. And after his first coast-to-coast tour they wanted him in Europe.

In Europe he had them leaping to their feet, crying "bravo" until their voices cracked. In Rome the women threw flowers onto the stage. When he came back to Carnegie Hall the seats had been sold out three months in advance. During that year when he was twenty-five, he gave four performances at Carnegie Hall.

In November of that year, he played at the Academy of Music in Philadelphia. He performed the Grieg *Concerto* and the audience was somewhat hysterical, some of them were sobbing, and a certain critic became incoherent and finally speechless. Later that night, Woodling gave a party in his suite at the Town-Casa. It was on the fourth floor. At a few minutes past midnight, Woodling came over to the pianist and said, "Where's Teresa?"

"She said she was tired."

"Again?"

"Yes." He said it quietly. "Again."

Woodling shrugged. "Perhaps she doesn't like these parties."

The pianist lit a cigarette. He held it clumsily. A waiter approached with a tray and glasses of champagne. The pianist reached for a glass, changed his mind and pulled tightly at the cigarette. He jetted the smoke from between his teeth, looked down at the floor and said, "It isn't the parties, Arthur. She's tired all the time. She's—"

There was another stretch of quiet. Then Woodling said, "What is it? What's the matter?"

The pianist didn't answer.

"Perhaps the strain of traveling, living in hotels—"

"No." He said it somewhat harshly. "It's me."

"Quarrels?"

"I wish it were quarrels. This is something worse. Much worse."

"You care to talk about it?" Woodling asked.

"That won't help."

Woodling took his arm and led him out of the room, away from the array of white ties and evening gowns. They went into a smaller room. They were alone there, and Woodling said, "I want you to tell me. Tell me all of it."

"It's a personal matter—"

"You need advice, Edward. I can't advise you unless you tell me."

The pianist looked down at the smoking cigarette stub. He felt the fire near his fingers. He moved toward a table, mashed the stub in an ashtray, turned and faced the concert manager. "She doesn't want me."

"Now, really—"

"You don't believe it? I didn't believe it, either. I couldn't believe it."

"Edward, it's impossible."

"Yes, I know. That's what I've been telling myself for months." And then he shut his eyes tightly, gritting it, "For months? It's been more than a year—"

"Sit down."

He fell into a chair. He stared at the floor and said, "It started slowly. At first it was hardly noticeable, as though she were trying to hide it. Like—like fighting something. Then gradually it showed itself. I mean, we'd be talking and she'd turn away and walk out of the room. It got to the point where I'd try to open the door and the door was locked. I'd call to her and she wouldn't answer. And the way it is now—well, it's over with, that's all."

"Has she told you?"

"Not in so many words."

"Then maybe—"

"She's sick? No, she isn't sick. That is, it isn't a sickness they can treat. If you know what I mean."

"I know what you mean, but I still can't believe—"

"She doesn't want me, Arthur. She just doesn't want me, that's all."

Woodling moved toward the door.

"Where are you going?" the pianist asked.

"I'm getting you a drink."

"I don't want a drink."

"You'll have one," Woodling said. "You'll have a double."

The concert manager walked out of the room. The pianist sat bent over, his face cupped in his hands. He stayed that way for some moments. Then he straightened abruptly and got to his feet. He was breathing hard.

He went out of the room, down the hall toward the stairway. Their suite was on the seventh floor. He went up the three flights with a speed that had him breathless as he entered the living room.

He called her name. There was no answer. He crossed the parlor to the bedroom door. He tried it, and it was open.

She was sitting on the edge of the bed, wearing a robe. In her lap was a magazine. It was open but she wasn't looking at it. She was looking at the wall.

"Teresa—"

She went on looking at the wall.

He moved toward her. He said, "Get dressed."

"What for?"

"The party," he said. "I want you there at the party."

She shook her head.

"Teresa, listen—"

"Please go," she said. She was still looking at the wall. She raised a hand and gestured toward the door. "Go—"

"No," he said. "Not this time."

Then she looked at him. "What?" Her eyes were dull. "What did you say?"

"I said not this time. This time we talk it over. We find out what it's all about."

"There is nothing—"

"Stop that," he cut in. He moved closer to her. "I've had enough of that. The least you can do is tell me—"

"Why you shout? You never shout at me. Why you shout now?"

"I'm sorry." He spoke in a heavy whisper. "I didn't mean to—"

"Is all right." She smiled at him. "You have right to shout. You have much right."

"Don't say that." He was turning away, his head lowered.

He heard her saying, "I make you unhappy, no? Is bad for me to do that. Is something I try not to do, but when it is dark you cannot stop the darkness—"

"What's that?" He turned stiffly, staring at her. "What did you mean by that?"

"I mean—I mean—" But then she was shaking her head, again looking at the wall. "All the time is darkness. Gets darker. No way to see where to go, what to do."

She's trying to tell me something, he thought. She's trying so hard, but she can't tell me. Why can't she tell me? She said, "I think there is one thing to do. Only one thing."

He felt coldness in the room.

"I say good-by. I go away—"

"Teresa, please—"

She stood up and moved toward the wall. Then she turned and faced him. She was calm. It was an awful calmness. Her voice was a hollow, toneless semi-whisper as she said, "All right, I tell you—"

"Wait." He was afraid now.

"Is proper that you should know," she said. "Is always proper to give the explanation. To make confession."

"Confession?"

"I did bad thing—"

He winced.

"Was very bad. Was terrible mistake." And then a certain brightness came into her eyes. "But now you are famous pianist, and for that I am glad."

This isn't happening, he told himself. It can't be happening.

"Yes, for that I am glad I did it," she said. "To get you the chance you wanted. Was only one way to get you that chance, to put you in Carnegie Hall."

There was a hissing sound. It was his own breathing.

"Woodling," she said.

He shut his eyes very tightly.

"Was the same week when he signed you to his contract," she went on. "Was a few days later. He comes to the coffee shop. But not for coffee. Not for lunch."

There was another hissing sound. It was louder.

"For business proposition," she said.

I've got to get out of here, he told himself. I can't listen to this.

"At first, when he tells me, is like a puzzle, too much for me. I ask him what he is talking about, and he looks at me as if to say, You don't know? You think about it and you will know. So I think about it. That night I get no sleep. Next day he is there again. You know how a spider works? A spider, he is slow and careful—"

He couldn't look at her.

"—like pulling me away from myself. Like the spirit is one thing and the body is another. Was not Teresa who went with him. Was only Teresa's body. As if I was not there, really. I was with you, I was taking you to Carnegie Hall."

And now it was just a record playing, the narrator's voice giving supplementary details. "—in the afternoons. During my time off. He rented a room near the coffee shop. For weeks, in the afternoons, in that room. And then one night you tell me the news, you have signed the paper to play in Carnegie Hall. When he comes next time to the coffee shop he is just another customer. I hand him the menu and he gives the order. And I think to myself, Is ended, I am me again. Yes, now I can be me.

"But you know, it is a curious thing—what you do yesterday is always part of what you are today. From others you try to hide it. For yourself it is no use trying, it is a kind of mirror, always there. So I look, and what do I see? Do I see Teresa? Your Teresa?

"Is no Teresa in the mirror. Is no Teresa anywhere now. Is just a used-up rag, something dirty. And that is why I have not let you touch me. Or even come close. I could not let you come close to this dirt."

He tried to look at her. He said to himself, Yes, look at her. And go to her. And bow, or kneel. It calls for that, it surely does. But—

His eyes aimed at the door, and beyond the door, and there was fire in his brain. He clenched his teeth, and his hands became stone hammerheads. Every fibre in his body was coiled, braced for the lunge that would take him out of here and down the winding stairway to the fourth-floor suite.

And then, for just a moment, he groped for a segment of control, of discretion. He said to himself, Think now, try to think. If you go out that door she'll see you going away, she'll be here alone. You mustn't leave her here alone.

It didn't hold him. Nothing could hold him. He moved slowly toward the door.

"Edward—"

But he didn't hear. All he heard was a low growl from his own mouth as he opened the door and went out of the bedroom.

Then he was headed across the living room, his arm extended, his fingers clawing at the door leading to the outer hall. In the instant that his fingers touched the door handle, he heard the noise from the bedroom.

It was a mechanical noise. It was the rattling of the chain-pulleys at the sides of the window.

He pivoted and ran across the living room and into the bedroom. She was climbing out. He leaped, and made a grab, but there was nothing to grab. There was just the cold empty air coming in through the wide-open window.

9

ON Front Street, as he stood on the pavement near the red-and-gold entrance to the five-and-dime, the Saturday shoppers swept past him. Some of them bumped him with their shoulders. Others pushed him aside. He was insensible. He wasn't there, really. He was very far away from there.

He was at the funeral seven years ago, and then he was wandering around New York City. It was a time of no direction, no response to traffic signals or changes in the weather. He never knew or cared what hour of the day it was, what day of the week it was. For the sum of everything was a circle, and the circle was labeled Zero.

He had pulled all his savings from the bank. It amounted to about nine thousand dollars. He managed to lose it. He wanted to lose it. The night he lost it, when it was taken from him, he got himself beaten. He wanted that, too. When it happened, when he went down with the blood spilling from his nose and mouth and the gash in his skull, he was glad. He actually enjoyed it.

It happened very late at night, in Hell's Kitchen. Three of them jumped him. One of them had a length of lead pipe. The other two had brass knuckles. The lead pipe came first. It hit him on the side of his head and he walked sideways, then slowly sat down on the curb. Then the others went to work with the brass knuckles. Then something happened. They weren't sure what it was, but it seemed like propeller blades churning the air and coming at them. The one with the lead pipe had made a rapid departure, and they wondered why he wasn't there to help them. They really needed help. One of them went down with four teeth flying out of his mouth. The other was sobbing, "gimme a break, aw, please—gimme a break," and the wild man grinned and whispered, "Fight back—fight back—don't spoil the fun." The thug knew then he had no choice, and did what he could with the brass knuckles and his weight. He had considerable weight. Also, he was quite skilled in the dirtier tactics. He used a knee, he used his thumbs, and he even tried using his teeth. But he just wasn't fast enough. He ended up with both eyes swollen shut, a fractured nose, and a brain concussion. As he lay there on the pavement, flat on his back and unconscious, the wild man whispered, "Thanks for the party."

A few nights later, there was another party. It took place in Central Park when two policemen found the wild man sleeping under a bush. They woke him up, and he told them to go away and leave him alone. They pulled him to his feet, asked him if he had a home. He didn't answer. They started to shoot questions at him. Again he told them to leave him alone. One of them snarled at him and shoved him. The other policeman grabbed his arm. He said, "Let go, please let go." Then they both had hold of him, and they were pulling him along. They were big men and he had to look up at them as he said, "Why don't you leave me alone?" They told him to shut up. He tried to pull loose and one of them hit him on the leg with a night stick. "You hit me," he said. The policeman barked at him, "Sure I hit you. If I want to, I'll hit you again." He shook his head slowly and said, "No, you won't." A few minutes later the two policemen were alone there. One of them was leaning against a tree, breathing hard. The other was sitting on the grass, groaning.

And then, less than a week later, it was in the Bowery and a well-known strong-arm specialist remarked through puffed and bleeding lips, "Like stickin' me face in a concrete mixer."

From someone in the crowd, "You gonna fight him again?"

"Sure I'll fight him again. Just one thing I need."

"What?"

"An automatic rifle," the plug-ugly said, sitting there on the curb and spitting blood. "Buy me one of them rifles and keep him a distance."

He was always on the move, roaming from the Bowery to the Lower East Side and up through Yorkville to Spanish Harlem and down and over to Brooklyn, to the brawling grounds of Greenpoint and Brownsville—to any area where a man who looked for trouble was certain to find it.

Now, looking back on it, he saw the wild man of seven years ago, and thought, What it amounted to, you were crazy, I mean really crazy. Call it horror-crazy. With your fingers, that couldn't touch the keyboard or get anywhere near a keyboard, a set of claws, itching to find the throat of the very dear friend and counselor, that so kind and generous man who took you into Carnegie Hall.

But, of course, you knew you mustn't find him. You had to keep away from him, for to catch even a glimpse of him would mean a killing. But the wildness was there, and it needed an outlet. So let's give a vote of thanks to the hooligans, all the thugs and sluggers and roughnecks who were only too happy to accommodate you, to offer you a target.

What about money? It stands to reason you needed money. You had to put food in your belly. Let's see now, I remember there were certain jobs, like dishwashing and polishing cars and distributing handbills. At times you were out of a job, so the only thing to do was hold out your hand and wait for coins to drop in. Just enough nickels and dimes to get you a bowl of soup and a mattress in a flophouse. Or sometimes a roll of gauze to bandage the bleeding cuts. There were nights when you dripped a lot of blood, especially the nights when you came out second best.

Yes, my good friend, you were in great shape in those days. What I think is, you were a candidate for membership in some high-off-the-ground clubhouse. But it couldn't go on like that. It had to stop somewhere. What stopped it?

Sure, it was that trip you took. The stroll that sent you across the bridge into Jersey, a pleasant little stroll of some hundred-and-forty miles. If I remember correctly, it took you the better part of a week to get there, to the house hidden in the woods of South Jersey.

It was getting on toward Thanksgiving. You were coming home to spend the holiday with the folks. They were all there. Clifton and Turley were home for the holiday, too. At least, they said that was the reason they'd come home. But after a few drinks they kind of got around to the real reason. They said there'd been some complications, and the authorities were looking for them, and this place deep in the woods was far away from all the guideposts.

The way it was, Turley had quit his job on the Philly waterfront and had teamed up with Clifton on a deal involving stolen cars, driving the cars across state lines. They'd been spotted and chased. Not that it worried them. You remember Clifton saying, "Yeah, it's a tight spot, all right. But we'll get

out of it. We always get out of it." And then he laughed, and
Turley laughed, and they went on drinking and started to tell
dirty jokes. . . .

That was quite a holiday. I mean, the way it ended it was
really something. I remember Clifton said something about
your situation, your status as a widower. You asked him not
to talk about it. He went on talking about it. He winked at
Turley and he said to you, "What's it like with a Puerto
Rican?"

You smiled at Clifton, you winked at Turley, and you said
to your father and mother, "It's gonna be crowded in here.
You better go into the next room—"

So then it was you and Clifton, and the table got knocked
over, and a couple chairs got broken. It was Clifton on the
floor, spitting blood and saying, "What goes on here?" Then
he shook his head. He just couldn't believe it. He said to
Turley, "Is that really him?"

Turley couldn't answer. He just stood staring.

Clifton got up and went down and got up again. He was
all right, he could really take it. You went on knocking him
down and he got up and finally he said, "I'm gettin' tired
of this." He looked at Turley and muttered, "Take him off
me—"

I remember Turley moving in and reaching out and then it
was Turley sitting on the floor next to Clifton. It was Clifton
laughing and saying, "You here too?" and Turley nodded solemnly and then he got up. He said, "Tell you what I'll do.
I'll give you fifty to one you can't do that again."

Then he moved in. He came in nice and easy, weaving. You
threw one and missed and then he threw one and his money
was safe. You were out for some twenty minutes. And later
we were gathered at the table again, and Clifton was grinning
and saying, "It figures now, you're slated for the game."

You didn't quite get that. You said, "Game? What game?"

"Our game." He pointed to himself and Turley. "I'm
gonna deal you in."

"No," Turley said. "He ain't for the racket."

"He's perfect for the racket," Clifton said quietly and
thoughtfully. "He's fast as a snake. He's hard as iron—"

"That ain't the point," Turley cut in. "The point is—"

"He's ready for it, that's the point. He's geared for action."

"He is?" Turley's voice was tight now. "Let him say it, then. Let him say what he wants."

Then it was quiet at the table. They were looking at you, waiting. You looked back at them, your brothers—the heist artists, the gunslingers, the all-out trouble-eaters.

And you thought, Is this the answer? Is this what you're slated for? Well, maybe so. Maybe Clifton has you tagged, with your hands that can't make music any more making cash the easy way. With a gun. You know they use guns. You braced for that? You hard enough for that?

Well, you were hard enough in Burma. In Burma you did plenty with a gun.

But this isn't Burma. This is a choice. Between what? The dirty and the clean? The bad and the good?

Let's put it another way. What's the payoff for the clean ones? The good ones? I mean the ones who play it straight. What do they get at the cashier's window?

Well, friends, speaking from experience, I'd say the payoff is anything from a kick in the teeth to the long-bladed scissors slicing in deep and cutting up that pump in your chest. And that's too much, that does it. With all feeling going out and the venom coming in. So then you're saying to the world, All right, you wanna play it dirty, we'll play it dirty.

But no, you were thinking. You don't want that. You join this Clifton-Turley combine, it's strictly on the vicious side and you've had enough of that.

"Well?" Clifton was asking. "What'll it be?"

You were shaking your head. You just didn't know. And then you happened to look up. You saw the other two faces, the older faces. Your mother was shrugging. Your father was wearing the soft-easy smile.

And that was it. That was the answer.

"Well?" from Clifton.

You shrugged. You smiled.

"Come on," Clifton said. "Let's have it."

"He's telling you," from Turley. "Look at his face."

Clifton looked. He took a long look. He said, "It's like— like he's skipped clear outa the picture. As if he just don't care."

"That just about says it," Turley grinned.

Just about. For then and there it was all connections split, it was all issues erased. No venom now, no frenzy, no trace of the wild man in your eyes. The wild man was gone, annihilated by two old hulks who didn't know they were still in there pitching, the dull-eyed, shrugging mother and the easy-smiling, booze-guzzling father.

Without sound you said to them, Much obliged, folks.

And later, when you went away, when you walked down the path that bordered the watermelon patch, you kept thinking it, Much obliged, much obliged.

The path was bumpy, but you didn't feel the bumps. In the woods the narrow, twisting road was deeply rutted, but you sort of floated past the ridges and the chug holes. You remember it was wet-cold in the woods, and there was a blasting wind, but all you felt was a gentle breeze.

You made it through the woods, and onto another road, and still another road, and finally the wide concrete highway that took you into the tiny town and the bus depot. In the depot there was a lush talking loud. He was trying to start something. When he tried with you, it was just no use, he got nowhere. You gave him the shrug, you gave him the smile. It was easy, the way you handled him. Well, sure, it was easy, it was just that nothing look—with your tongue in your cheek.

You took the first bus out. It was headed for Philadelphia. I think it was a few nights later you were in a mid-city ginmill, one of them fifteen-cents-a-shot establishments. It had a kitchen, and you got a job washing dishes and cleaning the floor and so forth. There was an old wreck of a piano, and you'd look at it, and look away, and look at it again. One night you said to the bartender, "Okay if I play it?"

"You?"

"I think I can play it."

"All right, give it a try. But it better be music."

You sat down at the piano. You looked at the keyboard. And then you looked at your hands.

"Come on," the bartender said. "Whatcha waitin' for?"

You lifted your hands. You lowered your hands and your fingers hit the keys.

The sound came out and it was music.

10

A VOICE said, "You still here?"

He looked up. The waitress was coming toward him through the crowd of shoppers. She'd emerged from the five-and-dime with a paper bag in her hand. He saw that it was a small bag. He told himself that she hadn't done much shopping.

"How long were you in there?" he asked.

"Just a few minutes."

"Is that all?"

"I got waited on right away," she asked. "All I bought was some toothpaste and a cake of soap. And a toothbrush."

He didn't say anything.

She said, "I didn't ask you to wait for me."

"I wasn't waiting," he said. "I had no place to go, that's all. I was just hanging around."

"Looking at the people?"

"No," he said. "I wasn't looking at the people."

She pulled him away from an oncoming baby carriage. "Come on," she said. "We're blocking traffic."

They moved along with the crowd. The sky was all gray now and getting darker. It was still early in the afternoon, just a little past two, but it seemed much later. People were looking up at the sky and walking faster, wanting to get home before the storm swept in. The threat of it was in the air.

She looked at him. She said, "Button your overcoat."

"I'm not cold."

"I'm freezing," she said. "How far we gotta walk?"

"To Port Richmond? It's a couple miles."

"That's great."

"We could take a taxi, except I haven't got a cent to my name."

"Likewise," she said. "I borrowed four bits from my landlady and spent it all."

"Well, it ain't too cold for walking."

"The hell it ain't. My toes are coming off."

"We'll walk faster," he said. "That'll keep your feet warm."

They quickened their pace. They were walking with their

heads down against the oncoming wind. It was coming harder, whistling louder. It lifted the snow from pavement and street and there were powdery flurries of the tiny flakes. Then larger snowflakes were falling. The air was thick with snow, and it was getting colder.

"Nice day for a picnic," she said. And just then she slipped on some hard-packed snow and was falling backward and he grabbed her. Then he slipped and they were both falling but she managed to get a foothold and they stayed on their feet. A store owner was standing in the doorway of his dry-goods establishment, saying to them, "Watch your step out there. It's slippery." She glared at the man and said, "Yeah, we know it's slippery. It wouldn't be slippery if you'd clean the pavement." The store owner grinned and said, "So if you fall, you'll sue me."

The man went back into the store. They stood there on the slippery pavement, still holding onto each other to keep from falling. He said to himself, That's all it amounts to, just holding her so she won't slide and slip and go down. But I guess it's all right now, I guess you can let go.

You better let go, damn it. Because it's there again, it's happening again. You'll hafta stop it, that's all. You can't let it get you like this. It's really getting you and she knows it. Of course she knows. She's looking at you and she—

Say, what's the matter with your arms? Why can't you let go of her? Now look, you'll just hafta stop it.

I think the way to stop it is shrug it off. Or take it with your tongue in your cheek. Sure, that's the system. At any rate it's the system that works for you. It's the automatic control board that keeps you way out there where nothing matters, where it's only you and the keyboard and nothing else. Because it's gotta be that way. You gotta stay clear of anything serious.

You wanna know something? The system just ain't working now. I think it's Eddie giving way to Edward Webster Lynn. No, it can't be that way. We won't let it be that way. Oh, Christ, why'd she have to mention that name? Why'd she have to bring it all back? You had it buried and you were getting along fine and having such a high old time not caring about anything. And now this comes along. This hits you and sets a spark and before we know it there's a fire started. A what? You heard me, I said it's a fire. And here's a flash just came in—it's blazing too high and we can't put it out.

We can't? Check the facts, man, check the facts. This is Eddie here. And Eddie can't feel fire. Eddie can't feel anything.

His arms fell away from her. There was nothing at all in his eyes as he gave her the soft-easy smile. He said, "Let's get moving. We got a long way to go."

She looked at him, and took a slow deep breath, and said, "You're telling me?"

Some forty minutes later they entered Harriet's Hut. The place was jammed. It was always busy on Saturday afternoons, but when the weather was bad the crowd was doubled. Against all snow and blasting wind, the Hut was a fortress and a haven. It was also a fueling station. The bartender rushed back and forth, doing his level best to supply the demand for antifreeze.

Harriet was behind the bar, at the cash register. She spotted the waitress and the piano man, and yapped at them, "Where ya been? What the hell ya think it is, a holiday?"

"Sure it's a holiday," the waitress said. "We don't start work till nine tonight. That's the schedule."

"Not today it ain't." Harriet told her. "Not with a mob like this. You shoulda known I'd need you here. And you," she said to Eddie, "you oughta know the score on this kinda weather. They come in off the street, the place gets filled, and they wanna hear music."

Eddie shrugged. "I got up late."

"Yeah, he got up late," Lena said. She spoke very slowly, with a certain deliberation. "Then we went for a ride. And then we took a walk."

Harriet frowned. "Together?"

"Yeah," she said. "Together."

The Hut owner looked at the piano man. "What's the wire on that?"

He didn't answer. The waitress said, "Whatcha want him to do, make a full report?"

"If he wants to," Harriet said, still looking quizzically at the piano man. "It's just that I'm curious, that's all. He usually walks alone."

"Yeah, he's a loner, all right," the waitress murmured. "Even when he's with someone, he's alone."

Harriet scratched the back of her neck. "Say, what goes on here? What's all this who-struck-John routine?"

"You get the answer on page three," the waitress said. "Except there ain't no page three."

"Thanks," Harriet said. "That helps a lot." Then, abruptly, she yelled, "Look, don't stand there giving me puzzles. I don't need puzzles today. Just put on your apron and get to work."

"First we get paid."

"We?" Harriet was frowning again.

"Well, me, anyway," the waitress said. "I want a week's wages and three in advance for this extra time today."

"What's the rush?"

"No rush." Lena pointed to the cash register. "Just take it out nice and slow and hand it to me."

"Later," the fat blonde said. "I'm too busy now."

"Not too busy to gimme my salary. And while you're at it, you can pay him, too. You want him to make music, you pay him."

Eddie shrugged. "I can wait—"

"You'll stay right here and get your money," Lena cut in. And then, to Harriet, "Come on, dish out the greens."

For a long moment Harriet didn't move. She stood there studying the face of the waitress. Then, with a backward gesture of her hand, as though to cast something over her shoulder to get it out of the way, she turned her attention to the cash register.

It's all right now, Eddie thought. It was tight there for a minute but I think it's all right now. He ventured a side glance at the expressionless face of the waitress. If only she leaves it alone, he said to himself. It don't make sense to start with Harriet. With Harriet it's like starting with dynamite. Or maybe that's what she wants. Yes, I think she's all coiled up inside, she's craving some kind of explosion.

Harriet was taking money from the cash register, counting

out the bills and putting them in Lena's palm. She finished paying Lena and turned to the piano man, putting the money on the bar in front of him. As she placed some ones on top of the fives, she was muttering, "Ain't enough I get grief from the customers. Now the help comes up with labor troubles. All of a sudden they go and form a union."

"That's the trend," the waitress said.

"Yeah?" Harriet said. "Well, I don't like it."

"Then lump it," Lena said.

The fat blonde stopped counting out the money. She blinked a few times. Then she straightened slowly, her immense bosom jutting as she inhaled a vast lungful. "What's that?" she said. "What'd you say?"

"You heard me."

Harriet placed her hands on her huge hips. "Maybe I didn't hear correct. Because they don't talk to me that way. They know better. I'll tell you something, girl. Ain't a living cat can throw that kinda lip at me and get away with it."

"That so?" Lena murmured.

"Yeah, that's so," Harriet said. "And you're lucky. I'm letting you know it the easy way. Next time it won't be so easy. You sound on me again, you'll get smacked down."

"Is that a warning?"

"Bright red."

"Thanks," Lena said. "Now here's one from me to you. I've been smacked down before. Somehow I've always managed to get up."

"Jesus." Harriet spoke aloud to herself. "What gives with this one here? It's like she's lookin' for it. She's really begging for it."

The waitress stood with her arms loose at her sides. She was smiling now.

Harriet had a thoughtful look on her face. She spoke softly to the waitress. "What's the matter, Lena? What bothers you?"

The waitress didn't answer.

"All right, I'll let it pass," the Hut owner said.

Lena held onto the thin smile. "You don't have to, really."

"I know I don't hafta. But it's better that way. Dontcha think it's better that way?"

The thin smile was aimed at nothing in particular. The waitress said, "Any way it goes all right with me. But don't do me any favors. I don't need no goddam favors from you."

Harriet frowned and slanted her head and said, "You sure you know what you're saying?"

Lena didn't answer.

"Know what I think?" Harriet murmured. "I think you got your people mixed."

Lena lost the smile. She lowered her head. She nodded, then shook her head, then nodded again.

"Ain't that what it is?" Harriet prodded gently.

Lena went on nodding. She looked up at the fat blonde. She said, "Yeah, I guess so." And then, tonelessly, "I'm sorry, Harriet. It's just that I'm bugged about something—I didn't mean to take it out on you."

"What is it?" Harriet asked. The waitress didn't answer. Harriet looked inquiringly at Eddie. The piano man shrugged and didn't say anything. "Come on, let's have it," Harriet demanded. "What is it with her?" He shrugged again and remained quiet. The fat blonde sighed and said, "All right, I give up," and resumed counting out the money. Then the money was all there on the bar and he picked it up and folded the thin roll and let it fall into his overcoat pocket. He turned away from the bar and took a few steps and heard Lena saying, "Wait, I got something for you."

He came back and she handed him two quarters, two dimes and a nickel. "From last night," she said, not looking at him. "Now we're squared."

He looked down at the coins in his hand. Squared, he thought. All squared away. That makes it quits. That ends it. Well, sure, that's the way you want it. That's fine.

But just then he saw she was stiffening, she was staring at something. He glanced in that direction and saw Wally Plyne coming toward the bar where they stood.

The big-paunched bouncer wore a twisted grin as he approached. His thick shoulders were hunched, weaving in wrestler's style. The grin widened, and Eddie thought, He's forcing it, and what we get next is one of them real friendly hellos, all sugar and syrup.

And then he felt Plyne's big hand on his arm, heard Plyne's

gruff voice saying, "Here he is, the crown prince of the eighty-eights. My boy, Eddie."

"Yeah," the waitress said. "Your boy, Eddie."

Plyne didn't seem to hear her. He said to the piano man, "I was lookin' for you. Where you been hiding?"

"He wasn't hiding," the waitress said.

The bouncer tried to ignore her. He went on grinning at Eddie.

The waitress pushed it further. "How could he hide? He didn't have a chance. They knew his address."

Plyne blinked hard. The grin fell away.

It was quiet for some moments. Then Harriet was saying, "Lemme get in on this." She leaned over from behind the bar. "What's cooking here?"

"Something messy," the waitress said. She indicated the bouncer. "Ask your man there. He knows all about it. He stirred it up."

Harriet squinted at Plyne. "Spill," she said.

"Spill what?" The bouncer backed away. "She's talkin' from nowhere. She's dreamin' or somethin'."

The waitress turned and looked at Harriet. "Look, if you don't wanna hear this—"

The fat blonde took a deep breath. She went on looking at Plyne.

"I hope you can take it," the waitress said to her. "After all, you live with this man."

"Not lately." Harriet's voice was heavy. "Lately I ain't hardly been living at all."

The waitress opened her mouth to speak, and Plyne gritted, "Close your head—"

"Close yours," Harriet told him. And then, to the waitress, "All right, let's have it."

"It's what they call a sellout," Lena said. "I got it straight from the customers. They told me they were here this morning. They bought a few drinks and something else."

Eddie started to move away. The waitress reached out and caught his arm and held him there. He shrugged and smiled. His eyes said to the bouncer, It don't bother me, so don't let it bother you.

The waitress went on, "It was two of them. Two ambassadors, but not the good-will type. These were the ugly kind, the kind that can hurt you. Or make you disappear. You get what I'm talking about?"

Harriet nodded dully.

"They were looking for Eddie," the waitress said.

Harriet frowned, "What for?"

"That ain't the point. The point is, they had a car and they had a gun. What they needed was some information. Like finding out his address."

The frown faded from Harriet's face. She gaped at Plyne. "You didn't tell them—"

"He sure as hell did," Lena said.

Harriet winced.

"They gave him a nice tip, too," the waitress said. "They handed him fifty dollars."

"No." It was a groan. Harriet's mouth twisted. She turned her head to keep from looking at the bouncer.

"I don't wanna work here no more," the waitress said. "I'll just stay a few days, until you get another girl."

"Now wait," the bouncer said. "It ain't that bad."

"It ain't?" Lena faced him. "I'll tell you how bad it is. Ever bait a hook for catfish? They go for the stink. What you do is, you put some worms in a can and leave it out in the sun for a week or so. Then open the can and get a whiff. It'll give you an idea of what this smells like."

Plyne swallowed hard. "Look, you got it all wrong—"

And the waitress said, "Now we get the grease."

"Will ya listen?" Plyne whined. "I'm tellin' you they conned me. I didn't know what they were after. I figured they was—"

"Yeah, we know," Lena murmured. "You thought they were census-takers."

The bouncer turned to Eddie. His arms came up in a pleading gesture. "Ain't I your friend?"

"Sure," Eddie said.

"Would I do anything to hurt you?"

"Of course not."

"You hear that?" The bouncer spoke loudly to the two women. "You hear what he says? He knows I'm on his side."

"I think I'm gonna throw up," Harriet said.

But the bouncer went on, "I'm tellin' you they conned me. If I thought they were out to hurt Eddie, I'da—why for Christ's sake, I'da ripped 'em apart. They come in here again, I'll put them through that plate-glass window, one at a time."

A nearby drinker mumbled, "You tell 'em, Hugger."

And from another guzzler, "When the Hugger tells it, he means it."

"You're goddam right I mean it," Plyne said loudly. "I ain't a man who looks for trouble, but if they want it they'll get it." And then, to Eddie, "Dontcha worry, I can handle them gunpunks. They're little. I'm big."

"How big?" the waitress asked.

Plyne grinned at her. "Take a look."

She looked him up and down. "Yeah, it's there, all right," she murmured. "Really huge."

The bouncer was feeling much better now. He widened the grin. "Huge is correct," he said. "And it's solid, too. It's all man."

"Man?" She stretched the word, her mouth twisted. "What I see is slop."

At the bar the drinkers had stopped drinking. They were staring at the waitress.

"It's just slop," she said. She took a step toward the bouncer. "The only thing big about you is your mouth."

Plyne grunted again. He mumbled, "I don't like that. I ain't gonna take it—"

"You'll take it," she told him. "You'll eat it."

He's eating it, all right, Eddie thought. He's choking on it. Look at him, look what's in the eyes. Because he's getting it from her, that's why. He goes for her so much it's got him all jelly, it's driving him almost loony. And there's nothing he can do about it, except take it. Just stand there and take it. Yes he's getting it, sure enough. I've seen them get it, but not like this.

Now the crowd at the bar was moving in closer. From the tables they were rising and edging forward so as not to miss a word of it. The only sound in the Hut was the voice of the waitress. She spoke quietly, steadily, and what came from her lips was like a blade going into the bouncer.

Really ripping him apart, Eddie thought. Come to think of

it, what's happening here is a certain kind of amputation. And we don't mean the arms or the legs.

And look at Harriet. Look what's happening to her. She's aged some ten years in just a few minutes. Her man is getting slashed and chopped. It's happening right in front of her eyes, and there ain't a word she can say, a move she can make. She knows it's true.

Sure, it's true. No getting away from that. The bouncer played it dirty today. But even so, I think he's getting worse than he deserves. You gotta admit, he's had some hard knocks lately, I mean this problem with the waitress, this night after night of seeing it there and wanting it, and knowing there ain't a chance. And even now, while she tears him to pieces, spits on him in front of all these people, he can't take his hungry eyes off her. You gotta feel sorry for the bouncer, it's a sad matinee for the Harleyville Hugger.

Poor Hugger. He wanted so much to make a comeback, some sort of comeback. He thought if he could make it with the waitress, he'd be proving something. Like proving he still had it, the power, the importance, the stuff and the drive, and whatever it takes to make a woman say yes. What he got from the waitress was a cold, silent no. Not even a look.

Well, he's getting something now. He's getting plenty. It's grief in spades, that's what it is. I wish she'd stop it, I think she's pushing it too far. Does she know what she's doing to him? She can't know. If she knew, she'd stop. If I could only tell her—

Tell her what? That the bouncer ain't as bad as he seems? That he's just another has-been who tried to come back and got himself loused up? Sure, that's the way it is but you can't put it that way. You can't sing the blues for Plyne; you can't sing the blues, period. You're too far away from the scene, that's why. You're high up there and way out there where nothing matters.

Then what are you doing standing here? And looking. And listening. Why ain't you there at the piano?

Or maybe you're waiting for something to happen. It figures, the bouncer can't take much more of this. The waitress keeps it up, something's gonna happen, sure as hell.

Well, so what? It don't involve you. Nothing involves you.

What you do now is, you shove off. You cruise away from here and over there to the piano.

He started to move, and then couldn't move. The waitress was still holding onto his arm. He gave a pull, his arm came loose, and the waitress looked at him. Her eyes said, You can't check out; you're included.

His soft-easy smile said, Not in this. Not in anything.

Then he was headed toward the piano. He heard the voice of the waitress as she went on talking to Plyne. His legs moved faster. He was in a hurry to sit down at the keyboard, to start making music. That'll do it, he thought. That'll drown out the buzzing. He took off his overcoat and tossed it onto a chair.

"Hey, Eddie." It was from a nearby table. He glanced in that direction and saw the yellow-orange dyed hair, the skinny shoulders and the flat chest. The lips of Clarice were gin-wet, and her eyes were gin-shiny. She was sitting there alone, unaware of the situation at the bar.

"C'mere," she said. "C'mere and I'll show you a trick."

"Later," he murmured, and went on toward the piano. But then he thought, That wasn't polite. He turned and smiled at Clarice, and walked over to the table and sat down. "All right," he said. "Let's see it."

She was off her chair and onto the table, attempting a one-armed handstand. She went off the table and landed on the floor.

"Nice try," Eddie said. He reached down and helped her to her feet. She slid back onto the chair. From across the room, from the bar, he could hear the voice of the waitress, still giving it to Plyne. Don't listen, he told himself. Try to concentrate on what Clarice is saying.

Clarice was saying, "You sure fluffed me off last night."

"Well, it just wasn't there."

She shrugged. She reached for a shot glass, picked it up and saw it was empty. With a vague smile at the empty glass she said, "That's the way it goes. If it ain't there, it just ain't there."

"That figures."

"You're damn right it figures." She reached out and gave him an affectionate pat on the shoulder. "Maybe next time—"

"Sure," he said.

"Or maybe—" she lowered the glass to the table and pushed it aside— "maybe there won't be a next time."

"Whatcha mean?" He frowned slightly. "You closing up shop?"

"No," she said. "I'm still in business. I mean you."

"Me? What's with me?"

"Changes," Clarice said. "I gander certain changes."

His frown deepened "Like what?"

"Well, like last night, for instance. And just a little while ago, when you walked in with the waitress. It was—well, I've seen it happen before. I can always tell when it happens."

"When what happens? What're you getting at?"

"The collision," she said. She wasn't looking at him. She was talking to the shot glass and the table top. "That's what it is, a collision. Before they know it, it hits them. They just can't avoid it. Not even this one here, this music man with his real cool style. It was easy-come and easy-go and all of a sudden he gets hit—"

"Say, look, you want another drink?"

"I always want another drink."

He started to get up. "You sure need it now."

She pulled him back onto the chair. "First gimme the low-down. I like to get these facts first hand. Maybe I'll send it to Winchell."

"What is this? You dreaming up something?"

"Could be," Clarice murmured. She looked at him. It was a probing look. "Except it shows. It's scribbled all over your face. It was there when I seen you comin' in with her."

"Her? The waitress?"

"Yeah, the waitress. But she wasn't no cheap-joint waitress then. She was Queen of the Nile and you were that soldier, or something, from Rome."

He laughed. "It's the gin, Clarice. The gin's got you looped."

"You think so? I don't think so." She reached for the empty glass, pulled it toward her on the table. "Let's have a look in the crystal ball," she said.

Her hands were cupped around the shot glass, and she sat there looking intently at the empty jigger.

"I see something," she said.

"Clarice, it's just an empty glass."

"Ain't empty now. There's a cloud. There's shadows—"

"Come off it," he said.

"Quiet," she breathed. "It's comin' closer."

"All right." He grinned. "I'll go along with the gag. Whaddya see in the glass?"

"It's you and the waitress—"

For some reason he closed his eyes. His hands gripped the sides of the chair.

He heard Clarice saying, "—no other people around. Just you and her. It's in the summertime. And there's a beach. There's water—"

"Water?" He opened his eyes, his hands relaxed, and he grinned again. "That ain't water. It's gin. You're swimmin' in it."

Clarice ignored him. She went on gazing at the shot glass. "You both got your clothes on. Then she takes off her clothes. Look what she's doin'. She's all naked."

"Keep it clean," he said.

"You stand there and look at her," Clarice continued. "She runs across the sand. Then she takes a dive in the waves. She tells you to get undressed and come on in, the water's fine. You stand there—"

"That's right," he said. "I just stand there. I don't make a move."

"But she wants you—"

"The hell with her," he said. "That ocean's too deep for me."

Clarice looked at him. Then she looked at the shot glass. Now it was just an empty jigger that needed a refill.

"You see?" he said. And he grinned again. "There ain't nothing happening."

"You leveling? With yourself, I mean."

"Well, if it's proof you need—" He put his hand in his pocket and took out the roll of money, his salary from Harriet. He peeled off three ones and put them on the table. "I'm paying you in advance," he said. "For the next time."

She looked at the three ones.

"Take it," he said. "You might as well take it. You're gonna work for it."

Clarice shrugged and took the money off the table. She slipped the bills under her sleeve. "Well, anyway," she said, "it's nice to know you're still my customer."

"Permanent," he said with the soft-easy smile. "Let's shake on it."

And he put out his hand. Just then he heard the noise from the bar. It was a growl, and then a gasp from the crowd. He turned his head and saw the crowd moving back, shoving and pushing to stay clear of the bouncer. The growl came again, and Harriet was coming out from behind the bar, moving fast as she attempted to step between the bouncer and the waitress. The bouncer shoved her aside. It was a violent shove, and Harriet stumbled and hit the floor sitting down. Then the bouncer let out another growl, and took a slow step toward the waitress. The waitress stood there motionless. Plyne raised his arm. He hesitated, as though he wasn't quite sure what he wanted to do. The waitress smiled thinly, sneeringly, daring him to go through with it. He swung his arm and the flat of his hand cracked hard against her mouth.

Eddie got up from the chair. He walked toward the crowd at the bar.

II

HE was pushing his way through the crowd. They were packed tightly, and he had to use his elbows. As he forced a path, they gasped, for Plyne hit the waitress a second time. This time it was a knuckle smash with the back of the hand.

Eddie kept pushing, making his way through the crowd.

The waitress had not moved. A trickle of red moved slantwise from her lower lip.

"You'll take it back," the bouncer said. He was breathing very hard. "You'll take back every—"

"Kiss my ass," the waitress said.

Plyne hit her again, with his palm. And then again, with the back of his hand.

Harriet was up from the floor, getting between them. The bouncer grabbed her arm and flung her sideways. She went sailing across the floor, landed heavily on her knees, and then twisted her ankle as she tried to get up. She fell back. She sat there rubbing her ankle, staring at Plyne and the waitress.

The bouncer raised his arm again. "You gonna take it back?"

"No."

His open hand crashed against her face. She reeled against the bar, recovered her balance and stood there, still smiling thinly. Now a thicker stream of blood came from her mouth. One side of her face was welted with fingermarks. The other side was swollen and bruised.

"I'll ruin you," Plyne screamed at her. "I'll make you wish you'd never seen me—"

"I can't see you now," the waitress said. "I can't look down that far."

Plyne hit her again with his palm. Then he clenched his fist.

Eddie was using his arms like scythes, a feeling of desperation on him now.

Plyne said to the waitress, "You're gonna take it back. You'll take it back if I hafta knock all your teeth out."

"That won't do it," the waitress said. She licked at her bleeding lip.

"God damn you." Plyne hissed. He hauled off and swung his fist at her face. His fist was in mid-air when a hand grabbed his arm. He jerked loose and hauled off again. The hand came down on his arm, holding tightly now. He turned his head to see who had interfered.

"Leave her alone," Eddie said.

"You?" the bouncer said again.

Eddie didn't say anything. He was still holding the bouncer's arm. He moved slowly, stepping between Plyne and the waitress.

Plyne's eyes were wide. He was genuinely astonished. "Not Eddie," he said. "Anyone but Eddie."

"All right," the piano man murmured. "Let's break it up."

"Christ," the bouncer said. He turned and gaped at the

gaping crowd. "Look what's happenin' here. Look who's tryin' to break it up."

"I mean it, Wally."

"What? You what?" And then again to the crowd, "Get that? He says he means it."

"It's gone far enough," Eddie said.

"Well I'll be—" The bouncer didn't know what to make of it. Then he looked down and saw the hand still gripping his arm. "Whatcha doin'?" he asked, his voice foggy with amazement. "Whatcha think you're doin'?"

Eddie spoke to the waitress. "Take off."

"What?" from Plyne. And then to the waitress, who hadn't moved, "That's right, stay there. You got more comin'."

"No," Eddie said. "Listen, Wally—"

"To you?" The bouncer ripped out a laugh. He pulled his arm free from Eddie's grasp. "Move, clown. Get outta the way."

Eddie stood there.

"I said move," Plyne barked. "Get back where you belong." He pointed to the piano.

"If you'll leave her alone," Eddie said.

Again Plyne turned to the crowd. "You hear that? Can you believe it? I tell him to move and he won't move. This can't be Eddie."

From someone in the crowd, "It's Eddie, all right."

And from another, "He's still there, Hugger."

Plyne stepped back and looked Eddie up and down. He said, "What goes with you? You really know what you're doin'?"

Eddie spoke again to the waitress. "Take off, will you? Go on, fade."

"Not from this deal," the waitress said. "I like this deal."

"Sure she likes it," Plyne said. "What she got was only a taste. Now I'm gonna give her—"

"No you won't." Eddie's voice was soft, almost a whisper.

"I won't?" The bouncer mimicked Eddie's tone. "What's gonna stop me?"

Eddie didn't say anything.

Plyne laughed again. He reached out and lightly patted Eddie's head, and then he said kindly, almost paternally,

"You're way outa your groove. Somebody musta been feedin' you weeds, or maybe a joker put a capsule in your coffee."

"He ain't high, Hugger," came from someone in the crowd. "He's got both feet on the floor."

From another observer, "He'll have his head on the floor if he don't get outa the way."

"He'll get outa the way," Plyne said. "All I hafta do is snap my fingers—"

Eddie spoke with his eyes. His eyes said to the bouncer, It's gonna take more than that.

Plyne read it, checked it, and decided to test it. He moved toward the waitress. Eddie moved with him, staying in his path. Someone yelled, "Watch out, Eddie—"

The bouncer swiped at him, as though swiping at a fly. He ducked, and the bouncer lunged past him, aiming a fist at the waitress. Eddie pivoted and swung and his right hand made contact with Plyne's head.

"What?" Plyne said heavily. He turned and looked at Eddie. Eddie was braced, his legs wide apart, his hands low.

"You did that?" Plyne asked.

Did I? Eddie asked himself. Was it really me? Yes, it was. But that can't be. I'm Eddie. Eddie wouldn't do that. The man who would do that is a long-gone drifter, the wild man whose favorite drink was his own blood, whose favorite meat was the Hell's Kitchen maulers, the Bowery sluggers, the Greenpoint uglies. And that was in another city, another world. In this world it's Eddie, who sits at the piano and makes the music and keeps his tongue in his cheek. Then why—

The bouncer moved in and hauled off with his left hand, his right cocked to follow through. As the bouncer swung, Eddie came in low and shot a short right to the belly. Plyne grunted and bent over. Eddie stepped back, then smashed a chopping left to the head.

Plyne went down.

The crowd was silent. The only sound in the Hut was the heavy breathing of the bouncer, who knelt on one knee and shook his head very slowly.

Then someone said, "I'm gonna buy new glasses. I just ain't seein' right."

"You saw what I saw," another said. "It was Eddie did that."

"I'm tellin' ya that can't be Eddie. The way he moved—that's something I ain't seen for years. Not since Henry Armstrong."

"Or Terry McGovern," one of the oldsters remarked.

"That's right, McGovern. That was a McGovern left hand, sure enough."

Then they were quiet again. The bouncer was getting up. He got up very slowly and looked at the crowd. They backed away. On the outer fringe they were pushing chairs and tables aside. "That's right," the bouncer said quietly. "Gimme plenty of room."

Then he turned and looked at the piano man.

"I don't want this," Eddie said. "Let's end it, Wally."

"Sure," the bouncer said. "It's gonna be finished in a jiffy."

Eddie gestured toward the waitress, who had moved toward the far side of the bar. "If you'll only leave her alone—"

"For now," the bouncer agreed. "Now it's you I want."

Plyne rushed to him.

Eddie met him with a whizzing right hand to the mouth. Plyne fell back, started forward, and walked into another right hand that landed on the cheekbone. Then Plyne tried to reach him with both arms flailing and Eddie went very low, grinning widely and happily, coming in to uppercut the bouncer with his left, to follow with a short right that made a crunching sound as it hit the damaged cheekbone. Plyne stepped back again, then came in weaving, somewhat cautiously.

The caution didn't help. Plyne took a right to the head, three lefts to the left eye, and a straight right to the mouth. The bouncer opened his mouth and two teeth fell out.

"Holy Saint Peter!" someone gasped.

Plyne was very careful now. He feinted a left, drew Eddie in, crossed a right that missed and took a series of lefts to the head. He shook them off, drew Eddie in again with another feinting left, then crossed the right. This time it landed. It caught Eddie on the jaw and he went flying. He hit the floor flat on his back. For a few moments his eyes were closed. He heard someone saying, "Get some water—" He opened his eyes. He grinned up at the bouncer.

The bouncer grinned back at him. "How we doin'?"

"We're doin' fine," Eddie said. He got up. The bouncer walked in fast and hit him on the jaw and Eddie went down again. He pulled himself up very slowly, still grinning. He raised his fists, but Plyne was in close and pushed him back. Plyne measured him with a long left, set him up against a table and then hit him with a right that sent him over the table, his legs above his head. He hit the floor and rolled over and got up.

Plyne had circled the table and was waiting for him. Plyne chopped a right to his head, hooked a left to his ribs, then hauled off and swung a roundhouse that caught him on the side of the head. He went to his knees.

"Stay there," someone yelled at him. "For Christ's sake, stay there."

"He won't do that," the bouncer said. "You watch and see. He's gonna get up again."

"Stay there, Eddie—"

"Why should he stay there?" the bouncer asked. "Look at him grinnin'. He's havin' fun."

"Lotsa fun," Eddie said. And then he came up very fast and slugged the bouncer in the mouth, in the cut eye, and in the mouth again. Plyne screamed with agony as his eye was cut again, deeply.

The crowd was backed up against a wall. They saw the bouncer reel from a smashing blow on the mouth. They saw the smaller man lunge and hit the bouncer in the belly. Plyne was wheezing, doubled up, trying to go down. The smaller man came in with a right hand that straightened Plyne. Then he delivered a whistling left that made a sickening sound as it hit the badly damaged eye.

Plyne screamed.

There was another scream and it came from a woman in the crowd.

A man yelled, "Someone stop it—"

Plyne took another left hook to the bad eye, then a sizzling right to the mouth, a left to the eye again, a right to the bruised cheekbone, and two more rights to the same cheekbone. Eddie fractured the bouncer's cheekbone, closed the eye, and knocked four teeth from the bleeding gums. The bouncer opened his mouth to scream again and was hit with a right to the jaw. He crashed into a chair and the chair fell apart. He reached out blindly, his chin on the floor, and his hand closed on a length of splintered wood, the leg from the broken chair. As he got up, he was swinging the club with all his might at the smaller man's head.

The club hit empty air. Plyne swung again and missed. The smaller man was backing away. The bouncer advanced slowly, then lunged and swung and the club grazed the smaller man's shoulder.

Eddie kept backing away. He bumped into a table and threw himself aside as the bouncer aimed again for his skull. The splintered cudgel missed his temple by only a few inches.

Too close, Eddie told himself. Much too close for health and welfare. That thing connects, you're on the critical list. Did you say critical? The shape you're in now, it's critical already. How come you're still on your feet? Look at him. He's gone sheer off his rocker, and that ain't no guess, it ain't no theory. Just look at his eyes. Or make it the one eye, the other's a mess. Look at the one eye that's open. You see what's in that eye? It's slaughter. He's out for slaughter, and you gotta do something.

Whatever it is, you better do it fast. We're in the home stretch now. It's gettin' close to the finish line. Yeah—he nearly got you that time. Another inch or so and that woulda been it. God damn these tables. All these tables in the way. But the door, the back door, I think you're near enough to make a try for it. Sure, that's the only thing you can do. That is, if you wanna get outa here alive.

He turned and made a dash toward the back door. As he neared the door, he heard a loud gasp from the crowd. He whirled, and looked, and saw the bouncer heading toward the waitress.

She was backed up against the bar. She was cornered there, blocked off. On one side it was the overturned tables. On the other side it was the crowd. The bouncer moved forward very slowly, his shoulders hunched, the cudgel raised. A low gurgling noise mixed with the blood dripping from his mouth. It was a macabre noise, like a dirge.

There was a distance of some twenty feet between the bouncer and the waitress. Then it was fifteen feet. The bouncer stepped over a fallen chair, hunched lower now. He reached out to push aside an overturned table. At that moment, Eddie moved.

The crowd saw Eddie running toward the bar, then vaulting over its wooden surface, then was hurling himself toward the food counter at the other end of the bar. They saw him arriving at the food counter and grabbing a bread knife.

He came out from behind the bar and moved between the waitress and the bouncer. It was a large knife. It had a stainless-steel blade and it was very sharp. He thought, The bouncer knows how sharp it is, he's seen Harriet cutting bread with it, cutting meat. I think he'll drop that club now and come to his senses. Look, he's stopped, he's just standing there. If he'll only drop that club.

"Drop it, Wally."

Plyne held onto the cudgel. He stared at the knife, then at the waitress, then at the knife again.

"Drop that stick," Eddie said. He took a slow step forward.

Plyne retreated a few feet. Then he stopped and glanced around, sort of wonderingly. Then he looked at the waitress. He made the gurgling noise again.

Eddie took another step forward. He raised the knife a little. He kicked at the overturned table, clearing the space between himself and the bouncer.

He showed his teeth to the bouncer. He said, "All right, I gave you a chance—"

There was a shriek from a woman in the crowd. It was Harriet. She shrieked again as Eddie kept moving slowly toward the bouncer. She yelled, "No Eddie—please!"

He wanted to look at Harriet, to tell her with his eyes, It's all right, I'm only bluffing. And he thought, You can't do that. You gotta keep your eyes on this one here. Gotta push him with your eyes, push him back—

Plyne was retreating again. He still held the cudgel, but now his grip on it was loose. He didn't seem to realize he had it in his hand. He took a few more backward steps. Then his head turned and he was looking at the back door.

I think it's working, Eddie told himself. If I can get him

outa here, get him running so's he'll be out that door and outa the Hut, away from the waitress—

Look, now, he's dropped the club. All right, that's fine. You're doing fine, Hugger. I think you're gonna make it. Come on, Hugger, work with me. No, don't look at her. Look at me, look at the knife. It's such a sharp knife, Hugger. You wanna get away from it? All you gotta do is go for that door. Please, Wally, go for that door. I'll help you get through, I'll be right with you, right behind you—

He raised the knife higher. He moved in closer and faked a slash at the bouncer's throat.

Plyne turned and ran toward the back door.

Eddie went after him.

"No—" from Harriet.

And from others in the crowd, "No, Eddie. Eddie—"

He chased Plyne through the back rooms of the Hut, through the door leading to the alley. Plyne was going very fast along the wind-whipped, snow-covered alley. Gotta stay with him, Eddie thought, gotta stay with the Hugger who needs a friend now, who sure as hell needs a chummy hand on his shoulder, a soft voice saying, It's all right, Wally. It's all right.

Plyne looked back and saw him coming with the knife. Plyne ran faster. It was a very long alley and Plyne was running against the wind. He'll hafta stop soon, Eddie thought. He's carryin' a lot of weight and a lot of damage and he just can't keep up that pace. And you, you're weighted down yourself. It's a good thing you ain't wearin' your overcoat. Or maybe it ain't so good, because I'll tell you something, bud. It's cold out here.

The bouncer was halfway down the alley, turning again, and looking, then going sideways and bumping into the wooden boards of a high fence. He tried to climb the fence and couldn't obtain a foothold. He went on running down the alley. He slipped in the snow, went down, got up, took another look back, and was running again. He covered another thirty yards and stopped once more, and then he tried a fence door. It was open and he went through.

Eddie ran up to the door. It was still open. It gave way to the small backyard of a two-story dwelling. As he entered the

backyard, he saw Plyne trying to climb the wall of the house.
Plyne was clawing at the wall, trying to insert his fingers
through the tiny gaps between red bricks. It was as though
Plyne meant to get up the wall, even if he had to scrape all
the flesh off his fingers.

"Wally—"

The bouncer went on trying to climb the wall.

"Wally, listen—"

Plyne leaped up at the wall. His fingernails scraped against
the bricks. As he came down, he sagged to his knees. He
straightened, looked up along the wall, and then he turned
slowly and looked at Eddie.

Eddie smiled at him and dropped the knife. It landed with
a soft thud in the snow.

The bouncer stared down at the knife. It was half hidden
in the snow. Plyne pointed with a quivering finger.

"The hell with it," Eddie said. He kicked the knife aside.

"You ain't gonna—?"

"Forget it, Wally."

The bouncer lifted his hand to his blood-smeared face. He
wiped some blood from his mouth, looked at his red-stained
fingers, then looked up at Eddie. "Forget it?" he mumbled,
and began to move forward. "How can I forget it?"

Easy now, Eddie thought. Let's take it slow and easy. He
went on smiling at the bouncer. He said, "We'll put it this
way—I've had enough."

But Plyne kept moving forward. Plyne said, "Not yet.
There's gotta be a winner—"

"You're the winner," Eddie said. "You're too big for me,
that's all. You're more than I can handle."

"Don't con me," the bouncer said, his pain-battered brain
somehow probing through the red haze, somehow seeing it
the way it was. "They saw me running away. The bouncer
getting bounced. They'll make it a joke—"

"Wally, listen—"

"They'll laugh at me," Plyne said. He was crouched now,
his shoulders weaving as he moved in slowly. "I ain't gonna
have that. It's one thing I just can't take. I gotta let them
know—"

"They know, Wally. It ain't as if they need proof."

"—gotta let them know," Plyne said as though talking to himself. "Gotta cross off all them things she said about me. That I'm just a washed-up nothing, a slob a faker a crawling worm—"

Eddie looked down at the knife in the snow. Too late now, he thought. And much too late for words. Too late for anything. Well, you tried.

"But hear me now," the bouncer appealed to himself. "Them names she called me, it ain't so. I got only one name. I'm the Hugger—" He was sobbing, the huge shoulders shaking, the bleeding mouth twisted grotesquely. "I'm the Hugger, and they ain't gonna laugh at the Hugger."

Plyne leaped, and his massive arms swept out and in and tightened around Eddie's middle. Yes he's the Hugger, Eddie thought, feeling the tremendous crushing power of the bear hug. It felt as though his innards were getting squeezed up into his chest. He couldn't breathe, he couldn't even try to breathe. He had his mouth wide open, his head flung back, his eyes shut tightly as he took the iron-hard pressure of the bouncer's chin applied to his chest bone. He said to himself, You can't take this. Ain't a living thing can take this and live.

The bouncer had him lifted now, his feet several inches off the ground. As the pressure of the bear hug increased, Eddie swung his legs forward, as though he was trying to somersault backwards. His legs went in between the bouncer's knees, and the bouncer went forward stumbling. Then they went down, and he felt the cold wetness of the snow. The bouncer was on top of him, retaining the bear hug, the straddled knees braced hard against the snow as the massive arms applied more force.

Eddie's eyes remained shut. He tried to open them and couldn't. Then he tried to move his left arm, thinking in terms of his fingernails, telling himself it needed claws and if he could reach the bouncer's face—

His left arm came up a few inches and fell back again in the snow. The snow felt very cold against his hand. Then something happened and he couldn't feel the coldness. You're going, he said to himself. You're passing out. As the thought swirled through the fog in his brain, he was trying with his right hand.

Trying what? he asked himself. What can you do now? His

right hand moved feebly in the snow. Then his fingers touched
something hard and wooden. At the very moment of contact,
he knew what it was. It was the handle of the knife.

He pulled at the knife handle, saying to himself, In the arm,
let him have it in the arm. And then he managed to open his
eyes, his remaining strength now centered in his eyes and his
fingers gripping the knife. He took aim, with the knife pointed
at Plyne's left arm. Get in deep, he told himself. Get it in
there so he'll really feel it and he'll hafta let go.

The knife came up. Plyne didn't see it coming. At that instant Plyne shifted his position to exert more pressure with
the bear hug. Shifting from right to left, Plyne took the blade
in his chest. The blade went in very deep.

"What?" Plyne said. "Whatcha do to me?"

Eddie stared at his own hand, still gripping the handle of
the knife. The bouncer seemed to be drifting away from him,
going back and sideways. He saw the blade glimmering red,
and then he saw the bouncer rolling and twitching in the
snow.

The bouncer rolled over on his back, on his belly, then
again on his back. He stayed there. His mouth opened wide
and he started to take a deep breath. Some air went in and
came out mixed with bubbles of pink and red and darker red.
The bouncer's eyes became very large. Then the bouncer
sighed and his eyes remained wide open and he was dead.

12

EDDIE sat there in the snow and looked at the dead man. He
said to himself, Who did that? Then he fell back in the snow,
gasping and coughing, trying to loosen things up inside. It's
so tight in there, he thought, his hands clasped to his abdomen, it's all squashed and outa commission. You feel it?
You're damn right you feel it. Another thing you feel is the
news coming in on the wire. That thing there in the snow,
that's your work, buddy. You wanna look at it again? You
wanna admire your work?

No, not now. There's other work we gotta do now. Them sounds you hear in the alley, that's the Hut regulars coming out to see what the score is. How come they waited so long? Well, they musta been scared. Or sorta paralyzed, that's more like it. But now they're in the alley. They're opening the fence doors, the doors that ain't locked. Sure, they figure we're in one of these backyards. So what you gotta do is, you gotta keep them outa this one here. You lock that door.

But wait—let's check that angle. How come you don't want them to see? They're gonna see it sooner or later. And what it amounts to, it's just one of them accidents. It ain't as if you meant to do it. You were aiming for his arm, and then he made that move, he traveled just about four or five inches going from right to left, from right to wrong. Sure, that's what happened, he moved the wrong way and it was an accident.

You say accident. What'll they say? They'll say homicide.

They'll add it up and back it up with their own playback of what happened in the Hut. The way you jugged at him with the knife. The way you went after him when he took off. But hold it there, you know you were bluffing.

Sure, friend. You know. But they don't know. And that's just about the size of it, that bluffing business is the canoe without a paddle. Because that bluff was perfect, too perfect. Quite a sale you made, friend. You know Harriet bought it, they all bought it. They'll say you had homicide written all over your face.

Wanna make a forecast? I think they'll call it second-degree and that makes it five years or seven or ten or maybe more, depending on the emotional condition or the stomach condition of the people on the parole board. You willing to settle for that kinda deal? Well, frankly, no. Quite frankly, no.

You better move now. You better lock that door.

He raised himself on his elbows. He turned his head and looked at the fence door. The distance between himself and the door was somewhat difficult to estimate. There wasn't much daylight. What sun remained was blocked off by the dark-gray curtain, the curtain that was very thick up there, and even thicker down here where it was mottled white with the heavy snowfall. It reminded him again that he wasn't wearing an overcoat. He thought dazedly, stupidly, Oughtta go back and get your overcoat, you'll freeze out here.

It's colder in a cell. Nothing colder than a cell, friend.

He was crawling through the snow, pushing himself toward the fence door some fifteen feet away. Why do it this way? he asked himself. Why not get up and walk over there?

The answer is, you can't get up. You're just about done in. What you need is a warm bed in a white room and some people in white to take care of you. At least give you a shot to make the pain go away. There's so much pain. I wonder if your ribs are busted. All right, let's quit the goddam complaining. Let's keep going toward that door.

As he crawled through the snow toward the fence door, he listened to the sounds coming from the alley. The sounds were closer now. The voices mixed with the clattering of fence doors on both sides of the alley. He heard someone yelling, "Try that one—this one's locked." And another voice, "Maybe they went all the way up the alley—maybe they're out there in the street." A third voice disagreed, "No, they're in one of these backyards—they could'na hit the street that quick."

"Well, they gotta be somewhere around."

"We better call the law—"

"Keep movin' will ya? Keep tryin' them doors."

He crawled just a little faster now. It seemed to him that he hardly moved at all. His open mouth begged the air to come in. As it came in, it was more like someone shoveling hot ashes down his throat. Get there, he said to himself. For Christ's sake, get to that door and lock it. The door.

The voices were closer now. Then one of them yelled, "Hey look, the footprints—"

"What footprints? There's more than two sets of footprints."

"Let's try Spaulding Street—"

"I'm freezin' out here."

"I tell ya, we oughtta call the law—"

He heard them coming closer. He was a few feet away from the fence door. He tried to rise. He made it to his knees, tried to get up higher, and his knees gave way. He was face down in the snow. Get up, he said to himself. Get up, you loafer.

His hands pushed hard at the snow, his arms straightening, his knees gaining leverage as he labored to get up. Then he was up and falling forward, grabbing at the open fence door. His hands hit the door, closed it, and then he fastened the bolt. As it slipped into place, locking the door, he went down again.

I guess we're all right now, he thought. For a while, anyway. But what about later? Well, we'll talk about that when we come to it. I mean, when we get the all-clear, when we're sure they're outa the alley. Then we'll be able to move. And go where? You got me, friend. I can't even give you a hint.

He was resting on his side, feeling the snow under his face, more snow coming down on his head, the wind cutting into his flesh and all the cold getting in there deep, chopping at his bones. He heard the voices in the alley, the footsteps, the fence doors opening and closing, although now the noise was oddly blurred as it came closer. Then the noise was directly outside the door, going past the door, and it was very blurred, it was more like far-off humming. Something like a lullaby, he thought vaguely. His eyes were closed, his head sank deeper into the pillow of snow. He floated down and out, way out.

The voice woke him up. He opened his eyes, wondering if he'd actually heard it.

"Eddie—"

It was the voice of the waitress. He could hear her footsteps in the alley, moving slowly.

He sat up, blinking. He raised his arm to shield his face from the driving wind and the snow.

"Eddie—"

That's her, all right. What's she want?

His arm came away from his face. He looked around, and up, seeing the gray sky, the heavy snowfall coming down on the roof of the dwelling, the swirling gusts falling off the roof into the backyard. Now the snow had arranged itself into a thin white blanket on the bulky thing that was still there in the backyard.

Still there, he thought. What did you expect? That it would get up and walk away?

"Eddie—"

Sorry, I can't talk to you now. I'm sorta busy here. Gotta check some items. First, time element. What time did we go to sleep? Well, I don't think we slept long. Make it about five minutes. Shoulda slept longer. Really need sleep. All right, let's go back to sleep, the other items can wait.

"Eddie—Eddie—"

Is she alone? he asked himself. It sounds that way. It's as though she's saying, It's all clear now, you can come out now.

He heard the waitress calling again. He got up very slowly and unlocked the door and pulled it open.

Footsteps came running toward the door. He stepped back, leaning heavily against the fence as she entered the backyard. She looked at him, started to say something, and then checked it. Her eyes followed in the direction of his pointing finger. She moved slowly in that direction, her face expressionless as she approached the corpse. For some moments she stood there looking down at it. Then her head turned slightly and she focused on the blood-stained knife imbedded in the snow. She turned away from the knife and the corpse, and sighed, and said, "Poor Harriet."

"Yeah," Eddie said. He was slumped against the fence. "It's a raw deal for Harriet. It's—"

He couldn't get the words out. A surge of pain brought a groan from his lips. He sagged to his knees and shook his head slowly. "It goes and it comes," he mumbled.

He heard the waitress saying, "What happened here?"

She was standing over him. He looked up. Through the throbbing pain, the fatigue pressing down on him, he managed to grin. "You'll read about it—"

"Tell me now." She knelt beside him. "I gotta know now."

"What for?" He grinned down at the snow. Then he groaned again, and the grin went away. He said, "It don't matter—"

"The hell it don't." She took hold of his shoulders. "Gimme the details. I gotta know where we stand."

"We?"

"Yeah, we. Come on now, tell me."

"What's there to tell? You can see for yourself—"

"Look at me," she said. She moved in closer as he raised

his head slightly. She spoke quietly, in a clinical tone. "Try not to go under. You gotta stay with it. You gotta let me know what happened here."

"Something went wrong—"

"That's what I figured. The knife, I mean. You're not a knifer. You just wanted to scare him, to get him outa the Hut, away from me. Ain't that the way it was?"

He shrugged. "What difference—"

"Get off that," she cut in harshly. "We hafta get this straight."

He groaned again. He let out a cough. "Can't talk now."

"You gotta." She tightened her grip on his shoulders. "You gotta tell me."

He said, "It's—it's just one of them screwed-up deals. I thought I could reason with him. Nothing doing. He was too far off the track. Strictly section eight. Comes running at me, grabs me, and then I'm gettin' squeezed to jelly."

"And the knife?"

"It was on the ground. I'd tossed it aside so he'd know I wasn't out to carve him. But then he's usin' all his weight, he's got me half dead, and I reach out and there's the knife. I aimed for his arm—"

"Yes? Go on, tell me—"

"Thought if I got him in the arm, he'd let go. But just then he's moving. He moves too fast and I can't stop it in time. It misses the arm and he gets it in the chest."

She stood up. She was frowning thoughtfully. She walked toward the fence door, then turned slowly and stood there looking at him. She said, "You wanna gamble?"

"On what?"

"On the chance they'll buy it."

"They won't buy it," he said. "They only buy evidence."

She didn't say anything. She came away from the fence door and started walking slowly in a small circle, her head down.

He lifted himself from the ground, doing it with a great deal of effort, grunting and wheezing as he came up off his knees. He leaned back against the fence and pointed toward the middle of the yard where the snow was stained red. "There it is," he said. "There's the job, and I did it. That's all they need to know."

"But it wasn't your fault."

"All right, I'll tip them off. I'll write them a letter."

"Yeah. Sure. From where?"

"I don't know yet. All I know is, I'll hafta travel."

"You're in great shape to travel."

He looked down at the snow. "Maybe I'll just dig a hole and hide."

"It ain't right," she said. "It wasn't your fault."

"Say, tell me something. Where can I buy a helicopter?"

"It was his fault. He messed it up."

"Or maybe a balloon," Eddie mumbled. "A nice big balloon to lift me over this fence and get me outa town."

"What a picnic," she said.

"Yeah. Ain't it some picnic?"

She turned her head and looked at the corpse. "You slob," she said to it. "You stupid slob."

"Don't say that."

"You slob. You idiot," talking quietly to the corpse. "Look what you went and done."

"Cut it out," Eddie said. "And for Christ's sake, get outa this yard. If they find you with me—"

"They won't," she said. She beckoned to him, and then gestured toward the fence door.

He hesitated. "Which way they go?"

"Across Spaulding Street," she said. "Then up the next alley. That's why I came back. I knew you hadda be in one of these yards."

She moved toward the fence door, and stood there waiting for him. He came forward very slowly, bent low, his hands clutching his middle.

"Can you make it?" she said.

"I don't know. I don't think so."

"Try," she said. "You gotta try."

"Take a look out there," he said. "I wanna be sure it's clear."

She leaned out past the fence door, looking up and down the alley. "It's all right," she said. "Come on."

He took a few more steps toward her. Then his knees buckled and he started to go down. She moved in quickly and caught hold of him, her hands hooking under his armpits. "Come on," she said. "Come on, now. You're doing fine."

"Yeah. Wonderful."

She held him on his feet, urging him forward, and they went out of the yard and started down the alley. He saw they were moving in the direction of the Hut. He heard her saying, "There's nobody in there now. They're all on the other side of Spaulding Street. I think we got a chance—"

"Quit saying we."

"If we can make it to the Hut—"

"Now look, it ain't we. I don't like this *we* business."

"Don't," she said. "Don't tell me that."

"I'm better off alone."

"Save it," she gritted. "That's corn for the squares."

"Look, Lena—" He made a feeble attempt to pull away from her.

She tightened her hold under his armpits. "Let's keep moving. Come on, we're getting there."

His eyes were closed. He wondered if they were standing still or walking. Or just drifting along through the snow, carried along by the wind. There was no way to be sure. You're fading again, he said to himself. And without sound he said to her, Let go, let go. Cantcha see I wanna sleep? Cantcha leave me alone? Say lady, who are you? What's your game?

"We're almost there," she said.

Almost where? What's she talking about? Where's she taking me? Some dark place, I bet. Sure, that's the dodge. Gonna get rolled. And maybe get your head busted, if it ain't busted already. But why cry the blues? Other people got troubles, too. Sure, everybody got troubles. Except the people in that place where it's always fair weather. It ain't on any map and they call it Nothingtown. I been there, and I know what it's like and I tell you, man, it was sheer delight and the pace never changed, it was you at the piano and you knew from nothing. Until this complication came along. This complication we got here. She comes along with her face and her body and before you know it you're hooked. You tried to wriggle off but it was in deep and it was barbed. So the hooker scored and now you're in the creel and soon it's gonna be frying

time. Well, it's better than freezing. It's really freezing out
here. Out where? Where are we?

He was down in the snow. She pulled him up. He fell
against her, fell away, went sideways across the alley and
bumped into a fence. Then he was down again. She lifted him
to his feet. "Damn it," she said, "come out of it." She bent
over and took some snow in her hand and applied it to his
face.

Who did that? he wondered. Who hit who? Who hit Cy in
the eye with an Eskimo Pie? Was that you, George? Listen
George, you take that attitude, it calls for a swing at your
teeth.

He swung blindly, almost hit her in the face, and then he
was falling again. She caught him. For a few moments he put
up a tussle. Then he was slumped in her arms. She went sliding around him to get behind him, her arms tight around his
chest, lifting him. "Now walk," she said. "Walk, damn you."

"Quit the shovin'," he mumbled. His eyes were closed.
"Why you gotta shove me? I got legs—"

"Then use them," she commanded. She was bumping him
with her knees to push him along. "Worse than a drunk," she
muttered, bumping him harder as he tried to lean back against
her. They went staggering along through the heavily falling
snow. They went past four fence doors. She was measuring
the distance in terms of the fence doors on the left side of the
alley. They were six fence doors away from the Hut when he
fell again. He fell forward, flat in the snow, taking her down
with him. She got up and tried to lift him and this time she
couldn't do it. She stepped back and took a deep breath.

She reached inside her coat. Her hand went under her
apron and came out holding the five-inch hatpin. She jabbed
the long pin into the calf of his leg. Then again, deeper. He
mumbled, "What's bitin' me?" and she said, "You feel it?"
She used the hatpin again. He looked up at her. He said, "You
havin' a good time?"

"A swell time," she said. She showed him the hatpin.
"Want some more?"

"No."

"Then get up."

He made an effort to rise. She tossed the hatpin aside and helped him to his feet. They went on down the alley toward the back door of the Hut.

She managed to keep him on his legs as they entered the Hut, went through the back rooms and then, very slowly, down the cellar steps. In the cellar she half-carried him toward the high-stacked whisky and beer cases. She lowered him to the floor, then dragged him behind the wooden and cardboard boxes. He was resting on his side, mumbling incoherently. She shook his shoulder. He opened his eyes. She said, "Now listen to me," in a whisper. "You'll wait here. You won't move. You won't make a sound. That clear?"

He gave a slight nod.

"I think you'll be all right," she said. "For a while, anyway. They'll search all over the neighborhood, lookin' for you and Plyne. It figures they're gonna find Plyne. They'll try the alley again and they'll find him. Then it's the law and the law starts lookin' for you. But I don't think they'll look here. That is, unless they make a brilliant guess. So maybe there's a chance—"

"Some chance," he murmured. He was smiling wryly. "What am I gonna do, spend the winter here?"

She looked away from him. "I'm hopin' I can getcha out tonight."

"And do what? Take a walk around the block?"

"If we're lucky, we'll ride."

"On some kid's roller coaster? On a sled?"

"A car," she said. "I'll try to borrow a car—"

"From who?" he demanded. "Who's got a car?"

"My landlady." Then she looked away again.

He spoke slowly, watching her face. "You must rate awfully high with your landlady."

She didn't say anything.

He said, "What's the angle?"

"I know where she keeps the key."

"That's great," he said. "That's a great idea. Now do me a favor. Forget it."

"But listen—"

"Forget it," he said. "And thanks anyway."

Then he turned over on his side, his back to her.

"All right," she said very quietly. "You go to sleep now and I'll see you later."

"No you won't." He raised himself on his elbow. He turned his head and looked at her. "I'll make it a polite request. Don't come back."

She smiled at him.

"I mean it," he said.

She went on smiling at him. "See you later, mister."

"I told you, don't come back."

"Later," she said. She moved off toward the steps.

"I won't be here," he called after her. "I'll—"

"You'll wait for me," she said. She turned and looked at him. "You'll stay right there and wait."

He lowered his head to the cellar floor. The floor was cement and it was cold. But the air around him was warm, and the furnace was less than ten feet away. He felt the warmth settling on him as he closed his eyes. He heard her footsteps going up the cellar stairs. It was a pleasant sound that blended with the warmth. It was all very comforting, and he said to himself, She's coming back, she's coming back. Then he fell asleep.

13

HE slept for six hours. Then her hand was on his shoulder, shaking him. He opened his eyes and sat up. He heard her whispering, "Quiet—be very quiet. There's the law upstairs."

It was black in the cellar. He couldn't even see the outlines of her face. He said, "What time is it?"

"Ten-thirty, thereabouts. You had a nice sleep."

"I smell whisky."

"That's me," she said. "I had a few drinks with the law."

"They buy?"

"They never buy. They're just hangin' around the bar. The bartender's stewed and he's been givin' them freebees for hours."

"When'd they find him?"

"Just before it got dark. Some kids came out of the house to have a snowball fight. They saw him there in the yard."

"What's this?" he asked, feeling something heavy on his arm. "What we got here?"

"Your overcoat. Put it on. We're going out."

"Now?"

"Right now. We'll use the ladder and get out through the grating."

"And then what?"

"The car," she said. "I got the car."

"Look, I told you—"

"Shut up," she hissed. "Come on, now. On your feet."

She helped him as he lifted himself from the floor. He did it very slowly and carefully. He was worried he might bump against the wooden boxes, the cardboard beer cases. He murmured, "Need a match."

"I got some," she said. She struck a match. In the orange flare they looked at each other. He smiled at her. She didn't smile back. "Put it on," she said, indicating the overcoat.

He slipped into the overcoat, and followed her as she moved toward the stationary iron ladder that slanted up to the street grating. The match went out and she lit another. They were near the ladder when she stopped and turned and looked at him. She said, "Can you make it up the ladder?"

"I'll try."

"You'll make it," she said. "Hold onto me."

He moved in behind her as she started up the ladder. He held her around the waist. "Tighter," she said. She lit another match and said, "Rest your head against me—stay in close. Whatever you do, don't let go."

They went up a few rungs. They rested. A few more rungs, and they rested again. She said, "How's it going?" and he whispered, "I'm still here."

"Hold me tighter."

"That too tight?"

"No," she said. "Still tighter—like this," and she adjusted his arms around her middle. "Now lock your fingers," she told him. "Press hard against my belly."

"There?"

"Lower."

"How's that?"

"That's fine," she said. "Hold on, now. Hold me real tight."

They went on up the ladder. She lit more matches, striking them against the rusty sides of the ladder. In the glow, he looked up past her head and saw the underside of the grating. It seemed very far away.

When they were halfway up, his foot slipped off the rung. His other foot was slipping but he clung to her as tightly as he could, and managed to steady himself. Then they were climbing again.

But now it wasn't like climbing. It was more like pulling her down. That's what you're doing, he said to himself. You're pulling her down. You're just a goddam burden on her back, and this is only the start. The longer she stays with you, the worse it's gonna be. You can see it coming. You can see her getting nabbed and labeled an accessory. And then they charge her with stealing a car. What do you think they'll give her? I'd say three years, at least. Maybe five. That's a bright future for the lady. But maybe you can stop it before it happens. Maybe you can do something to get her out of this jam and send her on her way.

What can you do?

You can't talk to her, that's for sure. She'll only tell you to shut up. It's a cinch you can't argue with this one. This is one of them iron-heads. She makes up her mind to do something, there ain't no way to swerve her.

Can you pull away from her? Can you let go and drop off the ladder? The noise would bring the law. Would she skip out before they come? You know she wouldn't. She'd stick with you right through to the windup. She's made of that kind of material. It's the kind of material you seldom run across. Maybe once in a lifetime you find one like this. Or no, make it twice in a lifetime. You can't forget the first. You'll never forget the first. But what we're getting now is a certain reissue, except it isn't in the memory, it's something alive. It's alive and it's here, pressing against you. You're holding it very tightly. Can you ever let go?

He heard the waitress saying, "Hold on—"

Then he heard the noise of the grating. She was lifting it.

She was working very quietly, coaxing it up an inch at a time. As it went up, the cold air rushed through and with it came flakes of snow, like needles against his face. Now she had the grating raised high enough for them to get through. She was squirming through the gap, taking him with her. The grating rested on her shoulders, then on her back, and then it was on his shoulders as he followed her over the edge of the opening. She held the grating higher and then they were both on their knees on the pavement and she was closing the grating.

Yellow light came drifting from the side window of the Hut, and glimmered dimly against the darkness of the street. In the glow, he saw the snow coming down, churned by the wind. It's more than just a snowstorm now, he thought. It's a blizzard.

They were on their feet and she held his wrist. They moved along, staying close to the wall of the Hut as they headed west on Fuller Street. He glanced to the side and saw the police cars parked at the curb. He counted five. There were two more parked on the other side of the street. The waitress was saying, "They're all empty. I looked before we climbed out." He said, "If one of them blueboys comes outa the Hut—" and she broke in with, "They'll stay in there. They got all that free booze." But he knew she wasn't sure about that. He knew she was saying it with her fingers crossed.

They crossed a narrow street. The blizzard came at them like a huge swinging door made of ice. They were bent low, pushing themselves against the wind. For another short block they stayed on Fuller, then there was another narrow street and she said, "We turn here."

There were several parked cars, and some old trucks. Half-way up the block there was an ancient Chevvy, a pre-war model. The fenders were battered and much of the paint was chipped off. It was a two-door sedan, but as he looked at it, the impression it gave was that of a sullen weary mule. A real racer, he thought, and wondered how she'd ever managed to start it. She was opening the door, motioning for him to get in.

Then he was leaning back in the front seat and she slid behind the wheel. She hit the starter. The engine gasped, tried to catch, and failed. She hit the starter again. The engine made a wheezing effort, almost caught, then faded and died. The waitress cursed quietly.

"It's cold," he said.

"It didn't gimme trouble before," she muttered. "It started up right away."

"It's much colder now."

"I'll get it started," she said.

She pressed her foot on the starter. The engine worked very hard, almost made it, then gave up.

"Maybe it's just as well," he said.

She looked at him. "Whaddya mean?"

"Even if it moves, it won't get far. They get a report on a stolen car, they work fast."

"Not on this job," she said. "On this one they won't get a report till morning, when my landlady wakes up and takes a look out the window. I made sure she was asleep before I snatched the key."

As she said it, she was pressing the starter again. The engine caught the spark, struggled to hold it, almost lost it, then idled weakly. She fed it gas and it responded. She released the brake and was reaching for the shift when two shafts of bright light came shooting in from Fuller Street. "Get down," she hissed, as the headlights of the other car came closer. "Get your head down—"

They both ducked under the level of the windshield. He heard the engine noise of the other car, coming in closer, very close, then passing them and going away. As he raised his head, there was another sound. It was the waitress, laughing.

He looked at her inquiringly. She was laughing with genuine amusement.

"They just won't give up," she said.

"The law?"

"That wasn't the law. That was a Buick. A pale green Buick. I took a quick look—"

"You sure it was them?"

She nodded, still laughing. "The two ambassadors," she said. "The one named Morris and—what's the other one's name?"

"Feather."

"Yeah, Feather, the little one. And Morris, the back-seat driver. Feather and Morris. Incorporated."

"You think it's funny?"

"It's a scream," she said. "The way they're still mooching around—" She laughed again. "I bet they've circled this block a hundred times. I can hear them beefing about it, fussing at each other. Or maybe now they ain't even on speakin' terms."

He thought, Well, I'm glad she's able to laugh. It's good to know she can take it lightly. But the thing is, you can't take it lightly. You know there's a chance they spotted her when she raised her head. They ain't quite the goofers she thinks they are. They're professionals, you gotta remember that. You gotta remember they were out to get Turley, or let's say a step-by-step production that put them on your trail so they could find Turley, so they could find Clifton, so that finally they'd reach out and grab whatever it is they're after. Whatever it is, it's in South Jersey, in the old homestead deep in the woods. But when you called it a homestead, they gave it another name. They called it the hide-out.

That's what it is, all right. It's a hide-out, a perfect hide-out, not even listed in the post office. You mailed all your letters to a box number in that little town nine miles away. You know, I think we're seeing a certain pattern taking shape. It's sort of in the form of a circle. Like when you take off and move in a certain direction to get you far away, but somehow you're pulled around on that circle, it takes you back to where you started. Well, I guess that's the way it's gotta be. On the city's wanted list right now you're Number One. Hafta get outa the city. Make a run for the place where they'll never find you. The place is in South Jersey, deep in the woods. It's the hiding place of the Clifton-Turley combine, except now it's Clifton-Turley-Eddie, the infamous Lynn brothers.

So there it is, that's the pattern. With a musical background thrown in for good measure. It ain't the soft music now. It ain't the dreamy nothing-matters music that kept you far away from everything. This music here is the buzzing of the hornets. No two ways about that. You hear it getting louder?

It was the noise of the Chevvy's engine. The car was moving now. The waitress glanced at him, as though waiting for him to say something. His mouth tightened and he stared ahead through the windshield. They were approaching Fuller Street.

He spoke quietly. "Make a right-hand turn."

"And then?"

"The bridge," he said. "The Delaware River Bridge."

"South Jersey?"

He nodded. "The woods," he said.

14

IN Jersey, twenty miles south of Camden, the Chevvy pulled into a service station. The waitress reached into her coat pocket and took out the week's salary she'd received from Harriet. She told the attendant to fill up the tank, and she bought some anti-freeze. Then she wanted skid chains. The attendant gave her a look. He wasn't happy about working on the skid chains, exposing himself to the freezing wind and the snow. "It's sure a mean night for driving," he commented. She said it sure was, but it was a nice night for selling skid chains. He gave her another look. She told him to get started with the skid chains. While he was working on the tires, the waitress went into the rest room. When she came out, she bought a pack of cigarettes from the machine. In the car, she gave a cigarette to Eddie and lit it for him. He didn't say thanks. He didn't seem to know he had a cigarette in his mouth. He was sitting up very straight and staring ahead through the windshield.

The attendant was finished with the skid chains. He was breathing hard as he came up to the car window. He cupped his hands and blew on them. He shivered, stamped his feet, and then gave the waitress an unfriendly look. He asked her if there was anything else she wanted. She said yes, she wanted him to do something about the windshield wipers. The wipers weren't giving much action, she said. The attendant looked up at the cold black sky and took a very deep breath. Then he opened the hood and began to examine the fuel pump and the lines coming off the pump and connecting with the wipers. He made an adjustment with the lines and said, "Try it now." She tried the wipers and they worked much faster than before. As she paid him, the attendant muttered, "You sure you got everything you need? Maybe you forgot something." The waitress thought it over for a moment. Then she said, "We could use a bracer." The attendant stamped his feet and shivered again and said, "Me too, lady." She looked down at the paper money in her hand, and murmured, "Got any to spare?" He shook his head somewhat hesitantly. She showed him a five-dollar bill. "Well," he said, "I got a pint bottle of something. But you might not like it. It's that homemade corn—"

"I'll take it," she said. The attendant hurried into the station shack. He came out with the bottle wrapped in some old newspaper. He handed it to the waitress and she handed it to Eddie. She paid for the liquor and the attendant put the money in his pocket and stood there at the car window, waiting for her to start the engine and drive away and go out of his life. She said, "You're welcome," and closed the car window and started the engine.

The skid chains helped considerably, as did the repaired windshield wipers. The Chevvy had been averaging around twenty miles an hour. Now she wasn't worried about skidding or running into something and she pressed harder on the gas pedal. The car did thirty and then thirty-five. It was headed south on Route 47. The wind was coming in from the southeast, from the Atlantic, and the Chevvy went chugging into it sort of pugnaciously, the weary old engine giving loud and defiant back talk to the yowling blizzard. The waitress leaned low over the steering wheel, pressing harder on the gas pedal. The needle of the speedometer climbed to forty.

The waitress was feeling good. She talked to the Chevvy. She said, "You wanna do fifty? Come on, you can do fifty."

"No, she can't," Eddie said. He was taking another drink from the bottle. They'd both had several drinks and the bottle was a third empty.

"I bet she can," the waitress said. The needle of the speedometer climbed toward forty-five.

"Quit that," Eddie said. "You're pushing her too much."

"She can take it. Come on, honeybunch, show him. Move, girl. That's it, move. You keep it up, you'll break a record."

"She'll break a rod, that's what she'll do," Eddie said. He said it tightly, through his teeth.

The waitress looked at him.

"Watch the road," he said. His voice was very tight and low.

"What gives with you?" the waitress asked.

"Watch the road." Now it was a growl. "Watch the goddam road."

She started to say something, held it back, and then focused her attention on the highway. Now her foot was lighter on the gas pedal, and the speed was slackened to thirty-five. It stayed at thirty-five while her hand came off the steering wheel, palm extended for the bottle. He passed it to her. She took a swig and gave it back to him.

He looked at the bottle and wondered if he could use another drink. He decided he could. He put his head back and tipped the bottle to his mouth.

As the liquor went down, he scarcely tasted it. He didn't feel the burning in his throat, the slashing of the alcohol going down through his innards. He was taking a very big drink, unaware of how much he was swallowing.

The waitress glanced at him as he drank. She said, "For Christ's sake—"

He lowered the bottle from his mouth.

She said, "You know what you drank just then? I bet that was two double shots. Maybe three."

He didn't look at her. "You don't mind, do you?"

"No, I don't mind. Why should I mind?"

"You want some?" He offered her the bottle.

"I've had enough," she said.

He smiled tightly at the bottle. "It's good booze."

"How would you know? You ain't no drinker."

"I'll tell you something. This is very good booze."

"You getting high?"

"No," he said. "It's the other way around. That's why I like this juice here." He patted the bottle fondly. "Keeps my feet on the floor. Holds me down to the facts."

"What facts?"

"Tell you later," he said.

"Tell me now."

"Ain't ready yet. Like with cooking. Can't serve the dish until it's ready. This needs a little more cooking."

"You're cooking, all right," the waitress said. "Keep gulping that fire-water and you'll cook your brains to a frazzle."

"Don't worry about it. I can steer the brains. You just steer this car and get me where I'm going."

For some moments she was quiet. And then, "Maybe I'll have that drink, after all."

He handed her the bottle. She took a fast gulp, then quickly opened the car window and tossed the bottle out.

"Why'd you do that?"

She didn't answer. She pressed harder on the gas pedal and the speedometer went up to forty. Now there was no talk between them and they didn't look at each other. Later, at a traffic circle, she glanced at him inquiringly and he told her what road to take. They were quiet again until they approached an intersection. He told her to turn left. It brought them onto a narrow road and they stayed on it for some five miles, the car slowing as they approached a three-pronged fork of narrower roads. He told her to take the road that slanted left, veering acutely into the woods.

It was a bumpy road. There were deep chugholes and she held the Chevvy down to fifteen miles per hour. The snow-drifts were high, resisting the front tires, and there were moments when it seemed the car would stall. She shifted from second gear to first, adjusting the hand throttle to maintain a steady feed of gas. The car went into a very deep chughole, labored to get up and out, came out and ploughed its way through another high snowdrift. There was a wagon path branching off on the right and he told her to take it.

They went ahead at ten miles per hour. The wagon path was very difficult. There were a great many turns and in places the line of route was almost invisible, blanketed under the snow. She was working very hard to keep the car on the path and away from the trees.

The car crawled along. For more than an hour it was on the twisting path going deep into the woods. Then abruptly the path gave way to a clearing. It was a fairly wide clearing, around seventy-five yards in diameter. The headlights beamed across the snow and revealed the very old wooden house in the center of the clearing.

"Stop the car," he said.

"We're not there yet—"

"D'ja hear me?" He spoke louder. "I said stop the car."

The Chevvy was in the clearing, going toward the house. He reached down and pulled up on the hand brake. The car came to a stop thirty yards from the house.

His fingers were on the door handle. He heard the waitress saying, "What are you doing?"

He didn't reply. He was getting out of the car.

The waitress pulled him back. "Answer me—"

"We split," he said. He wasn't looking at her. "You go back to Philly."

"Look at me."

He couldn't do it. He thought, Well, the booze helped a little, but not enough. You shoulda had some more of that liquor. A lot more. Maybe if you'd finished the bottle you'd be able to handle this.

He heard himself saying, "I'll tell you how to get to the bridge. You follow the path to that fork in the road—"

"Don't gimme directions. I know the directions."

"You sure?"

"Yes," she said. "Yes. Don't worry about it."

Again he started to get out of the car, hating himself for doing it. He told himself to do it and get it over with. The quicker it was done, the better.

But it was very difficult to get out of the car.

"Well?" the waitress said quietly. "Whatcha waitin' for?"

He turned his head and looked at her. Something burned into his eyes. Without sound he was saying, I want you with me. You know I want you with me. But the way it is, it's no dice.

"Thanks for the ride," he said, and was out of the car and closing the door.

Then he stood there in the snow and the car pulled away from him and made a turn and headed back toward the path in the woods.

He moved slowly across the clearing. In the darkness he

could barely see the outlines of the house. It seemed to him that the house was miles away and he'd drop before he got there. He was trudging through deep snow. The snow was still coming down and the wind sliced at him, hacking away at his face, ripping into his chest. He wondered if he ought to sit down in the snow and rest a while. Just then the beam of a flashlight hit him in the eyes.

It came from the front of the house. He heard a voice saying, "Hold it there, buddy. Just stay right where you are."

That's Clifton, he thought. Yes, that's Clifton. You know that voice. It's a cinch he's got a gun. You better do this very carefully.

He stood motionless. He raised his arms over his head. But the glare of the flashlight was too much for his eyes and he had to turn his face aside. He wondered if he was showing enough of his face to be recognized.

"It's me," he said. "It's Eddie."

"Eddie? What Eddie?"

He kept his eyes open against the glare as he showed his full face to the flashlight.

"Well, I'll be—"

"Hello, Clifton."

"For Christ's sake," the older brother said. He came in closer, holding the flashlight so that they could look at each other. Clifton was tall and very lean. He had black hair and blue eyes and he was fairly good-looking except for the scars. There were quite a few scars on the right side of his face. One of the scars was wide and deep and it ran from a point just under his eye, slanting down to his jaw. He wore a cream-colored camel's-hair overcoat with mother-of-pearl buttons. Under it he wore flannel pajamas. The pajama pants were tucked into knee-length rubber boots. Clifton was holding the flashlight in his left hand. In his right hand, resting back over his forearm, he had a sawed-off shotgun.

As they stood there, Clifton sprayed the ray of the flashlight across the clearing, spotting the path going into the woods. He murmured, "You sure you're alone? There was a car—"

"They took off."

"Who was it?"

"A friend. Just a friend."

Clifton kept aiming the flashlight across the clearing. He squinted tightly, checking the area at the edge of the woods. "I hope you weren't traced here," he said. "There's some people lookin' for me and Turley. I guess he told you about it. He said he saw you last night."

"He's here now? When'd he get back?"

"This afternoon," Clifton said. Then he chuckled softly. "Comes in all banged up, half froze, half dead, actually. Claims he hitched a few rides and then walked the rest of the way."

"Through them woods? In that storm?"

Clifton chuckled again. "You know Turley."

"Is he all right now?"

"Sure, he's fine. Fixed himself a dinner, knocked off a pint of whisky, and went to bed."

Eddie frowned slightly. "How come he fixed his own dinner? Where's Mom?"

"She left."

"Whaddya mean she left?"

"With Pop," Clifton said. He shrugged. "A few weeks ago. They just packed their things and shoved."

"Where'd they go?"

"Damned if I know," Clifton said. "We ain't heard from them." He shrugged again. And then, "Hey, I'm freezin' out here. Let's go in the house."

They walked across the snow and entered the house. Then they were in the kitchen and Clifton put a coffee pot on the stove. Eddie took off his overcoat and placed it on a chair. He pulled another chair toward the table and sat down. The chair had weak legs, loose in their sockets, and it sagged under his weight. He looked at the splintered boards of the kitchen floor, and at the chipped and broken plaster of the walls.

There was no sink in the kitchen. The light came from a kerosene lamp. He watched Clifton applying a lit match to the chunks of wood in the old-fashioned stove. No gas lines here, he thought. No water pipes or electric wires in this house. Not a thing to connect it with the outside world. And that makes it foolproof. It's a hide-out, all right.

The stove was lit and Clifton came over to the table and sat down. He took out a pack of cigarettes, flicked it expertly and two cigarettes came up. Eddie took one. They smoked for a while, not saying anything. But Clifton was looking at him questioningly, waiting for him to explain his presence here.

Eddie wasn't quite ready to talk about that. For a while, for a little while anyway, he wanted to forget. He took a long drag at the cigarette and said, "Tell me about Mom and Pop. Why'd they leave?"

"Don't ask me."

"I'm asking you because you know. You were here when they went away."

Clifton leaned back in his chair, puffed at the cigarette, and didn't say anything.

"You sent them away," Eddie said.

The older brother nodded.

"You just put them out the door." Eddie snapped his fingers. "Just like that."

"Not exactly," Clifton said. "I gave them some cash."

"You did? That was nice. That was sure nice of you."

Clifton smiled softly. "You think I wanted to do it?"

"The point is—"

"The point is, I hadda do it."

"Why?"

"Because I like them," Clifton said. "They're nice quiet people. This ain't no place for nice quiet people."

Eddie dragged at the cigarette.

"Another thing," Clifton said. "They ain't bullet-proof." He shifted his position in the chair, sitting sideways and crossing his legs. "Even if they were, it wouldn't help much. They're getting old and they can't take excitement like this."

Eddie glanced at the shiny black sawed-off shotgun on the floor. It rested at Clifton's feet. He looked up, above Clifton's head, to a shelf that showed a similar gun, a few smaller guns, and several boxes of ammunition.

"There's gonna be action here," Clifton said. "I was hoping it wouldn't happen, but I can feel it coming."

Eddie went on looking at the guns and ammunition on the shelf.

"Sooner or later," Clifton was saying. "Sooner or later we're gonna have visitors."

"In a Buick?" Eddie murmured. "A pale green Buick?"

Clifton winced.

"They get around," Eddie said.

Clifton reached across the table and took hold of Eddie's wrist. It wasn't a belligerent move; Clifton had to hold onto something.

Clifton was blinking hard, as though trying to focus on Eddie's face, to understand fully what Eddie was saying. "Who gets around? Who you talking about?"

"Feather and Morris."

Clifton released Eddie's wrist. For the better part of a minute it was quiet. Clifton sucked in smoke, expelled it in a blast, and gritted, "That Turley. That goddam stupid Turley."

"It wasn't Turley's fault."

"Don't gimme that. Don't cover for him. He's a nitwit from way back. There ain't been a time he hasn't screwed things up one way or another. But this deal tops it. This really tops it."

"He was in a fix—"

"He's always in a fix. You know why? He just can't do things right, that's why." Clifton dragged again at the cigarette. "Ain't bad enough he gets them on his tail. He goofs again and drags you into it."

Eddie shrugged. "It couldn't be helped. Just one of them situations."

"Line it up for me," Clifton said. "How come they latched on to you? How come you're here now? Gimme the wire on this."

Eddie gave it to him, making it brief and simple.

"That's it," he finished. "Only thing for me to do was come here. No other place for me to go."

Clifton was gazing off to one side and shaking his head slowly.

"What'll it be?" Eddie asked. "Gonna let me stay?"

The other brother took a deep breath. "Damn it," he muttered to himself. "Damn it to hell."

"Yeah, I know what you mean," Eddie said. "You sure need me here."

"Like rheumatism. You're a white-hot property. Philly wants you, Pennsy wants you, and next thing they do is call

Washington. You crossed a state line and that makes it federal."

"Maybe I'd better—"

"No, you won't," Clifton cut in. "You'll stay. You gotta stay. When you're federal, you can't budge. They're too slick. You make any move at all and they're on you like tweezers."

"That's nice to know," Eddie murmured. He wasn't thinking about himself. He wasn't thinking about Clifton and Turley. His thoughts were centered on the waitress. He was wondering if she'd make it back safely to Philly and return the stolen car to its parking place. If it happened that way, she'd be all right. They wouldn't bother her. They'd have no reason to question her. He kept telling himself it would be all right, but he kept thinking about her and he was worried she'd run into some trouble. Please don't, he said to her. Please stay out of trouble.

He heard Clifton saying, "—sure picked a fine time to come walking in."

He looked up. He shrugged and didn't say anything.

"It's one hell of a situation," Clifton said. "On one side there's this certain outfit lookin' for me and Turley. On the other side it's the law, lookin' for you."

Eddie shrugged again. "Well, anyway, it's nice to be home."

"Yeah," Clifton said wryly. "We oughtta celebrate."

"It's an occasion, all right."

"It's a grief, that's what it is," Clifton said. "It's—" And then he forced it aside. He grinned and reached across the table and hit Eddie on the shoulder. "You know one thing? It's good to see you again."

"Likewise," Eddie said.

"Coffee's boiling," Clifton said. He got up and went to the stove. He came back with the filled cups and set them on the table. "What about grub?" he asked. "Want some grub?"

"No," Eddie said. "I ain't hungry."

They sat there sipping the black sugarless coffee. Clifton said, "You didn't tell me much about the dame. Gimme more on the dame."

"What dame?"

"The one that brought you here. You said she's a waitress—"

"Yeah. Where I worked. We got to know each other."

Clifton looked at him closely, waiting for him to tell more.

For a while it was quiet. They went on sipping the coffee. Then Clifton was saying something that he heard only vaguely, unable to listen attentively because of the waitress. He was looking directly at Clifton and it appeared he was paying close attention to what Clifton was saying. But in his mind he was with the waitress. He was walking with her and they were going somewhere. Then they stopped and he looked at her and told her to leave. She started to walk away. He went after her and she asked him what he wanted. He told her to get away from him. She walked away and he moved quickly and caught up with her. Then again he was telling her to take off, he didn't want her around. He stood there watching her as she departed. But he couldn't bear it and he ran after her. Now very patiently she asked him to decide what they should do. He told her to please go away.

It went on like that while Clifton was telling him about certain events during the past few years, culminating in Turley's trip to Philadelphia, to Dock Street, with Turley trying to make connections along the wharves and piers where he'd once worked as a longshoreman. What Turley had sought was a boat ride for Clifton and himself. They needed the boat ride away from the continent, far away from the people who were looking for them.

The people who were looking for them were members of a certain unchartered and unlicensed corporation. It was a very large corporation that operated along the eastern seaboard, dealing in contraband merchandise such as smuggled perfumes from Europe, furs from Canada, and so forth. Employed by the corporation, Clifton and Turley had been assigned to the department that handled the more physical aspects of the business, the hijacking and the extortion and sometimes the moves that were necessary to eliminate competitors.

Some fourteen months ago, Clifton was saying, he'd decided that he and Turley were not receiving adequate compensation for their efforts. He'd talked it over with certain executives of the corporation and they told him there was no cause for complaint, they didn't have time to hear his complaints. They made it clear that in the future he was to keep away from the front office.

At that time the front office of the corporation was in Savannah, Georgia. They were always changing the location of the front office from one port to another, according to the good will or lack of good will between the executives and certain port authorities. In Savannah, an investigation was taking place and the top people of the corporation were preparing to leave for Boston. It was necessary to leave quickly because the investigators were making rapid strides, and so of course there was some confusion. In the midst of the confusion, Clifton and Turley resigned from the corporation. When they did it, they took something with them. They took a couple of hundred thousand dollars.

They took it from the safe in the warehouse where the front office was located. They did it very late at night, walking in quite casually and chatting with three fellow employees who were playing pinochle. When they showed guns, one of the card players made a move for his own and Turley kicked him in the groin, then hit him on the head with the gun butt sufficiently hard to finish him. The two other card players were Feather and Morris, with Morris perspiring as Turley hefted the gun to use the butt again, with Feather talking very fast and making a proposition.

Feather proposed that it would be better to do this with four than just two. With four walking out, the corporation would be faced with a serious problem. Feather made the point that tracing four men is considerably more difficult than tracing two. And also, Feather said, he and Morris were rather unhappy with the treatment they were getting from the corporation, they'd be grateful for this chance to walk out. Feather went on talking while Clifton thought it over, and while Turley used an acetylene torch to open the safe. Then Clifton decided that Feather was making sense, that it wasn't just a frantic effort to stay alive. Besides, Feather was something of a brain and from here on in it would take considerable brains, much more than Turley had. Another factor, Clifton reasoned, was the potential need for gun-handling, and in that category it would be Morris. He knew what Morris could do with a gun, with anything from a .38 to a Thompson.

When the money was in the suitcase and they walked out of the warehouse, they took Feather and Morris with them.

On the road going north from Georgia to New Jersey, they traveled at fairly high speed. In Virginia they were spotted by some corporation people and there was a chase and an exchange of bullets and Morris proved himself rather useful. The other car was stopped with a front tire punctured, and, later, on a side road in Maryland, another corporation effort was blocked by Morris, leaning out the rear window to send bullets seventy yards down the road and through a windshield and into the face of the driver. There were no further difficulties with the corporation and that night they were crossing a bridge into South Jersey and Feather was handling the car very nicely. As Clifton told him what turns to make, he kept asking where they were going. Morris also asked where they were going. Clifton said they were going to a place where they could stay hidden for a while. Feather wanted to know if the place was sufficiently safe. Clifton said it was, describing the place, the fact that it was far from the nearest town, that it was very deep in the woods and extremely difficult to locate. Feather kept asking questions and presently Clifton decided there were too many questions and he told Feather to stop the car. Feather looked at him, and then threw a glance at Morris who was in the back seat with Turley. As Morris went for his gun, Turley hauled off and put a fist on his chin and knocked him out. Feather was trying to get out of the car and Clifton grabbed him and held him while Turley tagged him on the jaw, just under his ear. Then Feather and Morris were asleep in the road and the car was going away.

"—shoulda made a U-turn and came back and run over them," Clifton was saying. "Shoulda figured what would happen if I let them stay alive. The way it worked out, they musta played it slick. That Feather's a slick talker. He musta known just what to tell the corporation. I guess he said it was a strong-arm deal, that they didn' have no choice and they hadda come along for the ride. So the corporation takes them in again. Not all the way in, not yet. First they gotta find me and Turley. It's like they're on probation. They know they gotta make good to get in solid again."

Clifton lit another cigarette. He went on talking. He talked about Turley's witless maneuvering and his own mistake in allowing Turley to make the trip to Philadelphia.

"—had a feeling he'd mess things up," Clifton was saying. "But he swore he'd be careful. Kept telling me about his connections on Dock Street, all them boat captains he knew, and how easy it would be to make arrangements. Kept selling me on the idea and finally I bought it. We get in the car and I drive him to Belleville so he can catch a bus to Philly. For that one move alone I oughtta have my head examined."

Eddie was sitting there with his eyes half closed. He was still thinking about the waitress. He told himself to stop it, but he couldn't stop it.

"—so now it's no boat ride," Clifton was saying. "It's just sitting around, wondering what's gonna happen, and when. Some days we go out hunting for rabbits. That's a good one. We're worse off than the rabbits. At least they can run. And the geese, the wild geese. Christ, how I envy them geese.

"I'll tell you something," he went on. "It's really awful when you can't budge. It gets to be a drag and in the morning you hate to wake up because there's just no place to go. We used to joke about it, me and Turley. It actually gave us a laugh. We got two hundred thousand dollars to invest and no way to have fun with it. Not even on a broad. Some nights I crave a broad so bad—

"It ain't no way to live, I'll tell you that. It's the same routine, day after day. Except once a week it's driving the nine miles to Belleville, to buy food. Every time I take that ride, I come near pissing in my pants. A car shows in the rear-view mirror, I keep thinking that's it, that's a corporation car and I'm spotted, they got me now. In Belleville I try to play it cool but I swear it ain't easy. If anyone looks at me twice, I'm ready to go for the rod. Say, that reminds me—"

Clifton got up from the table. He reached to the shelf, to the assortment of guns, and selected a .38 revolver. He checked it, then opened one of the ammunition boxes, loaded the gun and handed it to Eddie. "You'll need this," he said. "Keep it with you. Don't ever be without it."

Eddie looked at the gun in his hand. It had no effect on him. He slipped it under his overcoat, into the side pocket of his jacket.

"Take it out," Clifton said.

"The gun?"

Clifton nodded. "Take it outa your pocket. Let's see you take it out."

He reached under his overcoat, doing it slowly and indifferently. Then the gun was in his hand and he showed it to Clifton.

"Try it again," Clifton said, smiling at him. "Put it back in and take it out."

He did it again. The gun felt heavy and he was awkward with it. Clifton was laughing softly.

"Wanna see something?" Clifton said. "Watch me."

Clifton turned and moved toward the stove. He had his hands at his sides. Then he stood at the stove and reached toward the coffee pot with his right hand. As his fingers touched the handle of the coffee pot, the yellow-tan sleeve of his camel's-hair coat was a flash of caramel color, and almost in the same instant there was a gun in his right hand, held steady there, his finger on the trigger.

"Get the idea?" Clifton murmured.

"I guess it takes practice."

"Every day," Clifton said. "We practice at least an hour a day."

"With shooting?"

"In the woods," Clifton said. "Anything that moves. A weasel, a rat, even the mice. If they ain't showing, we use other targets. Turley throws a stone and I draw and try to hit it. Or sometimes it's tin cans. When it's tin cans it's long range. We do lotsa practicing at long range."

"Is Turley any good?"

"He's awful," Clifton said. "He can't learn."

Eddie looked down at the gun in his hand. It felt less heavy now.

"I hope you can learn," Clifton said. "You think you can?"

Eddie hefted the gun. He was remembering Burma. He said, "I guess so. I've done this before."

"That's right. I forgot. It slipped my mind. You got some medals. You get many Japs?"

"A few."

"How many?"

"Well, it was mostly with a bayonet. Except with the snipers. With the snipers I liked the forty-five."

"You want a forty-five? I got a couple here."

"No, this'll be all right."

"It better be," Clifton said. "This ain't for prizes."

"You think it's coming soon?"

"Who knows? Maybe a month from now. A year from now. Or maybe tomorrow. Who the hell knows?"

"Maybe it won't happen," Eddie said.

"It's gotta happen. It's on the schedule."

"You know, there's a chance you could be wrong," Eddie said. "This place ain't easy to find."

"They'll find it," Clifton muttered. He was staring at the window. The shade was down. He leaned across the table and lifted the shade just a little and looked out. He kept the shade up and stayed there looking out and Eddie turned to see what he was looking at. There was nothing out there except the snow-covered clearing, then the white of the trees in the woods, and then the black sky. The glow from the kitchen showed the woodshed and the privy and the car. It was a gray Packard sedan, expensive-looking, its chromium very bright where the grille showed under the snow-topped hood. Nice car, he thought, but it ain't worth a damn. It ain't armor-plated.

Clifton lowered the shade and moved away from the table. "You sure you ain't hungry?" he asked. "I can fix you something—"

"No," Eddie said. His stomach felt empty but he knew he couldn't eat anything. "I'm sorta done in," he said. "I wanna get some sleep."

Clifton picked up the sawed-off shotgun and put it under his arm, and they went out of the kitchen. In the parlor there was another kerosene lamp and it was lit, the flickering glimmer revealing a scraggly carpet, a very old sofa with some of the stuffing popped out, and two armchairs that were even older than the sofa and looked as though they'd give way if they were sat on.

There was also the piano.

Same piano, he thought, looking at the splintered upright that appeared somewhat ghostly in the dim yellow glow. The time-worn keyboard was like a set of decayed, crooked teeth, the ivory chipped off in places. He stood there looking at it, unaware that Clifton was watching him. He moved toward the keyboard and reached out to touch it. Then something pulled his hand away. His hand went under his overcoat and into the pocket of his jacket and he felt the full weight of the gun.

So what? he asked himself, coming back to now, to the sum of it. They take the piano away and they give you a gun. You wanted to make music and the way it looks from here on in you're finished with that, finished entirely. From here on in it's this—the gun.

He took the .38 from his pocket. It came out easily, smoothly, and he hefted it efficiently.

He heard Clifton saying, "That was nice. You're catching on."

"Maybe it likes me."

"Sure it likes you," Clifton said. "It's your best friend from now on."

The gun felt secure in his hand. He fondled it. Then he put it back into his pocket and followed Clifton toward the rickety stairway. The loose boards creaked as they went up, Clifton holding the kerosene lamp. At the top of the stairs, Clifton turned and handed him the lamp and said, "Wanna wake up Turley? Let him know you're here?"

"No," Eddie said. "Let him sleep. He needs sleep."

"All right." Clifton gestured down the hall. "Use the back room. The bed's made up."

"Same bed?" Eddie murmured. "The one with the busted springs?"

Clifton gazed past him. "He remembers."

"I oughtta remember. I was born in that room."

Clifton nodded slowly. "You had that room for twelve-thirteen years."

"Fourteen," Eddie said. "I was fourteen when they took me off to Curtis."

"What Curtis?"

"The Institute," Eddie said. "The Curtis Institute of Music."

Clifton looked at him and started to say something and held it back.

He grinned at Clifton. He said, "Remember the sling-shots?"

"Slingshots?"

"And the limousine. They came for me in a limousine, them people from Curtis. Then in the woods it was you and Turley, with slingshots, shooting at the car. The people didn't know who you were. One of the women, she says to me, 'Who are they?' and I say, 'The boys, ma'am? The two boys?' She says 'They ain't boys, they're wild animals.' "

"And what did you say?"

"I said, 'They're my brothers, ma'am.' So then of course she tries to smooth it over, starts talking about the Institute and what a wonderful place it is. But the stones kept hitting the car, and it was like you were telling me something. That I couldn't really get away. That it was just a matter of time. That some day I'd come back to stay."

"With the wild animals," Clifton said, smiling thinly at him.

"You knew all along?"

Clifton nodded very slowly. "You hadda come back. You're one of the same, Eddie. The same as me and Turley. It's in the blood."

That says it, Eddie thought. That nails it down for sure. Any questions? Well yes, there's one. The wildness, I mean. Where'd we get it from? We didn't get it from Mom and Pop. I guess it skipped past them. It happens that way sometimes. Skips maybe a hundred years or a couple hundred or maybe three and then it shows again. If you look way back you'll find some Lynns or Websters raising hell and running wild and hiding out the way we're hiding now. If we wanted to, we could make it a ballad. For laughs, that is. Only for laughs.

He was laughing softly as he moved past Clifton and went on down the hall to the back room. Then he was undressed and standing at the window and looking out. The snow had stopped falling. He opened the window and the wind came in, not blasting now. It was more like a slow stream. But it was still very cold. Nice when it's cold, he thought. It's good for sleeping.

He climbed into the sagging bed, slid between a torn sheet and a scraggly quilt, and put the gun under the pillow. Then he closed his eyes and started to fall asleep, but something tugged at his brain and it was happening again, he was thinking about the waitress.

Go away, he said to her. Let me sleep.

Then it was like a tunnel and she was going away in the darkness and he went after her. The tunnel was endless and he kept telling her to go away, then hearing the departing footsteps and running after her and telling her to go away. Without sound she said to him, Make up your mind, and he said, How can I? This ain't like thinking with the mind. The mind has nothing to do with it.

Please go to sleep, he told himself. But he knew it was no use trying. He opened his eyes and sat up. It was very cold in the room but he didn't feel it. The hours flowed past and he had no awareness of time, not even when the window showed gray and lighter gray and finally the lit-up gray of daylight.

At a few minutes past nine, his brothers came in and saw him sitting there and staring at the window. He talked with them for a while and wasn't sure what the conversation was about. Their voices seemed blurred and through his half-closed eyes he saw them through a curtain. Turley offered him a drink from a pint bottle and he took it and had no idea what it was. Turley said, "You wanna get up?" and he started to climb out of the bed and Clifton said, "It's early yet. Let's all go back to sleep," with Turley agreeing, saying it would be nice to sleep all day. They went out of the room and he sat there on the edge of the bed, looking at the window. He was so tired he wondered how he was able to keep his eyes open. Then later his head was on the pillow and he was trying hard to fall asleep but his eyes remained open and his thoughts kept reaching out, seeking the waitress.

Around eleven, he finally fell asleep. An hour later he opened his eyes and looked at the window. The full glare of noon sunlight, snow-reflected, came in and caused him to blink. He got out of bed and went to the window and stood there looking out. It was very sunny out there, the snow glittering white-yellow and across the clearing the trees, laced with ice, were sparkling like jeweled ornaments. Very pretty, he thought. It's very pretty in the woods in the wintertime.

There was something moving out there, something walking in the woods, coming toward the clearing. It came slowly, hestitantly, with a certain furtiveness. As it edged past the trees, approaching closer to the clearing, a shaft of sunlight found it, lit it up and identified it. He shook his head and rubbed his eyes. He looked again, and it was there. Not a vision, he thought. Not wishful thinking, either. That's real. You see it and you know it's real.

Get out there, he said to himself. Get out there fast and tell her to go away. You gotta keep her away from this house. Because it ain't a house, it's just a den for hunted animals. She stumbles in, she'll never get out. They wouldn't let her. They'd clamp her down and hold her here for security reasons. Maybe they've spotted her already, and you better take the gun. They're your own dear brothers but what we have here is a difference of opinion and you damn well better take the gun.

He was dressed now, pulling the gun from under the pillow, putting it in his jacket pocket, then slipping into the overcoat as he went out of the room. He moved quietly but hastily down the hall, then down the steps and out through the back door. The snow was high, and he churned his way through it, running fast across the clearing, toward the waitress.

15

SHE was leaning against a tree, waiting for him. As he came up, she said, "You ready?"

"For what?"

"Travel," she said. "I'm taking you back to Philly."

He frowned and blinked, his eyes flicking questions.

"You're cleared," she told him. "It's in the file. They're calling it an accident."

The frown deepened. "What're you giving me?"

"A message," she said. "From Harriet. From the crowd at the Hut, the regulars. They're regular, all right."

"They're backing me?"

"All the way."

"And the law?"

"The law bought it."

"Bought what? They don't buy hearsay evidence. This needs a witness. I don't have a witness—"

"You got three."

He stared at her.

"Three," she said. "From the Hut."

"They saw it happen?"

She smiled thinly. "Not exactly."

"You told them what to say?"

She nodded.

Then he began to see it. He saw the waitress in there pitching, first talking to Harriet, then going out to round up the others, ringing doorbells very early in the morning. He saw them all assembled at the Hut, the waitress telling them the way it was and what had to be done. Like a company commander, he thought.

"Who was it?" he asked. "Who volunteered?"

"All of them."

He took a deep breath. It quivered somewhat, going in. His throat felt thick and he couldn't talk.

"We figured three was enough," the waitress said. "More than three, it would seem sorta phony. We hadda make sure it would hold together. What we did was, we picked three with police records. For gambling, that is. They're on the list as well-known crapshooters."

"Why crapshooters?"

"To make it look honest. First thing, they hadda explain why they didn't tell the law right away. Reason is, they didn't wanna get pinched for gambling. Another thing, the way we lined it up they were upstairs, in the back room. The law wantsa know what they're doing up there, they got a perfect answer, they're having a private session with the dice."

"You briefed them on that?"

"We went over it I don't know how many times. At seven-thirty this morning I figured they were ready. So they go to the law and spill it and then they're signing the statements."

"Like what? What was the pitch?"

"The window in the back room was the angle we needed. From the window you look down on a slant and you can see that backyard."

"Close enough?"

"Just about. So the way they tell it to the law, they're on the floor shooting crap and they hear the commotion from downstairs. At first they don't pay it no mind, the dice are hot and they're betting heavy. But later it sounds bad from downstairs, and then they hear the door slamming when you chase him out to the alley. They go to the window and look out. You getting it now?"

"It checks," he nodded.

"They give it to the law like a play-by-play, exactly the way you told it to me. They said they saw you throwing the knife away and trying to talk to him but he won't listen, he's sort of off his rocker and he comes leaping in. Then he's got you in the bear hug and the way it looks, you won't come outa there alive. They said you made a grab for the knife, tried to stick him in the arm to get him off you, and just then he shifts around and the blade goes into his chest."

He gazed past her. "And that's it? I'm really cleared?"

"Entirely," she said. "They dropped all charges."

"They hold the crapshooters?"

"No, just called them names. Called them goddam liars and kicked them outa the station house. You know how it is with the law. If they can't make it stick, they drop it."

He looked at her. "How'd you get here?"

"The car."

"The Chevvy?" frowning again. "Your landlady's gonna—"

"It's all right," she said. "This time it's rented. I slipped her a few bucks and she's satisfied."

"That's good to know." But he was still frowning. He turned and looked across the clearing, at the house. He was focusing on the upstairs windows. He murmured, "Where's the car?"

"Back there," she said. "In the woods. I didn't want your people to see. I thought if they spotted me, it might get complicated."

He went on looking at the house. "It's complicated already. I can't go away without telling them."

"Why not?"

"Well, after all—"

She took hold of his arm. "Come on."

"I really oughtta tell them."

"The hell with them," she said. She tugged at his arm. "Come on, will you? Let's get outa here."

"No," he murmured, still looking at the house. "First I gotta tell them."

She kept tugging at his arm. "You can't go back there. That's a hide-out. We'll both be dragged in—"

"Not you," he said. "You'll wait here."

"You'll come back?"

He turned his head and looked at her. "You know I'll come back."

She let go of his arm. He started walking across the clearing. It won't take long, he thought. I'll just tell them the way it is, and they'll understand, they'll know they got nothing to worry about, it stays a hide-out. But on the other hand, you know Clifton. You know the way he thinks, the way he operates. He's strictly a professional. A professional takes no chances. With Turley it's different. Turley's more on the easy side and you know he'll see it your way. I hope you can bring Clifton around. Not with pleading, though. Whatever you do, don't plead with him. Just let him know you're checking out with the waitress and give him assurance she'll keep her mouth shut. And what if he says no? What if he goes out and brings her into the house and says she's gotta stay? If it comes to that, we'll hafta do something. Maybe it won't come to that. Let's hope so, anyway. Let's see if we can keep it on the bright side. Sure, that's better. It's nice to think along the cheery lines, to tell yourself it's gonna work out fine and you won't be needing the gun.

He was a little more than halfway across the clearing, moving fast through the snow. He was headed toward the back door of the house, the door some sixty feet away and then fifty feet when he heard the sound of an automobile.

And even before he turned and looked, he was thinking, That ain't the Chevvy going away. That's a Buick coming in.

He pivoted, his eyes aiming at the edge of the woods where the wagon path showed a pale green Buick. The car came slowly, impeded by the snow. Then it gave a lurch, the snow spraying as the tires screeched, and it was coming faster now.

They followed her, he thought. They followed her from Philly. Kept their distance so it wouldn't give them away in the rear-view mirror. Score one for them. It's quite a score that's for sure. Maybe it's a grand slam.

He saw Feather and Morris getting out of the car. Morris circled the car and came up to Feather and they stood there talking. Morris was pointing toward the house and Feather was shaking his head. They were focused on the front of the house and he knew they hadn't seen him. But they will, he thought. You make another move and you're spotted. And this time it's no discussions, no preliminaries. This time you're on the check-off list and they'll try to put you outa the way.

What you need, of course, is a fox-hole. It would sure come in handy right now. Or a sprinter's legs. Or better yet, a pair of wings. But I think you'll hafta settle for the snow. The snow looks deep enough.

He was crouched, then flattened on his belly in the snow. In front of his face it was a white wall. He brushed at it, his fingers creating a gap, and he looked through it and saw Feather and Morris still standing beside the car and arguing. Morris kept gesturing toward the house and Feather was shaking his head. Morris started walking toward the house and Feather pulled him back. They were talking loudly now but he couldn't make out what they were saying. He estimated they were some sixty yards away.

And you're some fifteen yards from the back door, he told himself. Wanna try it? There's a chance you can make it, but not much of a chance, considering Morris. You remember what Clifton said about Morris and his ability with a gun. I think we better wait a little longer and see what they're gonna do.

But what about her? You forgetting her? No, it ain't that, you know damn well it ain't that. It's just that you're sure she'll use her head and stay right there where she is. She stays there, she'll be all right.

Then he saw Feather and Morris taking things from the car. The things were Tommy guns. Feather and Morris moved toward the house.

But that's no way to do it, he said to them. That's like betting everything on one card, hoping to fill an inside straight. Or it could be you're too anxious, you've waited a long time and you just can't wait any more. Whatever the reason, it's a tactical error, it's actually a boner and you'll soon find out.

You sure? he asked himself. You really sure they'll come out losers? Better give it another look and line it up the way it is. I think it's Clifton and Turley in bed asleep and of course you're hoping they heard the car when it came outa the woods and they ain't asleep. But that's only hoping, and hoping ain't enough. If they're still asleep, you gotta wake them up.

You gotta do it now. Right now. After all, it's only fifteen yards to the back door. Maybe if you crawl it— No, you can't crawl it. You don't have time for that. You'll hafta run. All right let's run.

He was up and racing toward the back door. He'd made less than five yards when he heard the blast of a Tommy and saw punctures in the snow in front of him, a few feet off to the side.

Nothing doing, he told himself. You'll never make it. You'll hafta pretend you're hit. And as the thought flashed through his brain he was already going down in simulated collapse. He hit the snow and rolled over and then rested on his side, motionless.

Then he heard the other guns, the shots coming from an upstairs window. He looked up and saw Clifton, with the sawed-off shotgun. A moment later it was Turley showing at another window. Turley was using two revolvers.

He grinned and thought, Well, anyway, you did it. You managed to wake them up. They're really awake now. They're wide awake and very busy.

Feather and Morris were running back to the car. Feather seemed to be hit in the leg. He was limping. Morris turned and let go a short blast at Turley's window. Turley dropped one of the revolvers and grabbed at his shoulder and ducked out of sight. Then Morris took aim at Clifton, started a volley and Clifton quickly took cover. It was all happening very fast and now Feather was on his knees, crawling behind the Buick to use it as a shield. Morris moved closer to the house and sent another blast at the upstairs windows, swinging the Tommy to get as many bullets up there as he could. Now from the house there was no shooting at all. Morris kept blasting at the upstairs windows. Feather yelled at him and he lowered the gun and walked backward toward the Buick. He stood at the side of the Buick, the Tommy still lowered but appearing ready as he looked up at the windows.

Some moments later the back door opened and Clifton came running out. He was carrying a small black suitcase. He was running toward the gray Packard parked near the wood-shed. As he neared the car, he stumbled and the suitcase fell open and some paper money dropped out. Clifton bent over to pick it up. Morris didn't see this happening. Morris was still watching the upstairs windows. Now Clifton had the suitcase closed again and was climbing into the Packard. Then Turley, holding a sawed-off shotgun and a revolver with one hand while his other hand clutched his shoulder, came out of the back door and joined Clifton in the Packard.

The motor started and the Packard accelerated very fast, coming out from the rear of the house and sweeping in a wide circle, cutting through the snow with the skid-chained tires getting full traction, the car now moving at high speed across the clearing, aiming at the wagon path leading into the woods. Morris was using the Tommy again but he was somewhat disconcerted and his shooting was off. He shot for the tire and he was short. Then he shot for the front side window and hit the rear side window. Feather was yelling at him and he kept shooting at the Packard, now running toward the Packard as it went galloping away from him. He was screaming at the Packard, his voice cracked and twisted, with the Thompson still blasting but no longer useful because he couldn't aim it, he was much too upset.

Feather was crawling along the side of the Buick, opening the door and climbing in behind the wheel. Morris had stopped running but was still shooting at the Packard. From the Packard there was a return of fire as Turley leaned out and used the sawed-off shotgun. Morris let out a yowl and dropped the Thompson and began to hop around, his left arm dangling, his wrist and hand bright red, the redness dripping. He kept hopping around and making loud noises. Then with his right hand he pulled out a revolver and shot at the Packard as it cut across the clearing headed for the wagon path. The shot went very wide and then the Packard was on the wagon path and going away.

Feather opened the rear door of the Buick and Morris climbed in. The Buick leaped into a turn and aimed at the wagon path to chase after the Packard.

Eddie sat up. He looked to the side and saw the waitress running out from the edge of the woods. She was coming fast across the clearing and he waved at her to get back, to stay in the woods until the Buick was gone. Now the Buick had slowed just a little and he knew they'd seen the waitress.

He reached into his jacket pocket and pulled out the .38. With his other hand he kept waving at her to get back.

The Buick came to a stop. Feather was using the Tommy, shooting at the waitress. Eddie fired blindly at the Buick, unable to aim because he wasn't thinking in terms of hitting anything. He kept pulling the trigger, hoping it would get the Tommy off the waitress. With his fourth shot he lured the Tommy to point in his direction. He felt the swish of slugs going past his head and he fired a fifth shot to keep the Tommy on him and away from her.

He couldn't see her now, he was concentrating on the Buick. The Tommy had stopped firing and the Buick was moving again. It picked up speed going toward the wagon path and he thought, It's the Packard they want, they're going away to go after the Packard. Will they get it? It really doesn't matter. You don't even want to think about it. You got her to think about. Because you can't see her now. You're looking and you can't see her.

Where is she? Did she make it back to the woods? Sure, that's what happened. She ran back and she's waiting there. So it's all right. You can go to her now. The hornets are gone and it's nice to know you can drop the gun and go to her.

He dropped the .38 and started walking through the snow. At first he walked fast, but then he slowed, and then he walked very slowly. Finally he stopped and looked at something half hidden in the deep snow.

She was resting face down. He knelt beside her and said something and she didn't answer. Then very carefully he turned her onto her side and looked at her face. There were two bullet holes in her forehead and very quickly he looked away. Then his eyes were shut tightly and he was shaking his head. There was a sound from somewhere but he didn't hear it. He didn't know he was moaning.

He stayed there for a while, kneeling beside Lena. Then he got up and walked across the clearing and went into the woods to look for the Chevvy. He found it parked between some trees near the wagon path. The key was in the ignition lock and he drove the Chevvy into the clearing. He placed the body in the back seat. It's gotta be delivered, he thought. It's just a package gotta be delivered.

He took her to Belleville. In Belleville the authorities held him for thirty-two hours. During that time they offered him food but he couldn't eat. There was an interval of getting into an official car with some men in plain clothes, and he guided them to the house in the woods. He was vaguely aware of answering their questions, although his answers seemed to satisfy them. When they found Tommy slugs in the clearing it confirmed what he'd told them in Belleville. But then they wanted to know more about the battle, the reason for it, and he said he couldn't tell them much about that. He said it was some kind of a dispute between these people and his brothers and he wasn't sure what it was about. They grilled him and he kept saying. "Can't help you there," and it wasn't an evasion. He really couldn't tell them because it wasn't clear in his mind. He was far away from it and it didn't matter to him, it had no importance at all.

Then, in Belleville again, they asked if he could help in establishing the identity of the victim. They said they'd done some checking but they couldn't find any relatives or records of past employment. He repeated what he'd told them previously, that she was a waitress and her first name was Lena and he didn't know her last name. They wanted to know if there was anything more. He said that was all he knew, that she'd never told him about herself. They shrugged and told him to sign a few papers, and when he'd done that, they let him go. Just before he walked out, he asked if they'd found where she lived in Philadelphia. They gave him the address of the rooming house. They were somewhat perplexed that he hadn't even known the address. After he walked out, one of them commented, "Claimed he hardly knew her. Then why's he taking it so hard? That man's been hit so hard he's goofy."

Later that day, in Philadelphia, he returned the Chevvy to its owner. Then he went to his room. Without thinking about it, he pulled down the shade and then he locked the door. At the wash basin he brushed his teeth and shaved and combed his hair. It was as though he expected company and wanted to make a presentable appearance. He put on a clean shirt and a necktie and seated himself on the edge of the bed, waiting for a visitor.

He waited there a long time. At intervals he slept, pulled from sleep whenever he heard footsteps in the hall. But the footsteps never approached the door.

Very late that night there was a knock on the door. He opened the door and Clarice came in with some sandwiches and a carton of coffee. He thanked her and said he wasn't hungry. She unwrapped the sandwiches and forced them into his hands. She sat there and watched him while he ate. The food had no taste but he managed to eat it, washing it down with the coffee. Then she gave him a cigarette, lit one for herself, and after taking a few puffs she suggested they go out for a walk. She said the air would do him good.

He shook his head.

She told him to get some sleep and then she went out of the room. The next day she was there again with more food. For several days she kept bringing him food and urging him to eat. On the fifth day he was able to eat without being coaxed. But he refused to go out of the room. Each night she asked him to go for a walk and told him he needed fresh air and some exercise and he shook his head. His lips smiled at her, but with his eyes he was begging her to leave him alone.

Night after night she kept asking him to go for a walk. Then it was the ninth night and instead of shaking his head, he shrugged, put on his overcoat and they went out.

They were on the street and walking slowly and he had no idea where they were going. But suddenly, through the darkness, he saw the orange glow of the lit-up sign with some of the bulbs missing.

He stopped. He said, "Not there. We ain't going there."

"Why not?"

"Nothing there for me," he said. "Nothing I can do there."

Clarice took hold of his arm. She pulled him along toward the lit-up sign.

Then they were walking into the Hut. The place was jammed. Every table was taken and they were three-deep and four-deep all along the bar. It was the same crowd, the same noisy regulars, except that now there was very little noise. Just a low murmuring.

He wondered why it was so quiet in the Hut. Then he saw Harriet behind the bar. She was looking directly at him. Her face was expressionless.

Now heads were turning and others were looking at him and he told himself to get out of here, get out fast. But Clarice had tightened her hold on his arm. She was pulling him forward, taking him past the tables and toward the piano.

"No," he said. "I can't—"

"The hell you can't," Clarice said, and kept pulling him toward the piano.

She pushed him onto the revolving stool. He sat there staring at the keyboard.

And then, from Harriet, "Come on, give us a tune."

But I can't, he said without sound. Just can't.

"Play it," Harriet yelled at him. "Whatcha think I'm payin' you for? We wanna hear some music."

From the bar someone shouted, "Do it, Eddie. Hit them keys. Put some life in this joint."

Others chimed in, coaxing him to get started.

He heard Clarice saying, "Give, man. You got an audience."

And they're waiting, he thought. They've been coming here every night and waiting.

But there's nothing you can give them. You just don't have it to give.

His eyes were closed. A whisper came from somewhere, saying, You can try. The least you can do is try.

Then he heard the sound. It was warm and sweet and it

came from a piano. That's fine piano, he thought. Who's playing that?

He opened his eyes. He saw his fingers caressing the keyboard.

THE REAL COOL KILLERS

by Chester Himes

I.

I'm gwine down to de river,
Set down on de ground;
If de blues overtake me,
I'll jump overboard an' drown . . .

Big Joe Turner was singing a rock-and-roll adaptation of *Dink's Blues.*

The loud licking rhythm blasted from the juke box with enough heat to melt bones.

A woman leapt from her seat in a booth as though the music had stuck her full of tacks. She was a lean black woman clad in a pink cotton jersey dress and red silk stockings. She pulled up her skirt and began doing a shake dance as though trying to throw off the tacks one by one.

Her mood was contagious. Other women jumped down from their high stools and shook themselves into the act. The customers laughed and shouted and began shaking too. The aisle between the bar and the booths became stormy with shaking bodies.

Big Smiley, the giant-size bartender, began doing a flat-footed locomotive shuffle up and down behind the bar.

The colored patrons of Harlem's Dew Drop Inn on 129th Street and Lenox Avenue were having the time of their lives that crisp October night.

A white man standing near the middle of the bar watched them with cynical amusement. He was the only white person present.

He was a big man, over six feet tall, dressed in a dark gray flannel suit, white shirt and blood red tie. He had a big featured sallow face with the blotched skin of dissipation. His thick black hair was shot with gray. He held a dead cigar butt between the first two fingers of his left hand. On the third finger was a signet ring. He looked to be about forty.

The colored women seemed to be dancing for his exclusive entertainment. A slight flush spread over his sallow face.

The music stopped.

A loud grating voice said dangerously above the panting

laughter: "Ah feels like cutting me some white mother-raper's throat."

The laughter stopped. The room became suddenly silent.

The man who had spoken was a scrawny little chicken-neck bantam-weight, twenty years past his fist fighting days, with gray stubble tinging his rough black skin. He wore a battered black derby green with age, a ragged plaid mackinaw and blue denim overalls.

His small enraged eyes were as red as live coals. He stalked toward the big white man stifflegged, holding an open spring-blade knife in his right hand with the blade pressed flat against his overalled leg.

The big white man turned to face him, looking as though he were caught in a situation where he didn't know whether to laugh or get angry. His hand strayed casually to the heavy glass ashtray on the bar.

"Take it easy, little man, and no one will get hurt," he said.

The little knifeman stopped two paces in front of him and said, "Ef'n Ah finds me some white mother-raper up here on my side of town trying to diddle my little gals Ah'm gonna cut his throat."

"What an idea," the white man said. "I'm a salesman. I sell that fine King Cola you folks like so much up here. I just dropped in here to patronize my customers."

Big Smiley came down and leaned his ham-size fists on the bar.

"Looka here, big bad and burly," he said to the little knife-man. "Don't try to scare my customers just 'cause you're bigger than they is."

"He doesn't want to hurt anyone," the big white man said. "He just wants some King Cola to soothe his mind. Give him a bottle of King Cola."

The little knifeman slashed at his throat and severed his red tie neatly just below the knot.

The big white man jumped back. His elbow struck the edge of the bar and the ash tray he'd been gripping flew from his hand and crashed into the shelf of ornamental wine glasses behind the bar.

The crashing sound caused him to jump back again. His second reflex action followed so closely on his first that he avoided the second slashing of the knife blade without even seeing it either. The knot that had remained of his tie was split through the middle and blossomed like a bloody wound over his white collar.

". . . throat cut!" a voice shouted excitedly as though yelling *Home Run!*

Big Smiley leaned across the bar and grabbed the red-eyed knifeman by the lapels of his mackinaw and lifted him from the floor.

"Gimme that chiv, shorty, 'fore I makes you eat it," he said lazily, smiling as though it were a joke.

The knifeman twisted in his grip and slashed him across the arm. The white fabric of his jacket sleeve parted like a bursted balloon and his black-skinned muscles opened like the Red Sea.

Blood spurted.

Big Smiley looked at his cut arm. He was still holding the knifeman off the floor by the mackinaw collar. His eyes had a surprised look. His nostrils flared.

"You cut me, didn't you," he said. His voice sounded unbelieving.

"Ah'll cut you again," the little knifeman said, wriggling in his grip.

Big Smiley dropped him as though he'd turned red hot.

The little knifeman bounced on his feet and slashed at Big Smiley's face.

Big Smiley drew back and reached beneath the bar counter with his right hand. He came up with a short handled fireman's axe. It had a red handle and a honed, razor-sharp blade.

The little knifeman jumped into the air and slashed at Big Smiley again, matching his knife against Big Smiley's axe.

Big Smiley countered with a right cross with the red-handled axe. The axe blade met the knifeman's arm in the middle of its stroke and cut it off just below the elbow as though it had been guillotined.

The severed coat-sleeved short-arm, still clutching the knife, sailed through the air, sprinkling the nearby spectators with drops of blood, landed on the linoleum tile floor, and skidded beneath the table of a booth.

The little knifeman landed on his feet, still making cutting motions with his half-an-arm. He was too drunk to feel the full impact of the shock. He saw that the lower part of his arm had been chopped off; he saw Big Smiley drawing back the red-handled axe. He thought Big Smiley was going to chop at him again.

"Wait a minute, you big mother-raper, 'til Ah find my arm!" he yelled. "It got my knife in his hand."

He dropped to his knees and began scrabbling about the floor with his one hand, searching for his severed arm. Blood spouted from his jerking stub as though from the nozzle of a hose.

Then he lost consciousness and flopped on his face.

Two customers turned him over; one wrapped a neck-tie about the bleeding arm for a tourniquet; the other inserted a chair leg to tighten it.

A waitress and another customer were twisting a knotted towel about Big Smiley's arm for a tourniquet. He was still holding the fireman's axe in his right hand and looking surprised.

The white manager stood atop the bar and shouted, "Please remain seated, folks. Everybody go back to his seat and pay his bill. The police have been called and everything will be taken care of."

As though he'd fired a starting gun, there was a race for the door.

When Sonny Pickens came out on the sidewalk he saw the big white man looking inside through one of the small front windows.

Sonny had been smoking two marijuana cigarets and he was tree top high. Seen from his drugged eyes, the dark night-sky looked bright purple and the dingy smoke-blackened tenements looked like brand new skyscrapers made of strawberry colored bricks. The neon signs of the bars and pool rooms and greasy spoons burned like phosphorescent fires.

He drew a blue-steel revolver from his inside coat pocket, spun the cylinder and aimed it at the big white man.

His two friends, Rubberlips Wilson and Lowtop Brown, looked at him in popeyed amazement. But before either could restrain him, Sonny advanced on the white man, walking on the balls of his feet.

"You there!" he shouted. "You the man what's been messing around with my wife."

The big white man jerked his head about and saw the pistol. His eyes stretched and the blood drained from his sallow face.

"My God, wait a minute!" he cried. "You're making a mistake. All of you folks are confusing me with some one else."

"Ain't going to be no waiting now," Sonny said and pulled the trigger.

Orange flame lanced toward the big white man's chest. Sound shattered the night.

Sonny and the white man both leapt straight up into the air simultaneously. Both began running before their feet touched the ground. Both ran straight ahead. They ran head on into one another at full speed. The white man's superior weight knocked Sonny down and he ran over him.

He plowed through the crowd of colored spectators, scattering them like nine pins, and cut across the street through the traffic, running in front of cars as though he didn't see them.

Sonny jumped to his feet and took out after him. He ran over the people the big white man had knocked down. Muscles rolled on bones beneath his feet. He staggered drunkenly. Screams followed him and car lights came down on him like shooting stars.

The big white man was going between two parked cars across the street when Sonny shot at him again. He gained the sidewalk unhit and began running south along the inner edge.

Sonny followed between the cars and kept after him.

People in the line of fire did acrobatics diving for safety. People up ahead crowded into the doorways to see what was happening. They saw a big white man with wild blue eyes and a stubble of red tie which looked as though his throat were cut, being chased by a slim black man with a big blue pistol. They drew back out of range.

But the people behind who were safely out of range joined the chase.

The white man was in front. Sonny was next. Rubberlips and Lowtop were running at Sonny's heels. Behind them the spectators stretched out in a ragged line.

The white man ran past a group of eight Arabs at the corner of 127th Street. All of the Arabs had heavy black grizzly beards. All wore bright green turbans, smoked glasses, and ankle-length white robes. Their complexions ranged from stove-pipe black to mustard tan. They were jabbering and gesticulating like a cage of frenzied monkeys. The air was redolent with the pungent scent of marijuana.

"An infidel!" one yelled.

The jabbering stopped abruptly. They wheeled after the white man in a group.

The white man heard the ejaculation. He saw the sudden movement through the corner of his eyes. He leaped forward from the curb.

A car coming fast down 127th Street burnt rubber in an earsplitting shriek to keep from running him down.

Seen in the car's headlights, his sweating face was bright red and muscle-ridged; his blue eyes were black with panic; his grayshot hair in wild disorder.

Instinctively he leaped high and sideways from the on-coming car. His arms and legs flew out in grotesque silhouette.

At that instant Sonny came abreast of the Arabs and shot at the leaping white man while he was still in the air.

The orange blast lit up Sonny's distorted face and the roar of the gunshot sounded like a fusillade.

The big white man shuddered and came down limp. He landed face downward in a spread-eagle posture. He didn't get up.

Sonny ran up to him with the smoking pistol dangling from his hand. He was starkly spotlighted by the car's headlights. He looked at the white man lying face downward in the middle of the street and started laughing. He doubled over laughing, his arms jerking and his body rocking.

Lowtop and Rubberlips caught up. The eight Arabs joined them in the beams of light.

"Man, Jesus Christ, what happened?" Lowtop asked.

The Arabs looked at him and began to laugh.

Rubberlips began to laugh too, then Lowtop.

All of them stood in the stark white light, swaying and rocking and doubling over with laughter.

Sonny was trying to say something but he was laughing so hard he couldn't get it out.

A police siren sounded nearby.

2.

THE TELEPHONE rang in the captain's office at the 126th Street precinct station.

The uniformed officer behind the desk reached for the outside phone without looking up from the record sheet he was filling out.

"Harlem precinct. Lieutenant Anderson," he said.

A high-pitched proper-speaking voice said, "Are you the man in charge?"

"Yes, lady," Lieutenant Anderson said patiently and went on writing with his free hand.

"I want to report that a white man is being chased down Lenox Avenue by a colored man with a gun," the voice said with the smug sanctimoniousness of a saved sister.

Lieutenant Anderson pushed aside the record sheet and pulled forward a report pad.

When he had finished taking down the essential details of her incoherent account, he said, "Thank you, Mrs. Collins," hung up and reached for the closed line to central police on Centre Street.

"Give me the radio dispatcher," he said.

Two colored men were driving east on 135th Street in the wake of a crosstown bus. Shapeless dark hats sat squarely on their clipped kinky heads and their big frames filled up the front seat of a small battered black sedan.

Static crackled from the shortwave radio and a metallic voice said:

Calling all cars. Riot threatens in Harlem. White man running South on Lenox Avenue at 128th Street. Chased by drunken Negro with gun. Danger of murder.

"Better goose it," the one on the inside said in a grating voice.

"I reckon so," the driver replied laconically.

He gave a short sharp blast on the siren and gunned the small sedan in a crying U-turn in the middle of the block, cutting in front of a taxi coming fast from the direction of the Bronx.

The taxi tore its brakes to keep from ramming it. Seeing the private license plates, the taxi driver thought they were two smalltime hustlers trying to play bigshots with the siren on their car. He was an Italian from the Bronx who had grown up with bigtime gangsters and Harlem hoodlums didn't scare him.

He leaned out of his window and yelled, "You ain't plowing cotton in Mississippi, you black son of a bitch. This is New York City, the Big Apple, where people drive—"

The colored man riding with his girl friend in the back seat leaned quickly forward and yanked at his sleeve.

"Man, come back in here and shut yo' mouth," he warned anxiously. "Them is Grave Digger Jones and Coffin Ed Johnson you is talking to. Can't you see that police antenna stuck up from their tail."

"Oh, that's them," the driver said, cooling off as quickly as a showgirl on a broke stud. "I didn't recognize 'em."

Grave Digger had heard him but he mashed the gas without looking around.

Coffin Ed drew his pistol from its shoulder sling and spun the cylinder. Passing street lights glinted from the long nickel-plated barrel of the special-made .38 calibre revolver, and the five brass-jacketed bullets looked deadly in the six chambers. The one beneath the trigger was empty, but he kept an extra box of shells along with his report book and handcuffs in his greased-leather lined right coat pocket.

"Lieutenant Anderson asked me last night why we stuck to these old-fashioned rods when the new ones were so much better. He was trying to sell me on the idea of one of those new hydraulic automatics that shoot fifteen times; said they were faster, lighter and just as accurate. But I told him we'd stick to these."

"Did you tell him how fast you could reload?"

Grave Digger carried its mate beneath his left arm.

"Naw, I told him he didn't know how hard these Negroes' heads were in Harlem," Coffin Ed said.

His acid-scarred face looked sinister in the dim panel light.

Grave Digger chuckled. "You should have told him that these people don't have any respect for a gun that doesn't have a shiny barrel a half a mile long. They want to see what they're being shot at with."

"Or else hear it, otherwise they figure it can't do any more damage than their knives."

When they came into Lenox, Grave Digger wheeled southward through the red light with the siren open, passing in front of an eastbound trailer truck, and slowed down behind a sky blue Cadillac Coupe de Ville trimmed in yellow metal, hogging the southbound lane between a bus and a fleet of northbound refrigerator trucks.

It had a New York State license plate numbered B-H-21. It belonged to Big Henry who ran the "21" numbers house. Big Henry was driving. His bodyguard, Cousin Cuts, was sitting beside him on the front seat. Two other rugged looking men occupied the back seat.

Big Henry took the cigar from his thick-lipped mouth with his right hand, tapped ash in the tray sticking from the instrument panel and kept on talking to Cuts as though he hadn't heard the siren. The flash of a diamond from his cigar hand lit up the rear window.

"Get him over," Grave Digger said in a flat voice.

Coffin Ed leaned out of the right side window and shot the rear view mirror off the door hinge of the big Cadillac.

The cigar hand of Big Henry became rigid and the back of his fat black neck began to swell as he looked at his shattered mirror. Cuts rose up in his seat, twisting about threateningly, and reached for his pistol. But when he saw Coffin Ed's sinister face staring at him from behind the long nickel-plated barrel of the .38 he ducked like an artful dodger from a hard-thrown ball.

Coffin Ed planted a hole in the Cadillac's left front fender.

Grave Digger chuckled. "That'll hurt Big Henry more than a hole in Cousin Cuts' head."

Big Henry turned about with a look of pop-eyed indignation on his puffed black face, but it sunk in like a burst balloon when he recognized the detectives. He wheeled the car frantically toward the curb without looking and crumpled his right front fender into the side of the bus.

Grave Digger had space enough to squeeze through. As they passed, Coffin Ed lowered his aim and shot Big Henry's gold lettered initials from the Cadillac's door.

"And stay over!" he yelled in a grating voice.

They left Big Henry giving them a how-could-you-do-this-to-me look with tears in his eyes.

When they came abreast the Dew Drop Inn they saw the deserted ambulance with the crowd running on ahead. Without slowing down they wormed between the cars parked haphazardly in the street and pushed through the dense jam of people with the siren open. They dragged to a stop when their headlights focused on the macabre scene.

"Split!" one of the Arabs hissed. "Here's the Things."

"The monsters," another chimed.

"Keep cool, fool," the third admonished. "They got nothing on us."

The two tall lanky loose-jointed detectives hit the pavement in unison, their nickel-plated .38 specials gripped in their hands. They looked like big-shouldered plow-hands in Sunday suits at a Saturday night jamboree.

"Straighten up!" Grave Digger yelled at the top of his voice.

"Count off!" Coffin Ed echoed.

There was movement in the crowd. The morbid and the innocent moved in closer. Suspicious characters began to blow.

Sonny and his two friends turned startled popeyed faces.

"Where they come from?" Sonny mumbled in a daze.

"I'll take him," Grave Digger said.

"Covered," Coffin Ed replied.

Their big flat feet made slapping sounds as they converged on Sonny and the Arabs. Coffin Ed halted at an angle that put them all in line of fire.

Without a break in motion, Grave Digger closed on Sonny and slapped him on the elbow with the barrel of his pistol.

With his free hand he caught Sonny's pistol when it flew from his nerveless fingers.

"Got it," he said as Sonny yelped in pain and grabbed his numb arm.

"I ain't—" Sonny was trying to say but Grave Digger shouted, "Shut up!"

"Line up and reach!" Coffin Ed ordered in a threatening voice, menacing them with his pistol. He sounded as though his teeth were on edge.

"Tell the man, Sonny!" Lowtop urged in a trembling voice, but it was drowned by Grave Digger thundering at the crowd, "Back up!" He lined a shot overhead.

They backed up.

Sonny's good arm shot up and his two friends reached. He was still trying to say something. His Adam's apple bobbed helplessly in his dry wordless throat.

But the Arabs were defiant. They dangled their arms and shuffled about.

"Reach where, man?" one of them said in a husky voice.

Coffin Ed grabbed him by the neck, lifted him off his feet.

"Easy, Ed," Grave Digger cautioned in a strangely anxious voice. "Easy does it."

Coffin Ed halted his pistol on the verge of shattering the Arab's teeth and shook his head like a dog coming out of water. Releasing the Arab's neck, he backed up one step and said in his grating voice,

"One for the money . . . and two for the show . . ."

It was the first line of a jingle chanted in the game of hide-and-seek as a warning from the "seeker" to the "hiders" that he was going after them.

Grave Digger took the next line, "Three to get ready . . ."

But before he could finish it with "And here we go," the Arabs had fallen into line with Sonny and had raised their hands high into the air.

"Now keep them up," Coffin Ed said.

"Or you'll be the next ones lying on the ground," Grave Digger added.

Sonny finally got out the words, "He ain't dead. He's just fainted."

"That's right," Rubberlips confirmed. "He ain't been hit. It just scared him so he fell unconscious."

"Just shake him and he'll come to," Sonny added.

The Arabs started to laugh again, but Coffin Ed's sinister face silenced them.

Grave Digger stuck Sonny's revolver into his own belt, holstered his own revolver, and bent down and lifted the white man's face. Blue eyes looked off at nowhere with a fixed stare. He lowered the head gently and picked up a limp warm hand, feeling for a pulse.

"He ain't dead," Sonny repeated. But his voice had grown weaker. "He's just fainted, that's all."

He and his two friends watched Grave Digger as though he were Jesus Christ bending over the body of Lazarus.

Grave Digger's eyes explored the white man's back. Coffin Ed stood without moving, his scarred face like a bronze mask cast with trembling hands. Grave Digger saw a black wet spot in the white man's thick black grayshot hair, low down at the base of the skull. He put his fingertips to it and they came off stained. He straightened up slowly, held his wet fingertips in the white headlights, and they showed red. He said nothing.

The spectators crowded nearer. Coffin Ed didn't notice; he was looking at Grave Digger's bloody fingertips.

"Is that blood?" Sonny asked in a breaking whisper. His body began trembling, coming slowly upward from his grasshopper legs.

Grave Digger and Coffin Ed stared at him, saying nothing.

"Is he dead?" Sonny asked in a terrorstricken whisper. His trembling lips were dust dry and his eyes were turning white in a black face gone gray.

"Dead as he'll ever be," Grave Digger said in a flat toneless voice.

"I didn't do it," Sonny whispered. "I swear 'fore God in heaven."

"He didn't do it," Rubberlips and Lowtop echoed in unison.

"How does it figure?" Coffin Ed asked.

"It figures for itself," Grave Digger said.

"So help me, God, boss, I couldn't have done it," Sonny said in a terrified whisper.

Grave Digger stared at him from agate hard eyes in a petrified face, and said nothing.

"You gotta believe him, boss, he couldn't have done it," Rubberlips vouched.

"Nawsuh," Lowtop echoed.

"I wasn't trying to hurt him, I just wanted to scare him," Sonny said. Tears were trickling from his eyes.

"It were that crazy drunk man with the knife that started it," Rubberlips said. "Back there in the Dew Drop Inn."

"Then afterwards the big white man kept looking in the window," Lowtop said. "That made Sonny mad."

"But I was just playing a joke," Sonny said.

The detectives stared at him from blank eyes. The Arabs were motionless.

"He's a comedian," Coffin Ed said finally.

"How could I be mad about my old lady," Sonny argued. "I ain't even got any old lady."

"Don't tell me," Grave Digger said in a hard flat unrelenting voice, and handcuffed Sonny. "Save it for the judge."

"Boss, listen, I beg you, I swear 'fore God—"

"Shut up, you're under arrest," Coffin Ed said.

3.

A POLICE CAR siren sounded from the distance. It came from the east; it started like the wail of an anguished banshee and grew into a scream. Another sounded from the west; it was joined by others from the north and south, one sounding after another like jets taking off from an aircraft carrier.

"Let's see what these real cool Moslems are carrying," Grave Digger said.

"Count off, you sheiks," Coffin Ed said.

They had the case wrapped up before the prowl cars arrived and the pressure was off. They felt cocky.

"Praise Allah," the tallest of the Arabs said.

As though performing a ritual, the others said, "Mecca," and all bowed low with outstretched arms.

"Cut the comedy and straighten up," Grave Digger said. "We're holding you for witnesses."

"Who's got the prayer?" the leader asked with bowed head.

"I've got the prayer," another replied.

"Pray to the great monster," the leader commanded.

The one who had the prayer turned slowly and presented his white-robed backside to Coffin Ed. A sound like a hound dog baying issued from his rear end.

"Allah be praised," the leader said, and the loose white sleeves of their robes fluttered in response.

Coffin Ed didn't get it until Sonny and his friends laughed in amazement. Then his face contorted in black rage.

"Punks!" he grated harshly, kicked the bowed Arab somersaulting, and leveled on him with his pistol as though to shoot him.

"Easy man, easy," Grave Digger said, trying to keep a straight face. "You can't shoot a man for aiming a fart at you."

"Hold it, monster," a third Arab cried, and flung liquid from a glass bottle toward Coffin Ed's face. "Sweeten thyself."

Coffin Ed saw the flash of the bottle and the liquid flying and ducked as he swung his pistol barrel.

"It's just perfume," the Arab cried in alarm.

But Coffin Ed didn't hear him through the roar of blood in his head. All he could think of was a con man called Hank throwing a glass of acid into his face. And this looked like another acid thrower. Quick scalding rage turned his acid burnt face into a hideous mask and his scarred lips drew back from his clenched teeth.

He wired two shots together and the Arab holding the half-filled perfume bottle said, "Oh," softly and folded slowly to the pavement. Behind, in the crowd, a woman screamed as her leg gave away beneath her.

The other Arabs broke in wild flight. Sonny broke with them. A split second later his friends took off in his wake.

"Goddammit, Ed!" Grave Digger shouted and lunged for the gun.

He made a grab for the barrel, deflecting the aim as it went off again. The bullet cut a telephone cable in two overhead and it fell into the crowd, setting off a cacophony of screams.

Everybody ran.

The panicstricken crowd stampeded for the nearest doorways, trampling the woman who was shot and two others who fell.

Grave Digger grappled with Coffin Ed and they crashed down on top of the dead white man. Grave Digger had Coffin Ed's pistol by the barrel and was trying to wrest it from his grip.

"It's me, Digger, Ed," he kept saying. "Let go the gun."

"Turn me loose, Digger, turn me loose. Let me kill 'im," Coffin Ed mouthed insanely, tears streaming from his hideous face. "They tried it again, Digger."

They rolled over the corpse and rolled back.

"That wasn't acid, that was perfume," Grave Digger said, gasping for breath.

"Turn me loose, Digger, I'm warning you," Coffin Ed mumbled.

While they threshed back and forth over the corpse, two of the Arabs followed Sonny into the doorway of a tenement. The other people crowding into the doorway got aside and let them pass. Sonny saw the stairs crowded and kept on through, looking for a back exit. He came out in a small back courtyard, enclosed with stone walls. The Arabs followed him. One put a noose over his head, knocking off his hat, and drew it tight. The other pulled a switchblade knife and pressed the point against his side.

"If you holler you're dead," the first one said.

The Arab leader joined them.

"Let's get him away from here," he said.

At that moment the patrol cars began to unload. Two harness cops and Detective Haggerty hit the deck and were the first on the murder scene.

"Holy mother!" Haggerty exclaimed.

The cops stared aghast.

It looked to them as though the two colored detectives had the big white man locked in a death struggle.

"Just don't stand there," Grave Digger panted. "Give me a hand."

"They'll kill him," Haggerty said, wrapping his arms about

Grave Digger and trying to pull him away. "You grab the other one," he said to the cops.

"To hell with that," the cop said, swinging his blackjack across Coffin Ed's head, knocking him unconscious.

The other cop drew his pistol and took aim at the corpse. "One move out of you and I'll shoot," he said.

"He won't move, he's dead," Grave Digger said.

The cop looked sheepish. "I thought it was him you were fighting," he said.

"Turn me loose, goddammit," Grave Digger said to Haggerty.

"Well, hell," Haggerty said indignantly, releasing him. "You asked me to help. How the hell do I know what's going on?"

Grave Digger shook himself and looked at the third cop. "You didn't have to slug him," he said.

"I wasn't taking no chances," the cop said.

"Shut up and watch the Arab," Haggerty said.

The cop moved over and looked at the Arab. "He's dead too."

"Holy Mary, the plague," Haggerty said. "Look after that woman then."

Four more cops came running. At Haggerty's order, two turned toward the woman who'd been shot. She was lying deserted in the street.

"She's alive, just unconscious," the cop said.

"Leave her for the ambulance," Haggerty said.

"Who're you ordering about," the cop said. "We know our business."

"To hell with you," Haggerty said.

Grave Digger bent over Coffin Ed, lifted his head and put an open bottle of ammonia to his nose. Coffin Ed groaned.

A redfaced uniformed sergeant built like a General Sherman tank loomed above him.

"What happened here?" he asked.

Grave Digger looked up. "A rumpus broke and we lost our prisoner."

"Who shot your partner?"

"He's not shot, he's just knocked out."

"That's all right then. What's your prisoner look like?"

"Black man, about five-eleven, twenty-five to thirty years, one-seventy to one-eighty pounds, narrow face sloping down to chin, wearing light gray hat, dark gray hickory striped suit, white tab collar, red striped tie, beige chukker boots. He's handcuffed."

The sergeant's small china blue eyes went from the big white corpse to the bearded Arab corpse.

"What one did he kill?" he asked.

"The white man," Grave Digger said.

"That's all right, we'll get him," he said. Raising his voice, he called, "Professor!"

The corporal who'd stopped to light a cigaret said, "Yeah."

"Rope off this whole goddamned area," the sergeant said. "Don't let anybody out. We want a Harlem-dressed zulu. Killed a white man. Can't have gotten far 'cause he's hand-cuffed."

"We'll get 'im," the corporal said.

"Pick up all suspicious persons," the sergeant said.

"Right," the corporal said, taking the cops and hurrying off toward the other cops that were arriving.

"Who shot the Arab?" the sergeant asked.

"Ed shot him," Grave Digger said.

"That's all right then," the sergeant said. "We'll get your prisoner. I'm sending for the lieutenant and the medical examiner. Save the rest for them."

He turned and followed the corporal.

Coffin Ed stood up shakily. "You should have let me killed that son of a bitch, Digger," he said.

"Look at him," Grave Digger said, nodding toward the Arab's corpse.

Coffin Ed stared.

"I didn't even know I hit him," he said as though coming out of a daze. After a moment he added, "I can't feel sorry for him. I tell you, Digger, death is on any son of a bitch who tries to throw acid into my eyes again."

"Smell yourself, man," Grave Digger said.

Coffin Ed bent his head. The front of his dark wrinkled suit reeked with the scent of dime store perfume.

"That's what he threw. Just perfume," Grave Digger said. "I tried to warn you."

"I must not have heard you."

Grave Digger took a deep breath. "Goddammit, man, you got to control yourself."

"Well, Digger, a burnt child fears fire. Anybody who tries to throw anything at me when they're under arrest is apt to get shot."

Grave Digger said nothing.

"What happened to our prisoner?" Coffin Ed asked.

"He got away," Grave Digger said.

They turned in unison and surveyed the scene.

Patrol cars were arriving by the minute, erupting cops like an invasion. Others had formed blockades across Lenox Avenue at 128th and 126th Streets, and had blocked off 127th Street on both sides.

Most of the people had gotten off the street. Those that stayed were being arrested as suspicious persons. Several drivers trying to move their cars were protesting their innocence loudly.

The packed bars in the area were being rapidly sealed by the police. The windows of tenements were jammed with black faces and the exits blocked by police.

"They'll have to go through this jungle with a fine tooth comb," Grave Digger said. "With all these white cops about, any colored family might hide him."

"I want those gangster punks too," Coffin Ed said.

"Well, we'll just have to wait now for the men from homicide."

But Lieutenant Anderson arrived first, with the harness sergeant and Detective Haggerty latched on to him. The five of them stood in a circle in the car's headlights between the two corpses.

"All right, just give me the essential points first," Anderson said. "I put out the flash so I know the start. The man hadn't been killed when I got the first report."

"He was dead when we got here," Grave Digger said in a flat toneless voice. "We were the first here. The suspect was standing over the victim with the pistol in his hand—"

"Hold it," a new voice said.

A plainclothes lieutenant and sergeant from downtown homicide bureau came into the circle.

"These are the arresting officers," Anderson said.

"Where's the prisoner?" the homicide lieutenant asked.

"He got away," Grave Digger said.

"Okay, start over," the homicide lieutenant said.

Grave Digger gave him the first part, then went on:

"There were two friends with him and a group of teenage gangsters standing around the corpse. We disarmed the suspect and handcuffed him. When we started to frisk the gangster punks we had a rumble. Coffin Ed shot one. In the rumble the suspect got away."

"Now let's get this straight," said the lieutenant. "Were the teenagers implicated too?"

"No, we just wanted them as witnesses," Grave Digger said. "There's no doubt about the suspect."

"Right."

"When I got here Jones and Johnson were fighting, rolling all over the corpse," Haggerty said. "Jones was trying to disarm Johnson."

Lieutenant Anderson and the men from homicide looked at him, then turned to look at Grave Digger and Coffin Ed in turn.

"It was like this," Coffin Ed said. "One of the punks turned up his ass and farted toward me and—"

Anderson said, "Huh!" and the lieutenant said incredulously, "You killed a man for farting?"

"No, it was another punk he shot," Grave Digger said in his toneless voice. "One who threw perfume on him from a bottle. He thought it was acid the punk was throwing."

They looked at Coffin Ed's acid burnt face and looked away embarrassedly.

"The fellow who was killed is an A-rab," the sergeant said.

"That's just a disguise," Grave Digger said. "They belong to a group of teenage gangsters who call themselves Real Cool Moslems."

"Hah!" the homicide lieutenant said.

"Mostly they fight a teenage gang of Jews from the Bronx," Grave Digger elaborated. "We leave that to the welfare people."

The homicide sergeant stepped over to the Arab corpse and removed the turban and peeled off the artificial beard. The face of a colored youth with slick conked hair and beardless cheeks stared up. He dropped the disguises beside the corpse and sighed.

"Just a baby," he said.

For a moment no one spoke.

Then the homicide lieutenant asked, "You have the gun?"

Grave Digger took it from his pocket, holding the barrel by the thumb and first finger, and gave it to him.

The lieutenant took it in a handkerchief and examined it for some moments curiously. Then he wrapped it in his hand-kerchief and slipped it into his coat pocket.

"Had you questioned the suspect?" he asked.

"We hadn't got to it," Grave Digger said. "All we know is the homicide grew out of a rumpus at the Dew Drop Inn."

"That's a bistro a couple of blocks up the street," Anderson said. "They had a cutting there a short time earlier."

"It's been a hot time in the old town tonight," Haggerty said.

The lieutenant raised his brows enquiringly at Lieutenant Anderson.

"Suppose you go to work on that angle, Haggerty," Anderson said. "Look into that cutting. Find out how it ties in."

"We figure on doing that ourselves," Grave Digger said.

"Let him go on and get started," Anderson said.

"Right-o," Haggerty said. "I'm the man for the cutting."

Everybody looked at him. He left.

The homicide lieutenant said, "Well, let's take a look at the stiffs."

He gave each a cursory examination. The teenager was shot once in the heart.

"Nothing to do with them but wait for the coroner," he said.

They looked at the unconscious woman.

"Shot in the thigh, high up," the homicide sergeant said. "Loss of blood but not fatal—I don't think."

"The ambulance will be here any minute," Anderson said.

"How did she get shot?" the homicide lieutenant asked.

"Ed shot at the gangster twice," Grave Digger said. "It must have been then."

"Right."

No one looked at Coffin Ed. Instead, they made a pretence of examining the area.

Anderson shook his head. "It's going to be a hell of a job finding your prisoner in this dense slum," he said.

"There isn't any need," the homicide lieutenant said. "If this was the pistol he had, he's as innocent as you and me. This pistol won't kill anyone." He took the pistol from his pocket and unwrapped it. "This is a .37 calibre blank pistol. The only bullets made to fit it are blanks and they can't be tampered with enough to kill a man. And it hasn't been made over into a zip gun."

They stared at him as though stupefied.

"Well," Lieutenant Anderson said at last. "That tears it."

4.

THERE WAS a rusty sheet-iron gate in the concrete wall between the small back courts. The gang leader unlocked it with his own key. The gate opened silently on oiled hinges.

He went ahead.

"March!" the henchman with the knife ordered, prodding Sonny.

Sonny marched.

The other henchman kept the noose around his neck like a dog chain.

When they'd passed through, the leader closed and locked the gate.

One of the henchmen said, "You reckon Caleb is bad hurt?"

"Shut up talking in front of the captive," the leader said. "Ain't you got no better sense than that."

The broken concrete paving was strewn with broken glass, bottles, rags and divers objects thrown from the back windows; a rusty bed spring, a cotton mattress with a big hole burnt in the middle, several worn out automobile tires, and the half dried carcass of a black cat with its left hind foot missing and its eyes eaten out by rats.

They picked their way through the debris carefully. Sonny

bumped into a loose stack of garbage cans. One fell with a loud clatter. A sudden putrid stink arose.

"Goddammit, look out!" the leader said. "Watch where you're going."

"Aw, man, ain't nobody thinking about us back here," Choo-Choo said.

"Don't call me *man*," the leader said.

"Sheik then."

"What you jokers gonna do with me?" Sonny asked.

His weed jag was gone; he felt weak-kneed and hungry; his mouth tasted brackish and his stomach was knotted with fear.

"We're going to sell you to the Jews," Choo-Choo said.

"You ain't fooling me, I know you ain't no A-rabs," Sonny said.

"We're going to hide you from the police," Sheik said.

"I ain't done nothing," Sonny said.

Sheik stopped still and they all turned and looked at Sonny. His eyes were white halfmoons in the dark.

"All right then, if you ain't done nothing we'll turn you back to the cops," Sheik said.

"Naw, wait a minute, I just want to know where you're taking me."

"We're taking you home with us."

"Well that's all right then."

There was no back door from the hall as in the other tenement. Decayed concrete stairs led down to a basement door. Sheik produced a key on his ring for that one also. They entered a dark passage. Foul water stood on the broken pavement. The air smelled like molded rags and stale sewer pipes. They had to remove their smoked glasses in order to see.

Halfway along, feeble yellow light slanted from an open door. They entered a small filthy room.

A sick man clad in long cotton drawers lay beneath a ragged horse blanket on a filthy pallet with burlap sacks.

"You got anything for old Badeye," he said in a whining voice.

"We got you a fine black gal," Choo-Choo said.

The old man raised up on his elbows. "Whar she at?"

"Don't tease him," Inky said.

"Lie down and shut," Sheik said. "I told you before we

wouldn't have nothing for you tonight." Then to his hench-men, "Come on, you jokers, hurry up."

They began stripping off their disguises. Beneath their white robes they wore sweat shirts and black slacks. The beards were put on with makeup gum.

Without their disguises they looked like three high school students.

Sheik was a tall yellow boy with strange yellow eyes and reddish kinky hair. He had the broad-shouldered, trim-waisted figure of an athlete. His face was broad, his nose flat with wide, flaring nostrils, and his skin freckled. He looked disagreeable.

Choo-Choo was shorter, thicker and darker, with the short-cropped egg-shaped head and flat, mobile face of the natural born joker. He was bowlegged and pigeon-toed but fast on his feet.

Inky was an inconspicuous boy of medium size, with a mild, submissive manner, and black as the ace of spades.

"Where's the gun?" Choo-Choo asked when he didn't see it stuck in Sheik's belt.

"I slipped it to Bones."

"What's he going to do with it?"

"Shut up and quit questioning what I do."

"Where you reckon they all went to, Sheik?" Inky asked, trying to be peacemaker.

"They went home if they got sense," Sheik said.

The old man on the pallet watched them fold their disguises into small packages.

"Not even a little taste of King Kong," he whined.

"Naw, nothing!" Sheik said.

The old man raised up on his elbows. "What do you mean, naw? I'll throw you out of here. I'se the janitor. I'll take my keys away from you. I'll—"

"Shut your mouth before I shut it and if any cops come messing around down here you'd better keep it shut too. I'll have something for you tomorrow."

"Tomorrow? A bottle?"

"Yeah, a whole bottle."

The old man lay back, mollified.

"Come on," Sheik said to the others.

As they were leaving he snatched a ragged army overcoat from a nail on the door without the janitor noticing. He stopped Sonny in the passage and took the noose from about his neck, then looped the over coat overtop the handcuffs. It looked as though Sonny were merely carrying an overcoat with both hands.

"Now nobody'll see those cuffs," Sheik said. Turning to Inky, he said, "You go up first and see how it looks. If you think we can get by the cops without being stopped, give us the high sign."

Inky went up the rotten wooden stairs and through the doorway to the ground floor hall. After a minute he opened the door and beckoned.

They went up in single file.

Strangers who'd ducked into the building to escape the shooting were held there by two uniformed cops blocking the outside doorway. No one paid any attention to Sonny and the three gangsters. They kept on up to the top floor.

Sheik unlocked a door with another key on his ring, and led the way into a kitchen.

An old colored woman clad in a faded blue Mother Hubbard with darker blue patches sat in a rocking chair by a coal burning kitchen stove, darning a threadbare man's woolen sock on a wooden egg and smoking a corn cob pipe.

"Is that you, Caleb?" she asked, looking over a pair of ancient steel-rimmed spectacles.

"It's just me and Choo-Choo and Inky," Sheik said.

"Oh, it's you, Samson." The note of expectancy in her voice died to disappointment. "Whar's Caleb?"

"He went to work downtown in a bowling alley, Granny. Setting up pins," Sheik said.

"Lord, that chile is always out working at night," she said with a sigh. "I sho hope God he ain't getting into no trouble with all this night work, 'cause his old Granny is too old to watch over him as a mammy would."

She was so old the color had faded from her dark brown skin in spots like the skin of a dried speckled pea, and her once-brown eyes had turned milky blue. Her bony cranium was bald at the front and over the ears and the speckled skin

was taut against the skull. What remained of her short gray
hair was gathered into a small tight ball at back. The outline
of each fingerbone plying the darning needle was plainly visible through the transparent parchment-like skin.

"He ain't getting in to no trouble," Sheik said.

Inky and Choo-Choo pushed Sonny into the kitchen and
closed the door.

Granny peered over her spectacles at Sonny. "I don't know
this boy. Is he a friend of Caleb's too."

"He's the fellow Caleb is taking his place," Sheik said. "He
hurt his hands."

She pursed her lips. "There's so many of you boys coming
and going in here all the time I sho hope you ain't getting
into no mischief. And this new boy looks older than you
others is."

"You worry too much," Sheik said harshly.

"Hannh?"

"We're going on to our room," Sheik said. "Don't wait up
for Caleb. He's going to be late."

"Hannh?"

"Come on," Sheik said. "She ain't hearing no more."

It was a shotgun flat, one room opening to the other. The
next room contained two small white enameled iron beds
where Caleb and his grandmother slept, and a small potbellied
stove on a tin mat in one corner. A table held a pitcher and
washbowl; there was a small dimestore mirror atop a chest of
drawers. Like in the kitchen, everything was spotlessly clean.

"Give me your things and watch out for Granny," Sheik
said, taking their bundled-up disguises.

Choo-Choo bent his head to the keyhole.

Sheik unlocked a large old cedar chest with another key
from his ring and stored their bundles beneath layers of old
blankets and house furnishings. It was Granny's hope chest
where she stored things given her by the white folks she
worked for to give to Caleb when he got married. Sheik
locked the chest and unlocked the door to the next room.
They followed him and he locked the door behind them.

It was the room he and Choo-Choo rented. There was a
double bed where he and Choo-Choo slept, chest of drawers

and mirror, pitcher and bowl on the table, as in the other room. The corner was curtained off with calico for a closet. But a lot of junk lay around and it wasn't as clean.

A narrow window opened to the platform of the red-painted iron fire escape that ran down the front of the building. It was protected by an iron grill closed by a padlock.

Sheik unlocked the grill and stepped out on the fire escape. "Look at this," he said.

Choo-Choo joined him; Inky and Sonny squeezed into the window.

"Watch the captive, Inky," Sheik said.

"I ain't no captive," Sonny said.

"Just look," Sheik said, pointing toward the street.

Below, on the broad avenue, red-eyed prowl cars were scattered thickly like monster ants about an anthill. Three ambulances were threading through the maze, two police hearses, and cars from the police commissioner's office and the medical examiner's office. Uniformed cops and men in plain clothes were coming and going in every direction.

"The men from Mars," Sheik said. "The big dragnet. What you think about that, Choo-Choo?"

Choo-Choo was busy counting.

The lower landings and stairs of the fire escape were packed with other colored people watching the show. Every front window on both sides of the street as far as the eye could see was jammed with black heads.

"I counted thirty-one prowl cars," Choo-Choo said. "That's more than was up on Eighth Avenue when Coffin Ed got that acid throwed in his eyes."

"They're shaking down the buildings one by one," Sheik said.

"What we're going to do with our captive?" Choo-Choo asked.

"We got to get the cuffs off first. Maybe we can hide him up in the pigeon's roost."

"Leave the cuffs on him."

"Can't do that. We got to get ready for the shakedown."

He and Choo-Choo stepped back into the room. He took Sonny by the arm, and pointed toward the street.

"They're looking for you, man."

Sonny's black face began graying again.

"I ain't done nothing. That wasn't a real pistol I had. That was a blank gun."

The three of them stared at him disbelievingly.

"Yeah, that ain't what they think," Choo-Choo said.

Sheik was staring at Sonny with a strange expression. "You sure, man?" he asked tensely.

"Sure I'm sure. It wouldn't shoot nothing but .37 calibre blanks."

"Then it wasn't you who shot the big gray stud?"

"That's what I been telling you. I couldn't have shot him."

A change came over Sheik. His flat freckled yellow face took on a brutal look. He hunched his shoulders, trying to look dangerous and important.

"The cops are trying to frame you, man," he said. "We got to hide you now for sure."

"What you doing with a gun that don't shoot bullets?" Choo-Choo asked.

"I keep it in my shine parlor as a gag is all," Sonny said.

Choo-Choo snapped his fingers. "I know you. You're the joker what works in that shoe shine parlor beside the Savoy."

"It's my own shoe shine parlor."

"How much marijuana you got stashed there?"

"I don't handle it."

"Sheik, this joker's a square."

"Cut the gab," Sheik said. "Let's get these handcuffs off the captive."

He tried keys and lockpicks but he couldn't get them open. So he gave Inky a triangle file and said, "Try filing the chain in two. You and him sit on the bed." Then to Sonny, "What's your name, man?"

"Aesop Pickens but people mostly call me Sonny."

"All right then, Sonny."

They heard a girl's voice talking to Granny and listened silently to rubbersoled shoes crossing the other room.

A single rap, then three quickly, then another single rap sounded on the door.

"Gaza," Sheik said with his mouth against the panel.

"Suez," a girl's voice replied.

Sheik unlocked the door.

A girl entered and he locked the door behind her.

She was a tall sepia-colored girl with short black curls, wearing a black turtleneck sweater, plaid skirt, bobby sox, and white buckskin shoes. She had a snub nose, wide mouth, full lips, even white teeth, and wide-set brown eyes fringed with long black lashes.

She looked about sixteen years old, and was breathless with excitement.

Sonny stared at her.

"Hell, it's just Sissie. I thought it was Bones with the gun," Choo-Choo said.

"Stop beefing about the gun. It's safe with Bones. The cops ain't going to shake down no garbage collector's house. His old man works for the city same as they do."

"What's this about Bones and the gun?" Sissie asked.

"Sheik's got—"

"It's none of Sissie's business," Sheik cut him off.

"Somebody said an Arab had been shot and at first I thought it was you," Sissie said.

"You hoped it was me," Sheik said.

She turned away, blushing.

"Don't look at me," Choo-Choo said to Sheik. "You tell her. She's your girl."

"It was Caleb," Sheik said.

"Caleb! Jesus!" Sissie dropped onto the bed beside Sonny. She looked stunned. "Jesus! Poor little Caleb. What will Granny do?"

"What the hell can she do," Sheik said brutally. "Raise him from the dead?"

"Does she know?"

"Does it look like she knows?"

"Jesus! Poor little Caleb. What did he do?"

"I gave old Coffin Ed the stink gun and—" Choo-Choo began.

"You didn't!" she exclaimed.

"The hell I didn't."

"What did Caleb do?"

"He threw perfume over the monster. It's the Moslem salute for cops. I told you about it before. But the monster must have thought Cal was throwing some more acid into his eyes. He blasted so fast we couldn't tell him any better."

"Jesus!"

"Where's Sugartit?" Sheik asked.

"At home. She didn't come in to town tonight. I phoned her and she said she was sick."

"Yeah. Did you have any trouble getting in here?"

"No. I told the cops at the door that I lived here."

They heard the signal rapped on the door.

Sissie gasped.

Sheik looked at her suspiciously. "What the hell's the matter with you?" he asked.

"Nothing."

He hesitated before opening the door. "You ain't expecting nobody?"

"Me? No. Who could I expect?"

"You're acting mighty funny."

"I'm just nervous."

The signal was rapped again.

Sheik stepped to the door and said, "Gaza."

"Suez," a girl's lilting voice replied.

Sheik gave Sissie a threatening look as he unlocked the door.

A small-boned chocolate-brown girl dressed like Sissie slipped hurriedly into the room.

At sight of Sissie she stopped and said, "Oh!" in a guilty tone of voice.

Sheik looked from one to the other. "I thought you said she was at home," he accused Sissie.

"I thought she was," Sissie said.

He turned his gaze on Sugartit. "What the hell's the matter with you? What the hell's going on here?"

"A Moslem's been killed and I thought it was you," she said.

"All you little bitches were hoping it was me," he said.

She had sloe eyes with long black lashes which looked se-cretive. She threw a quick defiant look at Sissie and said, "Don't include me in that."

"Did you tell Granny?" Sheik asked.

"Of course not."

"It was your lover, Caleb," Sheik said brutally.

She gave a shriek and charged at Sheik, clawing and kicking.

"You dirty bastard!" she cried. "You're always picking at me."

Sissie pulled her off. "Shut up and keep your mouth shut," she said tightly.

"You tell her," Sheik said.

"It was Caleb all right," Sissie said.

"Caleb!" Sugartit screamed and flung herself face-downward across the bed. She was up in a flash, hurling accusations at Sheik. "You did it. You got him killed. On account of me. 'Cause he had the best go and you couldn't get me to do what you made Sissie do."

"That's a lie," Sissie said.

"Caleb!" Sugartit screamed at the top of her voice.

"Shut up, Granny will hear you," Choo-Choo said.

"Granny! Caleb's dead! Sheik killed him!" she screamed again.

"Stop her," Sheik commanded Sissie. "She's getting hysterical and I don't want to have to hurt her."

Sissie clutched her from behind, put one hand over her mouth and twisted her arm behind her back with the other.

Sugartit looked furiously at Sheik overtop Sissie's hand.

"Granny can't hear," Inky said.

"The hell she can't," Choo-Choo said. "She can hear when she wants to."

"Let me go!" Sugartit mumbled and bit Sissie's hand.

"Stop that!" Sissie said.

"I'm going to him," Sugartit mumbled. "I love him. You can't stop me. I'm going to find out who shot him."

"Your old man shot him," Sheik said brutally. "The monster, Coffin Ed."

"Did I hear some one calling Caleb?" Granny asked from the other side of the door.

Sheik closed his hands quickly about Sugartit's throat and choked her into silence.

"Naw, Granny," he called. "It's just these silly girls arguing about their cubebs."

"Hannh?"

"Cubebs!" Sheik shouted.

"You chillen make so much racket a body can't hear herself think," she muttered.

They heard her shuffling back to the kitchen.

"Jesus, she's sitting up waiting for him," Sissie said.

Sheik and Choo-Choo exchanged glances.

"She don't even know what's happening in the street," Choo-Choo said.

Sheik took his hands from about Sugartit's throat.

5.

How soon can you find out what he was killed with?" the chief of police asked.

"He was killed with a bullet, naturally," the assistant Medical Examiner said.

"You're not funny," the chief said. "I mean what calibre bullet."

His brogue had begun thickening and the cops who knew him best began getting nervous.

The assistant M.E. snapped his bag shut with a gesture of coyness and peered at the chief through magnified eyeballs encircled by black gutta-percha.

"That can't be known until after the autopsy. The bullet will have to be removed from the corpse's brain and subjected to tests—"

The chief listened in red-faced silence.

"I don't perform the autopsy. I'm the night man. I just pass on whether they're dead. I marked this one down as D.O.A. That means dead on arrival—my arrival, not his. You know more about whether he was dead on his arrival than I do, and more about how he was killed too."

"I asked you a civil question."

"I'm giving you a civil answer. Or, I should say, a civil service answer. The men who do the autopsy come on duty at nine o'clock. You ought to get your report by ten."

"That's all I asked you. Thanks. And damn little good that'll do me tonight. And by ten o'clock tomorrow morning the killer ought to be hell and gone to another part of the United States if he's got any sense."

"That's your affair, not mine. You can send the stiffs to the morgue when you've finished with them. I'm finished with them now. Good night, everyone."

No one answered. He left.

"I never knew why we needed a goddamned doctor to tell us whether a stiff was dead or not," the chief grumbled.

He was a big weatherbeaten man dressed in a lot of gold braid. He'd come up from the ranks. Everything about him from the arm full of gold hash stripes to the box-toed special made shoes said, "Flat foot." Behind his back the cops on Centre Street called him Spark Plug after the tender-footed nag in the comic strip, *Barney Google*.

He formed the hub of the group near the white man's corpse, which, by then, had grown to include, in addition to the principals, two deputy police commissioners, an inspector from homicide, and nameless uniformed lieutenants from adjoining precincts.

The deputy commissioners kept quiet. Only the commissioner himself had any authority over the chief, and he was at home in bed.

"This thing's hot as hell," the chief said at large. "Have we got our stories synchronized?"

Heads nodded.

"Come on then, Anderson, we'll meet the press," he said to the lieutenant in charge of the 126th Street precinct station.

They walked across the street to where a group of newsmen were being held in leash.

"Okay, men, you can get your pictures," he said.

Flashlights exploded in his face. Then the photographers converged on the corpses and left him facing the reporters.

"Here it is, men, the dead man has been identified by his papers as Ulysses Galen of New York City. He lives alone in a two-room suite at Hotel Lexington. We've checked that. They think his wife is dead. He's a sales manager for the King Cola Company. We've contacted their main office in Jersey City and learned that Harlem is in his district."

His thick brogue dripped like milk and honey through the

noisy night. Stylos scratched on pads. Flashbulbs went off around the corpses like an anti-aircraft barrage.

"A letter in his pocket from a Mrs. Helen Kruger, Wading River, Long Island, begins with, *Dear Dad*—. There's an unposted letter addressed to Homer Galen in the sixteen hundred block on Michigan Avenue in Chicago. That's a business district. We don't know whether Homer Galen is his son or another relation—"

"What about how he was killed?" a reporter interrupted.

"We know that he was shot in the back of the head by a Negro man named Sonny Pickens who operates a shoe shine parlor at 134th Street and Lenox Avenue. Several Negroes resented the victim drinking in a bar at 129th Street and Lenox—"

"What was he doing at a crumby bar up here in Harlem?"

"We haven't found that out yet. Probably just slumming. We know that the barman was cut trying to protect him from another colored assailant—"

"How did the shine assail him?"

"This is not funny, men. The first Negro attacked him with a knife—tried to attack him; the bartender saved him. After he left the bar Pickens followed him down the street and shot him in the back."

"You expect him to shoot a white man in the front."

"Two colored detectives from the 126th Street precinct station arrived on the scene in time to arrest Pickens virtually in the act of homicide. He still had the gun in his hand," the chief continued. "They handcuffed the prisoner and were in the act of bringing him in when he was snatched by a teenage Harlem gang who call themselves Real Cool Moslems."

Laughter burst from the reporters.

"What, no Mau-Maus?"

"It's not funny, men," the chief said. "One of them tried to throw acid in one of the detective's eyes."

The reporters were silenced.

"Another gangster threw acid in an officer's face up here about a year ago, wasn't it?" a reporter said. "He was a colored cop too. Johnson, Coffin Ed Johnson, they called him."

"It's the same officer," Anderson said, speaking for the first time.

"He must be a magnet," the reporter said.

"He's just tough and they're scared of him," Anderson said. "You've got to be tough to be a colored cop in Harlem. Unfortunately, colored people don't respect colored cops unless they're tough."

"He shot and killed the acid thrower," the chief said.

"You mean the first one or this one?" the reporter asked.

"This one, the Moslem," Anderson said.

"During the excitement, Pickens and the others escaped into the crowd," the chief said.

He turned and pointed toward a tenement building across the street. It looked stark naked and indescribably ugly in the glare of a dozen powerful spotlights. Uniformed police stood on the roof; others were coming and going through the entrance; still others stuck their heads from front windows to shout to other cops in the street. The other front windows were jammed with colored faces, looking like clusters of strange purple fruit in the stark white light.

"You can see for yourselves we're looking for the killer," the chief said. "We're going through those buildings with a fine tooth comb, one by one, flat by flat, room by room. We have the killer's description. He's wearing toolproof handcuffs. We should have him in custody before morning. He'll never get out of that dragnet."

"If he isn't already out," a reporter said.

"He's not out. We got here too soon for that."

The reporters began then to question him.

"Is Pickens one of the Real Cool Moslems?"

"We know he was rescued by seven of them. The eighth was killed."

"Was there any indication of robbery?"

"Not unless the victim had valuables we don't know anything about. His wallet, watch and rings are intact."

"Then what was the motive? A woman?"

"Well, hardly. He was an important man, well off financially. He didn't have to chase up here."

"It's been done before."

The chief spread his hands. "That's right. But in this case both negroes who attacked him did so because they resented his presence in a colored bar. They expressed their resentment in so many words. We have colored witnesses who heard them. Both negroes were intoxicated. The first had been drinking all evening. And Pickens had been smoking marijuana also."

"Okay, chief, it's your story," the dean of the police reporters said, calling a halt.

The chief and Anderson recrossed the street to the silent group.

"Did you get away with it?" one of the deputy commissioners asked.

"Goddammit, I had to tell them something," the chief said defensively. "Did you want me to tell them that a $15,000.00 a year white executive was shot to death on a Harlem street by a weedhead negro with a blank pistol who was immediately rescued by a gang of Harlem juvenile delinquents while all we got to show for the efforts of the whole goddamned police force is a dead adolescent calling himself a Real Cool Moslem?"

"Sho nuff cool now," Haggerty slipped in soto voce.

"You want us to become the laughing stock of the whole goddamned world," the chief continued, warming up to his subject. "You want it said the New York City police stood by helpless while a white man got himself killed in the middle of a crowded nigger street?"

"Well, didn't he?" the homicide lieutenant said.

"I wasn't accusing you," the deputy commissioner said apologetically.

"Pickens is the one it's rough on," Anderson said. "We've got him branded as a killer when we know he didn't do it."

"We don't know any such a goddamned thing," the chief said, turning purple with rage. "He might have rigged the blanks with bullets. It's been done, goddammit. And even if he didn't shoot him, he hadn't ought have been chasing him with a goddamned pistol that sounded as if it was firing bullets. We haven't got anybody to work on but him and it's just his black ass."

"Somebody shot him, and it wasn't with any blank gun," the homicide lieutenant said.

"Well, goddammit, go ahead and find out who did it!" the chief roared. "You're on homicide; that's your job."

"Why not one of the Moslems," the deputy commissioner offered helpfully. "They were on the scene, and these teenage gangsters always carry guns."

There was a moment of silence while they considered this.

"What do you think, Jones?" the chief asked Grave Digger. "Do you think there was any connection between Pickens and the Moslems."

"It's like I said before," Grave Digger said. "It didn't look to me like it. The way I figure it, those teenagers gathered about the corpse directly after the shooting, like everybody else was doing. And when Ed began shooting, they all ran together, like everybody else. I see no reason to believe that Pickens even knows them."

"That's what I gathered too," the chief said disappointedly.

"But this is Harlem," Grave Digger amended. "Nobody knows all the connections here."

"Futhermore, we don't have but one of them and that one isn't carrying any gun," Anderson said. "And you've heard Haggerty's report on the statement he took from the bartender and the manager of the Dew Drop Inn. Both Pickens and the other man resented Galen making passes at the colored women. And none of the Moslem gang were even there at the time."

"It could have been some other man feeling the same way," Grave Digger said. "He might have seen Pickens shooting at Galen and thought he'd get in a shot too."

"These people," the chief said. "Okay, Jones, you begin work on that angle and see what you can dig up. But keep it from the press."

As Grave Digger started to walk away, Coffin Ed fell in beside him.

"Not you, Johnson," the chief said. "You go home."

Both Grave Digger and Coffin Ed turned and faced the silence.

"Am I under suspension?" Coffin Ed asked in a grating voice.

"For the rest of the night anyway," the chief said. "I want you both to report to the commissioner's office at nine o'clock tomorrow morning. Jones, you go ahead with your investigation. You know Harlem, you know where to go, who to see." He turned to Anderson. "Have you got a man to work with him?"

"Haggerty," Anderson offered.

"I'll work alone," Grave Digger said.

"Don't take any chances," the chief said. "If you need help, just holler. Bear down hard. I don't give a goddamn how many heads you crack; I'll back you up. Just don't kill any more juveniles."

Grave Digger turned and walked with Coffin Ed to their car.

"Drop me at the Independent Subway," Coffin Ed said.

Both of them lived in Jamacia and rode the E-train when they didn't use the car.

"I saw it coming," Grave Digger said.

"If it had happened earlier I could have taken my daughter to a movie," Coffin Ed said. "I see so little of her it's getting so I hardly know her."

6.

"LET HER loose now," Sheik said.

Sissie let her go.

"I'll kill him!" Sugartit raved in a choked voice. "I'll kill him for that!"

"Kill who?" Sheik asked, scowling at her.

"My father. I hate him. The ugly bastard. I'll steal his pistol and shoot him."

"Don't talk like that," Sissie said. "That's no way to talk about your father."

"I hate him, the dirty cop!"

Inky looked up from filing the handcuffs. Sonny stared at her.

"Shut up," Sissie said.

"Let her go ahead and croak him," Sheik said.

"Stop picking on her," Sissie said.

Choo-Choo said, "They won't do nothing to her for it. All she's got to say is her old man beat her all the time and they'll start crying and talking 'bout what a poor mistreated girl she is. They'll take one look at Coffin Ed and believe her."

"They'll give her a medal," Sheik said.

"Those old welfare biddies will find her a fine family to live with. She'll have everything she wants. She won't have to do nothing but eat and sleep and go to the movies and ride around in a big car," Choo-Choo elaborated.

Sugartit flung herself across the foot of the bed and burst into loud sobbing.

"It'll save us the trouble," Sheik said.

Sissie's eyes widened. "You wouldn't!" she said.

"You want to bet we wouldn't."

"If you keep on talking like that I'm going to quit."

Sheik gave her a threatening look. "Quit what?"

"Quit the Moslems."

"The only way you can quit the Moslems is like Caleb quit," Sheik said.

"If I'd ever thought that poor little Caleb—"

Sheik cut her off. "I'll kill you myself."

"Aw, Sheik, she don't mean nothing," Choo-Choo said nervously. "Why don't you light up a couple of sticks and let us Islamites fly to Mecca."

"And let the cops smell it when they shake us down and take us all in. Where are your brains at?"

"We can go up on the roof."

"There're cops on the roof too."

"On the fire escape then. We can close the window."

Sheik gave it grave consideration. "Okay, on the fire escape. I ain't got but two left and we got to get rid of them anyway."

"I'm going to look and see where the cops is at by now," Choo-Choo said, putting on his smoked glasses.

"Take those cheaters off," Sheik said. "You want the cops to identify you?"

"Aw hell, Sheik, they couldn't tell me from nobody else. Half the cats in Harlem wear their smoke cheaters all night long."

"Go 'head and take a gander at the avenue. We ain't got all night," Sheik said.

Choo-Choo started climbing out the window.

At that moment the links joining the handcuffs separated beneath Inky's file with a small clinking sound.

"Sheik, I've got 'em filed in two," Inky said triumphantly. "Let's see."

Sonny stood up and stretched his arms apart.

"Who's he?" Sissie asked as though she'd noticed him for the first time.

"He's our captive," Sheik said.

"I ain't no captive," Sonny said. "I just come with you 'cause you said you was gonna hide me."

Sissie looked bigeyed at the severed handcuffs dangling from his wrists.

"What did he do?" she asked.

"He's the gangster who killed the syndicate boss," Sheik said.

Sugartit stopped sobbing abruptly and rolled over and looked up at Sonny through wide wet eyes.

"Was that who he is?" Sissie asked in an awed tone. "The man who was killed, I mean."

"Sure, didn't you know," Sheik said.

"I done told you I didn't kill him," Sonny said.

"He claims he had a blank gun," Sheik said. "He's just trying to build up his defense. But the cops know better."

"It was a blank gun," Sonny said.

"What did he kill him for?" Sissie asked.

"They're having a gang war and he got assigned by the Brooklyn mob to make the hit."

"Oh, go to hell," Sissie said.

"I ain't killed nobody," Sonny said.

"Shut up," Sheik said. "Captives ain't allowed to talk."

"I'm getting tired of that stuff," Sonny said.

Sheik looked at him threateningly. "You want us to turn you over to the cops."

Sonny back-tracked quickly. "Naw, Sheik, but hell, ain't no need of taking advantage of me—"

Choo-Choo stuck his head in the window and cut him off, "Cops is out here like white on rice. Ain't nothing but cops."

"Where they at now?" Sheik asked.

"They're everywhere, but right now they's taking the house

two doors down. They got all kinds of spotlights turned on the front of the house and cops is walking around down in the street with machine guns. We better hurry if we're going to move the prisoner."

"Keep cool, fool," Sheik said. "Take a look at the roof."

"Praise Allah," Choo-Choo said, backing away on his hands and knees.

"Get off that coat and shirt," Sheik ordered Sonny.

When Sonny had stripped to his underwear shirt, Sheik looked at him and said, "Nigger, you sure are black. When you was a baby your mama must'a had to chalk your mouth to tell where to stick it."

"I ain't no blacker than Inky," Sonny said defensively.

"I ain't in that," Inky said.

Sheik grinned at him derisively. "You didn't have no trouble, did you, Inky? Your mama used luminous paint on you."

"Come on, man, I'm getting cold," Sonny said.

"Keep your pants on," Sheik said. "Ladies present."

He hung Sonny's coat with his own clothes on the wire line behind the curtain and threw the shirt in the corner. Then he tossed Sonny an old faded red shaker knit turtle-neck sweater.

"Pull the sleeve down over the irons and put on that there overcoat," he directed, indicating the old army coat he'd taken from the janitor.

"It's too hot," Sonny protested.

"You gonna do what I say, or do I have to slug you?"

Sonny put on the coat.

Sheik then took a pair of leather driving gauntlets from his pasteboard suitcase beneath the bed and handed them to Sonny too.

"What am I gonna do with these?" Sonny asked.

"Just put them on and shut up, fool," Sheik said.

He then took a long bamboo pole from behind the bed and began passing it through the window. On one end was attached a frayed felt pennant of the New York Giants baseball team.

Choo-Choo came down the fire escape in time to take the pole and lean it against the ladder.

"Ain't no cops on this roof yet but the roof down where they's shaking down is lousy with 'em," he reported.

His face was shiny with sweat and the whites of his eyes had begun to grow.

"Don't you chicken out on me now," Sheik said.

"I just needs some pot to steady my nerves."

"Okay, we're going to blow two now." Sheik turned to Sonny and said, "Outside, boy."

Sonny gave him a look, hesitated, then climbed out on the fire escape landing.

"Let me come too," Sissie said.

Sugartit sat up with sudden interest and pulled down her skirt.

"I want both you little jailbaits to stay right here in this room and don't move," Sheik ordered in a hard voice, then turned to Inky, "You come on, Inky, I'm gonna need you."

Inky joined the others on the fire escape. Sheik came last and closed the window. They squatted in a circle. The landing was crowded.

Sheik took two limp cigarets from the roll of his sweatshirt and stuck them into his mouth.

"Bombers!" Choo-Choo exclaimed. "You've been holding out on us."

"Give me some fire and less of your lip," Sheik said.

Choo-Choo flipped a dollar lighter and lit both cigarets. Sheik sucked the smoke deep into his lungs, then he passed one of the sticks to Inky.

"You and Choo-Choo take halvers and me and the captive will split this one."

Sonny raised both gloved hands in a pushing gesture. "Pass me. That gage done got me into more trouble now than I can get out of."

"You're chicken," Sheik said contemptuously, sucking another puff. He swallowed back the smoke each time it started up from his lungs. His face swelled and began darkening with blood as the drug took hold. His eyes became dilated and his nostrils flared.

"Man, if I had my heater I bet I could shoot that sergeant down there dead between the eyes," he said.

The marijuana cigaret was stuck to his bottom lip and dangled up and down when he talked.

"What I'd rather have me is one of those hard-shooting

long barrelled thirty-eights like Grave Digger and Coffin Ed have got," Choo-Choo said. "Them heaters can kill a rock. Only I'd want me a silencer on it and I could sit here and pick off any mother-raper I wanted. But I wouldn't shoot nobody unless he was a big shot or the chief of police or somebody like that."

"You're talking about rathers, what you'd rather have; me, I'm talking about facts," Sheik said, the cigaret dangling from his lips.

"What you're talking about will get you burnt up in Sing-Sing if you don't watch out," Choo-Choo said.

"What you mean!" Sheik said, jumping to his feet threateningly. "You're going to make me throw your ass off this fire escape."

Choo-Choo jumped to his feet too and backed against the rail. "Throw whose ass off where. This ain't Inky you're talking to. My ass ain't made of chicken feathers."

Inky scrambled to his feet in between them. "What about the captive, Sheik," he asked in alarm.

"Damn the captive!" Sheik raved and whipped out a bone-handled knife, shaking open the six inch blade with the same motion.

"Don't cut 'im!" Inky cried.

He knocked Inky into the iron steps with a backhanded slap and grabbed a handful of Choo-Choo's sweatshirt collar.

"You blab and I'll cut your mother-raping throat," he said. Violence surged through him like runaway blood.

Choo-Choo's eyes turned three-quarters white and sweat popped out on his dark brown skin like a fever breaking.

"I didn't mean nothing, Sheik," he whined desperately, talking low. "You know I didn't mean nothing. A man can talk 'bout his rathers, can't he?"

The violence receded but Sheik was still gripped in a murderous compulsion.

"If I thought you'd pigeon I'd kill you."

"You know I ain't gonna pigeon, Sheik. You know me better than that."

Sheik let go his collar. Choo-Choo took a deep sighing breath.

Inky straightened up and rubbed his bruised shin. "You done made me lose the stick," he complained.

"Hell with the stick," Sheik said.

"That's what I mean," Sonny said. "This here gage they sells now will make you cut your own mama's throat. They must be mixing it with loco weed or somethin'."

"Shut up!" Sheik said, still holding the open knife in his hand. "I ain't gonna tell you no more."

Sonny cast a look at the knife and said, "I ain't saying nothing."

"You better not," Sheik said. Then he turned to Inky and said, "Inky, you take the captive up on the roof and you and him start flying Caleb's pigeons. You, Sonny, when the cops come you tell them your name is Caleb Bowee and you're just trying to teach your pigeons how to fly at night. You got that."

"Yeah," Sonny said skeptically.

"You know how to make pigeons fly?"

Sonny hesitated. "Chunk rocks at 'em?"

"Hell, nigger, your brain ain't big as a mustard seed. You can't chunk no rocks up there with all these cops about. What you got to do is take this pole and wave the end with the flag at 'em every time they try to light."

Sonny looked at the bamboo pole skeptically. "S'posen they fly away and don't come back."

"They ain't going nowhere. They just fly in circles trying all the time to get back into the coop." Sheik doubled over suddenly and started laughing. "Pigeons ain't got no sense, man."

The rest of them just looked at him.

Finally Inky asked, "What you want me to do?"

Sheik straightened up quickly and stopped laughing. "You guard the captive and see that he don't escape."

"Oh!" Inky said. After a moment he asked, "What I'm gonna tell the cops when they ask me what I'm doin'."

"Hell, you tell the cops Caleb is teaching you how to train pigeons."

Inky bent over and started rubbing his shins again. Without looking up he said, "You reckon the cops gonna fall for that,

Sheik? You reckon they gonna be crazy enough to believe anybody's gonna be flying pigeons with all this going on all around here?"

"Hell, these is white cops," Sheik said contemptuously. "They believe spooks are crazy anyway. You and Sonny just act kind of simpleminded. They going to swallow it like it's chocolate ice cream. They ain't going to do nothing but kick you in the ass and laugh like hell about how crazy spooks are. They gonna go home and tell their old ladies and everybody they see about two simpleminded spooks up on the roof teaching pigeons how to fly at night all during the biggest dragnet they ever had in Harlem. You see if they don't."

Inky kept on rubbing his shin. "It ain't that I doubt you, Sheik, but s'posen they don't believe it."

"Goddammit, go ahead and do what I told you and don't stand there arguing with me," Sheik said, hit by another squall of fury. "I'd take me one look at you and this nigger here and I'd believe it myself, and I ain't even no gray cop."

Inky turned reluctantly and started up the stairs toward the roof. Sonny gave another sidelong look at Sheik's open knife and started to follow.

"Wait a minute, simple, don't forget the pole," Sheik said. "I've told you not to try chunking rocks at those pigeons. You might kill one and then you'd have to eat it." He doubled over laughing at his joke.

Sonny picked up the pole with a sober face and climbed slowly after Inky.

"Come on," Sheik said to Choo-Choo, "open the window and let's get back inside."

Before turning his back and bending to open the window, Choo-Choo said, "Listen, Sheik, I didn't mean nothing by that."

"Forget it," Sheik said.

Sissie and Sugartit were sitting silently side by side on the bed, looking frightened and dejected. Sugartit had stopped crying but her eyes were red and her cheeks stained.

"Jesus Christ, you'd think this is a funeral," Sheik said.

No one replied. Choo-Choo fidgeted from one foot to the other.

"I want you chicks to wipe those sad looks off your face,"

Sheik said. "We got to look like we're balling and ain't got a thing to worry about when the cops get here."

"You go ahead and ball by yourself," Sissie said.

Sheik lunged forward and slapped her over on her side.

She got up without a word and walked to the window.

"If you go out that window I'll throw you down on the street," Sheik threatened.

She stood looking out the window with her back turned and didn't answer.

Sugartit sat quietly on the edge of the bed and trembled.

"Hell," Sheik said disgustedly and flopped lengthwise on the bed behind Sugartit.

She got up and went to stand in the window beside Sissie.

"Come on, Choo-Choo, to hell with those bitches," Sheik said. "Let's decide what to do with the captive."

"Now you're getting down to the gritty," Choo-Choo said enthusiastically, straddling a chair. "You got any plans?"

"Sure. Give me a butt."

Choo-Choo fished two Camels from a squashed package in his sweatshirt roll and lit them, passing one to Sheik.

"This square weed on top of gage makes you crazy," he said.

"Man, my head already feels like it's going to pop open, it's so full of ideas," Sheik said. "If I had me a real mob like Dutch Schultz I could take over Harlem with the ideas I got. All I need is just the mob."

"Hell, you and me could do it alone," Choo-Choo said.

"We'd need some arms and stuff, some real factory-made heaters and a couple of machine guns and maybe some pine-apples."

"If we croaked Grave Digger and the Monster we'd have two real cool heaters to start off with," Choo-Choo suggested.

"We ain't going to mess with those studs until after we're organized," Sheik said. "Then maybe we can import some talent to make the hit. But we'd need some dough."

"Hell, we can hold the prisoner for ransom," Choo-Choo said.

"Who'd ransom that chickenshit nigger," Sheik said. "I bet his own mama wouldn't even pay to get him back."

"He can ransom hisself," Choo-Choo said. "He got a shine parlor, ain't he. Shine parlors make good dough. Maybe he's got a chariot too."

"Hell, I knew all along he was valuable," Sheik said. "That's why I had us snatch him."

"We can take over his shine parlor," Choo-Choo said.

"I got some other plans too," Sheik said. "Maybe we can sell him to the Stars of David for some zip guns. They got lots of zip guns and they're scared to use them."

"We could do that or we could swap him to the Porto Rican Bandits for Burrhead. We promised Burrhead we'd pay his ransom and they been saying if we don't hurry up and get 'im they're gonna cut his throat."

"Let 'em cut the black mother-raper's throat," Sheik said. "That chicken-hearted bastard ain't no good to us."

"I tell you what, Sheik," Choo-Choo said exuberantly. "We could put him in a sack like them ancient cats like the Dutchman and them used to do and throw him into the Harlem River. I've always wanted to put some bastard into a sack."

"You know how to put a mother-raper into a sack?" Sheik asked.

"Sure, you—"

"Shut up, I'm gonna tell you how. You knock the mother-raper unconscious first; that's to keep him from jumping about. Then you put a noose with a slipknot 'round his neck. Then you double him up into a Z and tie the other end of the wire around his knees. Then when you put him in the gunny sack you got to be sure it's big enough to give him some space to move around in. When the mother-raper wakes up and tries to straighten out he chokes himself to death. Ain't nobody killed 'im. The mother-raper has just committed suicide." Sheik rolled over on the bed laughing.

"You got to tie his hands behind his back first," Choo-Choo said.

Sheik stopped laughing and his face became livid with fury. "Who don't know that, fool!" he shouted. " 'Course you got to tie his hands behind his back. You trying to tell me I don't know how to put a mother-raper into a sack. I'll put you into a sack."

"I know you know how, Sheik," Choo-Choo said hastily.

"I just didn't want you to forget nothing when we put the captive in a sack."

"I ain't going to forget nothing," Sheik said.

"When we gonna put him in a sack?" Choo-Choo asked. "I know where to find a sack."

"Okay, we'll put him in a sack just soon as the police finish here, then we take him down and leave him in the basement," Sheik said.

7.

GRAVE DIGGER flashed his badge at the two harness bulls guarding the door and pushed inside the Dew Drop Inn.

The joint was jammed with colored people who'd seen the big white man die, but nobody seemed to be worrying about it.

The juke box was giving out with a stomp version of *Big Legged Woman*. Saxophones were pleading; the horns were teasing; the bass was patting; the drums were chatting; the piano was catting, laying and playing the jive, and a husky female voice was shouting:

> *". . . you can feel my thigh*
> *but don't you feel up high."*

Happy-tail women were bouncing out their dresses on the high bar stools.

Grave Digger trod on the sawdust sprinkled over the blood-stains that wouldn't wash off and parked on the stool at the end of the bar.

Big Smiley was serving drinks with his left arm in a sling.

The white manager, with the sleeves of his tan silk shirt rolled up, was helping.

Big Smiley shuffled down the wet footing and showed Grave Digger most of his big yellow teeth.

"Is you drinking, chief, or just sitting and thinking?"

"How's the wing?" Grave Digger asked.

"Favorable. It wasn't cut deep enough to do no real damage."

The manager came down and said, "If I'd thought there was going to be any trouble I'd have called the police right away."

"What do you calculate as trouble in this joint?" Grave Digger asked.

The manager reddened. "I meant about the white man getting killed."

"Just what started all the trouble in here?"

"It wasn't exactly what you'd call trouble, chief," Big Smiley said. "It was only a drunk attacked one of my white customers with his chiv and naturally I had to protect my customer."

"What did he have against the white man?"

"Nothing, chief. Not a single thing. He was setting over there drinking one shot of rye after another and looking at the white man standing here tending to his own business. Then he gets red-eyed drunk and his evil tells him to get up and cut the man. That's all. And naturally I couldn't let him do that."

"He must have had some reason. You're not trying to tell me he got up and attacked the man without any reason whatever."

"Nawsuh, chief, I'll bet my life he ain't had no reason at all to wanta cut the man. You know how our folks is, chief; he was just one of those evil niggers that when they get drunk they start hating white folks and get to remembering all the bad things white folks have ever done to them. That's all. More than likely he was mad at some white man that done something bad to him twenty years ago down South and he just wanted to take it out on this white man in here. It's like I told that white detective who was in here, this white man was standing here at the bar by hisself and that nigger just figgered with all these colored folks in here he could cut him and get away with it."

"Maybe. What's his name?"

"I ain't never seen that nigger before tonight, chief; I don't know what is his name."

A customer called from up the bar, "Hey, boss, how about a little service up here."

"If you want me, Jones, just holler," the manager said, moving off to serve the customer.

"Yeah," Grave Digger said, then asked Big Smiley, "Who was the woman?"

"There she is," Big Smiley said, nodding toward a booth.

Grave Digger turned his head and scanned her.

The black lady in the pink jersey dress and red silk stockings was back in her original seat in a booth surrounded by three workers.

"It wasn't on account of her," Big Smiley added.

Grave Digger slid from his stool and went over to her booth and flashed his badge. "I want to talk to you."

She looked at the gold badge and complained, "Why don't you folks leave me alone. I done already told a white cop everything I know about that shooting, which ain't nothing."

"Come on, I'll buy you a drink," Grave Digger said.

"Well, in that case," she said and went with him to the bar.

At Grave Digger's order Big Smiley poured her a shot of gin grudgingly and Grave Digger said, "Fill it up."

Big Smiley filled the glass and stayed there to listen.

"How well did you know the white man?" Grave Digger asked the lady.

"I didn't know him at all. I'd just seen him around here once or twice."

"Doing what?"

"Just chasing."

"Alone?"

"Yeah."

"Did you see him pick up anyone?"

"Naw, he was one of those particular kind. He never saw nothing he liked."

"Who was the colored man who tried to cut him?"

"How the hell should I know?"

"He wasn't a relative of yours?"

"A relation of mine. I should hope not."

"Just exactly what did he say to the white man when he started to attack him?"

"I don't remember exactly; he just said something 'bout him messing around with his gal."

"That's the same thing the other man, Sonny Pickens, accused him of."

"I don't know nothing about that."

He thanked her and wrote down her name and address.

She went back to her seat.

He turned back to Big Smiley. "What did Pickens and the white man argue about?"

"They ain't had no argument, chief. Not in here. It wasn't on account of nothing that happened in here that he was shot."

"It was on account of something," Grave Digger said. "Robbery doesn't figure, and people in Harlem don't kill for revenge."

"Nawsuh, leastwise they don't shoot."

"More than likely they'll throw acid or hot lye," Grave Digger said.

"Nawsuh, not on no white gennelman."

"So what else is there left but a woman," Grave Digger said.

"Nawsuh," Big Smiley contradicted flatly. "You know better'n that, chief. A colored woman don't consider diddling with a white man as being unfaithful. They don't consider it no more than just working in service, only they is getting better paid and the work is less straining. 'Sides which, the hours is shorter. And they old men don't neither. Both she and her old man figger it's like finding money in the street. And I don't mean no cruisers neither; I means church people and christians and all the rest."

"How old are you, Smiley?" Grave Digger asked.

"I be forty-nine come December seventh."

"You're talking about old times, son. These young colored men don't go for that slavery time deal anymore."

"Shucks, chief, you just kidding. This is old Smiley. I got dirt on these women in Harlem ain't never been plowed. Shucks, you and me both can put our finger on high society colored ladies here who got their whole rep just by going with some big important white man. And their old men is cashing in on it too; makes them important too to have their old ladies going with some bigshot gray. Shucks, even a hard working nigger wouldn't shoot a white man if he come home and found him in bed with his old lady with his pants down. He might whup his old lady just to show her who was boss, after he done took the money 'way from her, but he wouldn't sure 'nough hurt her like he'd do if he caught her screwing some other nigger."

"I wouldn't bet on it," Grave Digger said.

"Have it your own way, chief, but I still think you're barking up the wrong tree. Lissen, the only way I figger a colored man in Harlem gonna kill a white man is in a fight. He'll draw his chiv if he getting his ass whupped and maybe stab him to death. But I'll bet my life ain't no nigger up here gonna shoot down no white man in cold blood—no important white gennelman like him."

"Would the killer have to know he was important?"

"He'd know it," Big Smiley said positively.

"You knew him," Grave Digger said.

"Nawsuh, not to say knew him. He come in here two or three times before but I didn't know his name."

"You expect me to believe he came in here two or three times and you didn't find out who he was?"

"I didn't mean exactly I didn't know his name," Big Smiley hemmed. "But I'se telling you, chief, ain't no leads 'round here, that's for sure."

"You're going to have to tell me more than that, son," Grave Digger said in a flat, toneless voice.

Big Smiley looked at him; then suddenly he leaned across the bar and said in a low voice, "Try at Bucky's, chief."

"Why Bucky's?"

"I seen him come in here once with a pimp what hangs 'round in Bucky's."

"What's his name?"

"I don't recollect his name, chief. They driv up in his car and just stopped for a minute like they was looking for somebody and went out and driv away."

"Don't play with me," Grave Digger said with a sudden show of anger. "This ain't the movies; this is real. A white man has been killed in Harlem and Harlem is my beat. I'll take you down to the station and turn a dozen white cops loose on you and they'll work you over until the black comes off."

"Name's Ready Belcher, chief, but I don't want nobody to know I told you," Big Smiley said in a whisper. "I don't want no trouble with that starker."

"Ready," Grave Digger said and got down from his stool.

He didn't know much about Ready other than he operated uptown on the swank side of Harlem above 145th Street which the residents called Washington Heights.

He drove up to the 154th Street precinct station at the corner of Amsterdam Avenue and asked for his friend, Bill Cresus. Bill was a colored detective on the vice squad. No one knew where Bill was at the time. He left word for Bill to contact him at Bucky's if he called within the hour. Then he got into his car and coasted down the sharp incline to St. Nicholas Avenue and turned south down the lesser incline past 149th Street.

Outwardly it was a quiet neighborhood of private houses and five and six story apartment buildings flanking the wide black paved street. But the houses had been split up into bed-size one room kitchenettes, renting for $25 weekly, at the disposal of frantic couples who wished to shack up for a season. And behind the respectable looking façades of the apartment buildings were the plush flesh cribs and poppy pads and circus tents of Harlem.

The excitement of the dragnet hadn't reached this far and the street was comparatively empty.

He coasted to a stop before a sedate basement entrance. Four steps below street level was a black door with a shiny brass knocker in the shape of three musical notes. Above it red neon lights spelled out the word B U C K Y ' S.

He felt strange to be alone. The last time had been when Coffin Ed was in the hospital after the acid throwing. The memory of it made his head tight with anger and it took a special effort to keep his temper under wraps.

He pushed and the door opened.

People sat at white-clothed tables beneath pink-shaded wall lights in a long narrow room, eating fried chicken daintily with their fingers. There was a white party of six, several colored couples, and two colored men with white women. They looked well-dressed and reasonably clean.

The walls behind them were covered with innumerable

pink-stained small pencil portraits of all the great and the near-great who had ever lived in Harlem. Musicians led nine to one.

The hat check girl stationed in a cubicle beside the entrance stuck out her hand with a supercilious look.

Grave Digger kept on his hat and strode down the narrow aisle between the tables.

A chubby pianist with shining black skin and a golden smile dressed in a tan tweed sport jacket and white silk sport shirt open at the throat sat at a baby grand piano wedged between the last table and the circular bar. Soft white light spilled on his partly bald head while he played nocturnes with a bedroom touch.

He gave Grave Digger an apprehensive look and got up and followed him to the semi-darkness of the bar.

"I hope you're not on business, Digger, I pay to keep this place off-limits for cops," he said in a fluttery voice.

Grave Digger's gaze circled the bar. Its high stools were inhabited by a big dark-haired white man; two slim young colored men; a short heavy-set white man with blond crew cut hair; two dark brown women dressed in white silk evening gowns, flanking a chocolate dandy in a box back double-breasted tuxedo sporting a shoe-string dubonet bow; and a high yellow waitress with a tin tray waiting to be served. It was presided over by another tall slim ebony young man.

"I'm just looking around, Bucky," Grave Digger said. "Just looking for a break."

"Many folks have found a break in here," Bucky said suggestively.

"I don't doubt it."

"But maybe that's not the kind of break you're looking for."

"I'm looking for a break on a case. An important white man was shot to death over on Lenox Avenue a short time ago."

Bucky gestured with lotioned hands. His manicured nails flashed in the dim light.

"What has that to do with us here? Nobody ever gets hurt in here. Everything is smooth and quiet. You can see for yourself. Genteel people dining in leisure. Fine food. Soft music.

Low lights and laughter. Doesn't look like business for the police in this respectable atmosphere."

In the pause following, one of the marcelled ebonies was heard saying in a lilting voice, "I positively did not even look at her man, and she upped and knocked me over the head with a whiskey bottle."

"These black bitches are so violent," his companion said.

"And strong, honey."

Grave Digger smiled sourly.

"The man who was killed was a patron of yours," he said. "Name of Ulysses Galen."

"My God, Digger, I don't know the names of all the ofays who come into my place," Bucky said. "I just play for them and try to make them happy."

"I believe you," Grave Digger said. "Galen was seen about town with Ready. Does that stir your memory?"

"Ready!" Bucky exclaimed innocently. "He hardly ever comes in here. Who gave you that notion?"

"The hell he doesn't," Grave Digger said. "He panders out of here."

"You hear that!" Bucky appealed to the barman in a shrill horrified voice, then caught himself as the silence from the diners reached his sensitive ears. With hushed indignation he added, "This flatfoot comes in here and accuses me of harboring panderers."

"A little bit of that goes a long way, son," Grave Digger said in his flat toneless voice.

"Oh, that man's an ogre, Bucky," the barman said. "You go back to your entertaining and I'll see what he wants." He switched over to the bar, put his hands on his hips and looked down at Grave Digger with a haughty air. "And just what can we do for you, you mean rude grumpy man."

The white men at the bar laughed.

Bucky turned and started off.

Grave Digger caught him by the arm and pulled him back. "Don't make me get rough, son," he warned.

"Don't you dare manhandle me," Bucky said in a low tense whisper, his whole chubby body quivering with indignation. "I don't have to take that from you. I'm covered."

The bartender backed away, shaking himself. "Don't let

him hurt Bucky," he appealed to the white men in a frightened voice.

"Maybe I can help you," the white man with the blond crew cut said to Grave Digger. "You're a detective, aren't you?"

"Yeah," Grave Digger said, holding on to Bucky. "A white man was killed in Harlem tonight and I'm looking for the killer."

The white man's eyebrows went up an inch.

"Do you expect to find him in here?"

"I'm following a lead, is all. The man has been seen with a pimp called Ready Belcher who hangs out here."

The white man's eyebrows subsided.

"Oh, Ready. I know him. But he's merely—"

Bucky cut him off, "You don't have to tell him anything, you're protected in here."

"Sure," the white man said. "That's what the officer is trying to do, protect us all."

"He's right," one of the evening gowned colored women said. "If Ready has killed some trick he was steering to Reba's the chair's too good for him."

"Shut your mouth, woman," the barman whispered fiercely.

The muscles in Grave Digger's face began to jump as he let go of Bucky and stood up with his heels hooked into the rungs of the barstool and leaned over the bar. He caught the barman by the front of his red silk shirt as he was trying to dance away. The shirt ripped down the seam with a ragged sound but enough held for him to jerk the barman close to the bar.

"You got too goddamned much to say, Tarbelle," he said in a thick cottony voice, and slapped the barman spinning across the circular enclosure with the palm of his open hand.

"He didn't have to do that," the first woman said.

Grave Digger turned on her and said thickly, "And you, little sister, you and me are going to see Reba."

"Reba!" the woman said. "Who's she?" Turning to her companion, she asked, "You know any Reba."

"Reba?" her companion replied. "Do I know anybody named Reba. Lord no."

Grave Digger stepped down from his high stool.

"Cut that Aunt Jemima routine and get up off your ass," he said thickly. "Or I'll take my pistol and break off your teeth."

The two white men stared at him as though at a dangerous animal escaped from the zoo.

"You mean that?" the woman said.

"I mean it," he said.

She scrunched from the stool and said, "Gimme my coat, Jule."

The chocolate dandy took a coat from the top of the juke box behind them.

"That's putting it on rather thick," the blond white man protested in a reasonable voice.

"I'm just a cop," Grave Digger said thickly. "If you white people insist on coming up to Harlem where you force colored people to live in vice-and-crime ridden slums, it's my job to see that you are safe."

The white man turned bright red.

8.

THE SERGEANT knocked at the door. He was flanked by two uniformed cops and a corporal.

There was another searching party led by another sergeant at the door across the hall.

Other cops were in the corridors all the way down. They were starting at the bottom, working up, and sealing off the area they'd covered.

"Come in," Granny called in a querulous voice. "The door ain't locked." She bit the stem of her corncob pipe with toothless gums.

The sergeant and his party entered the small kitchen. It was crowded.

At sight of the very old woman working innocently at her darning, the sergeant started to remove his cap, then remembered he was on duty and kept it on.

"You don't lock your door, grandma?" he observed.

Granny looked at the cops over the rims of her ancient spectacles and her old fingers went lax on the darning egg.

"Nawsuh, Ah ain't got nuthin' for nobody to steal and ain't nobody want nuthin' else from an old 'oman like me."

The sergeant's beady blue eyes scanned the kitchen.

"You keep this place mighty clean, grandma," he remarked in surprise.

"Yessuh, it don't kill a body to keep clean and my old missy used to always say de cleaness is next to the Goddess."

Her old milky eyes held a terrified question she couldn't ask and her thin old body began to tremble.

"You mean goodness," the sergeant said.

"Nawsuh, Ah means Goddess; Ah know what she said."

"She means cleanliness is next to Godliness," the corporal interposed.

"The professor," one of the cops said.

Granny pursed her lips. "Ah know what my missy said; Goddess she said."

"Were you in slavery?" the sergeant asked as though struck suddenly by the thought.

The others stared at her with sudden interest.

"Ah don't rightly know, suh. Ah 'spect so though."

"How old are you?"

Her lips moved soundlessly; she seemed to be trying to remember.

"She must be all of a hundred," the professor said.

She couldn't stop her body from trembling and slowly it got worse.

"What for you white 'licemen wants with me, suh?" she finally asked.

The sergeant noticed that she was trembling and said re-assuringly, "We ain't after you, grandma; we're looking for an escaped prisoner and some teenage gangsters."

"Gangsters!"

Her spectacles slipped down on her nose and her hands shook as though she had the palsy.

"They belong to a gang in this neighborhood that calls itself Real Cool Moslems."

She went from terrified to scandalized. "We ain't no heathen in here, suh," she said indignantly. "We be Godfearing Christians."

The cops laughed.

"They're not real Moslems," the sergeant said. "They just call themselves that. One of them who's older than the rest, named Sonny Pickens, killed a white man outside on the street."

The darning dropped unnoticed from Granny's nerveless fingers. The corncob pipe wobbled in her puckered mouth; the professor looked at it with morbid fascination.

"A white man! Merciful hebens!" she exclaimed in a quavering voice. "What's this wicked world coming to?"

"Nobody knows," the sergeant said, then his manner changed abruptly. "Well, let's get down to business, grandma. What's your name?"

"Bowee, suh, but e'body calls me Granny."

"Bowee. How you spell that, grandma?"

"Ah don't rightly know, suh. Hit's just short for boll weevil. My old missy name me that. They say the boll weevil was mighty bad the year Ah was born."

"What about your husband, didn't he have a name?"

"Ah neber had no regular 'usban, suh. Just whosoever was thar."

"You got any children?"

"Jesus Christ, sarge," the professor said. "Her youngest child would be sixty years old."

The two cops laughed; the sergeant reddened sheepishly.

"Who lives here with you, Granny?" the sergeant continued.

Her bony frame stiffened beneath her faded Mother Hubbard. The corncob pipe fell into her lap and rolled unnoticed to the floor. The cops came to attention.

"Just me and mah grandchile, Caleb, suh," she said in a forced voice. "And Ah rents a room to two workin' boys; but they be good boys and don't neber bother nobody."

The cops grew sudden speculative looks.

"Now this grandchild, Caleb, grandma—" the sergeant began cunningly.

"He might be mah great-grandchile, suh," she interrupted.

He frowned. "Great, then. Where is he now?"

"You mean right now, suh?"

"Yeah, grandma, right this minute."

"He at work in a bowling alley downtown, suh."

"How long has he been at work?"

"He left right after supper, suh. We gennaly eats supper at six 'clock."

"And he has a regular job in this bowling alley?"

"Nawsuh, hit's just for t'night, suh. He goes to school— Ah don't rightly 'member the number of his new P.S."

"Where is this bowling alley where he's working tonight?"

"Ah don't know, suh. Ah guess youall 'ill have to ast Samson. He one of mah roomers."

"Samson, yeah." The sergeant stored it in his memory. "And you haven't seen Caleb since supper—about seven o'clock, say?"

"Ah don't know what time it was but it war right after supper."

"And when he left here he went directly to work?"

"Yassuh, you find him right dar on the job. He a good boy and always mind me what Ah say."

"And your roomers, where are they?"

"They is in they room, suh. Hit's in the front. They got visitors with 'em."

"Visitors?"

"Gals."

"Oh!" Then to his assistants he said, "Come on."

They went through the middle room like hounds on a hot scent. The sergeant tried the handle to the front room door without knocking, found it locked and hammered angrily.

"Who's that?" Sheik asked.

"The police."

Sheik unlocked the door. The cops rushed in. Sheik's eyes glittered at them.

"What the hell you keep your door locked for?" the sergeant asked.

"We didn't want to be disturbed."

Four pairs of eyes quickly scanned the room.

Two teenage colored girls sat side by side on the bed, leafing through a colored picture magazine. Another youth stood looking out the open window at the excitement on the street.

"Who the hell you think you're kidding with this phony stage setting?" the sergeant roared.

"Not you, Ace," Sheik said flippantly.

The sergeant's hand flicked out like a whip, passing inches in front of Sheik's eyes.

Sheik jumped back as though he'd been scalded.

"Jagged to the gills," the sergeant said, looking minutely about the room. His eyes lit on Choo-Choo's half-smoked package of Camel's on the table. "Dump out those fags," he ordered a cop, watching Sheik's reaction. "Never mind," he added. "The bastard's got rid of them."

He closed in on Sheik like a prizefighter and stuck his red sweaty face within a few inches of Sheik's dry freckled face. His veined blue eyes bored into Sheik's pale yellow eyes.

"Where's that A-rab costume?" he asked in a browbeating voice.

"What Arab costume? Do I look like an A-rab to you?"

"You look like a two-bit punk to me. You got the eyes of a yellow cur."

"You ain't got no prizewinning eyes yourself."

"Don't give me none of your lip, punk; I'll knock out your teeth."

"I could knock out your teeth too if I had on a sergeant's uniform and three big flatfeet backing me up."

The cops stared at him from blank shuttered faces.

"What do they call you, Mo-hammed or Nasser?" the sergeant hammered.

"They call me by my name, Samson."

"Samson what?"

"Samson Hyers."

"Don't give me that crap; we know you're one of those Moslems."

"I ain't no Moslem, I'm a cannibal."

"Oh, so you think you're a comedian."

"You the one asking the funny questions."

"What's that other punk's name?"

"Ask him."

The sergeant slapped him with his open palm with such force it sounded like a .22 calibre shot.

Sheik reeled back from the impact of the slap but kept his

feet. Blood darkened his face to the color of beef liver, on which the imprint of the sergeant's hand glowed purple red. His pale yellow eyes looked wildcat crazy. But he kept his lip buttoned.

"When I ask you a question I want you to answer it," the sergeant said.

He didn't answer.

"You hear me?"

He still didn't answer.

The sergeant loomed in front of him with both fists cocked like red meataxes.

"I want an answer."

"Yeah, I hear you," Sheik muttered sullenly.

"Frisk him," the sergeant ordered the professor, then to the other two cops said, "You and Price start shaking down this room."

The professor set to work on Sheik methodically, as though searching for lice, while the other cops started dumping dresser drawers onto the table.

The sergeant left them and turned his attention to Choo-Choo.

"What kind of Moslem are you?"

Choo-Choo started grinning and fawning like the original Uncle Tom.

"I ain't no Moslem, boss, I'se just a plain old unholy roller."

"I guess your name is Delilah."

"He-he, nawsuh, boss, but you're warm. It's Justis Broome."

All three cops looked about and grinned, and the sergeant had to clamp his jaws to keep from grinning too.

"You know these Moslems?"

"What Moslems, boss?"

"These Harlem Moslems in this neighborhood."

"Nawsuh, boss, I don't know no Moslems in Harlem."

"You think I was born yesterday? They're a neighborhood gang. Every black son of a bitch in this neighborhood knows who they are."

"Everybody 'cept me, boss."

The sergeant's palm flew out and caught Choo-Choo unexpectedly on the mouth while it was still open in a grin. It didn't rock his short thick body but his eyes rolled back whitely in their sockets. He spit blood on the floor.

"Boss, suh, please be careful with my chops, they're tender."

"I'm getting damn tired of your lying."

"Boss, I swear 'fore God, if I knowed anything 'bout them Moslems you'd be the first one I'd tell it to."

"What do you do?"

"I works, boss, yessuh."

"Doing what?"

"I helps out."

"Helps out what? You want to lose some of your pearly teeth?"

"I helps out a man who writes numbers."

"What's his name?"

"His name?"

The sergeant cocked his fists.

"Oh, you mean his name, boss. Hit's Four-Four Row."

"You call that a name?"

"Yessuh, that's what they calls him."

"What does your buddy do?"

"The same thing," Sheik said.

The sergeant wheeled on him. "You keep quiet; when I want you I'll call you." Then he said to the professor, "Can't you keep that punk quiet?"

The professor unhooked his sap. "I'll quiet him."

"I don't want you to quiet him; just keep him quiet. I got some more questions for him." Then he turned back to Choo-Choo. "When do you punks work?"

"In the morning, boss. We got to get the numbers in by noon."

"What do you do the rest of the day?"

"Go 'round and pay off."

"What if there isn't any payoff?"

"Just go 'round."

"Where's your beat?"

" 'Round here."

"Goddammit, you mean to tell me you write numbers in

this neighborhood and you don't know anything about the Moslems?"

"I swear on my mother's grave, boss, I ain't never heard of no Moslems 'round here. They must not be in this neighborhood, boss."

"What time did you leave the house tonight?"

"I ain't never left it, boss. We come here right after we et supper and ain't been out since."

"Stop lying, I saw you both when you slipped back in here a half hour ago."

"Nawsuh, boss, you musta seen somebody what looks like us 'cause we been here all the time."

The sergeant crossed to the door and flung it open. "Hey, grandma!" he called.

"Hannh?" she answered querulously from the kitchen.

"How long have these boys been in their room?"

"Hannh?"

"You have to talk louder, she can't hear you," Sissie volunteered.

Sheik and Choo-Choo gave her threatening looks.

The sergeant crossed the middle room to the kitchen door.

"How long have your roomers been back from supper?" he roared.

She looked at him from uncomprehending eyes.

"Hannh?"

"She can't hear no more," Sissie called. "She gets that way sometime."

"Hell," the sergeant said disgustedly and stormed back to Choo-Choo. "Where'd you pick up these girls?"

"We didn't pick 'em up, boss; they come here by themselves."

"You're too Goddamned innocent to be alive," the sergeant said frustratedly, then turned to the professor. "What did you find on that punk?"

"This knife."

"Hell," the sergeant said. He took it and dropped it into his pocket without a glance. "Okay, fan this other punk—Justice."

"I'll do Justice," the professor punned.

The two cops crossed glances suggestively.

They had dumped out all the drawers and turned out all the boxes and pasteboard suitcases and now they were ready for the bed.

"You gals rise and shine," one said.

The girls got up and stood uncomfortably in the center of the room.

"Find anything?" the sergeant asked.

"Nothing that I'd care even to have in my dog house," the cop said.

The sergeant began on the girls. "What's your name?" he asked Sissie.

"Sissieratta Hamilton."

"Sissie-what?"

"Sissieratta."

"Where do you live, Sissie?"

"At 2702 Seventh Avenue with my aunt and uncle, Mr. and Mrs. Coolie Dunbar."

"Ummm," he said. "And yours?" he asked Sugartit.

"Evelyn Johnson."

"Where do you live, Eve?"

"In Jamaica with my parents, Mr. and Mrs. Edward Johnson."

"It's mighty late for you to be so far from home."

"I'm going to spend the night with Sissieratta."

"How long have you girls been here?" he asked of both.

"About half an hour, more or less," Sissie replied.

"Then you saw the shooting down on the street?"

"It was over when we got here."

"Where did you come from?"

"From my house."

"You don't know if these punks have been in all evening or not."

"They were here when we got here and they said they'd been waiting here since supper. We promised to come at eight but we had to stay help my aunty and we got here late."

"Sounds too good to be true," the sergeant commented.

The girls didn't reply.

The cops finished with the bed and the talkative one said, "Nothing but stink."

"Can that talk," the sergeant said. "Grandma's clean."

"These punks aren't."

The sergeant turned to the professor. "What's on Justice besides the blindfold?"

His joke laid an egg.

"Nothing but his black," the professor said.

His joke drew a laugh.

"What do you say, shall we run 'em in?" the sergeant asked.

"Why not," the professor said. "If we haven't got space in the bullpen for everybody we can put up tents."

The sergeant wheeled suddenly on Sheik as though he'd forgotten something.

"Where's Caleb?"

"Up on the roof tending his pigeons."

All four cops froze. They stared at Sheik with those blank shuttered looks.

Finally the sergeant said carefully, "His grandma said you told her he was working in a bowling alley downtown."

"We just told her that to keep her from worrying. She don't like for him to go up on the roof at night."

"If I find you punks are holding out on me, God help you," the sergeant said in a slow sincere voice.

"Go look then," Sheik said.

The sergeant nodded to the professor. The professor climbed out of the window into the bright glare of the spotlights and began ascending the fire escape.

"What's he doing with them at night?" the sergeant asked Sheik.

"I don't know. Trying to make them lay black eggs, I suppose."

"I'm going to take you down to the station and have a private talk with you, punk," the sergeant said. "You're one punk who needs talking to privately."

The professor came down from the roof and called through the window, "They're holding two coons up here beside a pigeon loft. They're waiting on you."

"Okay, I'm coming. You and Price hold these punks on ice," he directed the other cops and climbed out of the window behind the professor.

9.

"GET IN," Grave Digger said.

She pulled up the skirt of her evening gown, drew the black coat tight, and eased her jumbo hams onto the seat usually occupied by Coffin Ed.

Grave Digger went around on the other side and climbed beneath the wheel and waited.

"Does I just have to go along, honey," the woman said in a wheedling voice. "I can just as well tell you where she's at."

"That's what I'm waiting for."

"Well, why didn't you say so. She's in the Knickerbocker Apartments on 145th Street—the old Knickerbocker I mean. She on the sixth story, 669."

"Who is she?" Grave Digger asked, probing a little.

"Who she is? Just a landprop is all."

"That ain't what I mean."

"Oh, I know what you means. You means who is she. You means you don't know who Reba is, Digger?" She tried to sound jocular but unsuccessfully. "She the landprop what used to be old Cap Murphy's go-between 'fore he got sent up for taking all them bribes. It was in all the papers."

"That was ten years ago and they called her Sheba then," he said.

"Yare, that's right, but she changed her name after she got in that last shooting scrape. You musta 'member that. She caught the nigger with some chippie or 'nother and made him jump buck naked out the third story window. That wouldn't 'ave been so bad but she shot 'im through the head as he was going down. That was when she lived in the Valley. Since then she done come up here on the hill. 'Course it warn't nobody but her husband and she didn't get a day. But Reba always has been lucky that way."

He took a shot in the dark. "What would anybody shoot Galen for?"

She grew stiff with caution. "Who he?"

"You know damn well who he was. He's the man who was shot tonight."

"Nawsuh, I didn't know nothing 'bout that gennelman. I don't know why nobody would want to shoot him."

"You people give me a pain in the seat with all that ducking and dodging every time some one asks you a question. You act like you belong to a race of artful dodgers."

"You is asking me something I don't know nothing 'bout."

"Okay, get out."

She got out faster than she got in.

He drove down the hill of St. Nicholas Avenue and turned up the hill of 145th Street toward Convent Avenue.

On the lefthand corner, next to a new fourteen story apartment building erected by a white insurance company, was the *Brown Bomber Bar*; across from it *Big Crip's Bar*; on the righthand corner *Cohen's Drug Store* with its iron-grilled windows crammed with electric hair straightening irons, Hi-Life hair cream, Black & White bleaching cream, SSS and 666 blood tonics, Dr. Scholl's corn pads, men's and women's nylon head caps with chin straps to press the hair while sleeping, a bowl of blue stone good for body lice, tins of Sterno canned heat good for burning or drinking, Halloween post cards and all of the latest in enamelware hygiene utensils; across from it *Zazully's Delicatessen* with a white-lettered announcement on the plate glass window: WE HAVE FROZEN CHITTERLINGS AND OTHER HARD-TO-FIND DELICACIES.

Going up the hill from *Cohen's* was a green fronted Chinese restaurant with fly-specked yellow curtains called *The New Manchu*; the *Alabama-Georgia Bar*; a small wooden shack built out from a crumbling brick house bearing a wooden sign reading *Slam's Real Cool Shoe Shine Parlor* above the front window which was filled with glossy portraits of blues singers, band leaders and prize fighters; and a green basement door with the plaque, *S. Zucker, M.D.*

Grave Digger parked in front of a big frame house with peeling yellow paint which had been converted into offices, got out and walked next door to a six story rotten-brick tenement long overdue at the wreckers.

Three cars were parked at the curb in front; two with upstate New York plates and the other from Mid-Manhattan.

He pushed open a scaly door beneath the arch of a concrete block on which the word KNICKERBOCKER was embossed.

An old grayhaired man with a looselipped mouth in a splotched brown face sat in a motheaten red plush chair just inside the doorway to the semi-dark corridor. He drew back gnarled feet in felt bedroom slippers to keep them from being trodden on and looked Grave Digger over with dull satiated eyes.

"Evenin'," he said.

Grave Digger flung him a glance. "Evenin'."

"Fourth story on de right. Number 421," the old man informed him.

Grave Digger stopped. "That Reba's?"

"You don't want Reba's. You want Topsy's. Dat's 421."

"What's happening at Topsy's?"

"What always happen. Dat's where the trouble is."

"What kind of trouble?"

"Just general trouble. Fightin' an' cuttin'."

"I'm not looking for trouble. I'm looking for Reba's."

"You're the man, ain't you?"

"Yeah, I'm the man."

"Then you wants 421. I'se de janitor."

"If you're the janitor then you know Mr. Galen."

A veil fell over the old man's face. "Who he?"

"He's the big Greek man who goes up to Reba's."

"I don't know no Greeks, boss. Don't no white folks come in here. Nothin' but cullud folks. You'll find 'em all at Topsy's."

"He was killed over on Lenox tonight."

"Sho nuff?"

Grave Digger started off.

The old man called to him, "I guess you wonderin' why we got them big numbers on de doors."

Grave Digger paused. "All right, why?"

"They sounds good." The old man cackled.

Grave Digger walked up five flights of shaky wooden stairs, knocked on a red-painted door with a round glass peephole in the upper panel.

After an interval a heavy woman's voice asked, "Who's you?"

"I'm the Digger."

Bolts clicked and the door cracked a few inches on the

chain. A big dark silhouette loomed in the crack, outlined by blue light from behind.

"I didn't recognize you, Digger," a pleasant bass voice said. "Your hat shades your face. Long time no see."

"Unchain the door, Reba, before I shoot it off."

A deep bass laugh accompanied chain rattling and the door swung inward.

"Same old Digger, shoot first and talk later. Come on in, we're all colored folks in here."

He stepped into a blue-lit carpeted hall reeking with the smell of incense.

"You're sure."

She laughed again as she closed and bolted the door.

"Those are not folks, those are clients."

Then she turned casually to face him. "What's on your mind, honey?"

She was as tall as his six feet two, but half again as heavy, with snow white hair cut short as a man's and brushed straight back from her forehead. Her lips were painted carnation red and her eyelids silver but her smooth unlined jet black skin was untouched. She wore a black sequined evening gown with a red rose in the V of her mammoth bosom which was a lighter brown than her face. She looked like the last of the Amazons blackened by time.

"Where can we talk," Grave Digger said. "I don't want to strain you."

"You don't strain me, honey," she said, opening the first door to the right. "Come into the kitchen."

She put a bottle of bourbon and a siphon beside two tall glasses on the table and sat in a kitchen chair.

"Say when," she said as she started to pour.

"By me," Grave Digger said, pushing his hat to the back of his head and planting a foot on the adjoining chair.

She stopped pouring and put down the bottle.

"You go ahead," he said.

"I don't drink no more," she said. "I quit after I killed Sam."

He crossed his arms on his raised knee and leaned forward on them, looking at her.

"You used to wear a rosary," he said.

She smiled, showing gold crowns on her outside incisors.

"When I got religion I quit that too," she said.

"What religion did you get?"

"Just the faith, Digger, just the spirit."

"It lets you run this joint?"

"Why not. It's nature, just like eating. Nothing in my faith 'gainst eating. I just make it convenient and charge 'em for it."

"You'd better get a new steerer, the one downstairs is simpleminded."

Her big bass laugh rang out again. "He don't work for us; he does that on his own."

"Don't make this hard on yourself," he said. "This can be easy for us both."

She looked at him calmly. "I ain't got nothing to fear."

"When was the last time you saw Galen?"

"The big Greek? Been some time now, Digger. Three or four months. He don't come here no more."

"Why?"

"I don't let him."

"How come?"

"Be your age, Digger. This is a sporting house. If I don't let a white John with money come here, I must have good reasons. And if I want to keep my other white clients I'd better not say what they are. You can't close me up and you can't make me talk, so why don't you let it go at that."

"The Greek was shot to death tonight over on Lenox."

"I just heard it over the radio," she said.

"I'm trying to find who did it."

She looked at him in surprise. "It said on the radio the killer was known. A Sonny Pickens. Said a teenage gang called the something-or-nother Moslems snatched him."

"He didn't do it. That's why I'm here."

"Well, if he didn't do it, you got your job cut out," she said. "I wish I could help you but I can't."

"Maybe," he said. "Maybe not."

She raised her eyebrows slightly. "By the way, where's your sidekick, Coffin Ed. The radio said he shot one of the gang."

"Yeah, he got suspended."

She went still, like an animal alert to danger.

"Don't take it out on me, Digger."

"I just want to know why you stopped the Greek from coming here."

She stared long into his eyes. She had dark brown eyes with clear whites and long black lashes faintly seen.

"I'll let you talk to Ready. He knows."

"Is he here now?"

"He got a little chippie whore here he can't stay 'way from for five minutes. I'm going to throw 'em both out soon. Would have before now but my clients like her."

"Was the Greek her client?"

She got up slowly, sighing slightly from the effort.

"I'll send him out here."

"Bring him out."

"All right. But take him away, Digger. I don't want him talking in here. I don't want no more trouble. I've had trouble all my days."

"I'll take him away," he said.

She went out and Grave Digger heard doors being discreetly opened and shut and then her controlled bass voice saying, "How do I know. He said he was a friend."

A tall evil-faced man with pockmarked skin a dirty shade of black stepped into the kitchen. An old razor scar cut a purple ridge from the lobe of his left ear to the tip of his chin. There was a cast in one eye, the other was reddish brown. Thin conked hair stuck to a doublejointed head shaped like a peanut. He was flashily dressed in a light tan suit. Glass glittered from two goldplated rings. His pointed tan shoes were shined to mirror brilliance.

At sight of Grave Digger he drew up short and turned a murderous look on Reba.

"You tole me hit was a friend," he accused in a rough, dangerous sounding voice.

She didn't let it bother her. She pushed him into the kitchen and closed the door.

"Well, ain't he?" she asked.

"What's this, some kind of frameup?" he began to shout.

Grave Digger chuckled at the look of outrage on his face.

"How can a buck as ugly as you be a pimp?" he asked.

"You're gonna make me talk about you mama," Ready said, digging his right hand into his pants pocket.

With nothing moving but his arm, Grave Digger back-handed him in the solar plexus, knocking out his wind, then pivoted on his left foot and followed with a right cross to the same spot, and with the same motion raised his knee and sunk it into Ready's belly as the pimp's slim frame jackknifed forward. Spit showered from Ready's fish-like mouth, and the sense was already gone from his eyes when Grave Digger grabbed him by the back of the coat collar, jerked him erect, and started to slap him in the face with his open palm.

Reba grabbed his arm, saying, "Not in here, Digger, I beg you; don't make him bleed. You said you'd take him out."

"I'm taking him out now," he said in a cottony voice, shaking off her hold.

"Then finish him without bleeding him; I don't want nobody coming in here finding blood on the floor."

Grave Digger grunted and eased off. He propped Ready against the wall, holding him up on his rubbery legs with one hand while he took the knife and frisked him quickly with the other.

The sense came back into Ready's good eye and Grave Digger stepped back and said, "All right, let's go quietly, son."

Ready fussed about without looking at him, straightening his coat and tie, then fished a greasy comb from his pocket and combed his rumpled conk. He was bent over in the middle from pain and breathing in gasps and a white froth had collected in both corners of his mouth.

Finally he mumbled, "You can't take me outa here without no warrant."

"Go ahead with the man and shut up," Reba said quickly.

He gave her a pleading look. "You gonna let him take me outa here?"

"If he don't I'm going to throw you out myself," she said. "I don't want any hollering and screaming in here scaring my white clients."

"That's gonna cost you," Ready threatened.

"Don't threaten me, nigger," she said dangerously. "And don't set your foot in my door again."

"Okay, Reba, that's the lick that killed Dick," Ready said slowly. "You and him got me outnumbered." He gave her a last sullen look and turned to go.

Reba walked to the door and let them out.

"I hope I get what I want," Grave Digger said. "If I don't I'll be back."

"If you don't it's your own fault," she said.

He marched Ready ahead of him down the shaky stairs.

The old man in the ragged red chair looked up in surprise.

"You got the wrong nigger," he said. "Hit ain't him what's makin' all the trouble."

"Who is it?" Grave Digger asked.

"Hit's Cocky. He the one what's always pulling his chiv."

Grave Digger filed the information for future reference.

"I'll keep this one since I got him," he said.

"Shit," the old man said disgustedly. "He's just a halfass pimp."

10.

STARK white light, coming from the street as though from a carnival midway, slanted upward past the edge of the roof and made a milky wall in the dark.

Beyond the wall of light the flat tar roof was shrouded in semi-darkness.

The sergeant emerged from the edge of light like a hammerhead turtle rising from the deep. He took one look at Sonny beating frantically at a flock of panicstricken pigeons with a long bamboo pole and Inky standing motionless as though he'd sprouted from the tar.

"By God, now I know why they're called tarbabies!" he exclaimed.

Gripping the pole for dear life with both gauntleted hands, Sonny speared desperately at the pigeons. His eyes rolled whitely at the red-faced sergeant. His ragged overcoat flapped in the wind. The pigeons ducked and dodged and flew in lopsided circles. Their heads were cocked on one side as they observed Sonny's gymnastics with one-eyed beady apprehension.

Inky stood like a silhouette cut from black paper, looking at nothing. The whites of his eyes gleamed phosphorescently in the dark.

The pigeon loft was a rickety coop about six feet high, made of scraps of chicken wire, discarded screen windows and assorted rags tacked to a frame of rotten boards propped against the low brick wall separating the roofs. It had a tarpaulin top and was equipped with precarious roosts, tin cans of rusty water, and a rusty tin dishpan for feeding.

Blue uniformed white cops formed a jagged semi-circle in front of it, staring at Sonny in silent and bemused amazement.

The sergeant climbed onto the roof, puffing, and paused for a moment to mop his brow.

"What's he doing, voodoo?" he asked.

"It's only Don Quixote in blackface dueling a windmill," the professor said.

"That ain't funny," the sergeant said. "I like Don Quixote."

The professor let it go.

"Is he a halfwit?" the sergeant asked.

"If he's got that much," the professor said.

The sergeant pushed to the center of the stage, but once there hesitated as though he didn't know how to begin.

Sonny looked at him through the corners of his eyes and kept working the pole. Inky stared at nothing with silent intensity.

"All right, all right, so your feet don't stink," the sergeant said. "What one of you punks are Caleb?"

"Dass me," Sonny said, without for an instant neglecting the pigeons.

"What the hell you call yourself doing?"

"I'se teaching my pigeons how to fly."

The sergeant's jowls began to swell. "You trying to be funny?"

"Nawsuh, I didn' mean they didn' know how to fly. They can fly all right at day but they don't know how to night fly."

The sergeant looked at the professor. "Don't pigeons fly at night?"

"Search me," the professor said.

"Nawsuh, not unless you makes 'em," Inky said.

Everybody looked at him.

"Hell, he can talk," the professor said.

"They sleeps," Sonny added.

"Roosts," Inky corrected.

"We're going to make some pigeons fly too," the sergeant said. "Stool pigeons."

"If they don't fly, they'll fry," the professor said.

The sergeant turned to Inky. "What do they call you, boy?"

"Inky," Inky said. "But my name's Rufus Tree."

"So you're Inky," the sergeant said.

"They're both Inky," the professor said.

The cops laughed.

The sergeant smiled into his hand. Then he wheeled abruptly on Sonny and shouted, *"Sonny! Drop that pole!"*

Sonny gave a violent start and speared a pigeon in the craw, but he hung on to the pole. The pigeon flew crazily into the light and kept on going. Sonny watched it until he got control of himself, then he turned slowly and looked at the sergeant with big white innocent eyes.

"You talking to me, boss?" His black face shone with sweat.

"Yeah, I'm talking to you, Sonny."

"They don't calls me, Sonny, boss; they calls me Cal."

"You look like a boy called Sonny."

"Lots of folks is called Sonny, boss."

"What did you jump for if your name isn't Sonny. You jumped halfway out of your skin."

"Most anybody'd jump with you hollerin' at 'em like that, boss."

The sergeant wiped off another smile. "You told your grandma you were going downtown to work."

"She don't want me messin' round these pigeons at night. She think I might fall off'n the roof."

"Where have you been since supper?"

"Right up here, boss."

"He's just been up here about a half an hour," one of the cops volunteered.

"Nawsuh, I been here all the time," Sonny contradicted. "I been inside the coop."

"Ain't nobody in heah but us pigeons, boss," the professor cracked.

"Did you look in the coop?" the sergeant asked the cop.

The cop reddened. "No I didn't; I wasn't looking for a screwball."

The sergeant glanced at the coop. "By God, boy, your pigeons lead a hard life," he said. Then turning suddenly to the other cops, he asked, "Have these punks been frisked?"

"We were waiting for you," another cop replied.

The sergeant sighed theatrically. "Well, who are you waiting for now."

Two cops converged on Inky with alacrity; the professor and a third cop took on Sonny.

"Put that damn pole down!" the sergeant shouted at Sonny.

"No, let him hold it," the professor said. "It keeps his hands up."

"What the hell are you wearing that heavy overcoat for?" The sergeant kept on picking at Sonny in a frustrated manner.

"I'se cold," Sonny said. Sweat was running down his face in rivers.

"You look it," the sergeant said.

"Jesus Christ, this coat stinks," the professor complained, working Sonny over fast to get away from it.

"Nothing?" the sergeant asked when he'd finished.

"Nothing," the professor said. In his haste he hadn't thought to make Sonny put down the pole and take off his gauntlets.

The sergeant looked at the cops frisking Inky.

They shook their heads.

"What's Harlem coming to," the sergeant complained.

The cops grinned.

"All right, you punks, get downstairs," the sergeant ordered.

"I got to get my pigeons in," Sonny said.

The sergeant looked at him.

Sonny leaned the pole against the coop and began moving. Inky opened the door of the coop and began moving too. The pigeons took one look at the open door and began rushing to get inside.

"IRT subway at Times Square," the professor remarked.

The cops laughed and moved off to the next roof, laughing and talking.

The sergeant and the professor followed Inky and Sonny through the window and into the room below.

Sissie and Sugartit sat side by side on the bed again. Choo-Choo sat in the straight-back chair. Sheik stood in the center of the floor with his feet wide apart, looking defiant. The two cops stood with their buttocks propped against the edge of the table, looking bored.

With the addition of the four others, the room became crowded.

Everybody looked at the sergeant, waiting his next move.

"Get grandma in here," he said.

The professor went after her.

They heard him saying, "Grandma, you're needed."

There was no reply.

"Grandma!" they heard him shout.

"She's asleep," Sissie called to him. "She's hard to wake once she gets to sleep."

"She's not asleep," the professor called back in an angry tone of voice.

"All right, let her alone," the sergeant said.

The professor returned, red-faced with vexation. "She sat there looking at me without saying a word," he said.

"She gets like that," Sissie said. "She just sort of shuts out the world and quits seeing and hearing anything."

"No wonder her grandson's a halfwit," the professor said, giving Sonny a malicious look.

"Well, what the hell are we going to do with them?" the sergeant said in a frustrated tone of voice.

The cops had no suggestions.

"Let's run them all in," the professor said.

The sergeant looked at him reflectively. "If we take in all the punks who look like them in this block, we'll have a thousand prisoners," he said.

"So what," the professor said. "We can't afford to risk losing Pickens because of a few hundred shines."

"Well, maybe we'd better," the sergeant said.

"Are you going to take her in too," Sheik said, nodding toward Sugartit on the bed. "She's Coffin Ed's daughter."

The sergeant wheeled on him. "What! What's that about Coffin Ed?"

"Evelyn Johnson there is his daughter," Sheik said evenly.

The cops turned as though their heads were synchronized and stared at her. None spoke.

"Ask her," Sheik said.

The sergeant's face turned bright red.

It was the professor who spoke. "Well, girl? Are you Detective Johnson's daughter?"

Sugartit hesitated.

"Go on and tell 'em," Sheik said.

The red started crawling up the back of the sergeant's neck and engulfed his ears.

"I don't like you," he said to Sheik in a constricted tone of voice.

Sheik threw him a careless look, started to say something, then bit it off.

"Yes I am," Sugartit said finally.

"We can soon check on that," the professor said, moving toward the window. "He and his partner must be in the vicinity."

"No, Jones might be but Johnson was sent home," the sergeant said.

"What! Suspended?" the professor asked in surprise.

Sugartit looked startled; Sheik grinned smugly; the others remained impassive.

"Yeah, for killing the Moslem punk."

"For that!" the professor exclaimed indignantly. "Since when did they start penalizing policemen for shooting in self defense?"

"I don't blame the chief," the sergeant said. "He's protecting himself. The punk was underage and the newspapers are sure to put up a squawk."

"Anyway, Jones ought to know her," the professor said, going out on the fire escape and shouting to the cops below.

He couldn't make himself understood so he started down.

The sergeant asked Sugartit, "Have you got any identification?"

She drew a red leather card case from her skirt pocket and handed it to him without speaking.

It held a black, white-lettered identification card with her photograph and thumb print, similar to the ones issued to policemen. It had been given to her as a souvenir for her sixteenth birthday and was signed by the chief of police.

The sergeant studied it for a moment and handed it back. He had seen others like it; his own daughter had one.

"Does your father know you're here visiting these hoodlums?" he asked.

"Certainly," Sugartit said. "They're friends of mine."

"You're lying," the sergeant said wearily.

"He doesn't know she's over here," Sissie put in.

"I know damn well he doesn't," the sergeant said.

"She's supposed to be visiting me."

"Well, do your folks know you're here?"

She dropped her gaze. "No."

"Eve and I are engaged," Sheik said with a smirk.

The sergeant wheeled toward him with his right cocked high. Sheik ducked automatically, his guard coming up. The sergeant hooked a left to his stomach underneath his guard, and when Sheik's guard dropped, he crossed his right to the side of Sheik's head, knocking him into a spinning stagger. Then he kicked him in the side of the stomach as he spun and when he doubled over, the sergeant chopped him across the back of the neck with the meaty edge of his right hand. Sheik shuddered as though poleaxed and crashed to the floor. The sergeant took dead aim and kicked him in the valley of the buttocks with all his force.

The professor returned just in time to see the sergeant spit on him.

"Hey, what's happened to him?" he asked, climbing hastily through the window.

The sergeant took off his hat and wiped his perspiring forehead with a soiled white handkerchief.

"His mouth did it," he said.

Sheik groaned feebly in unconsciousness.

The professor chuckled. "He's still trying to talk." Then he said, "They couldn't find Jones. Lieutenant Anderson says he's working on another angle."

"It's okay, she's got an ID card," the sergeant said, then asked, "Is the chief still there?"

"Yeah, he's still hanging around."

"Well, that's his job."

The professor looked about at the silent group. "What's the verdict?"

"Let's get on to the next house," the sergeant said. "If I'm here when this punk comes to I'll probably be the next one to get suspended."

"Can we leave the building now?" Sissie asked.

"You two girls can come with us," the sergeant offered.

Sheik groaned and rolled over.

"We can't leave him like that," she said.

The sergeant shrugged. The cops passed into the next room. The sergeant started to follow, then hesitated.

"All right, I'll fix it up," he said.

He took the girls out on the fire escape and got the attention of the cops guarding the entrance below.

"Let these two girls pass!" he shouted.

The cops looked at the girls standing in the spotlight glare. "Okay."

The sergeant followed them back into the room.

"If I were you I'd get the hell away from this punk fast," he advised, prodding Sheik with his toe. "He's headed straight for trouble, big trouble."

Neither replied.

He followed the professor from the flat.

Granny sat unmoving in the rocking chair where they'd left her, tightly gripping the arms. She stared at them with an expression of fierce disapproval on her puckered old face and in her dim milky eyes.

"It's our job, grandma," the sergeant said apologetically.

She didn't reply.

They passed on sheepishly.

Back in the front room, Sheik groaned and sat up.

Everyone moved at once. The girls moved away from him. Sonny began taking off the heavy overcoat. Inky and Choo-Choo bent over Sheik and each taking an arm began helping him to his feet.

"How you feel, Sheik?" Choo-Choo asked.

Sheik looked dazed. "Can't no copper hurt me," he muttered thickly, wobbling on his legs.

"Does it hurt?"

"Naw, it don't hurt," he said with a grimace of pain. Then he looked about stupidly. "They gone?"

"Yeah," Choo-Choo said jubilantly and cut a jig step. "We done beat 'em, Sheik. We done fooled 'em two ways sides and flat."

Sheik's confidence came back in a rush. "I told you we was going to do it."

Sonny grinned and raised his clasped hands in the prize-fight salute. "They had me sweating in the crotch," he confessed.

A look of crazed triumph distorted Sheik's flat freckled yellow face. "I'm the Sheik, Jack," he said. His yellow eyes were getting wild again.

Sissie looked at him and said apprehensively, "Me and Sugartit got to go. We were just waiting to see if you were all right."

"You can't go now, we got to celebrate," Sheik said.

"We ain't got nothing to celebrate with," Choo-Choo said.

"The hell we ain't," Sheik said. "Cops ain't so smart. You go up on the roof and get the pole."

"Who, me, Sheik?"

"Sonny then."

"Me!" Sonny said. "I done got enough of that roof."

"Go on," Sheik said. "You're a Moslem now and I command you in the name of Allah."

"Praise Allah," Choo-Choo said.

"I don't want to be no Moslem," Sonny said.

"All right, you're still our captive then," Sheik decreed. "You go get the pole, Inky. I got five sticks stashed in the end."

"Hell, I'll go," Choo-Choo said.

"No, let Inky go, he's been up there before and they won't think it's funny."

When Inky left for the pole, Sheik said to Choo-Choo, "Our captive's getting biggety since we saved him from the cops."

"I ain't gettin' biggety," Sonny denied. "I just want to get the hell outen here and get these cuffs off'n me without havin' to become no Moslem."

"You know too much for us to let you go now," Sheik said, exchanging a look with Choo-Choo.

Then Inky returned with the pole and he let up on Sonny. Pulling the plug out of the end joint, he shook five marijuana cigarets onto the table top.

"A feast!" Choo-Choo exclaimed. He grabbed one, opened the end with his thumb, and lit up.

Sheik lit another.

"Take one, Inky," he said.

Inky took one.

Everybody put on smoked glasses.

"Granny will smell it if you smoke in here," Sissie said.

"She thinks they're cubebs," Choo-Choo said, then mimicked Granny saying, "Ah wish you chillens would stop smokin' them coo-bebs 'cause they make a body feel moughty funny in de head."

He and Sheik doubled over laughing.

The room stunk with the pungent smoke.

Sugartit picked up a stick, sat on the bed and lit it.

"Come on, baby, strip," Sheik urged her. "Celebrate your old man's flop by getting up off of some of it."

Sugartit stood up and undid her skirt zipper and began going into a slow striptease routine.

Sissie clutched her by the arms. "You stop that," she said. "You'd better go on home before your old man gets there first and comes out looking for you."

In a sudden rage, Sheik snatched Sissie's hands away from Sugartit and flung her across the bed.

"Leave her alone," he raved. "She's going to entertain the Sheik."

"If her old man's really Coffin Ed you oughta let her go on home," Sonny said soberly. "You just beggin' for trouble messin' round with his kinfolks."

"Choo-Choo, go to the kitchen and get Granny's wire clothesline," Sheik ordered.

Choo-Choo went out grinning.

When he saw Granny staring at him with such fierce disapproval, he said guiltily, "Pay no tenshion to me, Granny," and began clowning.

She didn't answer.

He tiptoed with elaborate pantomime to the closet and took out her coil of clothesline.

"Just wanna hang out the wash," he said.

Still she didn't answer.

He tiptoed close to the chair and passed his hand slowly in front of her face. She didn't bat an eye. His grin widened.

Returning to the front room, he said, "Granny's dead asleep with her eyes wide open."

"Leave her to Gabriel," Sheik said, taking the line and beginning to uncoil it.

"What you gonna do with that?" Sonny asked apprehensively.

Sheik made a running loop in one end. "We going to play cowboy," he said. "Look."

Suddenly he threw the loop over Sonny's head and pulled on the line with all his strength. The loop tightened about Sonny's neck and jerked him off his feet.

"Grab him, men!" Sheik ordered.

They both jumped straddle him at once; Choo-Choo grabbed his arms and Inky his feet.

Sissie ran toward Sheik and tried to pull the wire from his hands. "You're choking him," she said.

Sheik knocked her down with a backhanded blow.

"You can let up on him now," Choo-Choo said. "We got 'im."

"Now I'm gonna show you how to tie up a mother-raper to put him in a sack," Sheik said.

II.

GRAVE DIGGER halted on the sidewalk in front of the yellow frame house next door to the Knickerbocker. It had been partitioned into offices and all of the front windows were lettered with business announcements.

"Can you read that writing on those windows?" Grave Digger asked Ready Belcher.

Ready glanced at him suspiciously. "'Course I can read that writing."

"Read it then," Grave Digger said.

Ready stole another look. "Read what one?"

"Take your choice."

Ready squinted his good eye against the dark and read aloud, "*Joseph C. Clapp, Real Estate and Notary Public.*" He looked at Grave Digger like a dog that's retrieved a stick. "That one?"

"Try another."

He hesitated. Passing car lights played over his pockmarked black face, brought out the white cast in his bad eye and lit up his flashy tan suit.

"I haven't got much time," Grave Digger warned.

He read, "*Amazing 100 year old Gypsy Bait Oil—MAKES CAT FISH GO CRAZY.*" He looked at Grave Digger again like the same dog with another stick.

"Not that one," Grave Digger said.

"What the hell is this, a gag," he muttered.

"Just read."

"*JOSEPH, The Only and Original Skin Lightener. I guarantee to lighten the darkest skin by twelve shades in six months.*"

"You don't want your skin lightened?"

"My skin suit me," he said sullenly.

"Then read on."

"*MAGIC FORMULA FOR SUCCESSFUL PRAYER . . .* That it?"

"Yeah, that's it. Read what it says underneath."

"*Here are some of the amazing things it tells you about: When to pray; Where to pray; How to pray; The Magic Formulas for Health and Success through prayer; for conquering fear through prayer; for obtaining work through prayer; for money through prayer; for influencing others through prayer; and—*"

"That's enough." Grave Digger took a deep breath and said in a voice gone thick and cottony again, "Ready, if you don't tell me what I want to know, you'd better get yourself one of those prayers. Because I'm going to take you over on 129th Street beside the Harlem River in that deserted jungle of warehouses and junk yards underneath the New York Central railroad bridge. You know where that is?"

"Yare, I know where it's at."

"And I'm going to pistol whip you until your own whore

won't recognize you again. And if you try to run, I'm going to let you run fifty feet and then shoot you through the head for attempting to escape. You understand me?"

"Yare, I understand you."

"You believe me?"

Ready took a quick look at Grave Digger's rage-swollen face and said quickly, "Yare, I believes you."

"My partner got suspended tonight for killing a criminal rat like you and I'd just as soon they suspended me too."

"You ain't asted me yet what you want to know."

"Get into the car."

The car was parked at the curb. Ready got into Coffin Ed's seat. Grave Digger went around and climbed beneath the wheel.

"This is as good a spot as any," he said. "Start talking."

" 'Bout what?"

"About the Big Greek. I want to know who killed him."

Ready jumped as though he'd been stung. "Digger, I swear 'fore God—"

"Don't call me Digger, you lousy pimp."

"Mista Jones, lissen—"

"I'm listening."

"Lots of folks mighta killed him if they'd knowed—" he broke off. The pockmarks in his skin began filling with sweat.

"Known what? I haven't got all night."

Ready gulped and said, "He was a whipper."

"What?"

"He liked to whip 'em."

"Whores?"

"Not 'specially. If they was regular whores he wanted them to be big black mannish looking bitches like what might cut a mother-raper's throat. But what he liked most was liddle colored school gals."

"That's it? That's why Reba barred him?"

"Yassuh. He proposition her once. She got so mad she drew her pistol on him."

"Did she shoot him?"

"Nawsuh, she just scared him."

"I mean tonight. Was she the one?"

Ready's eyes started rolling slowly in their sockets and the sweat began to trickle down his mean black face.

"You mean the one what killed him? Nawsuh, she was home all evening."

"Where were you?"

"I was there too."

"Do you live there?"

"Nawsuh, I just drops by for a visit now and then."

"Where did he find the girls?"

"You mean the school girls?"

"What other girls would I mean?"

"He picked 'em up in his car. He had a little Mexican bull whip with nine tails he kept in his car. He whipped 'em with that."

"Where did he take them?"

"He brung 'em to Reba's 'til she got suspicious 'bout all the screaming and carrying on. She didn't think nothing of it at first; these little chippies likes to make lots of noise for a white man. But they was making more noise than seemed natural and she went in and caught 'im. That's when he proposition her."

"How did he get 'em to take it?"

"Get 'em to take what?"

"The whipping."

"Oh, he paid 'em a hundred bucks. They was glad to take it for that."

"You're certain of that, that he paid them a hundred dollars?"

"Yassuh. Not only me but lots of chippies all over Harlem knew about him. A hundred bucks didn't mean nothing to him. They boyfriends knew too. Lots of times they boyfriends made 'em. There was chippies all over town on the lookout for him. 'Course one time was enough for most of 'em."

"He hurt them?"

"He got his money's worth. Sometime he whale hell out of 'em. I s'pect he hurt more'n one of 'em bad. 'Member that kid they picked up in Broadhurst Park. It were all in the paper. She was in the hospital three or four days. She said she'd been attacked but the police thought she was beat up by a gang. I believes she was one of 'em."

"What was her name?"

"I don't recollect."

"Where'd he take them after Reba barred him from her place?"

"I don't know."

"Do you know the names of any of them?"

"Nawsuh, he brung 'em and took 'em away by hisself. I never even seen any of 'em."

"You're lying."

"Nawsuh, I swear 'fore God."

"How did you know they were school girls if you never saw any of them?"

"He tole me."

"What else did he tell you?"

"Nuthin' else. He just talk to me 'bout gals."

"How old is your girl?"

"My gal?"

"The one you have at Reba's."

"Oh, she twenty-five or more."

"One more lie and off we go."

"She sixteen, boss."

"She had him too?"

"Yassuh. Once."

The sweat was coming in streamers down Ready's face.

"Once. Why only once?"

"She got scared."

"You tried to fix it up for another time?"

"Nawsuh, boss, she didn't need to. Hit cost her more'n it was worth."

"What were you doing with him in the Dew Drop Inn?"

"He was looking for a little gal he knew and he ast me to come 'long, that's all, boss."

"When was that?"

" 'Bout a month ago."

"You said you didn't know where he took them after he was barred from Reba's."

"I don't, boss, I swear 'fore—"

"Can that uncle toming crap. Reba said she barred him three or four months ago."

"Yassuh, but I didn't say I hadn't seed him since."

"Did Reba know you were seeing him?"

"I only seed him that once, boss. I was in the Alabama-Georgia bar and he just happen in."

Grave Digger nodded toward the three alien cars parked ahead, in front of the Knickerbocker.

"One of those cars his?"

"Them struggle buggies!" Scorn pushed the fear from Ready's voice. "Nawsuh, he had a dream boat, a big green Caddy Coupe de Ville."

"Who was the girl he and you were looking for?"

"I wasn't looking for her; I just went 'long with him to look for her."

"Who was she, I asked."

"I didn't know her. Some little chippie what hung 'round in that section."

"How did he come to know her?"

"He said he'd done whipped her girl friend once. That's how come he knew her. Said Sissie's boyfriend brought her to 'im."

"Sissie! You said you didn't know the names of any of them."

"I'd forgotten her, boss. He didn't bring her to Reba's. I didn't know nuthin' 'bout her but just what he said."

"What did he say exactly?"

"He just say Sissie's boyfriend, some boy they call Sheik, arrange it for him and he pay Sheik. Then he wanted Sheik to arrange for the other one but Sheik couldn't do it."

"What was the other one called? The one he and you were looking for?"

"He call her Sugartit. She was Sissie's girl friend. He'd seen 'em walking together down Seventh Avenue one time after he'd whipped Sissie."

"Where did you find her?"

"We didn't find her, I swear 'fore—"

"Does your girl know them?"

"I didn' hear you."

"Your girl, does she know them?"

"Know who, boss?"

"Either Sissie or Sugartit."

"Nawsuh. My gal's a pro and them is just chippies. I recollect him saying one time they all belonged to a kid gang over in that section. I means them two chippies and Sheik. He say Sheik was the chief."

"What's the name of the gang?"

"He say they call themselves the Real Cool Moslems. He thought it were funny."

"Did you listen to the news on the radio tonight?"

"You mean what it say 'bout him getting croaked? Nawsuh, I was lissening to the 1280 Club. Reba tole me 'bout it. She were lissening. That were just 'fore you come. She were telling me when the doorbell rang. She say the big Greek's been croaked over on Lenox Avenue and I say so what."

"You said before that lots of people might have killed him if they'd known about him. Who?"

"All I meant was some of those gal's pas. Like Sissie's or some of 'em. He might have been hanging 'round over there looking for Sugartit again and her pa might have got hep to it some kind of way and been layin' for him and when he seed him coming down the street might have lowered the boom on 'im."

"You mean slipped up behind him?"

"He were in his car, warn't he?"

"How about the Moslems—the kid gang?"

"Them! What they'd wanta do it for? He was money in the street for them."

"Who's Sugartit's father?"

"You mean her old man?"

"I mean her father."

"How am I gonna know that, boss? I ain't never heard of her 'fore he talk 'bout her."

"What did he say about her?"

"Just say she was the gal for him."

"Did he say where she lived?"

"Nawsuh, he just say what I say, boss. I swear 'fore God."

"You stink. What are you sweating so much for?"

"I'se just nervous, that's all."

"You stink with fear. What are you scared of?"

"Just naturally scared, boss. You got that big pistol and you mad at everybody and talkin' 'bout killin' me and all that. Enough to make anybody scared."

"You're scared of something else, something in particular. What are you holding out?"

"I ain't holding nothing out. I done tole you everything I know, I swear, boss, I swears on everything that's holy in this whole green world."

"I know you're lying. I can hear it in your voice. What are you lying about?"

"I ain't lying, boss. If I'm lying I hope God'll strike me dead on the spot."

"You know who her father is, don't you?"

"Nawsuh, boss. I swear. I done tole you everything I know. You could whup me 'til my head is soft as clabber but I couldn't tell you no more than I'se already tole you."

"You know who her father is and you're scared to tell me."

"Nawsuh, I swear—"

"Is he a politician?"

"Boss, I—"

"A numbers banker?"

"I swear, boss—"

"Shut up before I knock out your goddamned teeth."

He mashed the starter as though tromping on Ready's head. The motor purred into life. But he didn't slip in the clutch. He sat there listening to the softly purring motor in the small black nondescript car, trying to get his temper under control.

Finally he said, "If I find out that you're lying I'm going to kill you like a dog. I'm not going to shoot you, I'm going to break all your bones. I'm going to try to find out who killed Galen because that's what I'm paid for and that was my oath when I took this job. But if I had my way I'd pin a medal on him and I'd string up every goddamned one of you who were up with Galen. You've turned my stomach and it's all I can do right now to keep from beating out your brains."

12.

THE reception room of the Harlem Hospital, ten blocks south on Lenox Avenue from the scene of the murder, was wrapped in a midnight hush.

It was called an interracial hospital; more than half of its staff of doctors and nurses were colored people.

A graduate nurse sat behind the reception desk. A bronze shaded desk lamp spilled light on the hospital register before her while leaving her brownskin face in shadow. She looked up enquiringly as Grave Digger and Ready Belcher approached, walking side by side.

"May I help you," she said in a trained courteous voice.

"I'm Detective Jones," Grave Digger said, exhibiting his badge.

She looked at it but didn't touch it.

"You received an emergency patient here about two hours ago; a man with his right arm cut off."

"Yes?"

"I would like to question him."

"I will call Dr. Banks. You may talk to him. Please be seated."

Grave Digger prodded Ready in the direction of chairs surrounding a table with magazines. They sat silently like relatives awaiting word of a critical case.

Dr. Banks came in silently, crossing the linoleum tile floor on rubber-soled shoes. He was a tall, athletic-looking young colored man dressed in white.

"I'm sorry to have kept you waiting, Mr. Jones," he said to Grave Digger whom he knew by sight. "You want to know about the case with the severed arm." He had a quick smile and a pleasant voice.

"I want to talk to him," Grave Digger said.

Dr. Banks pulled up a chair and sat down. "He's dead. I've just come from him. He had a rare type of blood—type O—which we don't have in our blood bank. You realize transfusions were imperative. We had to contact the Red Cross blood bank. They located the type in Brooklyn, but it arrived too late. Is there anything I can tell you?"

"I want to know who he was."

"So do we. He died without revealing his identity."

"Didn't he make a statement of any kind before he died?"

"There was another detective here earlier, but the patient was unconscious at the time. The patient regained consciousness later, but the detective had left. Before leaving he examined the patient's effects, however, but found nothing to establish his identity."

"He didn't talk at all, didn't say anything?"

"Oh yes. He cried a great deal. One moment he was cursing and the next he was praying. Most of what he said was incoherent. I gathered he regretted not killing the man whom he had attacked—the white man who was killed later."

"He didn't mention any names?"

"No. Once he said 'the little one' but mostly he used the word *mother-raper* which Harlemites apply to everybody, enemies, friends and strangers."

"Well, that's that," Grave Digger said. "Whatever he knew he took it with him. Still I'd like to examine his effects too, whatever they are."

"Certainly; they're just the clothes he wore and the contents of his pockets when he arrived here." He stood up. "Come this way."

Grave Digger got to his feet and motioned his head for Ready to walk ahead of him.

"Are you an officer too?" Dr. Banks asked Ready.

"No, he's my prisoner," Grave Digger said. "We're not that hard up for cops as yet."

Dr. Banks smiled. He led them down a corridor smelling strongly of ether to a room at the far end where the clothes and personal effects of the emergency and ward patients were stored in neatly wrapped bundles on shelves against the walls. He took down a bundle bearing a metal tag and placed it on the bare wooden table.

"Here you are."

From the room adjoining an anguished male voice was heard reciting the Lord's Prayer.

Ready stared as though fascinated at the number "219" on the metal tag fastened to the bundle of clothes and whispered, "Death row."

Dr. Banks flicked a glance at him and said to Grave Digger, "Most of the attendants play the numbers. When an emergency patient arrives they put this tag with the death number on his bundle and if he dies they play it."

Grave Digger grunted and began untying the bundle.

"If you discover anything leading to his identity, let us

know," Dr. Banks said. "We'd like to notify his relatives." He left them.

Grave Digger spread the blood-caked mackinaw and overalls on the table. Ready's face turned gray at sight of the black clots of dried blood.

The contents of the pockets had been put into a cellophane bag. Grave Digger dumped it onto the table. It contained two incredibly filthy one dollar bills, some loose change, a small brown paper sack of dried roots, two Yale keys and a skeleton key on a rusty key ring, a dried rabbit's foot, a dirty piece of resin, a cheese-cloth rag that had served as a handkerchief, a putty knife, a small piece of pumice stone, and a scrap of writing paper folded into a small dirty square. The putty knife and pumice stone indicated that the man had worked somewhere as a porter, the putty knife being used to scrape chewing gum from the floor and the pumice stone for cleaning his hands. That didn't help much.

He unfolded the square of paper and found a note on cheap school paper written in a childish hand.

> "GB, you want to know something. The Big John hangs out in the Inn. How about that. Just like those old Romans. Bee."

Grave Digger folded it again and slipped it into his pocket. "Is your girl called Bee?" he asked Ready.

"Nawsuh, she called Doe."

"Do you know any girl called Bee—school girl?"

"Nawsuh."

"GB?"

"Nawsuh."

Grave Digger turned out the pockets of the clothes but found nothing more. He wrapped the bundle and attached the tag. He noticed Ready staring at the number on the tag again.

"Don't let that number catch up with you," he said. "Don't you end up with that tag on your fine clothes."

Ready licked his dry lips.

They didn't see Dr. Banks on their way out. Grave Digger stopped at the reception desk to tell the nurse he hadn't found anything to identify the corpse.

"Now we're going to look for the Greek's car," he said to Ready.

They found the big green Cadillac beneath a street lamp in the middle of the block on 130th Street between Lenox and Seventh Avenues. It had an Empire State license number UG-16 and it was parked beside a fire hydrant. It was as conspicuous as a fire truck.

He pulled up behind it and parked.

"Who covered for him in Harlem?" he asked Ready.

"I don't know, Mista Jones."

"Was it the precinct captain?"

"Mista Jones, I—"

"One of our councilmen?"

"Honest to God, Mista Jones—"

He got out and walked forward to the big car.

The doors were locked. He broke the glass of the left side windscreen with the butt of his pistol and reached inside past the wheel and unlocked the door. The interior lights came on.

A quick search revealed the usual paraphernalia of a motorist: gloves, handkerchiefs, Kleenex, half-used packages of different brands of cigarettes, insurance papers, a woman's plastic overshoes and compact. A felt monkey dangled from the rear view mirror and two medium sized dolls, a black-faced Topsy and a blonde Little Eva, sat in opposite corners on the back seat.

He found the miniature bull whip and a manila envelope of postcard size photos in the right hand glove compartment. He studied the photos in the light. They were pornographic pictures of nude colored girls in various postures, revealing a well developed technique of sadism. On most of the pictures the faces of the girls were distinct although distorted by pain and shame.

He put the whip in his leather-lined coat pocket, kept the photos in his hand, slammed the door, walked back to his own car and climbed beneath the wheel.

"Was he a photographer?" he asked Ready.

"Yassuh, sometime he carried a camera."

"Did he show you the pictures he took?"

"Nawsuh, he never said nothing about any pictures. I just seen him with the camera."

He snapped on the top light and showed Ready the photos. "Do you recognize any of them?"

Ready whistled softly and his eyes popped as he turned over one photo after another.

"Nawsuh, I don't know none of them," he said, handing them back.

"Your girl's not one of them?"

"Nawsuh."

Grave Digger pocketed the envelope and mashed the starter.

"Ready, don't let me catch you in a lie," he said again, letting out the clutch.

13.

HE PARKED directly in front of the Dew Drop Inn and pushed Ready through the door ahead of him. On first sight it looked just as he had left it: the two white cops guarding the door and the colored patrons celebrating noisily. He ushered Ready between the bar and the booths, toward the rear. The vari-colored faces turned toward them curiously as they passed.

But in the last booth he noticed an addition. It was crowded with teenagers, three schoolboys and four school-girls, who hadn't been there before. They stopped talking and looked at him intently as he and Ready approached. Then at sight of the bull whip all four girls gave a start and their young dark faces tightened with sudden fear. He wondered how they'd got past the white cops on the door.

All the places at the bar were taken.

Big Smiley came down and asked two men to move.

One of them began to complain. "What for I got to give up my seat for some other niggers."

Big Smiley thumbed toward Grave Digger. "He's the man."

"Oh, one of them two."

Both of the men rose with alacrity, picked up their glasses

and vacated the stools, grinning at Grave Digger obse-
quiously.

"Don't show me your teeth," Grave Digger snarled. "I'm no
dentist. I don't fix teeth. I'm a cop. I'll knock your teeth out."

The men doused their grins and slunk away.

Grave Digger threw the bull whip on top of the bar and sat
on the high bar stool.

"Sit down," he ordered Ready who stood by hesitantly. "Sit
down, goddammit."

Ready sat down as though the stool were covered with cake
icing.

Big Smiley looked from one to another, smiling warily.

"You held out on me," Grave Digger said in his thick cottony voice of smoldering rage. "And I don't like that."

Big Smiley's smile got a sudden case of constipation. He
threw a quick look at Ready's impassive face, found nothing
there to reassure him, then fell back on his cut arm which he
carried in a sling.

"Guess I must be runnin' some fever, Chief, 'cause I don't
remember what I told you."

"You told me you didn't know who Galen was looking for
in here," Grave Digger said thickly.

Big Smiley stole another look at Ready, but all he got was
a picture of a black pockmarked face and two blank reddish
brown eyes with a cast in one which told him nothing. He
sighed heavily.

"Who he were looking for? Is dat what you ast me?" he
stalled, trying to meet Grave Digger's smoldering hot gaze.
"I dunno who he were looking for, Chief."

Grave Digger rose up on the bar stool rungs as though his
feet were in stirrups, snatched the bullwhip from the bar and
slashed Big Smiley across one cheek after another before Big
Smiley could get his good hand moving.

Big Smiley stopped smiling. Talk stopped suddenly the
length of the bar, petered out in the booths. In the vacuum
left by the cessation of talk, Lil Green's whining voice issued
from the juke box at front:

> *Why don't you do right*
> *Like other mens do . . .*

Grave Digger sat back on the stool, breathing hard, struggling to control his rage. Arteries stood out in his temples, growing out of his short cropped kinky hair like strange roots climbing toward the brim of his kicked back misshapen hat. His brown eyes laced with red veins generated a steady white heat.

The white manager who'd been working the front end of the bar hastened down toward them with a face full of outrage.

"Get back," Grave Digger said thickly.

The manager got back.

Grave Digger stabbed at Big Smiley with his left forefinger and said in a voice so thick it was hard to understand, "Smiley, all I want from you is the truth. And I ain't got long to get it."

Big Smiley didn't look at Ready any more. He didn't touch his cheeks on which welts rose beneath his greasy black skin like tunnels of psychopathic moles. He didn't smile. He didn't whine.

He said, "Just ast the questions, Chief, and I'll answer 'em to the best of my knowledge."

Grave Digger looked around at the teenagers in the booth. They were listening with open mouths, staring at him with popping eyes. His breath burned from his flaring nostrils. He turned back to Big Smiley. But he sat quietly for a moment to give the blood time to recede from his head.

"Who killed him?" he finally asked.

"I don't know, Chief."

"He was killed on your street."

"Yassuh, but I don't know who done it."

"Do Sissie and Sugartit come in here?"

"Yassuh, sometimes."

Out of the corners of his eyes Grave Digger noticed Ready's shoulders begin to sag as though his spine were melting.

"Sit up straight, goddammit," he said. "You'll have plenty of time to lie down if I find out you've been lying."

Ready sat up straight.

Grave Digger addressed Big Smiley. "Galen met them in here?"

"Nawsuh, he met Sissie in here once but I never seen him with Sugartit."

"What was she doing in here then?"

"She come in here twice with Sissie."

"How'd you know her name?"

"I heard Sissie call her that."

"Was Sheik with her when he met her?"

"You mean with Sissie, when she met the big man? Yassuh."

"He paid Sheik the money?"

"I couldn't be sure, Chief, but I seen money being passed. I don't know who got it."

"He got it. Did they both leave with him?"

"You mean both Sheik and Sissie?"

"That's what I mean."

Big Smiley took out a blue bandana handkerchief and mopped his sweating black face.

The four schoolgirls in the booth began going through the motions of leaving. Grave Digger wheeled toward them.

"Sit down, I want to talk to you later," he ordered.

They began a shrill cacophony of protest: "We got to get home . . . got to be at school tomorrow at nine o'clock . . . haven't finished homework . . . can't stay out this late . . . get into trouble . . ."

He got up and went over and showed them his gold badge. "You're already in trouble. Now I want you to sit down and keep quiet."

He took hold of the two girls who were standing and forced them back into their seats.

"He can't hold you 'less he's got a warrant," the boy in the aisle seat said.

Grave Digger slapped him out of his seat, reached down and lifted him from the floor by his coat lapels and slammed him back into his seat.

"Now say that again," he suggested.

The boy didn't speak.

Grave Digger waited for a moment until they had settled down and got quiet, then he returned to his bar stool.

Neither Big Smiley nor Ready had moved; neither had looked at the other.

"You didn't answer my question," Grave Digger said.

"When he took Sissie off Sheik stayed in his seat," Big Smiley said.

"What kind of a goddamned answer is that?"

"That's the way it was, Chief."

"Where did he take her?"

Rivers of sweat poured from Big Smiley's face. He sighed. "Downstairs," he said.

"Downstairs! In here?"

"Yassuh. They's stairs in the back room."

"What's downstairs?"

"Just a cellar like any other bar's got. It's full of bottles an' old bar fixtures and beer barrels. The compression unit for the draught beer is down there and the refrigeration unit for the ice boxes. That's all. Some rats and we keeps a cat."

"No bed or bedroom?"

"Nawsuh."

"He whipped them down there in that kind of place?"

"I don't know what he done."

"Couldn't you hear them?"

"Nawsuh. You can't hear nothin' through this floor. You could shoot off your pistol down there and you couldn't hear it up here."

Grave Digger turned a look on Ready. "Did you know that?"

Ready began to wilt again. "Nawsuh, I swear 'fore—"

"Sit up straight, goddammit! I don't want to have to tell you again."

He turned back to Big Smiley. "Did he know it?"

"Not as far as I know, unless he told him."

"Is Sissie or Sugartit among those girls over there?"

"Nawsuh," Big Smiley said without looking.

Grave Digger showed him the pornographic photos. "Know any of these?"

Big Smiley leafed through them slowly without a change of expression. Three he laid aside from the others.

"I've seen them," he said.

"What's their names?"

"I don't know only two of 'em." He separated them gingerly with his fingertips as though they were coated with external poison. "Them two. This here one is called Good Booty, t'other one is called Honey Bee. This one here, I never heard her name called."

"What are their family names?"

"I don't know none of 'em's square monickers."

"He took these downstairs?"

"Just them two."

"Who came here with them?"

"They came by theyself, most of 'em did."

"Did he have appointments with them?"

"Nawsuh, not with most of 'em anyway. They just come in here and laid for him."

"Did they come together?"

"Sometime, sometime not."

"You just said they came by themselves."

"I meant they didn't bring no boyfriends."

"Did he know them before?"

"I couldn't say. When he come in if he seed any of 'em he just made his choice."

"He knew they hung around here looking for him?"

"Yassuh. When he started comin' here he was already known."

"When was that?"

"Three or four months ago. I don't remember 'zactly."

"When did he start taking them downstairs?"

"'Bout two months ago."

"Did you suggest it?"

"Nawsuh, he propositioned me."

"How much did he pay you?"

"Twenty-five bucks."

"You're talking yourself into Sing-Sing."

"Maybe."

Grave Digger examined the note addressed to GB and signed Bee he'd taken from the dead man's effects; then passed it over to Big Smiley.

"That came from the pocket of the man you cut," he said.

Big Smiley read the note carefully, his lips spelling out each word. His breath came out in a sighing sound.

"Then he must be a relation of her," he said.

"You didn't know that?"

"Nawsuh, I swear 'fore God. If I'd knowed that I wouldn't 'ave chopped him with the axe."

"What exactly did he say to Galen when he started toward him with the knife?"

Big Smiley wrinkled his forehead. "I don't remember exactly. Something 'bout if he found a white mother-raper trying to diddle his little gals he'd cut his throat. But I just took that to mean colored women in general. You know how our folks talk. I didn't figure he meant his own kin."

"Maybe some other girl's father had the same idea with a pistol," Grave Digger suggested.

"Could be," Big Smiley said cautiously.

"So evidently he's the father and he's got more girls than one."

"Looks like it."

"He's dead," Grave Digger informed him.

Big Smiley's expression didn't change. "I'm sorry to hear it."

"You look like it. Who went your bail?"

"My boss."

Grave Digger looked at him soberly.

"Who's covering for you?" he asked.

"Nobody."

"I know that's a lie but I'm going to pass it. Who was covering for Galen?"

"I don't know."

"I'm going to pass that lie too. What was he doing here tonight?"

"He was looking for Sugartit."

"Did he have a date with her?"

"I don't know. He said she was coming by with Sissie."

"Did they come by after he'd left?"

"Nawsuh."

"Okay, Smiley, this one is for keeps. Who was Sugartit's father?"

"I don't know none of 'em's kinfolks nor neither where they lives, Chief, like I told you before. It didn't make no difference."

"You must have some idea."

"Nawsuh, it's just like I say, I never thought about it. You don't never think 'bout where a gal live in Harlem, 'less you goin' home with her. What do anybody's address mean up here."

"Don't let me catch you in a lie, Smiley."

"I ain't lying, Chief. I went with a woman for a whole year once and never did know where she lived. Didn't care neither."

"Who are the Real Cool Moslems?"

"Them punks! Just a kid gang around here."

"Where do they hang out?"

"I don't know 'zactly. Somewhere down the street."

"Do they come in here?"

"Only three of 'em sometime. Sheik, I think he's they leader; and a boy called Choo-Choo and the one they call Bones."

"Where do they live?"

"Somewhere near here, but I don't know 'zactly. The boy down the street on t'other side. I don't know his name but he got a pigeon coop on the roof."

"Is he one of 'em?"

"I don't know for sure but you can see a gang of boys on the roof when he's flying his pigeons."

"I'll find him. Do you know the ages of those girls in the booth?"

"Nawsuh, when I ask 'em they say they're eighteen."

"You know they're underage."

"I s'pect so but all I can do is ast 'em."

"Did he have any of them?"

"Only one I knows of."

Grave Digger turned and looked at the girls again.

"What one?" he asked.

"The dark one in the green tam." Big Smiley pushed forward one of the three photos. "She's this one here, the one called Good Booty."

"Okay, son, that's all for the moment," Grave Digger said.

He got down from the stool and walked forward to talk to the manager.

As soon as he left, without saying a word or giving a warning, Big Smiley leaned forward and hit Ready in the face with his big ham-size fist. Ready sailed backward from his stool, crashed into the wall and crumpled to the floor.

Grave Digger looked down in time to see his head disappearing beneath the edge of the bar then turned his attention to the white manager across from him.

"Collect your tabs and shut the bar; I'm closing up this joint and you're under arrest," he said.

"For what?" the manager challenged hotly.

"For contributing to the delinquency of minors."

The manager sputtered, "I'll be open again by tomorrow night."

"Don't say another goddamned word," Grave Digger said and kept looking at him until the manager closed his mouth and turned away.

Then he beckoned one of the white cops on the door and told him, "I'm putting the manager and the bartender under arrest and closing the joint. I want you to hold the manager and some teenagers I'll turn over to you. I'm going to leave in a minute and I'll send back the wagon. I'll take the bartender with me."

"Right, Jones," the cop said, as happy as a kid with a new toy.

Grave Digger walked back to the rear.

Ready was down on the floor on his hands and knees, spitting out blood and teeth.

Grave Digger looked at him and smiled grimly. Then he looked up at Big Smiley who was licking his bruised knuckles with a big red tongue.

"You're under arrest, Smiley," he said. "If you try to escape, I'm going to shoot you through the back of the head."

"Yassuh," Big Smiley said.

Grave Digger shook a customer loose from a plastic covered chair and sat astride it at the end of the table in the booth, facing the scared, silent teenagers. He took out his notebook and stylo and wrote down their names, addresses, numbers of the public schools they attended, and their ages as they replied in turn to his questions. The oldest was a boy of seventeen.

None of them admitted knowing either Sissie, Sugartit, the big white man, Galen, or anyone connected with the gang of Real Cool Moslems.

He called the second cop down from the door and said, "Hold these kids for the wagon."

Then he said to the girl in the green tam who'd given her name as Gertrude B. Richardson, "Gertrude, I want you to come with me."

One of the girls tittered. "You might have known he'd take Good Booty," she said.

"My name is Beauty," Good Booty said, tossing her head disdainfully.

On sudden impulse Grave Digger stopped her as she was about to get up.

"What's your father's name, Gertrude?"

"Charlie."

"What does he do?"

"He's a porter."

"Is that so? Do you have any sisters?"

"One. She's a year younger than me."

"What does your mother do?"

"I don't know. She don't live with us."

"I see. You two girls live with your father."

"Where else we going to live."

"That's a good question, Gertrude, but I can't answer it. Did you know a man got his arm cut off in here earlier tonight?"

"I heard about it. So what? People are always getting cut around here."

"This man tried to knife the white man because of his daughters."

"He did." She giggled. "He was a square."

"No doubt. The bartender chopped off his arm with an axe to protect the white man. What do you think about that?"

She giggled again, nervously. "Maybe he figured the white man was more important than some colored drunk."

"He must have. The man died in Harlem Hospital less than an hour ago."

Her eyes got big and frightened. "What are you trying to say, Mister."

"I'm trying to tell you that he was your father."

Grave Digger hadn't anticipated her reaction. She came up

out of her seat so fast that she was past him before he could grab her.

"Stop her!" he shouted.

A customer wheeled from his bar stool into her path and she stuck her fingers into his eye. The man yelped and tried to hold her. She wrenched from his grip and sprang toward the door. The white cop headed her off and wrapped his arms about her. She twisted in his grip like a panicstricken cat and clawed at his pistol. She had gotten it out the holster when a colored man rushed in and wrenched it from her grip. The white cop threw her onto the floor on her back and sat straddle her, pinning down her arms. The colored man grabbed her by the feet. She writhed on her back and spat in the cop's face.

Grave Digger came up and looked down at her from sad brown eyes. "It's too late now, Gertrude," he said. "They're both dead."

Suddenly she began crying hysterically.

"What did he have to mess in it for?" she sobbed. "Oh, pa, what did you have to mess in it for?"

14.

Two uniformed white cops standing guard on a dark rooftop were talking.

"Do you think we'll find him?"

"Do I think we'll find him? Do you know who we're looking for? Have you stopped to think for a moment that we're looking for one colored man who supposedly is handcuffed and seven other colored men who were wearing green turbans and false beards when last seen. Have you turned that over in your mind? By this time they've long since got rid of those phony disguises and maybe Pickens has got rid of his handcuffs too. And then what does that make them, I ask you. That makes them just like eighteen thousand or one hundred and eighty thousand other colored men, all looking alike. Have you ever stopped to think there are five hundred thousand colored people in Harlem—one half of a million people with black skin. All looking alike. And we're trying to pick eight out of them. It's like trying to find a cinder in a coal bin. It ain't possible."

"Do you think all these colored people in this neighborhood know who Pickens and the Moslems are?"

"Sure they know. Every last one of them. Unless some other colored person turns Pickens in he'll never be found. They're laughing at us."

"As much as the chief wants that coon, whoever finds him is sure to get a promotion," the first cop said.

"Yeah, I know, but it ain't possible," the second cop said. "If that coon's got any sense at all he would at least have filed those cuffs in two a long time ago."

"What good would that do him if he couldn't get them off?"

"Well, he could wear heavy gloves with gauntlets like— Hey! Didn't we see some coon wearing driving gauntlets?"

"Yeah, that halfwit coon with the pigeons."

"Wearing gauntlets and an old ragged overcoat. And a coal black coon at that. He certainly fits the description."

"That halfwitted coon. You think it's possible that he's the one."

"Come on! What are we waiting for?"

Sheik said, "Now all we've got to do is get this mother-raper past the police lines and throw him into the river."

"Doan do that to me, please, Sheik," Sonny's muffled voice pleaded from inside the sack.

"Shhhh," Choo-Choo cautioned. "Chalk the walking Jeffs."

The two cops leaned over head by head and peered in through the open window.

"Where's that boy who was wearing gloves?" the first cop asked.

"Gloves!" Choo-Choo echoed, going into his clowning act like a chameleon changing color. "You means boxing gloves?"

The second cop sniffed.

"A weed pad!" he exclaimed.

They climbed inside. Their gazes swept quickly over the room.

The room reeked with the scent of marijuana smoke. Everyone in it was high. The ones who hadn't smoked were high from inhaling the smoke and watching the eccentric motions of the ones who had smoked.

"Who's got the sticks?" the first cop demanded in a bullying tone of voice.

"Come on, come on, who's got the sticks?" the second cop echoed, looking from one to the other. He passed over Sheik who stood in the center of the floor where he'd been arrested in motion by Choo-Choo's warning and stared at them as though trying to make out what they were; then over Inky who was caught in the act of ducking behind the curtains in the corner and stood there half in and half out like a billboard advertisement for a movie about bad girls; and landed on Choo-Choo who seemed the most vulnerable because he was grinning like an idiot. "You got the sticks, boy?"

"Sticks! You mean that there pigeon stick," Choo-Choo said, pointing at the bamboo pole on the floor beside the bed.

"Don't get funny with me, boy!"

"I just don't know what you means, boss."

"Forget the sticks," the first cop said. "Let's find the boy with the gloves."

He looked about. His gaze lit on Sugartit who was sitting in the straightbacked chair and staring with a fixed popeyed expression at what appeared to be a gunny sack filled with huge lumps of coal lying in the middle of the bed.

"What's in that sack?" he asked suspiciously.

For an instant no one replied.

Then Choo-Choo said, "Just some coal."

"On the bed?"

"It's clean coal."

The cop pinned a threatening look on him.

"It's my bed," Sheik said. "I can put what I want on it."

Both cops went suddenly still and stared at him.

"You're a kind of a lippy bastard," the first cop said. "What's your name?"

"Samson."

"You live here?"

"Right here."

"Then you're the boy we're looking for. That's your pigeon loft on the roof."

"No, that's not him," the second cop said. "The boy we want is blacker than he is and has another name."

"What's a name to these coons?" the first cop said. "They're always changing about."

"No, the one we want is called Inky. He was the one wearing the gloves."

"Now I remember. He was called Caleb. He was the one wearing the gloves. The other one was Inky, the one who couldn't talk."

The second cop wheeled on Sheik. "Where's Caleb?"

"I don't know anybody named Caleb."

"The hell you don't! He lives here with you."

"Nawsuh, you means that boy what lives down on the first floor," Choo-Choo said.

"Don't tell me what I mean. I mean the boy who lives here on this floor. He's the boy who's got the pigeon loft."

"Nawsuh, boss, if you means the Caleb what's got the pigeon roost, he lives on the first floor."

"Don't lie to me, boy. I saw the sergeant bring him down the fire escape to this floor."

"Nawsuh, boss, the sergeant taken him on by this floor and carried him down on the fire escape to the first floor. We seen 'em when they came by the window. Didn't we, Amos?" he called on Inky.

"That's right, suh," Inky said. "They went right past that window there."

"What other window could they go by?"

"None other window, suh."

"They had another boy with 'em called Inky," Choo-Choo said. "It looked like they had 'em both arrested."

The second cop was staring at Inky. "This boy here looks like Inky to me," he said. "Aren't you Inky, boy?"

"Nawsuh—" Inky began, but Choo-Choo quickly cut him off, "They calls him Smokey. Inky is the other one."

"Let him talk for himself," the first cop said.

The second cop pinned another threatening look on Choo-Choo. "Are you trying to make a fool out of me, boy?"

"Nawsuh, boss, I'se just tryna help."

"Leave up off him," the first cop said. "These coons are jagged on weed; they're not strictly responsible."

"Responsible or not, they'd better be careful before they get some lumps on their heads."

The first cop noticed Sissie standing quietly in the corner, holding her hand to her bruised cheek.

"You know them, Caleb and Inky, don't you, girl?" he asked her.

"No sir, I just know Smokey," she said.

Suddenly Sonny sneezed.

Sugartit giggled.

The cop wheeled toward the bed, looked at the sack and then looked at her.

"Who was that sneezed?"

She put her hand to her mouth and tried to stop laughing.

The cop turned slightly pinkish and drew his pistol.

"Some one's underneath the bed," he said. "Keep the others covered while I look."

The second cop drew his pistol.

"Just relax and won't anybody get hurt," he said calmly.

The first cop got down on his hands and knees, holding his cocked pistol ready to shoot, and looked underneath the bed.

Sugartit put both hands over her mouth and bit into her palm. Her face swelled with suppressed laughter and tears overflowed her eyes.

The cop straightened to his knees and braced himself on the edge of the bed. There was a perplexed look on his blood red face.

"There's something funny going on in here," he said. "There's someone else in this room."

"Ain't nobody here but us ghosts, boss," Choo-Choo said.

The cop threw him a look of frustrated fury, and started to his feet.

"By God I'll—" His voice was dried up by choking sounds issuing from inside the sack.

He jumped upward and backward as though one of the ghosts had sure enough groaned. Leveling his pistol, he said in a quaking voice, "What's in that sack?"

Sugartit burst into hysterical laughter.

For an instant no one spoke.

Then Choo-Choo said hastily, "Hit's just Joe."

"What!"

"Hit's just Joe in the sack."

"Joe!"

Gingerly the cop leaned over, holding his cocked pistol in his right hand, and untied the cord closing the sack with his left. He drew the top of the sack open.

A gray-black face containing a protruding purple-red tongue stared up at him from white-walled popping eyes.

The cop drew back in horror. His face turned white and a shudder passed over his big solid frame.

"It's a body," he said in a choked voice. "All trussed up."

"Hit ain't no body, hit's just Joe," Choo-Choo said with no intention whatsoever of sounding funny.

The second cop hastened over to look.

"It's still alive," he said.

"He's choking!" Sissie cried and ran over and began loosening the noose about Sonny's neck.

Sonny sucked in breath with a gasp.

"My God, what's he doing in there?" the first cop asked in amazement.

"He's just studying magic," Choo-Choo said. He was beginning to sweat from the strain.

"Magic!"

The second cop noticed Sheik inching toward the window and aimed his pistol at him.

"Oh no you don't," he said. "You come over here."

Sheik turned and came closer.

"Studying magic!" the first cop said. "In a sack?"

"Yassuh, he's trying to learn how to get out, like Houdini." Color flooded back into the cop's face.

"I ought to take him in for indecent exposure," he said.

"Hell, he's wearing a sack, ain't he," the second cop said, amused by his own wit.

Both of them grinned at Sonny as though he were a harmless halfwit.

Then the second cop said suddenly, "It ain't possible! There can't be two such halfwits in the whole world."

The first cop looked closely at Sonny and said slowly, "I

believe you're right." Then to the others at large, "Get that boy out of that sack."

Sheik didn't move, but Choo-Choo and Inky hastened over and pulled Sonny out while Sissie held the bottom of the sack.

The cops stared at Sonny with awe.

"Looks like barbecued coon, don't he," the first cop said.

Sugartit burst into renewed laughter.

Sonny was buck naked. His heels were pulled tight against his buttocks and his knees were jackknifed up to his chin. The wire clothesline ran from a noose about his neck out between his legs, was looped loosely about each knee with a slipknot between the loops, then down to his ankles, binding them tightly, and finally up his back where the remainder was wrapped several times about his wrists. His black skin had a gray pallor as though dusted over lightly with wood ashes. He was shaking like a leaf.

The second cop reached out and turned him around.

Everyone stared at the handcuff bracelets clamped about each wrist.

"That's our boy," the first cop said.

"Lawd, suh, I wish I'd gone home and gone to bed," Sonny said in a moaning voice.

"I'll bet you do," the cop said.

Sugartit couldn't stop laughing.

15.

THE BODIES had been taken to the morgue. All that remained were chalk outlines on the pavement where they had lain.

The street had been cleared of private cars. Police tow trucks had come and carried away those that had been abandoned in the middle of the street. Most of the patrol cars had returned to duty. Only those remained that were blockading the area.

The chief of police's car occupied the center of the stage. It was parked in the middle of the intersection of 127th Street and Lenox Avenue.

To one side of it the chief, Lieutenant Anderson, the lieutenant from homicide and the precinct sergeant who'd led one of the searching parties were grouped about the boy called Bones.

The lieutenant from homicide had a zip gun in his hand.

"All right then, it isn't yours," he said to Bones in a voice of tried patience. "Whose is it then? Who were you hiding it for?"

Bones stole a glance at the lieutenant's face and his gaze dropped quickly to the street. It crawled over the four pairs of big black copper's boots. They looked like the 6th Fleet at anchor. He didn't answer.

He was a slim black boy of medium height with girlish features and short hair almost straight at the roots parted on one side. He wore a natty shot topcoat over his sweat shirt and tight fitting black pants above shiny tan pointed-toed shoes.

An elderly man, a head taller, with a black face grizzled from hard outdoor work, stood beside him. Kinky hair grew like burdock weeds about his shiny black dome; and worried brown eyes looked down at Bones from behind steel-rimmed spectacles.

"Go 'head, tell 'em, son, don't be no fool," he said; then he looked up and saw Grave Digger approaching with his prisoners. "Here comes Digger Jones," he said. "You can tell him, cain't you?"

Everybody looked about.

Grave Digger had Big Smiley and Ready Belcher handcuffed together walking in front of him; and he held Good Booty by the arm.

He looked at Anderson and said, "I closed up the Dew Drop Inn and gave the manager and some juvenile delinquents to the officers on duty to hold. You'd better send a wagon up there."

Anderson whistled for a patrol car team and gave them the order.

"What did you find out on Galen?" the chief asked.

"I found out he was a pervert," Grave Digger said.

"It figures," the homicide lieutenant said.

The chief turned red. "I don't give a goddamn what he was," he said. "Have you found out who killed him?"

"No, right now I'm still guessing at it," Grave Digger said.

"Well, guess fast then. I'm getting goddamned tired of standing up here watching this comedy of errors."

"I'll give you a quick fill-in and let you guess too," Grave Digger said.

"Well, make it short and sweet and I damn sure ain't going to guess," the chief said.

"Lissen, Digger," the colored civilian interposed. "You and me is both city workers. Tell 'em my boy ain't done no harm."

"He's broken the Sullivan law concerning concealed weapons by having this gun in his possession," the homicide lieutenant said.

"That little thing," Bones' father said scornfully. "I don't b'lieve that'll even shoot."

"Get these people away from here and let Jones report," the chief said testily.

"Well, do something with them, sergeant," Lieutenant Anderson said.

"Come on, both of you," the sergeant said, taking the man by the arm.

"Digger—" the man appealed.

"It'll keep," Grave Digger said harshly. "Your boy belonged to the Moslem gang."

"Naw-naw, Digger—"

"Do I have to slug you," the sergeant said.

The man allowed himself to be taken along with his son across the street.

The sergeant turned them over to a corporal and hurried back. Before he'd gone three steps the corporal was already summoning two cops to take charge of them.

"What kind of city work does he do?" the chief asked.

"He's in the sanitation department," the sergeant said. "He's a garbage collector."

"All right, get on, Jones," the chief ordered.

"Galen picked up colored school girls, teenagers, and took them to a crib on 145th Street," Grave Digger said in a flat toneless voice.

"Did you close it?" the chief asked.

"It'll keep; I'm looking for a murderer now," Grave Digger

said. Taking the miniature bullwhip from his pocket, he went on, "He whipped them with this."

The chief reached out silently and took it from his hand.

"He paid them $100 for each whipping," Grave Digger said.

"You're sure he didn't pay to get whipped," the homicide lieutenant said.

"No, he whipped them. He was a sadist."

"At that price, it's usually the other way around," the homicide lieutenant said. "Sadists are usually cheap."

"He hurt some of them pretty bad," Grave Digger said.

The chief hefted the bull whip and tested it against his leg.

"It's got a sting all right," he said. "Have you got a list of them, Jones?"

"What for?"

"There might be a connection."

"I'm coming to that—"

"Well, get to it then."

"The landprop, a woman named Reba—used to call herself Sheba, the one who testified against Captain Murphy—"

"Ah, that one," the chief said softly. "She won't slip out of this."

"She'll take somebody with her," Grave Digger warned. "She's covered and Galen was too."

The chief looked at Lieutenant Anderson reflectively.

The silence ran on until the sergeant blurted, "That's not in this precinct."

Anderson looked at the sergeant. "No one's charging you with it."

"Get on, Jones," the chief said.

"Reba got scared of the deal and barred him. Her story will be that she barred him when she found out what he was doing. But that's neither here nor there. After she barred him Galen started meeting them in the Dew Drop Inn. He arranged with the bartender so he could whip them in the cellar."

Everyone except Grave Digger appeared embarrassed.

"He ran into a girl named Sissie," Grave Digger said. "How doesn't matter at the moment. She's the girl friend of a boy called Sheik, who is the leader of the Real Cool Moslems."

Sudden tension took hold of the group.

"Sheik sold Sissie to him. Then Galen wanted Sissie's girl-friend, Sugartit. Sheik couldn't get Sugartit, but Galen kept looking for her in the neighborhood. I have the bartender here and a two-bit pimp who has a girl at Reba's who steered for Galen. I got this much from them."

The officers stared appraisingly at the two handcuffed prisoners.

"If they know that much, they know who killed him," the chief said.

"It's going to be their asses if they do," Grave Digger said. "But I think they're leveling. The way I figure it is the whole thing hinges on Sugartit. I think he was killed because of her."

"By who?"

"That's the jackpot question."

The chief looked at Good Booty. "Is this girl Sugartit?"

The others stared at her too.

"No, she's another one."

"Who is Sugartit then?"

"I haven't found out yet. This girl knows but she doesn't want to tell."

"Make her tell."

"How?"

The chief appeared embarrassed by the question. "Well, what the hell do you want with her if you can't make her talk?" he growled.

"I think she'll talk when we get close enough. The Moslem gang hangs out somewhere near here. The bartender here thinks it might be in the flat of a boy who has a pigeon loft."

"I know where that is!" the sergeant exclaimed. "I searched there."

Everyone, including the prisoners, stared at him.

His face reddened. "Now I remember," he said. "There were several boys in the flat. The boy who kept the pigeons, Caleb Bowee is his name, lives there with his grandma; and two of the others roomed there."

"Why in the hell didn't you bring them in?" the chief asked.

"I didn't find anything on them to connect them with the Moslem gang or the escaped prisoner," the sergeant said, defending himself. "The boy with the pigeons is a halfwit—he's harmless; and I'm sure the grandma wouldn't put up with a gang in there."

"How in the hell do you know he's harmless?" the chief stormed. "Half the murderers in Sing-Sing look like you and me."

The homicide lieutenant and Anderson exchanged smiles.

"They had two girls with them and—" the sergeant began to explain but the chief wouldn't let him.

"Why in the hell didn't you bring them in too?"

"What were the girls' names?" Grave Digger asked.

"One was called Sissieratta and—"

"That must be Sissie," Grave Digger said. "It fits. One was Sissie and the other was Sugartit. And one of the boys was Sheik." Turning to Big Smiley, he asked, "What does Sheik look like?"

"Freckled-faced boy the color of a bay horse with yellow cat eyes," Big Smiley said impassively.

"You're right," the sergeant admitted sheepishly. "He was one of them. I should have trusted my instinct; I started to haul that punk in."

"Well, for God's sake get the lead out of your ass now," the chief roared. "If you still consider yourself working for the police department."

"Well, Jesus Christ, the other girl, the one Jones calls Sugartit, was Ed Johnson's daughter," the sergeant exploded. "She had one of those souvenir police ID cards signed by yourself and I thought—"

He was interrupted by the flat whacking sound of metal striking against a human skull.

No one had seen Grave Digger move.

What they saw now was Ready Belcher sagging forward with his eyes rolled back into his head and a white cut two inches wide in the black pockmarked skin of his forehead, not yet beginning to bleed; and Big Smiley rearing back on the other end of the handcuffs like a dray horse shying from a rattlesnake.

Grave Digger had his nickel-plated thirty eight gripped by

the long barrel, making a club out of the butt. The muscles were corded in his rage swollen neck like rigging ropes and his face was distorted like a maniac's. An effluvium of violence came out of him like the sudden smell of death.

Looking at him, the others were caught up and suspended in motion as though turned to stone.

Before their startled eyes had time to blink, he struck again. Beneath the pistol butt the top of Ready's four dollar conked head caved in like a softboiled egg. A small gush of breath slipped from Ready's slack mouth and he sunk like a stone.

Big Smiley shied again and Grave Digger struck him across his injured arm hard enough to break it, mouthing out the words like cotton spewing from the gin, "Keep still, you're moving him!"

The irises of Big Smiley's eyes disappeared, leaving slits of dirty whites barely visible between his half-closed eyelids.

"Stop him, goddammit!" the chief roared. "He'll kill them."

Grave Digger kicked at Ready's prone head, missed and clubbed Big Smiley in the middle of the spine as he went off balance.

The sculptured figures of the police officers came to life. The sergeant grabbed Grave Digger from behind in a bear hug. Grave Digger doubled over forward and sent the sergeant flying over his head toward the chief, who ducked in turn and let the sergeant sail on by.

Lieutenant Anderson and the homicide lieutenant converged on Grave Digger from opposite directions and each grabbed an arm while he was still in a crouch and lifted him upward and backward.

Ready was lying prone on the pavement, blood tricking from the two dents in his skull, a slack arm drawn tight by the handcuffs attached to Big Smiley's wrist. He looked already dead.

Big Smiley gave the appearance of a terrified blind beggar caught in a bombing raid; his giant frame trembled from head to foot.

Grave Digger had just time enough to kick Ready in the face before the officers jerked him out of range.

Ready's jawbone broke with a stomach retching sound and his lower jaw swung out at an angle that exposed one whole row of his bottom teeth and the edge of his white coated tongue swimming in blood.

"Get him to the hospital quick!" the chief shouted; and in the next breath added, "Rap him on the head!"

Grave Digger had carried the lieutenants to the ground and it was more than either could do to rap him on the head.

The sergeant had already picked himself up and at the chief's order set off at a gallop.

"Goddammit, phone for it, don't run after it!" the chief yelled. "Where the hell is my chauffeur anyway."

Cops came running from all directions.

"Give the lieutenants a hand," the chief said. "They have got a wild man."

Four cops jumped into the fray. Finally they pinned Grave Digger to the ground.

The sergeant climbed into the chief's car and began talking into the telephone.

Coffin Ed appeared suddenly. No one had noticed him approaching from his parked car down the street.

"Great God, what's happening, Digger!" he exclaimed.

Everybody got quiet. Their embarrassment was noticeable.

"What the hell!" he said, looking from one to the other. "What the hell's going on."

Grave Digger's muscles relaxed as though he'd lost consciousness.

"It's just me, Ed," he said, looking up from the ground at his friend. "I just lost my head is all."

"Let him go," Anderson ordered his helpers. "He's back to normal now."

The cops released Grave Digger and he got to his feet.

"Cooled off now?" the homicide lieutenant asked.

"Yeah, give me my gun," Grave Digger said.

"Give it to him," the chief said.

The lieutenant gave him back his gun.

Coffin Ed looked down at Ready Belcher's mangled head.

"You too, eh, partner," he said. "What did this rebel do?"

"I told him if I caught him holding out on me I'd kill him."

"You told him no lie," Coffin Ed said. Then asked, "Is it that bad?"

"It's dirty, Ed. Galen was a rotten son of a bitch."

"That doesn't surprise me. Have you got anything on it so far?"

"A little, not much."

"What the hell do you want here?" the chief said testily. "I suppose you want to help your buddy kill some more of your folks."

Grave Digger knew the chief was trying to steer the conversation away from Coffin Ed's daughter, but he didn't know how to help him.

"You two men act as if you want to kill off the whole population of Harlem," the chief kept on.

"You told me to crack down," Grave Digger reminded him.

"Yeah, but I didn't mean in front of my eyes where I would have to be a witness to it."

"It's our beat," Coffin Ed spoke up for his friend. "If you don't like the way we handle it why don't you take us off."

"You're already off," the chief said. "What in the hell did you come back for anyway?"

"Strictly on private business."

The chief snorted.

"My little daughter hasn't come home and I'm worried about her," Coffin Ed explained. "It's not like her to stay out this late and not let us know where she is."

The chief looked away to hide his embarrassment.

Grave Digger swallowed audibly.

"Hell, Ed, you don't have to worry about Eve," he said in a tone of voice he hoped sounded reassuring. "She'll be home soon. You know nothing can happen to her. She's got that police ID card you got for her on her last birthday, hasn't she?"

"I know, but she always phones her mother if she's going to stay out."

"While you're out here looking for her she's probably gone home. Why don't you go back home and go to bed. She'll be all right."

"Jones is telling you right, Ed," the chief said brusquely.

"Go home and relax. You're off duty and you're in our way here. Nothing is going to happen to your daughter. You're just having nightmares."

A siren sounded in the distance.

"Here comes the ambulance," Lieutenant Anderson said.

"I'll go and phone home again," Coffin Ed said. "Take it easy, Digger, don't get yourself docked too."

As he turned and started off a fusillade of shots sounded from the upper floor of some nearby tenement. Ten shots from regulation .38 calibre police specials were fired so fast that by the time the sound had reached the street it was chained together.

Every cop within hearing distance froze to alert attention. They strained their ears in almost superhuman effort to place the direction from which the shots had come. Their eyes scanned the fronts of the tenements until not a spot escaped their observation.

But no more shots were fired.

The only signs of life left were the lights going out. With the rapidity of the gun shots, one light after another went out until only one lighted window remained in all the totally dark dingy buildings. It was on the top floor behind a fire escape landing of the tenement a half block up the street.

All eyes focused on that spot.

The grotesque silhouette of something crawling over the window sill appeared in the glare of light. Slowly it straightened and took the shape of a short husky man. It staggered slowly the three foot width of the grilled iron footing and leaned against the low outer rail. For a moment it swayed back and forth in a macabre pantomime and then slowly, like a roulette ball climbing the last hurdle before the final slot, it fell over the railing, turning slowly in the air, missing the second landing by a breath, but turned sufficiently for the head to strike the railing of the third, which started it to spinning faster. It landed with a resounding thud on top of a parked car and lay there with one hand hanging down beside the driver's window as though signaling for a stop.

"Well, goddammit, get going!" the chief shouted in a stentorian voice, then on second thought added quickly, "Not

I'm holding a razor-edged butcher knife against her throat with my right hand. If you try to take me I'll cut her mother-raping head off before you can get through the door."

"All right, Sheik, you got us by the balls, but you know you can't get away. Why don't you come out peaceably and give yourself up like a man. I give you my word that no one will abuse you. The officer you shot ain't seriously hurt. There's no other charge against you. You ought to get off with five years. With time off for good behavior, you'll be back in the big town in three years. Why risk sudden death or the hot seat just for a moment of playing the big shot?"

"Don't hand me that mother-raping crap. You'll hang a kidnapping charge on me for snatching your prisoner."

"What the hell! You can keep him. We don't want him anymore. We found out he didn't kill the man. All he had was a blank pistol."

"So he didn't kill the man?"

"No."

"Who killed him?"

"We don't know yet."

"So you don't know who killed the Big Greek, do you?"

"All right, all right, what's that to you? What do you want to get mixed up in something that don't concern you?"

"You're one of those smart mother-rapers, ain't you? You're going to be so smart you're going to make me cut her mother-raping throat just to show you."

"Please don't argue with him, Mr. Chief, please," said a small scared voice from within. "He'll kill me. I know he will."

"Shut up!" Sheik said roughly. "I don't need you to tell 'im I'm going to kill you."

Beads of sweat formed on the ridge of the chief's red nose and about the blue bags beneath his eyes.

"Why don't you be a man," he urged, filling his voice with contempt. "Don't be a mad dog like Vincent Coll. Be a man like Dillinger was. You won't get much. Three years and no more. Don't hide behind an innocent little girl."

"Who the hell do you think you're kidding with that stale crap. This is the Sheik. Can't no dumb cop like you make a fool out of the Sheik. You got the chair waiting for me and you think you're going to kid me into walking out there and sitting in it."

"Don't play yourself too big, punk," the chief said, losing his temper for a moment. "You shot an officer but you didn't kill him. You snatched a prisoner but we don't want him. Now you want to take it out on a little girl who can't defend herself. And you call yourself the Sheik, the big gang leader. You're just a cheap tin horn punk, yellow to the core."

"Keep on, just keep on. You ain't kidding me with that mother-raping sucker bait. You know mother-raping well it was me killed him. You've had me tabbed ever since you found out that chickenshit nigger was shooting blanks."

"What!" The chief was startled. Forgetting himself, he asked Grave Digger, "What the hell's he talking about?"

"Galen," Grave Digger said with his lips.

"Galen!" the chief exclaimed. "You're trying to tell me you killed the white man, you chicken-livered punk?" he roared.

"Keep on, just keep on. You know mother-raping well it was me lowered the boom on the Big Greek." He sounded as though he bitterly resented an oversight. "Who do you think you're kidding? You're talking to the Sheik. You think 'cause I'm colored I'm dumb enough to fall for that rock-a-bye baby crap you're putting down."

The chief had to readjust his train of thought.

"So it was you who killed Galen?"

"He was just the Greek to me," Sheik said scornfully. "Just another gray sucker up here trying to get his kicks. Yeah, I killed him." There was pride in his voice.

"Yeah, it figures," the chief said thoughtfully. "You saw him running down the street and you took advantage of that and shot him in the back. Just what a yellow son of a bitch like you would do. You were probably laying for him and were scared to go out and face him like a man."

"I wasn't laying for the mother-raper no such a goddamn thing," Sheik said. "I didn't even know he was anywhere about."

"You were nursing a grudge against him."

"I didn't have nothing against the mother-raper. You must

be having pipe dreams. He was just another gray sucker to me."

"Then why the hell did you shoot him?"

"I was just trying out my new zip gun. I saw the mother-raper running by where I was standing so I just blasted at him to see how good my gun would shoot."

"You goddamned little rat," the chief said, but there was more sorrow in his voice than anger. "You sick little bastard. What the goddamned hell can be done with somebody like you?"

"I just want you to quit trying to kid me, 'cause I'd just as soon cut this girl's throat right now as not."

"All right, *Mister* Sheik," the chief said in a cold quiet voice. "What do you want me to do?"

"Is Grave Digger come yet?"

Grave Digger nodded.

"Yeah, he's here, *Mister* Sheik."

"Let him say something then, and you better can that *Mister* crap."

"Eve, this is me, Digger Jones," Grave Digger said, spurning Sheik.

"Answer him," Sheik said.

"Yes, Mr. Jones," she said in a voice so weightless it floated out to the tense group listening like quivering eiderdown.

"Is Sissie in there with you?"

"No sir, just Granny Bowee and she's sitting in her chair asleep."

"Where's Sissie?"

"She and Inky are in the front room."

"Has he hurt you?"

"Quit stalling," Sheik said dangerously. "I'm going to give you until I count to three."

"Please, Mr. Jones, do what he says. He's going to kill me if you don't."

"Don't worry, child, we're going to do what he says," he reassured her and then said, "What do you want, boy?"

"These are my terms: I want the street cleared of cops; all the police blockades moved—"

"What the hell!" the chief exploded.

"We'll do it," Grave Digger said.

"I want to hear the chief say it," Sheik demanded.

"I'll be damned if I will," the chief said.

"Please," came a tiny voice no bigger than a little prayer.

"What if she was your daughter," Grave Digger said.

"I'm going to give you until I count three," Sheik said.

"All right, I'll do it," the chief said, sweating blood.

"On your word of honor as a great white man," Sheik persisted.

The chief's red sweating face drained of color.

"All right, all right, on my word of honor," he said.

"Then I want an ambulance driven up to the door downstairs. I want all its doors left open so I can see inside, the back doors and both the side doors, and I want the motor left running."

"All right, all right, what else? The Statue of Liberty?"

"I want this house cleared—"

"All right, all right, I said I'd do that."

"I don't want any mother-raping alarm put out. I don't want anybody to try to stop me. If anybody messes with me before I get away you're going to have a dead girl to bury. I'll put her out somewhere safe when I get clear away, clear out of the state."

The chief looked at Grave Digger.

"Don't cross him," Grave Digger whispered tensely. "He's teaed to the eyes."

"All right, all right," the chief said. "We'll give you safe passage. If you don't hurt the girl. If you hurt her don't think that we're going to kill you. But you'll beg for us to. Now take five minutes and come out and we'll let you drive away."

"Who you think you're kidding?" Sheik said. "I ain't that big a fool. I want Grave Digger to come inside of here and put his pistol down on the table, then I'm going to come out."

"You're crazy if you think we're going to give you a pistol," the chief roared.

"Then I'm going to kill her now."

"I'll give it to you," Grave Digger said.

"You're under suspension as of now," the chief said.

"All right," Grave Digger said; then to Sheik, "What do you want me to do?"

"I want you to stand outside the door with the pistol held by the barrel. When I open the door I want you to stick it forward and walk into the room so the first thing I see is the butt. Then I want you to walk straight ahead and put it on the kitchen table. You got that?"

"Yeah, I got it."

"The rest of you mother-rapers get downstairs," Sheik said.

The two lieutenants and the sergeant looked at the chief for orders.

"All right, Jones, it's your show," the chief said, adding on second thought, "I wish you luck."

He turned and started down the stairs.

The others hesitated. Grave Digger motioned violently for them to leave too. Reluctantly they followed the chief.

Silence came from the kitchen until the sound of the officers' feet had diminished into silence below.

Grave Digger stood facing the kitchen door, holding the pistol as instructed. Sweat poured down his lumpy cordovan colored face and collected in the collar about his rage swollen neck.

Finally the sound of movement came from the kitchen. The bolt of the Yale lock clicked open, a hand bolt was pulled back with a grating snap, a chain was unfastened. The door swung slowly inward.

Only Granny was visible from the doorway. She sat bolt upright in the immobile rocking chair with her hands gripping the arms and her old milky eyes wide open and staring at Grave Digger with a fixed look of fierce disapproval.

Sheik spoke from behind the door, "Turn the butt this way so I can see if it's loaded."

Without looking around, Grave Digger turned the pistol so that Sheik could see the shells in the chambers of the cylinder.

"Go ahead, keep walking," Sheik ordered.

Still without looking around, Grave Digger advanced slowly across the room. When he came to the table he looked swiftly toward the small window at the far end of the back wall. It was on the other side of an old-fashioned home-made cupboard which partially blocked the view of the kitchen from the outside, so that only the half between the table and the side wall was visible.

He saw what he was looking for. He then leaned slowly forward and placed the pistol on the far side of the table.

"There," he said.

Raising his hands high above his head, he turned slowly away from the table and faced the back wall. He stood so that Sheik had either to pass in front of him to reach the pistol or go around on the other side of the table.

Sheik kicked the door shut, revealing himself and Sugartit, but Grave Digger didn't turn his head or even move his eyes to look at them.

Sheik gripped Sugartit's pony tail tightly in his left hand, pulling her head back hard to make her slender brown throat taut beneath the blade of the butcher knife. They began a slow shuffling walk, like a weird Apache dance staged in a Montmartre night club.

Sugartit's eyes had the huge liquid fatalistic look of a dying doe's, and her small brown face looked as fragile as toasted meringue. Her upper lip was sweating copiously.

Sheik kept his gaze pinned on Grave Digger's back while slowly skirting the opposite walls of the room and approaching the table from the far side. When he came within reach of the pistol he released his hold on Sugartit's pony tail, pressed the knife blade tighter against her throat and reached out with his left hand for the pistol.

Coffin Ed was hanging head downward from the roof with just his head and shoulders visible below the top edge of the kitchen window. He had been hanging there for twenty minutes waiting for Sheik to come into view. He took careful aim at a spot just above Sheik's left ear.

Some sixth sense caused Sheik to jerk his head around at the exact instant Coffin Ed fired.

A third eye, small and black and sightless, appeared suddenly in the exact center of Sheik's forehead between his two startled yellow cat eyes.

The high powered bullet had only cut a small round hole in the window glass, but the sound of the shot shattered the whole pane and blasted a shower of glass into the room.

Grave Digger wheeled to catch the fainting girl as the knife clattered harmlessly onto the table top.

Sheik was dead when he started going down. He went straight down in total collapse and landed crumpled up beside Granny's immobile rocking chair.

The room was full of cops.

"That was too much of a risk, too much of a risk," Lieutenant Anderson said, shaking his head with a dazed expression.

"What isn't risky on this job," the chief said authoritatively. "We cops got to take risks."

No one disputed him.

"This is a violent city," he added belligerently.

"There wasn't that much risk," Coffin Ed said. He had his arm about his daughter's trembling shoulders. "They don't have any reflexes when you shoot them in the head."

Sugartit winced.

"Take Eve and go home," Grave Digger said harshly.

"I guess I'd better," Coffin Ed said, limping painfully as he guided Sugartit gently toward the door.

"Geeze," a young patrol car rookie was saying. "Geeze. He hung there all that time on just some wire tied around his ankles. I don't know how he stood the pain."

"You'd have stood it too if she'd been your daughter," Grave Digger said.

"Forget what I said to you about being under suspension, Jones," the chief said.

"I didn't hear you," Grave Digger said.

"Jesus Christ, look at that!" the sergeant exclaimed in amazement. "All that noise and it hasn't even waked up grandma."

Everybody turned and looked at him. They were solemn for a moment.

"Nothing's ever going to wake her up again," the lieutenant from homicide said. "She must have been dead for hours."

"All right, all right, all right," the chief shouted. "Let's clean up here and get away. We've got this case tied up tighter than Dick's hat band." Then he added in a pleased tone of voice, "That wasn't too difficult, was it?"

17.

IT WAS eleven o'clock the next morning.

Inky and Bones had spilled their guts.

It had gone hard for them and when the cops got through with them they were as knotty as fat pine.

The remaining members of the Real Cool Moslems—Camel Mouth, Beau Baby, Punkin Head and Slow Motion—had been rounded up and questioned and were now being held along with Inky and Bones.

Their statements had been practically identical:

They had been standing on the corner of 127th Street and Lenox Avenue.

Q. What for?

A. Just having a dress rehearsal.

Q. What? Dress rehearsal?

A. Yassuh. Like they do on Broadway. We was practising wearing our new A-rab costumes.

Q. And you saw Mr. Galen when he ran past.

A. Yassuh, that's when we seed him.

Q. Did you recognize him?

A. Nawsuh, we didn't know him.

Q. Sheik knew him.

A. Yassuh, but he didn't say he knew 'im and we'd never seen him before.

Q. Choo-Choo must have known him too.

A. Yassuh, must 'ave. Him and Sheik usta room together.

Q. But you saw Sheik shoot him?

A. Yassuh. He said, "Watch this," and pulled out his new zip gun and shot at him.

Q. How many times did he shoot?

A. Just once. That's all a zip gun will shoot.

Q. Yes, these zip guns are single shots. But you knew he had the gun?

A. Yassuh, he'd been working on it for 'most a week.

Q. He made it himself?

A. Yassuh.

Q. Had you ever seen him shoot it previously?

A. Nawsuh. It were just finished. He hadn't tried it out.

Q. But you knew he had it on his person?

A. Yassuh, he were going to try it out that night.

Q. And after he shot the white man, what did you do?

A. The man fell down and we went up to see if he'd hit him.

Q. Were you acquainted with the first suspect, Sonny Pickens?

A. Nawsuh, we seed him for the first time too when he come past there shootin'.

Q. When you saw the white man had been killed, did you know Sheik had shot him?

A. Nawsuh, we thought the other fellow had did it.

Q. What one of you, er, ah, passed the wind?

A. Suh?

Q. What one of you broke wind?

A. Oh, that were Choo-Choo, suh, he the one farted.

Q. Was there any special significance in that?

A. Suh?

Q. Why did he do it?

A. That were just a salute we give to the cops.

Q. Oh! Was the perfume throwing part of it?

A. Yassuh, when they got mad Caleb threw the perfume on them.

Q. To allay their anger, er, ah, make them jolly?

A. Nawsuh, to make them madder.

Q. Oh! Well, why did Sheik kidnap, snatch, the other suspect, Pickens?

A. Just to put something over on the cops. He hated cops.

Q. Why?

A. Suh?

Q. Why did he hate cops? Did he have any special reason to hate cops?

A. Special reason? To hate cops? Nawsuh. He didn't need none. Just they was cops is all.

Q. Ah, yes, just they was cops. Is this the zip gun Sheik had?

A. Yassuh. Leastwise it looks like it.

Q. How did Bones come to be in possession of it?

A.   He give it to Bones when we was running off. Bones's old man work for the city and he figgered it was safe with Bones.

Q.   That's all for you, boy. You had better be scared.

A.   Ah is.

That was the case. Open and shut.

No complicity was established linking Sonny Pickens with the murder. He was being temporarily held on a charge of disturbing the peace while a district attorney's assistant was studying the New York State criminal code to see what other charge could be lodged against him for shooting at a citizen with a blank gun.

His friends, Lowtop Brown and Rubberlips Wilson, had been hauled in as suspicious persons.

The cases of the two girls had been referred to the probation officers, but as yet nothing had been done. Both were supposedly at their respective homes, suffering from shock.

The bullet had been removed from the victim's brain and given to the ballistics bureau. No further autopsy was required. Mr. Galen's daughter, Mrs. Helen Kruger of Wading River, Long Island, had claimed the body for burial.

The bodies of the others, Granny and Caleb, Choo-Choo and Sheik, lay unclaimed in the morgue. Perhaps the Baptist church in Harlem, of which Granny was a member, would give her a decent Christian burial. She had no life insurance and it would be financially inconvenient for the church, unless the members contributed to defray the costs.

Caleb would be buried along with Sheik and Choo-Choo in potter's field, unless the medical college of one of the universities obtained their bodies for dissection. No college would want Choo-Choo's, however, because it had been too badly damaged.

Ready Belcher was under an oxygen tent in Harlem Hospital, in the same ward where Charlie Richardson whose arm had been chopped off had died earlier. His condition was critical, but the staff was doing everything possible to keep him alive at the request of the police. He would never look the

same, however, and should his teenage whore ever see him
again she wouldn't recognize him.

Big Smiley and Reba were being held on charges of contributing to the deliquency of minors, manslaughter, operating a house of prostitution, and sundry other charges
collectively.

The woman who was shot in the leg by Coffin Ed was in
Knickerbocker Hospital. Two ambulance chasing shysters
were vying with each other for her consent to sue Coffin Ed
and the New York City police department on a fifty-fifty split
of the judgement, but her husband was holding out for a 60%
cut.

That was the story; the second and corrected story. The
late editions of the morning newspapers had gone hog wild
with it:

The prominent New York Citizen hadn't been shot, as first
reported, by a drunken Negro who had resented his presence
in a Harlem bar. No, not a little bit. He had been shot to
death by a teenage Harlem gangster, called Sheik, leader of a
Harlem teenage gang, called the Real Cool Moslems. Why?
Well, Sheik had wanted to find out if his zip gun would actually shoot.

The copy writers threw the book of adjectives at the bizarre
and Harlemistic aspects of the three ring murder; and meanwhile tossed a bone of commendation to the police department, the brave policemen who had worked through the small
hours of the morning, tracked down the killer in the Harlem
jungle and shot him to death in his lair within less than six
hours after the fatal shot had been fired.

The headlines read:

POLICE PUT THE HEAT TO REAL COOL MOSLEMS
DEATH IS THE KISSOFF FOR THRILL KILL
HARLEM MANIAC RUNS AMUCK
PANDEMONIUM UPTOWN

The hawkers cried:

"Read allabawt really cool muslims and zip gun murder
. . . allabawt cops kill three to one . . . allabawt ex-po-say of
Harlem vice . . . allabawt bloody nightmare . . ."

But already the story was a thing of the past, as dead as the four main characters.

"Kill it," the city editor of an afternoon paper ordered the composing room. "Someone else is already being murdered somewhere else."

Uptown in Harlem the sun shone on the same drab scenes it shone on every other morning at eleven o'clock, when it shone.

No one missed the few expendable colored people being held on their sundry charges in the big new granite skyscraper jail on Centre Street that had replaced the old New York City Tombs.

Not far off in the same building, in a room high up on the southwest corner with a fine clear view of the Battery and North River, all that remained of the case was being polished off.

Earlier the police commissioner and the chief of police had had a heart-to-heart talk about possible corruption in the Harlem branch of the police department.

"There are strong indications that Galen was protected by some influential person up there, either in the police department or in the city government," the police commissioner said.

"Not in the department," the chief maintained. "In the first place, that low license number of his—UG-16—tells me he had friends higher up than a precinct captain, because that kind of a license number is only issued to the specially privileged, and that don't even include me."

"Did you find any connections with politicians in that area?"

"Not connecting Galen; but the woman, Reba, telephoned a colored councilman this morning and ordered him to get down here and get her out on bail."

The commissioner sighed. "Perhaps we'll never know the extent of Galen's activities up there."

"Maybe not, but one thing we know," the chief said. "The son of a bitch is dead, and his money won't corrupt anybody else."

Afterwards the police commissioner reviewed the suspension of Coffin Ed which the chief had clamped on him the night before.

Grave Digger and Lieutenant Anderson were present along with the chief at this conference.

Coffin Ed had exercised his privilege to be absent.

"In the light of subsequent developments in this case, I am inclined to be lenient towards Detective Johnson," the commissioner said. "His compulsion to fire at the youth is understandable, if not justifiable, in view of his previous unfortunate experience with an acid thrower." The commissioner had come into office by way of a law practice and could handle those jawbreaking words with much greater ease than the cops who learned their trade pounding beats.

"What's your opinion, Jones?" he asked.

Grave Digger turned from his customary seat, one ham propped on the window ledge and one foot planted on the floor, and said, "Yes sir, he's been touchy and on edge ever since that con-man threw the acid in his eyes, but he was never rough on anybody in the right."

"Hell, I wasn't disciplining Johnson so much as I was just taking the weight off the whole goddamned police department," the chief said in defense of his action. "We'd have caught holy hell from all the sob sisters, male and female, in this town if those punks had turned out to be innocent pranksters."

"So you are in favor of his reinstatement?" the commissioner asked.

"Why not," the chief said. "If he's got the jumps let him work them off on those hoodlums up in Harlem who gave them to him."

"Right ho," the commissioner said, then turned to Grave Digger again: "Perhaps you can tell me, Jones; this aspect of the case has me puzzled. All of the reports state that there was a huge crowd of people present at the victim's death, and witnessed the actual shooting. One report states—" He fumbled among the papers on his desk until he found the page he wanted. " 'The street was packed with people for a distance of two blocks when deceased met death by gunfire.' Why is this? Why do the people up in Harlem congregate about a killing as though it were a three ring circus?"

"It is," Grave Digger said tersely. "It's the greatest show on earth."

"That happens everywhere," Anderson said. "People will congregate at a killing wherever it takes place."

"Yes, of course, out of morbid curiosity. But I don't mean that exactly. According to reports, not only the reports on this case, but all reports that have come into my office, this, er, phenomenon let us say, is more evident in Harlem than any place else. What do you think, Jones?"

"Well, it's like this, Mister Commissioner," Grave Digger said. "Every day in Harlem, two and three times a day, the colored people see some colored man being chased by another colored man with a knife or an axe or a club. Or else being chased by a white cop with a gun, or by a white man with his fists. But it's only once in a blue moon they get to see a white man being chased by one of them. A big white man at that. That was an event. A chance to see some white blood spilled for a change, and spilled by a black man at that. That was greater than Emancipation Day. As they say up in Harlem, that was the greatest. That's what Ed and I are always up against when we try to make Harlem safe for white people."

"Perhaps I can explain it," the commissioner said.

"Not to me," the chief said drily. "I ain't got the time to listen. If the folks up there want to see blood, they're going to see all the blood they want if they kill another white man."

"Jones is right," Anderson said. "But it makes for trouble."

"Trouble!" Grave Digger echoed. "All they know up there is trouble. If trouble was money, everybody in Harlem would be a millionaire."

The telephone rang. The commissioner picked up the receiver.

"Yes? . . . Yes, send him up." He replaced the receiver and said, "It's the ballistics report. It's coming up."

"Fine," the chief said. "Let's write it in the record and close this case up. It was a dirty business from start to finish and I'm sick and goddamned tired of it."

"Right ho," the commissioner said.

Some one knocked.

"Come in," he said.

The lieutenant from homicide who had worked on the case

came in and placed the zip gun and the battered lead pellet taken from the murdered man's brain on the commissioner's desk.

The commissioner picked up the gun and examined it curiously.

"So this is a zip gun?"

"Yes sir. It's made from an ordinary toy cap pistol. The barrel of the toy pistol is sawed off and this four inch section of heavy brass pipe is fitted in its place. See, it's soldered to the frame, then for greater stability it's bound with adjustable clamps of the kind used to hold small pipe or electrical cables in place. The shell goes directly into the barrel, then this clip is inserted to prevent it from backfiring. The firing pin is soldered to the original hammer. On this one it's made from the head and a quarter-inch section of an ordinary no. 6 nail, filed down to a point."

"It is more primitive than I had imagined, but it is certainly ingenious."

The others looked at it with bored indifference; they had seen zip guns before.

"And this will project a bullet with sufficient force to kill a man, to penetrate his skull?"

"Yes sir."

"Well, well, so this is the gun which killed Galen and led the boy who made it to be killed in turn."

"No sir, not this gun."

"What!"

Everybody sat bolt upright with stretched eyes and open mouths. Had the lieutenant said the Empire State Building had been stolen and smuggled out of town, he couldn't have caused greater stupefaction.

"What do you mean, not that gun!" the chief roared.

"That's what I came up to tell you," the lieutenant said. "This gun fires a .22 calibre bullet. It contained the case of a .22 calibre shell when the sergeant found it. Galen was killed with a .32 calibre bullet fired from a more powerful pistol."

"This is where we came in," Anderson said.

"I'll be goddamned if it is!" the chief bellowed like an enraged bull. "The papers have already gotten the story that he was killed with this gun and have gone crazy with it. We'll be the laughing stock of the world."

"No," the commissioner said quietly but firmly. "We have made a mistake, that is all."

"I'll be goddamned if we have," the chief said, his face turning blood red with passion. "I say the son of a bitch was killed with that gun and that punk lying in the morgue killed him, and I don't give a goddamned what ballistics show."

The commissioner looked solemnly from face to face. There was no question in his eyes, but he waited for some one else to speak.

"I don't think it's worth re-opening the case," Lieutenant Anderson said. "Galen wasn't a particularly lovable character."

"Lovable or not, we got the killer and that's the gun and that's that," the chief said.

"Can we afford to let a murderer go free?" the commissioner asked quietly.

"Who said anything about letting a murderer go free," the chief said.

The commissioner looked again from face to face.

"This one," Grave Digger said harshly. "He did a public service."

"That's not for us to determine, is it?" the commissioner said.

"You'll have to decide that, sir," Grave Digger said. "But if you assign me to look for the killer, I resign."

"Er, what? Resign from the force?"

"Yes sir. I say the killer will never kill again and I'm not going to track him down to pay for this killing even if it costs me my job."

"Who killed him, Jones?"

"I couldn't say, sir."

The commissioner looked grave. "Was he as bad as that?"

"Yes sir."

The commissioner looked at the lieutenant from homicide.

"But this zip gun was fired, wasn't it?"

"Yes sir. But I've checked with all the hospitals and the precinct stations in Harlem and there has been no gunshot injury reported."

"Some one could have been injured who would be afraid to report it."

"Yes sir. Or the bullet might have landed harmlessly against a building or an automobile."

"Yes. But there are the other boys who are involved. They might be indicted for complicity. If it is proved that they were his accomplices, they face the maximum penalty for murder."

"Yes sir," Anderson said. "But it's been pretty well established that the murder—or rather the action of the boy firing the zip gun—was not premeditated. And the others knew nothing of his intention to fire at Galen until it was too late to prevent him."

"According to their statements."

"Well, yes sir. But it's up to us to accept their statements or have them bound over to the grand jury for indictment. If we don't charge complicity when they go up for arraignment the court will only fine them for disturbing the peace."

The commissioner looked back at the lieutenant from homicide. "Who else knows about this?"

"No one outside of this office, sir. They never had the gun in ballistics; they only had the bullet."

"Shall we put it to a vote?" the commissioner asked.

No one said anything.

"The ayes have it," the commissioner said. He picked up the small lead pellet that had murdered a man. "Jones, there is a flat roof on a building across the park. Do you think you can throw this so it will land there?"

"If I can't, sir, my name ain't Don Newcombe," Grave Digger said.

18.

2702 Seventh Avenue was an old stone apartment house with pseudo-Greek trimmings left over from the days when Harlem was a fashionable white neighborhood and the Negro slums centered about San Juan Hill on West 42nd Street.

Grave Digger pushed open the cracked glass door and searched for the name of Coolie Dunbar among the row of mail boxes nailed to the front hall wall. He found the name on a flyspecked card, followed by the apartment number, 3-B.

The automatic elevator, one of the first made, was out of order.

He climbed the dark ancient stairs to the third floor and knocked on the left hand door at the front.

A middle-aged brownskin woman with a worried expression opened the door and said, "Coolie's at work and we've told the people already we'll come in and pay our rent in the office when—"

"I'm not the rent collector, I'm a detective," Grave Digger said, flashing his badge.

"Oh!" The worried expression turned to one of apprehension. "You're Mr. Johnson's partner. I thought you were finished with her."

"Almost. May I talk to her."

"I don't see why you got to keep on bothering her if you ain't got nothing on Mr. Johnson's daughter," she complained as she guarded the entrance. "They were both in it together."

"I'm not going to arrest her. I would just like to ask her a few questions to clear up the last details."

"She's in bed now."

"I don't mind."

"All right," she consented grudgingly. "Come on in. But if you've got to arrest her, then keep her. Me and Coolie have been disgraced enough by that girl. We're respectable church people—"

"I'm sure of it," he cut her off. "But she's your niece, isn't she?"

"She's Coolie's niece. I haven't got any wild ones in my family."

"You're lucky," he said.

She pursed her lips and opened a door next to the kitchen. "Here's a policeman to see you, Sissie," she said.

Grave Digger entered the small bedroom and closed the door behind him.

Sissie lay in a narrow single bed with the covers pulled up to her chin. At sight of Grave Digger her red, tear-swollen eyes grew wide with terror.

He drew up the single hard-back chair and sat down.

"You're a very lucky little girl," he said. "You have just missed being a murderer."

"I don't know what you mean," she said in a terrified whisper.

"Listen," he said. "Don't lie to me. I'm dogtired and you children have already made me as depressed as I've ever been. You don't know what kind of hell it is sometimes to be a cop."

She watched him like a half-wild kitten poised for flight.

"I didn't kill him. Sheik killed him," she whispered.

"We know Sheik killed him," he said in a flat voice. He looked weary beyond words. "Listen, I'm not here as a cop. I'm here as a friend. Ed Johnson is my closest friend and his daughter is your closest friend. That ought to make us friends too. As a friend I tell you we've got to get rid of the gun."

She hesitated, debating with herself, then said quickly before she could change her mind, "I threw it down a water drain on 128th Street near Fifth Avenue."

He sighed. "That's good enough. What kind of gun was it?"

"It was a thirty-two. It had the picture of an owl's head on the handle and Uncle Coolie called it an Owls Head."

"Has he missed it?"

"He missed it out of the drawer this morning when he started for work and asked Aunt Cora if she'd moved it. But he ain't said nothing to me yet. He was late for work and I think he wanted to give me all day to put it back."

"Does he need it in his work?"

"Oh no, he works in a garage in the Bronx."

"Good. Does he have a permit for it?"

"No sir. That's what he's so worried about."

"Okay. Now listen. When he asks you about it tonight, you tell him you took it to protect yourself against Mr. Galen and that during the excitement you left it in Sheik's room. Tell him that I found it there but I don't know whom it belongs to. He won't say any more about it."

"Yes sir. But he's going to be awfully mad."

"Well, Sissie, you can't escape all punishment."

"No sir."

"Why did you shoot at Mr. Galen anyway? You can tell me now since it doesn't matter."

"It wasn't on account of myself," she said. "It was on account of Sugartit—Evelyn Johnson. He was after her all the time and I was afraid he was going to get her. She tries to be wild and does crazy things sometimes and I was afraid he was going to get her and do to her what he did to me. That would ruin her. She ain't an orphan like me with nobody to really care what happens to her; she's from a good family with a father and a mother and a good home and I wasn't going to let him ruin her."

He sat there listening to her, a big tough lumpy-faced cop, looking as though he might cry.

"How'd you plan to do it?" he asked.

"Oh, I was just going to shoot him. I'd made a date with him at the Inn for me and Sugartit, but I wasn't going to take her. I was going to make him drive me out somewhere in his car by telling him we were going to pick her up; and then I was going to shoot him and run away. I took Uncle Coolie's pistol and hid it downstairs in the hall in a hole in the plaster so I could get it when I went out. But before time came for me to go, Sugartit came by here. I wasn't expecting her and I couldn't tell her I wanted to go out so it was late before I could get rid of her. I left her at the subway at 125th Street, thinking she was going home, then I ran all the way over to Lenox to meet Mr. Galen; but when I got over on Lenox I saw all the commotion going on. Then I saw him come running down the street and Sonny chasing him with a gun shooting at him. It looked like half the people in Harlem were running after him. I got in the crowd and followed and when I caught up with him at 127th Street I saw that Sonny was going to shoot at him again, so I shot at him too. I don't think anyone even saw me shoot; everybody was looking at Sonny. But when I saw him fall and all the Moslems in their costumes run up and gang around him I was scared one of them was going to see me, so I ran around the block and threw the gun in a drain then came back to Caleb's from the other way and made out like I didn't know what had happened. I didn't know then that Caleb had been shot."

"Have you told anyone else about this?"

"No sir. When I saw Sugartit come sneaking into Caleb's, I was going to tell her I'd shot him because I knew she'd come back looking for him. But Choo-Choo had let it slip out that Sheik was carrying his zip gun, and then after Sonny said his gun wouldn't shoot anything but blanks I knew right away it was Sheik who'd shot him; and I was scared to say anything."

"Good. Now listen to me. Don't tell anybody else. I won't tell anybody either. We'll just keep it to ourselves, our own private secret. Okay?"

"Yes sir. You can bet I won't tell anybody else. I just want to forget about it—if I ever can."

"Good. I don't suppose there's any need of me telling you to keep away from bad company; you ought to have learned your lesson by now."

"I'm going to do that, I promise."

"Good. Well, Sissie," Grave Digger said, getting slowly to his feet. "You made your bed hard, if it hurts lying on it, don't complain."

It was the visiting hour next day in the Centre Street jail.

Sissie said, "I brought you some cigarettes, Sonny. I didn't know whether you had a girl to bring you any."

"Thanks," Sonny said. "I ain't got no girl."

"How long do you think they'll give you?"

"Six months, I suppose."

"That much. Just for what you did."

"They don't like for people to shoot at anybody, even if you don't hit them, or even if they ain't shooting nothing but blanks like what I did."

"I know," she said sympathetically. "Maybe you're getting off easy at that."

"I ain't complaining," Sonny said.

"What are you going to do when you get out?"

"Go back to shining shoes, I suppose."

"What's going to happen to your shine parlor?"

"Oh, I'll lose that one, but I'll get me another one."

"You got a car?"

"I had one but I couldn't keep up the payments and the man took it back."

"You need a girl to look after you."

"Yeah, who don't? What you going to do yourself, now that your boyfriend's dead?"

"I don't know. I just want to get married."

"That shouldn't be hard for you."

"I don't know anybody who'll have me."

"Why not?"

"I've done a lot of bad things."

"Like what?"

"I'd be ashamed to tell you everything I've done."

"Listen, to show you I ain't scared of nothing you might have done, I want you to be my girl."

"I don't want to play around anymore."

"Who's talking about playing around. I'm talking about for keeps."

"I don't mind. But there's something I've got to tell you first. It's about me and Sheik."

"What about you and Sheik?"

"I'm going to have a baby by the time you get out of jail."

"Well, that makes it different," he said. "We'd better get married right away. I'll talk to the man and ask him to see if he can't arrange it."

BIOGRAPHICAL NOTES

NOTE ON THE TEXTS

NOTES

Biographical Notes

JIM THOMPSON   Born September 27, 1906, in Anadarko, Oklahoma
Territory. Father was a peace officer, later a lawyer, accountant, and
oil man; mother was a teacher. Raised in Oklahoma, Nebraska, and
Texas. Worked as bellboy at the Hotel Texas, Fort Worth, while in
high school; suffered nervous collapse partly precipitated by heavy
drinking (in later life suffered from alcoholism). As an itinerant
worker in the West Texas oil fields, joined the Wobblies in 1926. En-
rolled in the College of Agriculture of the University of Nebraska in
1929. Published folklore, sketches, stories, and poems in *Texas
Monthly*, *Prairie Schooner*, and *Cornhusker Countryman*. Married
Alberta Hesse in September 1931; daughter Patricia born in 1932. Returned to Fort Worth and worked as night doorman at the Worth
Hotel; wrote for *True Detective*, *Master Detective*, *Daring Detective*,
and other true crime magazines. Moved to Oklahoma City in 1936,
and joined the Oklahoma Federal Writers' Project. Second daughter,
Sharon, born in 1936, and son Michael in 1938. Appointed director
of the Writers' Project in 1938. Contracted with Viking to write *Always To Be Blest* (novel was never published). Left Writers' Project;
received fellowship from Rockefeller Foundation General Education
Board to write book about southwestern building trades, *We Talked
About Labor* (never published). Moved to San Diego in 1940, and
joined Ryan Aeronautical Company as stockroom clerk and book-
keeper. Published novel *Now and On Earth*, based closely on his
experiences at Ryan, in 1942. Took job as timekeeper at Solar Aircraft
Company in San Diego. Published *Heed the Thunder*, agrarian novel
based on history of mother's family, in 1946. Worked as reporter for
San Diego Journal and rewrite man for *Los Angeles Mirror*, 1947–48.
First crime novel, *Nothing More Than Murder*, published in 1949.
Moved to New York City in 1950 and worked as editor at *Saga* (1950–
51) and *Police Gazette* (1951–52). Wrote series of paperback originals
for Lion Books with strong encouragement of Lion editor Arnold
Hano: *The Killer Inside Me* (1952), *Cropper's Cabin* (1952), *Recoil*
(1953), *The Alcoholics* (1953), *Savage Night* (1953), *The Criminal* (1953),
The Golden Gizmo (1954), *A Swell-Looking Babe* (1954), *A Hell of a
Woman* (1954), *The Kill-Off* (1957), and two ostensible autobiogra-
phies, *Bad Boy* (1953) and *Roughneck* (1954); during same period also
published *The Nothing Man* (1954) with Dell and *After Dark, My
Sweet* (1955) with Popular Library. Worked on screenplays for two
films directed by Stanley Kubrick, *The Killing* (1955) and *Paths of
Glory* (1957). Published *Wild Town* (1957) with New American Library

and moved to Hollywood, where during the late 1950s and early 1960s he wrote teleplays for *Mackenzie's Raiders, Cain's Hundred*, and *Doctor Kildare*. Published *The Getaway* (1959), *The Transgressors* (1961), *The Grifters* (1963), *Pop. 1280* (1964), *Texas by the Tail* (1965), and *South of Heaven* (1967) as paperback originals. Was involved in various unproduced film projects, including hobo screenplays written for Tony Bill and Robert Redford; hired to write novelizations of television series *Ironside* (1967) and films *The Undefeated* (1969) and *Nothing But a Man* (1969). Published *Child of Rage* (1972) and *King Blood* (1973). *The Getaway* filmed by Sam Peckinpah in 1973; *The Killer Inside Me* filmed by Burt Kennedy in 1975. Played small role in *Farewell, My Lovely* (1975, directed by Dick Richards). Died in Los Angeles on April 7, 1977.

PATRICIA HIGHSMITH Born Patricia Plangman in January 19, 1921, in Fort Worth, Texas; parents divorced shortly after her birth, and she moved to New York City with mother and stepfather Stanley Highsmith; grew up mostly under care of maternal grandmother. Graduated Barnard College in 1942. In 1948 stayed at Yaddo, writers' colony in Saratoga, New York, along with Chester Himes, Truman Capote, and Katherine Anne Porter. Published first novel, *Strangers on a Train*, in 1950 (rights purchased for small amount by Alfred Hitchcock, whose film version, starring Farley Granger and Robert Walker, was released the following year). *The Price of Salt*, a novel with a lesbian theme, published under pseudonym Claire Morgan in 1952. Moved to Europe, living in Italy, England, and France; settled in a small village near Locarno, Switzerland, in 1981. Published series of novels including *The Blunderer* (1954), *The Talented Mr. Ripley* (1955), *Deep Water* (1957), *A Game for the Living* (1958), *This Sweet Sickness* (1960), *The Cry of the Owl* (1962), *The Two Faces of January* (1964), *The Glass Cell* (1964), *The Story-Teller* (1965), *Those Who Walk Away* (1967), *The Tremor of Forgery* (1969), *Ripley Under Ground* (1970), *A Dog's Ransom* (1972), *Ripley's Game* (1974), *Edith's Diary* (1977), *The Boy Who Followed Ripley* (1980), *People Who Knock on the Door* (1982), *Found in the Street* (1986), and *Ripley Under Water* (1992); also published a number of collections of short stories and a guide for writers, *Plotting and Writing Suspense Fiction* (1966). Her work was frequently adapted by European filmmakers including Rene Clement (*Purple Noon*, based on *The Talented Mr. Ripley*), Wim Wenders (*The American Friend*, based on *Ripley's Game*), Claude Chabrol (*The Cry of the Owl*), and Claude Miller (*This Sweet Sickness*). Besides writing she occupied herself with drawing, sculpture, and gardening. Died February 4, 1995, in Locarno, Switzerland. A final novel, *Small g: A Summer Idyll*, was published posthumously in 1995.

CHARLES WILLEFORD Born January 2, 1919, in Little Rock, Arkansas. Joined U.S. Army in 1936. Served as tank commander in Europe during World War II, earning Silver Star, Bronze Star, Purple Heart, and Luxembourg Croix de Guerre. Wrote radio serial "The Saga of Mary Miller" for Armed Forces Radio Service in 1948. First book, poetry collection *Proletarian Laughter*, published 1948. Married Mary Jo Norton in 1951 (divorced, 1976). First novel, paperback original *High Priest of California* (1953), followed by other novels written for small paperback imprints: *Pick-Up* (1955), *Wild Wives* (1954, also known as *Until I Am Dead*), *Lust Is a Woman* (1956), *Soldier's Wife* (1958), *Honey Gal* (1958, also known as *The Black Mass of Brother Springer*), and *The Woman Chaser* (1958, also known as *The Director*). Television play *The Basic Approach* broadcast by Canadian Broadcasting Corporation, 1956. Retired from military in 1956 with rank of master sergeant. After leaving military attended Palm Beach Junior College; obtained B.A. (1962) and M.A. (1964) from University of Miami, where he worked as instructor in humanities department, 1964–67. From 1967 served as English professor, and later chairman of English and philosophy departments, at Miami-Dade Junior College. Published further fiction including *Understudy for Love* (1961), *No Experience Necessary* (1962, in a version drastically revised by publisher), *The Machine in Ward Eleven* (1962), *The Burnt Orange Heresy* (1971), *Hombre from Sonora* (1972), *Cockfighter* (1962, revised 1972), and *Off the Wall* (1980). Also published *Poontang and Other Poems* (1967) and critical study *New Forms of Ugly: The Immobilized Man in Modern Literature* (1967). Achieved wider success with series of novels about Miami police detective Hoke Mosley: *Miami Blues* (1984), *New Hope for the Dead* (1985), and *Sideswipe* (1987). Also published memoir *Something About a Soldier* (1986). Died in Miami of a heart attack on March 27, 1988. The final Hoke Mosley book, *The Way We Die Now* (1988), the memoir *I Was Looking for a Street* (1988), and another novel, *The Shark-Infested Custard* (1990), were published posthumously.

DAVID GOODIS Born 1917 in Philadelphia. Attended University of Indiana in 1936 and Temple University, 1937–38; had already begun writing for the pulps and other magazines. First novel, *Retreat from Oblivion*, published 1938. Moved to New York in 1939; worked for advertising agencies and wrote for radio and the pulps. Married in 1942; his wife, Elaine, left him the following year. Became associate producer of radio program *Hap Harrigan of the Airwaves* in 1945. Second novel, *Dark Passage*, published in 1946 after being serialized in *The Saturday Evening Post*. Signed contract with Warner Brothers; worked on screenplays of *The Unfaithful* (1947, directed by Vincent

Sherman) and *Dark Passage* (1947, directed by Delmer Daves and starring Humphrey Bogart and Lauren Bacall); published novels *Behold This Woman* and *Nightfall* in 1947. *Dark Passage* appeared in French translation in 1949, and Goodis's books thereafter enjoyed great popularity and literary respect in France. After gradual decline of his screenwriting career, left Hollywood in 1950 and returned to his family home in Philadelphia, where he lived for the rest of his life. Published first paperback original, *Cassidy's Girl*, for Gold Medal in 1951; last hardcover novel, *Of Missing Persons*, published the same year. Continued to write novels for Gold Medal (*Street of the Lost*, 1952; *Of Tender Sin*, 1952; *The Moon in the Gutter*, 1953; *Street of No Return*, 1954; *The Wounded and the Slain*, 1955; *Down There*, 1956; *Fire in the Flesh*, 1957) and for Lion Books (*The Burglar*, 1953; *The Blonde on the Street Corner*, 1954; *Black Friday*, 1954). Film version of *Nightfall*, directed by Jacques Tourneur and starring Aldo Ray and Anne Bancroft, released in 1956. Collaborated with director Paul Wendkos, an old friend from Philadelphia, on film adaptation of *The Burglar*, starring Jayne Mansfield and Dan Duryea, that was released in 1957. Film version of *Down There*, directed by François Truffaut under title *Tirez sur le pianiste* (*Shoot the Piano Player*), starring Charles Aznavour, released 1960. Final Gold Medal novel, *Night Squad*, appeared in 1961. Met Truffaut in New York at American opening of *Shoot the Piano Player*. Sued producers of the television series *The Fugitive* in 1965, claiming it appropriated elements from *Dark Passage* (suit was settled out of court after Goodis's death). Died January 7, 1967, in Philadelphia. Last novel, *Somebody's Done For*, published later that year.

CHESTER HIMES Born July 29, 1909, in Jefferson City, Missouri. Moved with family in 1914 to Cleveland, Ohio, where father was chairman of Mechanical Arts Department of Alcorn College; family later lived in Georgia and Arkansas before returning to Cleveland in 1925. Attended Ohio State University, 1926–28. Left university and worked as bellhop. Arrested twice for armed robbery during 1928, and sentenced in December to 20–25 years of hard labor in Ohio State Penitentiary. Survived fire that killed over 300 inmates in 1930. While in prison, began publishing short stories in *Atlanta Daily World*, *Esquire*, and other periodicals. Paroled in April 1936; returned to Cleveland. Married Jean Johnson in August 1937. Worked at a variety of jobs, including writing assignments for the Federal Writers' Project and the CIO; wrote first version of prison novel later published as *Cast the First Stone*. Hired by novelist Louis Bromfield to work on his farm (Bromfield subsequently attempted to promote his literary career); formed friendship with novelist Richard Wright and his wife,

Ellen. Moved to Los Angeles and between 1940 and 1943 worked in war industries there and in San Francisco. Moved to New York City. First novel, *If He Hollers Let Him Go*, published in 1945, followed by *Lonely Crusade* (1947). Separated from wife in 1950. Published *Cast the First Stone* (1952), a novel based on his prison experience, before moving to France in 1953. Published *The Third Generation* (1954). *The End of a Primitive* published by New American Library in censored form in 1956 as *The Primitive*. Marcel Duhamel, editor of the Série Noire (crime fiction series published by Gallimard), asked Himes in 1956 to write a detective novel for the series. The novel was published in French as *La Reine des pommes* and in English as *For Love of Imabelle* and *A Rage in Harlem* (Himes's title, never used, was *The Five Cornered Square*); it won an important French prize, the Grand Prix de la Littérature Policière. It was the first of a series of novels featuring Harlem detectives Coffin Ed Johnson and Grave Digger Jones, a number of which appeared in French before they were published in America as paperback originals: *The Real Cool Killers* (1959), *The Crazy Kill* (1960), *The Big Gold Dream* (1960), *All Shot Up* (1960), *Cotton Comes to Harlem* (1965), *The Heat's On* (1966), and *Blind Man with a Pistol* (1969). Also published non-series novels: *A Case of Rape* (1963 in French only; first English-language publication 1984), *Pinktoes* (1965), and *Run Man Run* (1966). Met Malcolm X in Paris in 1962. Married Lesley Packard in 1965, and moved with her to Alicante, Spain, in 1968. Film version of *Cotton Comes to Harlem*, directed by Ossie Davis and starring Godfrey Cambridge and Raymond St. Jacques, released in 1970, followed by *Come Back Charleston Blue* (1972, based on *The Heat's On*), directed by Mark Warren with the same leading actors. Visited New York in 1972 and was honored by Carnegie Endowment for International Peace. His autobiography was published in two volumes as *The Quality of Hurt* (1972) and *My Life of Absurdity* (1976). Novel *Plan B* published in French in 1983 (English-language publication 1993). Died November 12, 1984, in Moraira, Spain.

Note on the Texts

This volume collects five American novels of the 1950s that have come to be identified with the "noir" genre of crime fiction: *The Killer Inside Me* by Jim Thompson (1952); *The Talented Mr. Ripley* by Patricia Highsmith (1955); *Pick-Up* by Charles Willeford (1955); *Down There* by David Goodis (1956); and *The Real Cool Killers* by Chester Himes (1959).

In the summer of 1952 Jim Thompson was introduced by Ingrid Hallen, his literary agent, to Arnold Hano, editor-in-chief of Lion Books, a paperback line begun in 1949 by Magazine Management Company, which also published Marvel Comics and a variety of pulp magazines. Lion Books issued original fiction in softcover as well as paperback reprints of hardcover titles; the firm often commissioned writers to develop novels from short synopses, usually about two-thirds of a page in length, that were prepared by Lion editors. Hano showed Thompson several of these story ideas, and Thompson chose to work from a synopsis, written by Lion editor Jim Bryans, for a novel about a New York City policeman who murders a prostitute he is involved with. Working at his home in Astoria, Queens, Thompson wrote the first twelve chapters of *The Killer Inside Me* in two weeks. After submitting them to Lion, he went to stay with Maxine and Joseph Kouba, his sister and brother-in-law, at their home on the marine base at Quantico, Virginia, where he completed the novel in another two weeks. *The Killer Inside Me*, Thompson's fourth published novel and the first of eleven books that he would publish with Lion between 1952 and 1954, was brought out by Lion Books in September 1952. Thompson did not revise the book after its initial publication. This volume prints the text of the first edition.

Patricia Highsmith recalled in an interview published in 1993 that she began to imagine the character of Tom Ripley when she saw a man walking along a beach in Positano, Italy. "I wondered why he was there alone at 6 A.M. Later I thought of a story about a man sent to Positano on a mission, and maybe he failed." *The Talented Mr. Ripley*, Highsmith's fourth novel, was published in 1955 by Coward-McCann, Inc. Highsmith did not revise the book after its initial publication. This volume prints the text of the first edition.

Charles Willeford wrote *Pick-Up*, his second novel, while serving as a sergeant in the United States Air Force. He sold the novel to Beacon Books, a paperback line established in 1954 by Universal Publishing and Distribution Corporation. (This corporation also owned

Royal Books, the paperback line that had published Willeford's first novel, *High Priest of California*, in 1953, after it had been rejected by Fawcett Gold Medal.) *Pick-Up* was published in 1955 as a "Beacon First Award Original Novel" and was the first of five Willeford novels, including a reissue of *High Priest of California*, to appear as a Beacon Book between 1955 and 1957. Willeford made no changes in the novel after its initial publication. This volume prints the text of the first edition.

David Goodis published five novels in hardcover between 1938, the year he graduated from Temple University, and 1950, when he left Hollywood and returned to Philadelphia to live with his parents. Goodis then began writing fiction for original paperback publication, and between 1951 and 1955 he published six novels with Gold Medal Books, a paperback line founded by Fawcett Publications in 1949, and three novels with Lion Books. *Down There*, his seventh novel for Fawcett Gold Medal, was published as a "Gold Medal Original" in November 1956. Goodis did not revise *Down There* after its initial publication. This volume prints the text of the first edition.

Chester Himes was living in Paris in 1956 when he met poet Marcel Duhamel while visiting Editions Gallimard, the publishing house. Duhamel had translated Himes's first novel, *If He Hollers Let Him Go*, into French; he was also the founder and editor of the Série Noire, a series of crime novels (established in 1945 and published by Gallimard) that presented work by French, British, and American writers. During their meeting, Duhamel asked Himes to write a crime novel for the Série Noire and suggested that he study the novels of Peter Cheyney (the British writer who created the series character Lemmy Caution), Raymond Chandler, and Dashiell Hammett. Himes agreed and began writing a story about a confidence game. He showed the first 80 pages of the manuscript to Duhamel, who told him that a crime novel should have police characters in it; Himes then introduced two detectives, Coffin Ed Johnson and Grave Digger Jones, into the story. Himes completed the novel, which he called *The Five Cornered Square*, early in 1957. It was published in France by Gallimard in 1958 as *La Reine des pommes* and in the United States by Fawcett Gold Medal in 1957 as *For Love of Imabelle* (a new American edition was published by Avon in 1965 under the title *A Rage in Harlem*).

Using the title *If Trouble Was Money*, Himes wrote his third novel for the Série Noire, and his third to feature the team of Coffin Ed and Grave Digger, in the summer of 1957 while staying in Hørsholm, a village outside of Copenhagen, Denmark. The novel was translated into French by Chantel Wourgraft and published by Gallimard in 1958 as *Il pleut des coups durs*. An American edition was published in paperback as an Avon Original by Avon Publications, Inc., in 1959 under the title *The Real Cool Killers*. Two typescripts of *The Real Cool Killers* are in the James Weldon Johnson Memorial Collection of the Beinecke Library at Yale University. One typescript, 205 pages in length, is complete; the other, 203 pages long, is missing the last two pages of the novel. Except for the retyping of the first page of the 205-page version, and the cancellation by overtyping in the 205-page version of passages cancelled by hand in the 203-page version, the typing of the two documents is identical. Both typescripts are titled "If Trouble Was Money"; the 205-page version has been re-titled "The Real Cool Killers," while the 203-page version has "Real Cool Killers" written above the original title.

The 203-page typescript contains handwritten revisions by Himes not found in the 205-page version, while the 205-page typescript, which was used as setting copy for the 1959 Avon edition, contains extensive handwritten revisions, not found in the 203-page version, that were made by someone other than Himes—most probably, by an editor working for Avon Publications. These editorial revisions, which were made throughout the novel and substantively alter the wording of many passages, were incorporated in the 1959 edition and in all subsequent American editions. For example, at 734.13–15 of this volume, where Himes wrote, "The big white man turned to face him, looking as though he were caught in a situation where he didn't know whether to laugh or to get angry," the Avon text reads, "The big white man turned to face him, looking as though he didn't know whether to laugh or to get angry"; at 735.36, where Himes wrote, "The severed coat-sleeved short-arm, still clutching the knife," the Avon text reads, "The severed arm in its coat sleeve, still clutching the knife"; and at 803.5–6 the passage "She stared long into his eyes. She had dark brown eyes with clear whites and long black lashes faintly seen" was changed to "She stared into his eyes. She had dark brown eyes with clear whites and long black lashes."

The second volume of Himes's autobiography, *My Life of Absurdity* (1976), contains evidence that these revisions were made in the 1959 Avon edition without the knowledge or approval of Himes. Regarding the publication of his detective novels in the United States in the early 1960s, Himes wrote, "By that time my books were published in America in paperback, but the American publishers didn't pay any more than Série Noire and they scrambled the books up in what they call editing and they were practically senseless." Himes also printed in his autobiography a letter written to him from the United States by his friend Herbert Hill on August 14, 1961; in this letter, Hill reports on his efforts to find and send to Himes a copy of *The Real Cool Killers*, suggesting that at the time Himes had not yet seen the

1959 Avon edition. Therefore, the text of *The Real Cool Killers* presented in this volume is taken from the two typescripts in the James Weldon Johnson Memorial Collection of the Beinecke Library: the text of the 203-page typescript is printed on pp. 733.1–875.26 of this volume, and the text of the last two pages of the 205-page typescript, which do not contain any editorial alterations, are printed on pp. 875.27–876.22. (These typescripts are reprinted by permission of the Yale Collection of American Literature, Beinecke Rare Book and Manuscript Library, Yale University.) In presenting the text of these typescripts, this volume accepts Himes's handwritten and typed revisions and corrects unmistakable typing errors.

This volume presents the texts of the original printings and typescripts chosen for inclusion here, but it does not attempt to reproduce features of their typographic design, such as display capitalization of chapter openings. The texts are printed without change, except for the correction of typographical errors. Spelling, punctuation, and capitalization are often expressive features, and they are not altered, even when inconsistent or irregular. The following is a list of typographical errors corrected, cited by page and line number: 57.26, bulls-eyes; 61.4, If fitted; 80.11, him.; 80.28, The. . . . ; 82.7, and. . . . ?; 98.18, They. . . . ; 100.31, he's; 120.18, here to; 144.3, as you; 189.37, *Ambassador*; 195.40, cartilege; 200.34, UM-hm; 202.19, Georgio's; 202.20, Georgio's; 362.6, him.; 383.25, screaching; 412.33, She; 419.12, He; 432.16, anyway; 434.32, She; 441.30, acadamic; 460.19, hospital; 468.12, He; 468.32, latrine,; 469.16, Jordan,; 470.23, patient's; 473.28, dishwasher,; 476.3, on,; 477.21, window,; 477.27, She; 478.32, See; 479.33, so,; 481.37, hand—'' whether; 482.11, you,; 488.22, Company; 490.27, seregant; 490.34, She; 491.27, The; 494.14, She; 494.34, She; 502.11, She; 505.26, However;; 506.8, said,; 506.21, colds,; 509.31, winow; 511.16, He; 513.19, He; 520.8, The; 520.21, Why; 522.13, He; 524.10, said,; 527.7, side; 528.5, tne; 530.31, idea.; 530.33, He; 531.16, He; 532.1, The; 534.16, it's; 538.19, Center.; 541.18, city;; 543.20, He; 545.27, He; 545.31, in; 548.18, your; 548.35, litttle; 550.18, He; 551.13, Nothing.; 551.34, nevously; 552.2, She; 552.24, then; 558.34, Meredith,; 562.13, He; 578.36, mens'; 634.35, reply.; 651.22, tuned; 651.23, that''; 651.24, mean''; 654.7, years,; 671.18, an; 682.5, fingers.''; 683.33, face—''.

Notes

In the notes below, the reference numbers denote page and line of this volume (the line count includes headings). No note is made for material included in standard desk-reference books such as Webster's *Collegiate*, *Biographical*, and *Geographical* dictionaries. For references to other studies and further biographical background than is contained in the Biographical Notes, see Robert Polito, *Savage Art: A Biography of Jim Thompson* (New York: Alfred A. Knopf, 1995); *Fireworks: The Lost Writings of Jim Thompson* (New York: Donald I. Fine, 1988), edited by Robert Polito and Michael McCauley; Philippe Garnier, *Goodis: La Vie en Noir et Blanc* (Paris: Editions du Seuil, 1984); Richard Gehr, "The Pope of Psychopulp: Charles Ray Willeford's Unholy Rites," *Voice Literary Supplement*, March 1989; Lou Stathis, "Charles Willeford: New Hope for the Living," in Charles Willeford, *High Priest of California/Wild Wives* (San Francisco: Re/Search Publications, 1987); Joan Dupont, "Patricia Highsmith: Criminal Pursuits," *New York Times Magazine*, June 12, 1988; Chester Himes, *The Quality of Hurt: The Autobiography of Chester Himes, Volume I* (New York: Doubleday & Co., 1972); Chester Himes, *My Life of Absurdity: The Autobiography of Chester Himes, Volume II* (New York: Doubleday & Co., 1976); *Conversations with Chester Himes* (Jackson: University of Mississippi Press, 1995), edited by Michel Fabre and Robert E. Skinner; Gilbert H. Muller, *Chester Himes* (Boston: Twayne Publishers, 1989); Geoffrey O'Brien, *Hardboiled America: Lurid Paperbacks and the Masters of Noir* (revised edition, New York: Da Capo Press, 1997); and Lee Server, *Over My Dead Body, The Sensational Age of the American Paperback: 1945–1955* (San Francisco: Chronicle Books, 1994).

THE KILLER INSIDE ME

61.37   ACTH]   Adrenocorticotropic hormone, a cortisone derivative.

108.34   *Max Jacobsohn on Degenerative Diseases*]   The New York physician Max Jacobson over a period of years prescribed Thompson injections of vitamins, amphetamines, and animal glands; Thompson had dedicated his novel *Nothing More Than Murder* (1949) to him. Jacobson, whose other patients included John F. Kennedy, Jacqueline Kennedy, Judy Garland, and Truman Capote, had his medical license revoked in 1975.

THE TALENTED MR. RIPLEY

192.29   "My Day"]   Syndicated newspaper column by Eleanor Roosevelt which began publication in 1935.

196.36   "Sempre seeneestra, seeneestra!"]   *Sempre sinistra*, Italian: Keep left, left!

214.20   "Subito, signor!"]   Italian: Right away, sir!

216.14   americanos]   Cocktails made with Campari and sweet vermouth, garnished with an orange slice.

217.5   "Grazie tante!"]   Italian: Thank you very much!

230.38–39   'voglio' . . . per esempio]   Italian: 'I want' . . . 'I want to present my friend Marge,' for example.

233.3   "Posso sedermi?"]   Italian: May I sit down?

234.8   "Niente, grazie]   Italian: Nothing, thank you.

252.14   FERMA]   Italian: Close.

254.15   "'Spetta un momento,"]   Italian: Wait a moment.

270.31–32   questura . . . Permesso di Soggiorno]   Italian: Police head-quarters. . . . Residency Permit.

274.15   "Ho . . . c'e arrivata]   Italian: I'm afraid he hasn't arrived.

289.1–2   "Qui parla . . . Fred-derick Mee-lays?"]   Italian: This is police station number 83. Are you a friend of an American named Fred-derick Mee-lays?

290.39   inamorata di te]   Italian: in love with you.

293.37   "Di niente!]   Italian: Not at all!

297.14–15   BARCA AFFONDATA . . . SAN REMO]   Italian: Sunken boat with traces of blood found in shallow water near San Remo.

298.9   Questo e questo e questo]   Italian: This and this and this.

311.15–16   *Papa non vuole . . . far' l'amor'?*]   Italian: Papa doesn't want it, Mama doesn't either, / So how can we ever make love?

311.29   Giuliano]   Salvatore Giuliano, notorious Sicilian bandit leader of the late 1940s, who gave interviews with the press and met with politicians while being sought by the police. He is believed to have been responsible for the murder of 11 left-wing demonstrators in Portella della Ginestra on May 1, 1947. Giuliano was assassinated by the Sicilian Mafia in 1950.

314.2–3   "Peccato . . . Grazie tante, signor."]   Italian: My mistake . . . Thank you so much, sir.

331.23   "Benone!"]   Italian: Very well!

338.38   il sparito . . . il assassinato]   Italian: the vanished . . . the murdered.

348.6   "Pronta la collazione, signor,"]   Italian: Lunch will be ready right away, sir.

356.25–30   "Mi dispiace, signor! . . . altro gondoliere!"]   Italian: "I'm sorry, sir! I have to return to San Marco! I have an appointment! . . . I will call another gondolier!"

395.18   Il te, per piacere, subitissimo!]   Italian: Tea, please, right away!

404.37–40   "A donda . . . il meglio!"]   Italian: "Where, where?" . . . "The best hotel. The best, the best!"

PICK-UP

430.4   Rocky Marciano]   Boxer (1923–69) who held the heavyweight title from 1952 to 1955, when he retired undefeated.

432.10   *Olympia*]   Painting (1863) by Edouard Manet.

459.22–25   *In a dim corner . . . the shifting gloom.*]   First stanza of "The Sphinx" by Oscar Wilde.

500.17–18   Van Gogh's pool table]   In *The Night Cafe* (1888).

536.21   T/5]   Rank of corporal in the U.S. army technical services.

DOWN THERE

611.10–13   Oscar Levant . . . Art Tatum . . . Walter Gieseking]   Levant (1906–72), composer and pianist; Tatum (1909–56), jazz pianist; Gieseking (1895–1956), French-born concert pianist.

625.28   Bud Powell]   Jazz pianist and composer (1924–66), a leading innovator in the bebop era whose compositions included "Un Poco Loco," "Parisian Thoroughfare," and "52nd Street Theme."

631.38   "Blue Suede Shoes,"]   Rock and roll hit (1956) written and performed by Carl Perkins.

642.33   Merrill's Marauders]   Popular name for the 5307th Provisional Regiment, an all-volunteer American infantry unit that fought the Japanese in northern Burma in 1944.

677.4–6   Henry Armstrong . . . Terry McGovern]   Armstrong (1912–88) who in the late 1930s held simultaneously the featherweight, welterweight, and lightweight titles; McGovern (1880–1918), boxer known as "Terrible Terry."

THE REAL COOL KILLERS

733.6   Joe Turner]   Blues singer (1911–85) who performed in his youth
with Kansas City musicians such as Bennie Moten and Count Basie, and later
recorded a series of hits including "Shake, Rattle and Roll" (1954) and
"Corrine Corrina" (1956).

777.25   Dutch Schultz]   Born Arthur Flegenheimer (1902–35); racketeer
and bootlegger assassinated by other underworld figures.

855.35–36   Vincent Coll . . . Dillinger]   Vincent "Mad Dog" Coll, New
York gangster murdered in 1932; John Dillinger (1902–34), bank robber killed
by FBI agents.

871.28   Don Newcombe]   Baseball player (b. 1926), star pitcher with the
Brooklyn Dodgers (1949–57).

Library of Congress Cataloging-in-Publication Data

Crime novels: American noir of the fifties.
     p.   cm. — (The library of America: 95)
  Contents: The killer inside me / Jim Thompson — The
talented Mr. Ripley / Patricia Highsmith — Pick-up /
Charles Willeford — Down there / Davis Goodis — The real
cool killers / Chester Himes.
  ISBN 1–883011–49–3 (alk. paper)
  1. Detective and mystery stories, American. 2. American
fiction—20th century. 3. Crime—Fiction. I. Thompson,
Jim, 1905–1977. Killer inside me. II. Highsmith, Patricia, 1921–
1995. Talented Mr. Ripley.   III. Willeford, Charles, 1919–1988.
Pick-up. IV. Goodis, David, 1917–1967. Down there.
V. Himes, Chester, 1909–1984. Real cool killers. VI. Series.
PS648.D4C697   1997
813'.087208054—dc21   97–2487
                                          CIP

THE LIBRARY OF AMERICA SERIES

This book is set in 10 point Linotron Galliard,
a face designed for photocomposition by Matthew Carter
and based on the sixteenth-century face Granjon. The paper is
acid-free Ecusta Nyalite and meets the requirements for permanence
of the American National Standards Institute. The binding
material is Brillianta, a woven rayon cloth made by
Van Heek-Scholco Textielfabrieken, Holland.
The composition is by The Clarinda
Company. Printing and binding by
R.R.Donnelley & Sons Company.
Designed by Bruce Campbell.

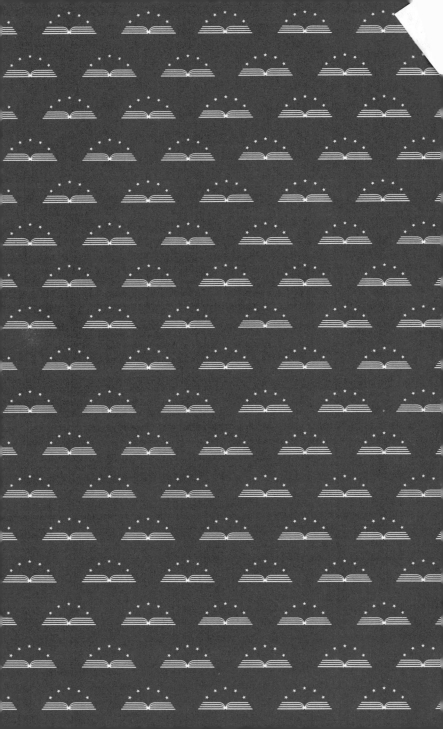